DARK ENEMY TRILOGY

THE CHILDREN OF THE GODS SERIES:BOOKS 4-6

I. T. LUCAS

CONTENTS

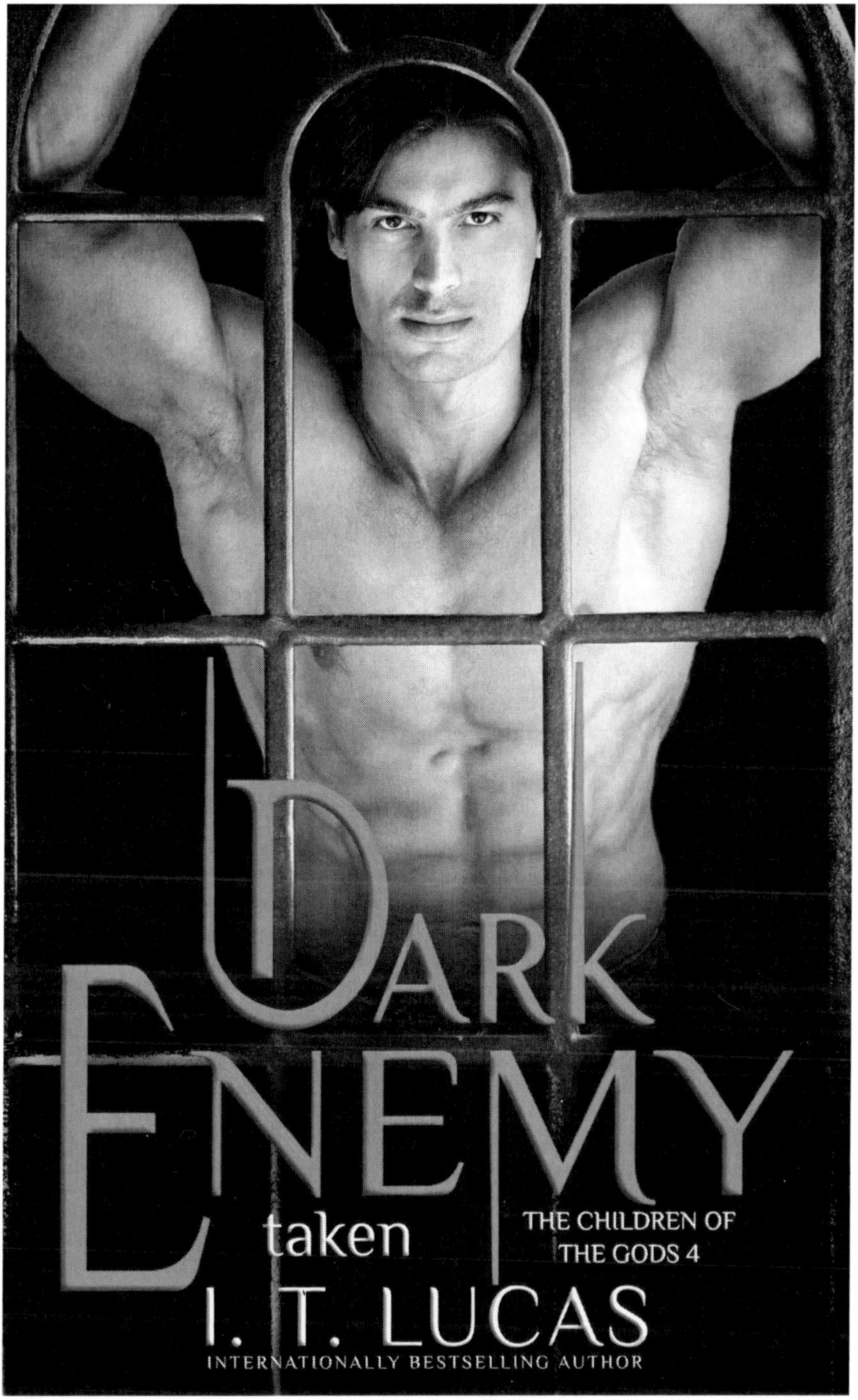
DARK
ENEMY
taken
THE CHILDREN OF
THE GODS 4
I. T. LUCAS
INTERNATIONALLY BESTSELLING AUTHOR

1

AMANDA

"Nice driving," Amanda said as Dalhu slammed on the brakes and took a sharp turn. The car swerved, skidding on the loose gravel, then finally coming to a full stop just inches away from a rusted metal gate.

After driving for hours through the dark forest, the Doomer had apparently reached his final destination. This private dirt road must've led to the mountain cabin he was planning to hide in.

Dear Fates, how could her life have taken such a sharp turn into the twilight zone in the span of just a few hours? In her craziest dreams, or rather worst nightmares, Amanda could not have foreseen being captured by a Doomer. No other female of their clan had ever fallen into the hands of their vicious enemy—the minions-of-all-that-is-evil—the Brotherhood of the *Devout Order Of Mortdh*—Doomers.

But why had the vengeful Fates doomed her to be the first? What had she done to earn their wrath? What wrong could she have possibly committed to deserve such punishment?

Everything had been going so well.

Maybe too well…

Enjoying too much success or too much happiness without giving the Fates credit for the good fortune they bestowed was never wise.

Amanda had been basking in the success of her research. She'd finally been able to identify two excellent potential Dormants and even managed to convince Kian, her stubborn and skeptic brother, to allow the process of their activation to begin. Amanda had high hopes for both. Syssi, her adorable lab assistant, was an exceptional seer, and Michael, a student, was an excellent receiving telepath. And what's more, Kian had fallen head over heels for Syssi, just as Amanda had known he would, and he was attempting the girl's activation himself.

Am I a fabulous matchmaker or what?

But the Fates were capricious and must've been angered by her vanity. She should've thanked them for their help and should've given them credit for her success.

Please forgive me? I want my old life back.

Only this morning, she'd taken Syssi on a fun day of beauty salons and shopping, after which they'd met with Andrew, Syssi's wickedly attractive brother, for lunch.

She should've stayed with them; she should've gone home with Syssi.

But Amanda had wanted to do something nice for Syssi.

She sighed; *no good deed goes unpunished.*

She'd wanted to commission a duplicate of the pendant Syssi had given her. The lovely diamond-encrusted heart was Andrew's gift to Syssi for her sixteenth birthday. Amanda wanted to prevent any unpleasantries between Andrew and Syssi in case he discovered that his sister had given away his gift. So she'd said goodbye, leaving them behind in the restaurant, and headed out on her own to the jewelry store, back to Rodeo Drive.

It had happened there.

She had been kidnapped. By a Doomer. In broad daylight. From the Beverly Hills jewelry store.

How is that for drama?

Though, unfortunately, not of her own making—for a change.

Dear Fates, Syssi and Kian must be going out of their minds with worry.

Or maybe not.

They're most likely busy declaring their love for each other over that romantic dinner Kian promised Syssi, or maybe they're already back at Kian's penthouse—making love...

Not that Amanda wasn't ecstatic for them. After all, it had been her brilliant matchmaking that had brought Syssi and Kian together.

She couldn't help worrying, though. Their happily-ever-after was far from guaranteed. If Syssi didn't turn immortal, their fairy-tale love story would end in tragedy.

Because letting Syssi go would destroy Kian.

Unfortunately, he'd be forced to do it. As much as Amanda would've wished for a different solution, she had to accept that there was no other way.

Even if they made an exception for Syssi, allowing her to keep knowledge of their existence, the sad fact was that her human life span was a blink of an eye compared to Kian's near immortal one. Kian would have no choice but to send her away and erase her memory—of him and everything else to do with the existence of immortals.

Though, in truth, what purpose could it serve for Syssi to retain her memories? Memories that would remind her of the great love she'd found and lost?

None.

Erasing them would be a mercy. There was no reason for Syssi to suffer along with Kian. Pity that there was no way to erase an immortal's memory—it could have saved him the anguish.

Unless...

Perhaps it was possible their mother could do it for him. As the only surviving pure-blooded goddess, Annani had the power to manipulate immortal minds—just as immortals had the power to manipulate those of humans. Maybe she'd be able to help him.

Except, Kian would most likely refuse. Knowing her brother, Amanda suspected that he would welcome the torment. The poor guy would believe that he deserved the punishment.

Though, if he wanted to assign blame, he should pick her.

Kian would've never attempted Syssi's activation if not for Amanda's insistence. Initially, he'd refused. Not that she could fault his reasoning. To the contrary, while Amanda was willing to bend clan law and her sense of honor for the greater good, Kian held himself to higher standards.

The act of seducing a potential dormant female and injecting her with venom to facilitate the activation of her dormant genes was morally iffy. Especially since, out of necessity, the attempted activation had to be done without her consent—her memory of it erased. Not to mention that the probability of it working was extremely low.

Nonexistent—in Kian's opinion.

Eventually, though, Kian's attraction to Syssi had overpowered his good conscience and honorable intentions and he'd seduced the girl. But somewhere along the line he'd fallen in love with her and had told her the truth.

About everything.

Yeah, if Syssi didn't turn, Kian would blame himself for lacking the willpower to stay away from her.

Dear Fates, please, let Syssi turn...

And please, help me get away from this crazy Doomer... Crazy, but, sigh, so incredibly handsome...

As Dalhu bent over the padlock, working to open it and remove the chain that held the gate fastened to the fence, his muscular arms flexed and his T-shirt clung to his strong back.

Amanda just couldn't help but admire what he was putting on display.

He must be at least six-seven or eight... Very appealing for a tall female like me...

Bad Amanda! Stop ogling the evil Doomer!

She averted her gaze when Dalhu returned and folded his huge frame inside. He drove the car a few feet past the gate, then stopped and got out to relock it behind them.

It was a little past midnight when he parked the car at the end of the long, private driveway, in front of the isolated mountain cabin.

Observing the so-called cabin, Amanda grimaced. Dalhu had obviously chosen the place based on how well hidden it was. Style, or even comfort, hadn't been factored in.

The place was dreadful. Calling it a cabin was a joke. She'd stayed at mountain cabins before, and this dingy shack didn't deserve the appellation. And what's worse, it was completely and utterly isolated. The last time she'd spotted signs of habitation, including power poles and power lines, had been over an hour ago. And it wasn't as if the electric cables were buried in the ground. At some point, the power lines had just veered away from the road and into the mountains, disappearing from view.

What had the Doomer been thinking? That she would gather wood and schlep water from a well?

Can you say delusional? Amanda humphed and crossed her arms over her chest.

Dalhu shot her an amused glance. "Come on, Professor, let's see what we got here."

She hated when he called her *Professor* in that mocking tone of his—as if she was delusional despite being well educated. "I asked you not to call me that..."

"Sorry, I just love saying it, *Professor...*"

Insufferable male...

He got out and walked up to the front porch—looking annoyingly cheerful. Evidently, the Doomer deemed this rundown shack to be just great. In his defense, though, she had no doubt this was a step up from what he'd been used to.

Whatever, she'd better take a good look around and check for anything that might give her some advantage—a way out. Trouble was, she had no idea what to look for.

Should've watched some adventure movies... about escape from captivity... Oh, well, should've and could've are not going to help me now.

Stepping out of the car, Amanda followed Dalhu—taking tiny, slow steps. It was dark. There was no artificial lighting coming out from the cabin, and the moon was obscured by heavy, dark clouds. Still, as an immortal, her night vision was excellent, and the little light filtering through the cover of clouds was enough. To her great relief, she saw that there would be no need for her to schlep wood or water to the cabin. Power was provided by a solar panel array that covered one side of the steep roof and a wind turbine that towered over the main building. There was another small structure a few feet away, probably storage, and what looked like a water well next to it. The contraption on top of the well must be an electrical pump. At least she hoped it was electrical... Amanda still remembered times when most people had to do with manual pumps—not that she'd ever done any pumping, that was what servants were for.

Oh, Fates, I miss Onidu.

Onidu, her loyal butler, who was always there for her, taking care of her and doing all of the boring housework tasks. Right now, if he were here, she would hug him and wouldn't let go—and it didn't matter at all that Onidu wasn't a real person, only a brilliant technological construct.

Fully aware that he had no real feelings, she loved him anyway. How could she not? Even though it was his programming that was responsible for all that he had done for her since she was little, like keep her company, take care of her, protect her...

Get a grip, Amanda! she commanded herself, fighting the tears that were stinging the back of her eyes. She had mere seconds to finish assessing her environment before Dalhu finished his breaking and entering and hauled her inside.

It seemed that, unfortunately, the cabin was self-sufficient and off the grid. The chances of anyone being able to follow her trail to this remote and isolated place were slim to none, and so were her opportunities to run or get help.

It took Dalhu no more than a few seconds to manipulate the lock and open the door. By the time she climbed the two steps leading up to the porch, he was already inside, flipping the light switch on.

The downstairs was only one room, with an ugly L-shaped kitchen and a narrow wooden staircase leading up to an open loft-style bedroom. Both were sparsely furnished with old, worn out furniture that was covered with a thick layer of dust and decorated with an appalling number of spider webs.

Ugh, so disgusting.

Standing by the entry, she clutched her twenty-thousand-dollar-plus purse close to her body, keeping it away from the grime, and glanced around in search of the bathroom. There was only one door in the whole place that looked like it could lead to another room, and it was upstairs in the loft bedroom.

She imagined the bathroom was just as dirty and disgusting as the rest of the place, but nature was calling, and crouching behind some bush in the middle of the night was not happening. "I'm going to pee and take a bath. In the meantime, you'd better start cleaning. The place is filthy." Amanda took the stairs up to the loft and strode into the bathroom.

She made sure to lock the door behind her.

Not that she had any illusions that it could keep Dalhu out if he decided he wanted in. But she hoped he would have the decency to get a clue and stay out. Until now, the Doomer had proven to be surprisingly courteous and civil—*for a kidnapper, that is, and a Doomer*. She was expecting him to behave like a gentleman, which probably meant that Dalhu wasn't the only one who was delusional here.

"Doomer" and "gentleman" just didn't belong in the same sentence.

"Pampered brat...," she heard him mumble under his breath as she wiped the dusty toilet seat with tissue paper. Thank heavens she'd found some that had been leftover by the previous occupant because she hadn't thought to bring it up from the car.

"I heard that!" she said, flushing it down.

The gall of the man, calling her a pampered brat. Not that he was wrong, necessarily—she was pampered... and a brat... but as her kidnapper, he had no right to expect her to be considerate.

Amanda slid a disgusted glance over the dirty tub and sighed. She would have to clean the thing herself. But how? She had never cleaned anything before.

Maybe filling it with water and then draining it would do the trick.

The rusty, old faucet made an ominous screeching sound when she forced it to turn, and waiting to see what would come out of it, Amanda held her breath. As she'd expected, the water was brown with rust from the old pipes and whatever other nasties. But when after a few seconds it ran clean, Amanda breathed out.

She flicked the toilet lid closed and sat down. Waiting for the tub to fill, she let her head drop back.

Oh, dear Fates, what am I going to do?

With her gone, there would be no one to continue her research.

All her hard work, the long years she'd spent studying and working toward earning her PhD. in neuroscience and then carving out a position for herself at the university—gone—because of one fateful coincidence. Why were the Fates so cruel to her? Just as she had finally found what she'd been searching for, they had taken it away from her.

The university would probably replace her with another

professor who would continue her lab's formal research. But there would be no one to conduct her unofficial experiments on mortals with paranormal abilities; no one to search for possible dormant carriers of her people's immortal genes. Amanda had been so close to finding a solution to her clan members' lonely existence. The matriarch of their clan, Annani, was the only known surviving full-blooded goddess, but that didn't mean that some of the immortal female descendants of other goddesses hadn't survived the cataclysm.

As long as Amanda was Dalhu's captive, she wouldn't know if Syssi and Michael did indeed descend from other goddesses. But if they'd transitioned, at least two members of her clan would gain life-long partners.

Amanda sighed. What if she'd been wrong?

Perhaps she'd been deluding herself.

Syssi most likely wasn't a Dormant, and neither was Michael. What if Amanda had given Kian false hope, condemning both her brother and Syssi to terrible heartache? Or worse?

Because if Syssi didn't turn, Kian would be devastated.

He would blame Amanda.

And he'd be right.

Long-term relationships between mortals and immortals weren't possible, not only due to the disparity in life spans, but also because of the risk of exposure. No one in the mortal world was allowed to know about the existence of immortals, no exceptions. It was an existential necessity.

Syssi, thank the merciful Fates, would be spared the pain because she wouldn't remember falling in love with Kian. But losing Syssi would destroy Kian.

At best, Kian and Syssi could have a couple of months together. Any longer and Syssi might suffer irreversible brain damage from having too many memories suppressed. And even if she were to escape neurological damage, she might be driven insane by the large chunk of time missing from her life and the inevitable surfacing of bits and pieces of confusing memories.

No!

This time, Amanda wasn't wrong. She could feel it in her gut. Syssi would turn, and so would Michael. And if she'd managed to find two potential Dormants just by conducting a few small-scale experiments in her university lab, then there must be many more out there.

At last she could ensure a better future for her clan and put an end to the lonely existence they had been forced to endure for centuries.

That's right; she would earn the respect of her family, transcending the image of a spoiled princess. Amanda's mood improved considerably. There was just one small obstacle she still had to overcome.

She had to escape.

2

DALHU

"I heard that!" Amanda called while flushing the toilet.

"Good!" he answered.

As he climbed up the rickety stairs with a load of shopping bags in each hand, Dalhu's full bladder demanded immediate attention. He dropped the bags on the dusty bed cover and waited for Amanda to be done.

But then, a squeak of an old faucet followed by the sound of water hitting the bottom of a tub made him realize that the selfish woman had started the water for a bath without giving a second thought to the fact that he might need to use the bathroom as well.

No big deal, he could take care of business outside.

Once that most pressing need was satisfied, Dalhu finished unloading the supplies he'd pilfered from the general store—well, it wasn't really pilfering since he'd left money on the counter to cover what he'd taken. After dropping the last load on the kitchen floor, he went back to the Honda and drove it off the driveway. Hiding it in the thicket, he made sure it was well covered with dense greenery—in case someone thought to do an aerial search for the missing car.

The keys went under the floorboards of the porch, safely hidden and out of Amanda's reach.

Back in the cabin, Dalhu appraised the thick layer of dust covering every exposed surface and the spider webs hanging from ceiling corners and between furniture legs. The place was indeed filthy, but it was so small that he would have no problem cleaning all of it while the spoiled princess soaked in the tub. And hopefully, by the time he was done, he would manage to work up a little sweat...

Imagining Amanda's lustful response to his half-naked, glistening body, he felt a surge of arousal. Since she'd admitted to fantasizing about him like that, he planned to exploit her weakness.

He was one lucky SOB. So lucky that he still had a hard time believing it.

For a change, the Fates had smiled kindly upon him, bringing him to the right place at the right time to snatch the first immortal female he'd ever encountered. And not just any immortal female, but the beautiful professor he'd been lusting after since the first time he'd seen her picture—the one in the autographed magazine article his men had found in the clan programmer's house.

The programmer whose assassination Dalhu had ordered.

But she didn't have to know this, did she? Not yet anyway. First, he was going to seduce her, then he was going to win her heart, and only after he was sure she was his would he come clean.

Damn. Maybe he should just keep it from her forever. Who knew how close Amanda had been to that programmer. After all, she'd signed that picture for the guy with a personal dedication. And even if they hadn't been close, family was still family, and she might not be able to get over that hurdle.

But he knew in his gut that keeping a secret like that would fester like a human's malignant wound.

His best bet was to seduce her and get her addicted to him. He'd heard rumors that the venom was addictive. True, the rumors had only talked about mortal females, but it made sense that the same would hold true for immortal ones. After all, if the venom was indeed addictive, the original purpose must've been to get immortal females bound to their mates.

He would prefer not to rely on such an underhanded method, but it could become necessary in case he failed for some reason to win Amanda's heart. She would get hooked on him no matter what. And anyway, it wasn't as if he could do anything to prevent it. With a wicked smile tugging at the corner of his mouth, Dalhu took off his shirt and went to work.

"Game on, Professor."

The first thing on his agenda was the dusty mattress. Dalhu climbed the stairs up to the loft and eyed the shopping bags he'd dumped on the bed.

Well, that hadn't been smart.

He took them down to the floor, then removed the bedding and dropped it over the railing down to the ground floor. Carefully, he hefted the mattress and lifted it over his head. It wasn't heavy, but maneuvering it down the narrow stairs and out the front door without banging into the walls forced him to go slower than he would've liked.

He left the mattress braced against the porch railing and jogged to the kitchen to grab a broom. As he pounded the mattress, he had to shield his nose and mouth with his other hand against the clouds of dust billowing out of it. The whole porch rattled and shook as he kept beating at the thing. Hopefully, the railing was sturdy enough to absorb the force of his strikes. When he was satisfied that no amount of additional pounding would cause the thing to release more dust, he hefted the mattress back up to the loft. But as he dropped it over the box spring, producing a new cloud, Dalhu realized that he should've given the boxspring the same treatment as the mattress. No time, though. There was still a lot to clean, and he wanted to be done before Amanda finished her bath.

With a quick jog down the stairs, he got to the pile of bedding he'd dropped and scooped it up from the floor. He headed toward what he thought was a utility room, but there was no washer in the broom closet next to the kitchen that he'd mistaken for one. If there was a washer in the cabin at all, it must've been stashed in the bathroom upstairs. He could think of no other place where it could've been hidden.

Maybe it was in the shack outside? He'd check later, but, for now, stuffing it in the broom closet would do. First, though, he had to take out the vacuum cleaner to make room for the bundle.

He was about to attack the floor with the ancient machine when it crossed his mind that the sofa was probably in no better shape than the mattress.

It took two more trips out to the porch and some more pounding with the broom to liberate the heavy layer of dust from the sofa cushions.

Back to the floors.

Though not much to look at, the simple vacuum cleaner was doing a decent job—for a little while. Dalhu stopped when the loud engine changed its tune from a drone to a whine, and a slight burning scent reached his nose.

Good that he had or the thing would've gone up in smoke. After examining the various components, he found a canister that needed emptying.

Live and learn.

Cleaned, the thing worked perfectly again. Once the floors looked passable, Dalhu wiped the rest of the surfaces with a couple of wet rags, then disposed of them the same way he did the bedding —into the broom closet.

Later, he planned to put everything in the washer. If there was one. If not, he was going to throw the stuff in the trash. As it was, he'd already exceeded his lifelong quota of domestic activity. Washing by hand was not going to happen unless the professor volunteered to do it…

Yeah... hell has a better chance of freezing over...

The things he was willing to do for a woman. At his home base, Dalhu wouldn't have been caught dead holding a broom. A warrior carried a rifle or a sword—only servants and trainees carried cleaning implements and did the kinds of jobs he had done tonight.

Dalhu rubbed his neck, his hand coming away oily with sweat. He smirked, wiping his palm on his dirty jeans.

Mission accomplished.

It was time to present himself to the bathing princess. Except, now that he was done, an insidious doubt drifted through his mind, and his plan suddenly seemed foolish. What if she screamed at him to get out? Or looked at him with disgust in her beautiful blue eyes?

After all, he'd kidnapped her, drugged her, and had cuffed her to a bed. It was a wonder Amanda was talking to him at all, or looking at him with anything other than fear, or even worse—loathing.

Dalhu sighed. It was what it was. He would do his best with the cards fate had dealt him—the good and the bad, and there was no place for doubts or second thoughts if he wanted to win the most important game of his life.

Winners didn't cower before a challenge.

They embraced it.

Amanda was going to be his.

Climbing the wooden stairs, he made sure to stomp his feet and make his approach as loud as possible. What little sense of propriety he possessed demanded that he at least let Amanda know he was coming and give the female a chance to cover herself before he barged in on her.

With his hand on the bathroom door's handle, Dalhu hesitated for a fraction of a moment before plastering a confident though totally fake grin on his face and forcing his way in. "Hello, princess," he said, the words he'd prepared on his way up.

It was good that he'd spoken as soon as he had, because the sight of Amanda's perfect body laid out in the bathtub in all its naked glory had rendered him speechless.

And the way she was looking at him, basking in the knowledge of the effect she had on him…

There was no shame in her eyes, no attempt to cover her perfect breasts with her hands. If anything, the woman seemed to feed off his stunned stupor.

"Dalhu, darling, as soon as you're done drooling, could you please bring me the toiletries and a towel? Don't forget the conditioner…"

He barely heard the words coming out of that gorgeous mouth.

What did she say? Soap and towel?

Damn, Dalhu swallowed, his brain short-circuiting from all the visual stimuli. Fully clothed, Amanda was stunning; naked, she was like a stroke of lightning—awe-inspiring and deadly. Because if he were mortal, his heart would have surely stopped.

Dalhu wiped a shaky hand over his mouth. Dimly aware that he had a plan coming up here and forcing his way into the bathroom, he struggled to remember what it was, but with most of his neurons misfiring it was hard to concentrate.

There was something that was supposed to turn her on…

Yeah… and I'm doing such a great job of it… as if gawking and drooling is going to do it for her…

Fuck! What a splendid personification of masculinity he was displaying…

Pull yourself together, you idiot!

Showing weakness wouldn't do with a woman like her…

Not a woman—a fucking goddess…

He'd better pull his shit together and project strength and confidence before he lost her respect…

If he'd ever had it to begin with.

At first, when he'd grabbed her in that jewelry store, she'd been terrified of him. But then, after he'd bitten her, overloading her system with his venom, she'd begged him to fuck her like a common slut. But that was the venom's doing; she'd been high on its aphrodisiac properties. He had no doubt that she would've never acted like that when sober. And that's why, as hard as it had been, he'd refused her pleas. In his mind, to oblige her would've been akin to rape.

Trouble was, the way she'd cussed at him for refusing her, Dalhu doubted his restraint had been appreciated. He wondered whether by treating her honorably he'd gained her respect or had lost it altogether.

Perhaps he'd been stupid for wanting her sober consent, but this was not about an easy lay. This woman was his future, and he'd be damned if he'd screw things up by taking advantage of her in a compromised state.

Hopefully, once she sobered up and remembered, she'd appreciate his gallantry.

Except, one could never know with women…

Still, even if she'd found his behavior gallant, it didn't mean she thought highly of him. Most likely, Amanda considered him beneath her.

Not nearly good enough.

And he wasn't—not by a long shot.

He was aware that Amanda found him attractive, but that was about it—his only redeeming quality. She was a professor while he was an uneducated mercenary. She was rich, and he wasn't. Not to mention the little issue of him kidnapping her and holding her prisoner with no intention of ever letting her go…

Or being her family's sworn enemy…

"The toiletries, Dalhu? And the towel?" she repeated, her eyes twinkling with amusement. The woman knew she had him by the balls… and not just figuratively…

"Coming right up, princess." Dalhu forced a smile before tearing his eyes away.

Damn. Now he was sweating worse than he had from the physical work he'd done before. Thank Mortdh, he'd been already covered in sweat when he'd come in… maybe she wouldn't notice it had gotten worse… because of her…

The woman had him wrapped around her little finger and doing her bidding as if she was the one calling the shots.

She was, though, wasn't she?

He would do anything to please her.

Except, Amanda might think she had gained the upper hand, but in the grand scheme of things, her victory was an illusion. It played right into his plan. Dalhu was fully committed to doing whatever was necessary to win her over, and to that end—to please her—he was willing to go places and do things he'd never endeavored before.

In the end, she would be his.

There was no way he was losing this most important campaign.

He took his time collecting Amanda's bathing paraphernalia—which was everything besides the soap, razor, and toothbrush that were his—the minute or two spent helping him get over the initial shock of seeing her naked. When he was done, Dalhu was ready to face her again.

Like a man…

"Thank you," she said when he came back with an armful of stuff he had no idea what she was going to do with. But what did he know? Perhaps all females required five different hair products and nine kinds of lotions.

"My pleasure." Leaning against the counter, he crossed his arms over his chest, purposefully. His bulging biceps producing the response he was hoping for. Amanda's appreciative glance had lingered before she shifted her gaze back to his face.

"Well, hand me the stuff and get out. The peep show is over."

"Which *staff* are you referring to?" Dalhu arched a brow.

Look at me, being all clever with the wordplay and all…

"Funny, aren't you?" Amanda feigned nonchalance, but couldn't help shooting a quick glance at the other bulging part of his body. "Just the soap, shampoo, and conditioner," she said a little throatily.

"You sure that's all you need, sweetheart?"

"Need and want in one hand, shit in the other—see what you get the most of…" She pinned him with her blue stare. "Get out, Dalhu, I mean it."

"Yes, ma'am." He saluted and pushed off the counter. "Don't take too long, though, I'm of a mind to get in there with you… As you can see, I'm dirty." He looked down his pecs, flexing, "Absolutely filthy." He winked and walked out.

Closing the door behind him was a no go because the handle was broken and the thing wouldn't stay closed, but he did the best he could, leaving it only slightly ajar.

He exhaled the breath he was holding and picked up his shirt from the floor, using it to wipe the sweat off his face and his chest. Well, that hadn't turned out a complete fiasco. When he'd finally been able to think with something other than his dick, he'd noticed the way Amanda had been struggling with her own lust.

Things were not going as smoothly as he'd anticipated, but then nothing ever did. All good things were worth waiting for, and though he didn't think he'd be waiting much longer, if need be, he would.

After all, time was on his side. The way he'd carefully covered their trail, no one was going to come to Amanda's rescue anytime soon.

3

AMANDA

As she heard Dalhu exhale a relieved breath from behind the bathroom door, Amanda smirked with satisfaction.

Dalhu's surprised expression when he'd burst into the bathroom had been priceless. Seeing her in all her nude glory with her body boldly displayed in the bath's clear water—not gasping or trying to cover herself as most women would—the guy had been rendered speechless.

But then she was nothing like what he was used to.

Not even close.

Amanda was the daughter of a goddess, for fate's sake.

He hadn't been the only one affected, though. As he'd devoured her with his hungry eyes, her body had responded, her nipples growing taut under his hooded gaze.

Ogling her, he'd wiped the drool off his mouth with the back of his dirty hand, looking just as awestruck as one of her students. But that was where the resemblance ended.

Dalhu was a magnificent specimen of manhood, and in comparison, all her former partners looked like mere boys. Shirtless and sweaty, he'd looked just as amazing as she'd imagined he would.

He was big; not even Yamanu was that tall, and Dalhu was more powerfully built. Nevertheless, his well-defined muscles were perfectly proportioned for his size with no excess bulk; he looked strong, but not pumped like someone who spent endless hours lifting weights at a gym.

Following the light smattering of dark hair trailing down the center of his chest to where it disappeared below the belt line of his jeans, she hadn't been surprised to find that he was well proportioned everywhere. And as he kept staring at her, mesmerized, his jeans growing too tight to contain him, she'd held her breath in anticipation of her first glimpse of that magnificent length.

Oh, boy, am I in a shitload of trouble.

There was just no way she could resist all that yummy maleness. Amanda knew she was going to succumb to temptation.

She always had.

Except, this time, she would be stooping lower than ever. Because she could think of nothing that would scream SLUT louder than her going willingly into the arms of her clan's mortal enemy…

Shit, damn, damn, shit… she cursed silently.

It had taken sheer willpower to kick him out. She so hadn't wanted to…

But she would've never been able to look at herself in the mirror if she'd succumbed to the impulse and had dragged him down into that bathtub to have her wicked way with him.

Hopefully, he'd been too busy hiding his own reaction to have noticed hers.

What was it about him that affected her so? Yes, he was incredibly handsome, and she was a lustful hedonist… but, come on, she had been a hair away from jumping the guy…

Was she one of those women that got turned on by bad boys?

Yep, evidently I am.

How shameful…

Her hand sneaked down to the juncture of her thighs, and she let her finger slide over the slick wetness that had nothing to do with the water she was soaking in. But after a quick glance at the door that wouldn't close, she gritted her teeth and pulled her fingers away from the seat of her pleasure.

She couldn't let Dalhu know how he affected her if she hoped to have a chance of keeping him off her.

And herself off him…

Damn!

She had to keep telling herself over and over again, repeating it like a mantra until it sunk in, that there was nothing that would scream SLUT louder than her going willingly into the arms of a Doomer.

Oh Fates, I'm such a slut...

But wait... this was it...the solution to her predicament...

If there was one thing that was sure to shatter Dalhu's romantic illusions, it was to find out that the woman he wanted for his mate had been with a shitload of others before him.

She was well acquainted with the Doomers' opinions about women and their place in society. Someone like her probably would get stoned to death in the parts of the world they controlled. And though Dalhu seemed smarter and better informed than the average Doomer, he no doubt believed in the same old double standard. It was perfectly okay for him to fuck a different woman every night because his body demanded it. But it was not okay for her.

She was supposed to suffer the pain like a good little girl because decent women were not supposed to want or enjoy sex…

Well, she not only wanted it and enjoyed it, but needed it to survive, just like any other near-immortal male or female.

But try explaining it to a Doomer…

Stupid. Blind. Deaf.

Members of the brotherhood of the "Devout Order Of Mortdh" were brainwashed to hate women and believed them to be inferior and unworthy. It was sad, really, how easy it was for Navuh and his propaganda to affect not only his followers, and not only the male population of the regions under his control, but also the women living there. They succumbed to the same beliefs, accepting that they were inferior, that being abused was their due, and that that was what their god wanted for them.

The poor things didn't know any better.

If a girl heard all throughout her life that she was worthless, and her education was limited to basic literacy at best, she was going to believe it, buying into the label she'd been given and perceiving herself that way.

Thinking back to her own youth in Scotland, and even later in their new home in America, the situation for women had been only slightly better. Though they were not as badly mistreated as their counterparts in Navuh's region, the prevailing attitude, sadly, had been similar up until recent times. Women had been considered not as smart and not as capable as men, but at least their mothering and homemaking skills had been appreciated. For most of her life, women had accepted these beliefs as immutable truths, treating the few that had tried to rise above them as bad mothers, misguided individuals, and an undesirable influence on their daughters.

Thank heavens this was changing. There was still discrimination in the workforce, with men getting better pay and faster promotions, but at least the West was on the right track.

Oh, well, her mother and the rest of their clan did what they could. But where Navuh had his clutches deeply in the hearts of mortals there was nothing to be done.

They were lost souls.

As was Dalhu.

The guy struggled against what he was, though, she had to hand him that. But could he break free after the centuries of brainwashing he'd suffered?

As a scientist, Amanda knew there was no hope for him. But as a person, as a woman... well... hope was for children and fools—as Kian was fond of saying.

She wasn't a child... so that left being a fool...

Still, hopeful or not, how was she going to get the guy disillusioned with her without getting him so enraged that he would chop her head off?

Dalhu was unstable, going from rage to affection in a heartbeat, and she was afraid of what he'd do if she told him the truth about whom he was planning to spend his life with.

Perhaps the smart thing to do was to bide her time and wait to be rescued.

But how would anyone even know where to look for her?

Damn. What to do... what to do...

Wait... but what if she let Dalhu have her...

Just so he wouldn't kill her... of course...

That wouldn't count as her going to him willingly, would it?

And if she didn't suffer horribly in the process... well...

Now that she'd come up with a semi-moral excuse for sleeping with the enemy—only if it became necessary of course—her mood improved, and she hurried to finish soaping, shampooing, and conditioning before Dalhu got tired of waiting and decided to jump in the tub with her.

Having the option didn't mean she should court that particular outcome, did it?

She finished drying off with the cheap, coarse towel and wrapped it around her body with a grimace. It was way too short, barely covering her butt.

Clutching the shitty towel so it would cover at least her nipples on top and the juncture of her thighs on the bottom, she walked out of the bathroom.

"Not a word, Dalhu. Not a fucking word..." she hissed at his ogling smirk, the cuss word feeling foreign and vulgar on her lips.

He arched a brow but said nothing. Grabbing a pair of gray

sweats, he tore off the price tags and ducked into the bathroom she'd just vacated.

There was another set of sweats folded on top of the bed… pink… and plain cotton panties… also pink…

Her lips twisted in distaste. "Oh, goody, that must be for me."

With a quick glance behind her, she made sure the bathroom door was closed, or as well as it could be, before dropping the towel. With a sigh, she reluctantly shimmied into the cheap panties and then pulled on the shapeless, polyester-blend sweats.

Her bare skin had never before touched anything as disgusting, and a glance at the mirror hanging over the bathroom door proved that she'd never before worn anything as ugly as this either.

She looked positively… well… blah.

The good news was that no one she knew was going to see her in this humiliating getup. Unfortunately, though, she was pretty sure that it didn't make her look ugly enough for Dalhu to lose interest either.

The bad news was that she had no idea how she was going to sleep with the horrible synthetic fabric irritating her skin. And sleeping naked was not an option—even if she made Dalhu sleep on the couch downstairs.

Sifting through the bags, she found the bedding she'd had him bring from the store. One scratchy sheet went over the naked mattress, then pillowcases over the two pillows, and another sheet under the comforter that, surprise, surprise, was also made from polyester…

Had there been nothing else in that store? Or had Dalhu chosen the worst stuff to torture her with…

Well, payback is a bitch.

Grabbing a pillow and a woven blanket, she hurried down the stairs and dropped them on the couch. The thing was too short for Dalhu's huge body, and hopefully, it was lumpy as well…

"Sleep tight… hope you get lots of bedbug bites…" she singsonged as she walked over to the kitchen.

The food supplies Dalhu had stolen from the store were on the floor, still in their paper bags, and as she began taking the stuff out and arranging it on the counter, her spirits sunk even further. Apparently, Dalhu's idea of nutrition was mostly canned meat, canned beans, a few cans of vegetables, sliced white bread, and peanut butter.

The only thing to brighten her mood was a can of ground coffee, but only momentarily—there was no coffeemaker.

Putting together a peanut butter sandwich was something even she could do, but making coffee without the benefit of a coffeemaker was above the level of her meager culinary skills.

A quick search through the cabinets yielded nothing more exciting than some pots and pans, but thank heavens, she found a can opener.

Scooping some of the coffee into a pot, Amanda filled it with water and turned on the electric stove. Trouble was, she had no idea what the ratio should be, or if it was even possible to make stovetop coffee.

Hopefully, it would be drinkable…

She was desperate for it.

As she arranged the rest of the supplies in the cabinets, the aroma wafting from the cooking coffee smelled delicious, and once it looked like it was done, she poured it into two cups and began making peanut butter sandwiches for Dalhu and herself.

4

DALHU

Dalhu glanced at the ridiculously short sweats he'd pulled on after showering. The sleeves reached a little below his elbows, and the shirt's bottom barely covered his bellybutton. He'd pulled and tied the waistband string as tight as it would go, but it was still too wide and the pants kept sliding down. The fucking double X must've been about the girth, not the length.

And it wasn't as if Dalhu was worried about flashing a pair of boxer shorts. He wasn't wearing any. He'd forgotten to include them in his supply procurement...

For a moment, he considered changing into one of the fancy designer jeans that he'd purchased at that Rodeo Drive boutique. The faggot salesman had insisted that they made Dalhu's ass look *fabulous*...

Fortunately, for the bastard, he'd been so helpful and pleasant before the *ass* remark that Dalhu had decided to let him live...

Had it been only this morning?

So much had happened since that he felt as if it had happened days ago.

How much had he paid for those jeans? A thousand? More?

At least he'd paid with a credit card and not cash. On the run, the card was useless and he was low on cash. He kept the card, though, just in case. Hopefully, the Brotherhood's bureaucrats wouldn't cancel it anytime soon.

The designer clothes he'd spent so much money on wouldn't be used for their original purpose, though, and the custom suit he'd ordered would remain unclaimed.

The only reason he'd needed those obscenely expensive clothes in the first place was to go hunting for the males of Amanda's clan in the lucrative nightclubs they frequented.

But he'd left that part of his life behind.

Hopefully, it wouldn't come chasing after him.

The reinforcements Dalhu had asked for were due to arrive any day now. Navuh was sending a large contingent this time, and he had no doubt someone higher up in the organization would be leading them. Dalhu had been a commander of a small unit. There was no way he would've been left to head the operation, regardless of the fact that discovering Annani's clan's elusive trail had been his achievement.

Whatever, it was of no consequence. He had abandoned the Brotherhood and its questionable crusade for good.

Heading for the staircase, he paused and looked at the two top windows flanking the fireplace. The exposed glass made him uneasy.

All the other windows had shutters, which he'd closed, but those two at the top had none. If there had been a tall ladder he could've used, he would've taped or nailed bed sheets over the glass, but as he'd searched the cabin and the attached woodshed, the only ladder he'd found was too short.

Those windows were a dead giveaway that someone was inside the cabin, and even though it was unlikely that anyone would be looking for Amanda out here in the mountains, Dalhu hated taking even that slight chance.

He would have to insist on as little lighting as possible.

With a curse, he jogged down the stairs, his scowl deepening as he took in the pillow and blanket the princess had prepared for him on the couch. Not for a moment did he entertain the notion that she'd intended to sleep there herself. But if she thought he would be a gentleman and cram himself into the thing, she had another thing coming.

Spoiled brat...

A beautiful, sexy, spoiled brat...

Standing barefoot at the counter, Amanda was a vision—looking amazing even in the plain pink sweats he'd gotten her. The pants waistband, which was clearly too wide for her narrow waist, was rolled over a couple of times, and the loose pants hung low on her hips, allowing him a glimpse of the curve of her creamy white ass each time she bent.

And she'd made coffee and sandwiches...

Maybe there was hope for her after all.

"You are beautiful," Dalhu breathed as he walked up to stand behind her and nuzzled her long, smooth neck.

Surprised, she shivered before ducking sideways. "Cut it out, Dalhu," she bit out. "Sit down and drink your coffee. I hope you like it black and bitter because you didn't get any sugar or creamer."

"That's so sweet of you, taking care of me like that," he said as he sat down and picked up the coffee mug.

"Don't get used to that."

As Dalhu took a sip, he barely made it to the sink in time to spit the thing out. "Are you trying to poison me, woman? What the hell did you do?" He rushed back to the table, grabbing a peanut butter sandwich and taking a quick bite to get rid of the gritty taste.

"There is no coffeemaker, okay? What did you expect?" The hurt expression on Amanda's face made it obvious that she didn't ruin the coffee just to spite him. Grabbing the pot by the handle, she dumped its contents in the sink, then braced her hands on the rim and dropped her head. Her delicate shoulders began trembling.

Was she crying? Did he make her cry?

Way to go, asshole...

"Don't worry about it. I'll make a new one." He got behind her and tried to turn her around.

A sob escaped her throat as she shrugged his hands off her shoulders. "Everything you got from that store is disgusting; the towels, the bedding, the clothes... everything... even the food. The bread tastes like cardboard, and everything else is canned yuck. And now I can't even have a decent cup of coffee. It's just too much... I can't take it anymore..." She began sobbing in earnest.

Dalhu felt helpless. What the hell was he supposed to do now?

"Please don't cry. If you make me a list, I'll go and get you whatever you need. I'm sorry that there was nothing better at that general store... Oh, hell..." Forcing her to turn, he wrapped his arms around her, crushing her to him—her cheek to his pec.

She struggled, but he held her tightly against him, rubbing his palm over her heaving back until she gave up and sagged in his arms. Crying and sobbing into his sweatshirt for what seemed like forever, Amanda was killing him.

And although he was well aware that the coffee was just the last straw that had broken this strong, amazing woman, the guilt of failing to provide for her, like he'd promised her he would, was eating him alive.

As the sobbing subsided, he reached for a paper towel, and still holding her with one arm, handed her the thing.

"Thank you." Amanda hiccupped and blew her nose into the towel. Pushing away from him, she threw it into the sink and wiped her face with her sleeve before glancing up at him. "I must be a mess. Red nose and blotchy eyes..."

"You're beautiful. Always. In any shape or form." He dipped his knees to look into the blue pools of her eyes, wanting to kiss her so bad it hurt.

She smiled a little. "You're just saying it to make me feel better..."

"No, I mean it. Come, sit down, relax, and I'll make you a good cup of coffee to cheer you up." He led her to the dining table and pulled out a chair for her.

"Good luck. There is no cream or sugar. So even if you manage to brew a decent coffee, I wouldn't like it."

"Oh, but you've missed something when you put the cans away. We have some condensed milk—it's both sweet and creamy."

5

AMANDA

The coffee Dalhu made turned out to be pretty good. And as hungry and thirsty as Amanda was, even the peanut butter sandwich was okay… well, edible… barely…

"Feeling better?" Dalhu peered at her from across the table.

"Much. Though I still hold you to your promise to get me everything I need."

"To the best of my ability. Though don't expect me to drive all the way to Rodeo Drive to buy you clothes. I know you're used to luxury, and at some point, hopefully soon, I'll be able to provide you with whatever you want. But for now, you'll have to lower your standards a little."

Amanda waved a dismissive hand. "At this point, I'll consider decent food and stuff not made from polyester a luxury."

"Tomorrow, I'll take care of it. I promise."

"Good."

In the silence that followed, Dalhu obliterated the rest of the sandwiches while Amanda sipped on her second cup of coffee, observing him from under her lashes. He wasn't the most graceful of eaters, stuffing his mouth with huge bites, half a sandwich at a time, and crumbs littered the table all around him. Still, it didn't bother her as it should have.

Usually, poor eating manners would immediately disqualify a guy from having a chance with her, but Dalhu wasn't just any other guy. For some reason, she thought he looked manly eating like a hungry beast, and instead of turning her off, his bad table manners were turning her on.

Damn, she was evidently so horny that anything and everything was a turn-on. She'd better get away from this hunk of a male before her resolve faltered and she jumped his bones.

The intensity with which she craved Dalhu wouldn't have been surprising if she had gone without sex for several days, but after only one? The night before the fateful lunch that had led to her abduction, she had been with two different guys in a row. It should've kept her sated at least for a couple of days.

Yeah, but they weren't Dalhu. An immortal male with an amazing physique, and fangs... Damn, the memory of that bite… it had been so erotic… *Shit, think of something else, quick before he scents my arousal... Famine, war...*

Amanda breathed out as the sad images did their job. "Well, I'm beat. I'm going up to bed. Good night, Dalhu." She pushed away from the table.

"You really expect me to sleep on that sofa?" Dalhu got up and took the dirty dishes to the sink.

"Yep." She headed for the stairs.

"Wait…" He followed behind her. "What if I promise to stay on my side of the bed like a good little boy? To make me sleep on that couch is a cruel and unusual punishment."

The big, bad Dalhu was eyeing her hopefully, but she had no intention of sleeping with the guy. Because one thing was sure, as horny as she was, if he got in that bed with her, she had no doubt they'd end up doing way more than sleeping.

"As I see it, you deserve a cruel and unusual punishment for kidnapping me and dragging me out here, and then torturing me with polyester."

Dalhu heaved a defeated sigh and hung his head for a moment, but then lifted it a little to look at her with a naughty smirk. "Okay, but I want a kiss. Just one kiss and I promise not to take it any further. A little reward for my gentlemanly sacrifice."

Oh, hell, one kiss. He was asking for just one kiss. Amanda wanted so much more than that…

Except, even though Dalhu had promised not to take it any further, Amanda was afraid a team of horses wouldn't be able to hold *her* back…

Oh, what the hell…

"Okay," she breathed and closed her eyes, tilting her head up.

His lips were incredibly soft and gentle as he brushed them against hers. Cupping her cheek with a tender palm, he kissed her, just a light stroke of mouth on mouth with hardly any pressure behind the contact. So sweet. Innocent.

A lover's kiss.

But it was enough to send an overwhelmingly erotic shudder through her, and she fought the urge to pull him down and kiss him the way a man like him should be kissed… Hard.

They both groaned, but it was Dalhu who pulled away first.

"For the love of Mortdh…" he hissed, turning around in a futile attempt to hide the tent that had sprouted in his sweatpants. "Please, just go. I want you so much, it hurts…"

Her eyes glued to the enormous erection he was trying to hide, Amanda was dimly aware that Dalhu was saying something.

Oh, dear Fates… that would feel so incredible inside me…

And the prospect of another bite…

As a flood of moisture pooled in her panties, Amanda closed her eyes. And as she relived that bite in her mind, the coiling sensation inside her got tighter and tighter, threatening to culminate in a climax.

Gritting her teeth, she fisted her hands and pushed the image away.

What the hell?

Fates knew that there had been plenty of times when she'd been horny, and a few days without sex would usually send her climbing up the walls—or the first attractive male she managed to snag—but she'd never orgasmed just from imagining it…

When Dalhu turned to her, he was all predator, his nostrils flaring with the scent of her arousal.

Oh, no…

No, no, no.

This was so bad…

They were both lost.

With Dalhu's fangs punching over his bottom lip and his eyes glowing, there was very little of the man left—he was mostly beast now—a beast who smelled a female in heat…

She had to stop him… and there was only one way she knew how…

"You're not the only one in pain. Do you know anything about immortal females?" She threw out a hand to stop him.

"I know everything I need to know…" he hissed through his fangs, his whole body somehow getting even bigger and scarier.

"Do you know that we are exactly like the males in our need for sex?"

"Good, then there is no reason for you to refuse me…" He smiled, though with his fangs out the smile wasn't exactly reassuring.

Here it goes...

Amanda swallowed audibly. It was now or never because she was already out of time. "I'm over two hundred years old, and since reaching the age of majority, which is seventeen among my people, I've been with a different guy almost every night…" she blurted in a hurry.

Dalhu looked as if someone had dumped a bucket of ice on his head. His fangs retracted and the tent in his pants deflated.

Which was good…

But the murderous look in his eyes was not… not good at all…

Whipping around, Amanda sprinted up the stairs—even though she had no clue where the hell she was going to hide from Dalhu's rage. But right now, getting away from him seemed like the smart thing to do.

The roar that left Dalhu's chest shook the cabin, and as she ducked under the comforter, she felt the cabin rattle again when he punched a wall—probably reducing it to dust by the sound of it.

A moment later, she heard the front door open and slam shut.

For long moments, Amanda lay huddled under the blanket, trembling as she listened to every tiny sound.

There were the chirps of crickets and the occasional hoot of an owl, and when the wind picked up, the rustle of leaves and branches swaying and rubbing against each other, but thankfully, no sounds of a madman stomping up the wooden porch steps.

What have I done?

This had been such an incredibly stupid idea. Who in their right mind told their abductor something that they knew would enrage him?

And to what end?

Like having sex with the guy would have been so bad… not! And who cared if she added him to her long list of partners.

As if one more would make a difference…

Though she had a feeling that this one would.

Big time.

Terrified, she waited for Dalhu to come back, fighting to stay awake until exhaustion won the battle.

6

DALHU

As he stormed out of the cabin, Dalhu didn't know what to do with himself or the rage consuming him. The familiar red haze was clouding his mind. Luckily, trained soldier that he was, he still had enough presence of mind to pull on his boots and then grab a knife and a gun from under the porch floorboards where he'd hidden his weapons.

Who knew what was hiding in this forest? As strong as he was, Dalhu was no match for a full-grown bear, and a pack of coyotes could inflict some serious damage.

On the one hand, he craved the confrontation. A brutal, hands-on fight against vicious beasts would be a great catharsis—a shortcut to getting rid of the raging storm inside his head. But on the other, he couldn't afford an injury. On the remote chance that Amanda's family or his own brethren were to locate them somehow, he needed to conserve his strength to fight them off, or at least give it all he had until they killed him. He wouldn't go down easy.

Unfortunately, he needed to find another way to work out his rage.

Crushing through the forest like an angry grizzly, it took him hours until his head cleared enough for him to think about what had gotten him so enraged.

He didn't know immortal females had a sex drive to match the males. How could he? They were as rare and mysterious as unicorns or honest politicians.

And why the hell had he gotten so mad? It's not like he was a blushing virgin, or even someone who had treated his own body with enough respect not to share it with hell only knew how many goddamned whores…

But that was the thing. He wanted a fresh start with Amanda—to forget what came before and start clean with someone he'd believed was purer.

It's not that he had any illusions about Amanda being a virgin, but to hear her say she'd been with a shitload of men was on a whole different level.

It had shattered his romantic fantasy.

Yeah, he was so goddamned romantic that his woman was terrified of him. Not that he could blame her. He had scared himself. Never in his life had he raised his hand to a woman, but he'd been too damn close to having done it tonight.

And for what? For admitting a truth that had nothing to do with him?

A truth about a physiology he was well familiar with and knew was impossible to deny.

He needed to go back and apologize.

Fuck, he shouldn't have left her alone in the first place—locking her in the cabin.

What if there was a fire and she was trapped inside?

Panic flaring to a bone-melting fear, Dalhu ran, his progress faster and easier on the path that he'd cleared trampling down the mountain before, even though he was going uphill this time.

As he got nearer and detected no smell of smoke, the vise around his heart eased, and as he got to the cabin's front door, he offered a prayer of thanks that nothing had happened to Amanda while he was gone.

It would never happen again.

Nothing was more important than Amanda, and he'd never allow his goddamned temper or anything else to jeopardize her safety.

Dalhu returned his weapons to their hiding place and took off his soiled boots. Leaving them out on the porch, he manipulated the lock with a few turns of the wire to get back inside.

Careful to close the door soundlessly behind him, he locked it, then tiptoed to the couch. Hopefully, Amanda was asleep, and he was too ashamed of himself to risk going upstairs for a change of clothes and waking her, having to face her. Instead, he dropped his dirty sweats on the floor and lay down, covering his naked body with the thin blanket Amanda had left for him.

But despite his physical and mental exhaustion, sleep eluded him as his thoughts kept running in circles.

He was failing miserably at this whole being a good mate thing. And to think he'd been so sure it would be easy—taking good care of Amanda, providing for her, keeping her safe.

He'd failed on all fronts on the first day.

She didn't have anything good to eat, nothing decent to wear, and he'd gotten her so terrified, he wasn't sure he would ever be able to make her feel safe with him again.

Who was he kidding—as if she ever had—him kidnapping her and all…

Then, he'd left her alone in a locked wooden structure, with no one around to come to her rescue if something went wrong.

He didn't deserve her.

Of course, he didn't.

But he'd make sure to do better tomorrow.

Because failure was not an option.

7

SHARIM

As Sharim emerged from the underground tunnel, the bright tropical sun blinded him momentarily before he swung the Range Rover to the left, where palm trees shaded the road. Slowing down, he leaned over to the glove compartment and pulled out his sunglasses.

Why, in the name of Mortdh, had his father chosen to live above ground?

The fucking tropical island was relentlessly hot and humid—the sun glaring without mercy day in and day out, all year round. Living in the underground complex on the other side of the island made so much more sense. No sun, no heat, no humidity. Perfect climate control twenty-four seven.

He didn't believe for a moment that his father chose to live topside because he loved the vivid green of the tropical vegetation and the magnificent view of the ocean, which was Losham's official excuse.

Sharim knew better.

Living in the plush villa adjacent to Navuh's mansion symbolized Losham's elevated status as their supreme leader's eldest son. And to live in the underground facility among the rest of the troops would have undermined his position, even though he would've been residing in the luxurious family wing.

In a way, it was stupid. Navuh's other sons had villas in the luxury resort as well, but for obvious reasons still spent most of their time in the underground. It was a lot more comfortable, not to mention necessary for keeping close tabs on the soldiers.

But his father wasn't a military commander like the others. He wasn't a soldier at all. His primary function was providing Navuh with an affable companion.

Soft-spoken and intelligent, Losham managed to appear as if he held some sway with their exalted leader, and maybe to some small extent he did, but the truth was that he was nothing more than a lackey.

Nevertheless, Losham's lofty aspiration had saved Sharim from becoming just another meaningless cog in Navuh's machine, prompting Losham to adopt Sharim as a way to further differentiate himself from Navuh's other sons—Losham's younger half brothers.

Praise Mortdh.

Besides Navuh, none of the other immortal males were allowed to father immortal sons. With Dormants being forbidden to them, the children they sired on mortal females were only mortal.

Sharim had been born to Losham's dormant sister—*the fucking bitch may she burn in hell.*

With some clever groveling, his father had gotten Navuh's permission to adopt Sharim—regrettably, though, only once Sharim was old enough to be taken to the training camp.

Sharim must've been the only boy who'd found living conditions in the camp to be a huge improvement over what he'd been used to in the Dormants' harem.

His mother—*the bitch may she burn in hell*—had hated him with rabid ferocity even before his birth, and it had taken the combined strength of five females to drag her away from the bucket she was trying to drown him in immediately thereafter.

Or so he'd been told.

But considering the way she'd treated him whenever she could put her hands on him, he had no reason to doubt the story.

He'd grown up sleeping in different nooks and crannies and eating scraps from the garbage. Not because the cooks hadn't wanted to feed him, and not because he hadn't been offered a bed to sleep in, but because whenever his bitch of a mother had found him, she'd made sure to let him know just how much she'd hated and despised him.

It had been a miracle he'd survived his mortal childhood to reach the age of transition, and getting there without any permanent deformities had been even a greater miracle. She must've broken nearly every bone in his body…

More than once…

Later, when he was old enough to put one and one together, he'd understood the why.

Not that that understanding had led to forgiveness.

Never.

The bitch had been Navuh's daughter, but unlike her brother Losham and her other half brothers who'd been turned immortal and become leaders, she'd been cast into a whorehouse, relegated to mortality and to serving mortal men with her body for as long as she had remained fertile.

Navuh's daughter hadn't accepted her fate as meekly as the other Dormants. She'd fought off every client, biting and scratching and kicking until overpowered. Consequently, she'd been assigned to males who relished beating and raping her. But though there was never a shortage of those, she'd needed weeks to heal after each assignation before being presentable enough to service the next client, which was probably why she'd only conceived once.

Bless the holy Mortdh.

Parking in his father's driveway, Sharim left his jeep in front of the entry, ascended the three wide steps leading up to the front door, and rang the bell.

One of his father's whores opened the door, her bright, welcoming smile turning into an involuntary cringe when she saw him. She recovered quickly, though, plastering a fake smile on her face. "Greetings, master." She inclined her head. "Please come in. Your father awaits."

Sharim smiled back, committing her features to memory. She was safe for as long as his father kept her around, but eventually Losham would tire of her and send her back.

Sharim would pay her a visit then.

Losham didn't share his son's sadistic proclivities, and after the one time he'd offered Sharim the use of one of his whores, he had never done it again.

Couldn't stomach the screams.

His father was such a soft male.

After all, it wasn't as if Sharim was inflicting permanent damage on the merchandise. The venom healed the bruises and welts in two days tops, and he was always careful not to break any bones or injure any internal organs. That kind of damage took much longer to heal, and he didn't want to be held accountable for all the lost profits from the time it took the whores to recover.

Compared to what his own mother had done to him, Sharim was tender...

Walking behind the whore, his eyes followed her swaying ass. With the two pale cheeks separated only by a narrow strip of red bikini and bouncing enticingly with each of her steps, he imagined adorning them with a different kind of red stripes—crisscrossing the welts—his cane striking mercilessly as she screamed and begged for mercy...

Mercy that he wasn't going to grant.

Whoa... He had to rein himself in.

To greet his father with dripping fangs and a hard-on would be a total lack of decorum…

Digging his nails into his palms hard enough to draw blood, he shifted his eyes away from that enticing ass and focused on the light reflecting from his shiny Dolce & Gabbana loafers.

As the whore pushed through the double doors to his father's study, Sharim wasn't surprised to find the guy seated on the couch with a pretty girl on each side.

"Good morning, Father." Sharim bowed his head a little.

"Come in, son." Losham kissed each pretty on the mouth before gently pushing them up. "Go, have some fun in the pool, girls." He got up and ushered the three out, closing and locking the doors behind them.

This is strange...

Why lock the doors?

"Let's play some chess." His father motioned to the table he'd dedicated to the game.

As always, the beautiful black and white ivory pieces were set up and ready for a new game, and Sharim took his place at the white army's side. His father, a true chess master, always insisted Sharim should have the advantage of making the first move.

Losham poured them each a shot of Macallan whiskey, and handing Sharim his glass, sat across from him in front of the black.

"I was surprised at your summons today, Father. Our game night was just a couple of evenings ago. May I assume you have more than chess on your mind?" Sharim pushed a pawn up.

"Naturally, but why waste an opportunity. It is always an exciting challenge to play against you, Sharim. You're a worthy opponent."

"Yet, you win every time."

"Yes, but it's getting harder. One of these days you are going to best me. And I think sooner rather than later."

"Thank you, I appreciate your confidence in my ability, but I'm afraid it would take another century or two for me to finally win, if ever. You've been winning for a millennium. Nothing has changed."

"Well, this is not entirely true. The name of the game has changed. It used to be Shatranj. Remember?"

"Certainly." Sharim waited patiently for his father to get to the real reason behind the meeting.

Losham made his move and leaned back in his chair. "I am sure you are aware of the success reported by our team in America, yes?"

"Of course."

"In light of his spectacular achievement, eliminating one of our enemies' main assets, the leader of the team requests reinforcements. He wants to go hunting for more of Annani's clan members."

"Yes, I'm well aware of that. But what does it have to do with me? Surely you don't think this kind of mission requires someone of my caliber..."

"Actually, I do. Dalhu got lucky. But this is above his pay grade. And besides, I have more in mind than a simple hunt." Losham smiled.

"Go on..."

"As you know, since the beginning, we have been using two main tactics in our war against Annani and her clan. The first was to support the enemies of her Western allies—those who didn't get to benefit from her stolen knowledge and envied those who did, eager to destroy them. The second was to sow seeds of destruction from the inside, nurturing them with clever propaganda until they grew and multiplied, eating up and destroying from within all of the progress previously achieved. Like we did in WWI and WWII, and many other smaller implosions."

Nothing new here, Sharim thought as he nodded, waiting to see where his father was leading with this simplified rehashing of their age-old strategies.

"But we have never been able to do it to the Americans. Unhindered, they had become the main power to contend with. Lately, though, it seems that the clever Americans lost some of their acuity, letting weeds of their own take root and grow unchecked. They are weakened from the inside."

Now it's getting interesting... Sharim edged closer to the table.

Losham continued, "The Americans losing their leadership position provides us with an amazing opportunity. If we help accelerate that trend, we will achieve WWIII in no time. Without the United States to protect it, the West is up for grabs. The world would revert to the dark ages." Losham's intelligent eyes shone with excitement as he waited for Sharim to make his move.

Sharim ventured with his knight though his mind wasn't on the chessboard anymore. It was now on the larger game at hand.

Losham was obviously letting himself get carried away on the wings of wishful thinking and his own imagination. The United States was still the strongest nation in the world, with the largest, most powerful army, and it would take a lot more than what his father was describing to weaken it. Still, planting weeds in that fertile soil was always a good strategy. One had to be careful about it, though. A few weeds here and there that grew hidden from watchful eyes and undermined the strong foundation that the country was built on were a better strategy than planting whole fields of them and attracting the watchers' attention.

"How do you propose we do it?"

"It is so easy, it is laughable. I do not even need to come up with creative ideas. They did it all for me. All we need to hasten their downfall is a gentle shove."

"I'm listening."

"Do you know why most of the European countries face bankruptcy despite their technology and their lofty democratic ideas?"

Sharim nodded, at the last moment refraining from snorting. "Everyone knows. Not enough people in the workforce to finance runaway government spending."

"Well, apparently not everyone knows because the United States is heading in the same direction, and China is nipping at their heels. Which is another issue we need to address. We need to start planting people there, but that's a discussion for another day."

"So why do we need to do anything? With the trajectory they are on, the American's downfall is inevitable. But then we will have to worry about China."

A cunning smile tugging at his lips, Losham braced his elbows on the table and steepled his fingers. "Yes, but we need to make sure they stay on that path. They could still turn things around. American workers are the most productive in the world, followed by the Germans and the Scandinavians. For now, their productivity keeps their economy from collapsing despite what's happening to their unmotivated and self-entitled younger generation."

He took a sip from his glass before continuing.

"So here is what I want you to do. Besides taking charge of the hunt, that is. You will start working on their media and their movie industry while your counterpart will work on Washington."

"I thought we were already doing that."

"Yes, but we did it in an indirect way, providing funds to organizations that supported our agenda, financing those student organizations in their learning institutions who voiced the views we wanted them to, providing shitloads of money for the campaigns of those we wanted to run their country."

Losham sighed. "The thing is, the big gears are moving, but not fast enough. Lord Navuh is getting impatient. He wants to quicken the pace."

"How?"

"On one front, by threatening and blackmailing anyone who is voicing opposition to the current social trends, and publicly demonizing those that we cannot get to. On the other front, we need to fill the minds of their young people with beliefs and attitudes that would make them the least productive generation that America has ever had. I want you to buy TV stations, cable stations, movie production companies, and controlling interest in news publications. We need to keep the American public's focus on nonsense and away from real issues."

Losham finished the last of his whiskey and got up to refill their glasses.

"I know I am asking a lot from you, son. But if anyone can pull it off without leaving a trail that can lead back to us, it is you. You have done it successfully before."

"What's my budget?"

"Basically unlimited. Lord Navuh is a hundred percent behind this, as are our deep-pocketed allies."

"I must say, I'm impressed with the scope of this campaign, and tremendously flattered to be one of the two entrusted with leading it."

"My part was the long term planning and assigning the right men to implement it. The rest is up to you and your counterpart in Washington. I've been teaching and grooming you for over a thousand years, and you're more than ready, my boy. The logistics and all the rest of the planning minutiae I leave to you."

Sharim pushed up from his chair, and as his father offered him his palm, he bowed and kissed the back of Losham's hand in a show of utmost respect.

"I will not disappoint you, Father."

"I know, my son." Losham pulled him into an embrace. "And if you are successful with this, your next project is going to be China. I don't have a plan yet, but I'm working on it. You and I both have lived long enough to see empires rise and fall. China is going to be the next superpower, and we have to be ready for it."

With his head buzzing with all he'd learned, Sharim got into his jeep and drove back to the base, his plans for spending some pleasant time in the whorehouse completely forgotten.

What a disrespectful fool he'd been for thinking his father was just a yes man for Navuh.

Losham was absolutely brilliant, and apparently Lord Navuh was well aware of the fact, keeping his eldest son at his side not because the man was a pleasant, agreeable companion, but because he was a great strategist.

And such modesty.

Thinking of the few times he'd alluded to his father's unimportant position in the organization, Sharim cringed. Losham had never bothered to correct him, smiling as if agreeing with the misguided perception, when, in fact, he was the one making all those smart plans in their exalted leader's name.

"Checkmate, Father. You win again." Sharim saluted as his headlights turned on, illuminating the dark tunnel leading back to the base.

He was so proud of his father…

So proud to be Losham's son.

8

AMANDA

With the morning's diffused sunshine warming her face, Amanda reluctantly opened her eyes and shifted to her back. The light was coming through the only windows that weren't shuttered, the two small glass triangles flanking the cabin's stone fireplace at its top. Looking out, all she could see were green treetops swaying gently against the cloudless, blue background.

It was a beautiful day.

Somewhere in the mountains...

So yesterday wasn't a bad dream. She really got kidnapped by an insane, huge Doomer, who initially had wanted her for his mate, but owing to her monumental stupidity had probably changed his mind and was going to kill her instead.

The good news was that Dalhu hadn't come back to chop off her head.

Yet...

And perhaps, if luck would have it, he wouldn't come back at all...

So why did she feel a ping of regret at the prospect of never seeing him again?

Because she was an idiot, who had the hots for a Doomer.

And to think that she'd actually started to like the brute. In a way, it was good that she'd discovered his true nature before doing something she would've regretted later. Not that doing the something that she had in mind with Dalhu would've been okay under any circumstances.

Luckily, it was off the table now. Hot or not, the guy was a ticking time bomb.

Scooting to the foot of the bed, she lifted to her knees and took a peek over the railing.

Shit.

Dalhu was sleeping on the couch with his long legs hanging over the armrest, one muscular arm resting on the couch's back, the other hanging down its side.

Naked.

Magnificent.

Unfortunately, the blanket covering his midsection robbed her of a full frontal view.

Bummer.

You are an idiot, Amanda.

This man, as mouth-watering as he was, was a killer.

With a sigh, she tore her eyes away from all that maleness, grabbed her purse, and tiptoed to the bathroom.

One look at the vanity mirror and her mood plummeted even lower. She looked just as awful as she felt. Or perhaps worse. There were dark circles under her eyes that had nothing to do with the black mascara smudges, her hair was a messed-up jungle and not half as glossy as it usually was after shampooing and conditioning with her custom-formulated hair products, and the pink sweats she was wearing were absolutely hideous.

Looking horrible, in addition to having a homicidal lunatic sleeping down on the couch, was utterly depressing.

Amanda sighed. There was nothing to be done about the pink polyester monstrosity, but she could do something about the hair and the face. Splashing cold water on her head helped to tame the wild mess into something manageable, and she felt a little better after washing her face and applying makeup.

Trouble was, once done with her morning routine, there was nothing to distract her from how parched she was or how empty her stomach felt. Going down to the kitchen, though, risked rousing the angry bear on the couch.

Another trip to the bathroom took care of the thirst problem. Though blah… drinking water from the faucet was a new low for her. Still, there was the issue of her growling tummy. A quick search through her purse yielded nothing edible—unless one counted the cherry-flavored lip gloss.

Oh, what the hell.

Slinking down the stairs, she did her best to avoid making any noise, putting as little weight as possible on the wooden stairs and bracing most of it on the wall-side railing.

She made it all the way down without waking Dalhu, but then couldn't resist getting a little closer for a better look.

Big mistake.

With him being so yummy, and her being so hungry—and not strictly for food—she had to shove a fist into her mouth and bite it to stifle the involuntary moan.

You're such a stupid slut, Amanda! Inching back, she turned around and tiptoed into the kitchen.

Another peanut butter sandwich coming up. Yippiee ki-yay.

Her cardboard-tasting creation in hand, Amanda leaned against the counter and eyed the cold pot of coffee Dalhu had made last night. But even though it was right there on the stove, she didn't dare heat it up. Turning on the electric stove would be soundless, but the boiling water was sure to make some noise. Even she knew as much.

Oh, hell. Old, cold coffee is better than none. Right?

Or maybe not.

The stuff tasted like mud. Not that she'd ever eaten dirt before... but if it quacked like a duck, it probably tasted like one too, and all that...

"I'll make you a new one." Dalhu's deep voice had her whip around so fast that she got dizzy and listed to the side, putting a hand out to steady herself.

In a flash, he was right next to her, propping her up by her elbow. "Easy there, girl."

Her heart up in her throat, Amanda scooted away and wedged herself into a corner of cabinets. Not that it offered any real shelter, but with Dalhu blocking the way she had nowhere to go.

He didn't move a muscle. Standing near the sink and clutching the blanket he wore like a sarong around his hips, he looked at her with dark, sorrowful eyes. "Please, Amanda, don't be afraid of me. I would never, ever, hurt you. I swear."

"Could've fooled me. Just take a look at the poor wall you took your anger out on. You demolished half of it with your bare fist." She motioned to the gaping hole in the wall across from the fridge. "I'm just glad it wasn't my face."

Dalhu winced. "I'm sorry. So sorry that I got angry. But I would've never raised my hand to you. You must believe that. You have nothing to fear. Walls, on the other hand, are a different story." He attempted a smile.

"The mindless beast that you turned into wasn't doing much thinking. You were completely out of control. After you left, I hid under the blanket for hours, afraid to fall asleep, just waiting for you to come back and chop off my head..." The expression of horror contorting his face stopped her mid-rant.

"Never! Oh, hell, Amanda, I would rather die a thousand horrible deaths than hurt you. You must believe me…" He reached for her cheek, but she flinched away.

"I'm so sorry." Dalhu let his hand drop by his side. "I'm going to get dressed. When I come back, I'll make you a new pot of coffee." He spun around and headed for the stairs.

Amanda remained glued to her spot until she heard the bathroom's floorboards squeak under Dalhu's weight. Releasing a relieved breath, she pushed away from the corner and with a shaky hand lifted her abandoned sandwich.

Unfortunately, as much as Amanda wanted to believe him, she couldn't trust Dalhu's promises. He might've meant each and every one, but then his intentions were not the problem.

The big question was whether his higher reasoning functioned at all when he raged. Unbalanced and combustive, he was like a stick of dynamite. She figured it wouldn't take more than a tiny spark to ignite him. And like the explosive, Dalhu wouldn't discriminate about what got caught in his circle of destruction.

Still, explosive or not, the man sure as hell was dynamite-hot, Amanda thought as Dalhu came down to the kitchen looking like a model from GQ magazine in a pair of Balmain jeans and a Tom Ford button-down. Not that he didn't look amazing with nothing more than a blanket tied around his hips, but damn… it was her turn to do a little drooling.

Except, where the hell did he get that designer getup? She frowned. "You certainly cleaned up nicely. Question is, how is it that you get to wear fancy stuff while I'm wearing cheap, butt-ugly sweats?" Indignation overriding trepidation, Amanda placed her hands on her hips and began tapping her bare foot on the linoleum floor.

"Everything is dirty, and I have nothing to wear aside from these faggot clothes. And the only reason I have this shit with me in the first place is that I'd been shopping for appropriate attire to wear to an exclusive club when I got sidetracked by my dream girl. But once the laundry is done, we can both go back to wearing what we had on yesterday."

"Don't get me wrong, you look very nice... not gayish at all, very manly in fact... Wait a second, what was that about laundry? Don't tell me you put my things in the washer!"

"Why? What's the problem? I know how to use one."

"My clothes are dry-clean only, you stupid man. You ruined them!" Amanda threw her hands in the air. "Where is that thing? Maybe I can still salvage something."

Dalhu didn't respond. Instead, he glared at her with a murderous expression on his face—his silence as loud and as terrifying as the worst of thunderstorms.

Oh, boy, I did it again, didn't I.

"I'm so sorry. You're not stupid. Really... it's just an expression. Please don't kill me..." Cringing, she backed into the corner again.

9

DALHU

What the hell was she apologizing for? He was the one that had failed her yet again, ruining her clothes. Would he ever do anything right for this woman? He'd thought it would be a nice surprise, getting her things clean so she could go back to wearing her fancy clothes. How was he supposed to know that her stuff wasn't washable? It wasn't as if he had ever done a woman's laundry before…

And what the fuck was the *"please don't kill me"* about?

"I'm the one who should be apologizing for ruining your things, not you, and I'm angry with myself, not you. But you've got to stop that cowering routine you got going on because *that* really pisses me off." Dalhu drew in a calming breath and hung his head. "And you are absolutely right. I'm stupid and incompetent. I want to take good care of you, but instead, I keep failing time and again."

He waited for the longest moment for Amanda to say something.

She didn't. Not even when she moved out of that damned corner, walked over to the dining table and plopped down on a chair.

Sitting as she did with her back to him, he couldn't see her face. Was she angry? Sad? Should he go to her? Leave her alone to stew?

But then her shoulders began heaving.

Oh, hell.

He rushed to her side, but she wasn't crying.

Soon, what had started as a soft chuckle turned into a bubbling laugh, her whole body shaking with it.

What the fuck?

Did she really think any of this was funny?

Or perhaps it was some form of hysterics, and any moment now her laughter would turn into sobs.

But as she kept at it, laughing and wiping the tears away with the sleeves of her sweatshirt, he got caught up in her madness and joined in, laughing so hard he had to sit down because he got a stitch in his side.

Dalhu couldn't remember the last time he'd laughed so hard, and it felt foreign—like a language he'd once known, but had forgotten. The sounds were familiar, but he found it difficult to form them in his throat, his mouth…

"Oh, Dalhu, what a mismatched pair we are," Amanda croaked once she caught her breath. "Yin and yang. Black and white. What are we going to do?" She regarded him warily, her eyes saying the things she was afraid to voice.

The same arguments she had from the start. That there was no way to bridge the differences between them. That there was no real chance for them to find common ground. That he was deluding himself if he thought they could build a life together.

But what she failed to understand was that he'd never give up, never stop trying. That he might fail over and over again, but in time he'd learn. And as he had all the time in the world for all the do-overs ever needed, in the end, he'd prevail.

If he'd learned one lesson in his long life, it was that perseverance was the key to success. It wasn't the smartest or the most talented who rose to positions of power, in business as well as in politics or even in the military—it was the one who kept pushing. The earth would not be inherited by the meek, and not even by those born with the advantage of superior intelligence or physical attributes. The earth was ruled by those who worked relentlessly toward achieving their goals, those who always got up after falling, those who never accepted defeat.

Like him.

Dalhu got to his feet and walked over to the other side of the table to stand beside her. "What we're going to do is talk, a lot. We are going to ask questions and get to know each other. But first, I'm going to make us a fresh pot of coffee and something to eat."

Gazing up at him, Amanda's huge blue eyes were red-rimmed from her tears, and her dark makeup was smeared all over her face. And still, the woman was a vision.

"It will be all right. You'll see." He smoothed her short, glossy hair with his palm. Bending down, he kissed her forehead, not trusting himself to kiss her lips again.

"Yeah, if you don't kill me first..." He heard her murmur under her breath as he moved over to the stove.

"Would you stop that already?" he grated as he dumped the old coffee in the sink.

The excessive force he'd used caused the dark slosh to splatter, getting all over the cabinets and staining his brand new, six-hundred-dollar shirt.

As a veil of red clouded his vision, Dalhu felt a roar pushing up from his gut.

That was it.

He couldn't take it anymore. He was going to explode.

The built-up pressure was seeking release, and it would just blow out of the top of his head and put an end to his misery.

A crazed chuckle escaped his throat as he thought of the irony of surviving countless battles only to be done in by a cold pot of coffee.

No.

Not again.

He couldn't explode like a fucking madman and terrify Amanda. He had to fight the rage. Dalhu gripped the edge of the sink with such force that the tiles under his fingers began crumbling.

"Breathe, Dalhu. It's okay. It's only a shirt. If you take it off, I'll wash it right away, and there'll be no stains."

The effect of Amanda's calm voice, combined with the feel of her delicate hand going up and down over the knotted muscles of his back was—for lack of a better word—miraculous. Like a gentle wave of cool water, it washed over the raging inferno consuming him, putting the fire out and soothing his raw nerves.

Dalhu closed his eyes and breathed in long and hard before letting the air back out, then did it again until his breathing evened out.

"Better?" Amanda asked quietly, her hand never ceasing its soothing up and down trek on his back.

"Yes, thank you," he breathed just as quietly.

"Is it okay if I wash your shirt now?"

"Yes." Dalhu spun around, facing Amanda, but that was as far as he was able to go. If she wanted his shirt, she'd have to take it off herself.

She peered up at him with worry in her big eyes. "Are you sure you're okay? You look a little dazed. Maybe you should sit down."

"No, I'm fine. I just need a moment..."

"Okay, big guy. Take your time." Amanda reached for the first button, then paused, waiting for his assent.

"Please." He nodded.

Going slowly, as if afraid to spook a wild animal, Amanda unbuttoned his shirt. She then spread the two halves and pushed it down his shoulders until he finally helped her by shrugging it off.

"I'll take it up to the bathroom and wash it there. You just take your time." Amanda dropped her eyes to the shirt she was holding and eased back.

"Wait..." Dalhu caught her arm. "Please, I need to feel your hand on me again." She regarded him quizzically, but didn't resist as he took her palm and placed it on his bare skin, right over where his heart was still hammering a crazy beat.

The effect was immediate, with that soothing calm washing over him once again. "You're an angel..." he breathed in awe, holding his palm over her hand and keeping it on him for as long as she would let him.

"I think you're a little confused... delirious. But thank you." Amanda blushed prettily.

What a strange and wonderful creature she was. An innocent compliment made her blush while talking about her numerous lovers left her completely unaffected. "I called you an angel because what you've been able to do for me is nothing short of a miracle."

"I'm glad. Now let me go before this shirt is a goner." She tried to pull away.

"Fuck the shirt... I'm sorry. I shouldn't use foul language around you."

"Don't be ridiculous, Dalhu. Stop trying so hard and just relax. I'm really not an angel, and a fuck here and there doesn't offend me —" She stopped and slapped a hand over her mouth, a shadow of fear crossing her eyes.

He chuckled. "It's okay. I'm over the shocking newsflash that immortal females have a healthy sex appetite to match that of their males. And I'm starting to get your twisted sense of humor as well. In fact, I love it." He closed his fingers over the hand she was covering her mouth with and lifted it to his lips for a light kiss. "I want you to feel free to say whatever is on your mind. Always. And if I get angry, again... Well, we have the antidote. All you need to do is touch me..."

"You sure? I have a really big mouth, and it has no filter."

"Positive."

"In that case... how long do I have to wait for a cup of coffee around here? I'm telling you, the service in this establishment is just subpar…" She winked.

Reluctantly, he let go of her hands. "It is, isn't it?"

"Well, get on it, big guy."

"Yes, ma'am."

10

SHARIM

By nightfall, Sharim had his two lieutenants and an administrative assistant for the mission selected. From the troop under his command, he'd chosen seventy-two of his best warriors.

Unlike the other commanders, who led by fear and intimidation, Sharim treated his men well and thus earned their loyalty. He spent time with them, knew each one by name and temperament, and knew exactly what could be expected from whom.

Those who knew him as a commander had a hard time believing that he was a self-proclaimed sadist and proud of it. Not surprisingly, they couldn't reconcile the charming, soft-spoken guy with someone who loved inflicting pain on others. Well, women in particular. Though, if needed, he had no problem torturing males for information. It just didn't turn him on.

Besides, he believed that if one was smart, one didn't mix business with pleasure, and what he did for sex during his free time had no bearing on his job.

Which brought his train of thought to the issue of scheduling a scene for tonight. After all that good work, he was in an exceptionally good mood—excited and full of energy. Hence, instead of selecting one of the newbies, he decided to call for the one hooker that actually enjoyed his kind of attention.

A quick text and he had it arranged. Once he was done in the office, Marla would be waiting for him, kneeling naked by the door the way he liked. After all, there were some advantages to dealing with an experienced sub—one who was well familiar with his particular preferences—instead of torturing some uninitiated tart...

Good, good, good... Sharim rubbed his hands and went over his list again.

It had been a productive day. An excellent utilization of time and resources—if he may say so himself.

After explaining how he wanted to go about it, Sharim had assigned the task of arranging the elaborate travel plans to his assistant.

There would be no more traveling in groups.

He had been appalled when he'd seen the travel arrangements for the small unit that had uncovered the clan's American location. They had been extremely lucky that airport security had not tagged them as suspects. Three groups of four men in the span of only two days. The least they could have done was to divide the groups unevenly. But this was what happened when travel arrangements were left to low-level bureaucrats.

The administrative branch of their army consisted of the least capable personnel, those who'd been deemed too inferior to be warriors. The best way to utilize their meager capabilities was to provide them with clear and precise step-by-step instructions. But apparently Dalhu, the leader of that group, had failed to do so.

Well, not really the guy's fault. An organization should keep examining and reexamining its procedures and install new ones when something didn't work as smoothly as it should. He would e-mail the head of that department and suggest that a new procedure be put in place for every commander to follow upon traveling on an assignment to the West. And just to be clear, he'd include his own clever travel plans as a blueprint.

Once the island's transport plane dropped them off at Kuala Lumpur, Malaysia, each man would fly to a different destination in the world, going through at least two other countries with a different fake passport for each leg of the trip before arriving at Los Angeles International Airport.

Sharim, one of his lieutenants, and his personal assistant would leave tomorrow morning. The zigzag route that he had planned for them would get them to their final destination in about seventy-two hours.

Starting two weeks later, the rest of the men would follow, trickling in over a period of several days.

He'd have plenty of time to take care of the rest of the logistics en route and then once he got to Los Angeles.

First and foremost on his agenda was securing a suitable place for a base and arranging for weapons and other supplies to be purchased and delivered for when the men arrived. The modifications and fortifications could be done while the men were already there, but the perimeter had to be secured with a proper fence and surveillance equipment beforehand.

With a few phone calls to the Brotherhood's contacts in Los Angeles, he'd arranged a search for appropriate properties—the promise of a five-figure cash commission and a bonus for fast delivery lighting a fire under the two Realtors' butts.

Hopefully, by tomorrow there would be some good properties lined up for him, and he'd be able to close a deal before reaching his next stop.

11

AMANDA

Check me out, playing house, like a good little woman…

Amanda hung the shirt she'd washed by hand on the shower curtain rod.

But what the hell, if Dalhu could cook and do laundry, she could deign to wash one shirt. And anyway, she was quite satisfied with herself for getting all the stains out.

Judging by the enticing smells coming from the kitchen, coffee was ready and Dalhu was cooking something that smelled pretty good. Unfortunately, being the one who'd unpacked their supplies, she was well aware of what he had to work with and doubted that she'd find the end product of his efforts edible.

If that man wasn't planning to starve her, he really needed to go shopping. And if she didn't want a repeat of the general store fiasco, she'd better make him a detailed list.

Amanda pulled a pen out of her purse and, for lack of other options, tore a big piece off one of the brown paper bags from the general store Dalhu had robbed.

Well, he did leave some money to cover the cost of what he took.

Wasted his money was more like it. It was all the worst quality of junk. As soon as he delivered the new supplies, she'd have him throw out all that stuff.

Everything except the pink monstrosity she was wearing.

That, she would burn and dance a victory dance around the fire. Though with all its polyester content, she wasn't sure if it would burn or melt.

"Breakfast is ready!" Dalhu called from the kitchen.

"Coming!"

Well, I wish I were... Naughty, naughty Amanda. Put a brake on your one-track mind...

Holding her pen and a piece of the brown paper bag, she jogged down the stairs.

Dalhu had the table set with two plates heaped with something unrecognizable and two cups of coffee… one already whitened with the condensed milk.

"Thank you," she said as she sat down next to where he'd placed it.

"You are welcome. I hope you like it." Dalhu smiled and sat across from her.

Amanda moved things around her plate with the fork, trying to guess what was in the weird mush. "You know how you said I should say whatever I want?"

"Yes. What's the matter? You haven't even tasted it yet…"

"No, I know. It's just that it's a sure thing I'm going to bitch about it, and I thought saying something nice first would be a good idea."

"Okay?" He cocked an eyebrow.

"First, thank you for remembering how I like my coffee, and for making this food, and setting the table, and everything… And for looking real fine without a shirt…"

Dalhu almost choked on what was in his mouth. "Really? Well… you're welcome… and thank you." He barely managed to get the words out. "Now, please, just taste it. It's not as bad as it looks."

"Okay. Here goes…" Amanda lifted a tiny amount of the slosh

with her fork, hesitating before bringing the stuff into her mouth. When it didn't trigger an immediate gag reflex, she gave chewing a try.

Dalhu's eyes were on her mouth, the poor guy forgetting to breathe as he awaited her verdict.

"It's edible. Which considering what you had to work with is an accomplishment. But unless you think I need to lose a lot of weight, you'd better go shopping." She was being generous. The stuff tasted just a tad better than throw-up, but she had no heart to tell him that.

"I don't want you to lose even an ounce. You're perfect the way you are. Make the list and I'll see what I can do. But for now this is all we have, and I don't want you to go hungry until I come back." He motioned to her plate and waited.

She forced herself to take a few forkfuls, washing down each one with generous gulps of coffee, but as soon as Dalhu shifted his attention to his own plate, she got busy making the list.

Taking into consideration that Dalhu had limited experience with shopping, she decided to group the items on her list by store and the department they could be found at. The clothing and undergarments, as well as cosmetics and skincare, were the easiest—she'd shopped for these herself and knew exactly where to get them. After all, it shouldn't matter that she had shopped at Bloomingdales and Saks while Dalhu would be lucky to find a Macy's. One department store shouldn't be all that different from another, at least as far as the configuration went. The rest of the stuff, the things Onidu took care of like bedding and food, she had to guess.

When she was done, the brown piece of paper was covered in her tight, messy script. "My handwriting is really messy. I think I should read it to you. Or better yet, come with you…" She glanced at him hopefully.

"Not a chance, princess, not this time."

"When, then? You can't keep me here forever. I'll go crazy. There is no TV, no Internet, nothing for me to do…"

"I realize that." Dalhu sighed. "I just need a little more time to figure out my next step. It's not like I had this whole thing planned out. And besides, I don't trust you not to run. Yet... I'm sorry."

With a huff, Amanda crossed her arms over her chest. "Well, it was worth a try."

The rest of the meal went by with her glaring at Dalhu and him polishing off both his plate and hers. She didn't offer to help him when he cleared the dishes, washed them, and wiped the table clean.

He didn't deserve it.

Once he was done, he came to stand beside her and offered her a hand up. "Come. Let's see that list."

"I'm mad at you." She shrugged.

"I know. But I'm sure getting the things on that list is more important to you than staying mad at me."

Well, when he put it like that...

She let him pull her up and walk her to the couch, where he had her sit beside him as he tried to decipher her scribbles.

12

DALHU

Amanda had no way of knowing that he was already familiar with her peculiar handwriting, and although he planned on telling her everything at some point in the future, that point wasn't now.

He had spent hours with her little notebook, the one his men had found in her lab, learning a lot from it. Her chicken scribbles, as he'd at first referred to her handwriting, were mostly about her research, both the official one that she had done for the university and the unofficial one she'd run on mortals with paranormal abilities. But not only. Between her random ideas and her little drawings he had glimpsed her unique personality, her mischievous streak, her loyalty to her clan, and how much their loneliness, as well as her own, weighed heavily on her.

Granted, it felt wrong to pretend he was having more trouble understanding what she'd written than he actually did, but as the saying went: all was fair in love and battle… or something along those lines.

As it was, though, Amanda must've been out of her mind if she thought he could get everything on her list, or that he even knew what some of the things were...

"Fifteen hundred TC organic Egyptian cotton bed sheets? What the hell does it even mean? Or that Japanese sounding moisturizer thing, Shiseido?"

"It's nothing complicated. Any decent department store will have all of those things. Look, I organized the list by departments; all you need to do is find a Nordstrom or a Bloomingdales or even a Macy's and ask a salesperson in each department to help you."

Was it a trick? A guy like him shopping for stuff like that and asking for help would be hard to forget. Was she planning to leave a trail for those searching for her? But his nose was telling him she was excited but not fearful, which she would have been if she was planning some subterfuge.

"Okay. I'll see what I can do. Let's move to the food list. What does good bread that doesn't taste like cardboard mean? How am I supposed to know which one tastes good to you without a brand name? And other than the bread, all I see is an assortment of cheeses, frozen pizzas, and fruits. Where is the rest of the stuff, like meat and eggs, fresh vegetables?"

"First of all, I'm a vegetarian. I don't eat meat. Second, my expertise at buying food is limited to picking stuff from a restaurant menu. And that goes for cooking as well..." Amanda leaned back and crossed her arms over her chest. "If you wanted someone to cook and clean for you, you certainly picked the wrong girl," she added with a snort.

"No, I wasn't looking for a maid. I was looking for a mate, a partner. I couldn't care less that you're challenged in these areas..." He flashed her a sideways grin.

Her eyes narrowed into slits and she pursed her lips, looking absolutely stunning despite her peeved expression.

Oh, man, did she have any idea what she was doing to him with those lush lips of hers puffed and begging to be kissed? If she didn't, she was soon going to find out.

Quick as a snake, he struck, taking those lips in a hungry kiss. When she didn't resist, he pushed her down on the couch and deepened the kiss, his tongue licking into the sweetness of her mouth.

Amanda moaned, grabbing his shoulders to bring him closer to her chest... Then, with a growl, she gave a strong shove and pushed him off.

Damn, she was strong for a woman. Which shouldn't have surprised him. It made perfect sense that if immortal males were stronger than their human counterparts, so were the females.

Amanda jumped off the couch. Holding the torn piece of paper with her list, she pointed at the door. "You need to get going. I don't know how far you need to drive to get me what I need, so you'd better hurry." She panted, her other hand resting over her racing heart.

"I will, in a moment. First, a little safety talk. I'm not going to lock you in because I don't want to risk you being trapped inside in case of a fire or an earthquake. But I don't want you wandering outside. And I'm not saying this to keep you from trying to escape. We are hours away from civilization and there are wild animals out there. So please, be smart about it and don't leave the cabin, not even to sit on the porch. And don't open the door to get fresh air in either—or any other such bright ideas. I'm serious." He pinned her with a hard stare.

"I got it. No going outside, and no opening the door. Now go..."

"Promise. I want you to swear on it."

Amanda rolled her eyes. "Sheesh! I promise! Swear to Bob and all that... I'm not stupid, you know."

When he still didn't move, she threw her hands in the air. "Men," she muttered under her breath before stomping away and climbing the stairs to the loft.

"I'll be back as soon as I can," he called after her.

Without looking back, she shrugged and then disappeared into the bathroom.

Dalhu almost made it out the door when he remembered he was shirtless.

Going up the stairs, he glanced toward the bathroom door, hoping to get a peek of what she was doing in there, but Amanda had propped something against it to hold it closed.

Damn.

He grabbed another one of the fancy shirts and shrugged it on, buttoning it on his way out.

Out on the porch, he lifted the loose plank and pulled out the car keys and his duffle bag. Not that he needed weapons and ammunition for his acquisition trip, or his laptop, but with Amanda left unsupervised and with plenty of time on her hands, she might get the urge to do some reconnaissance.

13

AMANDA

As the sun began its slow descent, Amanda got hungry again. But the thought of eating another peanut butter-covered cardboard was motivation enough to endure the hunger pangs for a little longer.

She could wait until Dalhu showed up with something edible.

What the hell was taking him so long? It had been more than six hours since he had left. For his sake, she hoped he'd come back with everything on her list, otherwise… what?

Well, she could ignore him. There wasn't much else she could do. It wasn't as if she could stomp her foot and walk out on him. With a *humph*. Except, being ignored would probably hurt Dalhu enough. The way he was desperate for every little crumb of affection she threw his way…

Poor guy.

Damn, she was hungry. What if he wouldn't be back for hours?

But she really couldn't stomach another sandwich. She'd rather starve.

Then again, maybe she could open a can of corn and another one of beans and mix them together.

Shouldn't be too bad...

Oh, how low the mighty have fallen...

Pulling the two cans down from the upper cupboard, she read the instructions.

Good, it said on the labels that the stuff didn't need cooking.

She scooped a little from each can and mixed the ingredients, then took the plate with her culinary creation to the table and set it down next to the book she'd been reading for the past couple of hours.

It wasn't that she found the history of jet fighter planes all that fascinating, but she was going out of her mind with boredom. And unfortunately, airplanes were the subject of each and every one of the small collection of books gathering dust over the fireplace mantel.

She'd already finished the one about the invention of modern flying machines, which had been kind of interesting, but the rest of the modest selection was mostly about famous jet fighter battles that were just too sad to read about, so she was stuck with the one in front of her.

Shoving a forkful of the mix into her mouth, she distracted herself from the bland stuff by trying to picture the cabin's owner. It was a guy, that was for certain, a bachelor or a widower, or someone that treated the cabin as his private man cave because the place was completely devoid of a woman's touch.

On the other hand, a man wouldn't have installed a claw-foot tub in the bathroom for himself. So he either had bought the cabin from a couple or had a woman and lost her... a long time ago. A widower then. Probably a veteran, maybe a survivalist...

As far as utilities, the cabin was self-sufficient, and if the guy were a hunter, he could choose to live up here indefinitely...

Oh, Fates. She hoped that wasn't what Dalhu had in mind when he brought her here.

Talk about cabin fever.

She'd rather take her chances with the bears and the coyotes and whatever else was lurking outside than stay cooped up in here and go slowly insane.

Forget slowly. It would take no more than one more day with nothing to do.

She had to find a way out.

If her assumptions about the guy who owned the cabin were true, then there was a good chance he had a rifle stashed somewhere around. Not that she planned to shoot Dalhu with it, though using it to clobber him over the head was an option…

She needed the rifle to make it to civilization without getting eaten on the way.

Why hadn't she thought about it sooner? With Dalhu gone for hours, she could've searched the place thoroughly at an easy pace.

Now, she might be already out of time.

It took her less than half an hour to conduct a frantic though thorough search to produce nothing more lethal than a broom.

She even knocked on the walls in the hopes of finding a hidden storage compartment. It wasn't completely out of left field. After all, the washer-dryer combo was hidden behind a panel in the bathroom. She would've never found it if not for the noise the machine was making. Which reminded her that the drying cycle was probably done a long time ago.

Whatever. First she had to finish the search before the sun set and before her kidnapper got back.

Opening the front door just a little more than a crack, she scanned the porch and the area around the cabin, even giving her sense of smell a go. Not that she'd ever sniffed for wild animals before, but she figured the smell of one predator ready to pounce shouldn't be all that different from another, and she was well acquainted with the smell of the most dangerous one—a male immortal. But if there was anything out there, it was too far away for her to smell.

Or at least she hoped so…

With a quick sprint, she dashed for the shed, then closed the door behind her and bolted it for good measure.

It was dark inside, but with the little light filtering through the cracks, she was able to see the single naked lightbulb hanging from the ceiling rafters. It took her a moment of searching for the light switch to realize that the string hanging down from the thing was the way to go about turning it on, and she pulled.

The good news, if one could call it that, was that there was enough wood stored in the shed to keep the cabin warm all winter long, and there were a couple of shovels in case they got snowed in. A few simple tools hung from pegs on the wall, and there was even an electric table saw. But the bad news was that there was no rifle.

Not ready to give up yet, she searched behind and under anyplace she could reach. When she didn't find anything useful, Amanda gave the shovels another glance. In a pinch, a shovel might prove handy… well, maybe against one predator, but certainly not a pack.

For clobbering Dalhu, though…

If she managed to knock him out for long enough, she could take the car. No need to fight off wild animals then.

But did she have the guts?

If she attacked him and failed, he might kill her despite all of his promises to the contrary. Though in truth? She was an immortal and not that easy to kill. Dalhu might get angry and go as far as inflicting some serious pain, but she'd never truly believed he would deliberately take the steps necessary to end her immortal life. One didn't sever a head or cut out a heart in a fit of anger.

At least she hoped not.

So why had she kept saying it? Because it sounded more dramatic than one hell of a beating, and besides, she'd gotten carried away, believing her own exaggerations.

Question was, where could she hide a shovel within easy reach?

Duh, under the couch, where else...

With the shovel in hand, she did the whole scan and sniff routine again before sprinting back to the cabin, then stashed the contraband under the couch…

Wait... that wouldn't work.

If Dalhu spent another night on the sofa, he might accidentally find it. And besides, it was stupid to hide the shovel where she would need to get close to Dalhu just to pull it out—and probably wake him before having a chance to do anything.

It would be better to hide it under the bed. Where she slept…

But wait… that wouldn't work either.

Damn.

With the new bedsheets she'd had him buy, he might offer to help her make the bed and discover the shovel hidden under it.

Oh, well, there was no other place that made sense. She had to chance it.

14

KRI

"Come on, Michael, stop torturing yourself and take the meds." Why were guys so stupid? There was no reason for him to suffer through the pain of growing fangs and venom glands. Not when Dr. Bridget offered to prescribe him perfectly safe painkillers and knock him out. At least until the worst part was over.

Thank the merciful Fates, though, that this was the extent of Michael's ordeal. Syssi had almost died going through hers.

Kian must've been to hell and back watching the woman he loved fighting for her life. Poor guy. And instead of celebrating Syssi's successful transition, he was heading out on a rescue mission to bring Amanda back.

Damn, I would've liked to be on that team... Not that Kian would've ever agreed to take a female Guardian on a mission like that. He was progressive, but not that progressive. And anyway, someone had to take care of Michael.

"No," Michael mumbled through the ice chips he'd stuffed in his mouth to numb the pain. "Ice is hepin..."

Poor baby, he couldn't even move his tongue to make the L

sound. Or the G. But whose fault was that? Maybe his mentor could talk some sense into that mulish head of his. She turned to Yamanu, who'd been grinning since this whole argument had started. "Talk to him. Maybe the stubborn ass will listen to you."

"He is a big boy." Yamanu shrugged. "There were no meds when I was a boy, and I lived through it. He can tough it out if he wants to."

Kri threw her hands in the air. "Argh, you men are all idiots."

Yamanu patted her shoulder. "Let the boy be a man, Kri, and witness his own transition. Would you like to be knocked out during the most transformative event of your life? Like maybe when you become a mother?"

"You can bet your ass, I would. I'm not as dumb as some of those women who want a *natural* birthing experience. If I ever deliver a baby, I want to have all the painkillers I can get. There is no glory in unnecessary suffering." Glaring at Yamanu, she crossed her arms over her chest.

Yamanu pushed away from the wall he'd been leaning against and gave Michael a pitying glance. "Well, boy, I did my best. You're on your own. See ya later." He waved and left Bridget's recovery room.

Kri sighed and sat down on the bed next to Michael. "I just can't stand seeing you in so much pain."

Michael reached for her hand and gave it a squeeze.

"How about you at least take the codeine, it's not going to knock you out cold, just take the edge off."

Michael closed his eyes for a moment, then nodded.

"Hallelujah! I'm going to get Bridget. Don't go anywhere!" She kissed his forehead, careful to stay away from his cheeks, then hurried out to search for the doctor.

Kri found Bridget in her office, busy typing furiously on her keyboard. "Dr. Bridget, I finally managed to persuade Michael to take the codeine. Could you give it to him? Like right now? I can't stand another minute of seeing him like that."

"Sure, give me a moment. I'll be right there."

"Thank you."

My poor, proud baby, Kri thought on her way back to Michael's room—the small recovery room in Bridget's clinic he'd been staying in since he'd begun his transition.

Which brought to mind the question of Michael's future accommodations. Now that he'd become an immortal there was no reason to keep holding him in the *Guest Suite*—as they called the fancy prison cell where Michael had been spending his time until now. Their secret was now his secret as well.

He should move in with me. I need to take care of him.

Not that she had any plans of letting him go once he got better. After his transition, Michael had become a most valuable asset—the first and, for now, only male immortal not from the same matrilineal descent as the rest of her clan, and she had no intention of allowing some other clan female to steal him away from her.

Andrew, Syssi's brother, was another potential candidate, but he was older. And as they had discovered with Syssi, the older the Dormant, the harder the transition went. He might decide not to risk it. And anyway, she liked Michael. The only problem? He was so damn young. But she was in no rush. She could wait for him to mature.

Best thing to do was to stake her claim, and the sooner, the better. She needed to talk to the chief Guardian and ask his permission to move Michael to her apartment. On second thought, she should also ask Onegus for some leave of absence to take care of her guy.

First, though, she needed to make some quick redecorations before she brought Michael to her place. It was just too girly. Living alone, and not in the habit of inviting anyone over, she didn't care if her place looked like the inside of a candy store. There was pink everywhere—pink walls, a pink coverlet on her queen-sized bed, and even pink cushions on the periwinkle sofa.

But the pink, though, wasn't as embarrassing as the posters.

Hunky actors and male models were her preferred wall ornaments. And she had quite a few.

She would die of embarrassment if anyone ever saw the inside of her apartment. She was supposed to be this tough cookie, and she was, on the outside. On the inside, she liked to be a girl, and not any girl, a girly-girl.

Michael was in for one heck of a surprise.

15

DALHU

While Dalhu chilled in the coffee shop across from the department store, the forty-something nothing-special he'd charmed the pants off was doing all the legwork of finding and buying the female-specific items on Amanda's list with the money he'd given her.

So, if Amanda hoped that a man like him shopping for bras and thongs and lotions would be too conspicuous to forget, Dalhu had managed to outsmart her.

Uneducated doesn't mean stupid, Professor...

The woman he'd chosen for the task had been more than happy to help poor, helpless him with the list of items his *little sister,* who was moving back home after graduating college, had asked him to buy for her.

When the woman came back, shopping bags galore, he thanked her, kissed her cheek, and promised to call.

Feeling a little guilty, he offered to pay her for her efforts, but she refused to accept the money...

Just as he'd known she would.

Her loss. He wouldn't be delivering the kind of payment he'd hinted on...

Next stop was the supermarket, where he did nothing more clandestine than slouching and drooping his shoulders to look smaller.

So all in all, he did well.

But it had taken him three hours to reach the nearest mall that had one of the department stores Amanda had listed, and about an hour and a half to complete all of the purchases. He had three more hours of driving to do.

It was getting dark by the time he drove up the steep incline of the private, unpaved road that lead up to the cabin.

Dalhu couldn't help the sense of excited anticipation as he imagined Amanda's happy welcome, especially upon discovering the gourmet cheeses he'd bought for her, not to mention the wine the lady at the cheese counter had suggested would accompany them nicely.

He'd bought four bottles. Just in case.

Except, as much as Amanda hated those pink sweats, she might go for the clothes first.

Hopefully, his personal shopper had done a good job with those. After all, he'd chosen her not for her looks, but for how well she'd been dressed.

At first, he'd intended to find a woman that looked wealthy—less chance of her running off with his money. But when his eyes had landed on, what was her name, Judy? he'd known she was exactly what he was looking for. In addition to her expensive-looking clothes, she was tall and slim and had Amanda's coloring. Though, that was where the resemblance ended. Where Amanda was a vision of beauty, poor Judy was more of a Plain Jane.

Telling her that she looked a lot like his *sister* had actually been the pickup line he'd used. And when he'd added that he liked what she was wearing and it was exactly the kind of stuff his sister would love, she had been his. Even before he'd told her to feel free to add to the list.

He hadn't bothered to check what was in the bags. Except one. He just couldn't help himself from going through the pink one from that lingerie store, Victoria's Closet, or something like that. Holding those tiny panties had given him a raging hard-on, especially the little white thong with a bow at the back. Picturing Amanda wearing it, with nothing else on, was the stuff of dreams. He imagined, in slow motion, unraveling that little knot and letting the tiny scrap of fabric flutter down to the floor…

Damn. He had no words.

Not that the woman wasn't amazing with whatever she had on—

Yeah...

Tonight was the night. Amanda would be grateful for all the nice things he'd bought her and reward him with at least a kiss. Though hopefully, he'd take that kiss and turn it into more.

As he crested the hill and the Honda's headlights swept over the dark cabin, his eyes immediately went up to the two exposed windows under the gabled roof. They kind of looked like the eyes of a crossed-eyed giant—with the brick chimney being his nose and the slanting roof-gable on each side its brows.

The cabin had only a few light fixtures, and the light coming from those windows was dim. But with nothing else for miles around, even this was a dead giveaway.

Right. There wasn't much he could do about it.

Parking parallel to the porch, he cut the engine, popped the trunk, and shoved the keys into his pocket—all along watching the front door and hoping Amanda would throw it open and come running to greet him…

Or not…

Yeah. Whatever. He'd told her not to open the door… she was just obeying his orders…

Right, in your dreams...

"Amanda, open up!" he gave a holler as he climbed the stairs with a bunch of shopping bags in each hand, then stood by the door, waiting...

Maybe she was in the bathroom...

Or maybe she wasn't there...

As panic fought for dominance with anger, Dalhu was about to kick open the door when she finally deigned to let him in.

"What took you so long?" she accused and sauntered back to the couch, then picked up some damn book she'd been apparently reading.

Jet fighters?

"The nearest mall is three hours away, and the stuff on your list wasn't exactly something I could find at a 7-Eleven," he bit out as he dropped the bags on the floor and went for another round.

Amanda didn't offer to help or begin putting things away, and she showed no sign of interest in what he'd bought either.

Of all the ungrateful, spoiled... princesses...

He was tempted to use a less flattering word, but even inside his own head, he refused to refer to her in a derogatory way. Their relationship would be built on mutual respect—starting with his choice of language.

"Thanks for all your help," he said sarcastically.

"You're welcome," she gritted without lifting her head.

"What's your problem?"

"You have to ask? Really?"

She had a point.

It wasn't like they were a couple on their honeymoon or anything. He'd kidnapped her and was holding her prisoner in an isolated cabin. But that was old news, and she'd been in a much better mood before he'd left. What the hell had gotten into her in his absence?

Well, glancing at the book in her hands, he had to admit that she must've been damn bored during the long hours he'd been gone to be desperate enough to read about the history of jet-fighters.

With that in mind, he switched gears. "I brought brie, and camembert, and gorgonzola, and goat cheese…" he singsonged, watching her expression change as he kept taking one fancy cheese after another out of the bag and putting them in the refrigerator.

Amanda pretended to be absorbed in the book, but she was practically salivating and trying to swallow without him noticing her do so.

"You don't have to wait until I put everything away, you could come and take a bite right now. I know you want it… come and get it…" he taunted, holding a wedge of Havarti cheese and unwrapping the top.

"Oh, damn." Amanda dropped the book on the coffee table and got up. "I have no willpower. None whatsoever…" she lamented as she got closer to the cheese, her eyes focused on the thing like a hungry cat on a mouse.

But as soon as she reached for it, he lifted his arm up and caught her around the waist with the other, bringing her close for a kiss.

Taken by surprise, she didn't have time to erect her defenses, giving in to the sensation for a moment. Only for a moment, though, and then he was shoved away and pinned with the blue stare of a hungry predator. A hissing, growling, angry jungle cat that was about to scratch his eyes out if he dared taunt her even a moment longer.

"Here you are, sweetheart. It's all yours." He quickly gave her the wedge.

With another hiss, she grabbed it, pivoted on her heel, and went back to sit on the couch with her prize. She peeled away the wrap, took a big bite, and began chewing.

The expression of bliss on her face was priceless.

"Aren't you curious to see all the nice things I've got for you? I know you don't want to spend another minute wearing those sweats..."

Her eyes darted to the Macy's bags piled next to the stairs, and he knew she was fighting the urge to go and check them out.

Slowly but surely he was chipping away at her defenses.

"Well?" He arched a brow.

"Stuff from Macy's is nothing to get excited about," she finally said over a mouthful of cheese.

Maybe so, but still, he knew she was dying to dive into those bags. "As you wish... I also brought some DVDs so we could watch a movie tonight," he threw over his shoulder as he pulled a bunch of thin cases from a supermarket bag.

"And how do you propose we watch them, Sherlock? There is no TV."

"On my laptop."

That shut her up. But only momentarily.

"That's right, I forgot you had one. Not that it crossed your mind that I might have used it to entertain myself while you were gone for most of the day."

"To do what? There is no Internet here. And if there was, you think I'd be stupid enough to let you use it?"

16

AMANDA

Amanda shrugged and took another bite of the cheese.

Damn, it was hard to keep all of that anger going on. Why did Dalhu have to be so amiable all of a sudden? Where was all that rage he had simmering just below the surface?

Did his new pleasant disposition have anything to do with him getting lucky with some chippy at the mall?

Well, that thought seemed to do the job—getting her good and angry as she imagined him pleasuring some slut with that amazing body of his…

Never mind that it proved that she was completely nuts…

Whatever, it didn't matter what caused it as long as it worked. She needed to keep up the anger for its pungent aroma to mask the scents of her anxiety and guilt. If Dalhu got a whiff of those, he might suspect something was up… as in up the stairs and under the bed…

Yep. She had lost it. Why the hell was she getting a knot in her gut every time she thought about that shovel she'd stashed upstairs?

Well, she wasn't a murderous bitch, that's why.

Not that a shovel to the head would kill Dalhu, but still, imagining his handsome face broken and bloody…

Oh, Fates, there is no way I could do it… no way!

"What's the matter?" Dalhu shot her a worried glance.

Great, now she'd given herself away.

"Nothing, I'm just antsy." She glared at him, trying to get herself angry again by imagining some other female's hands on him… unbuttoning his designer shirt, parting it to reveal his powerful chest… the tanned skin contrasting enticingly with the white fabric…

Shit. This was so not what she was going for…

"I can help with that." Dalhu's voice dropped to a growl as he breathed in, getting a lungful of the pheromones she'd just cast his way.

"No, you stay where you are… don't get any closer. I want none of that." Amanda shooed him away as he moved toward her.

"I beg to differ." Dalhu took another step, but then the panic in her eyes gave him pause, and he stopped, wiping a shaky hand over his mouth. "It's okay. I get it. Your body wants me, but your mind is still fighting it. I can wait. If what you've told me about immortal females is true, then you won't be able to hold off for much longer anyway." Dalhu swung around and began organizing the food supplies with deadly deliberation.

Unfortunately, he was right. And that was exactly why she needed to implement her plan.

Tonight.

Dalhu turned to look at her and frowned. "Why don't you take the stuff I bought you upstairs, relax with a nice bubble bath, and change into something pretty? I'm sure it would make you feel better. And by the time you're done, I'll have dinner ready."

Who was that man, and what had he done with Dalhu? Amanda shook her head in disbelief as she took a last bite of the cheese and got up. Leaving what was left of the wedge on the dining table, she grabbed as many shopping bags as she could carry and took them upstairs.

Instead of the misogynistic brute that she could easily hate, Dalhu was proving—against all odds—to be patient, respectful, and accommodating. If anyone had told her a Doomer was capable of this, she would've laughed in their faces and called them all kinds of stupid.

As she started the water for the tub, she glanced at the counter, making sure that there were a couple of fresh towels on hand.

Check her out, she was learning to be like a regular person. Yay!

And on that note, she even emptied the dryer, which had finished its cycle hours ago, and dumped the clothes on the bed. Her blouse had shrunk to something that wouldn't fit a ten-year-old, and although her pants looked fine, they were in desperate need of ironing...

She wondered if Dalhu knew how to do that.

Amanda wasn't sure she could manage even the folding. But that would wait for later. By now the tub was probably full.

Taking off the sweats, she debated between shoving them in the washing machine and dumping them in the trash, but in an uncharacteristic stroke of practicality, she decided on the machine. Who knew what Dalhu had in those bags, she thought as she slowly lowered her body into the water.

So what was his story? Was it all a very convincing act? But to what end? If he wanted to have sex with her, he could've done it already. And although she might've resisted initially, they both knew she would've quickly succumbed to her own need.

And besides, Dalhu didn't strike her as such a good actor.

But then, how the hell this walking-bomb-waiting-to-explode had managed to withstand her obnoxious act was baffling. And it wasn't as if this was all a show of admirable control either. She'd sensed only a mild surge of annoyance and disappointment when she hadn't greeted him with the excitement he'd been obviously hoping for, and then the familiar scent of determination she was starting to associate with him had quickly replaced even that.

Such a sexy combination.

A guy that was a tower of strength, physically and otherwise, and at the same time committed to making her happy in any way he could.

Except for letting her go, that is.

Shit. If he weren't a Doomer, he would've been the perfect male for her. How many guys out there would've tolerated her penchant for drama, the fact that she was a spoiled princess and was used to getting her way—always, and had a runaway mouth with no brakes.

Not to mention a history of partners as long as the list of animators in a Pixar movie.

Though be that as it may, it didn't mean she was willing to go along with his crazy plan. Staying with Dalhu meant never seeing her family again, and even if that weren't a line she drew in the sand, which of course it was, she couldn't spend her long life just as someone's mate and nothing more. She loved her job—the research, the teaching, the daily contact with minds that were hungry for knowledge. And other things…

None of that would be possible on the run.

Unfortunately, for Dalhu to keep his head attached to his shoulders, he had to keep running and hiding. If he were ever caught by his people, they would execute him for desertion, and she had no doubt Kian would tear him limb from limb for abducting her.

Her brother's deep-seated hatred for Doomers was well known.

Not that she could blame him when she felt the same.

Well, except for Dalhu.

With a sad sigh, Amanda reached for the soap.

Maybe she should have sex with the poor guy as a way to atone for later bashing his head in with a shovel as he slept. And maybe she could even leave him a note, explaining why she had to do it.

In the end, he would understand it was for the best... after healing from the injury, that is... and after reading her note.

With her gone, he would have no trouble disappearing somewhere where there was no chance of him accidentally bumping into his people. And she wasn't planning on telling Kian where she left Dalhu either, ensuring he was safe from her brother's wrath as well.

Finishing her bath in a hurry, she got out and wrapped herself in a towel, then tiptoed into the bedroom and lifted one of the paper bags.

Back in the bathroom, she tore off a good sized piece, then dropped her towel on the floor and pushed it with her foot, wedging it against the door to keep the thing closed.

Naked, she sat on the toilet to write the note. Her first attempt and the second got flushed down the drain. The third one she wrote standing up with the piece of paper lying flat against the hard surface of the counter so it would come out legible this time.

Dear Dalhu,

If you're reading this note, then my plan worked and I'm back home with my family.

Please forgive me for what I've done, and know that I'll always remember you fondly, regardless of how it all started and how it had to end.

You were nothing but kind and respectful, and it was with heavy heart that I've devised this plan to hurt you. But if you think it through, rationally, you'll realize that I did us both a service. Your plans for us, though sweet and romantic, were unrealistic.

I cannot live on the run and abandon my family and my work to be with you. I could never be happy with just being your mate, even if there were no ancient feud and hatred between our people.

You'll be safer without me and could start a new life somewhere far removed from the conflict.

Having to always look behind your back, waiting to be caught, is no way to live.

I'm not going to tell anyone about this cabin, so you have nothing to fear from my side. I'm going to invent a story of getting lost and confused and take them on a wild goose chase, giving you the time you need to heal and disappear.

Stay safe and live your life.

Wishing you the best of luck,

Amanda.

After reading it over, she folded the note several times and placed it under the pack of band-aids in the first aid kit.

This way, when Dalhu regained consciousness and went for the kit to treat his injuries, he'd find it.

Wasn't she a clever girl?

17

DALHU

Amanda came down in a pair of skin-tight jeans, a fitted, long-sleeved black T-shirt, and no bra, her beautiful breasts bouncing enticingly with each step she took. They weren't large, but like the rest of her, they were perfectly shaped—firm and yet soft, the hard little tips at their tops absolutely mouth-watering.

Damn. Dalhu swallowed hard. The woman was fine.

She took a seat next to the table he'd set up for their dinner and flashed him that gorgeous smile of hers.

"Thank you, Dalhu."

It seemed his efforts were well worth it.

"You're welcome," he said without sarcasm.

To see her smile at him with genuine affection in her eyes, he was willing to do much more than just put the groceries away and set a table.

What a shame there were no more dragons for him to slay or evil sorcerers to outsmart, and as it was, he was one of the not so imaginary bad guys.

Was being the imperative word.

But yeah…

Sitting across from Amanda, he watched with satisfaction as she piled her plate with chunks of assorted cheeses, crackers and some grapes, and then got to work.

A bunch of stinky cheeses wasn't what he would call a great meal —a juicy steak with some fries on the side would hit the spot for him —but for Amanda he was willing to turn off his sense of smell and even try to enjoy them.

"Aren't you going to eat?" Amanda waved her fork at his empty plate.

Dalhu reached for the bottle of wine. "I'm just taking a moment to watch you. I don't want to miss the expression of bliss on your face with each new bite you take." He pulled out the cork and filled two goblets to the rim.

"Cheers." He waited for her to lift hers and clink glasses with him.

"Not bad." She licked her lips, which sent a zing straight to his groin.

They ate in silence, with Amanda hungrily devouring everything on her plate and then going for seconds, and him mostly watching.

"Pour me another one, would you?" She raised her empty goblet.

"My pleasure." He filled it to the brim.

The woman had a healthy appetite and an impressive capacity for alcohol, drinking one-for-one with him. By the time the meal was over, they had emptied two bottles of wine.

"I'm stuffed." Amanda leaned back in her chair and rubbed her flat belly.

Oh man… in this position her breasts were clearly outlined, pushing against the fabric of her shirt, and as she let her head loll back, the pale expanse of her neck had his venom glands swell and his fangs drop down into his mouth.

Dalhu swallowed hard, his chest constricting from lack of oxygen as he forced his breathing to sound normal. Otherwise, it would've come out harsh and loud like a locomotive. "Time for a movie?" He got up and began to clear the table.

From the corner of his eye, he saw Amanda lift her arms over her head, which had her shirt stretch farther across her breasts and ride up to reveal the soft expanse of her middle.

She pushed away from the table and picked up their empty plates. "Let me help."

Stifling a groan, he took the things out of her hands. "No need, sweetheart. You go and sit on the couch. Pick a movie you'd like to watch while I finish here."

"Well, if you insist..." she slurred lazily, apparently having no problem following instructions when it suited her.

A few moments later he joined her on the couch. "So, what will it be?" He wrapped an arm around her shoulders. When she didn't protest, he was pleasantly surprised.

Maybe she didn't notice...

"I'm deliberating between *The Princess Bride* and *The Avengers*. Have you seen either of them?" She lifted the two movies for him to examine the covers.

"I've seen *The Avengers*, great movie, but not the other one. I picked it thinking a princess like you would like it..."

"I do like it. The guy only said *'as you wish'* to the girl. What's not to like?"

"*Princess Bride* it is, unless you'd rather watch *The Avengers*. I don't mind watching it again."

"No, I think you should watch the princess one. You could learn a thing or two." She smirked.

Dalhu freed the disk from the elaborate wrapping and popped it into his laptop's disk drive.

"I'm surprised you got to watch movies. I thought all *corrupt* Western media was forbidden."

"We were advised to watch with caution, and only action flicks. After all, how do you think I got to sound like I was born and raised in the US when, in fact, it's my first time here? Learning to speak like a native was the perfect excuse to watch shitloads of movies."

"Really? This is your first time here?" Amanda regarded him with what he hoped was newfound appreciation. "I must admit this is really impressive. I would've never guessed."

"Thank you." Dalhu felt like he'd just grown another inch or two.

"So tell me, did you learn to speak English so well just from watching movies? Or does the Brotherhood provide language courses?"

"No, not really." He chuckled. "The only education they provide are basic reading and writing skills, and even this is a recent development. They started it less than a hundred years ago, and only for the commanders. It took another twenty years until they realized that literacy was an essential skill in modern times, even for the rank and file. For foreign languages, they supply us with stuff like the Rosetta Stone courses, and we teach ourselves."

"Well, it's probably good enough. Our kind is uniquely talented in that department. Absorbing a new language is so easy for me, it takes me a couple of weeks at most of hanging with the locals in a new country to speak like a native, but I usually don't bother with the reading and writing. Not unless I have a good reason to." She smiled apologetically as if she was embarrassed to admit it.

Dalhu dipped his head to hide his grimace. What would Amanda think of him if she knew how limited his education was? That he had been illiterate for most of his life?

He wasn't going to tell her, and if she asked, he wouldn't flat out lie, but he wouldn't give her a straight answer either. She already had a pretty low opinion of him, and the last thing he needed was to dump this boulder on the negative side of the scale.

Luckily, she dropped the subject.

Things got even better as the movie started, and Amanda got comfortable, leaning back into his arm and completely stunning him by resting her head on his shoulder.

It was heaven to hold her close, her body soft and relaxed in his embrace. But it was hell to fight the urge to take this thing further.

There was no way she didn't know what she was doing to him. And not just because she was an immortal like him, who most likely could scent his lust, but because he couldn't control his breathing anymore, not without choking, and his breaths were coming in and going out, chuffing like a fucking locomotive. The cause would've been obvious to anyone.

Yeah, she was definitely aware.

She didn't remain unaffected, though. It seemed that as his breathing got heavier, hers was getting shallower, and he could've sworn her breasts were swelling, or maybe it was just the effect of her nipples getting harder and protruding farther.

He wasn't paying attention to the movie, and although Amanda had her eyes on the small laptop screen, pretending to watch, he suspected she paid it as much attention as he did.

The Princess Bride had just become his favorite movie of all times...

With gentle fingers, Dalhu took hold of Amanda's chin and tilted her head—so she was staring up at his eyes as he dipped down and kissed her lips, slowly.

Amanda didn't pull away.

She moaned, her chest heaving with pent-up desire as she parted her lips and invited him to deepen the kiss.

He brought them closer, kissing her harder, and still she didn't resist. Getting bolder, he reached under her T-shirt and rested his palm on the soft skin of her belly.

With a groan, Amanda covered his hand with her palm. But instead of pushing it away as he'd expected her to, she pushed it up to her breast—a shudder running through her upon contact.

Holy Mortdh, he didn't need a written invitation to get that he was just given the green light.

Gently, he lowered her down to the couch and pushed her T-shirt up and over her beautiful breasts, then pulled back to stare at the magnificent beauty he'd just unveiled.

He wanted to dive in and suckle her, to take turns with each puckered nipple until he got his fill...

Which could take a while...

Except, to pleasure her properly, he needed to take it slow and learn to play Amanda's body like one would learn to play a fine instrument, paying close attention to what she liked and what she did not. And that required two things he was in short supply of.

Patience and restraint.

Reaching to cup her breasts, he had a feeling that his hands shook a little, though if they did, it was barely perceptible. He groaned with pleasure. Perfect; the hard tips tickling the inside of his palms, and just the right size to fill his cupped hands but not overflow them.

Fighting the urge to descend on her with his lips and his tongue, he started slowly circling her turgid peaks with his thumbs, making contact only with the areola, teasing her, expecting her to urge him to do more. But besides arching her spine to push her breasts into his hands, she did nothing to protest his little teasing.

For some reason, Amanda was holding back.

Which troubled him.

By now he had a pretty good idea of the kind of woman she was, and meek wasn't it.

Dalhu had no problem with taking the lead, or with dominating the hell out of her, but only if this was what turned her on, and not because she was frightened.

Letting his senses probe deeper, he detected a hint of trepidation. But that was to be expected, it was no more than the thrill of a new partner, and nothing that would explain her timid response.

"We don't have to do this..." he murmured, even though it would kill him to stop.

"It's my first time... with an immortal..." She smiled a lopsided smile.

Aha... so that's her game...

No problem, he could play along…

"It's my first time as well... with one untried, that is… but you have nothing to fear, my sweet. I'll go slow and gentle and make sure it's good for you." He moved his thumbs back and forth across her hard tips before dipping his head and pulling one between his lips.

She bucked under him, but not to throw him off…

"Do you like this?" he breathed over her wet nipple.

"Oh, Fates, yeeees…" she mewled.

He suckled her other nipple, swirling his tongue around the tip and tugging gently with his fingers on its twin.

Dalhu took his time, alternating between using his fingers and his mouth, savoring each one of Amanda's throaty moans. When he sensed she'd had enough, he cupped her wet breasts and took her mouth in a hard kiss. She opened for him, drawing his tongue into her mouth.

When he came up for air, she grasped the hem of her T-shirt, yanked it over her head, and tossed it behind her.

Timid no more, she shifted up and reached for the buttons of his shirt, kissing him while she was at it, slipping her tongue between his lips and sweeping it against his.

Dalhu leaned back and Amanda moved to straddle him, her core hot over his rock-hard shaft even through the barrier of fabrics between them. Getting busy with the buttons, she rocked against him, kissing every little bit of skin she was exposing. He kept stroking her back and her waist and the sides of her bare breasts, running his ragged palms all over that soft, smooth skin.

When she parted the two halves, he helped her peel the shirt off his shoulders. And as she tugged on it, he leaned forward so she could pull it free. Giving the shirt a little spin over her head, Amanda sent the thing flying in the same direction her T-shirt went.

Admiring his bare chest, she looked like a triumphant goddess, as if he belonged to her—was hers to do with as she pleased.

Yes he was, and he had absolutely no problem with this.

After a moment, she hissed and latched on to his neck, licking, kissing, nibbling. And as she kept rocking and undulating her hips over his groin, her wet nipples rubbed against his chest.

The good news was that Amanda seemed to have forgotten that she wanted to play the shy virgin. The bad news was that with what she was doing, he wasn't going to last. With his fangs already down in his mouth, and precum wetting his jeans, he was either going to rip her pants off and plunge right in or explode in his pants.

Neither was acceptable.

Wrapping an arm tightly around her upper body and clamping a palm over her butt, he stilled her gyrations. "You have to stop... Unless you're ready to get straight down to business," he part hissed, part slurred through his fangs.

Amanda pulled back a little, gasping at the sight of him. "Can I touch them?" She kept her eyes on his fangs as she brought her pointer finger to hover a fraction of an inch away from the sharp tip.

"Yeah..." he breathed, his abdominals contracting in excited anticipation of her touch.

Very gently, she ran her finger all the way from his swollen gum down to the tip and pressed lightly, just enough for it to pierce her skin and draw a tiny drop of blood.

They both moaned when he swirled his tongue around her injured digit, the taste of her blood exploding over his senses as he healed the small nick.

"Fuck, Amanda..." His hips surged involuntarily, pressing his hard length up to her center. "This isn't helping..."

"I'm sorry," she whispered, wrapping her arms around him. With her slim palm holding on to his nape, she buried her nose in the crook of his neck. "I wanted to take it slow and savor this experience..." she mumbled against his skin. "Fates, I'm such a slut..." She sighed.

"Please don't..." Dalhu smoothed his palm over her bare back.

With the reminder of her sordid past, his arousal cooled as if a bucket of ice was dropped on the thing. At the same time, however, he hated that she felt this way. He wanted their first time to be all about her, her pleasure. Any guilt or shame, or whatever other negative feelings she might have, were unwelcome between them.

"No, it's true. With mortals, I take whatever I want, how I want it. I'm running the show… I use them." She chuckled, her exhale tickling his skin. "My boy toys…" she kept talking into his neck, holding on tight as if afraid he would push her away. "I wanted… heck… I'm not sure what I wanted… I wanted it to be different with you."

Something wet and warm slid down his neck—a tear.

"Oh, hell, Amanda, that's nothing to cry about. I know exactly what it's like, and all of those that came before, for you as well as for me, don't count. They were an upgraded version of a toy to masturbate with—a semi-decent substitute, but a substitute nonetheless. Did you ever have feelings for any of them? Or use them more than once or twice?"

She shook her head, rubbing her wet nose on his skin in the process. Not that he gave a fuck if she got some snot on him…

"You see? I'm right." Dalhu cupped her cheek and gently pushed her face up from her hiding place so she had to look into his eyes. "For real? This is like the first time for both of us, with the added advantage of actually knowing what the fuck we're doing. Right?"

"I guess… we sure do know how to fuck…" Amanda smiled her teasing smile, the spark of mischief once again glinting in her big, blue eyes.

Thank fuck.

18

SYSSI

As the blinking lights of the helicopter vanished in the distance, Syssi closed her eyes and let the tears flow freely. It had been such a struggle to keep the waterworks at bay for Kian and Andrew's sake. Not that she'd done such an admirable job of it. But now, standing alone on the roof of Kian's high-rise, in the middle of the night, there was no more need for pretense.

No one could see her.

Except, the tears weren't enough, she still felt like choking.

It was all too much, and the stress had finally gotten the better of her.

Or was it the transition?

According to Dr. Bridget, everything in Syssi's body was supposedly in flux, and that probably included her hormones. But whether she was being hormonal or not, she knew of only one way to get some small measure of relief, and it was to let it all go, break down completely and sob her heart out.

She did, noisily, hiccups and runny nose and all, using the bottom of her T-shirt to wipe her nose and the fountains of tears from her eyes. It was soaked.

Ugh, gross.

Ah, what the heck, the thing is beyond salvage anyway. She blew her nose on one side of the shirt and gave her face a good wipe down with the other. She then took a deep, shaky breath, and another.

Snap out of it, everything is going to be fine. Her brother and the two friends he'd brought on the mission were professionals—experts in hostage retrieval, and Kian's bodyguards, Brundar and Anandur, were obviously well-trained.

But what about Kian?

She wasn't sure about his fighting skills, but he'd surely carried that wicked-looking sword like it was an extension of his body, like it was nothing new to him. And he certainly was old enough to have lived at a time when men had waged war with swords.

She wondered if he'd fought in actual battles or just knew how to wield a sword for self-defense, or maybe for sport—fencing. But even as she thought it, deep down she knew the truth.

Don't be naive. Of course, he fought... he had to...

Kian had the bearing of a general, and it wasn't because he was Regent over the American part of his clan. Politicians, even presidents of countries, didn't have this particular aura around them—not unless they came from a military background.

But it was a good thing, right? As an experienced fighter, Kian was less likely to get injured.

Oh, God, what if...

Stop it. No one is going to get hurt. Well, except for that Doomer. Syssi shivered as she imagined what Kian would do to that guy.

As much as she loved him, there was still a lot she didn't know about Kian, and she suspected that there was a whole other side to him she had only caught glimpses of.

His beast, as he called it. As if there was some creature or separate entity living inside of him that was wild and untamable. Right. A convenient way to excuse lack of control. She had no doubt, though, that Kian was capable of killing. And she had the uneasy feeling that he wasn't beyond cruelty either.

Would it affect the way she felt about him if she knew that for a fact? Would she be wary of him?

Probably not.

Did she want to know?

No, not really.

Coward.

Yes, she was. War and its ugliness were, unfortunately, an integral part of life, and the strong had to do what needed to be done to defend the defenseless. While Kian had no choice but to fight against enemies that threatened his clan, killing and maybe even torturing for information, she had the luxury of hiding her head in the sand as one of the defenseless.

Still, even though she fully accepted Kian, darker side and all, she felt sorry for him. The man had selflessly sacrificed a part of his soul so others could live. Not that she would ever let him know that she did.

Kian was such a guy, so proud.

She smiled, remembering his smug expression when she'd called him Superman. Indeed.

I'm so lucky. I snagged such an incredible man... immortal...

Once he returned, victorious of course, and had a chance to catch up on his sleep, she was going to put his superhuman endurance to the test with her own new and improved body.

That's right, now that she was an immortal, Kian could really let go of his *beast* and ravage her to his heart's content. She was indestructible.

In a much better mood, Syssi got back inside the rooftop vestibule and pressed the button for the elevator. It was good that the penthouse level had one that was dedicated. She would've been mortified to encounter anyone and get caught looking like she did, with puffy red eyes, red wet nose, and a shirt covered in snot. Lucky for her, both of the penthouse occupants weren't there.

Oh, God! Lucky was such an inappropriate word. Amanda wasn't home because a dangerous Doomer held her captive, and Kian wasn't home because he was on his way to rescue his sister. The situation was as far from lucky as it could get.

Bad, bad Syssi.

And the floor wasn't completely deserted either. Annani, Kian's mother, was staying at Amanda's with her two servants. And there was Okidu, Kian's butler, and Onidu, Amanda's.

Kian had suggested that she wait for the team's return with Annani.

Not a bad idea, because she really didn't want to be alone, and Okidu wasn't exactly good company—the guy had the personality of a mannequin.

But first, a change of clean clothes was in order, and she had to do something about her blotchy face. On second thought, a quick fix wouldn't do. To look presentable enough for another audience with the goddess, Syssi would need to invest a lot more effort in sprucing up.

19

ANDREW

Andrew's stomach was giving him a hard time. Nothing new there, it always did on helicopter rides—no matter how many missions he'd flown.

Was it the noise? The change in altitude?

Because it sure as hell wasn't fear.

At least not for himself.

Hell, he prayed Amanda was all right.

But he knew better than to delude himself that she'd remained unharmed. The best he could hope for was that she was still alive and that whatever damage the motherfucker had done to her would heal. Except, rape was particularly hard to recuperate from. Probably impossible. Unlike injury or even torture, the part of one's soul that got ripped out by that particularly vile act of violence could never be fully restored.

Fuck. The worst part was not knowing.

It had been easier when he hadn't known the victim. It wasn't that he hadn't felt for the other abductees or their families, but to be a professional in this type of business one had to develop an emotional barrier—a numbness. Feelings led to mistakes—mistakes with life or death consequences. He imagined that surgeons had to develop a similar detachment. That's why they were advised to never operate on a family member.

Unless there was no other choice—like in this case. And besides, he wasn't a family member. Not yet. He'd met Amanda only once. Except, with a woman like her, the impact had been profound.

Andrew glanced at his watch again.

He estimated another fifteen minutes to touchdown, and then about two hours of trekking through the woods for a stealth attack.

Sitting next to him, Kian looked just as grim. Now that there was no more need to front confidence for Syssi's sake, the poor bastard looked tortured, probably by the same kinds of thoughts that were twisting Andrew's gut.

Not counting the pilot, they had four more guys on the rescue team, which should be more than enough if Kian was right in his assessment that Amanda was being held by a single guy.

But if Kian was wrong, they were fucked.

Jake and Rodney, the guys Andrew had brought on the mission, were buddies from his old unit and he knew he could count on their professionalism. But although Kian's guys, Brundar and his redheaded brother, gave off a vibe of experienced soldiers, they had no experience with hostage retrieval.

Fuck.

Between an overwrought brother and the two deadly cousins there were too many wild cards in the mix, but apparently he needed their special abilities.

The kidnapper wasn't the usual variety of scumbag.

He was a near-immortal.

Like them.

Andrew still had trouble wrapping his head around the immortal thing. Not that he doubted what he'd been shown, but man, what a trip down the rabbit hole.

It wasn't easy to adjust to the fact that the reality he was familiar with was only part of the story, and that besides governments and economic forces there were also two factions of immortals who manipulated the show from behind the cover of shadows.

The one good and the other evil—to put it in simplistic terms.

And the kicker was that apparently he and his sister belonged to this exclusive tribe, with the caveat that unless activated, those superior genes they were lucky enough to inherit from their mother would remain dormant.

Syssi had gotten activated by the big guy sitting next to him, but her transition hadn't gone as smoothly as Kian and his people had hoped it would. It had been touch and go for a while.

Thankfully, Andrew had been spared the gut-wrenching worry by showing up on the scene after the fact.

As big and as freaky as his sister's boyfriend was, he would've killed the bastard for putting her in harm's way…

Or at least given it his best try…

As he'd been told, killing one of these immortals was next to impossible, and Andrew had neither fangs nor venom, not yet anyway, and he wasn't armed with a sword to slice off a head or cut out a heart either.

Kian, on the other hand, was well prepared and fully equipped. Besides the deadly instruments he'd been born with, he'd brought a wicked-looking blade just for that purpose.

Gruesome, but effective.

Andrew wondered how it would feel to have deadly weapons as an integral part of his body. Was the experience different from that of an MMA fighter, or of how the knowledge affected any other guy who was deadly with his bare hands?

How would he feel after the transition?

Damn, having fangs would be so weird…

What was really surprising, though, was that he and his sister and only one other guy, Michael—a student at Amanda's university—were the first dormant carriers of those special genes that Kian's people had ever found. The rest of their clan members were all related to each other, descending from one single female and some anonymous mortal sperm donors.

The plan was, after they brought Amanda home, of course, for Andrew to go through the process as well. But he wasn't sure he was going to go for it. Not that becoming an invincible immortal didn't appeal to him, or that becoming a possible mate for Amanda wasn't as tempting as hell, but the flip side was that he might end up dead instead of immortal.

And that would really suck.

Given that Syssi, fourteen years his junior, had such a hard time transitioning, chances were good he wouldn't make it through the ordeal at all.

Good thing Kian didn't try to sugarcoat it for him, telling him the risks straight up.

Decent guy that immortal. Syssi could've done worse.

Glancing sideways at Kian, Andrew smiled a little. His future brother-in-law was one handsome motherfucker. No wonder he had Syssi wrapped around his little finger in such a short time…

True, no one was talking about a wedding yet, but they'd better, or else…

And besides, once they got hitched, there was a good chance they'd make him a little niece or a nephew, and that he wouldn't mind at all.

Not. At. All.

And if they had a boy, they could name him Jacob… after the brother he and Syssi had tragically lost.

20

KIAN

Touching. Kian glanced at Andrew's tough profile as he got a whiff of the guy's fear. It must be for Amanda because Andrew didn't strike him as one who had any qualms about jumping head-on into danger.

Unfortunately, it wasn't as if Kian could assuage Andrew's worry by telling him that Annani had seen her daughter unharmed—in a vision.

He himself had trouble putting much faith in his mother's mystical remote viewing, despite her proven record.

Knowing the kinds of animals the Doomers were, it was too much of a stretch for him to suspend belief.

Fuck! It was an insult to animals to equate them with that evil...

Still, he had to believe Amanda was alive. She was, after all, too valuable to kill.

Fates, he hoped she hadn't revealed her true identity. As an immortal female, she was valuable enough, but if the fucker were to discover that he was holding Annani's daughter, the consequences would be disastrous. Currently, the Doomer's agenda seemed to be of a personal nature—grab an immortal female and keep her for himself. But Annani's daughter was a ticket to fame and glory that the fucker might be tempted to cash, and surrender her to Navuh.

The Doomers could demand anything they wanted and get it in exchange for Amanda.

No, she wasn't that stupid. Though that being said, with his sister's runaway mouth, she might've been dumb enough to goad the fucker into a murderous rage…

Which she probably had…

No, he couldn't think this way. Amanda must be alive, and whatever else the fucker had done to her, she was strong enough to survive it.

She'd heal.

The fucker, on the other hand, was a dead man. Kian was going to kill that Doomer himself. And if Annani had a problem with that, tough. For this, he was more than willing to sacrifice his mother's approval and disregard her standing order to keep any Doomers they caught in stasis instead of offing them for good.

Unfortunately, with his venom glands swelling and his fangs pulsating within his mouth, Kian had a feeling the sword he'd brought specifically for the purpose of slicing the fucker's head off would remain unsullied in its scabbard.

Death by venom was too kind for that animal…

Tearing out the fucker's throat, though…

Fuck. He was reverting to a beast himself, wasn't he?

Kian heaved a sigh. If his sweet Syssi knew the kinds of thoughts he was harboring, she would run screaming.

Poor girl.

Instead of the romantic dinner he'd promised to take her on, she'd spent the night unconscious while her body had fought to survive the transition.

She could've died if his mother hadn't come to the rescue…

He would've never forgiven himself if she…

Yeah, better not go there.

Lately, it seemed that he couldn't make a move without it turning into a disaster.

His instructions to speed up the rate with which the clan had traditionally transferred information to mortals had resulted in Mark's exposure and subsequent murder by Doomers. Syssi almost dying was, of course, his fault. It had been his fangs and his venom that had facilitated her transition. Even Amanda's kidnapping was his fault. If he hadn't insisted on Syssi going shopping and taking Amanda with her, his sister would've never crossed paths with that Doomer.

The chances of the fucker bumping into her accidentally were so negligible that it almost seemed like the cursed Fates had a hand in it.

But why?

What had he or Amanda ever done to deserve such punishment?

Damn, he was losing his mind…

Fates...

Really...

Don't tempt the Fates, Kian, his mother's voice sounded in his head.

Yep, he was definitely losing it.

21

AMANDA

Dear Fates, the man was impossible.

As those big brown eyes of his gazed at her with such tender emotion, the idea of clobbering Dalhu with a shovel made her feel like dirt.

"I could never just fuck you." Dalhu's palms were still on her cheeks as he shifted up and placed a gentle kiss on her lips. "I will worship your body with mine, make love to you the way a rare treasure like you should be made love to," he breathed.

Okay, now he made her feel lower than dirt—more like a piece of dung.

To hide her perfidy, she kissed him back, funneling all of her guilt and self-loathing into the kind of desperate passion that had her cling to him as if she would never let go.

Only when the lack of oxygen made her dizzy did she release his mouth and buried her face in the crook of his neck. "I would like that," she whispered against his skin.

With his powerful arms wrapped around her, Dalhu held her to him, clinging just as desperately, his chest heaving as he gulped air into his oxygen-deprived lungs.

"I want to spend hours learning your body an inch at a time." He eased up on his tight hold as he moved his palm up and down her spine.

Such a lovely sentiment. Problem was, he'd drive her absolutely crazy like that, and in no time she'd take over and drive them home…

Except, she wanted this to go Dalhu's way, for this one time they had together to be about his pleasure. A parting gift so he'd remember her as something other than the underhanded, conniving slut that she was.

"You'd better tie me up, then…" she blurted in a hurry.

"What? No…! I would never do that." Dalhu sounded horrified by the suggestion. "I only want to bring you pleasure…" He pulled back a little and dipped his head to look into her eyes. "Whatever you want, however you want it."

What a sweet man... And to think she was talking about a Doomer…

Amanda palmed his scruffy cheek. "I want to experience something new—something different with you. But patience is not one of my strong points, nor is relinquishing even a tiny bit of control to another, and I don't want to spoil it for both of us by taking over and speeding things up. All I need is a reminder, like a T-shirt or some other piece of clothing tied around my wrists. You do know that I'm strong enough to rip it apart if I want to, right?"

"You are?"

"Dalhu, darling, you keep forgetting that I'm not a mortal. And just as you're stronger and faster than a mortal male, so am I compared to human females." She ran her hands over the sculpted perfection of his chest. "Though with that magnificent body of yours, I suspect you're stronger than most immortal males as well."

"Really… so you want to tell me that you could've gotten free from those handcuffs I used on you?" Dalhu's smile was conceited.

"Like I didn't know those were reinforced… Which begs the

question of why you had them in the first place…" She eyed Dalhu suspiciously. "You said my kidnapping wasn't planned. So what gives?"

"It wasn't. And the reason behind the cuffs is no longer relevant. Let's just forget it…"

"Tell me."

"I don't want to spoil the mood."

"If you don't spill, there'll be nothing to spoil."

Amanda felt like banging her head against a wall. She was such an idiot—so damn stupid it was criminal.

Here she was in a unique position to learn the enemy's dastardly plans for her family, but instead of using her head to pump Dalhu for information, all she could think about was the kind of pumping that involved both of them getting sweaty…

Dalhu sighed, his expression turning utterly despondent. "Before I answer, I just want you to know that everything is different now. I would never hurt you by hurting your family. But before I got to know you, before I pledged my future and myself to you, I was part of an organization that expected me to deliver certain results. I won't lie to you; I wasn't some big shot, but I wasn't just a mindless cog following orders either."

Wiping a nervous hand over his mouth, Dalhu sighed again. "I came up with the idea that males of your clan could be found where mortal females went searching for hookups. I planned on apprehending such a male to learn from him the location of your center of operation."

Deflated, he dropped his arms to his sides and leaned back against the couch cushions, his head falling back. But if he expected her to get off him, he was dead wrong. Up close and personal, bare chest to bare chest, she had the kind of leverage that would keep him talking.

"Would I be right to assume that this plan is still in effect without you?"

"Yes, the men I left behind are a bunch of incompetent morons, and they'll do nothing without me, but reinforcements are coming—a large contingent this time—and they are likely to send someone higher up on the chain of command to lead them."

Oh, that was just getting better and better…

"When are they going to get here?"

Dalhu lifted his head, a spark of hope lightening the pits of darkness his eyes had become.

"I don't know exactly, but the leader with a few men could arrive as early as tomorrow night. The good news is that a contingent this large will require a few days at the least to take care of the logistics before the rest of the men could get here, and then they'll need more time to get organized. It leaves plenty of time to warn your family to take preemptive measures."

"You would do that for me? For real?" Amanda searched Dalhu's eyes for signs of deception.

"You can write an e-mail to someone who knows you well and include something only you and that person are privy to, some anecdote or a private joke that'll convince them you sent it out of your own free will. Tomorrow, first thing in the morning, I'll drive to a Starbucks and use their free Wi-Fi to send it. I just hope you know somebody who will take it seriously and is in a position to do something about it."

"Do I know someone…" Amanda snorted, but then the red light in her addled brain flashed the stage-five alarm, and she closed her big mouth before blurting who she really was.

The way Dalhu kept calling her princess, it was easy to forget he had no clue she was Annani's daughter. And despite his professed loyalty to her, she'd be stupid to trust him with that piece of information.

After all, before pledging himself to her just thirty-something hours ago, he'd been a member of the Brotherhood for eight centuries. And he'd already proven that switching loyalties in a heartbeat wasn't a problem for him.

Finding out that he had Annani's daughter in his possession, he might come to the realization that she was more valuable to him as an asset he could surrender to Navuh in exchange for a prime position in the organization than the mate that he'd been fantasizing about.

"Who is it? Do you know a Guardian? It would be great if you do. A Guardian would be taken seriously."

"Yeah... that was exactly who I've been thinking of. I have a girlfriend on the force. We go clubbing together, a lot, so there are quite a few memories only she and I share..."

Dalhu looked stunned—his mouth gaping a little.

Oh, come on, like it was such a big revelation that she'd been clubbing.

"You guys have females on the force?" he gasped, apparently horrified not at the idea of her prowling for men at clubs, but that there were female Guardians.

Well, only one. For now...

And he didn't need to know that...

"Welcome to the twenty-first century, Dalhu," Amanda singsonged, not bothering to conceal her condescending tone.

"Are you guys out of your fucking minds? Who was the moron that came up with that brilliant idea?" Dalhu's eyes darkened again, the irises barely distinguishable from the pupils.

What the hell got his panties in a wad? Not that she thought he was wearing any... The guy was practically seething with rage, which proved that his theory about her touch's magically calming effect was complete crap.

"I know that Doomers still live in the dark ages, but come on, Dalhu, I'm surprised that you still hold on to these kinds of bullshit ideas. Women can run countries, fly jets, and aside from growing a set, they can do pretty much whatever males can do. With today's weaponry, one can be a soldier or a policewoman without having to be physically powerful."

He regarded her as if she was missing a couple of screws. "You think this is about some misogynistic crap? Are you blind to the kind of enemy you guys are sending those females against? Do you have any idea what a female would endure if she were captured? Any fucking idea?"

The vehemence in his voice was getting to Amanda, her gut clenching in a surge of fear and worry. "What?" she whispered, although her mind was already supplying the answer.

"The worst kind of hell imaginable. She would pray for the death that would never come. Should I say more? Or do you get the picture?"

Oh, she got the picture all right. Though knowing Kian, her brother would never risk sending Kri against Doomers. He used the girl primarily for situations that required—or were benefited by—a female taking care of things; like the handling of female clan offenders, and for other internal law enforcement matters.

That being said, though, it wasn't such a big stretch to imagine a situation in which Kri might be dragged into a fight with Doomers. Like when serving as a bodyguard for Amanda or Annani.

"I get the picture. Thank you very much. But the female Guardians perform only policing duties. No one in their right mind would send them against Doomers. We are well aware of the consequences."

"Thank heavens." Sinking back into the couch, Dalhu relaxed visibly, his body losing its rigidity. "Even before I met you, I would never, ever have surrendered a female immortal into the hands of my exalted leader. Never." From the way he'd hissed *my exalted leader,* Dalhu's opinion of Navuh was clear. "Nor to any of my brethren. In fact, I would've killed whoever needed killing to free her."

Dalhu kept surprising her at every turn. "My knight in shining armor." Amanda planted a loud kiss on his mouth.

Unless… it was one hell of an act to get her to like him…

Nah… To think that he was such an amazing actor was even more incredible than believing she was looking at the only Doomer with a conscience… a brain… and a heart.

Move aside, Wizard, and bow before Amanda—the new queen of Oz...

"You mean it? Or was it sarcasm I somehow missed …" Dalhu cocked a brow.

"No, I mean it. But you have to swear to me that you're going to send that e-mail tomorrow, first thing in the morning."

"I swear."

"Not good enough. I want you to make a binding oath."

"What do you want me to swear on? I'm sure you don't want to invoke Mortdh's name... unless you are calling on the devil, and as far as I know, you guys do not worship your matriarch that way. And anyway, it wouldn't mean anything to me."

He had a point. There was nothing the guy held sacred, nothing he believed in. Dalhu was mostly opportunistic and self-serving. Though, strangely, he was grounded in some internal moral code that against all odds, considering the attitude of the rest of his buddies, was very protective of women…

Eureka!

"Swear on your mother's memory."

His expression changed in a heartbeat. "How did you know?" he breathed.

"I listened when you told me about her, and it didn't require a degree in psychology to figure out that she meant a lot to you… I bet she still does. She is the flickering flame that kept your soul from being consumed by the darkness you were submerged in, the light that kept a tiny grain of hope alive in your heart. So yeah… I think you would never tarnish her memory by breaking an oath you took in her name."

"I think I've just fallen in love with you."

Did he just say that? Must've been only a figure of speech... Still, her heart fluttered a little. No one had ever said these words to her before.

No one.

"That's very sweet, but I still need the oath, Dalhu."

He took hold of her hand and placed it over his heart, then covered it with his. "I swear on my mother's memory, and that of my sister, that tomorrow morning I will send the e-mail you'll write to your friend, and with the exception of anything that might point to our location, I will make no changes to it."

"That's good. A very nice oath..." Amanda couldn't help but get a little teary... And it had nothing to do with being dramatic... for a change.

Dalhu's sincere vow touched her heart.

"I'm glad you approve." He lifted his finger and wiped away the tear that slid from the corner of her eye. "And I meant what I said before, about falling in love with you. You see me. The real me. The part that is hidden and protected by layers upon layers of heavy armor. The essence of me that no one aside from my mother and sister has ever gotten a glimpse of."

Lifting her hand to his lips, he kissed it, then did the same thing with the other. "Thank you."

Oh, boy, at this rate she'd be spouting the 'L' word back in no time...

Well, maybe not.

Nonetheless, there was no way in hell she was going to use that damned shovel now...

It was such a relief to forsake that abominable plan. She felt as if the darkness in her chest—that foreign evil thing that had taken residence inside her—got sucked up through the top of her head and dissipated.

Whatever, the important thing was that it was gone, and as she sagged against Dalhu and felt her muscles loosen, she became aware of the cramping in her legs.

With a sigh, she lifted her knee and shifted sideways to plop down on the couch.

Stretching like a cat, she lowered her legs over Dalhu's lap and her arms over the armrest, her naked breasts jutting as her body formed a gentle bow.

Dalhu's eyes zeroed right on target. "You still want me to tie you up?" The question was delivered with a rasp that suggested he no longer found the idea repugnant. In fact, he seemed quite eager.

In answer, Amanda crossed her wrists and wiggled her fingers.

"Go for it, big boy. I'm all yours."

22

SYSSI

After a quick shower, a fresh change of clothes, and a makeup job to make an undertaker proud, Syssi was ready to face Annani.

She was wearing a pair of designer jeans and a silk blouse, one of the new fancy outfits Amanda had made her buy, or rather bought for her using Kian's credit card. The whole stack of them must've been delivered sometime during Syssi's stay in Bridget's hospital room.

God, she still couldn't believe that she'd been so close to not making it through, or that she'd really transitioned. It all seemed like a dream, or a nightmare, depending on how this night would end.

With a sigh, she knocked on Amanda's door.

A moment later, Onidu opened it. "Mistress, please, come in. The Clan Mother has been expecting you." He bowed and waved his arm in invitation, pointing her toward the open terrace doors.

Strangely, Syssi heard several voices as she neared the terrace. Was Annani entertaining someone else at a time like this?

But as she stepped outside, the source of what she'd heard turned out to be a tablet. Annani was watching a comedy, and at one point even giggled like a schoolgirl.

God, what a strange family. Two of her children were facing deadly danger, and she was watching some silly sitcom. At a time like this, any normal mother would be pulling out hairs, or biting nails, or crying…

Well, Annani isn't a normal mother.

A normal mother didn't sit in a pool of her own illumination, one that was radiating from her own body, and her giggles didn't sound like the chiming of an angel. Nor was she more ancient than most civilizations yet looked like a seventeen-year-old girl.

Oh, boy, Annani was going to take some getting used to.

Lifting her head away from the screen, the goddess smiled. "Hello, my dear, come, join me."

"Thank you," Syssi said as she took a seat across from Annani.

"No, no, come and sit here beside me." Annani patted the chair next to her.

Reluctantly, Syssi did as she was told. It was still quite unnerving to get so close to all that freakish light.

Annani reached for Syssi's hand and clasped it. "Do not worry, Syssi, everything is going to be all right." She sounded confident.

"How can you be so sure?" Syssi's voice trembled a little.

"Because I know that boy is not going to hurt Amanda."

That boy? Was she calling that evil Doomer a boy? What was wrong with this woman, goddess, whatever?

Annani patted Syssi's hand. "Do not look so incredulous. When I saw Amanda, she did not look like a woman afraid for her life or even her safety. She had this smug smile on her face that could only mean she has that boy wrapped around her little finger like she does every other male."

"What do you mean, you saw her?"

"Remote viewing, of course," Annani said as if it should've been obvious.

Maybe it was one of the goddess's powers. Syssi had only a vague grasp on what Annani was capable of, and besides, she was the last person to doubt someone's special abilities. But then, if Annani's remote viewing were a real thing—a dependable source of information—Kian wouldn't have been so worried.

Apparently, the goddess was a little full of herself. Still, the last thing Syssi wanted to do was to challenge her conviction. If this misguided belief in her superpowers eased her, let her cling to it.

"I see," she said with a nod as if she'd accepted the explanation.

Annani wasn't fooled, though. "Kian is a skeptic. That is why he does not trust my visions, but I have a proven record of accurate remote viewings. And on top of those, I have a little of your talent, though in my case it is more of a gut feeling than a vision."

"Sometimes it's hard to tell the difference," Syssi admitted. "And your gut tells you no one will get hurt?"

"I did not say that. I just know that there will be no carnage tonight. And I am basing this on more than just my gut."

"Like what?" *That should be interesting.*

"As I said, I believe Amanda is in control of the situation, and the Doomer will not hurt her. As to the men on the team, they not only outnumber him six to one, but also have the element of surprise on their side."

"And what about the Doomer himself? What are his chances of getting out of this alive?" Syssi sincerely doubted the possibility. Kian intended to kill the guy. Otherwise, why carry a sword?

"His chances are good. I forbid unnecessary killings."

"What do you mean?"

"Exactly what I said. If an enemy is killed during a life and death fight, then his death is sanctioned. But I do not allow the execution of a subdued captive." Annani lifted her chin as if expecting Syssi to object.

In theory, Annani's approach was the morally right thing to do.

Except, if they didn't kill enemy warriors, what did they do with the men they captured?

Kian hadn't mentioned any war prisoners being held in the clan's jail even though some Doomers must've been captured recently. The guardians who'd defended both her and Michael from Doomers' attack had most likely taken some of their assailants prisoner. And if they had, where were they?

"I wasn't aware of any enemy prisoners being held down in your basement."

"Oh, Kian told you about the jail? I did not know that. But no, they are not in the jail. They are kept in the crypt."

Crypt? Like a burial chamber?

"I don't understand, you said they are taken alive…"

"Only barely. You see, an immortal can be held in stasis indefinitely. Which means a state in between, like the undead from your lore." Annani chuckled.

"How is it possible?"

"It is a precise art. The victim has to be injected with venom to a point when his heart slows down to almost nothing but still beats—a little more would kill him, a little less and he will revive in short order, regenerating his injuries."

"And that's what you order the Guardians to do?"

"Exactly. We call it injecting to the brink. Then we store them in the crypt." Annani looked like she had just revealed a most clever and marvelous plan.

"Why? What do you plan to do with them?"

Annani's face fell a little. "It is the same question Kian keeps asking me. He does not agree with my decree, and he chafes at having to obey it." Annani sighed. "But I just cannot allow it. There are so few of our kind left, and that includes the Doomers. I would be contributing to my own people's extinction if I let it happen. At this time, I have no solution for how to salvage these men. They have been brainwashed since birth and we do not have the resources and manpower to rehabilitate them or keep them as prisoners. So I did the only thing I could think of. I will keep them in stasis for as long as their leadership continues on its destructive path. But if one day something happens to Navuh, hopefully a coup, and the Brotherhood changes its objectives, maybe then I could order them revived."

"Your heart is so full of love... " Syssi said, when something occurred to her. "Are you by any chance the goddess of love?" Annani was, after all, ancient, and who was to say that she wasn't the mythological Venus? Or Aphrodite? Or Ishtar? Or any of the other names different cultures attached to the ideal of love and beauty?

"Maybe I am..." Annani winked.

She was kidding, right?

"Speaking of love, tell me how did you and Kian meet, and when did you fall in love? I adore a good love story. Especially when it involves my precious son."

Was Annani deflecting cleverly? Or did she just enjoy being mysterious? In any case, it wasn't like Syssi could pressure her for an answer.

"Well?" Annani motioned with a wave of her hand.

"We met at Amanda's lab at the university. Kian came to try to convince her it wasn't safe for her to stay there after the Doomers had murdered that programmer. She, of course, refused to listen to reason. But then his bodyguards called to warn about Doomers outside the lab, and he whisked us both away and brought us here."

"And what did you think of him when you first saw him? I want all the juicy details, not just the dry facts." Annani's eyes sparkled with excitement.

The goddess apparently not only looked like a teenager but had the mentality to match.

Syssi chuckled. "I thought he looked too good for a mere mortal, and I was right because as it turned out he wasn't."

Annani scooted on her chair to get closer. "Was it love at first sight? Did you know right away that he was the one?"

More like lust at first sight... Not that she was going to admit it to Annani. "I thought he was out of my league and tried to hide behind my computer monitor. I didn't want him to see me."

"Why on earth not? You are beautiful!"

"Thank you. But I'm well aware that compared to Kian and Amanda I'm just ordinary. Anyway, for some reason Kian walked over to my station and forced me to show myself." Syssi shrugged, pretending as if it had been nothing special when, in fact, she had almost fainted. And when he had taken her hand, she'd almost orgasmed just from that one little touch. But again, it was not something she wished to share with Kian's mother.

Except, judging by the knowing smirk on Annani's beautiful face, Syssi had a feeling the goddess wasn't fooled by her feigned nonchalance.

Annani sighed. "Oh, well, I see that you are uncomfortable sharing the exciting details with me. But at least tell me how it happened."

Thank God! That I can do.

"After we got to his apartment, Amanda made up a story to explain why we had to run. She told me that the attackers were some religious fanatics who believed our work was evil and had threatened her before. We had a drink and Kian took me home. Once we got there, he thralled me to forget everything that had happened, including himself, and sent me off to sleep." *But not before he kissed me senseless.*

"Then the next morning he showed up on my doorstep, introduced himself as Amanda's brother, and said I needed to come away with him. When I hesitated, he returned my memories."

"That must have been very confusing for you," Annani said.

"It was. I thought I was losing my mind. But anyway, he took me to his place and that was it."

Annani arched one perfect red brow. "That was when you fell in love with him?"

Syssi blushed. "I've been attracted to Kian from the first moment I saw him, but then any normal woman would be. He is so handsome and so impressive. But I realized that I loved him only after I got to know him better and discovered what a sweet and wonderful person he is."

Annani beamed like the proud mother she was. "Just do not ever tell him you think of him as sweet. I think my son will take offense."

Syssi chuckled. "I know. He is like a prickly pear, thorny on the outside, but sweet on the inside, and he doesn't want anyone to know he has a softer side."

Annani nodded. "As a leader, he is required to project strength and authority. Sweet will not cut it."

"No, I guess not."

23

KIAN

Trekking through the sparse forest on foot, Kian cursed. He hated that he was forced to slow down and wait for the mortals to catch up. Again.

He and the brothers could have been at the cabin by now.

It wasn't that the humans were out of shape or took it easy… they were simply outclassed…

Which seemed to rub Andrew the wrong way. As he hurried to close the distance, the murderous expression on the guy's face was like a promise of violence.

Bring it on, buddy... let's see what you're made of... just make it quick... Every minute that passed was another minute of Amanda enduring hell. Kian's hands hovered over his weapons, ready to disarm fast… Because if he accidentally killed the human…

Calm the fuck down... he is Syssi's brother... he is Syssi's brother... a good guy...

Kian took a deep breath and moved his hands behind his back, holding on tight.

"What the hell are you trying to prove, Kian? That you're faster? Stronger?" Andrew got in his face. "Well, fucking great for you."

Almost touching chests, Kian stared Andrew down from his superior height. "You'd better adjust your attitude, buddy."

Andrew didn't back down. "You are sabotaging the mission, dumbass!"

No one talked to Kian like that.

"Only Syssi's concern for you stays my fist from rearranging your face," he hissed through lengthening fangs as he took a step into Andrew.

"Holy fuck..." Andrew took a step back. "You are one scary motherfucker, aren't you?" Lifting his hand, he got closer again and reached a finger to touch one of Kian's fangs. "You're not fucking with my head this time, are you? Those things are like what? Two inches long? And your eyes... holy shit... they are glowing like a pair of fucking flashlights..."

Kian shook his head. Evidently, his future brother-in-law was insane. Anyone with any sense of self-preservation would have been at least cautious if not terrified by that display.

But not Andrew, there was no fear in the guy's scent. Not a trace.

"And you must be one of those psychos who get a hard-on from an adrenaline rush."

"Hold your horses." Anandur butted his head in between them, his crinkly beard scratching Kian's forehead. "Until you ladies are done complimenting each other, Brundar and I are going to take a piss, and we are taking Rodney and the other one with us. Do us all a favor and either kiss and make up or beat the crap out of each other, but get over yourselves." He flicked them both on the top of their heads before turning around and gesturing for the rest of the men to follow. "Five minutes," he threw over his shoulder as the bunch walked away.

Kian groaned. Anandur's intervention had been like a needle prick to the overinflated balloon of his aggression. For the big oaf to step in as the voice of reason, Kian must've been doing a really piss-poor job of handling things.

Yeah, he sighed, feeling his fangs retract.

The storm in his head, the rage, the worry, the deep-seated hatred, guilt… had clouded his head, allowing the mindless beast inside him to surface.

"You are right." Kian ran a hand through his hair, suddenly feeling a desperate need to light up. "You mind if I smoke?" He pulled the pack out of his shirt pocket.

"Not at all, but if you don't mind, I'm going to sit down." Andrew lowered himself to the ground.

After a moment, Kian followed him down. "Can I offer you one?"

"Thanks, but no. I live dangerously enough as it is." Andrew waved him off.

"That I believe." Kian chuckled as he lit up.

"I never take unnecessary risks. I don't know what gave you that impression."

"Could've fooled me." Kian exhaled a ring of smoke. "The way you got in my face, in the state I was in, wasn't smart. You saw me; I'm more beast than man when I get like that."

"Nah, I knew you wouldn't do anything to me."

"What if I was too far gone? You know next to nothing about me and my kind and what to expect from us."

"That's where you are wrong. I might not know exactly what you are, but I do know who you are. And anyway, I knew I could count on that redheaded Goliath to jump in if needed."

"Goliath… ha? I like it. Usually, I just call him a big oaf."

"Is he?"

"Nah, but he likes to pretend he is." In the silence that followed, Kian concentrated on the rings of smoke he was making. It was a little like meditating, relaxing.

"We agreed that it would be best for me to lead the mission. You need to slow the fuck down and let me set the pace. Got it?"

"Yeah."

"Wow, miracles do happen. I expected you to give me more crap over this."

"No, I have no problem admitting when I'm wrong." Kian pushed up to his feet and offered a hand-up to Andrew. "Though don't expect an apology…"

"Wouldn't dream of it." The man took what he was offered and pulled himself up, slapping Kian's shoulder before he let go.

"Oh, how touching. You girls made up. I have tears in my eyes." Anandur sniffled, placing a hand over his heart and batting his eyelashes.

Two hands flicked his head at the same time as Kian and Andrew got him between them.

Patting his messed-up curls, Anandur groaned, "I feel the love."

24

SHARIM

As the island's transport reached flight altitude, Sharim pulled out the stack of fake passports he and his two companions would be using on their way to Los Angeles.

Going over the different names he'd chosen for himself, he devised a little trick to remember who he was supposed to be on each leg of the trip. After all, it would look pretty suspicious for him to respond with a *huh*? Or a *what*? Or not at all, when addressed as Mr. So-and-so.

The trick was quite simple; he created a little backstory for each name and a character to go with it. Modeling the four made-up versions of himself either on men he knew or characters in films, he made a movie in his head. Each had not only a unique posture, his own hand gestures, and individual syntax and inflection, but also a completely disparate personality.

He chose the version he liked best to go with the name he decided to use throughout the remainder of this mission.

Sharim would become Sebastian Shar—a wealthy businessman looking to invest in movies, radio stations, and newspapers. A charming, easygoing Australian everyone liked. Especially the ladies…

Until they discovered his true nature, that is. Sharim chuckled.

Not that he planned on seducing any of his future female business associates. He'd flirt, of course, but only because it would help his interests. Many of the media industry executives were female, and his charm was an asset he planned on utilizing to its fullest.

In order to protect the image of his manufactured persona, though, his twisted preferences would have to be kept not only private but secret. If word got out regarding his sexual activities, it would have disastrous consequences on his business dealings. Until he got his hands on at least one piece of young flesh and had her imprisoned in the dungeon he was planning to build for just this purpose, he'd have to limit himself to escort services that specialized in his kind of kink. But the best solution was to renew his membership to that fancy BDSM club downtown. Tormenting willing partners was not as fun, but in the meantime, it would have to do.

"Here." He handed the men their passports. "Memorize the names and choose the one you like best for last. From the moment we embark on the final leg of the trip to Los Angeles, our old names will be left behind. We'll be reborn with these new ones, using them exclusively even among ourselves. You'd be smart to start practicing."

The best way to create a false identity was not to act like that person, but become him. He would think as Sebastian Shar, talk as Sebastian Shar, and eventually dream as Sebastian Shar.

Waiting impatiently for the men to choose theirs, he was eager to begin the game. But the guys were just simple soldiers, and although the two were fairly intelligent and capable, they had none of his special skills. Not to mention that he'd had a millennium of practice to perfect them that the much younger immortals hadn't.

Still, waiting patiently for others to catch up wasn't a skill he had full mastery of, yet.

The guys kept flipping between the dark booklets. Judging by their frowns and head-shaking, it appeared to be a tough choice to make.

His second was the first to be done. After tucking one of the passports in his shoulder bag, he inserted the others inside a special compartment in his suitcase.

"Robert Dowson." He offered his hand to Sharim.

"Sebastian Shar. It's a pleasure to make your acquaintance, Robert."

"The pleasure is all mine, Mr. Shar."

"Please, call me Sebastian."

"Yes, sir."

"You have to lose the *Yes sir,* Robert. And that rigid spine has to go as well. From now on you're not a soldier, but a corporate executive. Act like one."

"Yes, sir."

Sebastian rolled his eyes. "You want to try that again?"

"No problem."

"That's better." He wondered how long it would take until Robert would walk the walk and talk the talk...

The good news was that he expected the other guy to do better. His assistant was young, sharp, and liked watching a lot of American movies and goofing around.

The boy didn't disappoint.

"Damn, Sebastian. I wanted to be Robert. I asked you to put me down as Robert Downey Jr., but instead, you gave it to a guy that has no idea who the hell it is."

"It's bad enough that you look like that actor's doppelgänger. Using a similar name would've made you a caricature, not a real person. You feel me?"

"Yeah, I get it. But why did you have to give it to him?" He pointed at the tall soldier who looked nothing like the actor.

"So you'd be sure to remember it."

"Oh, hell, Tom Carson it is, then."

"Nice to meet you, Tom."

"Yeah, same here, but I still don't know who that Tom is supposed to be. Any suggestions?"

"You're fine as you are. You're an assistant to a successful businessman, and your flippant attitude is tolerated because you're so incredibly good at what you do."

The guy smiled, showing a lot of white teeth, and dipped his head in an impression of a bow. "Thank you, I appreciate the compliment, Sebastian."

"It's all settled then. Let's go over the travel plan one more time before we land."

The airports he'd chosen for the layovers were big and located in countries that had no reason to invest in face recognition technology.

Just in case.

Hopping from one airport to another and then taking a bus or train ride through Europe, they would each take different routes until they met again in Munich. They would travel the last leg of the trip on the same plane, but they wouldn't be sitting together.

Sebastian's route would take him from Kuala Lumpur to Sydney, then from Sydney to Istanbul. Flying first class, he would spend some of the twenty plus hours of that flight sleeping, so he would be fresh and ready to have a good time in Prague, which was his next destination. From there, it would be a bus to Munich, and then a direct flight to Los Angeles.

25

DALHU

Dalhu wrapped the sleeves of his dress shirt around Amanda's wrists and tied the ends in a loose bow.

"Make it tighter," Amanda commanded.

He did it again, a little snugger this time. "I think this is good enough. Any tighter and it will constrict your circulation."

The irony of Amanda still calling the shots, even in how she wanted to be restrained, wasn't lost on him. He didn't mind, though.

Their first time was going to be all about her.

He was going to pleasure her like she'd never been pleasured before, have her climb higher than she ever had, and erase the memory of all those mortals she'd bedded before him.

"You think?" Amanda gave a tug, and the whole thing fell apart.

"I have an idea. How about I tie it around your mouth instead of your hands? It will be more conducive to what you have in mind."

He was only half joking.

"Yeah, you might have a point. I'm being too bossy. Do it."

Now, that was hilarious… especially since she wasn't trying to be funny…

With the shirt wadded in his hand, he stretched on top of her, pinning her down with his weight. For a moment, he just gazed at her stunning face. Then he kissed her, licking at the seam between her lips, penetrating her mouth, tasting, taking…

Groaning, she gave as good as she got, her nails digging into his neck to hold him to her, her legs parting to welcome him between them.

Was he the luckiest male on the planet? Or what?

And then she started to grind against him.

Oh, hell, he wasn't going to last like that.

With an effort, he released her mouth, taking a moment to collect himself before lifting his head to look into Amanda's glowing blue eyes.

So feral—so clearly not human.

Hers were the eyes of a hungry predator—a tigress, a cougar—challenging her male to prove himself worthy…

"I'm not going to cover these lush lips of yours. I have plans for them." He smiled down at her. "Give me your hands."

Pushing back, he braced on his knees and straddled her narrow waist. Holding her wrists with one hand, he wrapped the shirt-sleeves around them—this time utilizing a serious knot—the kind he would have used on a prisoner…

Well, almost. There was a big difference between the luxurious fabric of his expensive dress shirt and a coarse rope…

"Try it now, princess." He smirked as she gave it a tug, then another one, stronger this time, and still the knot held. "You think you can get out of that?" he taunted.

"I bet I could if I needed to. But it's good." She sighed, stretching her arms over her head, her whole body loosening in surrender.

It finally dawned on him then.

Up until that moment, he'd assumed she was playing a game, amusing herself with something she hadn't experienced before.

But that wasn't what this was about.

Not at all.

This was about Amanda giving herself permission to let go. And she couldn't do so until it was out of her hands… literally.

Leaning back on his haunches, Dalhu gazed at all that magnificent beauty sprawled before him like an offering and felt unbelievably lucky.

Privileged.

The whole thing seemed unreal.

"You're so beautiful," he murmured, though what he really meant to say was *thank you*. And not only to Amanda, but to the Fates, or the universe, or whatever higher power had granted such a gift to someone as undeserving as him.

Hooded with passion, her eyes lingered on his face for a brief moment before going on a slow and deliberate tour of every muscle in his body. "You're not so bad yourself," she said.

Kind of made a guy feel eight feet tall. Not that his height wasn't impressive to begin with, but yeah…

In a sinuous wave, he lowered himself on top of her, and bracing his elbows by her sides, cupped her face in his palms.

She parted her lips, inviting him to take her mouth again.

He kissed her slow and deep. Moving one palm to encircle her throat, he kissed and nipped his way down her jawline to the spot on her neck where her pulse was beating fast between his splayed fingers.

Pulling in a ragged breath through her teeth, Amanda let loose a small whimper and turned her head in his gentle hold, providing him with more expanse of soft skin to kiss and nip at.

As he ran his lips down and up the column of her neck, his fangs scraping lightly against her skin, she shivered, though not because she was afraid. She trusted him… and he realized that by closing his hand over her throat he'd been testing her.

And what a heady feeling that was. Her trust was something he hadn't dared hope for, despite being compelled to seek it.

Sliding down, he released Amanda's throat, his palm drifting to her breast. He had neglected these beauties, letting them get chilled in the cold cabin, and it was about time he remedied this situation. Cupping his hand over one, he dipped his head and used his mouth to warm the other.

Amanda moaned, bucking up into him, and that was even before he began doing anything interesting. Which was about to change as soon as he deemed her perky breasts sufficiently warmed, starting with the one already in his mouth. Putting his tongue to work, he swirled it around the tight little nub, flicking and licking at it before giving it a hard pull as he hollowed his cheeks and sucked it in.

Then he did it again on her other side while his fingers paid attention to the one he'd just released. At first, he only circled his thumb round and round the wet, hard peak. But then, as he got serious about the sucking and the nipping on the other side, he caught her sensitive flesh between his thumb and finger. Pinching and tweaking, he increased the pressure he applied, gauging Amanda's response by her moans and the increased tempo of her gyrations.

The wild cat was loving it, and he would've lingered feasting on her breasts if he weren't so eager to get his mouth on another part of her anatomy.

Like right now…

Sliding even farther down her body, he kissed her belly button, then swirled the tip of his tongue inside it while his hands got busy with the button of her jeans. The zipper was next, and as he pulled it down a little bit at a time, he licked a trail down to the line of her pink cotton panties.

Surprisingly, it was one of the simple ones he'd picked for her in the general store, and not a fancy new one from the selection he'd bought for her at that lingerie store, or rather Plain Jane had. But he knew there was an even better surprise waiting for him under that cotton. Amanda was completely bare—he'd glimpsed it when he'd seen her in all her naked glory in that bathtub upstairs. Dalhu wondered if this was natural for a female of his kind or had she had it removed. In either case, he found it hot as hell. Imagining how soft and smooth that most intimate female flesh would feel under his lips and his tongue, he was impatient to get to it.

It was good then that her jeans were the kind that stretched; otherwise he would have torn them at the seams in his mad rush to yank them off Amanda's slender legs. The pink panties joined the ride and got tossed to the floor together with what had covered them. A split second later, he had his palm over what was his gateway to heaven.

Oh, man, the heat...

And she was so wet... drenched...

His mouth watered as he dipped his head to take his first taste.

As his long and dexterous tongue licked a path from the fountain of all that heavenly nectar up to the top of her wet folds—to the place where the key to her treasure was hidden—Amanda growled. The sound was more like that of a feral cat than a woman—the kind that would've scared a lesser man—a mortal.

Diving in for more of that ambrosia, he wondered if she'd ever made that sound for anyone but him...

The thought of his woman with some puny, weak human spurred his aggression, and his need to get inside her, to penetrate her became overwhelming...

He did...

With his tongue.

Shaping it into a spear, he thrust it deep inside her, penetrating her as he would with his shaft, fucking her rhythmically, forcefully. His palms clamped on her butt cheeks, he held her in place while he tongue-fucked her...

No... damn it.

He was supposed to be making love to his woman, not fucking her. And even though the difference was only in how he phrased it in his head, it struck him as a kind of sacrilege.

Fuck!

Damn it, he was starting to hate that word...

Even if it killed him, he was going to make love to Amanda slowly, tenderly—his body an extension of his heart.

Dialing back on his aggression, he began lapping leisurely.

Amanda's animal groans soon tapered down to a more human sounding moan, and she cranked her head up to get a better view of what he was doing.

Hot damn.

His mouth and nose buried between her wet folds, he gazed up at her eyes.

Seeing her beautiful face framed by the pair of her glorious breasts, flushed with lust as she watched him pleasuring her, was so fucking hot that he was afraid his mind would short-circuit.

As it was, his fangs reached their full length, pulsating with the urgent need to be sunk into his female whether his shaft was inside her or not.

"Do it," she breathed.

Oh, man, was he tempted. Licking a spot at the juncture of her inner thigh, he felt Amanda shiver in anticipation, the slight scent of her fear doing nothing to cool him down—on the contrary.

He was, after all, a predator, and for the first time in his long life he didn't have to wrestle with his nature to avoid hurting a female.

Amanda was not only just as feral as he, but she was practically indestructible.

Not to mention that after all her puny, mortal, boy toy lovers, she must crave that which only he could give her.

But biting her would be cheating, wouldn't it?

He wanted to make her climax before the venom did the work for him. And not just climax; he wanted her to fly higher than she had ever flown before and fall apart all over him, screaming his name. Or moaning it, or whispering it…

Whatever… as long as it was his name.

"Not yet, I want to make you come first… over…and…over… again…" he said in between long, wet laps of his tongue.

"Oh, hell…" She groaned and dropped back, the outpour of wetness he caught with his tongue the best kind of *yes* imaginable.

26

KIAN

Trekking behind Andrew, Kian gritted his teeth. Despite the fact that they were nearing their destination well ahead of time, the easy pace the guy was dictating was driving him insane.

Kian was well aware that his irritation was irrational, but he couldn't help it.

He was losing it big time.

Thankfully, it wasn't long before the cabin's steep roof came into view, and a few moments later Andrew motioned for them to halt.

The plan was for Kian and the brothers to wait some distance away from the cabin while Andrew and his buddies went ahead and planted small explosives around its perimeter. No need to risk the Doomer's innate immortal-male-alert waking him up prematurely, and ruin the tactical advantage of a surprise attack.

Hopefully, the fucker was a sound sleeper and wouldn't detect the faint scent emitted by the mortals. And besides, with the wind picking up, odds were that their scent would disperse before it had a chance to filter through the cabin's walls.

Not that it had done any good with the rest of the creatures inhabiting the forest. Judging by the howling frenzy of a nearby wolf pack, the wind wasn't all that effective in taking care of their team's smell. The fucking wolves were not only aware of the interlopers' presence, but the pack had been stealthily following them for some time now, getting vocal at the most inopportune time.

Unfortunately, as careful and as detailed as Andrew's plan was, there was no way to factor in nature's hindrance or conversely assistance.

Damn. Hopefully, the howling wouldn't alert the Doomer.

As Andrew led the group behind the cover of a slightly denser growth, he shrugged off his backpack and leaned it against the heavy roots of a tree. Crouching next to the green army issue, he pulled out a laser range meter and pointed it toward the cabin, took the measurement, then pointed it toward a large outcropping some five hundred yards away. "Kian, I need to time your guys' speed out here. Every fraction of a second counts. When I give the signal, I want you to sprint to that big rock over there." He motioned toward the rock formation. "It's the same distance from us as the cabin."

Readying for the next stage of the plan to commence, Kian's muscles were already coiled. "All three of us at once, or one at a time?"

"One at a time."

"I'll go first."

"Wait for my signal… And go!" As Andrew pressed a button on his watch, a corresponding red light flashed on Kian's.

He crossed the distance in seconds.

"Damn, you're fast," Andrew said as he recorded the time. "Okay, now you." He pointed at Anandur. "Go!"

Then it was Brundar's turn.

"And the winner is…" Andrew pointed at Kian.

Apparently, adrenaline had given him a boost. Kian had expected Brundar to win—the guy was their fastest runner.

"And you guys are not even breathing hard. Amazing." Andrew

shook his head. "Okay, listen up. I'm going to go over the details again."

"No need." Kian waved him off.

"Maybe yes, maybe not. But you're going to listen anyway."

Kian rolled his eyes but said nothing. Arguing with Andrew was pointless, and besides, he'd given his word that he would not interfere and would let the guy lead.

"Once the explosives are in place, I'll give the go signal, and you guys sprint for the cabin. Fifteen seconds later, I'll detonate the explosives. The timing is crucial. I timed your speed and calculated exactly how many seconds it takes you to cross the distance. The explosives will detonate precisely three seconds before you guys reach the cabin."

In addition to blowing a hole in the wall for unobstructed entry, the explosions would create a distraction, going off simultaneously in several spots around the perimeter and, hopefully, disorienting the Doomer.

If everything happened exactly as planned, the commotion would distract the fucker long enough for Kian to get to him before the Doomer had a chance to grab Amanda and put a knife to her throat.

Then it would be game over.

The Doomer was Kian's.

27

AMANDA

Holy hell.

The best sexual experience of her life, and this was just the foreplay. While expertly playing her body to a fever pitch with his mouth, Dalhu had kept his pants on, and she could only imagine how amazing that hard length she'd felt before through his jeans would feel inside her.

Amanda had expected sex with an immortal male to be different, but this was on a level she couldn't have even conceived.

In comparison, her prior experiences couldn't even qualify as masturbation.

What was it that cranked the dial on the erotic gauge all the way up? Immortal male's pheromones at work? The right chemistry? Was it Dalhu's magnificently powerful body?

Holding her in place, making her feel feminine, delicate, fragile...

Dominating her...

Gently, reverently...

The combination was so fucking hot—the novelty of being with a male who could overpower her with ease and yet never would without her permission.

Who knew that a male's dominance could be such a turn-on?

Well, not just any male, but still…

Even though Dalhu was more than strong enough to subdue her without tying her up, and even though she could've gotten free if she wished so, the make-believe restraint allowed her to give herself over to the pleasure. For once, she was allowing a male to take the lead and not thinking of what would be her next move.

Amanda didn't have even one submissive bone in her body, and though not quite the dominatrix, she was used to being the one in charge.

Maybe this was it. Maybe it was so hot because this was all new to her.

Different.

It felt like a new beginning.

A fresh start.

All thoughts ceased as she felt his thick finger slowly penetrating her. First one, then two… and as he began pumping, her body surged up to meet his lips.

He clamped a hand on her thigh, holding her down as he licked around her clitoris, his fingers moving in and out in maddeningly shallow thrusts.

She shifted up and heard herself say a word she'd never said during sex before."Pleeeease…"

Dalhu growled as he lifted his head. "Please what?"

His eyes glowing and his fangs fully extended, he looked feral, and instinctively, she knew the time to truly surrender was now. Behind those wild eyes, she saw little, if any, of the man. The beast had taken over, and it couldn't care less that she was impatient for him to bring her to a climax, and it certainly had never heard of women's lib.

The beast was asserting its dominance as it claimed its female.

Damn, it was hot.

As her body responded with an outpour of wetness, Amanda let her head drop back. Perhaps there was a little submissive bone somewhere in there after all.

Nah… Not me…

But as Dalhu kept her at a near boiling simmer, growling and nipping at her inner thighs whenever she wouldn't hold still, the coil inside her was winding impossibly tighter.

Amanda held on.

He wasn't going to let her come before he was good and ready, and once he did, she was going to shoot through the roof.

At first, the desperate sounds she was making—the mewls and the growls and the keening moans—embarrassed her. But as it became almost painful to be held over that elusive edge, she stopped thinking and let herself go wild. She didn't care anymore if Dalhu heard the tortured sounds he was wringing out of her, or that her head was thrashing side to side as her bound hands banged on the armrest.

Letting it all loose was liberating.

It felt amazing.

She was burning, and with her the whole world was going up in flames.

Let it burn. She didn't care.

Then Dalhu thrust his incredibly long fingers all the way inside her and curled them against that sweet spot on her front wall, at the same time sucking her clit between his lips, hard.

The orgasm exploded from her with the force of a volcanic eruption, and she screamed his name as she flew, soaring above as it went spewing out like lava, on and on, until there was nothing left inside her.

And with her, all around her, the world was exploding.

Boom! Boom! Boom!

Boom!

28

ANDREW

Andrew cleared the tree line and stopped. The cabin had approximately a hundred feet of open space around it, with only one mature oak in front to provide cover. But as he'd expected, the place was mostly dark. All but the two uppermost windows were shuttered, and some dim light was visible through those two small triangles of glass. Still, with the moonlight finally breaking through the heavy cover of clouds, the illumination was sufficient for him to take off his night-vision goggles.

Behind him, Jake and Rodney did the same.

He'd left the immortals who needed no help with night vision some distance away, where the forest was denser and provided better cover.

Stronger, faster, and the bastards can see perfectly in the dark.

Well, good for them. Hopefully, they could also do something about that bloody wolf pack because the fucking howling was getting on his nerves.

And what's worse, the wind was picking up at an alarming rate, which might render the helicopter useless for the return trip.

Fuck! Like he needed another complication.

He'd better hurry and assess the situation inside that cabin.

It would've been great if the immortals could also see through walls, but unlike Superman, they didn't have that ability.

Bummer, it could've saved him some time.

He would need to get close and check.

After all, it wouldn't be much of a rescue if they placed the explosives next to where Amanda was sleeping and blew her up. Though, if luck would have it, the perp was sleeping right next to a wall.

As Andrew approached the east side of the structure, he carefully lowered his heavy backpack to the ground, then pulled out the portable Xaver 800 Electromagnetic Radar. The thing was not as easy to operate as the smaller models, requiring a tripod, but it provided the most accurate picture of a room's interior, including placement of furniture, the exact location of live occupants, and their movements. With the tripod's legs extended, he placed the device next to the wall and turned it on.

Fucking hell.

The good news was that he had two live ones in there, which meant Amanda was okay. The bad news was that they were together… busy… and unless that Doomer was performing a medical exam, they were doing the horizontal mambo… And it didn't seem as if Amanda was struggling either…

Golly gee-fuckin'-whiz.

Thank God, Kian couldn't see through walls. No one would've been able to stop the guy.

If not for Andrew's many years of training, he would've been no better than Syssi's hotheaded boyfriend and would've charged inside himself.

This complicated everything. Not only was the perp awake, but it would be next to impossible to get to Amanda before the guy grabbed her.

At least the sofa he had Amanda on was practically in the middle of the room so the explosives could go wherever on the perimeter of the cabin.

Circling his finger, Andrew gave the sign for Rodney and Jake to go ahead and place the things at the spots they deemed best—no impediments to point out.

By the time he was finished folding the tripod and packing the Xaver in his backpack, the guys had everything in place. His men were the best.

Hefting the heavy load over his shoulders, he joined his buddies as they backed away, reluctantly clearing the stage for the immortals to do their thing.

They couldn't have been more than a few feet away from the cabin when he heard the scream. An ear-piercing sound that carried over the whistling wind and the howling wolves and straight into her brother's ears.

Fuck. Here goes the plan—

There was a terrifying roar, and as he fumbled with the remote-control detonator, Andrew had the impression of something hurtling toward him with the speed of a runaway car and the force of a locomotive.

No time to double-check the timing, he pressed the button and prayed to God the explosives would detonate before Kian reached the cabin.

A split second later, the explosions shook the structure behind him, and the three immortal titans passed him and his buddies, almost knocking them over as they galloped at what was an unbelievable speed even for them—they must've been faster than cheetahs.

Immortal or not, the perp was a dead man.

29

KIAN

The fucker is torturing Amanda!

Racing for the cabin, Kian felt like crossing that distance was taking forever, though it couldn't have been more than a few seconds.

And yet, as fast as he was running, his mind was going even faster.

Planning.

First, he was going to tear the Doomer's throat out.

With that out of the way, he'd make sure Amanda was safe before taking out of Andrew's hide every ounce of pain Amanda had suffered because he'd been dragging his feet. While Andrew was pacing them and forcing Kian to go slow, Amanda had been tortured.

Damn, he should have listened to his gut when it had urged him to push forward as fast as he could.

As he leaped over the smoking debris at the bottom of the large hole in the wall, the scene unfolding before him was even worse than what he'd been expecting.

Crouching with his arms spread wide and his elongated fangs

dripping venom, the Doomer was trying to block the view of Amanda's nude body laid out on the couch behind him.

The fucker had her wrists tied with some rags, and although Kian couldn't see any bruises, it looked like she was passed out.

This vile creature has tied and raped my little sister.

He is going to die... painfully.

With a roar, Kian attacked.

He expected the Doomer to rush ahead and use the momentum to add power to the clash, but the fucker didn't budge from his spot, waiting for Kian to come to him.

If he thought Kian would hesitate to tear him apart in front of Amanda, he was dead wrong. Very. Dead. Wrong.

But something was off.

On impact, the huge Doomer barely moved an inch, and Kian was starting to realize that he'd underestimated his opponent. But he couldn't count on Brundar and Anandur's help because he'd given them orders not to. They'd been assigned the important task of safeguarding Amanda.

And yet, besides keeping his neck out of reach of Kian's snapping fangs, the monster did nothing more than defend himself.

And guard Amanda.

But as the brothers circled around, approaching the couch from behind, the Doomer's attention was diverted for just long enough to provide Kian with the opening he needed, and he sank his fangs into the fucker's thick neck.

Kian's intention wasn't the merciful venom killing, though, not for this monster. He was going to rip out the fucker's throat, and as the Doomer was bleeding, go for his heart.

"Nooooo!"

Amanda's shrill scream was followed by the sound of ripping fabric, and then she was on Kian's back, clutching his torso between her naked thighs and pulling on his hair with both hands.

"Don't you dare harm him! Pull your fangs out of his throat! Now!"

She was ripping his fucking hair out, pulling on it with all her strength.

What the fuck?

"And do it slowly," she hissed in his ear. "If even a little of his skin tears… I'm never going to forgive you. Ever!"

Classic Stockholm syndrome...

Still, Kian did as she demanded. And not only because he believed she would deliver on her promise. He couldn't put his finger on it, but something was off with the scenario he'd created in his head.

"Why are you defending him? That monster had tied you down, tortured you, or raped you, or both, until you screamed and passed out from the pain." Kian held on to the Doomer, who stopped struggling.

"Not pain, you moron, pleasure. I screamed because I was having the best orgasm of my life. With your vast sexual experience, I would think you should be able to distinguish between a cry of pain and a cry of pleasure."

"But he had you tied up…"

Amanda got off his back and faced him, assuming her angry pose of hands on her hips and a foot tapping the floor.

With one significant difference—this time, she was doing it butt naked.

"It was a shirt. It took me how long to rip it apart? A second? You think I could be restrained with a piece of fabric?"

"I don't understand…"

"Really? Oh, wow, I never thought I'd have to explain sex games to you, Kian."

"Oh…"

Kian was speechless as he attempted to process what she was

telling him. Everything that felt off from the moment he had leaped into this room was starting to make sense.

There had been no bruises on her because the Doomer hadn't been abusing her. She had been having sex with that scum, willingly. And as incomprehensible as it was, the fucker hadn't attacked because he'd been protecting Amanda from perceived danger and then held back when he realized it was her family who'd come to rescue her.

Fucking unbelievable.

Amanda had a lot of explaining to do, and hopefully, it was along the lines of letting the scum touch her to prevent him from killing her… not because she'd wanted it.

Though, the way she'd protected that filth, she must have developed feelings for him.

Fucking hell.

Standing naked in a room full of males, Amanda was still glaring at him. It didn't faze the brothers, but the humans were staring at her with gaping, drooling mouths.

And that included Andrew.

"Get dressed, Amanda," Kian hissed, getting up and turning away from her.

Right now, he couldn't see the beauty the others were admiring.

Amanda disgusted him.

"Anandur, slap some cuffs on the scum. He is coming with us. And bag that laptop."

Leaving them all behind, on his way out Kian stepped over the debris and marched downhill toward the spot where the helicopter was supposed to be waiting for them. It was all he could do not to say—in front of a crowd—things Amanda would never be able to forgive.

Once they were alone, though, he was going to tell her exactly what he thought of her.

30

AMANDA

This was bad.

No, it was good—she was getting her old life back. But there was no place for Dalhu in it. And that was bad.

Ignoring Kian's order to get dressed, Amanda crouched over Dalhu instead. Slumped on the floor with his back propped against the sofa, his arms flopped uselessly at his sides. He wasn't moving.

He looked wasted.

But although his eyes were heavy-lidded, he didn't look venom-drugged or euphoric.

He looked defeated. Drained.

"Are you okay?" she whispered, aware of the five sets of eyes trained on her naked ass.

"It's over," he whispered back. "You are free, and I'm dead whether your people kill me or not. Just let them do it. It would be a mercy. There is no point for me to go on without you."

"Don't talk like that. Nothing is over until it's over. I'll figure something out."

"Even if you decide you want to keep me, they will never allow it. I saw how he looked at me."

"Who? Kian?"

"Yes."

"He was just angry. He thought you'd been hurting me. Once I explain what was going on, everything will be okay. Don't worry about it."

"You're wrong. You've explained and he believed you, but he still wanted me dead. And I saw the disgust in his eyes when he looked at you. Like you were dirty because I've touched you."

Yeah, she had seen it too. Not that Kian's reaction surprised her, but still, it hurt.

"He'll get over it. He always forgives me, no matter what I do."

"Not this time."

"He has no choice. I'm his little sister."

"I'm so sorry," Dalhu whispered as he closed his eyes. "You must tell him that it was just about survival—that you did it only because I'd threatened you. I don't want you to lose your brother on my account."

Anandur cleared his throat. "Sorry to interrupt, princess, but I suggest you get dressed. We need to get moving." He touched her shoulder.

"Get up," he addressed Dalhu in a much harsher tone. "Put on your boots and a shirt. Where are your clothes?"

"They are upstairs. I'll get them," Amanda said as she picked up her things from the floor and headed for the stairs.

"Didn't your mamas teach you not to stare, boys?" she threw over her shoulder to the three humans still ogling her naked butt.

"They will stop staring if you put some clothes on." Anandur chuckled.

Loath to leave Dalhu at Anandur's mercy, Amanda hurried into the bathroom, taking only a moment to clean up with a washcloth before getting dressed. She grabbed her purse and a shirt for Dalhu on her way down.

"Here you go." She handed it to him.

Anandur waited for Dalhu to put it on and button it up before cuffing him.

He was treating Dalhu better than she would've expected, not roughing him up or shoving him, and Amanda wondered if it was because she was watching. Otherwise, Anandur probably wouldn't have been as nice.

"Let's go," he said after Dalhu pulled on his boots.

The brothers led the small group out with Dalhu between them.

Amanda tried to squeeze in, wanting to be by his side, but Anandur shook his head, and she was relegated to walking behind them.

The three humans were apparently still in a state of shock from seeing her naked because none of them said a single word as they trailed after her.

Well, they would get over it. She had bigger problems than that.

What the hell was she going to do?

She knew Kian would forbid her having any contact with Dalhu, and if she insisted, he would eventually cave in but despise her for doing it.

What a mess.

She didn't want to forsake Dalhu, especially not to her brother's merciless clutches.

Fates, Kian was probably going to torture the poor guy. Which was entirely unnecessary since Dalhu had promised to reveal everything he knew voluntarily. But Kian wouldn't believe him and would torture him anyway.

But more than that, she wasn't ready to let the little flame that had sparked between them die before it had a chance to flare.

And if she was honest with herself, that flame wasn't so small.

It wasn't that she had fallen in love or anything, but for the first time in her life, there was a chance she might.

With a Doomer...

Fates, why? Why out of all the men in the universe had they

matched her with a Doomer? Was it some kind of a cosmic joke? A punishment? Was throwing the two of them together a source of amusement for the fickle Fates?

But was he even her match?

Who knew?

But after all, he was the only one out there she could have.

She felt more than saw as Andrew picked up his pace and sidled up to her.

"How are you holding up?" he asked with a sidelong glance at her face.

"Just peachy."

"I'm sorry Kian is being an ass to you, and I want you to know that I'm here for you. The whole ordeal must've been traumatic, but you've handled it beautifully. Survival justifies the use of any and every tool at your disposal. And as your beauty is your best weapon, I'm glad that you used it."

"Dalhu didn't force me. In fact, all the poor guy did was to pleasure me. We were interrupted before we had a chance to do the deed."

"I got that. But even if you had to seduce him to gain some kind of advantage, it was still a smart move. I would've advised my own sister to do the same."

Andrew was being such a sweetheart, so supportive at a time when she really needed a friend. Amanda was loath to tell him the truth and lose that support—as well as shatter his illusions.

"I'm so sorry, Andrew." She choked a little as tears welled in her eyes. His compassion was her kryptonite, making her weak. It was easier to be strong when there was no one to lean on.

"For what?"

"You're such a nice guy. Too nice for someone like me."

"What are you talking about?" He frowned.

"I did what I did because I wanted to. Not because I was afraid for my life or because Dalhu had threatened me or demanded anything other than being given a chance to woo me. So if it proves that I'm a slut and have absolutely no self-control, so be it. I never claimed otherwise. I'm not going to apologize for it."

"I see." Andrew dropped his head, keeping his eyes on his boots as they made their way downhill.

"Do yourself a favor and forget I ever flirted with you. It meant nothing. Not that you're not a great guy, you are. But there could've never been more than a casual hookup between us. We are, um… incompatible." She took a furtive peek at his hard face.

She had no idea how much he'd been told, and as the mortals had shown up after Dalhu and Kian's fangs had already retracted, they probably had seen nothing out of the ordinary.

Well, except for her in all her naked glory.

"Syssi has turned." He pinned her with a challenging stare.

"What?" Amanda froze, halting their little procession, and turned to face him.

"Sh… keep walking." He took her elbow, propelling her forward. "I know everything, but my men are on a need to know basis only. Kian is going to scramble their memories once we get back, but the less they know, the less he will have to mess with."

"When?" she whispered.

"It started at the restaurant we all had lunch at. Syssi began feeling sick right after you left and lost consciousness during the night. They were not sure she was going to make it. Lucky for me, I didn't find out until she pulled through, otherwise I would've tried to kill your obnoxious brother and we both know how that would've ended… Anyway, when I couldn't get a hold of her on the phone, I got worried, hoofed it to your building, and demanded to see her."

"How did you find where she was? Did you have her followed?"

"It was the necklace. I've known her location all along." He pointed to the small heart pendant Amanda was still wearing. "Syssi had no idea I had a tracking device installed inside the thing. That's how we were able to find you. You are very lucky that she gave it to you."

Amanda flashed him a sideways grin. "Or not. Dalhu grabbed me at the jewelry store where I went to have it duplicated. But be that as it may, I'm glad you're a paranoid, overprotective brother. Thank you."

"You're welcome."

For the next couple of minutes, they walked in silence. As the terrain got rougher, she stumbled a couple of times. The soles of the plain sneakers Dalhu had gotten her weren't providing much cushioning for her feet—she felt every little rock. Watching her step, she was slowing them down, and the gap between Dalhu and the Guardians and the rest of the group was widening.

"Do you want me to carry you? It seems you're suffering," Andrew offered.

Such a sweet guy.

She thought of dubbing him Andrew the Sweet, though not to his face, of course. It wouldn't sit well with his tough guy image.

Instead, she gave him an incredulous look. "Thank you. It is very sweet of you to offer. But really? You think? I'm not a small woman. I'm almost as tall as you. You'll fall, and both of us will end up tumbling down the hill. I'm fine, just being careful."

"Let me at least hold your hand. You scare the shit out of me every time you list to the side."

Rolling her eyes, she took the hand he offered. "Now that you know what I am, you should be aware that I'm not exactly fragile."

"Yes, I know. Just let me be a gentleman and deal with it."

Andrew's hand was large and warm, and his strong arm saved her from painfully twisting her ankle a few times. But for some reason, it felt awkward to hold it. He was really nice, and she liked him, but…

It felt as if she was being unfaithful… and how ridiculous was that.

Ridiculous or not, she nonetheless stretched on her tiptoes, trying to ascertain if Dalhu and the Guardians were indeed too far away to see or hear her exchange with Andrew.

"Don't worry about losing them. I know the way." Andrew misunderstood her concern.

Well, she wasn't going to explain what she was worried about—he would think she had lost her freaking mind. "I'm not worried. So, how is Syssi taking it? Being immortal, I mean."

"I don't think she's had time to process it yet. Right when she got back on her feet, she had to deal with your kidnapping and us going on a rescue mission."

"It seems that I always manage to steal the spotlight, providing all the drama and excitement. But at least it's never boring with me around. Right?" She grimaced.

"Of that I'm sure," Andrew's voice dropped, and he squeezed her hand, his hard face softening as he regarded her…

Fondly…

Fondly wasn't the right word for what she saw in his eyes, but she was going to stick with it anyway.

"Kian offered to activate my dormant genes…" Andrew glanced at her from under his long lashes.

That's right, she hadn't thought of that. As Syssi's brother, Andrew was also a Dormant. Her brain must've turned into mush. But who could blame her?

It is not every day that a girl gets kidnapped, starts developing feelings for her kidnapper, has him give her a brain-scrambling orgasm, gets rescued, and catches the eye of another sexy guy. All in the span of what? Thirty-six hours?

What a mess.

She smiled and gave his hand a little squeeze. "Congratulations, you must be very excited."

His answer surprised her. "I'm not sure I'm going to do it."

She halted. "Why the hell not? If I may ask?"

"Syssi is fourteen years my junior, and she barely got through it. I would rather live out the meager years I still have than die attempting immortality. Not unless I have one hell of a good reason to take such a risk." He looked at her pointedly.

Oh, boy, twist the knife, why don't you.

He couldn't have been more obvious if he'd spelled it out and submitted it in writing. So now she was responsible for him attempting or not attempting the change. Great.

What to do. What to do.

When in doubt, play it dumb.

"There is no rush. You can take your time and think it through. And if a compelling reason were to present itself, you could always change your mind. One never knows. The Fates are fickle."

Sadistic bitches is a better description... I'm sorry... please don't punish me... Amanda looked up, squinting, afraid of the bolt of lightning they might hurl her way.

"You sound like Syssi. Only when she says stuff like that, she scares the crap out of me. Her predictions always come true—one way or the other."

Thank you, sweet Fates. Andrew shifted away from dropping his boulder-sized hints to talking about his sister.

"When I tested her precognition ability and found how amazing she was, I suspected right away she might be a Dormant. That is the real story behind my research. I'm searching for people with special abilities in the hopes that some might be Dormants. Until now, I've only found Syssi and one other guy."

"Yes, I know, Michael. He transitioned at the same time as Syssi."

"I knew it! I was right!" Amanda couldn't help herself and did a little victory dance.

"Shush..." Andrew rolled his eyes toward the two mortals behind them.

"I can't help it. I'm so excited," she whispered. "I can't wait to get back to work and start searching for more Dormants. You have no idea what that means to us."

"I think I do. Good luck."

"Thanks."

The good news brought a new spring to Amanda's step. Forgotten were the little rocks poking at the soles of her feet, the look of disgust in Kian's eyes, and the whole mess with Dalhu. She felt invincible as she hurried to get to the helicopter as fast as she could without breaking a leg.

After all, if she had single-handedly found the solution to her people's greatest problem, how hard could it be to unravel the tangled knot of this mess?

Piece of cake.

31

DALHU

Plodding between the two Guardians with his hands cuffed behind his back, Dalhu contemplated his options—or lack thereof.

Running would achieve nothing except some serious damage from the big redhead's fists or a knife between his shoulder blades from the blond. Probably both.

Though in the mood he was in, he would have welcomed the pain.

Anything to override the horrible sense of loss, of failure—something to fill the empty hole in his chest.

Unfortunately, that required energy he couldn't muster in his current state. Maybe if he just goaded them, they would beat him up for mouthing off.

He wondered if that would work.

Nah. The brother, maybe, but not these guys. Guardians were not known to be hotheaded—too disciplined.

Was the brother a Guardian? It seemed he was in charge of this operation, which would suggest he was, and he was a strong motherfucker—well trained. But Amanda only mentioned the female Guardian; she said nothing about having a brother on the force.

Dalhu suspected he was missing some puzzle pieces.

And what was the story with the mortals they had brought with them? Since when did the Guardian Force employ humans? Was it some new strategy? A way to boost their measly ranks? And how the hell had the Guardians found him anyway?

Where had he gone wrong?

He had been so careful, thinking of every little detail, covering his tracks so meticulously…

It doesn't matter.

It is all over.

Amanda might have prevented his field execution, but she would not be able to keep her brother from locking him in a small dark cell and throwing away the key.

Which would be worse than death.

Even entombment was better than that. Though it took a long time, consciousness eventually faded at some point—not so with an indeterminate prison sentence.

Maybe he could goad the fucker to attack him. Call his sister some nasty names… that would certainly do it…

But Dalhu knew he wouldn't.

As it was, by allowing a Doomer to touch her and then making it worse by defending him, Amanda had already lost her brother's respect. There was no way he was making it even more difficult for her.

His only other option was to plead with the fucker to kill him…

Like hell.

No way would he give the arrogant, condescending, pretentious cocksucker the satisfaction.

Fuck him.

Dalhu was made of stronger stuff than that.

And brother or not, no one was looking down his nose at Amanda. No one.

He would challenge the fucker to a fight for making his own sister feel like crap.

There was nothing to justify such a sanctimonious attitude.

She hadn't stolen anything, hadn't harmed anyone or herself, and as the sole owner of her own body, she was free to do with it as she pleased—without prejudice or judgment.

That brother of hers was such a hypocrite. Where were his clan's lofty ideas of freedom and equality? Of a woman's right to choose whomever she pleased?

Supposedly, this whole ancient feud between their people was the result of the mother of their clan exercising that exact right, and choosing one male over another.

Amanda's brother was no better, in attitude if not in deeds, than the scum in Dalhu's part of the world who murdered their own daughters and sisters for putting a blemish on their family's honor.

The supposed *blemish,* more often than not, was the product of being a victim of rape.

It was ironic, really, that Dalhu, a Doomer, was going to teach that supposedly progressive jerk a thing or two about the respect he ought to show his sister.

Straightening his shoulders, Dalhu lifted his head and took a quick glance behind him, but Amanda and the mortals had fallen behind. He could dimly hear the murmur of their voices, but he couldn't see her.

32

KIAN

Barreling downhill, Kian waited till he walked off some of his anger before pulling out his sat phone to call his mother.

"We've got Amanda. Unharmed... perfectly fine, actually." Kian did his best to sound civil, hoping his mother wouldn't notice the bite he struggled to keep out of his tone.

"I told you she was fine. Never doubt me, Kian."

"I'm glad you were proven right. Is Syssi with you?"

"She is here by my side, waiting impatiently to talk to you."

"Could you put her on?"

"Here you go, sweetie," he heard his mother say as she handed the phone to Syssi.

"Oh, God, I'm so relieved. Is everybody okay? Did anyone get hurt?"

"Andrew's plan worked without a hitch, or rather despite a hitch or two..."

"Why? What happened?"

"Nothing I'm in the mood to discuss over the phone. I'll tell you when we get home."

There was a moment of silence. "You don't sound as happy as I thought you would be..." Syssi hesitated before whispering, "Did you kill the Doomer? Is that why you sound so strange?"

"No, I didn't. Though, not because I didn't want to or am such a forgiving kind of guy," he grated. "Amanda didn't let me. She practically pulled out chunks of my hair to stop me from—" *tearing his throat out.*

Oh, hell, he had almost blurted that out. Let her assume he only meant to put the fucker to sleep, permanently, with an overdose of venom... "Yeah, I probably have a few bald spots on my head."

"Oh, wow..."

"Yeah, wow is right. And that is not even the half of it. But I'll tell you the rest later."

"I guess Amanda is not next to you. Is she close by? I want to talk to her, see how she is coping, offer my support... She must be traumatized by the ordeal."

His sweet Syssi. She was on to him and was trying, very delicately, to bring him around to see things from a different perspective.

He sighed. "No, she is not. I had to get out of there and left Anandur and Brundar to deal with her and that thing."

"I hope that by 'to deal with' you don't mean 'to take care of' like in the gangster movies..."

He chuckled. "No, we are bringing the perp to the keep and rewarding him for kidnapping Amanda with indefinite free room and board in a small cell down in the basement."

"That's good... I can't wait for you guys to get home." Syssi paused and sighed. "Be nice to Amanda, Kian. She has been through enough."

He wanted to tell Syssi he would try, but that would have been a lie. Right now he couldn't even bring himself to look at his sister, let alone be nice to her. The best he might be able to pull off was to ignore her. And he wasn't sure he could do even that.

How the hell could she? Let that animal touch her? A cold-blooded murderer?

It might not have been this particular Doomer's fangs that had killed Mark, but he was part of the team that had done it. And even if that wasn't the case, he was a Doomer, for fuck's sake. A filthy, disgusting, evil creature.

"I need to speak with my mother. Could you pass her the phone?"

There was a silent pause before Syssi answered. "Yeah, sure."

She probably expected him to say he couldn't wait to hold her in his arms, or some other nice romantic thing, but he just couldn't. Not yet.

"You wish to speak with me?"

"We are bringing in the... the Doomer to be jailed in the basement. Permanently. On the remote chance that he will somehow manage to escape, or find a way to communicate with the other minions of evil, I don't want him to find out you're here. So please, don't wait for us on the roof."

"As you wish. I will await my daughter in her quarters."

Ending the call, Kian suspected that Annani humored him for now, but most likely was already planning on visiting the Doomer later on.

He could understand her desire to question the enemy, but there was no need for that. He would do the gruesome task for her, sparing her delicate sensibilities.

In fact, he was looking forward to it. And if that made him a bad guy, so be it. He had never claimed to be a saint.

Providing an apt ambiance for his malevolent intentions, the wolf pack that had hightailed it after the explosions was back, following him from a safe distance and howling like crazy.

He wasn't worried about them attacking him, and there were enough armed men with Amanda to ensure her safety. His brisk pace had nothing to do with the pack. But it brought him to his destination well ahead of the others.

The helicopter was parked at the spot they'd agreed on, where the narrow paved road had a little shoulder, providing just enough space for the thing not to block it completely. There was no traffic this late at night high up in the mountains. But on the remote chance that some random vehicle might be passing through, the pilot had placed small flares around the chopper and had left just enough space for a car to squeeze by. A truck would be shit out of luck.

Kian climbed inside and moved to sit up front with the pilot.

"How did it go?" the guy asked.

"Mission accomplished," Kian bit out. The pilot waited for him to elaborate. "They are on their way with an additional load of two hundred and something pounds. If this thing cannot take the added weight, I have no problem with disposing of it."

It took a moment for the pilot to catch his drift, and then his face paled. "No, it's okay. This bird is designed to take ten passengers, nine in the cabin and one more next to the pilot. We changed the configuration to make more space for cargo."

Bloody civilians. He should demand that all of the Guardians learn how to fly those things; himself included. Bringing uninitiated rookies on missions was a mistake.

What if someone had been injured? Would the guy faint at the sight of blood?

Kian sighed, running his hand through his hair and wincing as he pulled on a sore spot.

Truth was, he envied the guy.

Must be nice to be so naive, to still cringe at the sight of blood, or the mere thought of carnage. It was a luxury Kian had never been afforded. Since he was scarcely more than a boy, he had witnessed and participated in enough bloodbaths to fill a lake.

It was hard to maintain humanity, or rather what mortals referred to as humanity, after seeing how little of it there was in the world and how easily it was shed. The term no longer held the same meaning for him as it did for others. He knew how little it took to incite people into becoming murderous monsters that killed, maimed and raped everyone in their path. History recounted plenty of examples, too many of which Kian had witnessed firsthand.

Being nearly two thousand years old, he had a lot of shit to carry around in his head; shit he would've gladly forgotten.

The thing was, though, history had a nasty habit of repeating itself. And if one were foolish enough to forget the lessons of the past, one couldn't recognize the pattern—the chain of events that time and again had led to catastrophes of epic proportions.

The burden of his memories, his experiences, and his deeds had hardened him, like a sharp blade, annealing him until he became a formidable weapon. He had accepted his fate and was resigned to the sacrifices he had to make, paying with bits and sometimes chunks of his so-called immortal soul until he felt hollow on the inside.

It was his fate.

But sometimes, in moments of weakness, he wished for oblivion.

Dear Fates, he prayed that if he and Syssi were ever blessed with a child, it would be a daughter. Because, even though gender roles were changing, as a girl chances were better that she wouldn't have to go into battle and become a killer.

The act of killing tainted the soul.

It didn't matter if you killed in self-defense, or in defense of your family, or if your enemy was the lowest, evil scum that deserved to be eradicated from the face of the earth.

Once you killed another, something inside you died as well. And then it became easier and easier with each subsequent kill.

More than anything, he wished for his children to be spared that fate. And he would do his best to shield them and their mother from the ugliness of reality and his own disillusionment with humans and immortals alike.

Fucking Doomers.

It was all their fault.

Dimly, he was aware that it wasn't true. Mortals were perfectly capable of instigating wars and committing genocide without the Doomers stirring things up—as evidenced by the bloody history of the Maya and other primitive peoples that the Doomers had never given a fuck about.

Still, it was more gratifying to focus the blame on a particular group.

That way, he could still harbor an irrational shard of hope that without the Doomers to poison the minds and hearts of mortals, global peace and prosperity could be achieved, and the future was not as bleak as it seemed.

But whether true or not, there was no way to get rid of the Doomers, so it was a moot point. They were too powerful, and their evil tentacles reached too far, too wide, and too deep.

Stupid girl.

How could his own sister be so fucking stupid?

And she attacked him, her own brother, to defend that scum.

If it wasn't for the "If even a little of his skin tears, I'm never going to forgive you. Ever!" she had screamed in his ear, he might have still harbored hope that she was saving the Doomer for the information that could be extracted from him, and that the whole naked thing was about her pulling a Mata Hari.

The best orgasm of her life...

As he felt the bile rise in his throat, Kian took a big gulp from his water bottle, swallowed some, then gargled and spat out the rest.

He wished he had something stronger than water with him. But in a pinch, a cigarette would work.

Pulling the pack from his back pocket, he was surprised to see he had only two left. Evidently, the habit was back in full force.

Whatever, he had bigger problems than this insignificant addiction.

Stepping out of the chopper, he walked a few feet away and lit one of his remaining coffin nails, then took a long drag out of the thing.

Damn, it felt good.

And by the time the brothers showed up with the Doomer between them, Kian was on his second and last cigarette, and in a much calmer mood.

Which was lucky for the fucker.

"Did he give you guys any trouble?"

"Nah, he was doing the dead-man-walking thing most of the way." Anandur helped the Doomer climb inside… and buckled him in…

What the hell?

"Why are you so cordial with him?" Kian gestured with his cigarette.

"What? You wanted me to rough him up? You should have said something…" Anandur's red brows went in tight together.

"No, I'm just surprised. Usually, you're not as… reserved."

"For one, he didn't give us any trouble, and I'm not a bully who beats up prisoners. Second, he didn't harm our girl. And if she defended him, he obviously isn't some evil abomination. And third, he doesn't stink like some of the others. Besides, he looks so dead that it would've been like kicking a corpse. Which I don't do. Not unless they stink, that is."

"I never thought I would say this to you, but you are a better man than I, Anandur." Kian slapped the guy's thick bicep.

"I'll be damned. Did you hear that, Brundar? I want you to commit this to memory for future reference and back me up when no one believes me. I actually got a compliment from the big man himself."

Kian shook his head as he stubbed out what was left of his cigarette on the heel of his boot and returned it to join the other butts in the empty box. Anandur had a knack for making him smile. The big oaf… what was it that Andrew had dubbed him? The redheaded Goliath… Nah, that was a mouthful, he'd stick with oaf… The big oaf never took anything seriously.

Nevertheless, hard as he tried, Kian couldn't dismiss the guy's assessment or fault his logic. Who would have thought that while Kian's hatred for the enemy was turning him into a psychopath, Anandur was keeping his cool? On the other hand, it wasn't Anandur's sister who the fucker had kidnapped and defiled.

"Go and knock him out. I want him unconscious until he wakes up in the dungeon."

"And who is going to carry him in? Did you see the size of that guy? Why not just blindfold him?"

"We'll manage. I don't want him to have any idea where we're taking him. Not the distance traversed, not the sounds on the way, nothing."

"Got it. A blow to the head or a tranquilizer?"

"Whichever, I don't care."

33

AMANDA

As they cleared the trees and the chopper came into view, Amanda's eyes immediately went searching for Dalhu.

She found him, sitting between Anandur and Brundar, his huge body slumped forward, held in place by the seatbelt he was strapped in with.

Oh, no. She felt guilt slide over her, coating her with a layer of nasty self-reproach. She shouldn't have let Dalhu out of her sight, leaving him undefended with her brother and his sidekicks. Pulling her hand out from Andrew's grip, she tore across the narrow road and leaped up into the thing.

She grabbed for Dalhu's wrist even before her knees touched the helicopter's cabin floor, searching for his pulse as she went down to kneel in front of him.

Thank heavens; he wasn't dead. But he was out like a light.

"What have you done to him?" She glowered at the brothers.

"Just a tranquilizer, the boss's orders, princess."

She eyed Anandur suspiciously. "You didn't beat him up or anything, did you?"

"And earn your wrath? No, thank you very much." Feigning

offense, Anandur humphed and looked away, crossing his tree-trunk-sized arms over his chest.

"Stop bullshitting. If Kian had ordered you to do it, you would've done it in a heartbeat. My wrath, my ass… Now, move over, you two. I want to sit next to him."

Brundar got up and moved to sit in the row behind them, but Anandur ignored her, pretending to be absorbed by the view of the dark forest he was gazing at through the chopper's window.

"You too," she commanded.

"Sorry, no can do, princess. His body will soon neutralize the tranquilizer, and I'll have to dose him again. Take Brundar's seat."

"Fine." She plopped down next to Dalhu and crossed her arms over her chest.

Her feet hurt, and after a moment or two of pouting, she bent down and took her dirty sneakers off, along with the socks. Rubbing her toes, she glanced at the back of Kian's head.

The big jerk was ignoring her. Sitting up front with the pilot, he didn't even turn around to acknowledge her presence. *Would it kill him to say something nice? Like, I'm glad you are not dead, Amanda? Or, I was so worried about you, Amanda?*

Whatever, she was too tired to deal with the supercilious prick. Syssi must have the heart of an angel to put up with that. Poor girl.

Kian didn't deserve her.

And to think she was the one who had brought those two together.

Yet instead of showing his gratitude, her brother was being an ogre.

Tears stung the back of her eyes as she imagined the very different welcome she would get from Syssi. She had no doubt her friend was waiting anxiously for her to come home and would run to hug her and kiss her and tell her how worried she'd been, and how happy she was to have Amanda back safe and sound.

Syssi was such a sweet soul… and so was Andrew…

Following after his two friends into the craft, Andrew yanked the heavy sliding door shut, then gave her shoulder a little squeeze before heading back to join his friends in the last row.

The chopper lifted into the dark sky, barely disturbing the quiet as it kept climbing up and away.

Looking out the window, she spotted the cabin, the two upper windows still dimly illuminated by the one lamp they had left on.

For some inexplicable reason, she felt a tinge of sorrow seeing it go. And as she pondered the odd reaction, a dull ache settled in her chest.

She was going to miss it.

Heck, she missed it already.

She had been different there. Except, Amanda had a hard time putting her finger on what the difference was.

Then it hit her.

Intimacy.

It was such a foreign concept to her. Being with only one person, getting to know him, letting him see her naked.

And she wasn't referring to her body. Many had seen her unclothed. But the mask had always stayed on, her act shielding her better than any fabric ever could.

Dear Fates, sometimes she wasn't even sure that there was something real under the façade she was projecting. After fronting the diva persona for so long, what had been initially meant as a protective layer over her fragile inner self—the self that wasn't sure, the one that doubted she could be loved and accepted for who she really was—had become her.

Whoever that was.

She was going to miss the intimacy she had with Dalhu, his unrelenting efforts to win her heart, his complete acceptance of her.

But then, there was Andrew—the sweet—with his veiled and not so veiled hints.

If it hadn't been for Dalhu, she would've responded differently to him. After all, being confirmed as Dormant, his status had changed from a potential hookup to a potential mate.

Funny, in the span of two days, she had gone from having no options to having two.

The thing was, though, once Andrew's eligibility became known to the rest of the clan's females, he would get snagged real quick.

If she had any brains at all, she would grab him while he was still single and still interested and forget all about Dalhu and their doomed relationship.

Ha. Ha. Ha.

A doomed relationship with a Doomer...

Very funny...

Not.

34

ANDREW

As the chopper lifted and turned, Andrew's stomach lurched as usual upon takeoff, and he bit down the inside of his cheek to stop the rise of bile. Puking all over Amanda who was sitting right in front of him certainly wouldn't earn him favorable points.

Oh, God, the sight of her naked body. That image would forever be seared on his retinas. She was so damn perfect, she should be worshiped.

By him.

He had to have her.

Hell, he was going to.

She believed him to be such a nice guy; supportive, nonjudgmental. True, he was, though only with her… but not because he had such a cherubic disposition.

Oh, boy, she had him pegged all wrong.

Not that he was going to correct her misconception. After all, the whole point was to win her over, and he wasn't above taking advantage of her current emotional fragility. He was going to use whatever weapons were available to him.

So what if he was somewhat deceitful, or insincere? He had her best interests at heart… even if his tactics were questionable.

She would thank him later.

Her kidnapper was nothing but a lowlife scum that somehow managed to play her. And she fell for it.

Hook, line, and sinker.

Under normal circumstances, the guy could've never scored a woman like her, even if he wasn't a member of the deeply despised opposing team.

And besides, if Amanda had deluded herself into thinking Kian would allow anything between her and the Doomer, she had another thing coming.

Especially after the stunt she'd pulled attacking him to defend the guy.

Her brother harbored such deeply ingrained hatred for their clan's enemies that he would never be able to see that Doomer as anything but pure evil.

Not that Andrew could fault the guy for feeling that way, or disapprove—regardless of Amanda's misguided infatuation.

There was a good reason for Kian's rabid hatred. After all, these bastards' sole mission was to kill each and every member of Kian's family and while at it drag humanity back down into the dark ages.

Amanda obviously wasn't thinking clearly, no doubt suffering from a mild case of Stockholm Syndrome. But once she'd shaken it off and come to her senses, she would run away from that Doomer straight into the arms of her only relevant alternative—the one her family would approve of. The one who'd stood by her side, offering a supportive arm, a shoulder to cry on, and a nonjudgmental ear.

Andrew smiled. The Doomer didn't stand a chance.

Amanda & Dalhu's Story Continues in

Book 4 of The Children of the Gods series

Dark Enemy Captive

Is available on Amazon

Turn the page to read an excerpt.

Dear reader,

Thank you for joining me on the continuing adventures of the ***Children of the Gods***.

As an independent author, I rely on your support to spread the word. So if you enjoyed the story, please share your experience, and if it isn't too much trouble, I would greatly appreciate a brief review on Amazon.

Click here to leave a review

Love & happy reading,

Isabell

DARK
ENEMY
captive
THE CHILDREN OF
THE GODS 5
I. T. LUCAS
INTERNATIONALLY BESTSELLING AUTHOR

1

ANDREW

As the chopper began to descend, Andrew turned to the window and watched the bright helipad square on Kian's rooftop grow closer. There was a big letter A in its center that he hadn't noticed upon takeoff, and Andrew wondered what it stood for.

An A for Amanda? An A for awesome immortals?

Should be an F for fucking unbelievable...

The moment the craft touched down, Syssi rushed out from the cover of the vestibule onto the open rooftop—a gust of wind catching her long hair and blowing it around her head in a mad swirl. It looked like she was cold—the poor girl huddled inside her light jacket, tucking her chin and holding the collar against her cheeks.

That got her boyfriend moving fast.

With a muted curse, Kian threw the passenger's door open and jumped down. Ducking under the chopper's slowing blades, he ran out and wrapped his arms around Syssi.

It was good that the guy's wide back obscured what must've been a passionate kiss. As much as Andrew approved of Syssi's boyfriend, it didn't mean that he was okay with seeing his kid sister engaged in anything even remotely sexual.

It must have been pure hell for Kian to find Amanda as he had—spread out naked in postorgasmic bliss. Lucky for Andrew, he'd gotten on the scene a couple of minutes later, missing the main act of her and the Doomer getting it on.

It seemed to be his thing lately. He'd also been spared Syssi's almost fatal transition, learning about it only after the fact.

Thank God, she'd pulled through.

It was better that he hadn't been there. He would've gone crazy from worry and would've attacked Kian—consequences be damned. Someone must be watching over him, shielding him from stuff he couldn't stomach.

Though before shit had gone down at the cabin, Andrew had seen enough through the Xaver imaging equipment. He'd gotten more than an eyeful while scanning the cabin's interior. Thank God for the electromagnetic radar's crappy, pixelated display.

Unfortunately, the picture hadn't been hazy enough...

Fuck, he'd better not go there if he wanted to keep his shit together.

Besides, it was none of his business. Amanda was a big girl and could do whatever she pleased with whomever she chose—even if it was a scumbag Doomer who didn't deserve to lick the crap off the bottom of her shoes.

Andrew had no claim on her—of any kind.

Not yet.

God, seeing her naked had been like an electric shock. It had scrambled his brain and had refocused it into a singular objective—making this spectacular woman his. But he would've preferred not to have shared the experience with a bunch of other guys. Thank you very much.

The immortals he could've tolerated. After all, Kian was her brother and his bodyguards were her cousins. But not Rodney and

Jake, Andrew's own buddies. After the many years they had served together, the two were like brothers to him, but that didn't mean he'd been okay with them drooling over Amanda.

His only consolation was that they would remember nothing of tonight. Including Amanda's perfect, nude body. Before heading out, they had agreed to let Kian erase the whole rescue mission from their memories upon their return.

Andrew sneaked a glance at Syssi and Kian, hoping they were done with the kissing. Damn. Not only were their mouths still fused together in a heated smooch, but Kian had lifted Syssi and was trying to carry her inside.

An argument ensued, and she pushed at his chest in a futile attempt to make him put her down. After some more back and forth, it seemed a compromise had been reached. Syssi stayed outside, and Kian wrapped himself around her like a human coat. Well, not really human, close enough though.

Even when idling, the helicopter's engine was too loud to hear the particulars of their argument, but it had been easy to get the gist of it just by observing their body language. And it was obvious that Syssi had the big guy wrapped around her little finger.

Good, so Andrew wasn't the only one who was putty in her hands.

He'd learned a long time ago that his sweet kid sister's shy and demure demeanor was misleading. Syssi never backed down from what was important to her and somehow managed to bend even the toughest and the meanest to her will.

How did the saying go? The bigger they are, the harder they fall?

True, that.

Andrew smiled, glad that the lovebirds were getting along so well.

Kian was a wise man if he'd already discovered the magic of the two most important words in a guy's vocabulary—*yes, dear.*

As soon as Amanda stepped down and took a few steps away

from the helicopter, Syssi discarded the sheltering arms of her boyfriend and ran to hug her friend.

Evidently, that hug was exactly what Amanda needed, and long moments passed as the women stood in each other's arms.

It pained Andrew to see Amanda's shoulders heave as she cried in Syssi's embrace. The woman had abandoned her tough act at the first sign of loving compassion.

Kian was such a self-absorbed colossal jerk. Would it have killed him to give Amanda a hug?

When the heaving finally stopped, Amanda let go and swept a finger under her teary eyes. Casting a baleful glance at Kian, Syssi wrapped her arm around Amanda's waist and together they walked inside.

Andrew had a feeling the big guy was going to sleep in the proverbial doghouse tonight. Not that he didn't deserve it for treating Amanda like shit—regardless of the extenuating circumstances.

Judging by the murderous expression on Kian's face, he was well aware of his unfavored status, and Andrew was not going to let him mess with Rodney and Jake's memories until he had a chance to calm down.

The plan was to leave them with a memory of going on an unspecified, top-secret mission they'd agreed to be hypnotized to forget. It wasn't perfect, but the guys had to have a rational explanation, or they'd think they were losing their freaking minds. As it was, it would have been hard enough to explain the missing day. Explaining the large sum of money magically showing up in their bank accounts would have been even more difficult.

But until he made sure Kian was up to the task, Andrew's buddies would keep Brundar and Anandur company and wait in the chopper for the gurney to transport the prisoner to the dungeon.

How cool was it that they had a fucking dungeon down in their basement? Just to get a gander at that, he would've volunteered to escort the prisoner himself.

But he had to keep an eye on Kian while the guy did his thing with Jake and Rodney's memories, which might end up even more fascinating than the dungeon.

The basement could wait for some other time.

"Stay here. They may need your help," he told his friends on his way out, then headed toward Kian.

Rooted to the same spot where Syssi had left him, Kian looked like the statue of *The Thinker*—except for the sitting part.

Poor jerk.

"How are you doing, big guy?" Andrew took a furtive glance at Kian's face, checking for fangs and glowing eyes. But it seemed Kian was holding it together, as evidenced by the absence of what Andrew had learned were the telling signs of an immortal male ready for battle—or losing his cool.

"Not one of my better days, that's for sure. Though I feel like a complete ass for saying that. I should feel relieved, grateful..." Frustrated, Kian raked a hand through his hair.

"You need sleep, buddy. You're exhausted. Everything that seems bleak now will look better after a good night's rest. Trust me." Andrew gave Kian's shoulder a light squeeze. "Are you in any shape to take care of my guys' memories? Or should they crash somewhere around here for tonight, and you'll do it tomorrow?"

"No, I'm fine. The sooner it's done, the better."

"Where do you want to do it?"

"I promised them I'd take them home and erase today's events before they fell asleep. To minimize the damage to their brains it's best to do it as soon as possible, and falling asleep right after will make it even better for them."

"I'm sure they'll understand if we change it a bit; make it easier for you."

"I'm not in the habit of breaking promises."

"You are in no shape to go driving around town after not sleeping for how long? Two whole days? Or is it three?"

"I appreciate your concern, but it is going to go down exactly as I've promised them."

"Okay, but on one condition—I'm driving."

"You've got yourself a deal."

Once again, Kian surprised him. As stubborn and as obnoxious as he was, the guy wasn't above admitting weaknesses or accepting help.

A few minutes later, the gurney arrived, accompanied by a pretty petite redhead.

"Andrew, this is Bridget, our in-house physician," Kian introduced her. "Bridget, this is Andrew, Syssi's brother."

Andrew offered his hand and she took it, placing her tiny palm in his large one and giving it a short though surprisingly strong squeeze. "Welcome to our world, Andrew." The wide smile spreading across her face was as welcoming as her words. "We'll be seeing a lot of each other soon, I hope."

At first, Andrew assumed that she was coming on to him and reflexively straightened his shoulders and pulled in his abs. But then it occurred to him that it was highly unlikely—there was nothing flirtatious or coy in her demeanor.

Oh, right, she was referring to the transition.

Bummer.

"We'll see. I'm not sure about it, yet."

"No rush, take your time." She gave him a little pat on the arm and turned to go check on the prisoner.

The doctor had to wait a couple of moments as Jake and Rodney helped the brothers transport the unconscious guy out of the helicopter's cabin and onto the gurney.

She checked his vitals before letting the brothers wheel him away, then ambled up to Andrew.

Damn, he might have gotten it right the first time.

Bridget didn't bother to conceal the up and down look over she gave him. "Come and see me before you make up your mind. I'll give you a thorough check up to assess your general health. You'll want to know where you stand, health-wise, before deciding one way or the other."

"Sure will. Thank you."

This time, there was no doubt left in Andrew's mind that the pretty doctor wanted to get to know him better, and not strictly as a patient.

Hell, why not?

If things did not work out with Amanda, the petite redhead was an interesting alternative. Bridget was not bad at all. Quite fetching, indeed.

Andrew smirked. Either one was a definite step up from his usual. Not that he had been in the habit of dating bimbos, but a professor? A medical doctor?

He would've never considered even approaching one—out of his league.

True.

But hey, this was before discovering he was a rare specimen, coveted by beautiful immortal females.

And as it turned out, he had a thing for doctors.

2

AMANDA

Thank the merciful Fates for Syssi, Amanda thought as she stood in Syssi's arms and sobbed her heart out. At least one person gave a damn about her and was happy to see her come home unharmed.

She'd really needed that hug.

Leaving Dalhu behind in the helicopter wasn't easy. But he'd been out throughout the ride, and just before landing Anandur had tranquilized him again. Fates only knew how long it would take Dalhu to shake it off.

And besides, with Kian out of the chopper, Dalhu was in no immediate danger.

Later, though? Amanda could only hope that Kian would leave Dalhu alone for tonight.

"I have a surprise for you," Syssi whispered in her ear as she wrapped her arm around Amanda's waist and walked her toward the rooftop vestibule.

"I know, Andrew told me. I'm so happy for you!" Amanda pulled Syssi into another hug. It seemed as if she just couldn't get enough of those.

With Kian being a monumental jerk and giving her the cold shoulder, Syssi, with her concern and warm welcome, was treating Amanda more like family than Amanda's own brother.

Syssi punched the button for the elevator and glanced up at her. "How did Andrew.... oh, wait, you were talking about the transition?"

"Of course, silly, what did you think I was talking about?" Curiosity banishing her sad musings, Amanda ignored the ping preceding the quiet swish of the elevator doors opening.

"You'll see." Syssi pulled her inside. "The surprise is waiting for you in your apartment."

A moment later, as the doors slid open, Syssi pulled Amanda by the hand she was still holding, not letting go until they stood in front of Amanda's penthouse door. "Go ahead, open it..."

Arching a brow, Amanda turned the handle and slowly pushed open the door. Was there a Welcome Home banner hanging from the ceiling of her living room? Some balloons? Syssi was so sweet...

And what was that familiar, soothing scent?

It can't be...

"Ninni? Oh, sweet Fates, I can't believe it..." Amanda ran into her mother's open arms. The crack in the dam holding back the tears that had started in Syssi's arms became a gaping hole, and the waterworks resumed.

Amanda didn't know how long she'd cried. Vaguely, she remembered her mother pulling her to sit on the sofa and cradling her in her arms like a baby. But none of Annani's words had registered, only the effect of her soft, soothing voice.

When the last of the hiccups stopped, there was a mountain of used tissues on the floor, and a large margarita was sitting on the coffee table next to an oval platter of assorted cheeses and fruits.

One glance at the platter and Amanda started crying again.

"What is the matter, darling? You do not like the cheese? I can have Onidu take it away and replace it with another snack." Both her mother and Syssi regarded her with twin worried expressions on their faces.

"No, I like cheese, you know I do… It's just that Dalhu"—hiccup—"prepared a meal for me"—sniffle—"with cheeses and wine and fruit"—another sniffle.

"Oh, sweetheart, that does not sound so horrible. Did that Dalhu—I assume this is the name of your kidnapper—did he do something to hurt you after that meal? Is that why you are crying?"

"Noooo…" The *no* came out in a wail. But then after a few more sniffles and a hard blow into a tissue, Amanda dried her eyes and drained the margarita in two long gulps. She'd been babied enough. It was time to stop crying and behave like a grownup.

"He didn't do anything to hurt me. In fact, he was the most giving, the most attentive, the most accommodating male I have ever met. He treated me like a real princess, like I was precious, and certainly with more affection and respect than my own brother."

"I see." Annani nodded sagely.

Amanda braced herself for the lecture that was sure to follow. The one about how she wasn't thinking clearly and needed time to rest. Blah, blah, blah. "And don't think I'm suffering from Stockholm syndrome or some other psychological crap like that." Crossing her arms over her chest, she challenged her mother with a hard glare, then added a *humph* for emphasis.

"That is not what I was going to say. But I will not tolerate this kind of language or attitude in my presence. Uncross your arms, Amanda, you are not a toddler."

"I'm sorry. It's just that from the moment Kian saw me with Dalhu, he's been a jerk to me…" Amanda wasn't up for more rejection, especially not from her mother. It would destroy her completely. But she wasn't sure how Annani would react to the news flash that her daughter had let a Doomer have sex with her. Not that they'd actually gotten that far. But Amanda wasn't going to pull a Clinton and claim oral sex didn't count.

"I think you should start from the beginning and tell us everything that happened. Unless you are tired and prefer to do it tomorrow." Annani took her hand and covered it with her other palm. "You are my daughter, Amanda, and I love you no matter what. There is nothing you can say that will change how I feel. Do not be afraid to share your burden with me. This is what mothers are for." She leaned up and kissed Amanda's cheek.

"You promise not to get mad?"

"I promise. But you look exhausted, and it can really wait for tomorrow."

"I'm beat, but I won't be able to sleep until I know… until I'm sure that you're not going to hate me for what I've done." Amanda sniffled and dropped her head onto her hands.

"Come, child, no need to be so dramatic. You can tell me everything."

"Okay." Amanda wrapped her fingers around the stem of the second margarita glass Onidu had handed her. "Thank you." She reclined into the comfort of the sofa cushions and crossed her legs.

"After leaving Syssi and her brother Andrew in the restaurant, I headed to a jewelry store. My plan was to order a duplicate of the pendant Syssi gave me. You see, it was a present from Andrew for her sweet sixteen." She looked at her mother. "I didn't want her to get in trouble for giving it to me. But it must've been fated because that pendant is how they knew where to find me. Apparently, Andrew had a tracking device installed in it without Syssi's knowledge."

Amanda sighed and turned to Syssi. "He is so sweet. You are so lucky to have a brother who cares so much about you."

Syssi almost choked on her margarita. "Andrew? Sweet? Are we talking about the same guy?"

"Yes, he is a wonderful man. When Kian was treating me like dirt, Andrew was the one who asked me how I was holding up and offered his support."

"If you say so." Syssi chuckled.

"I know it was somewhat deceitful of Andrew not to tell you that he had a tracking device installed in the pendant. But he had only your best interest at heart. If it were you instead of me who was kidnapped, you would've been grateful to him for ensuring that you'd be found."

"Of course, I'm grateful. Realizing the tracker's significance, I even told Andrew he was my hero. Without it, we wouldn't have known where to even start looking for you."

"So that's that. You can think of him in any way you want, but to me, he is Andrew the sweet." Amanda shrugged. "But back to my story. So, I entered the store and immediately noticed a delicious scent, something male—enticing and calming at the same time—something that called to me like catnip to a cat. I looked around to see where it was coming from, and that was when I saw him—a gorgeous, huge male. It took only a moment for the clues to snap into place. He was an immortal, but not one of ours, therefore a Doomer. But that split second between realization dawning and my legs reacting to the command to move was more than enough for him. He pounced, his huge hand closing over my neck."

Amanda was getting into her story, enjoying the breathless anticipation of her small audience.

"I was terrified. I thought that he would tighten his grip and choke me at any moment. Instead, he bit me."

She paused to take another sip, her eyes darting between Syssi and her mother, who were scooting closer and closer to the edge of their seats with each new and exciting detail.

"It was incredible. I'd fantasized about an immortal male's bite for so long, but it was even better than I'd imagined. My legs turned into two useless noodles, and I leaned into him. I'm embarrassed to admit it, but I wanted his hands all over me."

Amanda smiled sheepishly. "I even begged him to touch me. But he refused, saying he wouldn't do it without my sober consent. Can you imagine that? He said no to *me*..." She pointed at herself, regarding their shocked expressions with a satisfied smirk. "Then he took care of the girl at the counter, thralling her without even looking her in the eyes. Impressive, right?"

Her mother nodded. "Indeed."

"After switching cars with some guy at the mall, he took me to this motel and cuffed me to the bed. Normally, I could have just broken the wooden slats to get free, but I was loopy from the venom and so horny I was going out of my mind."

Syssi sputtered, spraying the coffee table. "Sorry." She choked. "I keep forgetting how nonchalant you people are about these things."

"It is okay, sweetie. No harm done," Annani reassured her with a pat on her knee. "Go on, Amanda."

"So, I was going out of my mind with lust... you okay, Syssi?" Amanda cast her a glance. The poor girl's cheeks were so red they must've been burning.

"Yeah, I'm fine. Go on," she croaked, touching the cool margarita glass to her hot face.

"I even cussed him out for refusing to provide the relief I needed. The guy was completely clueless about immortal females, but when he realized that I was really suffering, he gave me a sedative, saying he needed to retrieve stuff from wherever he and the other Doomers were staying. He must've done it while I was out because he was back when I woke up. I asked him what he wanted from me."

Syssi rolled her eyes. "Duh—"

"Yeah, that's what I thought. But it wasn't sex. Dalhu had something else in mind."

"He didn't want that? Is he gay?" Syssi interrupted.

"No, he is not gay. He said he wanted a future with me, wanted me for his wife, his mate, to have children with him."

"And what did you reply?" her mother probed gently.

"I told him he was delusional, of course. That there was no way to bridge the differences between us." Amanda sighed. If that were the only obstacle in their way, she wouldn't be sitting here with her mother and Syssi and telling a story instead of enjoying her man. "And not to forget the fact that we are each other's worst enemy." Though, that was no longer true… Dalhu had pledged himself to her.

"You know what his answer was?"

"What?" Syssi and Annani asked in unison.

"He said he would do everything to win my heart. Abandon the Brotherhood, support our cause, do whatever I demand from him. Except let me go, that is."

"Wow, that's…. well… kind of romantic… delusional, but romantic." Syssi squinted as if afraid her words wouldn't be well received.

"I know, right? But still, I asked him how he thought to achieve that impossible goal. He said we would run away and hide some place where we could spend some time together and get to know each other. I thought he was completely nuts. But what choice did I have? Right? He drove us to this remote cabin high up in the mountains, and on the way he broke into a store for provisions. But wait for it…" She paused dramatically. "He paid for it. Left cash on the counter to cover the cost."

The surprised expression on Annani's face should've been gratifying, but it wasn't. Amanda's dramatic delivery failed to give her the usual kick. Worse, it made her feel immature and foolish. But apparently, old habits die hard. Amanda wouldn't be herself without the added flourish. "I didn't realize it at the time, but this was the turning point. His behavior intrigued me. I began asking questions, and he told me about himself. He didn't try to make himself sound good and admitted that he had done a lot of killing during his long life. But I glimpsed something remarkable in between his words. Despite all he had been through, there was still a small spark of light inside him. And honor."

"How old is he?" Annani asked.

"He is over eight hundred years old."

"For you guys, it's not that old," Syssi said.

"It is not young either. Go on, Amanda, I want to hear the rest of the story."

"We got to the cabin and, at least emotionally, it was a roller-coaster ride. There were moments I was terrified of him, and others when I was beginning to like him. Then for a little while, I was plotting to clobber him over the head with a shovel, but couldn't bring myself to do it because he was so incredibly nice to me. He even offered to send you a warning about the reinforcements his ex-bosses are sending to Los Angeles to hunt us down. Which reminds me that as much as I loathe to, I need to talk to Kian."

"What happened between Kian and you?" Annani asked.

"I'm getting there... Throughout our time together, Dalhu was doing exactly what he promised— everything he could to win my heart. And you know what? He was doing a damn good job of it. Obviously, it didn't hurt his efforts that he is so hot—very tall, beautifully built and sexy as hell—or the fact that my hormones went into overdrive whenever he got near me. I fought the attraction, but he was chipping away at the fragile wall of resistance I was struggling to keep up. Eventually, it crumbled last night, and I let Dalhu pleasure me. It wouldn't have ended at just that, but as I was coming down from the most fantastic completion I'd ever had, Kian blew a hole in the wall and leaped through it like some avenging demon."

"Oh, shit," Syssi blurted. "Sorry." She slanted a quick glance at Annani.

"No, 'oh shit' is appropriate in this case, Syssi." Annani got to her bare feet and began pacing. "I can guess what happened next, but please, continue."

"I must've screamed my head off when I climaxed, and Kian assumed I was being tortured."

Syssi snorted. "Sorry... I couldn't help it."

"And if my screaming wasn't enough to get Kian's blood boiling, I had Dalhu's shirt tied around my wrists... We were playing a game, you see..."

Amanda glanced sheepishly at Syssi and then at her mother. "Kian was already not thinking straight, so the moron didn't stop to think that a piece of fabric wasn't enough to restrain me for real. He attacked Dalhu, who was just defending himself while trying to protect me at the same time. It took me a moment to come down to earth, and as I did, Kian had his fangs embedded deep in Dalhu's throat and was about to tear it out."

Syssi gasped. "Oh, my god."

"I knew screaming at him would achieve nothing, not fast enough to save Dalhu, so I did the only thing I could. I tore out of the binding, jumped on Kian's back, and pulled at his head with all my strength while shouting and threatening him. Eventually, he let go. I tried to explain that the scream was one of pleasure, not pain, and that Dalhu didn't force me."

Recalling Kian's look of disgust, Amanda's gut twisted. She reached for her third margarita and drained it in one long gulp.

"You should have seen the way Kian looked at me," she whispered. "Like I was repulsive to him. Then, as if he couldn't stand the sight of me for even a moment longer, he issued a command to Anandur to cuff Dalhu and stormed out. He didn't say a word and hasn't looked at me since." Her chin began quivering, tears sliding down her cheeks.

Syssi moved to sit beside her and pulled her into a warm hug. "He'll get over it. You know he loves you."

"I'm not so sure. I gave him plenty of reasons to be mad at me before, but he never acted like this."

There was a long moment of silence, with her mother and Syssi deep in thought—no doubt trying to figure out a way to help her get back into Kian's good graces.

Yeah, good luck with that...

"The question is not if Kian would get over Amanda's liaison with the Doomer. The real question is whether Amanda would. How do you feel about it, dear?" Her mother regarded her with her ancient, knowing eyes.

Right, that was the real question, and while her mind was still struggling with it, her gut already knew the answer.

But was she going to fess up?

Yeah, she was.

Amanda wasn't one to chicken out and had no intention of pretending she was going to let it go when, in fact, she wasn't.

"No, I'm not going to get over it. Not yet, and not because Kian disapproves. I do not claim to have fallen in love with Dalhu, but I certainly felt something."

Amanda trained her eyes on Annani as she continued in a near whisper. "There was this intimacy, a connection I've never experienced with a man before."

She humphed. "Heck, the only thing I ever felt toward a guy was lust, and the moment my needs were satisfied, I couldn't wait to be rid of him."

Amanda pushed to her feet, walked over to the bar, and poured herself another drink. "It might be as simple as immortal pheromones at work, or as complicated as a budding relationship, but I would like to have the opportunity to find out."

With the drink in hand, she sat back down. "But how? It's such a complicated mess. Kian has Dalhu locked up somewhere in the dungeon. And even though I believe Dalhu was sincere in his promises to me, I'm in no way suggesting we should let a Doomer, even an ex-Doomer, roam free. Or that we should embrace him with open arms and invite him to join the family. I'm not that naive." Amanda reclined into the sofa's soft cushions and closed her eyes.

She was so damn tired.

Her mother's small palm caressed her cheek. "Do not despair, child. It is a difficult situation, but not an impossible one."

Annani clasped Amanda's hands. "The three of us, working

together, are powerful enough to conquer the world, right?" She waited for Amanda to nod. "Then unraveling this tangled knot should not be an obstacle too great for us to surmount. Do you agree?"

"Absolutely." Syssi stood up and joined Annani, placing her hand over hers. "Come on, Amanda. Put it here." They waited till she added her own hand to the pile.

"Thank you. Your support means the world to me." Amanda choked up. Her mother was right. Between the three of them, there was no way they wouldn't find a solution.

Annani pulled her hand out. "Although I'm sure both of you are eager, just as I am, to jump right in, our plans for world domination will have to wait for tomorrow. It is very late, and Amanda needs to recover from her ordeal." She winked and patted Syssi's hand, then gave Amanda's a tug. "Come, let us get you showered and then straight to bed."

Amanda didn't mind that Annani was pulling her by the hand like a small child, not at all, nor did she question why it felt so damn good to be ordered around by her tiny mother again.

"Good night, Syssi, whatever is left of it. We convene again tomorrow," Annani threw over her shoulder as she headed down the corridor to Amanda's bedroom.

"Good night," Syssi called after them, and a moment later Amanda heard her front door open quietly and close.

Syssi was such a good friend.

Maybe she could talk some sense into Kian. If anyone had a chance to break through his hateful attitude, it was Syssi. On the other hand, the girl was so timid, she might not be up to it. Syssi shied away from confrontations. Heck, she couldn't even bring herself to deal with David, who'd been tormenting her at work with rude, unwanted advances. It had gotten to the point where Syssi had been afraid to ask for his help with programming, even though she'd needed it desperately.

It might be a good idea to replace David with someone Syssi

would be more comfortable working with. Professor Goodfellow wouldn't mind taking the guy off Amanda's hands. After all, though unpleasant, David was a decent programmer, and there weren't many available. Anyone with a knack for computers was working for tech companies and making double what the university offered.

Good idea. And while she was at it, she should hire more staff to work on her paranormal side project, or rather the main project as far as she was concerned. But for the university administration's sake, she still needed to maintain appearances and show worthwhile results on her official research. Luckily, she had her own financial backing and didn't need to explain a bloated staff to anyone.

Now that her hypothesis about Dormants displaying paranormal abilities had been proven right, Amanda wanted to run with it, not walk.

Tomorrow, she would talk with Syssi and together they would plan a course of action to put the search for Dormants on a faster track.

3

DALHU

Dalhu woke up in a dark, dingy prison cell, or so he thought. But as he raised his arm to check the time on his watch, a harsh, blinding light flooded the place.

What the hell? Bloody motion detectors?

After a couple of seconds, his pupils adjusted to the bright illumination, and he swept a quick look around, taking stock of his surroundings. The windowless room was tiny, about seven feet wide by ten feet long, and bare—save for the mattress under him. At the back, a utilitarian bathroom area extended the space by another five feet or so and was separated from the main room by a low privacy wall made of semitransparent glass blocks.

Pretty standard for a single occupancy jail cell. Except for the door, which was a monster. The thing was at least twelve inches thick, and he knew this because there was a little glass door at the bottom of it and then another one about a foot away.

So he was in solitary confinement, and they planned to provide his meals through that contraption. Smart.

Still, he'd expected worse.

Hell, these accommodations were luxurious compared to some

of the places he'd stayed in. And not as a prisoner. The room was clean, free of mildew, and the mattress didn't stink. There was a clean sheet over it, and they even provided him with a warm blanket.

Both smelled new.

Other than that, there were the requisite cameras, mounted high up on the ceiling where even he, as tall as he was, couldn't reach them.

Real clever. There was nothing he could fashion a weapon from, and no real privacy.

He was going to lose his fucking mind in no time.

The situation reminded him of a scene from a silly movie he had once seen, *Rocketman,* if Dalhu remembered correctly. As part of his training for a space mission, the would-be astronaut was locked for twenty-four hours in a container about the size of this room. Passing the time singing nonstop and enacting puppet shows with his socks, he drove his competitor in the adjoining tank insane.

Maybe Dalhu could do the same. Trouble was, he didn't know any songs, and he wasn't wearing any socks.

Great, his only entertainment option was thinking about his impending torture and execution.

Or worse, torture and indefinite imprisonment.

With a muffled sigh, Dalhu got up and went to check out the facilities. Finding a new toothbrush and a battery-operated shaver inside the niche over the sink was a pleasant surprise. There was no mirror, but then he didn't need one to use either. He brushed, shaved, and showered, then got dressed, putting on his old clothes.

When he got back to the room, the first thing he noticed was the tray of food in the compartment behind the little glass door, and he took it out. Sitting on the mattress, he placed the tray on the floor in front of him. Again, he was pleasantly surprised—the coffee was excellent and the two sandwiches were loaded with cold cuts. A decent meal.

Who knew, maybe this was the worst his rich captors could dish out. He doubted anyone had taken pity on him or had cared to treat him kindly.

Unless this was meant to be his last meal. Though, if this were indeed the case, they should've at least served him a juicy steak. And a stiff drink.

Did he dare entertain hope that it had been Amanda's doing?

Nah. He knew her better than that. She would not have bothered with food. If anything, she would've been on the other side of this door, demanding to see him.

Yeah, as if there was a chance in hell she cared for him—enough to defy her brother.

Dalhu wondered whether she would visit him, at least one last time to say goodbye, or forget all about him and let him rot in here alone.

After all, she'd never claimed to have any feelings for him. And engaging in sexual activity was as meaningless for her as it used to be for him...

With her, though, it had been anything but. More like a life-altering experience. He'd been different with Amanda, and not just in the way he'd interacted with her, but on a more visceral level...

He felt as if he'd been reborn in that cabin, reshaped to become the man she needed him to be.

Still, it might have been all one-sided.

True, she'd defended him against her own brother. But there was a big difference between not wanting to see him dead and wanting to be with him.

Yeah.

It was time to wake up from the dream and face his grim reality. He needed to get back to the way he'd been before. Ruthless and cold would get him through this, romantic and soft would not. After sorting out his new cache of feelings and memories, he would lock it away inside the minuscule compartment dedicated to the good he'd experienced throughout his life.

Dalhu finished the last of the coffee and returned the tray to where he had found it, then went back to sit on the mattress.

With his back slumped against the wall and his elbows crossed over his up-drawn knees, Dalhu buried his face in his arms and delved into his cache of precious memories.

For a long time, it had been the memory of his mother and sister that had kept him from losing it and surrendering to the darkness around him.

The sound of his sister's giggles, the image of his mother's indulgent, loving smile—those memories had sustained him during other bleak times, and he'd desperately clung to them for decades. But inevitably, they were doomed to fade.

Amanda had gifted him with new ones.

He'd had so little time with her, and there had been precious few of them. But he cherished each and every one.

Aside from what he'd experienced with Amanda, and what was left of what he'd once had with his family, there was nothing else in his life worth remembering.

Hell, he would've paid good money to forget most of the crap he'd been through.

This new cache would have to sustain him for shit knew how long. Provided he escaped execution. But just in case he got to live, he wanted to preserve every little detail of his time with Amanda.

4

ANDREW

As he drove back to the high rise, Andrew barely managed to keep his eyes open, let alone concentrate on the road. And it didn't help that neither he nor Kian was in the mood to chat.

First, they'd dropped off Jake at his home and then Rodney. Despite being exhausted to the point of nearly passing out, Kian had insisted on waiting for each to shower and get in bed before doing his thing with their heads.

Just as he'd promised.

"You'd better crash at my place and get a few hours of sleep before heading home," Kian offered as they reached the underground parking.

For a moment, Andrew was tempted to play it tough and pretend he was perfectly fine to drive back to his place. But that would've been stupid.

And pointless.

In his youth, when impressing his friends had been paramount—safety and self-preservation a far-flung, distant notion—he would've said he was okay. He would've driven home even if it meant forcing his eyelids open with his fingers the entire time. But those days were long gone, as were the days when he could've pushed it, going without sleep for two or three full cycles while still functioning at close to optimal level.

He was getting old, and as much as he hated to admit it, particularly to himself, he could no longer pull the same shit he had been able to—with ease—a decade ago.

And wasn't that a bitch.

A midlife crisis before forty.

Reluctantly, he nodded, eased into an empty spot, and cut the ignition.

They made the trip up to the penthouse in silence. Kian unlocked his front door and headed down the hallway to his bedroom, just pointing to one of the doors he had passed to show Andrew where to crash.

The guy was operating on fumes. The difference was that it had taken Kian three days without shut-eye to reach this state. Andrew, on the other hand, had had a full night's sleep less than twenty-four hours ago.

It wasn't a good feeling—relatively young, but already over the hill—at least for any kind of active field duty, that is. Of course, he could still supervise, train, plan missions, spy—do all the things that required his knowledge and experience, but not physical strength, agility, and endurance.

It sucked balls.

Taking a perfunctory, one-minute shower, he got into bed naked and slid between the sheets. In his own home, it was standard operating procedure. As a guest? Yeah, not so much. But he didn't have a change of clothes and asking Kian to borrow some of his was not cool.

Most likely, the guy was already sleeping. And if he wasn't? Well, then he was probably busy doing other things… with Syssi…

Yeah… no need to go there.

Exhaustion taking over, Andrew's eyelids slid shut. But as soon as they did, the image of Amanda's naked perfection popped behind his closed lids, and he grew instantly hard.

Shit, his damn erection didn't give a rat's ass about the rest of his body not being on board for the wakey-wakey.

Reaching under the covers and fisting the bad boy, Andrew felt like a dirty old man. Though come on, occasionally, every guy whacked off to the image of a woman he wasn't involved with—even those who fronted the holier-than-thou attitude. The only men who didn't, couldn't, or took a turn at the self-serve station to the image of another guy.

Andrew chuckled. If Amanda were a famous star, her poster would be hanging over every teenager's bed, providing the boys with inspiration for endless hours of self-play.

Funny thing was, he had the distinct impression that she wouldn't mind. In fact, he was pretty sure she would love it.

What a woman.

Stroking himself, he pictured Amanda in all her naked glory.

She was magnificent, standing in the middle of that cabin with her hands on her hips and her foot tapping the floor, staring Kian down while ignoring the rest of her drooling audience. Hell, the woman couldn't have looked more confident if she were addressing a courtroom dressed to the nines in a power suit.

Having every detail of her stunning face and perfect body already memorized, Andrew tried to go a step further and imagine himself with her. But the face of that Doomer intruded on his fantasy, turning the hard club in his hand into a limp noodle.

He tried again, focusing only on Amanda, but it was no use.

Andrew sighed and turned on his side. It was probably nothing. The bad boy down-under had evidently gotten a bitching memo from management about him draining the last of the energy reserves and had finally agreed it was time to give it a rest.

It wasn't like the guy was malfunctioning or anything. He had never let Andrew down before. And there was no way in hell Andrew was accepting any other explanation.

5

KIAN

On his way to the bathroom, Kian glanced at his empty bed, regarding it with mixed feelings. He would've loved nothing better than to snuggle up to Syssi's warm body and have her lovely scent soothe his raw nerves. But it was good that she was with Amanda.

At a time when he couldn't even bring himself to look at his sister, let alone provide comfort, Kian was grateful to Syssi for being there for her. Not that he would've been capable of doing much good under normal circumstances—providing a shoulder to cry on wasn't his style. He was more of a kick to the butt kind of guy.

Amanda needed someone to unload her ordeal on—someone who cared for her and would listen and *ah* and *huh* at all the right places without passing judgment. True, their mother was with her as well, but Kian wasn't sure if Annani was any better at handling an emotional crisis than he was.

From his experience, it depended on his mother's mood. At times, she had been supportive and understanding, but more often than not she'd expected him to toughen up instead of seeking solace from her. But maybe Annani was more indulgent toward

Amanda. After all, no one expected the princess to assume a leadership position, which would have demanded a steel backbone of her. Unlike Sari and Kian, the princess was allowed some slack, and Annani might be more inclined to grant her some motherly comfort.

Still, there was no one better for the job than his sweet, empathetic Syssi.

During the long drive to Jake's place in Valencia, Kian had plenty of time to think, and it had helped clear his head. Not that he had a choice. He had to force himself to calm down in order to do a decent job of suppressing the guy's memories without damaging his brain. Later, after they had left Rodney at his home in Santa Clarita, Kian had done more soul searching on the drive back home.

As he'd sifted through their memories, watching the replay of what had happened over at the cabin and seeing himself through their eyes hadn't been easy. It had been a chilling eye-opener. And even though they had only seen the tail end of his attack, from the mortals' perspective he'd looked like an out-of-control madman raging at a traumatized, vulnerable, naked woman.

An incredibly beautiful, naked woman.

It had been no big surprise to witness the males' reaction to Amanda in her birthday suit, but he hadn't expected the almost worshipful reverence they had been hit with. The poor schmucks had been literally rendered stupid.

No wonder they'd immediately taken her side.

Nevertheless, as much as he would've liked to, he couldn't entirely dismiss Andrew's buddies' opinion as biased, or their assessment as inaccurate—regardless of the back story they had been missing.

Still, to be able to see things in a different light, he needed to let go of the rage.

Easier said than done, though. And in Kian's case—impossible.

His deep-seated hatred for his enemies was built upon two

millennia of witnessing their unimaginable cruelty and their complete disregard for human life.

True, the atrocities had been executed by the mortals under the Doomers' control. But to say it had been the mortals' fault was like blaming the finger for pulling the trigger and not the brain commanding it. But to be perfectly honest, he couldn't blame the Doomers for all of it. He was well aware that some of the *humans* hadn't needed any outside influence.

There were always those who thirsted for the rush of power they got from the killing and the raping and the terror and destruction they wreaked. In the past, bloodthirsty thugs had joined armies; nowadays, they joined terror organizations and *rebel* groups. The motive was the same, though—to indulge their evil appetites with impunity.

But when people who would've otherwise spent their entire lives without committing even one act of cruelty became monsters, there was influence behind it.

Some called it the Devil. Kian had another name for it—The Brotherhood of the Devout Order of Mortdh—The Doomers.

It wasn't a case of a different ideology, or a fierce competition between rivals, or even a personal vendetta. This was a battle over the fate of humanity. Kian and his clan wanted it to thrive; the Doomers wanted it to yield to their power.

And to that end, the Doomers were doing everything in their power to keep the human population divided, ignorant, and fearful.

So yeah, Kian felt well justified in his hatred. But be that as it may, he shouldn't have extended it to his own sister, despite her momentary lapse of judgment—even if it had been a monumental one.

In fact, the sex with her captor had probably been Amanda's way of coping with a terrifying situation, and convincing herself that she wanted it had made it tolerable.

But even though the shift in logic helped him see things in a different light, Kian still felt contaminated by the filth that had soiled Amanda.

Standing under the spray of the almost scalding water, he kept running the soap over his body, over and over, wishing he had one of those loofah things to better scrub with. In the recesses of his mind, Kian was aware that the stain he was trying to rub off was on the inside, but he couldn't help the compulsion.

His only consolation was that Syssi wasn't there to witness his slip into insanity.

6

AMANDA

"Where is he?" Amanda rounded on Anandur the moment his door cracked open.

The racket she'd made pounding on his door should've been enough to rouse the whole floor, and yet the guy had taken his sweet time getting his butt in gear.

Through the sliver of an opening, Anandur peeked at her with a tight-lipped stare. Then, after a long moment, he swung it open and turned back inside, flashing her his naked ass. She followed, waiting impatiently as she heard him flush the toilet and brush his teeth, then watched him plod to his bedroom to finally emerge wearing a pair of unbuttoned jeans.

Without sparing her a glance, Anandur continued to the kitchen and got busy making coffee.

Insufferable man.

Were all the males in her family jerks?

At last, as the coffeemaker spewed its few remaining drops, filling the two cups he'd shoved under it to the brim, Anandur pulled one for himself and handed her the other. "Milk is in the fridge, but I would check the date if I were you. Sugar is right over there." He pointed to the cluttered counter.

Amanda humphed in indignation but accepted the mug. After all, coffee was coffee and she needed her fix. After a horrible nightmare had awakened her way too early, she'd bolted up from bed, barely pausing to pull on a T-shirt and a pair of jeans, let alone stop for coffee.

Terror clawing through her, she'd grabbed her phone and texted Syssi.

Thank heavens, her friend had answered immediately. Syssi had reassured her that Kian had been sleeping soundly beside her. And that no, the clothes he had worn before coming to bed hadn't been bloodied.

Amanda had made Syssi check.

With panic shorting out her brain, it had been a miracle that the idea to ask Syssi had managed to surface from that disjointed swirl.

Even now, knowing it had been only a dream, the image of Dalhu's mangled body had her heart hammer a drumroll against her ribs. Hanging from chains bolted to a stone wall high above him, he'd been so beaten and bloodied that she'd barely recognized him. His manacled wrists had been broken, and his ankles had been secured by links bolted to the floor, his feet pointing in the wrong direction.

Amanda shivered. She hadn't needed to see the face of his tormentor to know it had been Kian. She'd heard his voice, distorted, demonic, while he'd tortured Dalhu for information, demanding more and more…

Except, Dalhu had had no more to give. He'd already told Kian everything.

Rationally, Amanda accepted that it hadn't been real, but she needed to see Dalhu with her own eyes to banish the last vestiges of that nightmare.

That being said, though, she could spare a few moments to drink her morning coffee.

The milk turned out to be fine, and she poured some into her cup, then added sugar. "Okay, enough stalling. Tell me where you dumped Dalhu. I want to see him."

Leaning against the counter and sipping his hot brew, Anandur just stared at her for a long moment before responding. "He is down in the dungeon. It's on the same level as the rest of the *guest rooms,* but in a section that is better secured and not as lavishly appointed."

"Take me to him."

"I can't, not without Kian's authorization. And frankly? Hell would freeze over before he allows it."

"Then we'll go over his head."

"What do you mean over his head? Kian is at the top of our food chain."

"Wrong. My mother is. Or did you forget that she is still the head of our clan? The fact that she lets Kian and Sari run things as they see fit and doesn't interfere with the day to day operations doesn't mean she can't or wouldn't. After all, we are not a democracy, and she has the final word."

"You've got a point there. You'll have to forgive me, though, if I demand to hear it from her own lips... or in writing. As it is, I'm in enough trouble with Kian already over that little incident with Syssi."

"Damn you, Anandur. Since when did you turn into a wuss? My mother is still sleeping, and I really need to see Dalhu now. I had this horrible nightmare about Kian torturing him. It was so bad that I didn't even brush my teeth before rushing down here."

Anandur arched a brow, but then his face softened. "You can rest easy. No one tortured your Doomer. Kian left with Andrew and his men, going straight from the helipad to the garage. And I'm sure he was too exhausted to torture anyone when he came back. But if you need to see your Doomer so badly, I have a solution that can ease your mind without getting me in trouble or waking a sleeping goddess and risking her wrath."

"Yeah? What is it?"

"We can go down to security and view him on the surveillance monitors."

"Anandur, you're a genius. Let's go." Amanda put her empty mug on the counter and reached up to kiss his cheek.

"I'll be damned, wonders never cease. First Kian, and now you? Two compliments in less than twenty-four hours." He shook his head as he headed for the bedroom. "I wish Brundar was here to hear it. He would never believe me."

"Why? Where is he?"

"Who knows?" Anandur answered from the bedroom. "He is a secretive bastard."

That was true. Brundar was the most tight-lipped guy she had ever met.

Anandur came out of the bedroom tugging on a T-shirt. "Let's go, princess. Your frog awaits."

"Does he do it a lot? Stay the night somewhere else, that is?" she asked as they entered the elevator. Amanda couldn't help her curiosity. Brundar was such an enigma that every morsel of information about him, no matter how small, was a rare treat.

"From time to time. Not often, though. I've learned not to ask because I never get an answer." Anandur crossed his arms over his chest and leaned against the elevator's panel.

"Care to hazard a guess?" Anandur had to know something. Not only was he Brundar's brother, but the two worked and lived together.

Anandur shrugged. "I assume it's sex. When we go clubbing, he doesn't go for the females, and I know he doesn't use paid services either, not any that I'm aware of, anyway. But he has to get it somewhere, right?"

The elevator stopped on the second floor and Amanda followed Anandur out. "Do you think he is gay?" she whispered.

"No, I know he isn't. His reaction to females is the same as any other heterosexual, horny immortal male's."

"So what do you think he's hiding?" she asked as they reached a set of gray double doors that were secured with a card-reader lock.

"I don't know. But if Brundar wants to keep his sex life private, it's his prerogative. Right?" Anandur slid his card through the scanner and pushed the left door open.

Amanda had never seen the place before, and as it turned out, Security was not what she had imagined. Instead of one room full of monitors and a guy watching them with a bored expression on his face, the Security Department was huge, occupying most of the second floor's office space and employing dozens of people—mortal and immortal.

Lording supreme over the whole thing was the gatekeeper—Rose the receptionist—a formidable elderly human.

She smiled at Anandur while Amanda got the tight-lipped who-is-that-floozy look-over. "I'm sorry. But Dr. Dokani doesn't have the necessary clearance. You'll have to go in by yourself, dear," Rose rasped in her smoker's voice.

It took some of Anandur's famous charm, or maybe it was the veiled threat of a possible retribution from the big boss that did the trick, but eventually the harpy relented and buzzed them in.

As they made their way down the long hallway, Anandur poked his head into the various rooms and explained their function. Besides several viewing rooms that were each in charge of monitoring a different section of the building, there was also a weapons room, the head of security's room, a changing room with rows of lockers, and even a small staff cafeteria that doubled as a rec room.

Greeting everyone by name, Anandur introduced Amanda as his *cousin*.

For some reason, the appreciative looks she got from the guys failed to thrill her—annoying her instead—and she was glad to reach the end of the tour.

Anandur swiped his access card to the only room in the security wing that was restricted to immortal personnel only. Not that the humans were aware of who their coworkers were, of course. As far as they were concerned, the restricted access only meant that a higher clearance was required.

Over there, surveillance tracked the floors occupied by the clan, including the private underground garage, the rooftop, and the entrances to the dedicated elevators. Though, if needed, they had access to all the other camera feeds as well.

Two guys and one girl were working the twelve-hour night shift, which would probably be over soon. Early dawn had been on the horizon when she'd left her apartment.

"Hi, Steve, how're you, buddy?" Anandur slapped hands with the guy. "How is our lone prisoner doing?"

"Sleeping, I think. Here, these are the two feeds from his room."

Amanda waited for the monitors to come online, but when nothing happened she got impatient. "Well? How long does it take to turn them on?"

"They are on. It's just dark in there. That's why I said he was probably sleeping."

Dark? Pitch black was more like it. If even she, with her enhanced eyesight, could see nothing, then there was absolutely no light in the room.

"Has he woken up at all since we brought him in?" Anandur placed a hand on Amanda's shoulder, halting the rant that was building up.

"Yeah, he did. Got up, used the bathroom, ate breakfast, then went back to sit on the mattress. But after five minutes of him pulling the Rodin, sitting motionless, the sensors turned the lights off. That was a little over an hour ago."

"Could you rewind the footage? Amanda wants to make sure he is okay."

Steve gave her a quizzical glance, then shrugged and did as Anandur had asked, starting the recording from the moment the brothers had brought the unconscious Dalhu into the room and had transferred him from the gurney to the mattress.

The room—if one could call it that, more like a closet—wasn't as bad as in her dream. The walls were painted a plain cream color, and there were no chains or even hooks to attach them to in sight. But other than that, it was shockingly small and bare.

A few minutes after the guys left and locked the door, the lights switched off, and the monitors went black.

"Speed it up," Anandur said.

Steve did just that, and once Dalhu woke up and the lights switched back on, he slowed the thing to only four times the normal speed.

As she watched Dalhu in the video while they fast forwarded, it was obvious he'd been aware of the cameras, and as his gaze had swept over every detail in the room, his expression had been guarded, revealing next to nothing. But Amanda knew him well enough to notice the little tell signs he had been working so hard to conceal.

He looked hopeless.

Not that she could blame him. Being locked in a small inescapable box, with no hope of ever getting out, who wouldn't feel despondent?

But he was wrong.

Dalhu underestimated what she could and would do for him, and more importantly, who she had in her corner.

When the recording ended, and the monitors returned to live feed, the little number at the top left corner of the screen showed it to be a little before seven in the morning. It was still too early, considering that Annani had gone to bed less than two hours ago. Nevertheless, she was going to risk rousing her mother.

"Thank you, Steve. Let's go, Anandur."

"I'm having Dalhu moved," she said once they were out of the security wing and back inside the elevator.

"You know I can't do it. Kian selected this cell specifically. That's where he wants him to stay."

"I know. I'm going to wake my mother."

"Oh, boy, the shit's gonna hit the fan."

Amanda glanced up at Anandur with a half-hearted smile. He was right. This was going to get real nasty, real fast. And for once, she wasn't looking forward to all the drama.

"Good luck," Anandur said as they reached his floor. "I'm going back to sleep. Don't wake me up unless an all-out war is raging."

She smiled. "Good night, or rather good morning."

He nodded, giving her the thumbs-up as the elevator doors were about to close.

Back in the penthouse, Amanda paced around her living room for a good ten or fifteen minutes. Before waking her mother, she needed to work on phrasing her request to sound as convincing and as respectful as possible.

Despite what she'd told Anandur, she wasn't certain at all Annani would agree to go over Kian's head. In fact, she was pretty sure her mother would take a lot of convincing.

True, Annani had promised her support, but her mother's idea of helping was probably talking with Kian and attempting to reason with him.

There was no doubt in Amanda's mind that her mother would balk at undermining Kian's authority over his own keep.

Shit. Amanda didn't like it either.

She had to find a way to have Dalhu transferred to a decent room without an all-out battle with Kian.

7

DALHU

The darkness didn't bother Dalhu, nor did the quiet. The lack of outside stimuli provided a blank canvas for his imagination. He filled the void with images of Amanda, painting them in vivid colors on the inside of his eyelids, and the silence with her voice, playing her spoken words like a soundtrack in his head.

He was committing to memory each and every nuance of her expressive face, her perfect body. The smiles. The way she tapped her foot on the floor when angry. The arch of her perfect dark brows when doubtful.

Her spirit.

She was such a passionate woman, and he wasn't referring to sex. Although, yeah... that too. She was just as enthusiastic about her work—finding a solution to her clan's plight.

Fuck. As Dalhu's head jerked up, activating the motion detectors, the harsh light flooded his cell again. Amanda would not be able to return to her work. Not as long as the men he had foolishly left behind—alive—knew who she was, where she worked, and what her face looked like.

Even if she were to change her name and establish a new research laboratory elsewhere, they'd still be able to find her.

As long as they lived, Amanda would never be safe.

Damn. He hadn't planned for the contingency of her ever going home, and therefore had never considered what would happen if she were to be rescued.

Amanda would want to return to her work at the lab as soon as possible.

He'd been careless. He'd fucked up and had failed to protect Amanda again. What the hell had he been thinking? What had possessed him to spare their lives? He should have eliminated each and every last thread leading to her.

I'm such a fucking idiot.

Dalhu pushed up from the mattress and began pacing. Like a caged animal, he walked in circles around his tiny jail cell, struggling to suppress the roar that was building up in his chest.

Up until that moment, he'd been careful to project a strong image for the benefit of the guys watching him on the surveillance cameras, refusing to give them the satisfaction of seeing him lose it.

Not anymore.

Lacing his fingers behind his head and pressing the heels of his palms into his temples, he didn't give a shit if his captors were watching.

Let them see his distress.

Let them gloat.

He had to talk to Amanda and warn her.

But how? How would he communicate with her?

The fuckers watching the monitors wouldn't tell her if he asked for her, and anyway, it wasn't likely that they were monitoring sound in addition to visual in this rattrap. If the room were ever to be used for interrogation, it would have been rigged with audio recording equipment. But Dalhu doubted a cell this size could accommodate such activity. Besides, there was no residual scent of blood. And it wasn't like prisoners in solitary confinement were known to talk to themselves and reveal secrets that were worth recording.

He had the passing thought that if he were to trash the place, someone would come to check on him. Except, there wasn't much to trash, and the room was probably soundproof. No one in the adjoining cells or the corridor would be able to hear him; only the guys in security would know anything was going on.

In the end, desperation drove him to employ a last-resort measure. He turned his face up to the camera and began miming.

From a warrior to a fucking mime.

How low the mighty had fallen.

Doing the chatting thing with his lips and the fingers of one hand, he pointed to his head with the other. Hopefully, the guards were better at charades than he was, and weren't mistaking his gestures to mean he was hearing voices in his head.

Asking to talk to someone in charge, Dalhu mouthed the words and gesticulated with his hands. Repeating his request, he even tried to shape his hands into something resembling a crown on his head.

Damn, he could only imagine the ridicule his performance was garnering.

8

AMANDA

"Ninni?" Amanda whispered and dipped her head to kiss her mother's warm cheek. "Are you awake?" she whispered again.

It was dark in Annani's bedroom. The closed shutters blocked all outside light from filtering through, and the room would have been pitch black if not for the lambent glow cast by the Goddess's luminous skin.

"No," Annani rasped, a small smile blooming on her delicate face. "I am still sleeping and dreaming my little Mindy is afraid of the dark and wants to crawl in bed with her Ninni. Come, child, get in and let me hug you." She lifted the comforter and scooched back a little, making room for Amanda.

Hesitating for all of two seconds, Amanda hopped in and snuggled up to her mother. And if anyone had a problem with a two-hundred-year-old woman wanting a little babying from her Ninni, they could shove it where the sun doesn't shine.

Annani let the comforter drop back, then lifted her palm to Amanda's cheek and cupped it gently. "What troubles you so early in the morning?"

"I had a bad dream."

Annani chuckled and shifted up, kissing Amanda's forehead. "Here, I kissed the bad dream away. All better?"

"You know what? It's funny, but it is."

"Of course it is. Love always brightens the mood."

Amanda sighed and moved to lie on her back. "I had a horrible nightmare. I dreamt that Dalhu had been tortured. It was so awful that I woke up with my heart up in my throat, and I just had to check on him to reassure myself that he was okay. But knowing Kian would never allow it, I tried to get Anandur to take me to see Dalhu. But Anandur refused to go over Kian's head and took me to security instead. I watched the recording from the surveillance cameras, all of it, from the moment they'd brought Dalhu in and up to that moment. As far as I could ascertain, he wasn't harmed. But his cell is tiny, with nothing but a mattress on the floor. He is a big guy, taller even than Anandur, he'll go crazy in there."

Amanda paused and sighed again, adding a soft sniffle for effect. "I don't know what to do, Ninni. I'm well aware that we can't risk letting a Doomer roam free about the keep, and I'm not suggesting it. But I can't stand the thought of Dalhu being locked up in that little empty box. Besides, I want to be able to visit him and spend some time with him without everyone in security watching and listening to everything that's going on. You know what I mean?"

She sniffled again, a little louder this time. "Talking with Kian will achieve nothing. In fact, the opposite is probably true. If I try to reason with him, he'll just get angrier and may take it out on Dalhu." As real tears slid down her temples, trickling into the crease between her shoulder and neck, Amanda covered her eyes with the palms of her hands.

Annani's reply was a long time in coming. "Do not worry, child, I will talk to him."

"Kian won't listen to reason, not even from you."

"Oh, but my dear Mindy, you underestimate me. By the time I am done with Kian, he will be convinced it was his own idea to move Dalhu to a better holding room."

"How? Are you going to use influence on him?"

It was a disconcerting thought. As far as Amanda knew, Annani had never used her power to manipulate her own children, but what if she had? As the only one capable of playing with the minds of immortals, she could've done so with no one any the wiser.

Except, why would she?

Whenever Annani wanted something from her children, or from any of the other members of her clan for that matter, all she had to do was ask. No one would dare defy her. And it wasn't as if the Goddess shied away from voicing her demands.

"No, of course not," Annani humphed. "I will simply do what every other mother does... well, maybe not every mother... just those with a flair for the dramatic." She winked. "I am, after all, a diva, and my loving son is obligated to cater to my whims, however bizarre."

Amanda smiled at her mother's wink. "What do you have in mind?"

"Patience, my dear, you will see."

9

ANANDUR

"What?" Anandur barked into his cell phone. What the hell could Steve want less than an hour after he and Amanda had left the control room? Interrupting Anandur's sleep for the second time this morning?

He'd only just managed to close his eyes when the incessant ringing forced him to answer the damn thing. "Steve, buddy," Anandur hissed, "unless we are under attack or there is a raging inferno in the building, I don't want to hear about it. I'm going back to sleep."

"Sorry, bro, I hate to do this to you, but it was you or Kian, and I chose the lesser of two evils. Our prisoner is trying to communicate... Excuse me for a moment," he said as rolling laughter sounded in the background. "Shut up, you morons!" Steve's admonition was muffled, indicating that his hand was covering the receiver. "Sorry about that, the idiots think it's funny—" He snickered. "I'm so sorry, it's just that the Doomer doesn't know we can hear him, and he's been miming for the past half an hour that he needs to talk to someone in charge. The poor bastard is getting more and more creative with each new charade." Steve snorted, then inhaled deeply to calm himself. "I think you should check what his problem is. He says it's a matter of life and death... Unless you want me to call Kian..."

"No, damn it, don't call him. I'll handle this."

"I thought so."

"Fucking Doomer," Anandur muttered under his breath as he threw off the covers and pulled on the jeans he'd dropped on the nightstand before getting back in bed. In the bathroom, he splashed his face with cold water and brushed his teeth, again. Looking up, he groaned. Not that he needed the damn mirror to show him that he looked like hell—with the color of his bloodshot eyes matching the color of his hair.

Damn, he'd better get some sleep before hitting the clubs tonight, or he'd scare the ladies away.

Nah, not going to happen.

Nothing short of his demonic illusion could keep females from lusting after him. Anandur flexed his impressive pectorals and smirked. They could never resist all of this.

Yeah, even with eyes that were red-rimmed and underlined by dark circles he was still one hell of a handsome devil. Getting closer to the mirror, he patted a few wayward curls in place. His beard needed a trim and so did his mustache, but it would have to wait. His barber was off today, and Anandur didn't trust himself with the task. It was too damn hard to manage the dense bush.

Shaving it off, however, was not an option. Without it his damn baby face, though pretty, looked too young. Absurd, considering the fact that he was over a thousand years old. Problem was, even though he loved an eyeful of young flesh as much as the next guy, he preferred to bed women, not girls. But experienced, older females preferred men in their thirties, not twenties, which was what he looked like without the beard.

This was the only concession he made, though. With his height and muscular build, it was more than enough. Anandur bought his clothes wherever he could find stuff his size and paid no attention to fashion trends or designer names. In fact, he liked shopping at discount stores even though he could afford better things. That way he knew for sure that the ladies were after his body and not his wallet. Besides, it was easier to just grab something at Walmart than get hassled by the sales people working at the fancier places.

Grabbing the T-shirt he'd left on the bathroom floor, he brought it up to his nose for a sniff. It was still fresh. After all, he'd put it on only this morning when Amanda had so rudely interrupted his sleep. Nevertheless, he tossed it into the hamper and headed back to his bedroom for a new one.

A male could never be too fastidious about his personal hygiene, especially body odor. The more virile the male, the more potent the stench, hence the more grooming required.

Not that Anandur's obsession with cleanliness extended to his and Brundar's apartment. The place would've looked like a pigsty if not for Okidu showing himself in, every couple of nights or so, to tidy up.

Pulling a plain, gray T-shirt over his chest, Anandur headed to Brundar's room. If he was lucky, his brother was back, and he would send him down to deal with the Doomer. Not that it was likely, but he could hope.

Nope, Brundar wasn't back yet.

Crap.

Anandur made himself a big mug of coffee, strapped a dagger to his calf, pocketed a wicked switchblade, and headed for the dungeon while cursing his good-for-nothing brother and the damn Doomer all through the elevator ride.

Besides the Doomer, the *guest* level had no other occupants at the moment. After his transition, Michael had moved in with Kri. And Kian had released Carol, who up until last night had been chilling in the same miserable cell they had thrown their new *guest* in.

Used for solitary confinement, it was the nastiest they had.

The poor girl had been begging pitifully to be released, promising she would never ever get drunk in a bar and yap so irresponsibly again. Kian would've probably kept her there for another twenty-four hours, but he'd needed the room and had called Onegus from the chopper to let her out.

When he reached the end of the corridor, Anandur stopped in front of the Doomer's room and punched in the code, engaging the mechanism to open the cell's heavy steel door. As the thing started its smooth, but slow swing-out motion, he rested his other hand on the switchblade in his pocket. Not that he expected any trouble from the Doomer, the guy seemed smarter than that. But as the saying went, better safe than sorry, or the other one about not trusting a scorpion or something like that.

As soon as the door fully opened, the Doomer backed away and raised his hands, palms facing out, to show he wasn't planning anything.

Anandur stepped in. "So, what is so urgent that I had to drag myself out of bed and come down here to look at your sorry face?" And a sorry face it was, the haunted look in the Doomer's eyes leaching out the bite from Anandur's tone.

"Thank you for coming. I would invite you to sit down, but as you can see, there is nowhere to sit. Unless you want to join me on the mattress."

"Sorry, dude, but you're not my type." Anandur heaved himself up on the half wall that delineated the bathroom area. "Okay, talk, I'm listening."

The Doomer didn't sit either. Instead, he leaned his back against the wall and crossed his arms over his chest.

"Are you in charge here? Or is it the other guy? Kian, Amanda's brother?"

Obviously, the Doomer had no clue who either Amanda or Kian was, or he wouldn't be asking who was in charge.

Smart girl, she didn't tell him.

"I'm all that you are going to get, so talk."

The Doomer regarded him for a split second longer, then dipped his head. "I made a mistake." He looked up. "When I ran with Amanda, I decided not to eliminate the men under my command. I thought it would look less suspicious to those in charge if only I went missing, not the entire team. I even left my men with the impression that I was going after a Guardian, so when I didn't return, they would assume I was taken out. That way, I thought, no one from my side would come looking for me. But now, because of my unforgivable miscalculation, Amanda is in danger. They know who she is and where she works."

His expression was blank, a guarded mask as he delivered his request. "You need to take my men out before the reinforcements arrive, and before they can share what they know with the others."

"Are you serious? You want us to kill your men?"

"Yes."

"Cold bastard, aren't you?" Anandur pinned him with a hard stare.

The man didn't flinch, his expression stony as he locked eyes with Anandur. "I am, but that's beside the point. These men are mindless cogs in Navuh's machine of destruction, and they are deemed disposable even by their own people. If given the chance, they will come after you and your family and relish killing your men and raping your women. So if I were you, I would not shed a tear at their demise."

"I definitely wouldn't. I'm just surprised at the nonchalant way you are offering me their heads on a platter."

"I don't give a damn who I have to off to keep her safe. Or to put it bluntly, other than Amanda, I just don't give a damn about anyone."

Shaking his head, Anandur chuckled. "I have to admit, it's kind of romantic. Gruesome, but heartfelt."

Dalhu's expression didn't change as he appraised Anandur.

"What would you have done in my place? If you were lucky enough to find a woman who meant everything to you, was there anything you wouldn't have done to keep her safe?"

Yeah, probably not, with the exception of sacrificing his family.

Well, that wasn't precisely true. Some members of his clan he wouldn't mind.

Still, he understood where the guy was coming from. Having an immortal female to form a lifelong bond with was every immortal male's dream, with maybe the exception of those who were gay. Not that the Doomer had a chance in hell of achieving it. But Anandur could sympathize with the guy's yearnings, delusional as they were.

Even if he weren't a coldhearted bastard, the Doomer had nothing and no one to care for. The Brotherhood of the Devout Order Of Mortdh wasn't exactly a nurturing organization.

No wonder the guy had no qualms about offing his brethren for Amanda's sake.

10

KIAN

"Kian, your mother is on the phone." Syssi ran a gentle palm up and down Kian's bicep.

He cracked one eye open and yawned. "What does she want?" Did it only feel like he'd gone to bed a few minutes ago? "What time is it?"

Holding her thumb over the phone's mic, Syssi whispered, "It's fifteen after eight. She says it's important."

What the hell could Annani want that couldn't wait until later? As in much later? After he had his fill of shut-eye and of Syssi? Or maybe the other way around…

Even in his exhausted state, Syssi's innocent touch had stirred him. But it wasn't as if he could refuse the call and have Syssi tell Annani to call later.

Stifling a groan, he reluctantly accepted the receiver from Syssi. "What is it, Mother?" Kian tried and failed to hide his irritation.

"I am sorry to disturb your much-needed slumber, Kian. But it is imperative that I talk to your prisoner as soon as possible. You can take care of it for me in less than a minute, without even leaving your bed. Just instruct Anandur to arrange the meeting and then go back to sleep."

It took a moment for her words to penetrate his sleep-addled brain. "What? Why the hell would you want to do that?" He jerked up to a sitting position and gripped the receiver, hard, easing up only when the plastic began to bend.

"I will forgive your slip, Kian, but only this one time," she said imperiously. "Anandur has just visited with the prisoner. The Doomer insists there is some sort of danger we need to address immediately before it is too late. I need to hear what he has to say."

With a sigh, Kian swung his legs over the edge of the bed. "I'll do it. I don't want you anywhere near that... that thing, Mother." There were some other choice adjectives he had in mind, but heeding her warning about language, he stopped himself in time.

"I understand your concern for my safety, my sweet boy. But I am in no danger, as you well know, and I wish to talk to the prisoner. It is a rare opportunity to have some of my questions about the Brotherhood answered and to learn about Navuh's future plans. I am not asking your permission, Kian. All I need is for you to make the arrangements."

Damn it. When Annani made up her mind, it was futile to try to reason with her. And it certainly sounded like she wouldn't budge on this one.

"I see that I have no choice, but I'm coming with you."

"Please do not. I have no need of a chaperone. Anandur will suffice as my protection. And you, Kian, need your sleep. You are no good to anyone when you are grumpy and snappy because you are exhausted."

This wasn't good. In Annani speak, she was telling him she didn't want him to be there, and there was nothing he could say or do to convince her otherwise.

But that didn't mean he couldn't take every precaution he could think of. She was right, of course. The Doomer, however big and strong, posed no real danger to her. She could immobilize him with one mental command. Nevertheless, imagining his tiny, delicate mother in the same room with that monster went against every protective instinct in him.

"Give me half an hour."

"Thank you. I will be awaiting your call."

With a groan, Kian heaved his legs back onto the bed and dropped his head against the headboard, then reached for the mug of fresh coffee Syssi was holding for him. "You're a life saver. Thank you."

"So, what's going on? What did she want?" Syssi sat on the bed and snuggled up to him, placing her palm over his bare chest.

He took a sip and cleared his throat. "She wants to talk to the Doomer."

"Is it a problem? You think he'll try something?"

"Not likely. Nevertheless, before I allow her in the same room with him, I'm going to make damn sure he's neutralized."

Syssi smirked as she stroked his chest, playing with the few hairs she found there. "I don't think your mother would appreciate seeing Dalhu chained to the wall. Or drugged. Her idea of interrogation is probably a pleasant chat over drinks and hors d'oeuvres."

"I know. This is exactly what I'm trying to figure out. How the hell am I going to secure a room in a way that will not offend her sensibilities? And without being too obvious about it?" Kian rubbed his brows.

Syssi leaned and planted a small kiss on his chest. "I'm sure you'll figure something out. Just be quick about it so you can go back to sleep and recharge." She extended her little pink tongue and licked at his nipple. "There are some promises"—lick—"you've made"—another swipe of her tongue—"that I'm still waiting for you to fulfill," she said, her voice husky.

He was tired, but not that tired.

Syssi squeaked as he pulled her up to lie on top of him, and tried to wiggle away. He captured her neck, holding her still and kissing her deep and slow.

She moaned, rubbing herself all over his erection.

"You just wait until I'm done taking care of this thing for my mother… then I'm going to take care of you."

"Not until you've gotten several hours of sound sleep." Once again, she tried to wiggle out of his arms.

Kian tightened his hold and in one swift move flipped Syssi, pinning her underneath him. "I don't think so," he growled, pressing down and letting her feel how hard she had gotten him.

She gasped, and her eyelids fluttered, her body softening in surrender.

"My sweet Syssi." He eased his hold and kissed her gently, then nuzzled at her neck, inhaling the intoxicating aroma of her arousal. "I love you," he whispered into her skin.

It was incredible, the way she made all his troubles seem trivial. With her thighs cradling him in a loving embrace, he gazed at her flushed, beautiful face and felt at peace with the world.

Unfortunately, the world was demanding his attention, and although he was tempted to tell it to go to hell and then make love to his woman, he couldn't.

Instead, he took one more quick kiss and rolled off her. "How about you stay here and wait for me?" he said as he got up and headed for the bathroom.

Syssi scrambled to get out of bed. "You need to sleep. And I can see that it's not going to happen as long as I'm here."

She was absolutely right. If he got back in bed and she was still there, sleep would be the furthest thing from his mind. He would pleasure her as he had promised until she screamed loud enough to…

"That reminds me," he called from the bathroom. "If you haven't noticed, Andrew stayed over and is sleeping in one of the spare bedrooms."

“The way he snores? I think everybody in the keep knows he is here. He sounds like a broken blender.” Syssi leaned against the door frame and watched Kian as he brushed his teeth, eating up his naked body with hungry eyes.

With a grin, Kian flexed a little.

Her breath hitched. She licked her lips.

Sweet.

“Like what you see?” he taunted, using a small washcloth to dry off the water drops from his face and chest—slowly.

“Oh, you’re a wicked, wicked man. I’m going to the kitchen.” She pushed away from the frame and left, the door swinging closed behind her.

Pity, he wanted to tease her for a little longer.

11

AMANDA

"Hi, Anandur, what's up?" Amanda glanced at Annani and clicked her phone's speaker button on.

"I don't know how you managed to pull it off, but Kian just called. He wants me to transfer your frog into the largest *guest room* and secure it for Annani's visit."

Yes! Amanda gave her mother the thumbs-up. "I had nothing to do with it. Kian must've realized on his own that Dalhu's tiny cell is inappropriate for any kind of visit, let alone Annani's. You know Kian, he would've never allowed her to be cooped up with a dangerous Doomer in such small quarters." She did her best to sound nonchalant. After all, the whole point of this maneuver was about preserving appearances and not challenging Kian's authority or undermining his status as the leader of this keep.

"Yeah, right... have it your way. Oh, and get a load of that, he asked me to lend the Doomer some of my clothes. Kian wants him to look presentable for her highness."

Looking at her mother with new appreciation, Amanda grinned. Everything worked like a charm. "You don't say... that's a good idea. And don't worry, I'll pay you back for the clothes."

"No need, princess. But I would take an IOU for a future favor."

"You got it. What should I tell Annani?"

"I'm on my way down to the dungeon. As soon as I'm done there, I'll come up and escort her to the prisoner. It seems she refused Kian's offer to do the honors, which by the way, he sounded quite peeved about. He wants me to stay glued to her side at all times."

"I'll tell her to be ready. See you later." Amanda terminated the call and turned to give her mother a hug.

"You did it, Ninni."

Annani's smug face had 'I told you so' written all over it. "I'm glad Anandur, and not Kian, will come to escort me down to the dungeon. I was not sure about Kian's compliance with this part of my request. "

"You mean, us," Amanda corrected.

"No, child, I am going to see the prisoner by myself. You can visit him after I come back."

"But why? Anandur is going to be there, and probably other Guardians as well," Amanda whined.

"Your presence there will distract Dalhu. I want his full and undivided attention, and I do not want him choosing his words carefully and omitting things on your account."

For a moment, Amanda considered producing a little sniffle or two to soften her mother's resolve. But as one drama queen to another, she suspected her antics wouldn't work on Annani.

And besides, she could use the time to choose an outfit and make herself pretty.

The tough part was to decide what look she was going for. Elegant and refined? Sexy? Casual?

What did she want to achieve on her first visit?

Sex, of course, was foremost on her mind. After the little taste Dalhu had given her at the cabin, she couldn't wait to finish what had been so harshly interrupted.

The memory of the incomparable pleasure he'd wrought out of

her was still so fresh, she felt her breasts grow heavy and her core spasm with need.

Amanda shivered.

She had the nagging suspicion that mortals just wouldn't do anymore.

After having been exposed to the exquisite taste of such rare wine, going back to the *meh* variety would be a serious letdown. Better go without than compromise for something subpar.

Trouble was, the rare wine came from a forbidden fruit.

It would have been so much easier if she had been able to forget all about Dalhu and give Andrew a chance. Andrew and Kian seemed to get along fabulously, and everyone else would welcome Syssi's brother into the family with open arms.

Heck, maybe she would. Fates knew the whole thing with Dalhu was tenuous.

Andrew was a great guy, and what's more, he obviously still wanted her, even after that talk they had on the way to the chopper, during which she'd made sure that he had no illusions as to the sort of woman he was pining for. He knew who and what she was. Except there was always the chance that, like most guys, Andrew had been blindsided by her beauty, but she didn't think so. Andrew wasn't the impressionable type.

Dalhu, on the other hand, believed Amanda could walk on water. And that was while he was still clueless about who she really was. Though not for long. After the chat he was going to have with her mother, the cat would be out of the bag. And heavens only knew how he'd react to that.

He might resent her for keeping this information from him, and there was the distinct possibility that he would be intimidated by her status.

Or, he might react the way she hoped he would, telling her that there was nothing that could change the way he felt about her.

Amanda chuckled. Dalhu had no idea how apt he'd been when

he'd called her *princess,* or how much this *Princess Buttercup* liked having her own *as-you-wish* guy.

She sighed. Sex would have to wait.

They needed to talk.

12

DALHU

Down at his cell, Dalhu tensed as the whiz of the pneumatic bolts retracting preceded the slow swing-out motion of his cell's door.

How heavy was that thing that an immortal male couldn't swing it open manually? Or were they just too spoiled to exert themselves by pushing it?

Figures, with all that money...

"It's your lucky day, frog." The redheaded Guardian walked in with a small bundle of clothes under his arm.

"Frog?"

Was this some new kind of insult he wasn't familiar with?

"You know, like in the princess and the frog story. The princess kisses a frog, and he turns into a prince. Though in your case, you're no prince, just a garden variety frog." Anandur handed him the small bundle. "Here, I brought you some fresh clothes."

"Why?" Dalhu was genuinely perplexed. The clothes Anandur was handing him didn't look like prison garb, and even though his captors were rich, it didn't mean that they were obliged to provide their enemies with anything more than the bare necessities. And it wasn't as if he was offending their sensibilities by wearing dirty or torn stuff. Hell, Dalhu was better dressed than the Guardian. The plain gray T-shirt the guy was wearing looked like something he had paid five bucks for at a discount store.

"Because I'm just nice like that." Anandur winked. "Go change, I'm moving you to a better room."

"Not that I don't appreciate the kindness, but I'm suspicious of what you would want in return." He regarded the redhead warily. The guy didn't strike him as gay, but maybe he was just very good at fronting a hetero. After all, not all gay men flamboyantly overdramatized femininity. Though, in Anandur's case, the Guardian would have to be a superb actor to project such a powerful masculine, heterosexual vibe.

Anandur snorted. "As I've said before, you're not my type. Get over it, dude, and go change. I promise not to peek." He winked again, this time licking his lips in an obvious leer.

The guy must be just messing with me... or is he?

Going behind the privacy wall, Dalhu hesitated before taking his clothes off. But a quick glance at the Guardian reassured him he had nothing to worry about. The guy was leaning against the wall and watching something on his phone.

Still, better to be quick about it.

Taking a one minute turn in the shower, Dalhu washed again. Not that he felt dirty, but he hated the idea of changing into fresh clothes without washing first.

"You're oddly fastidious, for a Doomer," Anandur commented as Dalhu came out dressed in the new, or rather used clothes.

Surprisingly, they fit, though barely, and he suspected that their original owner was the redhead. Anandur was almost the same size as Dalhu, maybe an inch or two shorter, but he was bulkier, probably outweighing Dalhu by a dozen pounds or so.

"You've got a problem with that?" Dalhu was used to taunts about what the other guys considered as his excessive bathing habits.

"No, not at all, to the contrary. It is just that I find it unusual for you guys." Anandur opened the door, and they stepped out into the wide corridor. "The others I had the displeasure of getting acquainted with stank to high heavens." The Guardian grimaced. "I hate stinkers," he grated, stopping in front of another door and punching a code into the panel.

Inside, two males, Guardians by the look of them, were seated at a round dining table, busy playing a card game. There was also a sofa and two armchairs as well as a flat-screen TV. No bed, though. But there was another door, maybe leading to a separate bedroom?

They gave him a suite?

What the hell was going on?

"These are my comrades, Bhathian and Arwel." Anandur made the introduction. The men nodded and went back to their game.

Evidently, there was no need to introduce Dalhu.

He turned to his unlikely new friend. Granted, referring to Anandur as a friend was a stretch, but at least the Guardian wasn't openly hostile and treated Dalhu decently. "Please, tell me what's going on? And why am I suddenly treated like royalty?"

"You're not, but your visitor is."

"What visitor?"

"And what? Spoil the surprise? No way."

Dalhu's heart skipped a beat. Was it Amanda? Was she coming to see him?

Except, why call her royalty…

Anandur had called her princess, but Dalhu had assumed the guy meant it as a form of endearment, same way he had. If not for the lavish suite and the additional guards, he would've dismissed the whole thing as Anandur's peculiar sense of humor. But now he wondered. Was Amanda someone important? Aside from the importance of her research, that is?

"Enough with the fish-out-of-water thing. Go plant your butt on that sofa. Do not get up or make any sudden movements until after your guest leaves. Am I clear?" Anandur was all business now, all traces of humor gone.

Dalhu didn't get the fish-out-of-water reference, but he had no problem understanding the rest. Anandur and the two other Guardians were there to ensure the mysterious guest's safety, and if Dalhu even twitched the wrong way, they were going to jump on him.

For the life of him, though, he couldn't understand why they didn't just put him in chains. Better yet, strap an electric collar around his throat and zap him if he made a suspicious move.

In their shoes, this was what he would've done.

The Guardians didn't carry any visible weapons either. They must be very confident in their hand-to-hand to forgo those while guarding him.

Not that he doubted their abilities. He had been at the receiving end of the Guardians' fighting skills time and again. Not personally, but they had proven their superiority over the men he had sent against them.

"I'm leaving you in the capable hands of my colleagues. Don't give them any trouble while I'm gone." Anandur pointed a finger at Dalhu and pulled open the door.

Dalhu nodded, and Anandur stepped out, closing it behind him.

Dalhu heard the whiz of the lock engaging. The door to this room was nothing like the monster securing his previous lodging, but he wasn't fooled by its slender profile. It was probably reinforced with thin titanium rods, which locked into a doorjamb that was probably enhanced as well. The Guardians were not stupid. They wouldn't put him in a room he could break out of.

Unless, this was only a temporary reprieve, and he would be returned to that tiny cell after his mysterious rendezvous was over.

Shortly after Anandur left him under the watchful eyes of the two Guardians, a stout, weird-looking butler brought in a tray of assorted appetizers and placed it on the coffee table in front of Dalhu.

The two Guardians eyed the thing with interest but refrained from sampling.

The butler walked up to the double door cabinet behind the dining area and opened it, revealing a well-stocked bar. He pulled out a carafe, filled it with some dark liquid from the fridge, and together with two crystal goblets brought it over to the coffee table.

The one named Arwel got up from his seat, leaving his cards face down on the table, and stepped up to the bar. He poured himself a drink.

"You want something?" he asked the other one.

"No. I don't drink before lunch," the surly one bit out.

Arwel shrugged. "Suit yourself." He sat down with his large drink in hand and picked up his cards.

No one thought to ask Dalhu. Not that he would've accepted. He didn't drink before lunch either. And anyway, it was imperative for him to stay sharp for the audience with his guest—whoever he might be. *Or she... hopefully, she...*

"Yeah. It's all good... No, nothing at all," Arwel said, though it didn't look like he was addressing Bhathian. The tone and the small pause indicated that he was talking to someone outside the room, and a quick glance confirmed the almost invisible earpiece hiding under the guy's hair.

Dalhu tensed. Watching the door, he squared his shoulders and forced his hands to stay loose on top of his knees—palms down.

He heard the mechanized buzz and then the click of the lock a moment before the door swung open.

Anandur stepped in and nodded his head once, approving of Dalhu's obedient pose, before stepping aside to let the *important guest* in.

Looking up, Dalhu almost missed the first clue, but following

Anandur's eyes, he glanced down and saw a dainty foot cross the doorjamb, followed by a tiny red-haired female in a long black dress.

She turned her face to him, and time stopped, then exploded like a bolt of lightning.

Later, when he'd think back to this moment, he'd remember that it felt like being shocked by a mighty bolt of electric power, but sans the pain, only the glory.

Forgetting Anandur's warning, Dalhu did what he was compelled to. He dropped to his knees and prostrated himself before the Goddess.

"It's okay. He's just awestruck." He dimly heard Arwel stopping Bhathian from lunging forward.

Awestruck could not begin to describe it.

She was the real thing—a real Goddess—and she was magnificent.

For some reason, whenever he thought of Annani, he imagined a female version of Navuh. A tall, dark, majestic woman, with an angry scowl permanently etched on her handsome face.

The real Annani was so far beyond whatever a mortal or an immortal could conjure in his imagination.

She was otherworldly.

Awesome power, indescribable beauty…

And love…

Dalhu felt guilt crushing down on him like an anvil—couldn't fathom how he could've ever hated this… this Goddess?

For the first time in his life, he understood the meaning of the word sacrilege. As one who had never believed in a higher power, he had sneered at those who were offended by what they perceived as disrespect for their deity.

But if he had known the real Annani, he would've been more than offended. He would've been outraged by any negative comment about her. And to think he'd been guilty of much worse? That he'd harbored hate in his heart for a goddess that was the material representation of love and beauty and all that was good?

"Oh, my dear boy, there is no need for that. Please rise." Her voice sounded like heavenly chimes.

More than anything, Dalhu wanted to obey, but he was frozen in place.

"Come on, frog. Up you go." Anandur's amused voice managed to break the spell, and Dalhu lifted to his knees.

The Goddess was so small that from his kneeling position he was almost eye to eye with her. He caught a glimpse of her smile before lowering his eyes.

"It is permitted to gaze upon my face, and you do not need to kneel either. Make yourself comfortable on the sofa. I wish to converse with you." She gave him a little pat on the top of his head.

Awkwardly, he pushed back to sit without standing first, afraid his towering height would somehow be offensive to her. Never mind that Anandur wasn't that much shorter than him. But then again, Anandur wasn't a hated enemy either.

As the Goddess gracefully lowered herself into one of the armchairs, from behind her Anandur pointed a finger at Dalhu in warning, then moved to join his friends at the card table.

"Lift your head and let me see you," she commanded.

He did, taking a furtive look at her impossible face, childlike and yet ancient.

She regarded him in silence, her smart eyes appraising. "I understand now what my daughter sees in you. You are very handsome, strong."

Daughter? Like a real daughter? Or did the Goddess refer to all of her progeny as her children?

She must've read his mind. "Yes, Dalhu, Amanda is my daughter." She smirked. "The youngest child of my womb," she clarified.

Struck by lightning, again.

Speechless.

Hopeless.

The little hope he had harbored that Amanda would somehow find a way for them to be together had just been pulverized.

"Do not look so despondent, Dalhu. Where there is a will, there is a way." She winked.

Annani, the only Goddess known to exist, had actually winked at him.

"Now, tell me more about the danger to my daughter."

Dalhu dropped his head. Choosing his words carefully, he swallowed and cleared his throat. "My men know that Amanda is an immortal and that she works at the university. It wouldn't have been an issue if she'd remained in hiding. With me—"

He swallowed again, his eyes flickering over to the Goddess's face. Her expression remained impassive.

"Now that she is back home, Amanda will want to resume her work. I know how important this research is to her… to all of you." Dalhu glanced at the Goddess again.

She nodded.

"Time is of the essence. Reinforcements are arriving shortly, and once they do, containing this will become impossible. We have a small window of opportunity to eliminate the threat."

"They might have already surrendered the information," she countered.

"I didn't inform my superiors about Amanda, and the men's low ranking prohibits them from calling headquarters directly. Besides, they will do nothing without being ordered to do so. They'll wait for me to come back or for my replacement to arrive."

"Are you sure about that?"

"Positive."

"Well, in that case, we definitely need to make our move quickly. However, I am not keen on using the extreme measures you suggest."

"Every member of the Brotherhood you get rid of is one less threat to you and your clan. If this were my family—and despite your opinion of me, I consider Amanda and by extension all of you as such—I would do everything I could to keep it safe."

In the background, he heard the snorts and *humphs* his proclamation had elicited, but he ignored the Guardians, focusing on the Goddess instead.

Annani was difficult to read, but he had a feeling she approved. And hers was the only opinion that mattered.

Still, minutes passed as she mulled it over before she spoke again. "I wonder. Is it common in the Brotherhood? This every-man-for-himself attitude? And I mean no offense by it, but I wonder how such an organization functions without its members being loyal to each other." She tilted her head a little, the mass of her big, red curls sliding over one delicate shoulder.

Dalhu lifted his hand to rub at his mouth, but then hastily dropped it back to his knee, heeding Anandur's warning. Besides, who knew what the Goddess considered as good manners, and avoiding unnecessary hand movements seemed like a safe bet. "No, it's not common. However, the chief loyalty of the simple soldiers is to the cause and to Navuh. Their own lives and those of their comrades are deemed inconsequential, and they are more than happy to make the ultimate sacrifice on the altar of the holy war," he bit out.

Out of respect for the Goddess, Dalhu suppressed the anger bubbling to the surface. How many years of his life had he spent being just as stupid as the others? Believing in a ridiculous cause that had nothing but hate and envy at its roots? A cause that preached destruction and death as an ultimate goal?

"For a long time, I've been just as blind and dumb as they are, but eventually, I figured it out. Navuh's agenda is the same as any other power-hungry despot's—world domination. And the only way he knows how to achieve it is to ensure that humanity is plagued by wars, ignorance, and superstition, therefore easy to manipulate. Are there others like me? I must assume I'm not the only sharp tool in the shed, but it is not like we could seek each other out and form a club. Unless it's the severed heads club," he chuckled.

Annani didn't smile at his clever pun. If anything, she looked saddened. "It is hard to overcome the relentless brainwashing, nay impossible. I am glad that you were able to break free of it, Dalhu, but I doubt there are more than a handful of males like you, if at all." She sighed. "I wish there were another way. After all, my clan and these immortal males are all that is left of our people."

Dalhu had no clever answer to that. It surprised him, though, that she still thought of members of the Brotherhood as *her people*.

Yes, they'd originated from the same seed, but they'd branched in opposite directions. Besides their unique genetics, they had nothing in common—polar opposites, black and white, good and evil.

It was as simple as that.

Not that he was going to correct the Goddess, but she was blindsided by her own goodness, mistakenly believing that there must be some good deep down in the hearts of her enemies.

There was none.

Breaking free of the brainwashing didn't mean Dalhu had miraculously become good. He was still as dark and as evil as he had been before.

His love for Amanda was the only good he had in him.

13

AMANDA

"So, how did it go?" Amanda pounced on Annani as soon as Anandur brought her mother back. The *little chat* had taken much longer than she had expected.

Her mother had been gone for over an hour.

With a sad little smile, Annani cupped Amanda's cheek. "Let us go out to the terrace." She let her arm drop and glided out through the open sliding doors.

Amanda's gut twisted. What was that melancholy look all about?

"I'll be back later to take you down to your frog," Anandur threw over his shoulder as he headed out. "Half an hour tops."

"It's okay. Take your time," she called after him. Right now, hearing all about her mother's conversation with Dalhu took precedence over seeing him.

Joining Annani on the terrace, Amanda drew out a chair and sat across from her mother at the round bistro table. "Well?"

"He is handsome, that is for sure. Tall and strong." Annani paused to wave Onidu over. "Could you please serve us some Perrier, Onidu?"

Amanda waited till the butler left. "And?" She crossed her arms and began tapping her fingers on her biceps.

"I know you want to hear that I approve of Dalhu. But based on only one conversation, I cannot. Not wholeheartedly."

Amanda's spirit sunk. "No, of course not," she mumbled.

"He seems really taken with you, and I believe him when he says he would do anything and everything to ensure your safety. But..."

Oh boy, here it comes. Amanda held her breath.

"He is obsessed with you. For him, the sun and the moon revolve around you. You may think it is a good thing, but it is not. This kind of passion forms an unhealthy attachment, one that has the potential of turning deadly. That being said, though, I have to consider that Dalhu's abnormal fixation on you might be temporary. He is desperate and sees you as his only lifeline. It is also reasonable that his worry for your safety is keeping him on edge." Annani accepted the glass of soda from Onidu and took a little sip.

"I don't understand. What are you trying to say?"

"I am saying that you should be careful. Go ahead and visit with him, indulge a little..." Annani winked. "But guard your heart, and do not tell him any more than he already knows."

Amanda snorted. "Yeah, right, as if I'm going to do anything in front of the surveillance cameras and provide the guys in security with homemade porn."

Her eyes sparkling, Annani smiled a mischievous little smile and leaned forward to whisper, "Anandur is taking care of it for you. There would be no camera feed from the bedroom, just the living room." With a smug expression on her beautiful face, her mother leaned back in her chair.

"How did you get him to agree to that?"

With a barely noticeable grimace, Annani shifted in her chair. "He agreed on the condition that he is going to be there with you, guarding."

Amanda's brows shot up. "Really?"

"You can close your mouth, Amanda. He is not going to be in the bedroom with you. He is going to wait in the living room." Annani made it sound like it was a nonissue.

"But he is going to hear everything! How am I supposed to even get in the mood with him eavesdropping? And you know Anandur, he will have a field day with this. The man is the worst kind of gossip."

Amanda was not shy about her sexual endeavors, but she balked at having an audience.

Annani looked hurt. Probably because Amanda wasn't as ecstatic over this arrangement as she had expected. "He promised he would keep your forays into the bedroom secret. And you should know that one does not make promises to me in vain. Besides, it is in Anandur's best interest that Kian never finds out about it. This was the best I could do. It was not easy to persuade Anandur to join in on our little conspiracy. You know how I hate bending my own grandchildren's will to my own. I'd rather they cooperate out of love and respect. Luckily for you, it appears that our Anandur is a romantic at heart."

Oh, hell. This was just peachy.

Why couldn't it have been someone else?

She would've been more comfortable with stoic Brundar on guard duty, or any of the other Guardians for that matter. Anandur was the least respectful of the bunch, and the fact that he had promised not to reveal her secret didn't mean he wouldn't use it to torment her mercilessly.

On the other hand, she was pretty sure none of the others would've agreed to cooperate, fearing Kian.

Admittedly, Annani had chosen their coconspirator wisely. Anandur was the only one brazen enough to risk Kian's wrath.

She'd take it. After all, beggars couldn't be choosers.

"Thank you." Amanda took her mother's small hand and gave it a gentle squeeze.

"You are welcome."

"So, what else did you talk about? You've been gone for an awfully long time."

Annani lifted her hand to her chest. "Oh dear, you would not believe the things he has told me."

"What? Is it about the danger he was talking about?"

"Among other things, but that wasn't the worst of it. Though, if you were ever to fall into their hands it definitely would have been the worst." Annani shivered. After a moment, she leaned and lifted the carafe, pouring herself more sparkling water.

Her mother wasn't a woman easily shaken, but she seemed distraught over what she had learned. After several long sips, Annani placed the glass back on the table and squared her shoulders, regaining her regal composure. "First, about the immediate danger to you. I do not know if Dalhu told you, but he was the leader of a small unit of Doomers. The men he left behind are aware of who you are and where you work. Not that you are my daughter, of course, but that you are an immortal. For now, he is adamant that his men will not do anything without being ordered, and that this knowledge is contained. But with reinforcements arriving shortly, your identity will become known throughout their organization. All the way to the top. You will be forced to remain in hiding indefinitely. No more teaching, and no more research. Not unless you conduct it in a private facility and erase your test subjects' memories as soon as you are done with them."

That would be a disaster. Amanda loved teaching and loved her lab. She even liked hanging out with the other professors. Not because any of them were hot, but because she enjoyed having an intelligent conversation with well-educated, smart people. "What does he suggest we do?"

"Eliminate them. He gave us the address of where his six remaining men are staying. We have already taken care of five out of the eleven he started with. He believes we killed them."

"Didn't we?"

"No, I forbade it. They are entombed in our crypt."

"Why? And how did you get Kian to agree to spare them?"

"I had to order him to do it. I knew he could never be persuaded. He would have never agreed. And as to why? I cannot bear the thought of destroying what is left of our kind. Even Doomers. Maybe one day, if the merciful Fates smile kindly upon us, their leader will somehow be eliminated and their organization will disperse. I cling to the hope that the effects will eventually fade without the relentless brainwashing."

"And then you will wake the sleepers?"

"Yes."

Amanda snorted. "An immortal version of the end-of-days prophecy."

Annani tilted her head and lifted her palms. "What can I say? I am an optimist, and I'd rather avoid the irreversible when there is a viable alternative."

"So, are we going to kill Dalhu's men… sorry… entomb them? I guess they are as good as dead while entombed, so why not. Less guilt is always good. Right?"

"I have another idea I want to run by Kian first."

"What is it?"

"You will have to wait. I need to think it through before I talk it over with Kian."

"Fair enough."

Sinking back in her chair, Amanda tilted her face up toward the morning sun. She welcomed the warmth.

Dalhu's cold disregard for the lives of his men shouldn't have surprised her. After all, he had told her as much himself. Still, it was a chilling reminder that the accommodating, romantic male she'd been with was a recent creation—a thin veneer of bright paint over scars that ran deep and long.

Scars that no amount of care and time could heal.

14

AMANDA

With all the hard questions buzzing around in Amanda's head, and no clear answers, by the time Anandur returned to escort her down to the dungeon, her stomach was churning, and she felt nauseated.

A quandary wasn't something Amanda experienced often. Most issues, she didn't care enough to give a damn about, and when addressing those that actually mattered to her, she found it easy to reach a decisive conclusion based on relevant information or even pure gut instinct.

Not this time, though.

During the ride down to the basement, she avoided Anandur's eyes, not ready to deal with the condescending smirk she was sure to find there. Instead, she checked herself in the elevator's mirror. Adjusting the collar of her silk blouse, Amanda regarded the conservative outfit she had chosen—one of her modest teacher getups. She looked good, of course, but not hot...well, relatively speaking... not hot by her own standards, but still...

In a way, her choice of outfit reflected her contemplative rather than lustful mood.

"Why so somber?" Anandur punched the dungeon's floor number. "I thought you'd be happier about finally seeing your frog. And by the way, you owe me, big time. If Kian ever finds out, he is going to go ballistic on my ass." For a change, Anandur wasn't joking. Thc big guy looked worried.

"I appreciate it. But if it comes to that, you can always drop it at Annani's feet. She will back you up."

His lips lifted in a sardonic smile. "That might help to keep my head attached to my neck, but that's about it. I would not be surprised to find myself the next occupant of that crappy cell."

"Yeah, you are probably right," she said as they stepped out into the corridor. "I'm curious, though, how did you manage to remove the camera feed from the bedroom?"

"I couldn't, not without pulling more people into this mess. You never know who might snitch."

"Oh, I see." Well, that was it for the sex then—even if she managed to get in the mood somehow…

"But"—he leaned to whisper in her ear—"there are no cameras in the bathroom. And I played with the one in the bedroom, repositioning it to observe only the bed. If you hug the wall as you enter and duck straight into the bathroom, the camera will not see you. I checked." He lifted his head. "Smart, huh?"

"The bathroom…" Amanda arched her brows.

"It's large, and I had Onidu schlep down a huge stack of towels." He winked. "You're welcome."

Okay, she could work with that—if needed.

"Thank you." She stretched on her toes and kissed his cheek, then grabbed his crinkly hair and pulled him down to whisper in his ear. "I truly appreciate what you've done for me, but if you ever tell anyone about any of this, Kian will be the least of your worries." She let him go.

"Don't worry, princess, your secrets are safe with me. Just remember, you owe me, big time."

"That I do. Whatever and whenever, I'm at your service." Not that she had a clue as to what he might need from her, but whatever it was, she owed him.

As they reached the door of the guest suite, Amanda grew nervous. Watching Anandur punch the code into the lock pad, she wiped her sweaty palms on her light gray trousers, then panicked, remembering they were silk and quickly checked for wet fingertips. Thank heavens, there were none. Tugging on the long sleeves of her white blouse, she held her breath as Anandur opened the door and went in first, keeping her behind him.

"I've got an early Christmas present for you, frog." He took a step to the side.

Dalhu's eyes widened as she came into view, and she heard his heartbeat speed up. He scrambled to his feet.

Anandur was on him immediately. "Take it easy." He pushed on Dalhu's shoulder until he sat back. "No sudden movements, buddy."

"Okay," Dalhu rasped. Eating her up with hungry eyes, he looked like a starved man who was just denied a juicy morsel of food.

"Hi," she said, running her hand through her hair. Why was it so awkward?

Anandur snorted and rolled his eyes. "Suddenly you two act like a couple of shy kids on a playdate when yesterday... well, you know." He wisely changed what he'd been planning to say next when Amanda pinned him with a hard stare. "Whatever. You go sit with your frog while I'll be over here, watching a movie, listening to it on my earbuds, full volume..." He pulled out a pair from his jean pocket and plugged it into his phone.

Making a show of twisting one of the dining chairs around to face the bar, he sat down with his back to them, plugged his ears, and lifted his booted feet to the bar's counter.

Anandur was turning out to be a real sweetheart. Who knew?

"Hi," Dalhu breathed as she sat down on the couch next to him.

"Are you okay?" He took her hand and enfolded it in his.

"I am. Are you?"

"Now that you're here… yes."

"I'm so sorry."

"Yeah, me too."

As they both stared at their entwined hands, there was no need to elaborate what they were sorry for.

All that could've been…

The what if…

When he reached a finger to wipe a tear from her cheek, she realized the mist in her eyes had coalesced.

"You look beautiful. This suits you." He brushed his fingers over her arm and then her thigh as if appreciating the luxurious fabrics.

Amanda chuckled. "You're just using it as an excuse to put your hands on me."

His eyes glinted with a fresh spark. "Guilty as charged, princess."

"About that…"

"Yeah, I know. No one could accuse me of aiming low, right?" He sighed.

"So you're not mad at me for not telling you?"

"No, why would I be? I can't blame you for not trusting me with this."

There was a stretch of uncomfortable silence as they sat close enough to touch yet so far apart—separated by the deep chasm of their pasts, their clans' millennia-long conflict, their disparate social standing, their heritage. The weight of their deeds.

Except, none of that mattered when all she wanted was to get closer, to have him pull her into his arms and feel the strong muscles of his chest against her breasts and his large hands on her back.

"Do you still want me?" she whispered, gazing into his dark eyes.

"More than anything," he said softly. Dalhu's eyes briefly darted to Anandur before he grabbed the back of her neck and pulled her to his mouth, his other arm shooting around her back to mold her to his chest.

He kissed her as if he'd go crazy if he didn't, as if he had already gone too long without, groaning as she opened for him and drew his tongue into her mouth.

"There are no cameras in the bathroom," she whispered against his lips, desperate for the feel of his big, warm hands on her naked skin.

"Should we risk it? Won't it anger the Goddess? Your mother?" Dalhu allowed a little space between them so he could look into her eyes. "It's bad enough that I caused a rift between you and your brother. I don't want you to alienate the rest of your family on my behalf."

Such a noble sentiment from such a ruthless man. She wished her mother could've heard him. Dalhu didn't sound like a male bent on possessing her at all costs with no regard for the consequences.

Well, not anymore.

Trouble was, she couldn't decide whether this change came about because Dalhu cared about her so much that he was willing to sacrifice his own needs and wishes for her happiness, or because he figured it would be easier for him to just give her up.

"My mother was actually the one to arrange this behind my brother's back." Amanda smiled despite the seeds of insidious doubt that were taking root in her mind. "She tried to have the bedroom free of surveillance, but the bathroom and a clear path to it was the best Anandur was able to arrange."

Dalhu's brows lifted in surprise, his eyes softening with some indescribable feeling. "If I felt like worshiping at your mother's tiny feet before, now I'm moved to kiss the soles of her shoes." He kissed Amanda instead, lingering on her lips, then he brushed his mouth against her cheeks and her ears and along her jawline. "I can't believe she would do this for me, or that Anandur would help. I don't deserve this," he whispered, his voice sounding tortured.

"Sorry to disappoint, but they didn't do it for you. They did it for me." Amanda suspected he would prefer this take on things.

"Nevertheless, I'm grateful."

"We are providing one hell of a show for the guys in security," she breathed as he nuzzled her neck, the soft scrape of his fangs sending shivers all the way down to the wet spot between her legs.

Dalhu lifted his head, his eyes smoldering as his gaze drifted to the hardened peaks clearly outlined by the soft silk of her white blouse. He looked as if he had already stripped her and was ogling her naked flesh. His fangs elongated, extending over his lower lip, and she moaned—the sight of them bringing back memories of incomparable pleasure, but at the same time making her feel oddly vulnerable.

15

DALHU

Amanda went first, sneaking past Anandur, who made like a statue and pretended not to notice a thing.

But as Dalhu followed, the Guardian grabbed his arm. "You've got fifteen minutes. If you're not out by then, I'm coming in," he issued his warning, his hard eyes promising retribution.

Dalhu nodded and pulled away. Fifteen minutes would have to do.

Ducking into the bathroom, he found Amanda leaning against a stretch of mirrored wall, her beautiful breasts heaving with her panting breaths.

Dalhu was on her in a flash, tugging the blouse out of her pants and palming the satin-covered mounds.

Not good enough.

With an impatient growl, he shoved her bra up to get to her naked skin.

They both sucked in a breath.

Beaded with tight, dark nipples, her breasts seemed to swell for him. He cupped them gently, and when he moved his thumb back and forth across one hard tip, Amanda groaned, arching her back and thrusting more of her flesh into his hands.

"More," she commanded as her fingers threaded through his hair to pull him down.

"With pleasure." His fingers rolling and tugging, he dipped his head and took her mouth in a hungry kiss.

When he pinched, a rugged groan rose up from her throat, the back of her head hitting the wall and her hands losing their hold on his head, dropping by her sides.

And as he pulled her blouse up and over her head, Amanda seemed boneless—her arms lifting like a string puppet's, then dropping back to her sides.

She watched him with hooded eyes as he unclasped her white satin bra, leaving her upper body gloriously bare. Soon, he'd remove every last scrap of fabric covering her, but first, he needed a moment to gaze at her perfection.

Under his hungry stare, her nipples puckered even more. "I need your mouth on me," she breathed.

With a groan, he looped his arm around her back, clutching her ass as he heaved her up and took one tight, little nipple into his mouth. He suckled, rolling his tongue around it, then suckled again.

As his fangs scraped the sensitive bud, Amanda cried out, her back arching sharply. He moved to her other nipple and gave it the same treatment. She gasped, lacing her fingers through his hair and tugging his head closer.

When he had his fill of feasting on her breasts, he trailed kisses up her throat, letting her slide down his body so he could take those lush lips of hers again.

She murmured something incoherent as he dropped to his knees in front of her and with one hard tug on the waistband of her pants bared her completely. Sliding down her narrow hips, her lacy thong came down along with the trousers, the luxurious fabrics pooling like liquid silk at her feet.

Very gently, he placed a soft, open-mouthed kiss over her mound. She shivered, her hips swiveling wantonly, and as he extended his tongue and licked, her knees gave out and she braced herself on his shoulders—as if without the support she would've crumpled onto the floor.

It gave him a wicked idea.

Freeing one of her legs of the tangle of clothes they were trapped in, he lifted her foot to his shoulder, exposing her wet core. Both hands clutching her smooth ass cheeks, his grip was firm as he tilted her pelvis up to his hungry mouth.

It was so damn hot, the way Amanda watched him go down on her, and he pleasured her with blissful abandon, savoring her taste and the velvety softness of her nether lips.

"Fates, yes, don't stop!" she groaned.

His woman loved what he was doing to her, and he loved doing it… loved her…

"I need—" she began.

Before she had a chance to finish the sentence, he slid a finger into her tight sheath, then withdrew and thrust back with two.

"Dear Fates…ahh, yes!" Amanda cried out, her head once again banging against the mirrored wall behind her.

He chuckled, replacing his tongue with his thumb and rubbing lightly over her swollen clitoris. "Shouldn't it be, dear Dalhu?"

Lifting her head, she looked down at him. Her eyes were hooded with lust, but there was also a hint of a wicked gleam sparkling in them when she purred, "Dalhu, darling"—and grabbed his head with both hands, pulling him to her core. She undulated her hips, urging him to use his mouth, to thrust harder…

His woman wasn't shy about asking for what she needed.

More like demanding.

He would've enjoyed tormenting her a bit longer, but time was running out, and he had no idea what was left of the fifteen minutes

Anandur had allotted him. He needed to bring her to a climax, and if there was any time left, maybe she could return the favor.

Sliding his fingers in and out of her, he pushed back in with a third, filling her, stretching her as he yearned to do with his shaft.

She let go of his head to pinch her own nipple and shoved a fist into her mouth to muffle the breathy moans which were gaining in volume.

Amanda was splendid, coming undone for him; a wanton, lustful, beautiful goddess.

And she was all his. Even if only for these stolen fifteen minutes.

With his eyes trained on hers, Dalhu closed his lips around the little bundle of nerves that was the seat of her pleasure and sucked it in.

As she orgasmed for him, she must've shoved that fist all the way inside her mouth, choking the scream that tore out of her throat. Still, he heard his name in that muffled shriek. And as her sheath kept rippling around his invading digits, he continued thrusting and suckling, wringing every last ounce of pleasure out of her until she pulled his head away.

With her fingers entwined in his hair, she tugged until she had him standing again, then kissed him, hard, her tongue invading his mouth.

He groaned, the idea of Amanda tasting herself on his tongue a major turn-on. Not that he needed the extra pressure. His cock was so engorged it was on the verge of exploding.

Her arms tightening around him, she pushed then pulled, turning them around, and it was Dalhu's turn to have his back pressed against the mirrored wall.

16

AMANDA

Amanda was far from done with Dalhu, the orgasm just whetting her appetite for more. Grinding her pelvis against his hard shaft, she all but fucked his mouth with her tongue, remembering to be careful around his fangs only after getting nicked.

She had some passing thought that her aggression might turn off a dominant male like him, but she just couldn't help herself. Everything inside her screamed, *more!*

She couldn't get enough of him.

Dimly aware that this lust was odd even for her, she cast the thought aside, her brain too scrambled with pheromones to think coherently.

Still, as she sank down on her knees and rubbed her cheek against his jean-clad erection, she had to accept that this was completely out of character for her.

No male had ever inspired her to pleasure him this way.

Amanda—the slut—had never given a blow job, not even once.

Why would she?

The guys she'd been with were of the disposable variety, and not entirely out of necessity. She had used them to get her fix and had deemed their services paid in full when they'd climaxed. Which of course, they all had.

Some, unfortunately, sooner than others.

The men, boys, had needed no extra stimulation, and she certainly had never felt close enough to any of them to perform such an intimate act just to reciprocate.

Dalhu's hands trembled as he cupped her face, lifting it away from his crotch. "You don't have to do this," he whispered.

"I want to." She kept her eyes on him as she popped his jean button free and began pulling the zipper down. Slowly.

"There is no time," he choked out.

No time? What the hell was he talking about? It wasn't as if he needed to be somewhere other than here. And she definitely wasn't late for anything—

"Time's up, frog, I'm coming in." Anandur rapped loudly on the door.

Oh, no he wouldn't.

Dalhu's muscles tensed and he swooped down, grabbing her arms in an attempt to get her up. She batted his hands away.

"Go away, Anandur," she hissed, her temper flaring. "I'll scratch your freaking eyes out if you dare to open this door."

There was a moment of silence before he responded. "As long as you're okay—"

"I'm fine. Now, get lost," she bit out.

Another moment passed.

"You're sure?"

"Fuck off, Anandur."

"Okay, no need to be rude, sheesh…"

She heard his soft footfalls as he left, and then the sound of the bedroom's door closing.

Dalhu let out a long breath and slid down the wall until his butt hit the floor, then scooped her into his arms and lifted her onto his lap.

"Did he ruin the mood?" she pouted.

Dalhu lifted up a little, pressing his hard-as-rock erection into her butt. "You think?"

"I still want to taste you," she purred, then averted her eyes, suddenly feeling shy. What if she sucked at it?

Sucked at it... She chuckled.

"What's so funny?"

"I was just thinking that I've never done this before and that I might suck at it. Get it? Suck?" She snorted.

Amanda felt his shaft jerk under her, growing even fuller. Tilting her head toward him with a finger under her chin, he whispered, "How is it possible?"

"How is it possible that I might suck at it? Or how is it possible that I've never done it before?" she taunted.

"The second one—"

She wanted to look away, but he held her chin firmly, forcing her to look into his dark eyes. "Tell me."

"I've never wanted to before." She shrugged, again trying to look away from those twin pools of darkness.

The smoldering heat and intense possessiveness made him look hard, ruthless, and she was suddenly very aware of being naked in his arms while he was still dressed.

Dalhu was scary, but in a good way—if it made any sense. Certain that he would never hurt her, his intensity and his ruthlessness titillated her, and she felt her core clench.

He sucked in a breath. "I..." He looked lost for words. "I'm humbled that you're choosing me for your first time," he whispered.

Amanda cupped his smooth cheek, lifting a little to press a kiss to his lips. "There is no one I would rather do it for."

He closed his eyes when she wiggled out of his arms and reached inside his still unzipped pants to free his erection, hissing as his shaft jerked into her palm.

When she began stroking him, he lifted a little and pulled his jeans and boxers past his hips to give her better access.

Yanking them down the rest of the way, she moved to straddle his muscular legs. He spread them a little, forcing her to move her knees farther apart, his hard rod jutting, pulsing, beckoning her to touch it, taste it.

Licking her lips, she seized his shaft. He groaned in bliss, lifting up into her stroking hand as she rubbed her thumb across the head, spreading his own moisture down the length of him.

Gaze locked on his, she bent at the hips, gauging his reaction as she followed the same path with her tongue. He sucked in a breath, his eyelids briefly dropping before snapping open again—as if he didn't want to miss any of it.

He tasted good—a little sweet and a little salty but mostly potent—like the man himself. She went for another taste, licking him down and up like a Popsicle before returning back to the crown and circling it all around with long licks.

Operating on pure instinct, she hoped she was doing it right.

It was somewhat embarrassing to admit, but aside from her own experience at being pleasured this way—which considering the differences in anatomy wasn't all that helpful—she was ignorant on the subject. Even in theory.

As a lustful immortal, she was constantly horny as it was. Reading or watching anything erotic would've been like dousing gasoline on an already raging fire. She could not allow herself to indulge.

Now, she wished she had.

Though judging by Dalhu's groans and hisses, she was doing something right—not that it served as a true testament to her skill. As one of the comedians she'd once heard on the radio had said, "Flick it with a newspaper and it will do it for a guy…" Not to mention that he'd been referring to humans, who were pale, watered down versions compared to an immortal virile male.

"Oh, fuck, it feels so good." Dalhu bucked up as she licked the slit, arched his back sharply when she wrapped her lips around the head, and growled like a wild beast when she sucked it in. And as she moaned around him and sucked him even deeper, he banged his fisted hands on the floor.

Dalhu was magnificent in the throes of passion—carnal, animalistic—his big body shuddering, his leg muscles bunching, his T-shirt dampening from sweat.

And his fangs, sharp and long, had fully descended.

She was soaking wet just from seeing him like that and tried to ease the ache by rocking her hips in synch with her suckling.

He was getting closer, and as his shaft thickened inside her mouth, his hand shot to her head to hold her in place. Bucking his hips harder and thrusting deeper, Dalhu's growls were beginning to sound less and less human.

And yet, even though he seemed too far gone to think of anything other than his own pleasure, he didn't neglect hers. Bending a knee, he raised his leg up to rub at her wet sex.

She rocked her hips, grinding against his muscled thigh, the coarse hair covering it providing a delectable friction where it was most needed.

One hand gripping the base of his shaft and the other gently holding her head, Dalhu began thrusting deeper and faster. But she was so turned on, that instead of gagging, her throat muscles went lax under the onslaught, and she moaned and groaned around him.

With a muffled cry, he ejaculated—the hot jets of his seed sliding down her throat and stifling her own cries of completion.

He wasn't done, though.

With a sharp tug on her hair, he pulled her head up, and she gasped… not so much from the pain in her scalp as at the sight of his wild, glowing eyes and dripping fangs.

There was only one thing left for her to do.

She tilted her head and submitted her neck.

In a split second, his fangs sank in, the twin pinpricks burning like hell for the whole of two seconds before the venom hit and euphoria took over.

She climaxed again.

It took a few seconds or maybe minutes—she wasn't sure—before Amanda became aware of Dalhu's strong arms holding her flush against him and his hot tongue lapping at her throat.

She smiled and shifted, making herself more comfortable on his lap, then sighed. She was blissed out, wiped out... and just overall out.

Immortal sex was out of this world.

Dalhu had bitten her before, and he had brought her to a climax before as well. But not at the same time. And as it turned out, the two were definitely not one plus one.

More like two to the tenth power.

Dalhu nuzzled the spot he had licked so thoroughly before. "I'm sorry I lost it there at the end," he whispered against her neck.

"It was incredible." She breathed in, smiling and stretching. "Don't let it get to your head, but it was the best sex I ever had—by a huge margin. And we didn't even get to the main act yet. Imagine what that would be like."

Dalhu's wet cock jerked to attention under her butt. "Fuck, yeah...," he hissed. "Still, I hate that I lost control. I behaved like a crazed animal. Fuck, I was a beast."

"A very sexy beast," she purred, "and all mine. Mine to command and to serve my every whim." She looped an arm around his neck, pulling his head down for a kiss. "Right?"

"As you wish." He smiled down at her.

"Oh, you say the sweetest things."

17

SEBASTIAN

At his first-class private suite on Emirates Airlines, Sebastian Shar powered up his laptop. The lovely flight attendant had just cleared the dishes from the truly superb five-star dinner he'd finished, and before calling it a day, he wanted to check on the lineup of, hopefully, suitable properties for his new base in California.

The first on the list was a defunct all-boy boarding school. It had lovely if neglected grounds, with a school building and dormitories that were serviceable. But it was too close to the town it was named after.

The second was so perfect that it was almost too good to be true.

A Buddhist monastery near Ojai was closing its gates after the number of monks had dwindled down to too few to manage the property.

At least this was the official story.

Sebastian suspected that running out of money had been the real reason behind it. He couldn't imagine that there was much demand for Buddhist retreats, and it didn't look like the monks had been producing anything for sale. Whatever, their mismanagement was his gain. The location was perfect, and the property was offered at a ridiculously low price.

The grounds, situated at the end of a long unpaved road, sprawled over gently sloping hills and were surrounded by a tall stone wall—topped with serpentine barbwire.

Apparently, a monk had gotten mauled by a mountain lion a few years back—the cat leaping with ease over the eight foot high stone wall. Following the attack, the monastery had added the barbwire, raising the height of the fence to well over twelve feet, and was now reassuring potential buyers that the wall was tall enough to keep mountain lions out.

Not really.

A big cat could jump over up to twenty feet. But this was not something that caused Sebastian concern. Predators were smart enough to stay away from more dangerous ones. There was no chance a cat would go after one of his warriors. A monk, on the other hand, must've been a tasty, defenseless treat.

The twelve-foot-high fence was good enough, and the place even came with a basement.

The monastery's few shortcomings were easy to fix. A new electric gate was needed, and on that note, it wouldn't hurt to electrify the barbwire as well. That way the place would be tightly secured—no uninvited guests getting in, and no prisoners getting out.

The main renovation, though, would be transforming the basement into a well-functioning dungeon. Used by the monks for storing produce and other staples, the basement was one big space, with random supporting walls and pillars strewn about.

Sebastian planned to turn it into living quarters for the girls he was going to provide his men with, applying the formula that worked so well for Passion Island to his own new stronghold.

There was no shortage of young, pretty junkies and runaways on the streets of LA. After all, other than the former Soviet Union, Los Angeles and New York were the main hubs for procuring fresh new flesh for the island—the typical customers showing a preference for the fair-skinned, blond, Slavic and American beauties.

For a short time, Sebastian would just divert the flow of supply to his new base.

Other than providing for the needs of his men, he envisioned turning a nice profit on the side. And as an added bonus, offering free and discreet sex services to his potential new business associates might be just the right sort of bribe—or in some cases extortion—to incentivize cooperation. In addition to the traditional monetary incentives, that is.

A few e-mails and phone calls later the deal was closed, and arrangements were made for the renovation work to start.

Now it was time for the fun part. Pulling out a crisp piece of white stationery paper, Sebastian began drawing a design for the dungeon.

He knew exactly how he wanted it. He was going to model it after an exclusive BDSM club in Amsterdam—one of his favorites. The club was housed in the basement of an old castle and was luxuriously appointed. Sebastian was not interested in replicating most of the common areas, but the layout and decor of the many private rooms was perfect for what he had in mind.

18

KIAN

It was late afternoon when Kian finally woke up.

Unbelievable.

He couldn't remember when was the last time he'd slept for so many hours straight. And as it turned out, his mother had been right—it was exactly what he'd needed. Without the exhaustion, last night's events and even her bizarre request to see the Doomer, although still troubling, no longer triggered an uncontrollable rage.

Instead, he wondered what she had learned.

But first thing first—he had some unfinished business with Syssi.

On that note, he was out of bed, showered, and dressed in a matter of minutes.

Well, the dressed part was an overstatement; he pulled on some pants to go look for her, but was planning on shucking them as soon as he found her.

Smirking, he freed the top button and headed for the kitchen. Maybe he would start on the fun right there.

Except, instead of his lovely Syssi, he found Andrew sitting at the kitchen counter, drinking coffee and reading the morning paper.

Kian's morning newspaper.

Great. So much for his plans to use the counter for something other than eating… Or better yet, feasting on something other than food.

"Morning," Andrew muttered from behind the newspaper.

"Don't you mean afternoon?" Kian pulled out a barstool and helped himself to some of the coffee from the stainless steel, thermal carafe.

"Nah, it's still morning for me as well. I woke up not so long ago."

"Where is Syssi?"

"She left a note." Andrew pushed over a folded piece of paper.

To my two best guys, it said on the top flap.

Hope you slept well. Coffee is in the Thermos on the counter, and Okidu's delicious walnut pancakes are in the warming drawer. I'll be over at Amanda's. Come join us when you're ready.

XOXO

Damn, how disappointing.

With a sigh, Kian got up and headed for the warming drawer.

"Want some?" he asked Andrew as he piled a plate for himself.

"Sure."

Kian dropped the two plates stacked with pancakes on the counter and got some jelly and a can of ready-made whipped cream from the fridge.

As he sat down, Andrew passed him the headline news section, while he moved on to sports. Together, they ate and read in companionable silence.

Strange, how at ease they were with each other after butting heads like two bucks only yesterday. But as pleasant as this camaraderie was, Kian would have preferred to have Syssi sitting next to him while he ate his breakfast, or better yet, on his lap.

He missed her.

Wolfing down his pancakes at a record speed, he poured himself another cup of coffee to wash it down with. "I'm going to get dressed and head over to Amanda's. You coming?"

"Yeah, just give me a moment to put on my boots."

A few minutes later they met by the front door and crossed the few feet between Kian and Amanda's apartments.

Halting in front of her front door, Kian turned to Andrew. "Before we go in, I just want to warn you. You are about to meet our Clan Mother, the only surviving goddess—"

"You're kidding me, a goddess?"

"That's right, I forgot you don't have the whole story, yet. So here is the very short version: the gods of old got wiped out by a nuclear bomb with only one goddess surviving. The mother of our clan. The bad guys, our enemies, are the descendants of another god, one who hated her. His son is their leader, and he carries on his father's mission to destroy her and the rest of us. The full version can wait for later."

"You keep saying that, but no one tells me anything. True?" Andrew arched a brow. "But whatever. What did you want to warn me about?"

"First and foremost, the fact that she is here is known only to a select few. She came when Amanda went missing, and to be with Syssi...Anyway, we can't risk our enemies finding out that she is here. So you talk to no one about it. Second, watch your language. Just behave as you would in the presence of a queen, and you'll be fine."

"What do I call her? Your highness? Your holiness?"

"No." Kian chuckled. "You can start with Clan Mother, and once she approves of you, she'll let you call her by her name, Annani."

"Got it."

"Ready?"

"Lead the way."

Kian rapped his knuckles on the door and pushed it open

without waiting for an invitation to come in. If no one was giving him the courtesy, why should he?

"Oh, good, you're up." Crossing into the living room from the terrace through the open sliding doors, Syssi walked up to them and gave each a kiss on the cheek.

Yeah, a damn kiss on the cheek—that's all I get for all my troubles. But no worries, he was going to collect later…

"How is Amanda doing?" Andrew asked, craning his neck to see if she was outside.

"Um, she is taking a nap." For some reason, Syssi's cheeks reddened.

Something was afoot. "A nap? In the middle of the afternoon?" Kian lifted a brow, pinning Syssi with a suspicious stare.

"She had a rough night. A nightmare woke her shortly after she got in bed, and she couldn't shake it off for a long while. But eventually, the fatigue sent her crashing."

Syssi was hiding something, but Kian knew she wouldn't dare an outright lie in front of Andrew—the human lie detector.

"Perfectly understandable after what she has been through," Andrew murmured.

"Yeah, it is. Please, join us outside."

Out on the terrace, his mother welcomed them with a radiant smile, rising to give Kian a hug. "Thank you for bringing Amanda safely home. And you too, Andrew." She hugged the speechless Andrew.

The guy was stunned even though Annani's natural luminescence wasn't as visible in daylight, and her ancient, knowing eyes were hidden behind a pair of dark sunglasses. Still, there was no mistaking her palpable power and perfect features as anything but otherworldly.

"Andrew, this is my mother, Annani." Kian nudged Andrew with his elbow.

It took the guy a moment to respond as he glanced between Kian and the misleadingly youthful goddess. He dipped his head. "I'm honored, Clan Mother."

"Please, call me Annani, Andrew. You are part of the family now, and there is no need for formality." She patted his cheek. "Come, boys, take a seat. We have a lot to discuss." She sat back down and poured each of them a cup of black coffee.

"Your mother?" Andrew whispered, locking stares with Kian.

"Yes."

"And Amanda's..."

"Yes."

"Damn... "

Annani cleared her throat.

"My apologies, Clan Mother." Andrew bowed his head, belatedly reminded of Kian's instructions.

"Yes, well, you are forgiven." She sighed. "It is most unfortunate, though, that foul language became so prevalent in this age. It used to be that only the lowborn uttered such profanities. Now it is everyone. Even my dear children—who should know better." She lifted her brows at Kian.

He chuckled. "You see, Andrew? A mother is a mother, even a queen or a goddess. No matter how old her children are, she always finds something in need of improvement."

Annani smiled indulgently. But then she lifted her palm to end the casual banter, her expression reverting to its regal composure.

"There is an urgent matter that I need to discuss with both of you," she began. "I spent over an hour this morning chatting with Dalhu, and I was greatly troubled by the things he told me. But first, we need to address the issue of Amanda's safety."

Kian stiffened. "She is perfectly safe here in the keep."

"Yes, she is. But she needs to go back to work. Unfortunately, her identity is known to the few men remaining from Dalhu's original unit. He suggests we eliminate them before the reinforcements he asked for are scheduled to arrive, which he estimates will be over the next few days. He does not know the exact date."

"What makes him think his superiors are still in the dark about Amanda?" Andrew asked.

"He was in charge of this unit, and he did not disclose the information. The way their organization works, his men will do nothing without him ordering it. They will wait for him to return, or his replacement to arrive."

"And you believe anything that leaves a Doomer's mouth?" Kian humphed, crossing his arms over his chest.

Andrew cleared his throat. "It's actually not uncommon in cult-like organizations—correct me if I'm wrong to assume that this is the case here." He glanced at Kian, then continued when Kian didn't refute his assessment. "The brainwashing of the rank-and-file into blind obedience effectively nullifies a simple soldier's decision-making ability."

"And besides," Annani said. "Dalhu would not lie about anything that has to do with Amanda's safety. He is completely enamored with her, and he is committed to doing whatever it takes to safeguard her." She injected power into her tone, suggesting that as long as she didn't doubt the Doomer's sincerity the subject wasn't open for debate.

Keeping his yap shut with difficulty, Kian met Annani's hard stare head-on.

She just smiled, shaking her head at him as if to mock his agitation. Then shifting her gaze to Andrew, she continued. "I believe that for the first time since this conflict began, we have a reliable source of information. Dalhu is more than willing to share with us all that he knows, shedding light not only on his former leader's machinations, but on what is going on in their backyard." Annani glanced briefly at Kian, anticipating a retort.

But as much as he hated to admit it, he was intrigued.

Annani sighed. "Except, for this information to remain relevant, it is imperative that his superiors never find out we have him, and that he is cooperating with us. With his whole unit gone missing—if we follow Dalhu's suggestion and take his men out—his superiors are going to suspect that someone was providing us with inside information."

"Yes, but what else can we do?" Syssi said in a small voice. "If you don't do as he says, Amanda will become a prisoner in here. She would hate it." She darted a nervous look at Kian, unsure she had a voice in this discussion.

Silly girl, of course she did. For better or worse, she was now a member of the crew. Reaching for her hand under the table, he clasped it and gave it a reassuring squeeze.

Annani smirked as if she was waiting for just this objection. "I gave it a lot of thought and came up with a plan."

Oh, hell. Kian knew he was not going to like it.

"Instead of taking them out, which will entail entombing them in our crypt, I will fuddle their memories so they will remember nothing of taking Amanda's picture from Mark's home or staking out Syssi and Michael, not even the raid on the lab."

Annani raised her hand to shush Kian's objections. "To fill the gap, I will double their memories of the search for immortal males in nightclubs. Which, by the way, is the reason reinforcements are coming."

Her eyes turning fierce, she looked at Kian. "They need more manpower to cover an area as large as Los Angeles and its adjoining cities. And on that note, we need to issue a warning for everyone to stay away from clubs that admit indiscriminately. With some added security, the higher class members-only clubs should still be fine."

His mother must've lost her mind completely. "If you think I'll let you anywhere near those animals, you have another thing coming. This is the most harebrained idea you've ever come up with, and that's saying a lot." He pushed to his feet and began pacing.

"There is no other way, Kian. Sit down, please."

Annani waited for him to obey her command. "I am the only one that can affect other immortals' minds, and I will not be going alone. Andrew will accompany me, and you together with the other Guardians will be nearby. Far enough so the Doomers will not sense your presence, but close enough if anything goes wrong. Not that I anticipate any trouble; their simple minds will be like putty in my hands. I am only suggesting the escort for your peace of mind."

"So you plan on just walking up to their front door and knocking?" Kian threw his arms in the air. "What then? What if one of them isn't there? What if this is an ambush?"

"I can ask the Doomer some questions," Andrew suggested. "If there is any subterfuge, he won't be able to hide it from me."

"And I am going to use a disguise," Annani chirped, excited by what she no doubt thought of as a fun game. "Do not assume that I have not thought this through. I have a great plan. Andrew will pretend to be a health inspector, checking the house for mold contamination, and I will be the nurse checking each of the occupants for signs of mold poisoning—erasing their memories while I am at it."

"What makes you think they will not slam the door in our faces?" Andrew asked.

"Easy, you will tell them the inspection was prearranged with Dalhu. If they refuse, they will have to vacate the house and be put in quarantine. A very aggressive mold is suspected, and if indeed detected, it must be neutralized before spreading to neighboring houses."

"Very clever. We can show them some fake documentation to validate our official status. Even an inspection order. With one phone call, I can have the real thing delivered here in less than an hour."

"Don't encourage her." Kian shot Andrew a murderous glare before shifting to Annani. "I am not going to allow it. We do not go to the extreme measures we do to keep you safe and to guard your whereabouts, only to have you march head first into danger, treating a potentially disastrous situation like some silly little game."

In the silence that followed, Andrew and Syssi held their breaths as Kian held his mother's angry gaze. Eventually, Annani smiled, but it was the insidious, ill-boding kind of smile he was, unfortunately, all too familiar with.

"It is going to be done, my son. Your options are to either offer me your help or not. Whatever you decide, it has no bearing on my decision. As I have stated before, I do not require your permission, nor your assistance."

Grinding his teeth as he struggled to contain his outrage and stifle the bellow in his throat, Kian felt his facial muscles tighten. Knowing nothing he could say would change her mind, and hating that he was helpless to prevent this new disaster in the making, he turned to Syssi and Andrew with the faint hope that they might have a better chance of talking some sense into her stubborn head.

But by their expressions, it was obvious he was on his own. He wasn't sure, though, whether they were siding with Annani because they agreed with her, or because they feared the Goddess's wrath.

19

ANDREW

"What health inspection?" The Doomer who'd opened the door was talking to Andrew, but his eyes were trained on Annani's seductive smile.

Andrew flipped closed his inspector badge, which the Doomer had summarily ignored, and stuffed it into his jacket's inner pocket. Apparently, it had been a waste of time and resources to bother with obtaining authentic documentation. All that had been needed was a pretty girl with a smile. Not that Annani was a girl, but she sure as hell looked like one. And she had a killer smile.

Well, it wasn't a complete waste. With the badge and inspection order made and delivered on such short notice, Andrew had gotten to show off his impressive resources and connections.

Puffing out his chest, Andrew cleared his throat. "It was all arranged with Mr. Dalhu. Could you please tell him that Mr. Wyatt from the health department and the nurse are here to check for the mold infestation? I've already explained everything once. I would rather not have to repeat myself." Andrew affected a haughty, impatient tone.

Without acknowledging Andrew, the Doomer smiled at Annani

and stepped back. "Mr. Dalhu is indisposed at the moment, but if you cleared this with him, then by all means, come in." He extended his arm and with a dip of his head invited Annani to go ahead. Following her inside, he left Andrew to trail behind.

"How can I be of assistance? Miss…?"

"Rebecca…" Annani pointed to the name tag pinned to the lapel of her short nurse's dress. "Nurse Rebecca McBrie."

Annani's outfit looked dangerously close to a naughty nurse's costume, even though it was the real thing and had been purchased from a de facto nursing supply store.

Cinched with a matching belt, the white dress accentuated Annani's tiny waist, and with its top buttons unfastened, the tops of her braless breasts were enough to cause a riot. White pantyhose and flat, white shoes completed the fetching outfit. She had tied her voluminous red hair in a loose bun, leaving a few wayward strands to frame her stunning face.

The Doomer was practically drooling, enthralled even before the Goddess used any of her formidable powers.

Apparently, she didn't need to.

Gazing up at the tall guy, Annani said, "Any room with a chair will do. And a door. I need to take skin and blood samples from each occupant." She smiled and winked. "In privacy." She touched the guy's chest.

The Doomer sucked in a breath. "Of course. Let me show you to the study." He reached for her arm.

"Hold on…" Andrew stayed the guy's hand. "First, I need to collect a few samples from the walls, and Nurse Rebecca is not allowed to draw blood unsupervised. Standard protocol." He'd promised Kian not to let her out of his sight. Not that he would've even without that promise. "Please, assemble the home's occupants first, and once everyone is here, we'll go ahead and test each one individually."

The Doomer narrowed his eyes and scrutinized Andrew for a

long moment as if just realizing that there was someone besides *Nurse Rebecca* in the room.

Andrew managed to look down his nose at the guy with all the self-importance of a pompous city official, but as the seconds ticked off, he tensed, expecting the Doomer to smarten up and turn them away.

"What is your name, big guy?" Annani touched the guy's bicep. "Oh, my, you must work out, like a lot. Look at those arms." She brought her other palm up and tried to connect the fingers of her tiny hands around the muscle he was now flexing for her. "I cannot encircle it even with both my hands… the fingers do not meet… so strong…," she gasped.

"Edward." The Doomer grinned like an idiot, Annani's somewhat odd speech pattern escaping his notice as he flexed both arms for *Nurse Rebecca* to squeeze and *ooh* and *ah* over.

Hell, with how he was ogling her, a gorilla could've been crapping in the middle of the room and he wouldn't have noticed.

"So, are there any other big, handsome boys like you in the house? Or are you the only one?" Annani batted her eyelashes.

Damn, she is overdoing it. And calling the Doomer 'boy'? A dead giveaway.

"You'll be the judge of that." The Doomer pulled out his phone and texted. "They'll be coming down shortly." He smirked as if sure that he was going to win the good looks contest.

Unbelievable, the guy was buying her act.

Annani stretched on her toes and pulled him down to whisper in his ear, "I am sure none is more handsome than you, Edward… I love this name… Edward… so masculine," she breathed.

Were all men so gullible? Or was this particular Doomer exceptionally stupid? Annani's acting was bad, like in a third-rate porn bad. Yet considering her vast experience, she must've known what she was doing.

But come on, Andrew would've never fallen for that.

Perhaps she had been utilizing that influence thing. Though if she had, Andrew hadn't detected a thing.

Well, instead of observing Annani's antics, he should get busy with the samples he was supposed to collect.

Andrew snapped on a pair of latex gloves and proceeded to scrape some paint and dust from the baseboards at the entry and the living room, depositing the samples inside little plastic bags and scribbling notes on the tags attached to them. All along, he kept Annani in his line of sight.

When all six Doomers surrounded tiny Annani, he got nervous. But he had nothing to worry about—the other five were just as dumb as the first.

Or maybe she was just that good.

"I'm done with the samples, gentlemen. Let's proceed with Nurse Rebecca's tests," he announced as he pushed through the wall of meat to get to Annani.

"I'm going first," Edward volunteered. "Wait here for your turn," he instructed the others.

As he took Annani's elbow and led her to the study, Andrew followed, closing the double doors behind him.

"Grab a chair, darling," Annani said, depositing her medical kit on the long table in the center of the room.

The study was more of a library, with shelves full of leather-bound books, a few oversized leather recliners, and two chairs at each side of the long mahogany table in its center.

The Doomer calling himself Edward sat next to where Annani arranged her tools and laid his forearm on the table.

She flicked on the closest reading lamp and trained the light on the crook of his arm, then leaned and touched his shoulder. "Are you nervous, big boy?"

Now Andrew could detect a faint hypnotic undercurrent in her melodic voice.

"Not at all, sweetheart." It took the Doomer a second or two to lift his stare up from her cleavage and gaze into her eyes.

He was hers the moment their eyes met.

The Doomer seemed paralyzed, not even blinking.

Annani said nothing as she looked into the guy's eyes, absent-mindedly brushing her fingers through his hair as if to soothe him while she played with his memories.

Fascinated, Andrew watched the Doomer's face. There was something familiar about the guy, and he had a nagging feeling that he had seen him somewhere before.

Andrew would've dismissed it as a strange déjà vu, but as each of the Doomers took his turn submitting to Annani's ministrations, the feeling grew stronger.

It took all six for his brain to make the connection. Without their beards, they were not as readily recognizable, but eventually it all snapped into place.

As it turned out, the twelve recent visitors from Maldives he'd been searching for were Dalhu and his men.

Serendipitous or what? Finding the answer to the mystery was an unexpected bonus to this little stint.

And who said good deeds went unrewarded…

Once the Goddess was done, she closed her medic case and waved the six stupefied guys goodbye.

"Piece of pie." Annani high-fived Andrew the moment he closed the front door behind her, then pumped her small fist and whooped like a cheerleader whose team had won.

She was bursting with energy as they entered his car and all through the drive back to the keep, excited over what she perceived as a wonderful adventure. "A refreshing break from my routine," she confided in him. "Oh, Andrew, I cannot remember when was the last time I had this much fun. I have been stifled in this role I have been stuck in: playing the queen mother, hiding away in a remote place with barely any mortals to play with."

She sighed. "It is not who I am on the inside. I crave adventure, excitement."

If she weren't who she was, he would have patted her knee for reassurance. But come on, she was a freaking goddess, for God's sake, and for all he knew, she might've smote him for daring to touch her.

But as she continued without pause, he realized she only wanted his ear and wasn't expecting a response.

In this, Annani was a typical woman.

Finally, she stopped long enough for him to ask the question that was bothering him. "I'm curious. What exactly will these Doomers remember and what will they forget?"

Annani shrugged. "They will remember nothing about Amanda. I erased, or rather muddled, their memory of ever seeing her picture or even taking it from Mark's home. I also muddled their memories of going after Michael and Syssi, and of searching Amanda's lab. Other than these, I didn't mess with anything else."

"Did you leave them the memory of our visit? And why? Isn't it dangerous? They will know what you look like."

"Think about it. When I was done with one of them and proceeded to the next, we were still there for the first one to remember." She said it as if he was a little dimwitted for not figuring it out. "If it were possible to thrall them all at once, then maybe I might have been able to do it. But one at a time? No. And besides, they are males. So they will only remember that Nurse Rebecca had a lovely bosom. Not much more than that. No thralling required." She smirked.

Andrew chuckled, she had a point.

"Today was great. I feel alive." Annani threw her hands in the air and began singing a merry tune in a foreign language he couldn't place.

Not that he cared. Her siren voice was so beautiful, he could've listened to her endlessly. Andrew idly wondered if that voice of hers could be used as a weapon. Probably. It had an enthralling quality, powerful enough to lure men to follow wherever she wanted to lead them.

A smile tugged at Andrew's mouth. Was that the real story behind the siren's song legend? The voice of a goddess? Or goddesses?

As he parked in the underground garage, Annani didn't wait for him to open the door for her. She was out of the car before he even cut the engine. No doubt running to tell Amanda the good news.

Andrew waited for Kian and the other Guardians to file out of their SUV before heading up.

The Goddess's ebullient mood evidently hadn't waned in the short time it had taken Andrew and Kian to get up to Amanda's penthouse. Prancing around in her short nurse's dress, and tiny, white nurse's flat-soled shoes, she was in the middle of recounting the story for Amanda's eager ears.

Andrew found that he was fond of the Clan Mother. With how she looked now, exuberant, like a young girl in a Halloween costume, it was easy to forget that Annani was the most powerful being on earth.

Earlier, as they'd readied to embark on this evening's information containment mission, Andrew had braced himself for having a lousy time in her company, expecting the Goddess to have a condescending diva attitude. But it turned out that she was a riot to be around. And besides her little tiff with profanity, the Goddess seemed to embrace contemporary culture wholeheartedly and was surpassingly well versed in many of its nuances.

Though somewhat intimidating, Annani was a lively and pleasant companion. In fact, if she were an agent, he wouldn't have minded having her as a partner. He had always known the power a beautiful woman had over men, but he'd underestimated to what extent. Someone like her would have made his work so much easier, keeping men stupefied and easy to manipulate.

Andrew sighed. If he were ten years younger, he would've petitioned his superiors for a drop-dead-gorgeous female partner. But his time as a field operative was a thing of the past, and he had no need for a partner. Gorgeous or not.

Sitting on Amanda's deep-cushioned couch, Kian glared at his mother. Probably still sulking over her flagrant disregard for her own safety. Or maybe it was her brushing off his protests and overriding his authority that had him fuming. Most likely both. Andrew sympathized. If it were his mother or his sister, he would've felt the same.

The guy was holding Syssi glued to his side as if he feared she might get infected by Annani's recklessness.

It didn't seem to bother the Goddess, though. "You should have seen Andrew, flashing his fake inspector badge with such pompous superiority, just as a city official would. Your brother is a fantastic performer, Syssi," Annani chirped as she paced around, too excited to sit down.

Andrew lifted off the chair to offer a mock bow. "Thank you, thank you all." He affected a snobbish British accent to everyone's delight.

Except Kian's.

It seemed that a scowl would be the guy's only expression for the foreseeable future.

Pushing up from her chair, Amanda wiped a stray tear from her eye. "You have no idea how much I appreciate what you have done for me. I love you all. Thank you." She sniffled, first reaching for her mother and pulling her in for a hug, then Syssi and the reluctant Kian—saving the biggest hug for Andrew. "I'm sorry that I missed your command performance." She flashed him her beautiful smile.

Damn woman, why did she have to get this close?

As her soft breasts pressed against his chest, and her belly brushed against his arousal, the contact sizzled through his skin as if it was branding him.

And that smile…

Oh, God, that smile...

The heat sliding through his veins crept all the way up his neck and was about to engulf his ears. Great, just what he needed. Blushing like a schoolboy for everyone to see because a girl that had a crush on someone else had smiled at him.

Been there, done that, wrote the book, sold the rights to the movie.

That first time, he'd been only ten years old. Not that being a kid had made it any less traumatic. Karina, he was never going to forget her name, the girl he had a crush on since kindergarten, had seemed to like him too, giving him false hope. But by the end of fifth grade, she'd told everyone she liked Ben Brook and had obliterated Andrew's young heart.

Lesson learned: until Amanda made up her mind one way or the other, he was not going to succumb to her considerable charms.

No siree, Bob.

Easier said than done, though. No man in his right mind could help wanting a woman like her. Andrew detested the useless pining. As the saying went, want in one hand, shit in the other… Andrew had a bad feeling about which one he was going to get.

Desperate to divert attention away from himself, he gently dislodged Amanda's arms and turned to face Annani. He cleared his throat. "I don't want to spoil your good mood, but I am curious to hear what else the Doomer had to say, specifically about their organization."

"Well, yes," she said, plopping down onto one of the overstuffed armchairs. "First, I need something to drink. I feel a little parched. Would you be a dear, Kian? And pour me something sweet and tangy? You know what I like."

"Sure." Kian managed not to sound surly. He pushed off the sofa. "Anyone else?" he asked as he headed to the bar.

"I'll pass," Andrew said.

Amanda lifted her hand. "A margarita for me."

"Syssi? Anything for you?"

"I'll have the same."

After mixing the three margaritas, Kian handed one to Annani, then delivered the other two to Syssi and Amanda.

Annani waited patiently for Kian to pour himself some scotch and go back to his seat next to Syssi.

Sweeping a quick gaze over her audience, she made sure everyone's eyes were trained on her before she began. "Navuh has his own little island somewhere in the Indian Ocean, and no one aside from him and his sons knows exactly where it is. The mortal pilots transporting people and goods to and from the island are heavily thralled to guard the secret, and the planes they fly are windowless. Everyone and everything is carefully checked for tracking devices before being allowed on board, then checked again upon arrival."

"Clever…," Andrew muttered.

"Indeed." Annani nodded gravely and continued. "The island serves as the home base for his army of immortals, which just as we had suspected has close to ten thousand brutally trained warriors."

"Damn," Kian bit out.

Ignoring his slip, Annani sighed and took a long sip of her drink. "The island is also known as Passion Island; a large-scale, lucrative brothel, secretly serving a select clientele of very rich, powerful mortals. The women, serving these clients and the soldiers are snatched off the streets from all over the world and forced into servitude. They can choose, however, between sexual service or manual labor as cooks, maids, servers and the like. Once enslaved, they are never allowed to leave the island. A highly guarded portion of this brothel is a prison within the larger prison, segregating the Dormants from the rest of the compound. Paired with mortal clients who possess traits valuable to Navuh, mainly physical size and brutality, they are bred to produce boys to be turned and serve in Navuh's army, and girls who remain Dormant and serve in the brothel once they turn fifteen, continuing their mothers' task of producing the next generation."

Amanda sucked in a breath. "That's terrible. No wonder Dalhu was appalled by the idea of a female Guardian."

"Well, Doomers' opinion of women is not exactly a newsflash," Kian snorted. "Inferior, and good for serving males and breeding only." He pinned her with a condescending look.

"No, that is not why he was so aghast. Though before I gave him a chance to explain, I too accused him of misogyny."

"Then what?" Syssi lifted a brow.

"He asked who was the moron that came up with the brilliant idea of employing females in the Guardian force, considering the kind of enemy we're facing." Amanda shot Kian an accusing look.

He shifted uncomfortably.

"He said that even before he met me and switched loyalties, if it were up to him, he would have never, ever allowed an immortal female to fall into the clutches of his brethren. He even went as far as saying that he would have killed whoever needed killing to free her. And this is a direct quote." With a small satisfied smirk, Amanda held Kian's gaze until he looked away.

Andrew chuckled. *Score one for Amanda.*

But wait, the Doomer looking good was the opposite of what was good for Andrew... Nevertheless, the guy had just gained esteem in Andrew's eyes.

Kian wasn't ready to concede, though. "And you believed him? That's the other thing we all know about Doomers—they are obdurate liars—they say whatever they think you want to hear because they have absolutely no regard for you, no respect. For them it is like lying to a dog or a cow—it doesn't count!"

The guy had a point. Some of Andrew's missions had taken him into that part of the world, and he had personal experience with this kind of culture. Being a good liar and successfully pulling one over on your enemy was something to be proud of, a badge of honor. And the inferior fool who believed the lie deserved what he got. Be it being cheated out of something, or death.

Well, score one for Kian.

But the match wasn't over yet, and Amanda wasn't ready to fold. Getting up and marching to stand in front of her brother, she pointed a finger at Kian. "Yes, I did. You might think me a fool, but I am far from it. And you, who did not exchange even one word with Dalhu, still think you know him better than I do. He is not like the others."

"That is enough, children," Annani cut in. "Amanda is correct. Before you pass judgment, Kian, you might want to go and talk with Dalhu because we just cannot afford to dismiss everything he says as a lie. The information he disclosed is too valuable. And although I have no idea what we could do for these poor women, we are still their only hope. Maybe, if we all put our heads together, we could come up with a rescue plan."

Kian crossed his arms over his chest, glaring at his mother and sister in stubborn silence.

"I could go with you," Andrew offered reluctantly. "Provide my human lie detector services."

The last thing he wanted was to help Dalhu, his number one rival for Amanda's affection. But Andrew had a feeling the guy had been forthright, and if so, the information he was providing was invaluable. And the only way Kian would act on it was if he was assured of its veracity.

Hence, Andrew felt morally obligated.

Damn.

Amanda turned to him. "Lie detector? What do you mean?"

Syssi snorted. "Yeah, he is really good at that. You have no idea how hard it was to grow up with him. On the rare occasion that I tried to hide something, he always knew. I just assumed that I was a terrible liar."

"You are." Andrew chuckled. "But even the best cannot deceive me face to face. I don't know how, but I'm never wrong. Except, over the phone. I'm not so good without visual clues."

Rubbing her chin with her thumb and forefinger, Amanda made an *hmm* sound. "Interesting, most immortals have some special ability—some even more than one. This was actually my hypothesis for identifying potential Dormants, and you've just reinforced it. Syssi has strong precognition ability, Michael is a good telepath, and you, Andrew, are the lie detector."

Annani clapped her hands. "Problem solved, then. With Andrew's special talent to aid you, you will have your proof of Dalhu's loyalty." She looked pointedly at Kian.

That frown he had going on rode the guy's brow even harder, turning his face into a cruel mask. "As you all gang up on me, caviling my hostility toward that Doomer, you forget something. That male, the one you are all rooting for with such enthusiasm, is Mark's murderer. It might not have been his fangs that delivered the deadly dose of venom, but they might've just as well. He was in charge—the one who ordered it."

Kian looked each of them in the eyes before pinning Amanda with a hard glare. "Face it, sister mine; that Doomer you seem so taken with, the one you allowed access to your body, murdered your beloved nephew."

In the silence that followed, Amanda's eyes widened with consternation and her tall body began to tremble. She slapped a palm over her mouth as if she was about to retch.

On a surge, Annani got up and reached for her daughter, pulling her into her arms. Too short to reach over Amanda's shoulder, she leaned sideways to glare at Kian with eyes that could freeze lava. "Explain the realities of war to my son, Andrew," she bit out.

It was an exceedingly awkward situation. On one hand, Andrew's rival had been dealt a potentially fatal blow. Score one for Andrew. On the other hand, Kian was being a total jerk, and Amanda looked devastated.

The facts of war, as Annani had so succinctly put it, were that shit like this happened. Warring factions made peace, and former enemies became allies—often to join forces against a common adversary. But be that as it may, in this case, it was too close and personal.

"No one needs to explain the facts of war to me," Kian grated as he heaved himself off the sofa. "Come, Syssi, let's go home." He offered her his hand.

With an apologetic glance at Amanda, Syssi let him walk her out.

"I am sorry you got caught up in this drama, Andrew." Annani sighed. "I just want you to know that I am grateful for all your help. It was fun." She smiled a little before leading Amanda out of the room.

Letting himself out, Andrew walked up to the single elevator door and punched the button to call it up. The few things he had left over at Kian's could be picked up some other time. This evening, it was time to go home and do some serious thinking.

Or soul searching as it were.

Question was, would he do the right thing and try to talk some sense into Kian? Or would he do the selfish thing and let Kian cool down on his own?

And while Kian was taking his time to come to terms with the situation, Andrew's rival would be temporarily out of the race, giving Andrew the opportunity to make his move for Amanda.

It might be his only chance.

20

AMANDA

The storm of conflicting emotions that kept Amanda tossing and turning all through the night eventually had given her one hell of a headache.

Or maybe it was all that crying before she'd finally fallen asleep. After Kian had forced her to face the fact that her paramour was responsible for her nephew's murder, she'd cried for hours.

To be frank, the thought had flitted through her mind before, but she'd shoved it aside, doing the cowardly thing and refusing to let it sink in. And until Kian had shoved it in her face, she'd gotten away with it.

Same way she usually got away with ignoring almost everything she considered potentially disturbing.

After her son's tragic death… was it almost two centuries ago? It still hurt so bad… it had been the only way she'd managed to keep herself afloat and not sink into depression. Except, with time, she became so adroit at this strategy that anything disconcerting or unpleasant no longer registered at all.

It was like she was wearing a coat of Teflon—nothing stuck.

And nothing got absorbed either.

Which, come to think, might have been the reason behind the hollowness she felt inside.

Nothing about her was real. She was a made-up persona. Most of the time she thought nothing of it; on the contrary, she thought of herself as larger than life. But the truth was that she was kind of cartoonish.

Pretty on the outside, empty on the inside.

The problem was, she had no idea who she really was.

After pretending for so long, she had forgotten. And what's worse, Amanda feared she wouldn't like the *real her* if she ever found her.

The persona she had created was great, and she liked being that woman. Carefree, dramatic, lustful, smart, not to mention beautiful… pretty cool, if she may say so herself. Unfortunately, the pretense didn't run deep enough—more than skin deep, but not all the way down to her shriveled soul.

With a sigh, she gave up on sleep and got up.

Dawn was on the horizon, the wispy rosy-pink like a whisper of hope against the backdrop of gloomy darkness. Donning a warm robe, Amanda opened the sliding door to the terrace and stepped out into the chilly air. As the cold seeped through the fleece, giving her goose bumps, she tightened the robe against her body.

A faint ocean scent was riding on the breeze, cutting through the morning fog and evoking a strange longing for the sea—a voyage that would take her far away from this place and the hard choices that were weighing her down.

Choices.

Not really, more like lack of.

Now that Mark's murder was firmly pinned on Dalhu, Amanda couldn't stomach the idea of being anywhere near the guy.

The thing was, she couldn't imagine going back to her old life either. Or living without what Dalhu had given her…

The intimacy, the sense of connection, the mind-blowing pleasure…

The unrelenting devotion.

What were the chances of her ever finding something like this again? A man who made her feel like a princess for real? Forever…

Andrew?

Yeah, there was some attraction there. But she was well familiar with this kind of superficial connection. Amanda had nearly two centuries of experience with it.

It didn't reach all the way down to the essence of her.

Heck, it wasn't even skin deep.

And though Andrew might believe differently at the moment, it wasn't the real thing for him either.

Trouble was, until he found it, Andrew would not know that this wasn't it, and would keep trying to win her.

If only she had never crossed paths with Dalhu, she wouldn't have known better and could've been happy with Andrew.

Everything would have been so much simpler then…

Until… one of them happened to find the real thing, and then their lives would've turned into a nightmare…

Yeah.

Syssi had been absolutely right when she'd said that relationships were complicated, people were complicated, and not everything could be resolved with great sex.

Amanda leaned over the railing and breathed in, searching for the faint ocean scent that was quickly dispersing along with the morning fog.

She needed to get away.

But five o'clock in the morning was too early to make calls.

To pass the time she took a long bath and then spent a couple of mindless hours shopping for shoes on the Internet.

At eight, she phoned Alex.

Still too early for a guy that worked nights, but whatever, he owed her.

As the phone kept ringing and ringing, she almost hung up, but then Alex finally answered. "What's going on?" he rasped.

"Morning. Sorry to wake you up, but I need a favor."

"Amanda? Thank the merciful Fates you're okay. Everyone was looking for you. I didn't know you'd been found. What happened?"

Damn, she didn't know how much he knew. "Yeah, they found me. Though I wish they didn't." It wasn't a lie, wasn't the truth either, but good enough. "That's why I'm calling. Can I borrow your yacht for a few days? I need some time alone, and with my intrusive family that's not going to happen unless they can't reach me. Like in the middle of the ocean."

His answer came after a short pause. "Sure, though I'd appreciate you telling them where you're going this time."

"I will. Promise. So is it okay with you? Or do you have plans for it yourself?"

"No, not for the next couple of weeks. How long do you need it for?"

"Only a few days, less than a week for sure. On Monday, I'm going back to work. So I'll be back Sunday evening at the latest. Does it work for you?"

"Yeah…" He hesitated.

"Don't worry, you know I'll cover all the expenses." Alex was such a miser. On the other hand, fuel for a boat this size was expensive, and she shouldn't expect him to pay for it. Loaning her the boat with its crew was enough.

"Good, but that's not the problem."

"Then what?"

"You know my crew is all female, right?"

"No, I didn't know that, you naughty boy."

"And although I have no problem with you there, I would appreciate it if you didn't bring any guys with you. My girls are not for sharing."

"No worries. It's actually perfect for what I have in mind. I'm taking a break from men."

Alex snorted. "Why? What happened?"

"Long story, but yeah… no guys."

"When should I tell my captain to expect you? And where would you be heading? She needs to stock up on supplies."

"I don't really care where, just out to sea. Maybe down the coast toward Baja. Would a couple of hours be enough time for her to prepare?"

"I'll call Geneva right away—not the city, my captain—and if she needs more time, I'll call you."

"Wonderful, thank you. The name of your yacht is Anna, right?"

"The one and only, my pride and joy."

With that settled, Amanda scribbled a quick note for Annani and left it on the kitchen counter.

Hopefully, her mother would understand why she needed to get away and forgive Amanda for not spending more time with her during her rare visit.

Amanda promised to make it up to Annani as soon as she regained some sanity.

Half an hour later, she was out the door with a large satchel over her shoulder and a carry-on rolling behind her.

Thank heavens the penthouse's elevator could be made to go straight down to the lobby without stopping at any of the other floors. The last thing she needed was for one of her relatives to come along for the ride and start asking questions.

Waving the security guys goodbye, she hurried into the taxi waiting for her in front of the building.

"Good morning, Miss. Marina del Rey? Right?" The cabbie verified the destination she had given his dispatch as he loaded her luggage into the trunk.

"Yes, thank you." She waited until he opened the door for her.

Once the taxi pulled out, Amanda relaxed into the seat.

Mission accomplished, she was free.

Fates, it felt good.

To be free to do whatever she wanted. With no one to censor her, no one to criticize her or her choices, and no one to answer to.

No angry brother. No enemy lover.

Free as a bird.

What a shame Captain Geneva couldn't head out to sea right away.

Well, the important thing was that she managed to flee the coop without getting caught, and she didn't mind spending the hour or so eating breakfast in the café overlooking the water while the captain and her crew prepared the *Anna* for the trip down to Baja. Or maybe to Catalina, she could decide later. As long as the boat was out of the marina, with her onboard, the destination didn't really matter.

21

SYSSI

"Don't go." Syssi caught Kian's arm as he tried to sneak out of bed.

"I'm just going down to the gym." He bent to kiss her cheek, expecting her to let go. Instead, she grabbed on and pulled him back.

Wow, cool. She hadn't expected him to budge.

Hey, this was new. She was growing stronger. There was no way she could've done this before her transition. Still, she was pretty sure that if her new and improved physique hadn't taken Kian by surprise, it wouldn't have been so easy. Next time, he would be ready for her increased strength.

"You're not going anywhere. I hate waking up in an empty bed." She pouted and snuggled up to him, her hands going to his warm, bare chest.

Last night, Kian had made good on his word and then some, and the only reason she wasn't sore all over this morning was the venom's magical healing properties.

Or maybe it was her new, better, and stronger body.

Hey, she might be faster too. She should join Kian in the gym and test her speed on a treadmill.

"I thought I exhausted you last night."

"What gave you that idea?" Her hand trailed lower.

"The T-shirt and panties said it all."

"Yeah? What did they say?"

"Get away from me, you brute. I need to sleep, you insatiable sex machine...," he said in a high-pitched voice.

Syssi laughed. "True. True. And how surprisingly perceptive of you."

He rolled on top of her, bracing his weight on his forearms. "When you returned from the bathroom wearing these things, crawled into bed and started snoring right away, it would've been impossible even for an insensitive jerk like me not to get a clue."

"I don't snore." Syssi felt her cheeks warm. *Bummer,* she thought Kian's sexcapades had cured her of her embarrassing tendency to blush, but apparently not.

"Yes, you do. And your little kitten snores are as cute as the rest of you."

"A cute kitten? That's what you think of me?" She took hold of his erection and began stroking. *How about that for cute...*

Kian smirked before dipping his head and taking her mouth in a hungry kiss. That was all it took for her nipples to pebble and her cotton panties to get moist.

"How about my little sex kitten?" He nuzzled her neck.

She pushed up her hips to rub her hot and achy core against his shaft. "That's better...," she breathed as he scraped his fangs up and down her neck.

Damn, Kian knew all of her triggers by now, every erogenous point. He could probably get her from zero to orgasm in under a minute.

"My kitten is hungry for more?" Kian's hand trailed under her T-shirt to palm her breast.

Suddenly, she didn't want any barriers between them. "Take it off." She wiggled under him in an effort to free the shirt from under her butt.

"Hungry and impatient. I like it." He gave her nipple a little tweak before helping her out of the shirt.

Once he bared her, Kian took a moment to ogle her nakedness. "I can never have enough of this. If I had my way, you would wear nothing when we are alone… all day long."

"Absolutely nothing? Not even stilettos?" she taunted.

His erection twitched. "Uh, that's one hell of an image, you naughty girl. I'll allow the high heels, and a diamond wedding ring and choker to go with them…"

The vivid picture he painted in her head had her flood her panties. "Is that a pervy proposal?"

"I'm not asking, I'm stating a fact. You're mine." He cupped her through the soaking wet cotton.

"And I have nothing to say about it?"

"You already did." He sneaked a finger under the edge, stroking her swollen, wet flesh before pushing the thick digit inside her.

Syssi moaned, arching, her hips going up for more.

"I'll take it as a yes…," Kian's voice deepened with his arousal. He didn't wait for her answer. Instead, he dipped his head and took a nipple between his lips, suckling and finger fucking her into a frenzy.

"Yes, oh yesss…," Syssi hissed as his teeth gently closed around her nipple.

She was going to come like that, but it was okay. Before this was over, her wonderful man would make her come again. And again…

22

ANDREW

On his way to the office, Andrew stopped by the Beverly Hills mansion.

"Hello, Edward." He flashed his inspector badge again. "Remember me? I'm Inspector Wyatt with the health department. I was here yesterday to collect mold samples."

"What do you want?"

"I need to collect a few more samples."

"Why?"

Without Annani to scramble the guy's brain, he wasn't as eager to cooperate. Well, maybe the Doomer would respond better to a different approach.

Dropping the condescending mannerism, Andrew ran his fingers through his hair. "Who the hell knows. The guys in the lab don't give a shit if I need to drive an hour out of my way to collect some more dirt for them to play with. You know how it is. I'm just following orders."

The Doomer still didn't give any indication that he was going to let Andrew in. Evidently, friendly wasn't going to cut it, but a threat might.

"Look, Edward, the test results came inconclusive. I either bring them more samples to test, or they are going to put in a request for the guys in hazmat suits to quarantine the house."

That did the trick. "Okay, but be quick about it."

Problem was, with the Doomer breathing down his neck throughout the *inspection,* Andrew barely managed to plant one tiny listening device in the living room.

Better one than none, though.

With the anticipated reinforcements arriving soon, someone would no doubt make contact with Dalhu's remaining crew. And when it happened, Andrew might learn something.

It was a shame he had not thought of the idea until this morning. It would've been easier yesterday when all of the Doomers had been busy drooling over Annani.

But no harm done.

From now on, Andrew's little spy would keep transmitting, and anything that was said in its vicinity would be recorded.

Hopefully, he could learn of the Doomers' new location.

Andrew felt a twinge of guilt over the unauthorized use of government resources for his private sting. But it wasn't as if he could tell his bosses what was going on and get them on board with the fight against this new and bizarre threat.

He'd be sent to a psych evaluation and suspended from his job before his boss finished rolling his eyes.

But the clan needed his help.

Andrew didn't have the whole story yet, but it was obvious his new relatives were outnumbered and outmuscled by their enemies. They could really use his particular expertise.

Perhaps he should quit the agency and go work for them.

Kian would love to have him, and the pay would most definitely be better.

Some of the operatives he had known had chosen to move into the private sector. Instead of accepting a glorified desk job once they were deemed too old for the field, they were still out there and making shitloads of money.

But if he quit, he would lose access to the most valuable of resources—information.

True, he had friends that would do him a favor here and there, but it would be just crumbs. Compared to the vast pool of data he had access to with his high-security clearance, it would be a drop in the bucket.

No, quitting the agency wasn't an option. But Kian would have to fund some equipment. Using his access to government data to help the clan was one thing, using its gadgets was another.

A tracker here and there or one simple listening device he could get away with, but more missing equipment would trigger a red flag at accounting, and he'd have internal affairs on his ass.

Still, keeping his job and at the same time helping the clan would be a tough gig to pull. He'd be working endless hours. And if he were to run missions for the clan, he'd have to miss work days at the agency.

As he had done for Amanda's rescue.

The long hours didn't bother him. It wasn't as if he had anything better to do with his life. Always better to keep busy than go home to an empty house and stare at the stupid tube until it was time to sleep.

The problem would be taking time off.

True, Andrew hadn't used his vacation days in God knows how many years, and he had accumulated quite a lot. Nevertheless, he would run out of them pretty quick if he went on missions for the clan.

He would have to make it work, somehow, because for the first time in God knows how long, Andrew was excited about something, anything, and it felt good.

23

SYSSI

"Come in," Annani chimed.

Syssi would never get used to the quality of that voice.

Heavenly. As befitting a goddess.

"Good morning," she said as she opened the door to Amanda's apartment.

"And a lovely morning to you too. Did you have breakfast already, my dear?"

Judging by the dark sunglasses perched on her pert nose, Annani was about to take her breakfast out on the terrace.

It seemed the Goddess couldn't get enough of Southern California's sunshine. Not a big surprise considering her home was in Alaska. Still, with her sensitivity to the bright light, it must've been a mixed bag of goods.

"Yes, I did, but I would gladly have another cup of coffee." Syssi followed Annani out, joining her at the table that was being set by... not Onidu, but someone who must've been his brother.

More like a twin.

"How many brothers are there?" Syssi reached for the coffee

press while sneaking a surreptitious glance at the guy, but she only got his profile.

"Brothers?" Annani tilted her head, her dark red brows arching above the black frame of her sunglasses.

"Onidu and Okidu and now... I'm sorry, I don't know your name..." As he turned, Syssi looked up at Annani's butler, searching his face for dissimilarities between him and his two other brothers.

"Oridu, madame, at your service." He bowed at the waist. "Would there be anything else Mistress might require?" he addressed Annani.

"No, thank you." Annani sounded like she was choking down giggles.

"What's so funny?" Syssi asked as soon as Oridu disappeared inside.

"I see that Kian did not tell you. He must have forgotten in all the excitement," Annani chortled.

"Didn't tell me what?"

"The Odus, they are not brothers, well, at least not in a strict interpretation of the term, though they were probably made by the same person."

Wasn't that the definition of brothers? Or half-brothers at the least?

Annani must've realized Syssi's confusion. "What I mean by made, is manufactured, constructed, not born of a mother and father."

"Like clones?" Syssi scooted to the edge of her seat. This was so exciting, though somewhat morally disturbing. But to see a living proof that cloning humans was possible? Mind-boggling.

"No." Annani paused to think. "I guess their creator might have used some genetic material to build their outer shell. And if I would hazard another guess, it was probably his own."

She chuckled. "Funny, I often tried to imagine the genius behind the Odus, and yet, it never crossed my mind that he might have created them in his own image."

What Annani was trying to say was starting to sink in.

Except, no way...

"You mean that they are some kind of robot? It's impossible... or more accurately, impossible with current technology." But God only knew how... *now, that's funny...* how advanced the gods' technology had been.

"You are right. We do not have the technology either. The Odus are marvelous, practically indestructible, invaluable. They were a wedding present from my Khiann, and they were considered an ancient relic even then."

Khiann must have been the young husband Annani had lost so long ago. Her voice had faltered when she'd said his name. For her to mourn his death thousands of years later, their love must've been indeed legendary.

"And speaking of weddings"—Annani perked up—"it is time we started to plan yours."

"Oh, no, Kian and I haven't discussed anything yet. It is way too early to be even talking about a wedding, let alone planning it."

"You mean to tell me that there is any doubt in either of your minds? Or that the subject did not come up?"

"No... and yes..." The damn blush was taking over her face again.

"I do not understand. Is it a no, or a yes?"

Oh boy, how to answer when she wasn't sure herself. "No, I don't have any doubts, and I'm pretty sure Kian doesn't either. And yes, the subject came up... sort of..."

"What do you mean, sort of? Has Kian proposed or not?" The Goddess leaned forward, her displeasure evident even behind the dark sunglasses.

Why? Oh, why? Did she have to probe like this? Like I'm going to tell her about Kian's pervy proposal.

Oh, hell, here goes nothing.

"He did, but I think it was meant as a joke." Syssi's ears were so hot they were in danger of catching fire.

Annani smiled and leaned back. "Then it is settled."

"But what if he was only joking?"

"Trust me, child, men do not joke about things like that."

Most men wouldn't. But Kian's kinky mind had been busy imagining her in nothing but stilettos and a collar, and attempting to make it sound less pervy, he had exchanged it for a diamond choker, throwing in the wedding ring as a bonus.

"I see you are still unsure." Annani pursed her lips and produced a smartphone from a hidden pocket in her dress. Before Syssi had time to process her intentions, the Goddess's small fingers flew over the screen and she pressed send.

"What have you done?" She would be so humiliated if Kian laughed at the idea. And why wouldn't he? It was absurd to talk about marriage so soon.

"Do not worry, my dear. I only asked Kian when and where he wants to hold the wedding."

As Syssi's mouth did an imitation of a fish out of water, Annani's phone pinged with a return message.

"That was quick." Annani smiled as she lifted the phone from the table. "Let me read it to you: As soon as you can make the arrangements and get all the clan members here. First wedding. We celebrate big."

"Can I see that?" Syssi wouldn't have put it past Annani to invent this.

The Goddess handed her the phone.

Yep, there it was, black on-screen. "I don't know what to say." Syssi cradled the device. "Could you send me a screenshot? I want to save this."

"As soon as you give me my phone back." Annani chuckled.

Reluctantly, Syssi did. "Is Amanda still sleeping? I need to talk to her..." Syssi felt like she was falling down the rabbit hole again. She needed Amanda to keep her from going into full panic mode.

Why was all this talk about a wedding making her so anxious? It wasn't about second thoughts. Syssi had none. Kian was the only man she would ever want. It was just that everything was moving too fast.

What was the rush?

She wasn't pregnant, so why the shotgun wedding?

"No, Amanda is not here. My daughter decided to take some time off by herself." Annani sighed. "Poor girl."

"Where? When?"

And how could she? The deserter. Apparently when the going gets tough, Amanda splits, probably to go shopping.

"She did not say. But Amanda has her phone with her so you can call her with the good news. I am sure she will love to help us plan the joyous event."

Planning any grand party, and Syssi's wedding in particular, was definitely something Amanda would love to sink her claws into, and she was much better suited for that than Syssi. Problem was, Syssi didn't feel ready for a wedding, even if someone else took over the preparations.

"Why the rush, though? I don't understand. Is it about propriety? I would have thought that your…" She corrected herself. "…our people don't concern themselves with things like that."

Annani sighed and leaned to take hold of Syssi's hand—the one holding a spoon and endlessly stirring creamer into her coffee. "My dear Syssi, I understand that you are overwhelmed and that everything is moving too fast. And considering that you and Kian have all the time in the world, literally, you do not understand why I am rushing you."

"Exactly."

"In part because it is my nature. Once I make up my mind about something, I do not procrastinate, I do not examine and question my decision, I move forward. I trust my intuition because it is smarter than me."

Annani's eyes shone with ancient wisdom as she patted Syssi's hand. "Action is a forward movement, fear and procrastination are not. You have already made the decision to tie your life with my son's. Do not let fear hold you from moving forward."

"It's not about fear..."—*yeah, it's totally about fear*—"I just prefer to progress at a slower pace."

Annani wasn't fooled. "Do not fret, child, trust your instincts."

Syssi sighed, she was going nowhere with the Goddess, and it seemed that resistance was futile when dealing with Annani. "So what is the other reason for the rush? You said it was only in part about moving forward."

"Excitement, hope. Do you realize that yours and Kian's will be the first clan wedding? The best cause for celebration we've had in ages? This is why Kian wants to invite everybody, and why the party we are going to plan must be grand—unforgettable."

Syssi felt herself relax a little. That kind of a party would take months to plan, maybe even a year, which would give her time to get used to the idea. And in the meantime, Kian would get to know her better, and hopefully still want to stay with her. The worst scenario she could imagine was if Kian regretted his decision. Which he still might, once they spent more time together.

"How long do you think planning and producing an unforgettable party will take?" *Please say a year...*

"To plan a ball for close to six hundred people, including travel arrangements for those who will come from out of town, we will need at least two weeks."

"Two weeks?" Syssi croaked.

"Maybe I could shave off a day or two, but no less than ten days."

Oh, boy, it was getting hard to breathe through the surge of panic. "My parents... are in Africa..." she managed a whisper, or rather a whimper… "My mother is a doctor, she cannot just get up and go on such short notice, and travel is complicated."

"It is not a problem. We will send another doctor to cover for her in her absence and charter a private jet to bring your parents here. Same for their return trip."

Evidently, enough money could move things forward very quickly, and Annani was going to move mountains to have her grand celebration in two weeks or less. If Syssi wanted a say in her own wedding, she'd better stop chickening out.

If you can't fight them, join them. Right?

"What are we going to tell my parents?"

"About what, dear?"

"Who you are, who I am now, why the shotgun wedding?"

"We can pretend to be mortals, and you could tell them that you fell in love with a Scot, who comes from a large family, a clan, and that you are rushing the wedding because his mother has to return home, which is true. I cannot stay here indefinitely."

Syssi snorted. "Yeah, right. I can just imagine introducing you as Kian's mother. You look younger than him. And the rest of the clan? You think my parents wouldn't notice that everyone seems to be no older than thirty-five?"

"Yes, I see, you are right. Which means that you will have to tell them the truth, and then before they go home, someone will have to thrall them."

"Maybe I shouldn't invite my parents at all. Instead, I could send them a postcard from my fake honeymoon in Hawaii, informing them that I've eloped." Her parents would most likely prefer for her to do it this way. She would save them from being inconvenienced by their only daughter's wedding.

Bitter, much?

"It is up to you. Whatever you choose to do, Kian and I will support your decision. But if you decide not to invite them, just bear in mind that you are only getting married once, and later on you might regret not having them witness your wedding."

Yeah, Annani had a point. After all, it wasn't as if Syssi was estranged from her parents, or didn't love them. She shouldn't let her resentment over petty grievances cloud her judgment or influence such important decisions.

But on the other hand, the issue of them attending the wedding wasn't the only thing to worry about regarding her parents. In the long run, the real problem would be how to explain why she wasn't aging.

Makeup?

Refrain from seeing them altogether?

"I need to think about it."

"You do that, dear. But do not take too long, because if you decide to invite them, we will need time for the travel arrangements."

"Yes, I know."

"How about we ring Amanda now? If we are to pull it off successfully, we need her on board." Annani handed Syssi the phone. "Go ahead, call her," she prompted.

Syssi narrowed her eyes at the Goddess. "I see what you're doing. You want to lure her back with the wedding plans."

"But of course, what is wrong with that?"

"Absolutely nothing."

24

AMANDA

On board the *Anna,* Amanda lounged on the top deck with a martini in one hand and a tablet in the other—reading the same paragraph for the third time.

Her mind just refused to stay focused on the romance novel, even though it was the latest release by one of her favorite authors. And it wasn't as if reading about someone else's love tribulations was upsetting her. After all, misery liked company. However, unlike the novel's protagonist, Amanda's problems wouldn't get resolved at the end of the three hundred and some pages, and her story had no chance of culminating with a happily-ever-after.

But her troubles, as grave and as daunting as they were, weren't the reason for her inattention.

Since her first moment onboard, Amanda couldn't shake the feeling that there was something fishy about Captain Geneva and her crew. And if these females were Alex's type, then there was something wrong with the guy as well.

The *Anna's* all female crew was an unpleasant bunch of butch lesbos if she ever saw one. The vibe they projected was absolutely nasty.

The gay part didn't bother her, and it wasn't as if anyone could accuse Amanda of having a prejudice against her own gender. To the contrary. Although she loved men for sex, she preferred the company of other women. And not only because she could carry on an intelligent conversation without lust scrambling her brain.

In her experience, and contrary to popular belief, women were by far more honest and trustworthy than men.

Unless they were vying for the attention of the same guy. Then all bets were off. But when chasing tail, men weren't any better, and the whole bros-before-hoes was another urban legend.

At first, Amanda had thought she was imagining the nasty looks. Then, as Captain Geneva had made the introductions, and Amanda had realized all six women were Russian, she had speculated that cultural differences might've been responsible for the cold welcome.

Then again, she had known quite a few Russians in her day, and although a scowl was the Russians' most popular expression, the people she had met were also easy to joke and laugh with once they'd grown comfortable around her, especially after a few drinks. Not these girls, though. They'd remained unfriendly, if not outwardly hostile.

Apparently, onboard the *Anna*, the cold war was still on.

Except, she hadn't tried to get them drunk yet.

Hmm, alcohol might improve their disposition. If she wanted to enjoy her trip, she should throw a party and get the bitches drunk. Hopefully, the free booze would cure their hostility.

"Hey, Lana," she called the one who was supposed to be a stewardess. A tall, leggy blonde that kept an eye on her as if suspecting Amanda of planning to abscond with the silverware.

"What you want?"

Now, how is that for polite?

"Do you have a karaoke on board?"

"Why?" Lana of the many words asked.

"Maybe I want to throw a party, get you girls to loosen up a bit so you'll pull the sticks out of your butts."

"Ha, you lucky Alexander said to treat you nice."

"Or what?" *Bring it on, bitch...*

"Or you find out what happens to stupid American girls like you." Lana smiled menacingly.

"Lana!" Geneva barked. "*Zat'knis*!" Shut up.

"*Shto?*" What? Lana shrugged. "*Ona nie ponimayu.*" She doesn't understand.

Oh, she understands all right, suka—bitch.

"*Idi suyda,*" come here, Geneva commanded.

"*B'lyad...*" Fuck, Lana muttered and stomped up to Geneva.

The captain said nothing besides glaring and pointing a finger toward the stairs leading down. Once Lana disappeared down the stairwell, Geneva walked over to Amanda.

"I apologize for Lana's rudeness. She will be punished." Geneva dipped her head then pivoted on her heel.

"Wait..."

"What?"

"What are you going to do to her?"

"What disciplinary action I decide on is none of your concern, Dr. Dokani."

Oh, so now I am Dr. Dokani...how cordial.

"Look, Captain, Geneva, I don't know what's going on, but I don't understand why you are all so, how to put it nicely, bitchy. Did everyone go into her period at the same time or something? I heard it happens when several females live together."

"Again, I apologize. Is there anything I can do to make you feel more welcome?" Her eyes colder than a Siberian winter, Geneva looked like she was holding herself in check by a thread.

"Yeah, give everyone a bottle of vodka, I'll gladly pay for it. But seriously, what have I done to earn such animosity? I'm a pretty cool chick once you get to know me."

Geneva dipped her head and took in a long breath. "It's not really about you. Please don't tell Alexander I told you this, but we were promised two weeks off. And believe me, the crew needs it."

Alex had mentioned something about not needing the *Anna* for the next couple of weeks. But Amanda had a feeling the captain was deflecting with a convenient excuse.

For now, though, Amanda would give her the benefit of the doubt.

"I see, sorry I've ruined your vacation plans. Now I can understand why you guys are pissed off at me. How about I double your pay for the time I'm here? Will that improve everyone's mood?'

"You'll do that?"

"Sure, I want to enjoy myself and I am willing to pay for it. Give me the names and numbers, and I'll wire the money to each girl's account. And put the vodka on my tab as well." Suddenly, Amanda was struck by a brilliant idea. "One bottle for each girl and one for me. I bet a hundred that this American can outdrink all of you Russians."

Geneva's smile was the first Amanda had seen since getting on board. "In that case, American, you will have to pay for at least three bottles of vodka for each. One bottle is not a challenge for a Russian."

Yeah, like these girls could handle three bottles.

Amanda pretended being horrified for about five seconds, then narrowed her eyes at Geneva and smiled. "You are on, suka." She watched as Geneva's eyes widened.

"You speak Russian?"

"Nah, just a few curse words." No need to reveal her cards, yet, or ever. For some reason, Amanda suspected there was more going on than met the eye on board the *Anna*.

Things didn't add up.

Why hire a graceless, foreign crew for a luxury blue water yacht that must've cost Alex something in the range of twenty-five million?

Save some chump-change on wages?

Come to think of it, where did he get the kind of money needed to buy a boat like this?

His share in the clan profits was enough to keep him in style, but not this kind of style, and his club, although successful, wasn't making this kind of money either.

Was Alex really dealing drugs as Kian had insinuated?

Well, tonight, she was going to get the crew drunk and ask some questions. With an immortal's high tolerance for alcohol, even the infamous Russians had no chance of besting her in a drinking competition.

25

SEBASTIAN

It was late evening when Sebastian's plane taxied up to the sleeve at Tom Bradley International Terminal in Los Angeles.

Immigration took forever, but everything went without a hitch. An hour and a half later, he and his assistants walked up the ramp where they were greeted by a uniformed limo driver with a sign that read "Mr. Sebastian Shar."

Slugging along the freeway in LA's infamous traffic, it took another hour to reach their accommodations for the night—the renowned Beverly Hills Hotel.

"Nice," Robert said as he looked around the elegant lobby.

"Wait until you see the suites I've reserved for us, each with a bedroom, a separate living room, and a balcony." Tom glanced at Sebastian. "You said to go for the best..."

"Yes, I did." He'd meant for himself, but what the hell, it wasn't like the cost was going out of his own pocket. Let the men enjoy. "Only the best for my team. Go settle down. I'll see you tomorrow morning." Sebastian pocketed the card-key to his suite.

"Eh, boss..." Tom stopped him. "What about some ass? I don't know about you, but I need some, and so does Robert. He is just too shy to say anything."

"Call the concierge, tell him you're with me and you need special accommodation. He'll know what to do."

"Sweet."

Sebastian had tried the service before. Unfortunately, it couldn't provide for his particular tastes. And it wasn't a good idea to indulge with an unreceptive hooker anywhere other than the island. Even with the fast healing the venom facilitated, it took time for the evidence to disappear, and the last thing he needed was to call attention to himself by getting arrested.

Besides, in a hotel, there was no way to contain the screams other than gagging his victim, which he preferred not to do. It was like watching a movie without the sound.

And what fun was that...

Which meant no room service for Sebastian. He had to scratch his itch elsewhere.

But as the saying went; where there was demand, for the right amount of money, there was supply.

The first time Sebastian had visited LA, he had found a club catering to his extreme tastes and had been a loyal member, or customer as it were, since.

"Tomorrow, nine, my suite. Until then, I bid you good night," he told his men and headed to his room.

Let them think what they would.

Sebastian waited until the bellboy brought his luggage, then grabbed a quick shower, changed into something appropriate for his planned activity, and called for a taxi to take him to the club.

26

DALHU

The passage of time progressed at a different pace in rooms without windows, Dalhu reflected as he stared at the ceiling. Or maybe it was the isolation and lack of activity that made it seem as if he'd been stuck in there forever. Though in reality, it was less than forty-eight hours since he had been imprisoned.

And twenty-one hours thirty-two minutes since he'd last seen Amanda.

But who was counting?

Fuck.

Why had she abandoned him?

She could've at least called. There was a phone in his fancy prison. And although it wasn't connected to the outside world, only to some guy in security, she could've obtained the number with ease.

Or not.

Maybe her brother had forbidden it.

Probably.

It was the most likely explanation.

Amanda had loved their bathroom interlude, and Dalhu could think of no reason for her to stay away unless she had no choice.

He was going out of his mind with worry.

And boredom...

How many movies could a guy watch?

The only other entertainment option was a large assortment of video games, but he'd never learned how to play.

Not that he had any desire to.

Grown men shouldn't entertain themselves with boys' games.

By now, he'd hoped Amanda would come see him again. But the only visitor he'd had for the past day and a half was the stoic butler who had been bringing in his meals.

Strange that they were sending the small man by himself with no Guardian backup. Not that Dalhu had any intention of hurting the guy, still, they had no way of knowing it. And although the Goddess hadn't seemed to regard Dalhu as a murderous abomination, her son definitely had.

Not that the fucker was wrong necessarily.

But the butler didn't appear to have a problem with Dalhu. Polite, as if serving an honored guest, the stout little man wasn't nervous around him at all.

Getting some information out of the guy, though, had been a no go. Same for the significantly less cordial guy in security.

No one would tell Dalhu anything.

Still, when the butler showed up again with the evening snack, Dalhu gave it another try.

"Hey, my man, does anyone plan on seeing me tonight?"

"I do not know, sir."

"And Amanda, is she well?"

"As I have said before, I do not know."

Well, it was worth a try.

But then the butler added, "I have not seen the mistress today to ask about her well-being."

"Why? Where did she go?"

"I do not know, sir."

Fuck, the guy didn't deny that Amanda was gone.

Had her brother had something to do with it? Had he sent her away to prevent any further contact between them?

Anger rising to the surface, Dalhu managed to appear calm until the little guy left. Once he was alone, though, the urge to destroy everything in his vicinity became almost overpowering. He didn't. All that trashing the room would have achieved, aside from releasing the excess steam, would have been to prove Kian's point, and Dalhu was not about to give the fucker the satisfaction.

Still, the barely contained rage needed an outlet.

A good, rigorous fight would've helped, or even a long run, but as those were not an option, Dalhu dropped to the floor and began a series of fast push-ups.

He slowed the pace after the first thousand, but kept going without rest until he was drenched in sweat.

It wasn't enough, though.

It took another three thousand sit-ups until he was finally ready to quit and hit the shower.

27

KIAN

"Have you talked with Amanda?" Kian asked, giving the comforter a tug from his side and stretching it nice and flat over the bed the way Syssi liked it.

For some unfathomable reason, Syssi had insisted on making the bed herself instead of leaving the task to Okidu.

It wasn't like the butler needed help with the house chores; after all, he never tired and never slept, which thanks to Annani, Syssi was now well aware of.

Kian still couldn't believe he hadn't explained about Okidu. But the truth was that he'd never regarded his butler as anything other than a person, often catching himself giving Okidu incomplete instructions because it was so damn easy to forget the guy's limits.

And besides, considering the whirlwind of events following Syssi's transition and Amanda's kidnapping, no wonder the subject had never come up.

It had slipped his mind.

Not that Syssi had made a big deal out of it. In fact, Syssi was not the type to make a big deal out of anything other than the really important stuff.

His sweet Syssi, he smiled at her from across the bed. He was so lucky to have her.

And he had to admit that doing this little morning chore together felt kind of nice. Intimate, in a familiar sort of way. Kian was looking forward to countless mornings just like this one.

Each time he'd woken up with Syssi's warm body in his arms, Kian had thanked the Fates for the gift of her—the happiness and gratitude setting a positive tone for the rest of his day.

And whether it was her chest or her back that was pressed to his front, he had no particular preference—both were equally enticing.

Now that Syssi wasn't allowing him out of bed before she was up, he was making love to her every morning as well as every night.

Good times. Good times indeed.

"No, I'm giving her space. I wanted to call her yesterday, you know, after your mother sprang that whole wedding thing on me, but then I decided to wait. Amanda didn't get away just to have me heap my troubles on top of hers. She has enough stuff to sort out."

Troubles?

"I'll pretend I didn't just hear you say that."

"What?"

"Marrying me is trouble?"

"Oh, you know what I mean. But here…" Syssi climbed on top of the just-made bed and crab-walked on her knees to where he was standing on the other side. Grabbing him by his shirt, she pulled him to her mouth and kissed him until they were both starved for breath. "Better?" she panted.

"A little…" Kian lifted her in his arms then spread her out on the bed, covering her with his body like a blanket. "Now, this is better." He began trailing kisses, starting with her sweet lips, going down to her chin, then her neck, until he reached her breasts. Cupping her through her shirt, he pushed them together and licked the valley in between.

Syssi giggled. "Oh, shoot, now we'll have to make the bed again."

"We could wait, you know…" Kian gazed into her smiling eyes, so full of love, so adoring. "I want our wedding to be a source of joy for you, not anxiety."

"I know, right? My heart is fully on board with it, but I can't stop thinking about how little we know each other. And after a lifetime of cautiously examining each and every decision, no matter how trivial, I'm having trouble with just jumping headlong into the most important one. It's not like I'm having doubts. You know my heart belongs to you, forever. I'm just a big, fat, chicken, that's all."

"First of all, you're not big and not fat. And as to being a chicken, well, you are my scrumptious, hot chick." Kian gave the valley between her breasts another long lick. "Yummy." He smacked his lips.

"How come you're not freaking out? I thought men were supposed to be the commitment-phobes."

"I've waited for you for close to two thousand years, and now that I have you, I'm done with waiting. I love you, will always love you, and will never stop loving you. I know it like I know that the sun will rise in the morning and set in the evening, and that spring will lead to summer. No doubts. You were, are, and will be the only one for me."

Syssi's eyes misted with tears. "Wow, I have no words."

"You don't have to say anything. Your eyes and your body tell me all I need to know. For now. Later, when you find the words, you'll tell me." He quoted her own words back to her. The words she'd spoken to him that first night they had spent together.

Her eyes foggy with tears, she reached a hand to cup his cheek and smiled. "Well, my love, it seems you found the most beautiful words. And to think you claimed you're not a romantic."

"I had professed to be an uncouth brute, and a crude, insensitive jerk. I've never said anything about not being romantic. Though, I'm just telling it as it is."

"I love you so much," Syssi whispered.

"I know."

"No more doubts, I don't need any more time, let's do it—a grand wedding to eclipse them all."

"What have I done? I've created a monster!" Kian gasped in mock horror, then kissed the living daylights out of her. "But seriously," he said after letting her take a breath, "if you need more time, that's okay. Just not too long—I'm not a patient guy."

"No, I'm diving in, headlong. And if it means that Amanda's little vacation is cut short, tough. I'm calling her, and she'd better pack her bags and come home right away. I need her."

"That's my girl." Kian kissed Syssi's forehead. "Beautiful, lush, smart, and brave."

"Brave?"

"Yes, brave. Bravery is not about the absence of fear. It's about facing it and conquering it."

The little smirk on her face told him that she liked his compliment, but then she said, "If this is so, my love, you need to back your words with actions. It's time you faced your own fears and conquered them."

This was not the answer he'd been expecting.

And what did she mean by that?

"Did you just call me a coward?" Kian pinned her arms to her sides.

"I wouldn't dream of it." A mischievous smile was tugging at her lips. "You might spank me if I did," she breathed.

Imp.

"I'm going to spank you anyway…because you fucking love it."

"When?"

"Not before you tell me what that facing my fears is all about."

Turning serious, Syssi sighed, and with a little shrug freed her arms. She then cupped his cheeks with her soft palms. "In your case it is not about fear. It's about facing the demons of your past and rising above them. You need to go talk to Dalhu."

And wasn't that a complete mood spoiler.

Damn Doomer.

"I know. And later today I will. But I want Andrew to be there. Without him to verify it, I won't believe anything that comes out of that scum's mouth."

"Text him, I'm sure Andrew would gladly offer his lie detector services."

28

ANDREW

Andrew closed the Maldives file with mixed feelings. He hated that there was nothing for him to report, or rather nothing he could report. The war between the two immortal factions was not a threat to national security, and therefore not something his agency was concerned with.

Under normal circumstances, he would've forwarded the file to the police or the FBI, but there sure as fuck was nothing ordinary about this.

But be that as it may, the new file assigned to him was so massive that he was glad to be rid of the old one. Someone higher up had either been tipped off, or just had the smarts to realize that airport security should include in its screening not only the travelers, but also the thousands upon thousands of employees; from cleaning crews, mechanics, and other service personnel, to flight attendants and pilots.

Right now, he had close to two hundred employee files to investigate, and that was only the initial sweep of potential suspects from just one airport.

If his boss had thought Andrew could do it all by himself, the guy was delusional.

And as if Andrew hadn't had enough on his plate, this morning Kian had texted him, asking Andrew to stop by any time that worked for him. Today. Apparently, his unique talent was required for verifying the Doomer's story.

There would be no overtime for Andrew this evening, at least not on his official job.

At five sharp, he headed out, ignoring the raised brow or two his coworkers sported. They would have to get used to him no longer being the last one to leave the office.

Gone were the days when he had stayed late because there had been nothing and no one waiting for him at home, and he would work, or hit the downstairs gym, until it was late enough for him to join his friends for some drinks at the bar.

Now, he had a whole bloody clan that needed him. And surprisingly, the added responsibility felt good. Or maybe it was the sense of belonging—of being part of a tribe.

Even if only on its fringes, he thought as he eased into the designated guest parking of the luxury high-rise. Andrew wondered what it would take for him to get access to the private one underground.

Hell, he still didn't even know Kian's last name.

True, with a name like that it wasn't as if the security guard manning the reception desk at the lobby would ask Kian who?

As soon as Andrew said he was there to see Kian, the two guys at the front desk snapped to attention. One got busy on the phone while the other pointed Andrew to the waiting area. "Someone will be here shortly to escort you upstairs."

Ignoring the guard's suggestion, Andrew did a little walk about the lobby, taking in the opulence he'd been too agitated to notice the first time he'd been here. The space, some thirty feet tall and spanning most of the building's footprint, was all marble, glass and mirrors. Dotted with contemporary leather sofas and chairs that were grouped around glass tables, and big, green trees he wasn't sure were real or fake, it looked like the lobby of a high-end hotel.

But what interested him most were the extensive security measures.

There were the requisite cameras, though as well hidden as they were, it took someone who knew what to look for to find them.

The reception slash guard station, as well as any point of entry into the building proper, was separated from the lobby by thick, bulletproof glass. And the only door to the other side had none of the standard key-card entry pads or even a handle. The only way for the thing to open was for a security guy to buzz you in or out.

Clever.

But it didn't end there. Besides the three elevators visible through the glass partition, Andrew knew there were three more on the other side. Though to get to them from the lobby, one had to not only be buzzed in but have a key-card to another inconspicuous door—labeled *Maintenance.*

Waiting for his escort, Andrew didn't watch the bank of elevators this time, but the beautiful flower arrangement farther away at the back wall, or rather the alcove to its right.

The one leading to a short corridor and the door labeled *Maintenance.*

He didn't have to wait long until a burly guy emerged from that alcove, but not one of the Guardians Andrew had met before. Still, the man, or immortal, had no trouble figuring out who Andrew was. Though not necessarily because he knew who to look for, but simply because Andrew was the only one on the other side of the glass.

"Bhathian." The guy offered his hand.

Apparently, no one here bothered with last names. Which kind of made sense for those hundreds of years old. Last names were, after all, a recent invention, evolving from the medieval naming practice which had been based on an individual's occupation, or where they were from, or the name of their clan.

"Andrew." Shaking Bhathian's hand, Andrew omitted his own surname. When in Rome, do as the Romans do… and all that.

The big guy wasn't one for small talk, and they made their way to the private bank of elevators in silence.

After getting out on basement level three, Bhathian stopped in front of the first door that was made of glass as opposed to the solid metal of the other doors they'd passed by. "First, let me check if Kian is ready to see you."

Behind the double door was a large, nicely kitted-out office, with a conference table in its center, and a desk at the back, where Kian was busy on the phone.

He cast Andrew an apologetic glance.

"Let's go." Bhathian pulled out his phone and lifted it up for Kian to see, then waited until Kian nodded. "You hungry?" he asked, heading down the same corridor.

"It depends on what you're offering."

The guy's scowl deepened. "If you like all that crappy veggie stuff, then you're going to love it, but if you were hoping for meat, you're shit out of luck."

"I'm fine with the veggies."

"Good, because that is all Okidu is cooking."

"You have a cook?"

"No, not really."

Andrew waited to hear the rest, but evidently it was all Bhathian was going to say.

Surly son of a bitch.

The guy was built like a pro-wrestler and had the nasty disposition to match. Tall, he was about Kian's height, but probably outweighed Syssi's boyfriend by at least a hundred pounds.

Still, despite his intimidating size and his bushy, dark eyebrows being clenched in what appeared to be a permanent scowl, Bhathian wasn't a bad-looking dude. In fact, the ladies probably found him attractive, particularly those who were into the big, tough, silent types.

"Take a seat." Bhathian motioned to a barstool as they entered the huge, commercial-style kitchen.

There was no dining table per se, only a long stainless steel prep area with several barstools thrown in at one end.

Bhathian pulled out a half-empty pan of lasagna from a warming drawer and a couple of beers from the fridge, and brought the loot to the table, then went back for plates and utensils.

"Dig in," he said after scooping half of the leftover lasagna onto his plate.

As Andrew piled his plate with the rest of it, Bhathian wolfed down several forkfuls, then took a swig from his beer. "So, you're Syssi's brother…," he said.

"Yeah?"

"And you're some kind of commando or Special Ops as they call it today, right?"

"Not anymore, retired. Now I'm a desk jockey. Though still in the same field."

"Retired? At your age?"

Andrew was starting to like the guy. "Too old for active duty."

"Anandur told me he was impressed with your skills, you know, on both missions."

The guy was either trying to make conversation or working up to something.

"Old age has one advantage. It entails a lot of experience."

Bhathian snorted. "Old age… you're forgetting who you're talking to. Compared to me you're an infant."

Now, that was a tad offensive…

"Yeah, well, I do have a lot of experience in particular kinds of situations, which makes me a valuable asset to my government even from behind a desk."

"That you are. You're a valuable asset to us as well." Bhathian rubbed his neck, his eyebrows riding even lower. "I...," he started and stopped, "I need a favor...," he gritted, cupping the back of his almost shaved skull with his huge hand.

Andrew waited for the guy to continue.

Bhathian avoided Andrew's eyes when he spoke. "There is something I've been trying to find for nearly thirty years and reached a dead end at each turn. But you... you might have access to information I don't even know exists."

He sucked half his beer on a oner, then faced Andrew. "I've never told anyone, and whether you can, or will help me or not, I need to know that this will stay between us."

"No problem."

Bhathian's gray eyes were trained on Andrew's for a long moment before he nodded.

29

SYSSI

"Get out of here!" Amanda gasped.

"I know, two weeks, crazy... right?"

"Yeeeee..." All Syssi heard was the yeeping and the swish of wind.

It was easy to picture Amanda pirouetting on deck with the phone in hand.

Apparently, her friend, or rather her future sister-in-law, was cruising down the California coast on a luxury yacht.

The deserter...

"Yeah, I bet it's very exciting to hear about it, but planning a wedding that is supposed to be the most memorable event in the clan's history, not so much. I'm getting an anxiety attack like every five minutes."

"Fear not, Amanda the great to the rescue."

Syssi's shoulders sagged in relief. "Oh, thank you. You can't imagine how much I appreciate your coming back to help me."

The long stretch of silence had Syssi tense all over again.

"I can't, not yet. But I'm going to work on it from here. We can divide the tasks between the three of us, with you having the last say on all final decisions, of course." Amanda's idea sounded reasonable, but after Syssi had her hopes up, the disappointment stung.

Still, she was being selfish, wasn't she? Amanda needed to be away just as much as Syssi needed her to be back.

On the other hand, this wedding was a once in a lifetime affair, while Amanda could go on her vacation whenever. "Yeah, sure. But it's not the same. I need you here to keep me from falling apart."

Amanda sighed. "Oh, sweetie, I know. I'll try to come back as soon as I can. But I need a little more time."

Syssi chewed on her lower lip, debating if she should bring up the thorny subject. But Amanda needed to know. "Kian is finally going to talk to Dalhu sometime later today, and he asked Andrew to be there when he does."

"That's good... Yeah...," Amanda whispered.

"Talk to me. What's going on with you?" Syssi wanted to kick herself. Obviously, Amanda wasn't in a good place despite the cheerful confidence she was fronting. And all Syssi had been concerned with were her own petty problems and her needs. She hadn't paused to think that maybe it was Amanda who needed her help and not the other way around.

Some friend you are...

And Syssi's problems? What problems? Those were happy problems...

"Hold on...," Amanda said. "Hey, Lana, go scrub some toilets, would you? I want to talk with my bestie without you eavesdropping." She shooed this Lana away.

"Who is Lana?"

"One of Alex's crew of Russian lesbos." Amanda snorted.

Syssi chuckled. "That sounds interesting, Russian lesbians? How would you know?"

"Well, the Russian accents give them away."

"The lesbian part, you witch!"

"I'm just kidding, or maybe not, who knows? It's just that they are so butch. Same short haircut, like really boy short, and muscles that would put most guys to shame. Not to mention a complete lack of manners. Not that their peculiar social graces have anything to do with sexual orientation, it's just the cherry on top of this crew's overall *feminine, ladylike* bearing."

"I see. But if they are so rude, what are you still doing there?"

"I'm curious," Amanda whispered, though this time it wasn't a sad, choked-up whisper, more like conspiratorial. "Tonight, I'm going to get them drunk and find out what's going on." Her whisper was barely audible.

"Good luck with that." Amanda had an impressive capacity for alcohol, but compared to the legendary Russians? She would be drunk way before them.

"Don't worry. I got it."

She probably did. After all, Amanda had some pretty nifty abilities in her bag of tricks. "Are you going to compel them? Or thrall them? Or whatever you call the thing you do?"

"I wish it was that easy. But thralling and influencing work only on unsuspecting, receptive minds. Compelling people to do something they are actively resisting is nearly impossible—except for the really weak minded. And in the case of suspicious, stubborn Russians, I don't think even Yamanu is powerful enough to compel them to spill. But shitloads of vodka might do it."

"Okay, Mata Hari. Now tell me where you're at."

Amanda sighed. "I'm in limbo. I can't stand the sight of Dalhu, knowing he is responsible for Mark's murder, but I can't stand being without him either. Even the thought of getting it on with some random guy makes me want to retch. So yeah, I'm screwed, and not in a good way."

Yeah, that was one hell of a conundrum. "You must've known he was associated with the murder. It shouldn't have been such a big shock."

"I know. What can I say, I blocked it. And associated is not the same as being the one who ordered it."

Damn. What was she supposed to say to that? What would she do in Amanda's place? Probably the same thing—run as far and as fast as she could.

"Maybe you should talk with your mother. If anyone has a chance to find a way to reconcile this, it is her."

Way to go, Syssi, drop it at someone else's feet.

But she had no words of wisdom to offer.

"I suppose, though I don't think I'm ready to listen to anything one way or the other."

"I understand completely. Remember the night at the club? When Kian came to get me?"

"Yeah?"

"I don't think I've ever told you, but just before he showed up, I was convinced that you guys were mafia and that he was the boss."

"What? Why?"

"Well, what do you think? You and Kri kept taking guys to the back rooms, and after you were done with whatever you were doing there, they just walked away without as much as a wave goodbye. I thought you were selling them drugs. Then Arwel and Bhathian show up, looking like bodyguards, saying that they came to keep an eye on us, but couldn't sit with me because they didn't want to infringe on your turf. Combined with the attack at the lab, the secrecy… you get the picture."

"Oh, wow, totally… So what did you do?"

"I tried to make a run for it, but Alex—who by the way is a total creep—got in my way. I really don't understand how you can be friends with someone like that. Just saying. Then Kian showed up, and I was freaking out because being involved with a mafia boss felt like a death sentence. I was terrified. And yet, when he dragged me onto the dance floor and held me tight, I couldn't help wanting him like crazy. I was so confused. I couldn't understand how I could possibly feel safe in his arms while suspecting he was the worst kind of criminal."

"Fascinating story, and I get what you're trying to say, but it's not the same. There is no denying that Dalhu is a murderer, and Kian isn't really a mafia boss."

"Here is the thing, though, I'm not sure I would have been able to walk away from Kian even if he turned out to be a criminal. And as to Dalhu, if he is a murderer, then every soldier who has ever killed is a murderer too."

After a long pause Amanda responded. "No, Syssi, you are wrong. I wish you weren't, but unfortunately you are. Soldiers fight other soldiers on the battlefield; it is ugly and sad and horrible, but not as horrible as the premeditated, cold-blooded murder of an unarmed man in his own home."

Sadly, Amanda was absolutely right.

30

SEBASTIAN

After the swarm of construction workers had left, Sebastian surveyed the job site. The plumbing and electrical in the basement were already in place, and the partition walls for the small rooms—each with its own bathroom—were up and covered in drywall.

The building above was being repainted inside and out, and all the old bathroom fixtures were piled in a huge dumpster outside. Tomorrow, the new fixtures would get delivered and installed, first in the thirty-eight upstairs bathrooms, then once they were ready, in the twenty-one down in the basement.

The only significant change Sebastian had made, besides the basement conversion, was to combine several rooms on the third floor for his own use, adding a luxurious bathroom and a balcony.

In three to four days most of the place would be ready for furniture, except for his suite of rooms, which would take longer to complete.

After all, luxury demanded time and attention to detail.

The speed with which things were being done could have never been achieved legally. The basement, full of rooms without windows, would have never been permitted, and the rest of the work, although not violating city codes, would have raised suspicion.

Not to mention the time and money it would have taken to pull the countless permits or the delays caused by waiting for inspections.

Still, even though the old monastery was isolated, with that many workers and deliveries of building material, there was a good chance some city official would eventually show up at the site.

Not that the inspector would have anything to report after meeting Sebastian.

Thank Mortdh, he possessed a strong thralling gift. Influencing the minds of the over fifty construction workers at the end of each day would've been time-consuming and exhausting otherwise.

It wasn't that he was concerned that they would report to the city officials. The illegal workmen his contacts had supplied could not and would not talk to the authorities. But without him planting a suggestion that they really didn't want to talk about their work, they were bound to gossip to friends and family.

Tom thought Sebastian was being overly cautious, and that it would have sufficed to muddle their memories once the basement was completed, but Sebastian refused to take the chance of the workmen blabbering in the meantime about the underground facility he was building. And anyway, there was the issue of the electric fence, the new massive gate, and the surveillance cameras that were being installed not only all over the facility and its grounds, but also along the road leading up to it.

Sebastian had no doubt that even the lowly workmen had figured out that this kind of security was excessive for an *Interfaith Spiritual Retreat*.

31

BHATHIAN

"Okay, so here is the story." Bhathian sucked back the rest of his beer and set the empty bottle down.

One beer would not cut it if he were to tell that shameful tale. He got up and came back with two more.

"I see it's going to be a long one." Andrew saluted with his mostly full bottle, a smirk catching one side of his mouth.

Bhathian felt his glower deepen. It was hard enough to get this story out without snide remarks. "You want to listen or not?"

"Sorry, man, I was just making a joke."

"Okay." Bhathian popped the cap off his second beer. "So, thirty-something years ago, on a flight from Edinburgh to LA, the flight attendant I was flirting with invited me to join her for drinks at this little-known bar next to the airport. As it turned out, the place was, still is, a favorite watering hole for many of the transcontinental flights' stewardesses and pilots."

Bhathian took a swig of his beer, then wiped his mouth with the back of his hand. "The place was packed with beautiful women, and due to the nature of its transient clientele, unlike the other bars and clubs, there was a never-ending supply of fresh lovelies."

And the best part? None of the other males in his family had known about it.

He had struck gold.

His private hunting ground.

Andrew saluted with his bottle. "Sweet, my kind of place."

"That's where I met Trish." One of the most beautiful women he had ever met. "Patricia Evans, a first-class flight attendant on the now-defunct TWA."

Bhathian palmed his bottle. "We went back to her hotel room." And she had been incomparable. In more ways than one.

"Trish turned out to be one of those rare mortals who cannot be thralled."

"Not at all? Or just resistant?" Andrew asked.

"I don't know. I'm not great at it, but I had no trouble with anyone before or since. But anyway, luckily, I figured it out before biting her, otherwise... yeah, it would've been one hell of a fuckfest."

"What did you do?"

"What do you think? I didn't bite her. We said our goodbyes, and I thought it was the end of it, that I would never see her again."

It had hurt because for the first time ever Bhathian had wanted more with a woman.

"But you did."

"A month later, she found me at the bar. And I figured, sweet, why not."

Bhathian closed his eyes at the memory, her image still as vivid as it had been thirty years ago. "I didn't get to bite her, but she was so fucking gorgeous—with that banging body of hers, and hair so black it was almost blue, and so long it was kissing the top curve of her perfect ass." He felt his face redden, and he looked away, embarrassed by what he'd said out loud. Too late to take it back, though.

"We went back to her room again, but instead of shucking her clothes, she pulled out one of those miniature whiskey bottles and handed it to me."

"You'll need it," she told him, a beautiful blush climbing up her cheeks.

He gulped it and lifted a brow.

"I'm pregnant."

Oh, hell. This was so not what he had been expecting.

"And you think it's mine?"

"I know it is, I've been with no one else for months." Trish didn't look upset. If anything, she seemed to glow with joy.

He hated himself for it, but he said it anyway. "I want you to abort it. I'll pay whatever expenses and loss of income you'll incur, but there is nothing more I can offer you. I'm sorry."

Trish looked as if he had slapped her, and in a way, he felt like he had. Though what did she expect? Even if he chose to believe her, and for some reason he did, this pregnancy was the result of a one-night stand, for heaven's sakes.

"I'm not going to abort my child," she whispered.

"Trish, be reasonable. I am not what you need, I can't be. A beautiful woman like you should have no trouble finding a good man. One that will make you happy, be a proper father to your children."

Damn, he would've loved nothing more than a chance to be that man.

"You don't understand, this is a miracle. I'm forty-five, and I haven't been on contraceptives for years because I couldn't get pregnant. And here I am, with a child growing inside me..." Tears began sliding down her cheeks.

"Oh, hell, Trish..." He took her in his arms. "I didn't know..." She was forty-five? She looked no older than thirty, and even that was a stretch.

"It's okay. I didn't come here expecting anything from you, just thought you'd be happy to know that you've created a child... and maybe... maybe put your name on the birth certificate when the time comes..."

Fuck, he couldn't do even that. All he could do was offer money, and although Trish would no doubt hate it, she would need it.

"I'm sorry, I can't do that."

"Oh my God, you're married, aren't you?"

"No, I didn't lie about that... it's just that I have some legal issues." It was

kind of true... "But I can give you money, enough so you and your child will never lack anything."

Yes, this was good. He could help support her, and maybe get to watch over her and the kid from afar.

"Thank you, that's very generous of you."

32

ANDREW

"Did she take the money?"

Bhathian closed his eyes and shook his head. "I haven't heard from her since. I kept hoping she'd call, kept going to that bar, but she never came back."

"Did you try to find her?"

"For a time. I got a hold of her employment record, so I had her address and social security number. I also discovered that she quit her job shortly after talking to me. But when I went looking for her at the address she provided, the place was already rented out to someone else. The manager said that she was never there, and he doubted she ever really lived there. The rent money, however, he said, was arriving in the mail like clockwork until about the same time she quit the airline. Other than that, I wasn't able to find anything else. It was like she never existed before applying for the job at TWA, and she vanished after quitting it."

Bhathian rubbed his neck. "Eventually, I gave up and tried not to think about the child I might have somewhere or how Patricia was managing, raising that child by herself. But from time to time I still wonder, you know?"

He cast Andrew a sad look. "When I heard about your connections, I thought maybe you could find out for me—working for the government as you do, and having access to information I wasn't able to get to."

Poor guy. The woman had probably used a fake name and social to get the job and had changed it again after quitting it. It wasn't that unusual. She might have been running from an abusive boyfriend or husband, or maybe even from the law. Or she might've been an illegal immigrant. In any case, it would be next to impossible to pick up a trail that was thirty years old. Especially when all he had to go on were a fake name and social, and an approximate age.

Andrew finished what was left of his beer. "You don't happen to have a picture of her, do you?"

"No."

"If I hook you up with a forensic artist, could you describe her well enough for him to draw one?"

"Yes, though what good would it do? If she is still alive, Patricia would be seventy-five now."

"I know, but that's all we have. A name and social that were probably fake, Patricia's approximate age, and that of her child, and your memory of her."

"Fuck." Bhathian sagged on his barstool and popped the cap off his third beer. "Well, it was worth a shot."

"Do you still have that social?"

"Yeah, and the address as well."

"Good. Don't get your hopes up, but I'm going to look into it. And I'll hook you up with the forensic artist."

"Thank you." Bhathian offered his hand.

Andrew shook on it and clapped the guy's shoulder. "No problem."

Damn, the thing was like solid rock—muscles on top of muscles.

Bhathian shifted in his seat, then pushed to his feet. "I'm going to see what's keeping Kian." With his head hung low, he pivoted on his heel and strode away.

By the looks of him, the guy wasn't used to talking about himself, and confiding in another—especially a mortal—must've rankled.

Andrew shook his head as he tried to put himself in the guy's shoes.

To know that he had a son or a daughter that he'd never gotten to see, never gotten to support, to protect, must've festered inside Bhathian for the past thirty years.

But then, it would've been the same for any decent human being—or immortal.

Kian walked into the kitchen. "Thank you for coming, Andrew. Sorry that I kept you waiting." He offered his hand.

Apparently, Bhathian's escort duty was finished.

"No problem, Bhathian took good care of me." Andrew motioned to the empty lasagna pan and the lineup of beer bottles.

"Good. You ready to go?" Kian waited for Andrew to get up, and together they headed out.

"Any instructions before we talk to the Doomer?" Andrew asked.

"I trust your judgment. Mostly, I want you there to detect his lies. But feel free to ask the Doomer questions if you feel like I'm overlooking something."

"If I catch him lying, do you want me to tell you later or give you a sign right away? I'd rather not say anything about it. It's better if he doesn't know I can do this."

They stopped in front of the elevator, and Kian punched the down button. "I want to know right away. How about tapping your shoe? Or clearing your throat? I don't want to chance missing a visual cue."

"When he lies, I'll tap my shoe twice."

Kian gave a nod, and as the elevator door opened with a ping, they got inside, then exited a few seconds later—four levels below.

Down the corridor, Anandur was leaning against the wall next to one of the doors with his arms crossed over his chest.

Andrew slanted a look at Kian. "You think we need him there? Between the two of us, I'm sure we can handle one prisoner."

The guy grimaced. "Standard protocol. As Regent, I'm supposed to have a bodyguard at all times. I get away with not always following it, but in this case, Anandur insisted."

"Aren't you the one making the rules?"

"Nope. This one was Annani's doing. And as such, it is set in stone."

"I see." Andrew chuckled.

As he had already figured, the Goddess had the ultimate say.

Tough little lady.

"Good evening, gentlemen, ready to proceed?" Anandur punched the security code into the keypad, and the door began its inward swing.

"After you." Kian motioned for Andrew to enter.

The Doomer was sitting on the couch with his palms down on his thighs, his nonthreatening pose belied by the way he was eyeing them with thinly veiled hostility.

But the Doomer had nothing on Kian.

The guy's hands curled into tight fists, and his eyes began their eerie glow.

Andrew put a hand on Kian's tight shoulder. "Easy, my man," he whispered, warily watching Kian's lips for those monstrous fangs to make an appearance.

With an apparent effort, Kian uncurled his fists and walked over to the bar. "Scotch, anyone?" When no one answered, he poured himself a glass and downed it on a oner, then poured another before sitting down in an armchair across from the Doomer.

Anandur walked over to the small dining table near the bar and planted his butt in a chair.

As Andrew sat next to Kian in the other armchair, he took a

quick look around. The room was a far cry from the prison cell he had imagined. In fact, it was a lot fancier than his own living room, and through the open door he glimpsed an adjoining bedroom as luxurious as any high-end hotel's.

Complete with a large screen television and a game console, the Doomer's accommodations were fit for a king. He had no reason to look so pissed off.

"Where is Amanda? What have you done with her?" the Doomer bit out.

Aha, so that's why...

Andrew wasn't even aware Amanda was gone. Had Kian sent her away? Or what was more likely, she was still here but had smartened up enough to stay away from Dalhu.

"None of your damn business. But I don't mind telling you that she left of her own volition, not because I forced her to. She finally woke up and realized what a piece of shit you are and doesn't want to see you."

The Doomer could not have looked worse if Kian had shot him. He closed his eyes and slumped back into the couch cushions.

Andrew actually felt pity for the bastard. There was nothing worse than shattered hopes.

"I'm going to ask you some questions," Kian said.

"Why should I tell you anything." It was more of a statement than a question.

And it wasn't about defiance either.

The Doomer simply didn't seem to care about anything. Which wasn't going to do them any good. He had to give the guy something to hold on to.

Leaning forward, Andrew peered into Dalhu's dark eyes. "Because even if Amanda never wants to see you again, you still want to make sure she is safe."

Dalhu sighed and shifted up. "You're right, even if it's the last thing I do."

From the corner of his eye, Andrew caught Kian looking down at the shoe he hadn't tapped, and a smirk tugged at his mouth.

The Doomer hadn't lied, though, he'd meant what he'd said.

"Did you take out my men?"

"It was all taken care of," Kian said in a surprisingly conversational tone.

Was he mellowing out toward the Doomer?

"Good. She can return to her work now. She loves it..." Dalhu's voice petered out to a near whisper at the end.

It had the opposite effect on Kian. "Tell me about the incoming reinforcements and what is their plan of action," he barked.

In the silence that followed, the Doomer's internal conflict was barely perceptible on his hard face, but in the end, his eyes narrowed on Kian as he decided to speak his piece. "I don't give a fuck if you believe me or not, but just for the record... the set of rules I'd been operating under before meeting Amanda no longer applies."

"Noted," Kian bit out.

Dalhu nodded. "I wasn't told how many are coming, but if I were to guess, at least fifty, but no more than a hundred. And with a contingent this big, someone higher up on the chain of command will be leading them."

Andrew pulled out his phone and began recording, even though he had no doubt he could later retrieve everything from security. But having his own would save him a trip, not to mention having to deal with whatever paperwork was required to obtain copies. "Can you make a list of probable candidates for the leader position? There shouldn't be too many at that level."

"Probably, but what good will it do?"

"The names alone, none. But compiling a file for each of the top players in the game, including a physical description, a set of attributes, a style of command, and any other information you can think of is a critical first step."

Kian cast Andrew an approving look. "You really know your shit, don't you?"

"This is elementary. Information is the most valuable asset there is, and you should always gather as much of it as you can about your adversaries, as well as your allies. True?"

"True," the Doomer agreed. "Give me a pen and some paper, and I'll give it my best shot."

Kian again glanced at Andrew's motionless foot before returning his eyes to the Doomer. "I'll do better than that, I'll give you a laptop."

"A laptop will be great, but I still need a pen and paper if you want me to sketch their portraits for you."

Andrew snorted. "No offense to your doodling skill, my man, but I'd rather have you describe them to a forensic artist."

The Doomer seemed more amused than offended. "Anyone have a piece of paper and a pen?"

"I think I have something." Anandur pushed to his feet and pulled out a folded green piece of paper from his back pocket, then straightened what turned out to be some sort of flyer and handed it to Dalhu. "You can use the back."

Andrew rolled his eyes but produced a pen from his jacket's inside pocket. "Here, knock yourself out."

Dalhu placed the flyer face down on the coffee table and ran his hand over it a couple of times to smooth out the creases, then went to work.

Anandur crouched next to him, while Kian and Andrew leaned forward, all three observing the image Dalhu's fast pen strokes were creating.

"I'll be damned." Anandur was the first to say something as Amanda's face took shape on paper, and Andrew was tempted to echo the sentiment.

It was brilliant, and not only because the depiction was strikingly true. Amanda's spirit—her playful haughtiness, the stubborn tilt of her chin, the shadow of old pain in her eyes—it was all there, black pen strokes on green paper as if the Doomer had glimpsed her soul.

"What? Did I get something wrong?" Dalhu voice was hesitant as he lifted his head to look at Anandur.

"No, nothing. This is fucking amazing." Anandur took the sketch and handed it to Kian. "Take a look at this."

Kian looked at it for a long moment, then handed it back to Dalhu. "Very good. You proved your point. You've got talent."

The guy had proved his point and then some, and Andrew wasn't referring to the Doomer's sketching skill.

Dalhu swallowed. "It's nothing, just a good visual memory and attention to detail, that's all. Useful…" His body began swelling with aggression as his eyes darted between them.

The guy acted as if he had been caught wearing lipstick or ladies' undergarments. Evidently, in Dalhu's camp, artistic ability was not considered as befitting a fighter.

"I sing." Anandur caught on fast. "And I'm damn good." He began a merry tune in what sounded like Old Norse, and by the sparkle in his eyes and expressive hand gestures was about the female form.

He had a good, deep, rumbling voice that only enhanced his masculinity. It wasn't helping.

Well, what the hell. Andrew joined the effort. "Unfortunately, I have no special talent, but I wish I did."

Kian regarded them as if they were idiots. "What these two are trying to say is that your talent is a gift, not something to hide and be embarrassed about. Not here, and not even for a warrior."

Dalhu shrugged. "If you say so, I've never looked at it as anything other than a useful tool."

Anandur clapped the Doomer's back. "I'm no expert, but this is good."

"Enough about that." Kian waved at Anandur to go back to his seat. "I'll get you a laptop and some sketching supplies. Now tell me about the plan."

33

DALHU

For a moment, Dalhu contemplated playing down his part.

But it seemed he had gained some ground with Kian; the waves of hatred the guy had been emitting had subsided, if only marginally. It would be lost once Dalhu admitted to being the mastermind behind this new threat to Kian's family. Except, Dalhu had already admitted everything to the Goddess, and even the slightest subterfuge would undermine his credibility.

And besides, he didn't really care what Kian or the rest of them thought of him. The only one whose opinion he valued had already decided he wasn't worthy.

And yet, even though he knew it to be the honest truth, so had Amanda when she had accepted him before. She'd had no illusions as to who and what he was. So why the change of heart? What had made her flee without even giving him the courtesy of a see-you-in-hell goodbye?

Maybe Kian had lied. Maybe he'd found out about her visit and had made sure it wouldn't happen again.

Yes, that was the only thing that made sense. And if this was indeed the case, all was not lost.

Amanda would find a way.

As he felt the dark cloud of despair lift, Dalhu fought hard to keep his expression impassive. No reason to tip his hand and let Kian suspect he was on to him.

"Start from the beginning. From what you and your team were sent to do and why, to the reason you asked for reinforcements, and what they are planning to do," Andrew clarified.

At first, Dalhu hadn't understood what use the clan could possibly have for a mortal. But he was starting to realize that the guy was a valuable asset. Andrew seemed to know what he was doing and was levelheaded, methodical and thorough—unlike the hot-headed Kian.

Dalhu nodded. "It was retaliation for that computer virus you helped your allies develop. I was to find the team of programmers that made it happen and take out the best one. It was supposed to send you a message; you mess with ours, we will mess with yours. Nothing new there."

"How did you find them?" Andrew asked, and Dalhu noticed just then that the guy was recording everything on his phone.

Smart.

"We had an informant. Not in the programming unit, but somewhere higher up in the defense department. I can't give you a name, though, or even a description, because I never dealt with the guy. The info went to my superior first, and he passed it down to me."

Andrew's brows furrowed. "You guys managed to bribe someone high ranking in the defense department? These people have to go through an extensive vetting process, and I'm sure their finances are closely monitored."

Dalhu shrugged. "I wasn't privy to that kind of information. I was just a field commander of a small unit. But from what I've gathered over the years, there are several ways the Brotherhood goes about it. The best is to raise a mole from the ground up. The Brotherhood recruits promising young boys, who are then brainwashed into supporting whatever cause they invent for them. The recruiters then help them and their families in ways that are hard to detect—ensuring the parents get well-paying jobs, and the boys and their siblings get scholarships to the best universities. Then the Brotherhood waits patiently for them to climb up the ranks. Eventually, a few of the many that were nurtured make it to critical positions."

Andrew whistled. "That's a very long-term approach. Makes sense, though. Time considerations are different for immortals."

Kian got up to refill his glass. "And the other methods?"

"The run-of-the-mill bribes and blackmails."

"Go on. So what happened next?" Kian asked.

Damn, now was the part Dalhu was dreading. "We had the name of the civilian programming unit—the one masquerading as a gaming company—but their offices had the kind of security we had no chance of breaching. And we had no idea who their top programmer was. So we surveyed the building and followed them around for a couple of days. Until one evening, they all went to celebrate at a bar. From there it was easy. Pinpointing the one they were all saluting, following him home, and taking him out."

As Dalhu cast a longing look at Kian's drink, he couldn't help but notice the guy's fingers tightening around the glass. Any moment, the thing would shatter in his hand.

"And no one stopped to question him before killing him? You had an untrained male from your enemy's clan. Why waste such a rare opportunity?" Andrew asked.

"We didn't know he was one of yours. And the guy sent after him had his orders. Fortunately for you, Doomers don't question their orders. Otherwise, your location would have been already compromised."

Although true, he regretted his choice of words. To use the word fortunate in this context had been a mistake. Except, he wasn't a diplomat, and his mastery of the English language didn't include a rich vocabulary.

Judging by the baleful expression on Kian's face, Dalhu wouldn't live long enough to expand it either.

"Indeed." Andrew cast a somber glance at Kian. "I'm sorry for your loss, Kian, but at least the man hadn't been tortured. True?" He pinned Dalhu with a hard stare.

"Just fangs and venom." Dalhu glanced briefly at Kian and felt a pang of guilt.

And envy.

Kian, the leader of Annani's clan, wasn't just angry about losing a great programmer, he was mourning the guy's death. In contrast, no one ever gave a damn about a Doomer's demise.

No one would mourn Dalhu.

Still, the fact was that the clan got more than even. "You took out eleven of mine and have me down here. I think your loss has been avenged."

Damn, it was again the wrong thing to say. Kian looked ready to tear out his throat. "Just do yourself a favor, Doomer, and don't try to equate the two. Clear?" he hissed through his fangs.

As much as Dalhu hated the supercilious jerk, Kian was right. It wasn't the same. Unlike Dalhu and his men, the programmer had not been a fighter. Dalhu bowed his head. "My apologies, you are right."

That seemed to somewhat mollify the guy, and the dangerous glow in his eyes subsided. "How did you know where to find Amanda, though?"

"My men found a framed article about Amanda's research, with a personal dedication from her to the programmer. When they brought it back to me, I had a hunch she was related to the guy and decided to check it out. The presence of Guardians at her lab confirmed my suspicion. But running into her that day on the street was purely coincidental."

A very lucky, fated coincidence.

Kian's face hardened. "How did you know it was her? Did you sense she was an immortal?"

"No, of course not. There is no way to detect immortal females." Dalhu paused as he remembered that he had been compelled to follow Amanda even before recognizing her. "To tell you the truth, I'm not sure. I knew her face from the picture in the article, but I felt the urge to go after her even though all I saw was her retreating back. And not only because she is exquisite from any angle."

The mortal eyed him with open curiosity. "What made you run and leave everything you knew behind, instead of delivering her to your leader?"

"First of all, I would have never handed over an immortal female to my brethren. Second, would you have done differently?"

The guy chuckled. "Good point. Though I'm not in the habit of abducting women when they refuse to come willingly."

Yeah, the human probably had no trouble finding willing candidates for his affections. Still… "You also have no shortage of possible mates. There are probably millions of them in this city alone. I, on the other hand, had this one and only chance, and I was not going to let it get away, even if it went against my own code of honor."

"Wasn't aware Doomers had any," Kian gritted.

"First of all, I'm no longer a Doomer. And second, honor is subjective. And even those who others consider monsters sometimes cling to their own notion of honor."

Kian wasn't impressed. "Good, I see you have no illusions as to what you are."

The condescending prick.

"I might be a monster, but I would have never treated my own sister the way you did yours. No matter what."

As Dalhu's barb hit home, Kian's wince was deeply satisfying.

"We are getting off track here, guys." Andrew raised his palm to halt Kian's retort. "So what happened next?"

Dalhu rubbed his neck. "After the first team encountered Guardians at Amanda's lab, the same night I sent another to search it for clues. They found her journal, which I learned a lot from."

Kian snorted. "Yeah, like the names of her top test subjects, who you tried to snatch."

"Yes. But also that you guys adhere to the old taboo against in-line mating, and with no Dormants of other lines, are all the descendants of one female. Which finally explained your age-old tactic of hiding instead of facing the Brotherhood head-on. There just aren't enough of you."

"So, you decided it wouldn't be all that difficult to hunt us into extinction." The hatred wafting off of Kian was not only pungent but felt like a tangible force—pervasive and oppressive.

Not that Dalhu could fault the guy. He sighed. "Actually, my first response was a grudging respect. Achieving all that you had with so few members is damn impressive."

Kian shifted in his chair. "Glad you approve," he hissed.

"Not at all. In my opinion, you're wasting your efforts. Mortals are not worth it. Their herd mentality is ill-suited for democracy. They're better off being led and controlled. But this is neither here nor there. Anyway, after being bested by your Guardians time and again, I did some thinking and figured that their presence indicated a clan stronghold somewhere around LA. But to find it I didn't need to catch a Guardian. Any immortal would do. And where better to hunt for immortal males than the places they frequent hunting for hookups—bars and clubs. But as there are hundreds of those in this city, I needed more men to conduct an adequate search."

Andrew frowned. "But from what you've said before, your superiors were not sending you more men to command, but replacing you with a higher ranking officer."

34

KIAN

The Doomer chuckled. "I knew they wouldn't leave such an important mission to me, but I hoped to get credit for the idea, maybe even a larger and better-trained unit under my command."

Kian didn't know if he hated the guy more or less for his dispassionate recounting, or for being so absolutely, fucking honest. Andrew's foot hadn't tapped even once, and he'd been watching the thing like a hawk.

Plotting the demise of Kian's family had been just a job for the Doomer, an assignment, an opportunity for advancement. The guy was a cold, opportunistic bastard, nothing more.

What the hell did Amanda see in that thing?

And yet, the Doomer wasn't cold when it came to her. That sketch, more than anything he might have said, proved that the guy not only had feelings for Amanda, but had somehow gotten to know her pretty damn well in the short time he'd had her. And not only in the biblical sense.

And what's worse, Kian had to admit, if grudgingly, that a soulless creature couldn't have imbued his rendering of Amanda with so much life, emotion, and insight.

Andrew touched his phone to stop the recording and got up. "I'm ready for a drink. What can I get you, Dalhu?"

The Doomer looked grateful. "Whatever you're having."

Andrew glanced at Kian. "A refill?"

"Yeah." He got up and handed Andrew his empty glass.

What an asset the guy was turning out to be. How had he managed all this time without him? Andrew practically took over the interrogation and was doing a much better job than Kian would have done.

Evidently, there was something to be said for emotional distance—or maybe proper training.

Dalhu drained his glass, and Andrew poured him another before going back to his chair.

"Okay, let's move on to your fascinating home base." Andrew touched his phone's screen to restart the recording.

"I assume the Goddess has told you what I've told her."

"Yes, we know about the Brotherhood's underground facility, and the world-class brothel your leader runs on the other side of that island. From what I understood, the security is extremely tight, but I want to hear more. Everything from facts to suspicions to guesses. No place is airtight. There must be a way to infiltrate the island."

With Andrew conducting the questioning, Kian leaned back in his chair, not at all minding being relegated to the role of a passive observer.

As far as he was concerned, there was nothing to be gained from this line of questioning anyway.

He wasn't planning on storming his enemy stronghold, no matter how much he despised Doomers, or how much he pitied the enslaved females—mortal and Dormant alike. It just wasn't feasible, and Kian wasn't in the habit of indulging in make-believe scenarios.

"A single human may have a chance, but not an immortal." Dalhu looked at Andrew. "The immortal guards would sniff another immortal right away. He wouldn't get through the first line of security. And although the only way to get in, which is even remotely conceivable, would be as a client, I have no idea how one would go about getting an invitation or even being in the know."

"Who are the typical customers?"

"The rich, powerful and corrupt. From all over the world."

"That doesn't tell me much, could you be more specific?"

"It's not as if I went around asking questions and mingling with the guests. But the girls aren't required to be as tight-lipped with the soldiers as they are with the other clients, and they like nothing more than a piece of juicy gossip. Then again, it's not like the johns introduce themselves by name and title. From what I've garnered, though, they are a diversified crowd; drug lords, arms dealers, oil tycoons, officers of large corporations, politicians, judges, professors, and even the occasional royal."

Andrew frowned. "I bet that it isn't only money your leader collects from his distinguished clientele. Information and favors most likely bring an even greater profit."

No doubt.

Kian was starting to wonder if he hadn't deluded himself over the years, thinking the clan had at least a financial advantage over the Doomers. From what Dalhu was telling them, it seemed Navuh created his own fountain of gold.

But again, although enlightening, the information was useless. "Where are you going with this, Andrew? It's not like we can do anything about it. Even if we can get a mortal in there, what could one guy do?"

"Information, as I've said before, is priceless. And you need as much of it as you can get because you never know when it will become handy. Knowing who the Brotherhood has in its pockets is in itself vital. And even if we can't do anything to help the women already trapped there, maybe we can do something about the supply end of it."

Apparently, there was such a thing as an information addiction, and Andrew had it bad. "I'm sorry, Andrew, but from where I stand, the risk is not worth the potential gain. To me anyway. Our clan is not the government."

Andrew's brows drew tight. "I'm not sure you're right about that. I'll collect what I can from Dalhu and analyze it." He smiled. "You know I would love to sink my teeth into this."

Okay, the guy is both information and adrenaline junkie. "Even if I were willing to risk you on a suicide mission like this, which I'm not, your sister would kill me if I did. So when you think of a plan, don't include yourself in it. Not going to happen."

Andrew pinned him with a hard stare. "Syssi wasn't privy to my missions before, and she is not going to be in the future. And last I checked, I'm not working for you, and you have no authority over me."

"Ahem." Anandur cleared his throat.

Damn. Kian really liked the guy, but Andrew was a pain in the ass —with an iron will and no respect for authority.

Still, he was right about the independent agent status, and it was something Kian intended to remedy as soon as possible. If putting the guy on payroll was going to make him more manageable, Kian would hire him in a heartbeat. "We will discuss this later."

Andrew nodded and turned back to the Doomer.

And what do you know, it was the first time Kian had seen Dalhu smiling.

"Wipe that smirk off your face," Kian barked at him. "And you too." He pointed a finger at Anandur.

"Yes, sir." Anandur saluted and turned his face to the wall, but his heaving shoulders betrayed him.

The Doomer had his head bowed down as if concentrating real hard on the scuff on his boot.

Damn, what did a guy have to do to get some respect…

35

ANDREW

Three hours, God knows how many drinks, and a platter of munchies later, Andrew was finally satisfied that he'd squeezed out of Dalhu all there was to squeeze.

To follow were the profiles of the top players in Navuh's camp, and a map of the island, or rather the parts Dalhu was familiar with.

Not that an infiltration seemed likely.

Unfortunately, Andrew had to agree with Kian. Aside from a spying solo mission, gathering information of a doubtful strategic value, there wasn't much to be gained considering what he'd be risking. Like his head.

Still, he was itching to go.

It was dangerous, and finding who he could blackmail into getting him on the guest list might prove difficult if not impossible. But the idea filled him with renewed vigor and excitement the likes of which he hadn't felt in a long time.

He craved adventure, and Amanda's rescue hadn't even come close to providing enough of a challenge to sate it.

The need to get back the vitality that he felt was leaching out of him at his desk job grabbed him so hard, it overshadowed what he had believed was his quest for Amanda's affections, making a mockery out of it.

Given a choice, he would take the mission and dump Amanda in Dalhu's lap, wishing them the best of luck with a big smile on his face.

And wasn't that a revelation.

Yeah, she was beyond gorgeous, and hot. And competing for her with another man had been a challenge, which he had to admit was part of the lure. But she had not touched his soul the way she had obviously touched Dalhu's. So, even though he still believed himself to be a far better choice for Amanda than the Doomer, and even though with time a deeper connection might've been forged between them, he would be deceiving her and himself if he pretended she had won his heart.

Perhaps she was better off with a lesser man, yet one who loved her with everything he had.

But then, there was Kian.

A big, stubborn obstacle in both Andrew and Amanda's way.

During the long hours of questioning, Kian's attitude toward Dalhu had improved somewhat, and a couple of times he'd even addressed the guy by name instead of spitting the derogative *Doomer*. Yet to hope that he would come around and allow anything between Amanda and Dalhu was ludicrous.

And unless Andrew could come up with a very convincing rationale behind his quest to infiltrate Passion Island, that wasn't going to happen either.

He would most definitely be facing an uphill battle, and so would Amanda if she was still interested in Dalhu.

Though if she was, Andrew doubted even Kian would be able to keep her away from what she wanted. Blood would spill, and Annani would have to put her little, yet formidable foot down to keep her children from tearing each other's throats out.

On a more positive note, Kian had invited Andrew to stop by

tomorrow to discuss the possibility of Andrew's inclusion in the clan's organization. Kian had also instructed Anandur to take Andrew to William, where he'd been given a transmitter to install in his car that would allow him access to the clan's underground parking, and his thumbprint had been taken and encoded into the reader of the clan's private elevators.

So progress had been made—he'd been officially accepted into their inner circle—as evidenced by the fact that he was strolling down the corridor of the basement's top level, unescorted, on his way to the clinic.

Now that he'd decided not to pursue Amanda, nothing prevented Andrew from visiting the lovely Dr. Bridget and letting her give him a checkup, or check him out, or anything else she'd had in mind when she'd invited him the other night to stop by.

In fact, Andrew felt quite proud of himself. Bowing out from the competition was the right thing to do.

He wished Amanda good luck.

Though not a religious man by any stretch of the imagination, he felt like offering her a blessing to echo his own epiphany. *May you find the wisdom to realize your heart's desire, the strength to acknowledge it, and the courage to pursue it.*

DARK
ENEMY
redeemed
THE CHILDREN OF
THE GODS 6
I. T. LUCAS
INTERNATIONALLY BESTSELLING AUTHOR

1

AMANDA

"Are you sure? Not a single karaoke machine?"

Freaking Lana probably hadn't bothered to even look for it.

"*Niet,* I found one in a bar, but the owner not want to sell."

"How much did you offer?"

"Two thousand."

"You should've offered more."

"We buy the vodka and the fish you want, and this was all the money left from what you give me."

While the *Anna* moored for the night in Avalon harbor, Amanda had sent Lana and Sonia with instructions to buy supplies and find a karaoke—whatever the cost. Because c'mon, a party wasn't a party without one.

Especially since this one would be missing the most important element—hunky guys.

Regrettably, though, twenty-three hundred and some change in cash had been all she'd had on her, and the Russians had refused to take her credit card.

The obvious solution would've been to go with them, but she preferred to stay on board—not only because their company was such a dubious pleasure, but because she dreaded encountering horny males and their lustful, leering looks.

Which was sure to happen if she were to grace the streets of Avalon.

There was a price to be paid for beauty, and enduring leering glances from men wasn't even the worst of it—heck, most of the time she didn't mind.

Topping the list were the resentful looks from other females, followed closely by the presumption that all beautiful women were airheads.

Come to think of it, most people, males and females alike, found her looks intimidating.

So yeah, she had been enduring leering glances since she was scarcely a pubescent girl, but they hadn't bothered her before—on the contrary, most times she'd found them arousing.

But nothing was as it used to be.

She was horny, but at the same time felt nauseated by the prospect of a meaningless hookup. And earlier, during her afternoon *nap*, when she'd given self-pleasuring a halfhearted try, it had been more of the same.

Because there was only one male she was able to fantasize about, but the guilt and loathing associated with her attraction to Dalhu weren't exactly conducive to that particular activity.

Shit. It was hell, and it seemed she was going to be stuck in this purgatory for the foreseeable future.

Oh, well, there was nothing to be done about it, except giving it time.

Besides, as the *Anna* swayed gently on the pull and ebb of the tide, lying on a lounger on her top deck wasn't exactly a torment. And the fishy, salty smell of the murky waters wasn't all that bad either. Actually, it could have been quite pleasant if not for the diesel fumes wafting up from the boat's engines.

Fates, how she missed the era of old-fashioned sailboats. The experience had been completely different—the ocean had smelled wonderful—unpolluted.

On the other hand, there was something to be said for the speed, luxury, and modern amenities of the *Anna.*

This was the thing about life—nothing was ever perfect, and to gain one thing you often had to sacrifice another.

And wasn't that the inconvenient truth.

She'd found spending the day with a good book relaxing and would've loved to keep on reading, but the sun was getting low on the horizon, and even though the drop in temperature wasn't all that significant, it was getting too chilly for lounging in a string bikini.

With a sigh, Amanda closed her book and padded inside.

Back in her cabin, she eyed her laptop. Maybe she should check her e-mail to see if the design ideas for Syssi's wedding gown were ready.

Joann had been amazing, as always, and had contacted all of her designer friends, asking if they'd be willing to do a rush job. But with less than two weeks from idea to final fitting, only two had accepted the challenge of creating an original, breathtaking masterpiece for Amanda's best girl.

Nothing less than spectacular would do for Syssi.

With a frown, Amanda wondered if anyone had remembered Kian. After all, the groom also needed something new and fabulous for the event. Unless her brother was planning on showing up at the altar in his fancy Regent robe.

Yeah, right, she chuckled. In her opinion, he looked dashing in it, regal, but she was well aware that Kian detested the thing.

Maybe she should call him and suggest the robe. At first, Kian would blow up, but then he'd realize it was a joke and they would have a good laugh about it.

Or maybe not.

Amanda plopped down on the king-sized bed and crossed her arms over her eyes. She was dimly aware that the suntan oil she was covered with would leave a sticky imprint on the sheets, but she just didn't give a damn.

Who cared about bed linens when she was contemplating the depressing prospect of never regaining the easygoing, loving relationship she and Kian had enjoyed prior to this whole ugly mess.

Her hand reached for the phone, and she was tempted to hit his number.

But what would she say to him? Ask for his forgiveness?

If she believed it would mend things between them, she would've done it in a heartbeat. Pride, or who was right and who was wrong, was of no consequence when the stakes were so high.

Amanda just wanted her brother back.

Instead, she selected Syssi's number.

"Just a sec"—Syssi answered after the first ring—"let me get someone off the other line."

"Take your time."

Syssi came back after a few moments, puffing as if she'd been running. "I'm all yours."

"What's going on? You sound harried."

"You think? You try planning a wedding for six hundred guests. Neither your mother nor I have any experience in organizing events. And before you ask, no wedding coordinator worth her salt will take the job on such short notice. Ugh, it's going to be a disaster."

Amanda smiled. "Who's the drama queen now? Relax, it's going to be amazing. It shouldn't be all that difficult to arrange for good food, lively music, tasteful decorations, and most importantly—a gorgeous wedding dress."

"Yeah? The way things are going it seems Okidu will have to cook, decorate, and sew the dress. Because every caterer and florist

I've called has practically laughed in my face. I had no idea these people are booked months in advance—some even years."

"This is actually a splendid idea. Between Okidu and Onidu and my mother's two, the Odus will have no problem pulling it off. All you need to do is give them a menu, including the recipes, show them pictures of how you want it to look, and they will take it from there."

"You must be kidding, right?"

"I'm dead serious. They can do all of it, except for the dress, which I've got covered."

"Oh, yeah? Do tell."

"Hold on, I'm checking my e-mail. Joann, bless her soul, found not one, but two designers who were willing to take on the challenge, and I'm waiting for the initial sketches." She quickly scrolled through her inbox, but there was nothing from Joann. "Nope... nothing yet. As soon as I have something, I'll forward it to you."

"That's wonderful, thank you. Joann has impeccable taste, I trust her completely."

"Good, I was afraid you'd hate me for not checking with you before talking to her."

"Nah, after outfitting me with an entire wardrobe of fabulous, I trust her to come up with something I can't even imagine. I'm all for letting the pros do their thing. One less item to worry about."

"Poor Syssi, you sound as excited about this wedding as if it was somebody else's."

"I know, right? I hate big events, and being at the center of one is my personal idea of hell. If it were up to me, it would've been just Kian and me, you, Andrew, and Annani. That's it."

"Really? What about your parents? And my sisters Sari and Alena? And the Guardians? And William and Bridget?"

"Okay, them too, but that's it, no one else."

"Oh, sweetie, don't you see? You might be happy with only our immediate families and the few people you know and care for witnessing your joining, but Kian wants, needs, each and every member of the clan to be there."

"I know. That's why I'm still here and not running off screaming." Syssi let out a huff.

"By the way, speaking of Kian, did anyone remember to get him fitted for a tux for the wedding? If you leave it up to him, he'll show up wearing one of his old business suits."

"You're right. God, I can't believe I didn't think of it." Syssi heaved a sigh. "Just another reminder of how little I know about the man I'm going to marry in thirteen days."

"You know everything that really matters, and you have endless time to learn the rest. So, stop fretting. Kian is a great guy—bad temper and all."

"Yeah, I know... but speaking of your brother's *sunny* disposition,",Syssi switched to a whisper, "Kian spent the entire evening with Dalhu and came back... well, I wouldn't say happy, but not enraged either. I think it's an encouraging sign."

Amanda chuckled. "I guess it is—by Kian's standards. Did you ask him what they talked about?" She wasn't curious, not at all...

"He gave me no chance, planting one hot kiss on my mouth and heading straight to his office to grab a file for his next meeting. But I'll grill him later tonight and report to you tomorrow."

In spite of herself, Amanda felt her heart give a little flutter. Kian must've been in at least a decent mood if the first thing he had done after spending hours with Dalhu was to kiss Syssi.

"Deal. First thing in the morning."

"Are you sure you want me to call you that early? You might be too hungover to talk after your drinking party with the Russians."

"Oh, please, I'll be fine. I'll have them drunk and singing in more ways than one before I'm even tipsy."

Syssi snorted. "If you say so."

"I've got it covered."

Well, almost. Without the karaoke, she would have to make a playlist on her phone and hook it up to the sound system in the grand salon, then hand out printouts of the lyrics to the girls.

Russian songs would have been the best, but unfortunately, although she spoke it with decent fluency, Amanda never bothered to learn to read the Cyrillic script—and mastering it in a span of a couple of hours was a feat that even she couldn't pull off.

2

ANDREW

As Andrew knocked on the clinic's door, it crossed his mind that it was late and chances were that Dr. Bridget had already gone home.

Disappointed, he gave it one last go and knocked again, then waited. After all, he was already there, and it wasn't as if there was somewhere else he needed to be.

Calling it a night and heading back to his empty house was no more appealing than standing in this deserted corridor and waiting for a woman that might not even be there to let him in.

Kind of pathetic.

The life of a bachelor was not everything the married guys believed it to be.

True, he was free to shag whomever he was able to seduce—and there was no shortage of those—but most nights it just meant that he ended up going home alone.

That's why Syssi's news about the wedding hadn't been such a big surprise—not for him anyway—he'd been expecting it. Though maybe not so soon. He could empathize with Kian's desire to end his lonely bachelor life the moment he'd found the right woman to spend eternity with.

Andrew couldn't even imagine what it must have been like for the guy, spending endless years without someone to share his life with.

He was happy for them, he really was, but he couldn't help feeling a little jealous—even though his single status wasn't anybody's fault but his. And the excuse of his chosen occupation precluding meaningful relationships was just that—an excuse. Somehow it hadn't stopped his comrades from tying the knot.

Problem was, he'd never dated a woman he could imagine spending his life with, and not because none were good enough. Andrew suspected that the flaw was within him—he was either emotionally stunted or just too picky.

Another minute passed, and he was about to turn on his heel and head back when the door finally opened to reveal a surprised Dr. Bridget—the red handbag clutched under her arm betokening that she was on her way out.

Wow! Can you say sexy?

Gone was the conservative doctor, and the woman that had taken her place was hot. Bridget looked ready for action—with her wavy red hair loose around her shoulders and her curvy figure encased in a pair of skin-tight jeans and a clingy red T-shirt. But what had really done it for him were the red, fuck-me heels.

Evidently, Bridget loved to flaunt her red.

Trying hard to look into her pretty eyes and not glance down to peer at her ample cleavage, Andrew ran his hand over his mouth. Who could've guessed the petite physician had been hiding all of this under her doctor's coat?

"I'm sorry, I should have realized it was late. I'll stop by some other time, earlier in the day."

Her eyes widened, and she grabbed his hand, giving a strong tug. "Nonsense, you are coming with me." She pulled him behind her as she went inside and flipped the lights back on. There was a sly little smile on her lovely face as she turned around and looked up. "I'm not going to waste the opportunity of you coming to see me of your own volition. I thought I'd have to drag you here by force."

Andrew was about to snort at the ridiculous idea of her forcing him to do anything when it occurred to him that although tiny, she might be stronger than him. He hadn't resisted when she'd pulled, but still, it had been one hell of a tug.

Did it make her any less appealing? Hell, no, quite the opposite. "You underestimate your charms, Dr. Bridget. There is nowhere I'd rather be than here, with you."

A lovely blush blossomed over her pale porcelain cheeks, and she glanced away. But that sly smile was still there when she returned her eyes to his face. "Quite the charmer, aren't you? I bet you make all the ladies swoon."

Andrew chuckled. "Hardly." He let her lead him to an examination table and sat down.

"Take off your jacket and your shirt," she said and reached for her stethoscope.

"What? Already? I was hoping for a nice dinner and a pleasant conversation before you got me to undress for you," he teased as he shrugged off his jacket, folded it, and put it beside him on the table, then tackled the buttons on his shirt.

Bridget smiled, the pink blush refusing to abandon her face. "I'll take you up on the offer of dinner and flirtatious chitchat, but first, I'm going to check you out." She winked, her blue eyes sparkling with mischief.

"I'm all yours, Doctor." Andrew shrugged his shirt off, making sure to suck in his gut and flex as he exposed his torso to her gaze. He was in good shape and carried no excess fat. Nevertheless, he didn't have the body of a twenty-year-old either. Not to mention the many scars—some small, some large—scattered over his chest and abdomen as well as his back. And the sparse hair on his chest wasn't enough to hide even the smaller ones.

Bridget let go of the stethoscope and let it hang around her neck. Getting closer, she reached with gentle fingers to touch an old bullet scar. "You lived dangerously, didn't you?" she whispered, trailing her fingers over some of the others.

Thank God, it hadn't been pity that he'd heard in her voice, more like admiration. Or at least he hoped it was the latter. "You could say so."

"You know, once you turn, your body would probably heal these, even the older ones." She let her hand drop, but her eyes trailed over his front, making a tally, and she glanced behind him to look at the scars on his back.

"Would you like me better without them?" he teased, her scrutiny making him uncomfortable.

"I like you either way, with or without, how about that?" She plugged her ears and palmed the chest piece of the stethoscope. "Okay, breathe in... breathe out..."

He did as instructed, using the opportunity to sniff her hair as she leaned over him. Nice, some mild flowery scent, sweet and feminine, like Bridget herself. There was something very attractive about a soft, small woman that at the same time was a capable physician with a no-nonsense attitude and a strong personality.

"Perfect." She took the earpieces out and put the stethoscope away. "Okay, now shuck the pants."

"What? Why?" If Bridget was thinking about administering a prostate exam, she should think again.

"Got you!" She giggled. "You should have seen your face... the sheer horror... Though come on, it's not like you have something I haven't seen before."

Devilish woman. "First of all, how do you know I don't?" He cocked a brow.

"Yeah, yeah, I'm sure you're hung like a horse..." Bridget pushed at his chest to have him lie down. "And what's the second thing?"

"If I'm to let you poke me where the sun doesn't shine, it would only be after I've been naked in your bed first and have done some poking of my own."

Her cheeks pinked again. "My, oh my, what a naughty boy you are...," she murmured as she palpated his abdomen.

"You have no idea." He caught her hand and gave a tug, pulling her down on top of him. "Permission to kiss the doctor," he breathed a fraction of an inch away from her mouth.

"Permission granted," she said against his lips, then kissed him.

Tentative at first, it was no more than a brush of her lush lips against his, but as he closed his palm around her nape and drew her closer, she let out a moan and licked into his mouth.

His hands gentle as he caressed her back, Andrew wrestled with the urge to grab hold of Bridget and flip her under him. But she was so tiny compared to him, and he was afraid that letting out his hunger might overwhelm her.

Better let her set the pace.

Except, he wasn't sure how long his restraint would hold under Bridget's onslaught. She was kissing him and writhing on top of him with the abandon and urgency of a woman who knew exactly what she wanted and was starved of it. Her fingers seeking purchase on his short hair, she held him as she kissed him, her hips rocking over his hard shaft, setting him on fire.

"God, Bridget, I need you naked," he heard himself murmur against her lips as his arms tightened around her.

Fuck, he hadn't meant to say it out loud, and he hadn't meant to squash her to him either. But damn, it felt good— feeling her sweet little nipples getting so hard that they rubbed at his bare chest through her clothes. With a herculean effort, he eased his hold.

"Your wish is my command," she purred and reared up to her knees. Straddling his hips—her seductive smirk promised anything but demure obedience. She grabbed the hem of her red T-shirt and tugged it over her head, revealing creamy breasts covered by a sheer red bra that left nothing to the imagination. A moment later, it joined the shirt on the floor.

As if possessing a mind of their own, his hands reached and palmed the perky beauties.

"You're gorgeous."

She leaned into his touch, her eyes hooded. "Hold nothing back, Andrew, I'm a lot tougher than I look."

Okay...

She was under him in a flash.

"Better?" He smiled down at her before dipping his head to nuzzle her neck.

"Yes..." She arched into him, rubbing her breasts against his chest. "Oh, yes...just like that," she groaned as he slid down and licked around one nipple, then gasped as he sucked it in. "But it would be even better without the pants."

"Under one condition." He blew on her swollen, wet peak.

She arched a brow.

"The fuck-me red shoes stay on."

3

AMANDA

"*Salute!*" Geneva raised her glass with an annoyingly steady hand.

Not quite drunk yet, Amanda might've been in better shape than her drinking buddies, but she was on her way to seriously tipsy. It was all good, though. Her plan was working—the atmosphere in the grand salon was becoming decidedly cheerful.

Situated on the main deck, the place was truly grand—in size as well as luxury. The sleek sofa in winter-white-colored leather was a custom-built beauty that could easily seat six, and it faced a glass coffee table of enormous proportions. Two brown overstuffed leather chairs completed the sitting area.

An oblong milky glass top and a wooden pedestal shaped like a tree trunk with sinewy branches comprised the dining table. Fourteen chairs, done in the same winter-white leather as the sofa, surrounded it.

The party had started with dinner, and the crew's mood had been steadily improving thanks to the bottle and a half of vodka she and her new friends had gone through—each.

Amanda could've enjoyed herself for real, if not for the stink coming off the grilled fish. The requisite butter-smothered potatoes didn't smell good, but not as bad.

As for her own culinary preferences, she'd been served a dish of string beans along with Renata's disgusted sneer. Apparently, green wasn't a color the crew appreciated anywhere near their plates. Renata's grilled tilapia, however, had been a big success with the girls.

A vegetarian hanging out with a bunch of Russians was like a nun in a bikers' bar—a page out of a find-the-one-thing-that-doesn't-belong game.

After dinner, they moved to the sitting area for the entertainment portion of the evening, and the girls humored her by giving a couple of the songs she'd prepared a halfhearted try. But then Sonia dropped the printed page on the glass table and began bellowing an old Russian Red Army song. Kristina and Lana joined her, and the three tried to harmonize.

They were either drunker than they looked or tone deaf. Except, it seemed that the painful cacophony didn't bother anyone but Amanda—the girls were having fun.

The only one who remained somber was Marta, a stocky woman with thick arms and wide shoulders and a scowl that was impressive even for a Russian. Her bushy brows, which looked like they'd never been touched by a pair of tweezers, were drawn tight despite the amount of alcohol she'd poured into her belly.

"Salute!" Amanda tossed back another shot, schooling her face not to show a grimace. The fact that she could handle a lot of vodka didn't mean she liked it—not unless it was mixed with something sweet and fruity. But to gain the Russians' respect, she had to drink it the way they did—straight up.

Pushing up to her feet, Amanda held onto the table as she refilled her glass—more for show than any real need. Her balance was still fine, thank you very much.

"To Alex! A great boss!" *Let's see what they think of their employer.*

"To Alexander!" The women all stood up for this one and tapped each other's glasses with loud clinks.

Interesting, they seem to like him.

Amanda plopped down on her chair, exaggerating her movements only a little—after all, good acting required subtlety. "So, tell me, Geneva, how did the bunch of you end up working for my cousin?"

"You are Alexander's cousin? He didn't tell me." Geneva eyed her with suspicion.

"What did he tell you then? That I'm his girlfriend?" Amanda snorted.

"No, just that you are an important guest and to be nice to you."

"Don't tell me you treat his other guests even worse. Because if that's the best you can do, well..."

Lana harrumphed which earned her a scowl from Geneva.

Amanda pretended not to notice. But c'mon, were they supposed to be nasty to Alex's guests?

Geneva waved a dismissive hand. "Alexander doesn't have guests."

"What, not even girlfriends?" That was weird. What was the point of having a luxury yacht if not to impress others? Especially women?

Kristina giggled, Sonia snorted, and even Geneva was trying to hide a smile.

"What? I know he isn't gay. I've seen him with enough females to fill a stadium, so there is no way."

That statement seemed to sour their good mood. "No, Alexander is definitely not gay," Geneva bit out, then reached for her bottle, refilled her glass, and tossed it back without a salute.

Holy Fates, Alex must've really meant it when he'd said they were his girls. He was really screwing his crew, and not out of wages.

Amanda narrowed her eyes and looked from one face to another, but none would meet her gaze. "So, which one of you is he shagging, or is it all of you?"

"Why? What do you care? You're supposed to be his cousin, not his girlfriend." Geneva crossed her muscular arms over her chest, leveling a pair of intense gray eyes on Amanda.

Tough cookie, and quite pretty if one looked past the scowl, the very short hair, and the lack of makeup. Like those of a lot of Russians, her lips were full and fleshy. High, defined cheekbones hinted at some Asian genes in the mix, as did the almost pure black of her hair and the lack of a defined separation between the lower and upper lid. The rest was typical Slavic though—the very pale skin and big gray eyes, as well as the large breasts and the narrow hips.

"I don't. As far as I'm concerned, you can all be having big, multi-limb orgies. It's just that I thought you girls were into other girls, not guys, or a particular guy as it seems to be the case here."

Geneva snorted, then her wide shoulders began shaking, and she burst out laughing. Soon, the whole table was shaking as the other women joined in, laughing and banging their hands on the table.

"You think we lesbians?" Lana managed between giggles. "Why?"

"Duh, the buzz cuts, the big muscles..."

"Ah..." Lana exchanged smug looks with her shipmates. "Is because we are wrestlers." She banged her fist on her chest. "Strong muscles for fighting, and no long hair to grab...*Dah*?"

"Like in the Olympics? I didn't know they had women wrestling."

"Not in the Olympics"—Geneva chuckled—"in the mud."

"Mud wrestling? Get out of here!"

"Mud wrestling good money in Russia," Marta said with a heavy accent—her first words ever to Amanda.

"How did a team of Russian mud-wrestlers end up as crew on an American yacht?"

"Russian yacht. Alexander bought her in St. Petersburg."

"And?"

"We were working in a club, and Alexander came to watch," Kristina said with a quick glance at Geneva.

The captain lifted her palm to reassure her no harm was done. "It's okay. I'll tell the story."

"We were working nights in the club. A lot of men come to watch —Russians and foreigners. It is a very popular thing, more popular than strip clubs, better money too. The men think it's hot—strong women, practically naked in the mud, fighting each other, not just for show, but for real. They place bets, and some pay for private services later on."

"Just say it," Lana interfered. "They pay for sex. It's really good money, and working as a *prostitutka* is not a big deal in Russia. No shame."

Geneva shrugged. "Alexander came to watch one evening and paid for all of us to come to his hotel suite after we were done. We laughed on our way there. Crazy American, what was he going to do with the six of us? Sonia thought that he might want to watch us with each other. Some men do, you know..." She glanced at Amanda.

"Sure." Amanda nodded, stifling a smile. She could just imagine their surprise when Alex had shagged each and every one of them and then had gone for seconds.

"But Alexander is not an ordinary man—" Geneva shook her head.

You have no idea...

Renata harrumphed, "A sex machine..."

"Yes, so after he pleasured us, one at a time, two at a time, then again and again, he let us sleep over at his luxurious suite. It was the largest one in the hotel, top floor, two bedrooms, two bathrooms, a living room, kitchen, dining room, everything. In the morning, when he had breakfast delivered to us, we were ready to worship him as God." Geneva smirked.

"And sing ballads to his glorious manhood." Lana saluted with another drink.

"Over breakfast, he said he would like us to come work for him on his yacht. I asked as what? Prostitutes for his guests? I thought he planned to have a floating brothel. Not a bad idea, by the way. But he said he wasn't going to offer us to any other men, we were to operate his new yacht and serve only him. I asked how much he would pay. His offer was good, especially since he promised to take care of our legal status in the United States." Geneva ended her tale with another shrug. "And here we are."

Obviously, this wasn't the whole story. Alex had no need for a personal harem. There were plenty of readily available females at the club who were more than willing to share his bed. And besides, he was not known as a generous employer. For his offer to be good enough to cover what the women had been making from prostitution, he must've expected more than sex from them—and running the yacht as an added bonus wasn't it, or at least not entirely.

The question was what? And how to get them to spill? Geneva was still perfectly lucid despite the second bottle of vodka.

"I don't understand, though. It's not like being a captain of a vessel this size is something one learns in a day."

"No, I already had a license, and the club owner must've told Alexander. Not that it was a big secret or anything; everybody knew I was saving up to buy a small cruiser. I was planning to run dinner tours out of St. Petersburg. That's why I was working at the club. It was the only way to make enough money for it. Renata was saving up too. She was going to be my partner and the chef."

"Then Alex's offer must have seemed like a godsend to you guys."

"Exactly."

Geneva's choice of adjective indicated certainty, but her tone didn't, and a barely perceptible shadow of regret crossed her impassive face.

But why?

This job was a big step up from her previous one, and several steps closer to her dream.

Perhaps she resented having to sleep with Alex as part of her new job description. Except, the woman seemed genuinely impressed with the guy's bedroom skills.

"Is sharing him okay with you, though?"

Geneva shrugged again. "It's not as if any of us has fallen in love with him or anything. And none of us is in a big hurry to find a decent man of her own—if such a creature even exists. It's just business. Just until we make enough money to make a new life for ourselves here. We like it in America. We want to stay. But with a fresh start—leave our old lives behind and start over clean."

Amanda nodded and poured another shot. "To new beginnings!" She saluted, and the women joined her with an enthusiastic one of their own.

Fascinating story, but what did it hint at? Other than Alex's fetish for mud-covered females, that is?

The most likely scenario she could think of was that he was using the yacht to smuggle drugs. Alex must've figured that an all female crew would be less suspicious—or, that as females with a shady past and questionable legal status the Russians would be easier to control.

And in case the *Anna* ran into trouble, they were certainly not helpless either.

But for some reason, she had a nagging suspicion that it wasn't about drugs, at least not exclusively. There were much easier ways, not to mention less costly, to smuggle illegal substances.

Then what?

Maybe illegal aliens?

Except, she was pretty sure that smuggling illegals wasn't all that profitable.

Unless, the illegal aliens were the big money types, who liked to travel in style.

Drug lords? Mafiosi?

Recalling her conversation with Syssi, Amanda chuckled. *Kian a mafioso, really...* as if her uptight, do-gooder brother fit the profile. But Alex kind of did. And although Amanda thought he was okay,

Syssi's opinion of the guy differed—she thought he was a major creep.

So yeah, that must've been the story behind the *Anna* and her peculiar crew. Alex was using the boat to smuggle wealthy criminals in and out of the United States, and probably drugs too.

She had no proof, though.

Unlike Kian, Amanda wasn't a do-gooder and, therefore, didn't feel morally outraged at Alex's alleged criminal activity. Not that she condoned it, but still, Alex was a friend who'd graciously loaned her the use of his boat.

Should she share her suspicions with Kian? Or should she keep them to herself—at least until she uncovered some solid evidence?

After all, to add fuel to her brother's antipathy toward Alex—based on a mere hunch—wouldn't be the right thing to do either.

Or would it?

To tattle on Alex without proof was bad. Except, how on earth was she going to get it? And even if she looked and failed to find any incriminating evidence, it wouldn't necessarily mean that there was none. After all, she was not an investigator.

If she chose not to confide in Kian because she had no proof, no one would even know that there was something fishy going on that required further looking into.

Damn, once again she was torn between two options—neither of them good.

Not that telling or not telling on Alex was in the same category as her other dilemma—it was like comparing shoplifting to armed robbery. Because craving the man who had ordered her nephew's murder was worse than any alleged smuggling. It was disgraceful, even revolting, but on the other hand, keeping away from him was hell.

4

SYSSI

Damn, the man is fine, Syssi thought for the umpteenth time as she watched Kian walk into the bedroom with nothing but a towel wrapped around his hips. From the harsh lines of his gorgeous face to the ripple of his muscles, as he moved with that unnatural fluidity of his, he was so sexy that he took her breath away.

With all this glorious, male perfection scrambling her brain into a horny mush, her plan to ask about his meeting with Dalhu was shoved aside.

After all, a girl had to have her priorities straight, and as a blast of desire hit her breasts and landed between her thighs, guess what made it to the top of the list?

"Come here," she breathed, beckoning him to her with a crooked finger.

Kian dropped the towel. "Like what you see, sweet girl?"

Oh, yes, she liked.

Fully erect and ready for action, her man was magnificent. "You know I do. You are such a show-off," she teased.

"And you're not naked." Kian stalked closer.

"That could be easily remedied." She pulled her nightshirt over her head and tossed it to the floor, then shimmied out of her panties. "Catch." She aimed at his smirking face.

He caught them, shaking his head at the simple undergarment dangling from his fingers. "Cotton?"

What's wrong with that? Did he expect her to sleep in a lacy thong? *Not this girl.*

"Cotton is breathable and comfortable."

With a wicked smile, he mounted her, his hands pinning her wrists over her head. "But not as breathable as having nothing on at all. If I can't have you naked all of the time, I want you to at least sleep in the nude."

She parted her legs to cradle him between her thighs. "If I wear nothing to bed, you wouldn't let me sleep at all."

"True, that." He pressed a kiss to the side of her neck, then licked the same spot.

As his hot shaft rubbed against her mound, his hips surging and retreating, Syssi closed her eyes and let herself slide into submission—her body liquefying under his. She no longer had to struggle to find that special place inside her head that allowed her to let go. Like a meditative state, once attained, she could now ease into it effortlessly.

The effect was almost euphoric.

"My sweet Syssi," Kian breathed, his tender, loving voice prompting her to lift her lids and look at him.

His beautiful eyes were glowing, but even their otherworldly luminescence wasn't as breathtaking as the love shining through.

"I love you," she whispered, wishing there was a word not as overused to express the magnitude of what was in her heart. Like an all-consuming fire, it was more than the physical attraction, more than appreciation for this amazing man, more than her need to be with him—begrudging every moment of his time away from her—and even more than his feelings for her that ran just as deep.

It was like the sum was greater than the parts. And what's more, the maelstrom of emotion no longer terrified her.

Maybe it was the upcoming wedding that had finally put her fears and insecurities to rest—their bond solidifying once the decision to have their commitment to each other witnessed and confirmed had been made.

But why?

What power did a piece of paper have? One that she was pretty sure wouldn't even be deemed legal in any mortal court?

Shouldn't their pledge to each other be enough? What additional validation did a marriage ceremony provide?

She used to believe that marriage was about a legal contract spelling out the obligations and responsibilities of two people engaged in the business of raising a family and sharing a household. But apparently, there was some metaphysical aspect to this age-old tradition as well.

And yet, observing the many corrosive relationships and failed marriages, she had to wonder if this elusive aspect had been either absent from them to begin with or just too easily broken.

She and Kian must be among the uniquely blessed—those who God or fate or dumb luck joined in a true love match.

Yeah, she was one lucky girl.

"What is this secretive smile all about, my love?"

"I'm happy that we are getting married."

"Yeah? What brought that about? Seeing my sexy body? My impressive size?" he teased, giving his hips a wicked twist that had the aforementioned sizable part rub her just the right way.

She arched into him. "All of the above and more. I'm just glad you are mine to keep."

"And you are mine." He nuzzled her neck. "To keep." His mouth trailed south. "To love." He licked at her nipple. "And to hold." He licked the other one. "And to make love to, again, and again…"

5

AMANDA

"O *bo´ze moy, o bo´ze moy, o bo´ze moy, ya ydu hority v pekli...*" —Oh my God, oh my God, oh my God, I'm going to burn in hell—Marta was chanting over and over in Ukrainian, clutching her knees and rocking back and forth on the floor. Early into her third bottle, the woman had broken down, scooting into a corner to sob her heart out.

Renata had gone to sit with her, whispering calming words into her ear until the tears had dried out, but the chanting hadn't ceased.

Was Marta lamenting her whoring days? Or fearing her god's punishment for participating in drug trafficking?

Geneva ignored her fallen comrade. "You are going to lose, American," she said and pounded back another shot.

"Not a chance, Ruska." Amanda followed with her own.

She had been pretending to be wasted for the past hour or so, as she and Geneva—the last two standing, or rather sprawling as it were—had gone one to one on their third bottle of vodka.

Not that she had remained unaffected, but with her higher tolerance for alcohol and lesser need for sleep, there had been no doubt in her mind that the mortal would succumb first to the powerful combination of alcohol and exhaustion.

Mercifully, the chanting stopped, and Marta's head fell on Renata's shoulder.

Only two more shots to go. Amanda eyed her nearly empty bottle.

She had been sure Geneva would pass out by now, but the woman was proving to be stubbornly resilient.

"I finish first." Geneva's mumble was barely audible as her last empty glass clunked against the table.

Amanda emptied hers as well. "It's a draw," she slurred.

Closing her eyes and pretending to sleep, she waited until the captain slumped against Lana, joining her friend in a snoring duet.

With the crew finally asleep, passed out over sofas and chairs and the floor of the grand salon, Amanda was presented with a perfect opportunity to search for proof of Alex's illicit endeavors.

Trouble was, by now she was way beyond tipsy and into really drunk territory, not to mention exhausted. It was nearly morning, and outside the main deck's windows the sky was already pinking with the rising sun.

Okay, Mata Hari, time to investigate.

Amanda pushed to her feet and stood on legs that felt like two rubber noodles. Carefully, she took the stairs down, holding on to the banister as she placed one bare foot in front of the other. Her head was spinning, and the sway of the boat was not helping with her rising nausea. Still, she somehow made it to the lower deck without puking all over the pretty glass staircase.

Since Amanda had appropriated Alex's cabin—the large and luxurious master suite on the main deck—she'd been down to the lower deck only once to check out the fitness room that was right by the staircase. But she remembered Geneva telling her that the four guest cabins were in the front and the three crew cabins were in the back, or stern—if she remembered her boating terminology.

She decided to investigate the guest cabins first. Two were

outfitted with queen beds and the other two with two twins each, but from the looks of things no one had slept in either of them since the yacht had been bought and redecorated. There were no towels or even toilet paper in the bathrooms, and although the beds were made with clean bedding and elegant duvets, it was obvious that the things were brand new and had never been washed. The sheets and pillowcases still had creases from the original packaging and stank of the formaldehyde the fabrics had been treated with.

After checking the closets and banging on the walls, the floors, and the ceilings, she had to accept that there was nothing hidden in the guest portion of the lower deck, and moved on to the crew cabins. Naturally, those looked lived in, and though a far cry from the fancy guest rooms, they were nonetheless comfortable. Each cabin had an adjacent bathroom. Those were small, with just a shower stall, a sink and a toilet.

Two of the rooms were shared, and one was a single. Recognizing the particular scent of each woman, Amanda had no trouble figuring out who slept where. Renata and Marta shared one, Sonia and Kristina the second, and surly Lana had a cabin of her own—probably because no one wanted to room with her and her attitude.

Unfortunately, Amanda's snoop of the crew cabins didn't produce any hidden compartments either.

Going for another round, she checked that the dividing walls corresponded to the cabin sizes with no significant gaps in between them.

But everything seemed kosher.

There was no space that could accommodate a hiding place big enough for one person, let alone several.

Geneva's captain cabin was on the upper deck next to the wheelhouse, but there was little chance Amanda would find what she was looking for up there—too public.

It didn't make sense.

Not unless she was wrong and Alex didn't smuggle people.

Because even if there was a small secret compartment she hadn't discovered yet, it would have been used only in the rare occurrence of the yacht being boarded for inspection. At all other times, the guest or guests would have been staying in the cabins, which they obviously hadn't.

Unless they were staying with Alex at his master cabin. Which was ludicrous. Wealthy master criminals were almost exclusively male, and Alex didn't swing that way.

That left only the under deck.

Taking the narrow stairs down to the service area, Amanda ducked into the engine room, then continued to survey everything from the stabilizer fins, bow-thrusters, and other machinery, to the washers, dryers, refrigerators, and she even poked her head into the large double door freezer.

Nothing.

Shit.

She climbed the stairs back to the main deck, bypassing the salon where her drinking buddies were still sprawled out, and heading straight for her cabin. Maybe a shower would clear her head and lift the drunken fog, because there was no doubt in her mind that she was missing something.

Shimmying out of her jeans and thong, she dropped them in the pullout laundry bin. Her T-shirt was next.

Cold water would have been best, but Amanda was in no shape for self-inflicted torture. A warm shower would have to do. The hot spray was divine, and she braced her arms against the marble wall, dipping her head and letting the water pound her spine.

If Alex had been smuggling people, they must've stayed in the master cabin…

Of course, she slapped her hand on her forehead. It was so simple that she must have been really drunk not to figure it out right away.

While a guest stayed in Alex's cabin, Alex stayed with Geneva at hers.

It probably wasn't as luxurious as this one, but it was most likely just as spacious and elegant as the guest cabin—captain's quarters on a boat this size usually were. Or, he might have even taken over her cabin and sent her down to room with Lana. There was a spare bed in her cabin.

That way, if the yacht were boarded for inspection, it would look as if no one aside from the owner and his crew were aboard. The guest would be rushed into some hiding nook—without the need for a mad shuffle to clean up his cabin and eliminate all evidence of him ever being there.

Simple and smart.

Except, she still had no evidence one way or the other, and this whole mental exercise could be nothing more than an interesting hypothesis.

If she wanted proof, she needed to find that hidden compartment.

Amanda was pretty certain it wasn't on the lower deck or the under deck. She had been quite thorough in searching those. Which left the main and upper decks.

The main deck housed the master cabin she was occupying and the grand salon. The salon wasn't accessible at the moment and the master cabin she could search later at her leisure.

Shit, she should hurry and check out the upper deck before the crew woke up.

Problem was, she was operating on fumes. Between the alcohol, the lack of sleep, and the effect of the hot shower, she was barely able to keep her eyes open.

With a hard resolve and a wince, Amanda turned the temperature dial all the way down, cringing as she waited for the cold water to hit her.

But the water wasn't just cold, it was freezing.

Damn, this is awful!

Unable to tolerate more than a few seconds, she jumped out and grabbed a towel, wrapped it tightly around herself first, and only then reached to turn the water off.

She was miserably cold and shivering, her teeth rattling like a pair of castanets, but hey, she was fully awake.

Eyeing the thick terry bathrobe hanging from a hook behind the bathroom's door, she hesitated for about a second. The thing must've belonged to Alex. It was an ugly mushroom color, and the idea of putting on something that had touched Alex's naked body was gross. But style and even personal hygiene be damned—she needed to get warm.

Wrapped in the double layer of bathrobe and towel, her teeth no longer banging against each other, she plodded back to the cabin and glanced at the bed with longing.

Hell, do I really need to be doing this? I'm no Mata Hari... More than anything, she wanted to crawl under the warm duvet and let sleep claim her.

Come on, Amanda, don't be a wuss.

With a sigh, she said goodbye to the lovely bed and stepped inside the large walk-in closet. After pulling on a pair of yoga pants, both towel and bathrobe still on, she grabbed the only long-sleeve warm top she had with her—a black, lightweight cashmere turtleneck. It required some acrobatic-level twisting to manage to get it over her head, while holding onto the towel until it was fully on.

A pair of red Uggs warming her feet, she left the cabin and tiptoed past the salon, counting the heads to make sure that they were all still there, before climbing the stairs to the upper deck.

Emerging up in the top grand salon, she passed the sitting area and the bar, disregarding them as potential hiding places, and headed straight for Geneva's cabin.

It was unlocked.

Size wise, it was similar to the smaller guest cabins, but the furnishings and their placement had been chosen for utility, not style. The queen-sized bed was covered with a generic, purple comforter and pushed against the side wall to make room for an oak desk and a small bookcase. Both pieces looked like something one would find discarded on a street of a shitty neighborhood or pay a buck and a half for at a Goodwill store.

Next to the bed, instead of a nightstand, a tall cherry wood dresser provided extra storage space. Inside, there were the standard panties and a couple of bras, socks, a few T-shirts, a beanie and some scarves, but not a shred of the personal memorabilia Amanda had hoped would shed light on the kind of person Geneva was.

Over at the bookcase, she flipped through a few of Geneva's books and shuffled through the disk cases that were stacked one on top of the other. Most were related either to boating or the mastering of American English—which explained her fluency and good accent compared to the rest of the crew. A few disks even tackled basic, spoken Spanish. Other than that, there were several Russian titles that seemed to be novels, but lacking the ability to read Cyrillic script, Amanda couldn't tell for sure. She flipped through them nonetheless, searching for photos or other documents that might have been hiding between the pages.

Nada, zilch.

The utilitarian theme continued inside the small clothes closet: A few pairs of jeans and khakis, some long, some short; four polo shirts; three button-downs; two jackets—one light and one warm; two pairs of shoes, one pair of boots, and no heel in sight.

How boring.

In the bathroom, Amanda finally found some small concessions to femininity; a lavender-scented soap, shampoo and conditioner, and lo and behold—a brown pencil eyeliner and black mascara.

There was only one toothbrush, and no razor, which meant first and foremost that Geneva's bare legs and armpits were laser-treated or waxed—shocking for a Russian—though it might have been a requirement of her mud wrestling job. And secondly, no male had shared her bathroom recently.

Not that there was even a sliver of a chance that Alex would have deigned to grace Geneva's spartan cabin, but neither had any other male.

Just to make sure, Amanda gave the bedding a thorough sniffing.

There was nothing besides the lavender soap scent, Geneva, and a laundry detergent. So unless the bedding was brand new, the woman had been sleeping alone.

Bummer. Yet another dead end.

Oh, well, she must've been wrong, inventing a whole bogus scenario built on nothing more than suspicion and conjecture.

Trouble was, she knew she wasn't. For Alex to make the kind of money needed to buy and run this yacht, he must've been doing a lot more than running a club and selling some drugs.

But if indeed that was all, then he must have been a major distributor.

Whatever.

She was too tired to think straight. Her investigation would have to wait for another day, or better yet, the proper authorities.

6

SYSSI

"Last night, before I got distracted by your sexy body and impressive size." Syssi leaned against the bathroom's doorframe and ogled Kian as he brushed his teeth, naked. "I wanted to ask you how your meeting with Dalhu went."

Even though they'd just made love, watching the interplay of muscles on his sculpted back, she felt her nipples pebble.

Down, girls. She crossed her arms over her chest. But as he dipped his head to spit out the toothpaste, his strong thigh muscles flexing, she dropped her arms in surrender and let out a soft sigh. "You're doing it again..."

"What?"

"Distracting me."

"It's not going to work."

"What's not going to work?"

"I'm not going back to bed to satisfy your insatiable appetite. I have work to do, woman." Kian was trying for a severe tone, but was losing the battle to the twitch in his lip and the smile that was threatening to foil his show.

"What? Is there anything more important than taking care of your fiancée's needs?" Syssi taunted.

Kian was on her between one heartbeat and another. "Absolutely nothing," he whispered in her ear, then caught the soft flesh of her earlobe between his teeth and pressed.

She shivered and he picked her up, then carried her back to their bed.

"How about you take this off?" He tugged at the hem of her nightshirt.

"Seriously? Even my new and improved physique is not up to a third time. It's just that you're so sexy I can't take my eyes off you, you big, arrogant oaf."

"Is that so?" He kissed her nose.

"It is. You know you're gorgeous."

"As long as you think so, I'm good." He pressed another kiss to her forehead and pushed off the bed. "Regretfully, I need to get going. But you're welcome to join me in the closet. You can admire my body to your heart's content while I'm getting dressed."

Following after him, she did just that.

"So? How did it go?" Inside the walk-in closet, Syssi pulled out a footstool and sat down, straddling it.

"The Doomer didn't lie, but he didn't know much either. Apparently, he was just a lowly commander of a small unit. Leave it to Amanda to aim lower than low, falling for a Doomer that isn't even an important one. The girl needs to work on her self-esteem."

Curiously, Syssi didn't detect much bite in Kian's tone. He sounded almost conversational. Was he losing some of his animosity toward Dalhu? Or was it just the effect of postcoital bliss?

"Did you learn anything new, though?" she probed, not sure which direction her questions should take.

"A little." Kian shrugged as he buttoned his shirt.

Now, she knew for sure that there was something he wasn't telling her. "Come on, do I have to beg for crumbs?"

Kian paused with his fingers hovering over the top button of his shirt. "Wait here," he said and walked out of the closet in a pair of gray socks, a pale blue dress shirt, and no pants—no doubt the only man on the planet who could pull off that look with such tremendous success.

After a quick visit to the bathroom, he came back with a folded piece of green paper in his hand. "Take a look." He handed it to her.

Curious, she unfolded what looked like a flyer for a rock band concert and arched a brow.

"Turn it over."

She did and gasped. "Oh my God, this is amazing. Who drew it?"

"Dalhu."

Her eyes shot up to Kian's. "He is good, very good."

"I know. Not that I'm an expert on art or even know what to look for, but it's quite evident. And it took him no more than a minute or two."

"How did it come about? I don't suppose that just out of the blue he decided to draw Amanda's picture for you?"

"The Doomer was trying to prove he can sketch. Andrew suggested that we compile files on the top players in Navuh's camp. Dalhu offered to supply the information and even to draw their portraits for us. When we sneered at him, with Andrew saying that this was a job for a forensic artist, Dalhu drew the picture to show off his skill."

Kian walked over to the suit section of his closet and removed a pair of slacks off a hanger.

A suit, right. She'd almost forgotten. "Are your suits custom made?"

"Yes, why?"

"You need a nice one for the wedding, maybe a tuxedo?"

"Not a chance."

Syssi let out a soft chuckle. "Why am I not surprised… but anyway, do you go to a tailor or does he come to you? I want to arrange a fitting. We don't have much time." Now was not the time to argue about the tux. She would approach that subject again later.

"You have enough on your plate. I'll have Shai do it. He is the one who decides when I need new clothes and either buys them himself or invites Mr. Fentony to measure me for suits and dress shirts." Kian grimaced at a blemish he'd noticed on the pair of slacks he was holding and cast them aside, then reached for a different pair. "Though I have no idea why he needs to come, it's not as if my measurements change from one fitting to another. He probably does it just to justify his inflated prices." Kian chuckled.

Syssi felt her cheeks heat up though this time the cause wasn't embarrassment. Shai would not fight Kian over the tux. He would just do whatever Kian told him to. But there was more to it than that.

She was angry.

Why had such a trivial thing upset her so? Was it because Kian should've realized it was no longer his secretary's job to take care of him?

Don't be an idiot. The man has been on his own for literally forever, and you want him to adapt just like that? "I'll get Mr. Fentony's number from Shai and call him myself."

"Why?" Kian cast her a quizzical look.

"Because I want to." *Let him figure out the why himself.*

"Okay." He shrugged as if it was a nonissue.

Not that he was wrong, necessarily. It was just that she wanted to take care of him in any way she could, needed to, and there was so little she could do for him.

Someone else made sure Kian had new clothes and kept him company in the office; another cooked his meals and did his laundry. Not that she wasn't grateful for Okidu. She was so busy with the wedding plans that preparing a meal or stuffing the washer would've been all she could've managed.

And as for joining Kian in the office and learning about the conglomerate he was running, so she could eventually be of some help, it would have to wait until after the party.

Trouble was, Amanda wanted her back in the lab. But even though Syssi enjoyed the research, she hated the idea of being away from Kian for so many hours a day. Neuroscience was more exciting than administrative work, but sharing Kian's office and easing some of his load was more appealing to her.

Why?

Because she loved him, and people who loved each other wanted to be together and take care of each other.

It was as simple as that.

Syssi looked down at the crumpled piece of green paper she was still holding. Smoothing out the creases, she ran her fingers over the outline of Amanda's face. There was so much feeling in the eyes staring at her from the picture, and she wondered if Amanda had truly gazed at Dalhu like this, or had he drawn what he was yearning for.

But one thing was certain, only a man in love could've captured the beauty of Amanda's spirit, shining through the breathtaking perfection of her face, the way Dalhu had done in his sketch.

"He loves her… you realize that, don't you?" she murmured.

"Yeah, so what?"

"And she loves him back…"

"No, she doesn't."

"How can you say that? You haven't talked to her even once since the rescue. How would you know if she does or does not?"

"Because it's Amanda." Kian pulled on the pair of dark gray slacks and tucked the shirt inside. "She is frivolous, and like a succubus for drama, she feeds on it—the more, the better—but even she must realize that the Doomer is beneath her." He zipped up his pants, then moved over to the dresser and pulled out the top drawer—the one with his favorite ties. There were many more, taking up that whole bank of drawers. And yet, looking at his many options, Kian's brows dipped. He couldn't decide, or perhaps for some reason, none of them met with his approval this morning.

"Here, let me." Syssi shooed him over, looking through the tie selection for the one that would match the colors of what he was wearing. "I don't think social status has anything to do with love. Why is he beneath her? Is he stupid? Uneducated? Uncouth?" She held up a gray-and-blue-striped tie to Kian's pale blue shirt.

"I don't think he is educated, Doomers typically aren't, but it's not about that. I'm not educated either. But even though he seems intelligent and is well spoken, he is tainted by his past, and there is nothing he or she can do about it."

"Not a great believer in redemption, are you?" Syssi looped the tie around Kian's neck.

"Nope."

"You realize that it's not really up to you. You can huff, and you can puff, and still, when all is said and done, Amanda will do as she pleases." Syssi finished the knot and smoothed the tie over Kian's shirt, then placed her palms over his hard pecs.

He covered her hands with his and held them against his chest. "It is true that I have little control over Amanda, but I have complete control over the Doomer. And I'm not letting him out of that cell."

7

ANDREW

"I'll have a double espresso and these." Andrew handed the tuna sandwich and the cup of fruit to the Starbucks barista.

Since he'd started the new desk job, he'd been having his breakfast at this same Starbucks every morning on his way to work. He knew everyone there by name, but this one was new. Brea—it said on her name tag—a slightly chubby girl with a pretty face and lots of makeup.

"Sure, will there be anything else, sir?" She smiled, revealing a set of small white teeth covered with shiny metal braces.

Damn, they were getting younger and younger, while he was getting older and older. And this morning in particular, his body felt like a used and abused forty-year-old truck. "No, thank you, Brea." Like some old fart, he'd been tempted to substitute *honey* for her name.

Not yet, buddy. He managed a tight smile as she swiped his credit card.

The place was packed with the morning crowd, but as most of the patrons were either standing in line to order their coffee or hovering around the other side to collect it once it was ready, he found an empty stool at the counter facing the window—his favorite spot. Unwrapping his sandwich, he listened for his name to be called out.

Hell, after last night, that double shot of espresso should be classified as medicinal. Andrew needed the stimulant to get his tired old ass in gear.

A sly smirk tugged at his lips as he thought back to his eventful visit to the good doctor. Bridget had introduced him to sex like he had never experienced before—mind-blowing intensity, insatiable, and the endurance to match.

It had been humbling.

While he had felt like he'd been through a marathon after climaxing for the fourth time—which was quite impressive for any male over twenty thank-you-very-much, though potentially life threatening for someone his age—Bridget had tried to hide her disappointment.

Her apology had made it worse. As if admitting that she hadn't been with a man for a while and then explaining the sexual appetite of immortal females was supposed to make him feel better.

With a smirk, he wondered if by literally sucking the life out of him the doctor had been violating her Hippocratic Oath to do no harm.

But hey, what was he complaining about? As if there was a better way to go than croaking from too much sex—he would have arrived on the other side with a big smile on his face.

Tonight, he was going back for seconds, but not before taking a nap and chugging an energy drink or two. Having a decent bed instead of the hard, narrow exam table would no doubt help matters as well. That bloody table must've been the source of most of his aches and pains.

Yeah, keep telling yourself that...

Should he bring flowers?

Bridget had invited him to dinner at her place, and showing up empty-handed seemed rude. On the other hand, neither of them had any illusions as to what this was all about, so flowers might not be appropriate—too romantic. God knew there was no romance involved, and chances were good that they would skip the meal altogether and jump straight into bed.

Wine would be a better choice.

Pulling out his phone, Andrew added it to his shopping list. But then, wine seemed like not enough for a woman that had rocked his world.

He added a box of Godiva chocolates to the list.

Not that this was enough either, but again, anything more would imply feelings that just weren't there, and might send Bridget running. After all, the woman made it clear she was just after his body.

Which was perfectly fine with him, she was welcome to use him for as long as he wished to be used.

"Double espresso for Andrew," he heard the barista call out.

On his way to collect his double shot of energy, he passed by several young women—mostly college students—sitting around the small tables with their laptops and their coffees.

They had no idea how lucky they were, and how inconsequential their troubles were compared to those of women their age in other parts of the world.

That thought pulled him away from the pleasant subject of Bridget and flowers to the disturbing one of Passion Island and the women imprisoned there. To do nothing about it went against everything he stood for, but the hard truth was that the idea of invading the island was indeed ludicrous.

Even if he succeeded in convincing someone in the government that something must be done about it, no one in their right mind would consider attacking a foreign country to free a bunch of women. And even if anyone did, there was the issue of an army of immortal warriors to contend with.

The sad reality was that as miserable as the lives of those women were, they were not worth the lost lives of thousands of soldiers or the havoc an international incident like that would cause.

The only thing to do was to make it damn hard for the Doomers to collect new flesh for their bazaar—at least from the States. And he could talk to a buddy of his on the Russian side about doing something about it on their front.

In truth, though, Andrew was well aware that he was indulging in mental masturbation. Nothing could stop the worldwide plague of kidnapping and sexual enslavement of women and girls—not as long as there was demand and big money could be made from the trade.

Regrettably, he had a hard time envisioning a future in which this age-old, loathsome market had been eradicated.

8

AMANDA

"Hey, American! You alive in there?"

"Go away!" Amanda barked and covered her head with a pillow.

What the hell possessed Lana to bang on her door at this ungodly hour? And as far as she was concerned, it was an ungodly hour, even if it was two in the afternoon.

"Geneva said to check on you, so I did."

"Grrr…" Amanda tightened the pillow over her ears.

Shit.

Now that she had been so rudely awakened, the effects of last night's binge were making themselves known. Her head felt like it had doubled in size and was filled with sharp needles that were poking at her temples and her eye sockets from the inside.

I'm going to strangle her. Though, which her? Geneva for sending Lana? Or Lana for making a racket?

I'll strangle them both; problem solved.

With a grunt, Amanda threw the pillow at the door and shoved off the bed. Assessing the damage as she got vertical, she found that the dizziness had passed, and only a faint echo of nausea remained.

The headache was a bitch, though, and a glance at the time explained why she was still suffering from last night's drinking fest effects.

Are these fucking Russians insane? Seven-thirty in the morning? Really? She'd just gotten into bed a couple of hours ago for heaven's sake.

She'd better take something for that pounding headache before she went postal on the bunch. Maybe Alex kept some painkillers in his bathroom. Though why he would, she couldn't imagine. It wasn't as if immortals needed to have them on hand.

And yet, as she shuffled over to the vanity, she had her hopes up.

Catching her reflection in the mirror, Amanda winced. Since when did she wake up with dark shadows under her eyes? And what was with that hair? Her normally sleek, short hair, looked like a frizzy, messy nest.

She'd need to shower again just so it would dry properly. But first, a comb and a splash of water on her face were in order.

Done taking care of the necessities, she turned to search the drawers for something to relieve her headache. She found several brand new bottles of Tom Ford and Kilian perfumes for men, a few tubes of toothpaste, and several bars of soap, but no painkillers.

Damn, she'd have to ask the mortals for it, or just tough it out.

Or better yet, go home.

But she wasn't ready to face what she had run away from. Not yet. With no new insight or brilliant inspiration, she was exactly at the same place she had been before fleeing.

So what was the point?

With her hands on the counter, Amanda leaned and dropped her head. It had been fun to play detective, but with no evidence, she could no longer justify the distraction. It was time to do some hard thinking.

And as a last resort, maybe ring her mother.

Heaving a sigh, she pushed herself off the vanity and trudged back to the cabin. Inside the walk-in closet, the few remaining clean items of clothing out of all that she'd brought with her took up a tiny section at the front of it. And as she was in no mood to lounge on deck in a bikini or a sundress, her options were limited to one clean pair of jeans, one skirt, and two T-shirts.

Another reason to go home.

A sudden impulse had her look at the back of the closet, where Alex's incredible selection of designer clothes was either hanging from luxury hangers or folded neatly on shelves. Separated into casual and dressy, each section was color coordinated, with matching footwear on the lower shelves.

Considering Alex's metrosexual style, some of it might even look good on her. He might be a couple of inches taller, but then her legs were longer.

Not that she was going to put on something that he had already worn—even laundered, it would be gross. She still cringed thinking about that bathrobe of his she had been desperate enough to borrow. But knowing Alex, half of the stuff was probably brand new with the tags still attached.

The man was a major clotheswhore.

Amanda let out a chuckle as she sifted through the hanging garments, most of which had either a store tag dangling from a sleeve or a label or a tailor's note pinned on.

Taking into account the fact that Alex didn't spend all of his time cruising, the size of the wardrobe he kept on his yacht was impressive even by her standards. The guy was totally obsessed if he kept the one at his Malibu estate as fully stocked as this one.

Wondering if that included his extensive jewelry collection, she pushed aside the clothes to peek at the back wall in search of a safe.

The wall was decorated with fabric-covered padded panels in a nice beige and burgundy paisley design, each about thirty inches wide.

Running her palms over the fabric, Amanda patted the padded

panels from top to bottom, squeezing herself between the wall and the hanging garments as she kept going from one panel to the next. But from one end to the other, her patting didn't discover any hard surface in the shape of a safe.

She repeated the process on the side walls with the same results. Or rather lack thereof.

Come on, open sesame. She pressed on each of the panels' sides as well as other random places, but none clicked open or even hinted at being anything but glued to the wall.

Back at the section that she had cleared of clothes, Amanda stood with arms akimbo and glared at the wall.

It wasn't about finding the safe anymore. It was about her instincts firing hot, hot, hot as she faced the wall, and cold, cold, cold as she took a step back.

Okay, Amanda, calm down, close your eyes and focus on your other senses, because they are trying to tell you something.

It wasn't easy with a pounding headache still drilling holes inside her head, but she closed her eyes and breathed in, slowly.

Then again, and again.

She caught a very faint scent, which was what must've alerted her subconscious in the first place. Feminine, a trace of perfume or body lotion… no… not one…Now that she was focusing, she was able to detect several different barely there scents coming from behind the paneled wall.

Straining, she tried and failed to catch any residual whiff of emotions. Unfortunately, even though her sense of smell was much better than that of a human, it wasn't as strong as an immortal male's. Still, something feminine had been stashed in there at some point in time.

Except, from this side of the wall, she couldn't tell whether it had been actual women or just their belongings that had left that scent behind.

Sesame open?

Hey, it was worth a try, maybe the magic words worked in reverse order.

Nepo emases? Emases nepo?

Backward didn't seem to work either.

Come on, Amanda, stop fooling around and think!

Trouble was, her brain was still kind of fuzzy.

Okay, it's probably not a pressure mechanism if pressing didn't work. How about prying it open?

The problem with this idea was that she had no tools. Going to look for one would, first of all, alert the crew to the fact that she was awake but hadn't gone out to sit on one of the decks—which by now they would know was not like her—and second, would raise suspicion as to why she needed it.

With one last sad look at her manicured nails, she attacked the panels with her fingers, or rather her long nails, barely managing to wedge them in the tiny grooves between the panels. Pulling was out of the question, as they would just break off. Instead, she tried to wiggle the panel a little to see if there was any give.

There was none.

But then, she couldn't apply much force. She needed a tool—something that was thin enough to fit in the grooves, but strong enough not to bend or break.

About to leave the closet and go search the cabin for a letter opener, she stopped as her eyes landed on something better. Down on the bottom shelf, a metal shoehorn was sticking from one of Alex's shoes.

Perfect.

It worked like a charm, and the first panel she tried popped out quite easily. But what she discovered behind it was nothing nefarious, just more shelf space.

Weird. Unless this hidden part of the closet was used to store the drugs she suspected Alex of smuggling. But after a few sniffs, she had to discard that hypothesis. The only scents lingering on the empty, padded shelves were those faint traces of feminine products.

No drug residue.

She pried open another panel just to make sure there wasn't anything else hiding there.

It was just more shelf space.

Come to think of it, the shelving was kind of peculiar, and not just because it was hidden behind a cleverly constructed false wall. It was deeper than standard, about the width of the panels, and peeking farther inside she saw no dividers, just long, deep shelves, padded and covered in the same fabric as the wall panels. In fact, it looked as if the same panels that made the wall were used to construct the shelves.

With not a lot of vertical space between them, the height of the wall allowed for five levels, and it seemed like they ran the length of the closet wall.

Kind of reminded her of the crypt underneath the keep. Except, the crypt's stone shelves were much deeper and spaced farther apart vertically to accommodate the bulky sarcophagi.

Amanda snorted. *So that must be it; Alex is smuggling dead bodies.*

Seriously, though, was this hidden compartment used to smuggle rich criminals from south of the border into the United States?

Female rich criminals?

Amanda took a step closer and sniffed again, making sure she hadn't missed anything, but the only scent was still female, and there was no residual scent of emotions. Which again didn't mesh with her hypothesis. If people had been hiding there while the yacht was being inspected, by whatever agency did those things, they would've felt fear or at least stress, and both emotions produced strong scents that would've lingered long after they were gone.

Unless they'd been dead...which would explain the lack of emotions, but then she was pretty sure that there was no profit to be made from transporting dead bodies.

As it was, it seemed that only inanimate objects had ever graced those shelves, which made perfect sense considering the fact that this was a closet.

Possibly, Alex didn't like how the yacht's previous owners designed the space and blocked off that rear section to square it off. Or he might have even bought it like this and wasn't aware that there was anything behind the closet's back wall.

Oh, well. So much for my conspiracy theory. Amanda shrugged and picked up one of the two panels she had pried off their metal guides. Pushing it back in place took some effort, and she had to lean on it to force it in. It wasn't perfectly aligned with its neighbor, but she decided to wait with the final adjustments until the other one was back in place as well.

Banging on the panel sides with the heel of her palm was painful, but that was the least of her worries. She was making such a racket that there was no way the crew didn't hear it, and at any moment someone might burst in, demanding to know what the hell was going on.

Exercising—and she was going to stick to it—kick-boxing.

The panels must've warped a bit from her prying them out with the shoehorn because nothing she did managed to restore the wall to its former condition. The tight seams between those she had taken out were no longer as uniform as those between the others.

The best she could do was to slide the hangers over and hide the incriminating evidence behind the clothes.

Hopefully, Alex wouldn't notice.

Whatever, plausible deniability was the name of the game. If he asked, she would play dumb and say she had no idea what he was talking about.

Amanda returned the shoehorn to the same shoe she had found it in, and wiped her sweaty, throbbing palms on her yoga pants.

Oh, well, she had been so certain she would find something, but on the other hand, it was also a relief to find nothing incriminating about Alex. He was, after all, her friend.

Back in the cabin, she added her sweaty clothes to the pile of dirties in her carry-on and headed for the bathroom.

Surprisingly, no one came banging on her door.

After a quick shower, she put on her last clean pair of jeans and a red T-shirt. As she left her cabin and headed for the grand salon, she hoped Renata had left coffee and breakfast for her.

Thank heavens it wasn't ten yet. Otherwise the woman would've cleared the table already.

As it was, Amanda found the thermal carafe full and the coffee still hot. "I love you, Renata," she murmured, promising herself to be nicer to the cook from now on.

Watching the ocean while drinking coffee never got old, but it wasn't as relaxing as it had been the last time she sat here alone. She just couldn't shake the uncomfortable feeling that she was missing some important clue, or rather the insight to piece all the clues she had gathered into a cohesive picture.

Oh, heck, enough of that. She pulled her phone from her front pocket and called Syssi.

"Hi," Syssi chirped, then added in a whisper, "Sorry, forgot you're probably nursing a hangover."

"Just a pounding headache, but I'm drinking coffee and gazing at the ocean, so it's all good. How about you?"

Syssi snorted. "I'm fine, I'm not the one who has been drinking all night with a bunch of Russians. How did it go? Learn anything interesting?"

"Lots, but I'll tell you all about it when I come home."

"When?"

Amanda sighed. "Hopefully this evening."

"That's wonderful! But I thought you planned on staying longer, what happened?"

"I ran out of clothes."

"No, seriously."

"I'm very serious. I'm on my last clean pair of jeans. And you know me. Laundry is not something I do."

"Okay, be like that. If you don't want to tell me anything, it's fine, but I have something for you."

Syssi sounded eager to share the news. Must be something good. "Yeah? What is it?"

"I had to practically squeeze it out of him, but I got Kian to tell me about his meeting with Dalhu."

Excitement swirled through Amanda's gut. "And?"

"And, I have a feeling that Kian is softening toward Dalhu or at least easing up on the hostility. He even referred to him by name a couple of times instead of spitting out 'The Doomer' with murder in his eyes."

"Wow, miracles never cease."

"I know, right? But that's not all... Did you know that your Dalhu is a talented artist?"

My Dalhu... go ahead, twist the knife in my bleeding heart, why don't you?

"First of all, he's not mine, and second, what the hell are you talking about? To the best of my knowledge, killing is his only skill." She couldn't keep the bitterness out of her voice.

"Nope, not the only one. He draws, really well. He sketched your portrait and it is stunning. Want to see?"

Duh, of course she wanted to see it... "Show me."

"Hold on..." She heard Syssi take a few steps. "Okay, here it is. I'm going to switch to camera for a moment and send it to you... I'm adjusting the zoom... here, perfect." There was a click. "Go ahead, check your messages. I'm waiting."

At first glance, Amanda was impressed, then zooming in, her eyes teared. Not only because Dalhu's sketch was beautifully done, and not only because it was achingly obvious that he'd gotten to know her better than most—despite the short time they'd had together.

But because the face staring at her from the small screen looked happy—excited, hopeful, and maybe even a little in love. It was a reminder of the one time she hadn't been faking it, but had actually felt this way.

"Are you crying?" Syssi asked softly.

"Just a little..." She must've sniffled.

Oh, what the hell, just go with it. Amanda let out a few louder ones, then blew her nose in the cloth napkin.

Gross, I need to remember to throw it in the trash.

"Are those sad tears? Or happy tears?"

"Happy-sad tears."

"Huh?"

"I don't know. It's lovely... I look so... happy. And Dalhu... well, I knew how he felt about me, but this just drove it home. And I've realized that I might've been falling in love with him as well." The waterworks started again.

Shit.

"So why sad?"

"Because it's all in the past, gone, kaput." She had to blow her nose again.

"It doesn't have to be...," Syssi said so softly it came out in a whisper. Then she added with more passion, "It's obvious that he loves you, and you feel strongly about him, maybe even love him... the rest is just background noise."

Amanda snorted. "More like a marching band parade."

"Ignore it... get out of your head for a moment and listen to your gut. A wise woman once told me that she always lets her instinct guide her because it's smarter than her."

"Yeah? And how did it work out for her?"

"Ask her yourself, it was your mother."

"First, I need to figure out what to do. I feel like I'm in a maze of one-way-street turns and can't get anywhere no matter which route I take. I'm going in never-ending circles in my head."

"See? You just reinforced what I said. You need to get out of that loop altogether. Stop thinking and just feel. What do you have to lose? Dalhu wouldn't harm you even if he could, which he can't because he is imprisoned in your stronghold. He can't leave you either. Again, because he is not free to go. And if you're thinking about Kian, don't. He'll come around if he has to. He loves you too much to stay mad forever. So, the way I see it, you hold all the cards in your hands."

"And what about my heart?" Amanda placed her hand on her chest. "What if I fall for him but then realize that I can never forget or forgive?"

"So you're telling me you'd rather play chicken? That doesn't sound like you."

Syssi was right, and what's worse, it reminded Amanda of a similar conversation she'd had with Kian. Only then, Kian had been the one who was afraid to take the plunge, and she the one giving advice and pushing him to jump off that proverbial diving board.

Hypocrite, anyone?

"You're right. It's about time I stopped being a chicken and unleashed the cougar."

"You go, girl! Sharpen those claws!"

"Grrourr…"

"I'll see you tonight, cat woman."

"Wait, don't tell Kian I'm coming home."

"Sure, but why not?"

"It will be hard enough to face Dalhu, and I'd rather save the inevitable confrontation with Kian for another day. One battle at a time is all I can handle right now." Amanda chuckled. "I guess this cougar is just a little one, with itsy bitsy claws."

"I've seen those claws, and they looked damn lethal to me."

9

DALHU

"I come bearing gifts." Anandur waltzed in with a big cardboard box under each arm. "Something to keep you busy, frog." He dropped them on the coffee table.

"What's in there?"

Anandur dipped his hand inside the smaller one and pulled out a laptop. "This is for your memoirs. And as you naturally have no Internet access, William, our tech guy, has already downloaded a dictionary and an encyclopedia for your use. So no excuses for sloppy work." He handed Dalhu the device, then pulled a long, white cord from the box. "And here is the charger."

"Thank you." Dalhu lifted the incredibly thin laptop, weighing it in his hand. "This is really light."

Anandur grinned. "Yeah, the newest something-air. Only the best for our resident frog."

"This frog thing is getting old. Why not mix things up? Make it interesting with a couple of new derogatory nicknames for me." Dalhu connected the charger to the laptop, then plugged it into the wall socket.

"Nah, this one is so clever it's perfect, if I may say so myself. And it's not meant as an insult. On the contrary, it means you've got potential."

"I don't understand."

Anandur sat on the couch and started pulling out smaller boxes from the larger one. "Of course you don't. This fairy tale didn't exist when your poor mama was reading you bedtime stories."

"My mother was illiterate," Dalhu grated.

Anandur cast him a sad look, then shrugged. "Yeah… I forgot how old you are. Hardly anyone was literate back then."

Nice save.

Except, Dalhu had no doubt that Anandur and the others had been taught to read and write as children, and probably much more, regardless of when they had been born. And what's more, the guy's mother was probably still around, pretty and healthy, and not rotting in some unmarked grave after aging prematurely from hard use and then dying a broken woman.

That thought brought about a bitter dose of jealousy, which in turn supercharged the rage he had so far managed to control.

Get a grip, it's not the guy's fault that he had it better than you.

Fisting his hands, Dalhu forced his tone to what he hoped sounded bored, if not conversational. "If you insist on calling me a frog, at least tell me that damn fairy tale you keep alluding to."

Anandur's grin spread wide. "The princess and the frog… I may botch the story a little because I don't remember exactly how it goes, but you'll get why I think of you as the frog, and Amanda as the princess, obviously."

"Obviously…"

"Once upon a time… just so you know, all fairy tales start like that… a beautiful princess was playing with her favorite ball by a pond, but then it slipped from her hand and fell into the water, sinking fast. She tried to reach it, but the pond was too deep. 'Please, I'll give all my riches to have my ball back,' she cried." With a hand over his heart, Anandur enacted the princess in a high-pitched voice while batting his eyelashes.

Dalhu chuckled. "You missed your calling, my man."

"I know. But back to the story. Then the princess heard a tiny voice. 'I don't want your riches, but if you take me home and let me eat from your plate and sleep on your pillow, I'll get the ball back for you,' was the promise the ugly, slimy frog made to her."

Dalhu grimaced. "Now I get it. I'm the ugly frog who tricked the princess into taking him home with her."

"Would you let me finish?" Anandur rolled his eyes.

"Please, I can't wait to hear the end."

"The princess wanted her ball back, so, even though she was disgusted by the creature, she agreed and took the frog home. For three days the frog ate from her plate, and for three nights he slept on her pillow. And during that time, as they talked and played together, the princess grew fond of the frog. So much so that on the last night she kissed him good night on his ugly, slimy, green cheek. Then the following morning, in place of the frog the princess found a handsome prince sleeping next to her."

Dalhu snorted. "Then the beautiful princess screamed for her guards who rushed in and hastily killed the presumptuous prince. The end."

Anandur frowned. "Maybe in the story's adaptation for Doomers—"

Dalhu harrumphed and crossed his arms over his chest. "As if any woman who went to sleep with a pet and woke up with a man next to her wouldn't have screamed murder."

"Hello? A talking frog? Fairy tale?"

"Okay, go on…"

"The prince told her that he had been cursed by an evil witch and only the kindness of a good-hearted maiden who would let a frog eat from her plate and sleep on her pillow could've broken the curse."

"And?"

"And what?"

"What did she say?"

"At this point, the fairy tale ends with the unlikely couple getting married and riding off into the sunset to live happily ever after."

"I don't get it. So what's the moral of the story? Show kindness to a frog and it will turn into a prince?"

Anandur rolled his eyes again. "I can't believe I'm explaining a fairytale—to a Doomer. It depends on how you want to look at it. The moral could be that you should be kind to everyone, even to a lowly creature, because it might be more than it seems. Or, be careful what you wish for and who you make promises to because rarely anyone turns out to be a prince, and most times you'll end up stuck with a frog."

"I see..." Not really, though. What was Anandur trying to say? That Dalhu might be a cursed prince? Not likely. Probably more along the lines of Amanda wishing for a prince, but getting stuck with a frog. Which was true, but an insult nonetheless, and Anandur had claimed it wasn't.

Still, Dalhu wasn't about to ask Anandur for further clarification. As it was, the guy already thought him ignorant. He didn't want to add stupid to the impression.

"Here, frog, your chance to morph into a prince." Anandur handed him the largest notebook Dalhu had ever seen. The thing looked to be a foot and a half wide and two feet long.

"What is this?" He took it and read the cover—*Drawing*—which made his question sound stupid.

"I also got you charcoal sticks, charcoal pencils, drawing pencils, erasers, sharpeners—in other words, the works." Anandur piled the boxes one on top of the other as he listed what was inside them. "And if you want to dabble in acrylics or oil paints, I would gladly take another trip to that art store for you. They have very helpful staff if you know what I mean." Anandur winked.

Dalhu was rendered momentarily speechless, expressing his amazement with a whistle. "When Kian said he would bring me sketching supplies, I imagined a few sheets of paper and some pencils."

Anandur harrumphed. "I bet he did as well. I went wild in that store. You see…" He shifted to get closer and glanced both ways as if to check for eavesdroppers—strange, because they both knew that the place was bugged—then continued in a hushed voice. "The sales-girl had an incredible ass, and I made her run all over the store—following closely behind of course. It would've been rude not to buy all the things that she worked so hard on fetching."

Yeah, good story, but for whose benefit? Dalhu's or Anandur's? Was the guy reluctant to admit his kindness? Maybe he sought to protect his tough-guy reputation. Or, maybe he attempted to make it easier on Dalhu to accept the thoughtful gift and not feel weird about it or obligated in any way.

In either case, Anandur had proven himself to be one hell of a guy, a true prince among men.

"Thank you. I appreciate it." Dalhu offered his hand.

Anandur shook it. "You're welcome. I'll collect the payment later."

What the hell?

"Payment? I have no money."

"I'll take it in the form of marketable goods. A signed drawing would do, preferably of a nude female…just make sure that she doesn't resemble Amanda in any way." He winked and clapped Dalhu's shoulder. "Go, knock yourself out. I expect to see some production when I come back."

"You've got yourself a deal."

10

SEBASTIAN

"Mr. Shar, would you please sign here." The driver of the delivery truck handed Sebastian a clipboard.

The fixtures for the upstairs bathrooms had arrived later than promised, but it was all good. Despite the slight delay, the additional crews he'd hired would help install everything by tonight.

Any other day, the two hours of pay for the workmen to just sit and wait would have chafed even though it wasn't money out of his pocket, but Sebastian was in a good mood. And not only because the first shipment of weapons had arrived on schedule in the early hours of the morning and was now stored safely in the outbuilding he'd dedicated as an armory.

Well, maybe in part it was. The quality of the few items he had inspected had exceeded his expectations. But mainly, his good mood had to do with the uniquely pleasing evening that he'd spent at his club—with a particularly loud sub.

The woman had not been a beauty by any stretch of the imagination, or even as young as he usually liked them, but she had been an excellent screamer. And the begging... beautiful, it had been music to his ears. He should thank the club owner personally for the suggestion. Without it, he could've overlooked a very pleasing sub in favor of a better-looking one.

How did the American saying go? Never judge the book by its binding? Or something to that effect.

He might even schedule another round with her. If she was up to it...

Maybe in a couple of days.

Or sooner.

The woman must've been amazed at how little damage she had actually sustained. Sebastian had been very careful to leave the memories of pain and humiliation intact, submerging only the memory of his bite.

For a masochist like her, a sadist like him must've seemed like a godsend.

Sebastian chuckled. Now, this was a term he had never expected a woman to associate with him. And yet, it was true. Who else could've healed the damage he'd caused so she could indulge in her kink much sooner than she normally would?

The novelty of having an enthusiastic partner—one that was up to almost all that he liked to dish out, and not because it was part of her job, but out of her own free will—had been unexpectedly pleasing, even satisfying.

For a moment, Sebastian entertained the idea of keeping her for himself, making her the first occupant of his dungeon.

He would not share her, though. A woman of that caliber was too good for the others.

He had even enjoyed her quick mind and, surprisingly, her sense of humor during the pre-assignation negotiations. The woman was intelligent, a lawyer by occupation, and had very few hard limits.

Still, had he enjoyed this new experience enough to shift his preference to willing partners?

Only one way to find out—follow up with his usual fare of

victims. There were pros and cons to both, and he was curious which way the scale tilted.

Regrettably, he had to concede that even if the masochist won, his partner from last night wasn't right for his dungeon. She didn't fit the profile of an easy abductee—one with no family, friends, or coworkers who would notice her missing and report to the authorities.

The lawyer was a partner in a large firm, and her absence would be noted immediately. And anyway, a smart cookie like her might figure a way to escape.

Too risky.

In his experience, the prudent approach was to stick to what had been tested and proven to work well, and not gamble on something new unless it was absolutely necessary.

"Robert." Sebastian turned to his assistant.

"Yes, sir." The man's spine snapped into a straight line, but he managed to check himself at the last moment before adding a salute. "Sorry, Se... bastian."

The man was a lost cause. "Did you call the commander of the other team? What was his name?"

"Dalhu, sir."

"Robert, Robert, Robert, whatever shall we do with you..."

"I'm sorry, I'll try harder."

"Don't try, just do."

"Yes..." The man swallowed hard, choking down the compulsion to finish with the requisite sir. "I've talked with his second. Apparently, Dalhu was one of the warriors who were taken out by the Guardians. But I forwarded your instructions to the second, and he was happy to hear that they were going home."

"What about the house they've been renting?"

"Tom already took care of it. The whole deal has been brokered from the start through our trade partners here in Los Angeles, so there was no paperwork to bother with. All it took was letting them know the men will be vacating the place by tomorrow."

"Good, well done, Robert."

Sebastian was glad to be rid of that team. The men he had chosen to join him were loyal to him, and he knew they were the right ones for the job. He had no intention of bringing in outsiders whom he hadn't personally vetted.

Still, he'd decided to wait a few days after arrival before arranging for their transport back to base.

He wasn't worried about anyone questioning his decision to send the other team home. But impressions mattered, and it was important not to look as if he feared outsiders. It might raise unnecessary suspicions when, in fact, he had nothing to hide. So he took his time.

His grandfather—the exalted leader of the Brotherhood of the Devout Order Of Mortdh—was brilliant, but unfortunately, he was also paranoid. And although Sebastian was loyal to the core, there was no convincing Navuh of that.

The man trusted no one.

11

KIAN

Kian's phone chimed with the sound of bells—the ringtone he'd assigned to his mother.

"Good afternoon, Mother."

"Indeed, it is a splendid afternoon. I have just convinced Gerard to help. He is going to design a menu and even prepare part of it in his restaurant. The rest he will give Okidu the recipes for—provided in strict confidentiality, of course."

"You sure the Odus will be able to handle Gerard's elaborate creations for such a big dinner? What works for his restaurant might not work for a large scale production."

"I am sure an experienced chef like him will take it into consideration. But I did not call you to discuss the wedding menu. There was something important I wanted to ask you but had to wait until your lovely bride excused herself to go powder her nose."

Kian smiled, wondering if he should tell Annani that no one powdered their nose anymore.

Nah... "Ask away."

"Did you buy a wedding ring for Syssi? Or even an engagement ring?"

Fuck, how could he have forgotten an important thing like that? "No, I didn't."

"Just as I thought. Hurry up and buy both. And may I offer a suggestion?"

A suggestion, right. Kian rolled his eyes. Annani didn't offer suggestions, she issued diktats. "Yes, of course, Mother."

"Take your sweet fiancée out to dinner and present her with the ring in a romantic setting. I would think the girl deserves at least one date as your fiancée before becoming your wife."

"Can't argue with that logic." Did he feel like an ass or what? What was he? Twelve? That he needed his mother to point out the obvious?

"Do not forget that you need an appointment if you want a high caliber jeweler, which I am sure you do."

Hell, how was he supposed to know that? "Can you suggest one? I'm really out of my element here."

"But of course. I will do better than that. I will call the one I use and arrange for an appointment within an hour. Without my influence, any respectable establishment would demand at least a fortnight's notice to see you."

"Thank you, you're a lifesaver."

"No need to thank me. That is what mothers are for."

"How about, I love you."

There was a sniffle. "That is perfect."

Kian chuckled. "So why are you crying?"

"Because it has been ages since the last time you said you love me."

That can't be—

Actually, he couldn't remember telling her he loved her ever since he was a boy.

Regardless of how many times Annani had referred to herself as a mother, in his mind she was first and foremost the head of their clan, and, as such, deserving of his respect and deference. But her station aside, Annani was pure heart and valued love above all.

He should've been mindful of that.

"I'm sorry I've neglected to tell you I love you. I promise that from now on you will hear it more often from me."

Annani chuckled. "Do not make promises you are not going to keep, Kian. And I do not need daily affirmations to know that you love me. But once in a while, it is nice to hear."

And… the head of the clan was back. "As you wish."

"Call Syssi and tell her you are taking her out. Make it late evening in case the purchase takes longer than expected."

"Yes, she who must be obeyed."

Annani laughed, the chiming sound more beautiful than anything ever recorded. "Indeed," she said before disconnecting.

Kian swiveled his chair to face Shai.

The guy sighed. "I know, reschedule all your phone conferences and e-mail everyone waiting for a response from you to let them know they will have to wait a little longer."

"You read my mind."

"Don't I always?"

"Yes, you do."

"But before you go, there are a few quick items Onegus asked me to run by you. All I need is a couple of minutes."

"Shoot."

"He wanted to let you know that everyone who received the warning e-mail that he sent out confirmed that they got it and are going to take precautions." Shai chuckled. "He said that judging by the panicky responses, escort services are going to see an unprecedented spike in business. There were even a few who suggested that we should have our own private brothel…" He lifted a brow in question.

As if Kian was going to stoop to the fucking Doomers' level. "Not going to happen. Next."

"The first self-defense class is scheduled for seven this evening, and Onegus wondered if you'd like to come and say a few words. But obviously that's not going to happen either."

"No. But I'll try to make it to the next one."

"I'll let him know. And lastly, which left me somewhat puzzled, Onegus wants me to schedule a mandatory class for all our boys between the ages of thirteen and eighteen about sex and consent. And he wants Bhathian to teach it?"

"Yeah, after the fiasco with Jackson got resolved, we've decided it's a good idea. And Bhathian is just the right guy to scare the shit out of them."

"I thought Jackson was found innocent."

"He was. But the whole thing stunk. First, we got the accusation, then after Onegus e-mailed the accuser back and explained the consequences, the little chickenshit e-mailed an apology saying he misunderstood and that the blow job was consensual. Onegus decided to investigate anyway, but although he confirmed that Jackson was indeed innocent, he was alarmed by the boys' cavalier attitude. Hence the class."

"Okay... But did anyone ask Bhathian if he's willing to teach it?"

Kian smirked. "He can't wait to terrorize a bunch of boys out of their self-entitled attitude."

Shai nodded. "Good, I didn't want to be the one to ask the grouch."

"Is that all?"

"You want more? I have plenty..."

Kian swiveled his chair away from his assistant, letting him know he was done, and pulled out his phone to call Syssi. But looking at the picture of her beautiful, smiling face on his home screen, he opted for a more personal delivery.

The girl was a saint for putting up with him and all his blunders, and topping that long list was forgetting to buy her a ring.

He hoped to atone for his lack of finesse with some sinful kisses and a really big diamond.

12

ANDREW

Andrew closed yet another airport employee file and stretched his arms over his head to release some of the tension that had accumulated in his shoulders. He'd been hunched over his desk since morning, but at four in the afternoon the big stack was only marginally shorter than it had been at the start of his day. And he hadn't even taken a lunch break. Instead, he'd grabbed a sandwich from the vending machine.

Blah. He could still taste the eggs on his tongue.

Damn, on a day like this, the idea of quitting and going to work for Kian looked better than ever.

If there was a way to tap into the government data without working for Uncle Sam, he would do it in a heartbeat. Nearly twenty years of dedicated service was more than enough to do for one's country. True?

Definitely.

Not that he had regrets, he'd loved his job up until the powers that be had decided to chain him to a desk.

Pushing away from the damned thing, Andrew got up to get himself coffee.

There was a new caricature taped to the wall above the counter in the break room, this time of Rick, and Andrew wondered when Tim would get around to his. Not that he was looking forward to it. The guy was vicious, blowing up each and every flaw—from yellowing teeth to a double chin and thinning hair.

And Tim didn't spare the female agents either. Nothing was off limits, wrinkles and sagging breasts included. One day they were going to gang up on him and take their revenge.

Andrew's lip curled in a smirk. He'd better hurry up and ask the guy to make a forensic sketch of Bhathian's long-lost lover before someone arranged an unfortunate accident for Tim. And considering the background of Tim's many slighted coworkers, it wasn't such a far-flung scenario.

Coffee mug in hand, Andrew wended his way through the maze of cubicles looking for Tim's—the one with pages upon pages of black and white caricatures pinned to every surface of the divider panels delineating his space.

The guy had definitely too much free time on his hands.

"Andrew, my man, what brings you to my humble little cube?" Tim begrudged Andrew his spacious office, even though he was sharing it with three other agents—or analysts according to what it said on the plaque on the door. Thank God. If he were forced to work out of a cubicle, Andrew would have gone insane.

"I have a favor to ask."

"It would be my pleasure to draw your portrait." There was an evil gleam in Tim's eyes.

"Not if you want to keep your nimble fingers in one piece. It's not for me. I need you to make a forensic sketch for a friend of mine."

"What's in it for me?"

"Helping a guy to find his long-lost love out of the goodness of your heart?"

"Nope."

"A couple of beers?"

"You've got a deal." Tim offered his hand, then quickly withdrew it. "These babies are too important to be squashed in your paw." He wiggled his long, elegant fingers.

"Tomorrow? Barney's at seven?"

"Fine, but I also want their grande nachos and pizza to go with my beers."

Andrew rolled his eyes. He had no doubt that before the evening was out Tim would renegotiate the deal. "No problem."

It wasn't as if it was coming out of his pocket. And spending a few bucks was a good deal for Bhathian even if nothing came out of the search. At the very least, the guy would have a picture of the alleged mother of his child.

Back at his desk, Andrew texted Bhathian the time and place.

Damn, he was itching to do a little preliminary investigation based on the woman's fake social. But knowing himself, chances were that he would get sucked into it, and hours would pass with him glued to the monitor before he realized six had come and gone.

Not something he should do while on the clock.

A quick look was one thing, spending hours working on a private investigation was another—it was unethical.

Better to wait for the forensic sketch, and once it was done dedicate an evening to the search—maybe even a weekend.

No big deal, he was used to working evenings and weekends.

But today, he was going to leave early, well, early for him. He needed to stop by the supermarket and buy wine and chocolates for Bridget before heading home to shower and change. And chug those energy drinks…

Unfortunately, there would be no time for a nap.

13

AMANDA

The *Anna* had left Avalon an hour ago, but at her current speed, she was still at least an hour away from the mainland marina. Supposedly, plenty of time to think and plan—if one wasn't running in mental circles, that is.

Drinking coffee and snacking on pieces of cut fruit, Amanda appeared calm and collected when she was anything but. The Russians were suspicious enough as it was, and looking distraught might give them ideas.

Besides, projecting a façade was her default state.

There were the nagging suspicions about Alex—his lavish lifestyle that couldn't be reconciled with his legitimate finances, the unusual choice of crew, and the hidden section of the closet. Nothing added up, but she was no closer to solving this mystery than she had been yesterday—and not ready to chuck the whole thing as a product of her overactive imagination either.

Maybe she could've done better if her brain had stayed focused on solving the puzzle instead of constantly wandering to a towering hunk of a man with warm brown eyes and big gentle hands.

What was she going to say to him when she returned? *Hi, I'm back, let's pick up where we left off?*

Not likely.

Some form of heart-to-heart was in order. Trouble was, she didn't know what to think, let alone what to say. Seven years of intense academic study and she was fumbling for words like a high-school girl.

Perhaps she should see her mother first and listen to some words of wisdom before trying to organize the jumble of thoughts that were bouncing around in her head like a bunch of agitated molecules.

Like, how could she consider a murderer as her perfect mate? And what did it say about her? That she was insane? Insecure? Desperate?

But how could she deny her gut—the instinct that was relentlessly tugging at her to return to Dalhu?

Then again, maybe it wasn't her gut or her instinct at all that was doing the talking, but her hormones. If there was one thing that was beyond contestation, one thing that was perfect between them, it was the sex.

Fates, the sex.

Even not fully consummated, it had been the best she'd ever had. Amanda wanted more of that.

Heck, she was starved for it, would never have enough.

If only she could turn off her brain and forget all about Dalhu's rotten baggage—his sordid past that was stinking up what could've been as close to perfect as she was ever going to get.

But how?

How could she forget about Mark? Dishonor his memory by joining with the one who had ordered his murder?

Apparently, sleeping with the enemy wasn't the lower than low she had believed it to be: falling for the murderer of her nephew was worse—way worse.

Help!

She felt like taking a page from Marta's book—finding a corner and rocking back and forth on the floor while chanting, *oh my God, oh my God, I'm going to burn in hell.*

Trouble was, Amanda didn't believe in Marta's God or her biblical hell.

But then, the hell of her own making—the one burning her gut, cutting her heart, and incinerating her brain—was bad enough.

14

DALHU

As he scanned the room for an empty spot for the drawing he'd just finished, Dalhu rubbed a charcoal-stained palm over his mouth.

Ever since Anandur had left him with the supplies, he'd been drawing like a man possessed. The black and white sketches were spread out over every available surface of the small living room.

It started with the various pencils and charcoals, tempting him to give them a try. But then one stroke had led to another, and before long Amanda's eyes were gazing at him from a dozen or so drawings —smiling, deep in thought, sitting in a chair, reclining on a sofa, dressed, and undressed...That one, though, he'd stashed under his bed.

As it was, by neglecting to work on the profiles he'd promised to compile, he was already courting Kian's wrath. To add a nude depiction of Amanda's perfection on top of that had the potential of pushing her brother into a full-blown murderous rage.

Hopefully, the guys watching the feed from the security cameras hadn't been paying close attention to what he'd been sketching.

Though if they had, so be it. There was nothing he could do about it now.

Propping his latest creation against the wall, Dalhu stepped back to admire his work.

Damn, he needed some sticky tape or some pushpins to tack his drawings onto the wall. Save for the woman herself, there was nothing else Dalhu would rather stare at.

Though not as good as an actual photograph, he believed he'd managed to do justice to Amanda's beauty. But was he really as talented as the men had claimed he was? Or had they been simply impressed by his impeccable memory and his ability to reproduce on paper the snapshots that he'd taken with his visual cortex?

But then, producing an accurate rendition was more of a skill than an art, and he had no idea what that special something extra was that differentiated between the two.

He cast a guilty glance at the bar where the laptop sat still unopened on top of the counter. It wasn't smart to delay the profiles he'd promised Kian. He'd better stop with the drawing and get to work on those.

And yet, clutching the charcoal pencil in his hand, he couldn't bring himself to let go of it.

Hell, he didn't want to.

For those couple of hours or so that he'd been consumed by the sketching frenzy, he'd felt alive, and to open that laptop would be like dying again. Because the only way he could deal with diving back into the cesspool that had been his life over the hundreds of years of service in the Brotherhood was to get back to feeling nothing—numb—dead on the inside.

On the other hand, as gratifying as it had been to immerse himself in creating them, dozens of Amanda's portraits would get him nowhere. If he were right to assume that she'd abandoned him on her brother's orders, and not of her own free will, then Dalhu's first priority should be gaining favor with Kian. And he sure as hell wasn't going to achieve this by producing even more sketches of Amanda.

True, Kian had been impressed with that first sketch, and subsequently his attitude toward Dalhu had improved somewhat. But it wasn't enough to overcome the guy's hatred, or to influence his decision to disallow contact between Dalhu and Amanda.

As much as he loathed having to do it, Dalhu had to prove himself to the sanctimonious prick. And the only way he could attempt it in his current situation was to compile the fucking portfolios and sketch the goddamned portraits of Navuh's army's top commanders.

He'd better do an outstanding job on those and impress the hell out of the asshole. Perhaps this would convince Kian that Dalhu could be trusted.

Yeah, as if there is a chance in hell that's going to happen.

Still, there was nothing else he could do to improve his position, and it was worth the effort even for the less than slim chance that it might make a difference.

Closing his fist around the piece of charcoal, he crushed it to dust, then headed to the bathroom to wash his hands.

15

KIAN

"You want to take me out tonight?" Syssi asked, her voice sounding a little panicky.

Kian shifted the phone to his other ear as he turned on the ignition of the Lexus and shifted into gear. "Why? Is that a problem? I figured that I still owe you a date." It was a shame he couldn't ask her in person like he'd wanted to, but there was a jeweler waiting for him behind an unmarked storefront in Beverly Hills.

According to Annani, those interested in the best jewels in the world were referred to LaBurg Jewelers by other distinguished clients. No signage identified the place.

Syssi chuckled. "Yeah, I guess we should go on at least one before getting married. It's just that I'm drowning in work with all the preparations for the wedding. But I'll make time for this. When do you want to go, and where?"

"I made a reservation for eight at *By Invitation Only.*"

"Oh, that's actually perfect. We can sample Gerard's creations before he finalizes the menu—an opportunity to make last minute changes if we find something we really like or conversely do not."

"Hey, that's great, that way no one can claim that I haven't taken part in the planning. Correct?"

Syssi hadn't asked for his help, but he had a feeling that it wasn't because she had no need, but because she'd known what his answer would be. And it wasn't only on account of his busy schedule. Truth was, he had nothing to contribute, and didn't really care about the details. Whatever made Syssi happy was fine with him. Well, that wasn't entirely true—eloping and skipping the big party altogether would've made her happier.

"Your only job is to show up looking handsome. Which reminds me, Mr. Fentony will be here tomorrow at twelve. I figured that scheduling him for lunchtime will work best for you, but if it's a problem, I can call him and move the appointment. For you, the guy would reschedule the president."

"It's fine. Noon tomorrow works for me."

"I love you."

"Love you more. Be ready by seven thirty." Smiling, Kian ended the call before Syssi had a chance to respond with an I-love-you-more of her own.

It was silly, competing for who said it last and won. But it was fun, and if it made him feel like a stupid teenager, it wasn't necessarily a bad thing for a two-thousand-year-old fart.

As he rolled down the freeway at a snail's pace, he tried to imagine the perfect ring for Syssi and drew a blank. Perhaps he should not have kept it a secret and asked her to come with him? Let her choose what she liked best?

Except, knowing his sweet, unassuming Syssi and her frugal disposition, she would've chosen something simple and argued with him endlessly about spending too much money on a proper ring.

Hell, she would've never agreed, and the outing would've ended in a big fight. Because there was no way he would've compromised on that one. His girl deserved only the best—even if she didn't want it—and he certainly could afford to give it to her.

Some impatient idiot honked the horn, interrupting Kian's musing. Where did the moron think he could go? He fought the urge to open the window and flip the guy off. They were all stuck on this endless ribbon of asphalt-covered concrete, and the only way off was to find an exit. Trouble was, the surface streets were just as clogged.

Kian sighed and turned on the radio, which was tuned to his favorite classical station. As Mozart's Concerto Number 21 filled the Lexus's interior with its timeless sound, Kian relaxed into his seat, his grip on the steering wheel relaxing.

If Amanda were back home, he would've brought her along to help with the selection. Except, he doubted she would've gone anywhere with him after the way he'd treated her. And frankly, he wasn't sure he was ready for her company either. It was so damn difficult to get rid of that bitter feeling he'd come to associate with her.

Disappointment. Betrayal. Taint.

The steering wheel groaned as Kian's grip tightened again.

On some level, he was aware that his lingering resentment toward Amanda no longer made sense. After spending time with the Doomer, Kian had to concede, albeit grudgingly, that he wasn't pure evil. Not to mention that it was glaringly obvious the guy was in love with Amanda and would do anything and everything for her.

Same way I would for Syssi.

Damn, where did this come from? Kian hated that his brain had spewed out such nonsense. Comparing his feelings for Syssi to what the Doomer felt for Amanda? Ludicrous.

But was it?

Kian's gut, or perhaps it was his conscience, insisted that the difference existed only in his head, tinted by his perception of who and what Dalhu was.

An enemy. A killer. A heartless, cruel creature with no conscience or morality. A self-centered, self-absorbed opportunist.

Or was he?

Casting a glance at Brundar's stoic face, Kian shook his head. There would be no words of wisdom coming from that direction. The guy was there only because Kian had promised his mother he'd go nowhere without his bodyguards, and not because he needed the guy's advice or his opinion. And it wasn't as if he would've gotten any if he asked. Brundar would've just arched his blond brows and returned to staring ahead.

It was easy to forget that he was even there.

Weird guy. But a goddamned excellent fighter. If Kian ended up buying a million dollar ring for Syssi, which was his intention, he wanted an extra pair of capable hands to guard it on the way home. And besides, having a passenger allowed him to make use of the carpool lane if one was available.

The drive that should've taken no more than ten minutes stretched to double that, and as he left the SUV with the valet, he was already five minutes late for his appointment with the renowned Mrs. LaBurg. A few seconds later, the reinforced glass door was opened by a courteous employee in a three-piece suit who introduced himself as Pierre. Kian wondered if the French names were real. Probably not. More likely a sly attempt to add a flair of sophistication meant to impress the high-class patrons of the place.

"Please, follow me. Mrs. LaBurg will see you in the private viewing room." Pierre dipped his head in a perfunctory bow and motioned for them to follow through a cleverly concealed metal detector. The main showroom was not as large as Kian had expected, but it was classy and understated. A pale Aubusson rug covered the hardwood floor, and several small oil paintings in substantial, yet minimally adorned, wooden frames hung on the walls. Small light fixtures cast soft illumination on the surfaces of the paintings, but little else.

The lack of bright light was a peculiar choice for a place that was supposed to showcase diamonds. But what did he know, perhaps this was the standard for jewelry stores.

As Pierre opened the door to the back room, an older lady rose to greet them. She was wearing a conservative beige suit that even Kian recognized as signature Chanel, and her small stature was aided by a pair of high-heeled shoes that seemed too tall for a woman who looked like somebody's grandma.

Her intake of breath as she got a good look at him was audible, but then her eyes drifted to Brundar and a tiny smirk lifted her thin lips. "Welcome, Mr. Kian." She offered her slightly wrinkled hand.

"Just Kian." He shook it. Damn, he really needed to come up with a last name for situations like these. He hated the generic "Smith" Shai had used for his driver's license and other official documents.

"And you are?" She offered Brundar a warm smile as he took her offered hand.

Fuck. Obviously, she thought Brundar was the one Kian was purchasing the ring for. Not that he could blame the old girl for her misconception. With the guy's smooth-shaven pretty face, and his fucking blond hair reaching his mid back, it was no wonder she assumed he was the fiancé. After all, this was Los Angeles.

"His bodyguard," Brundar clarified.

"Oh, yes, but of course. Very prudent of you, Mr. Kian." She quickly recovered like the pro she was.

"Though we would've gladly delivered your purchases to your home ourselves. Most of our clients opt to have it done this way. No need to take unnecessary risks. Unfortunately, it's not unheard of for criminals to observe an establishment such as ours and follow a client home." She was looking Brundar over from head to toe, no doubt searching for a concealed weapon—something that the metal detector up front had missed.

But heeding Annani's advice, Brundar had left his daggers stashed under the Lexus's back seat instead of surrendering them to Pierre upon entering the store. Even unarmed, however, Brundar was a deadly weapon—the daggers just one more accessory in his arsenal.

"It's very kind of you to offer, but as you can see, there will be no need. Can we please move on to the selection? I'm somewhat in a rush." Kian sat down and motioned for Brundar to do the same.

"Yes, right away, sir." She took a seat across from them. "Pierre? Could you please bring the selection for Mr. Kian?"

He'd wondered about that. There were no display cases in the private viewing room. It was set up as a parlor—with a thick Persian rug covering the hardwood floor, and a sitting arrangement comprised of a dainty sofa, two matching armchairs, and a dark-mahogany coffee table. A few pictures hung on the fabric-covered walls, the largest one a portrait, no doubt of the late Mr. LaBurg—the proud founder of LaBurg Jewelers.

Only the microscope and the powerful LED lamp sitting on top of the coffee table hinted at the type of business taking place in this room. To the side, a cart stood on two short legs in front and two large wheels in the back and held an ice bucket with a wine bottle chilling inside it. Kian wondered if the two crystal glasses on the tray next to the bucket were there for Mrs. LaBurg and him, or for the happy couple.

Pierre got busy at the sizable wall safe that was hidden behind Mr. LaBurg's portrait, pulling out a velvet-covered tray. His steps were small and measured as he brought the tray over and gently placed it on the coffee table. There were only four simple rings on top of that tray, but each held a diamond that was anything but, and as Mrs. LaBurg flicked on the LED lamp, the light reflecting off those stones was blinding.

Kian was impressed. The lady had asked for his preferences over the phone and had delivered exactly what he had in mind—a simple, elegantly designed ring with one extraordinary stone.

The modest design was the only concession he was willing to make on account of Syssi's aversion to extravagance—but the stone would be the best this jeweler had to offer. And as this was the most prominent establishment of its kind on the West Coast, it meant that it was the best there was.

"Can I pour you some wine while you examine the selection?" She pulled out the bottle from the ice bucket and presented it to him.

As if he was going to check the label. "No, thank you."

Kian lifted each of the rings one at a time, examining them under the LED light and then returning them to the tray before checking out the next. They were all equally beautiful.

"These are the best we have and, naturally, each diamond is certified by the two leading grading agencies. The GIA, the Gemological Institute of America. And the AGS, the American Gemological Society," Mrs. LaBurg whispered with reverence. "You will not find diamonds of this size and quality anywhere else on the West Coast, you have my word. At least not from a reputable establishment."

Did he believe her? Perhaps. But that wasn't important for him to have the absolute best. The best available, with certificates, would have to do because he was out of time. Besides, he knew next to nothing about diamonds.

"They are all beautiful. Which one would you say is the best?"

Mrs. LaBurg picked up the one he had his eye on. It seemed to be slightly larger than the others, but it wasn't the only reason he gravitated toward it. There was something about the ring's design and the stone itself. It just seemed like the one. "This is a flawless, nine-point-five-carat emerald-cut, D color. I think it's the most beautiful of the four."

He had to agree. "How much?"

"The best I can do is one million seven hundred and fifty thousand."

Not too bad. From what his mother had told him, he'd expected it to be more than two million. But that didn't mean he wasn't going to negotiate. If for no other reason than to tell Syssi that he got it at a bargain price without having to lie.

"If I have the money transferred to your account right now, can you do one and a half?"

Mrs. LaBurg didn't even blink. Evidently, he wasn't the first client to offer cash payment. She smiled, her veneered teeth gleaming. "You've got yourself a deal, Mr. Kian." She offered her hand.

From there it was a matter of getting her banking information to Shai and having him wire the money directly there.

Pierre produced a fancy box to house the even fancier little box he'd put the ring in, then wrapped everything and placed it in a small, black fabric bag together with the certificates the diamond came with. There was no logo or any other indication that the bag came from a store. Discreet.

"Of course, if there is any problem with the sizing, we will do all of the necessary adjustments." She handed Kian the little bag. "I hope your fiancée loves it, but if she is not happy with the ring for some reason, we would gladly exchange it."

"Thank you, I'm sure there will be no need."

The ring was stunning, and the only problem Syssi would have with it was its price. Kian was prepared for a long and hard argument.

Funny, here he was with a beautiful engagement ring, and instead of expecting a big thank-you he was worried that his fiancée would march him back to the store to return it because it was too extravagant.

Still, if this was all they would ever fight about, they were good.

When he stood up, Mrs. LaBurg offered her hand again.

"It was a pleasure doing business with you, Mr. Kian. Is there anything else I can interest you in? Maybe a set of matching earrings? Or a necklace?"

Well, in fact, there was. After all, his *pervy* proposal included a diamond choker to go with the ring, right?

16

AMANDA

Standing on the top deck of the *Anna,* Amanda watched the sunset as the massive boat glided into Marina del Rey.

It wouldn't be long now before she docked in her spot. Not long enough, anyway. Amanda wasn't ready to face Dalhu yet.

Hell, she would probably never be.

For the past two hours, she'd been mulling over what to say to him—the thoughts running in circles in her head. Problem was, she still didn't know how she felt about him.

Liar... Her subconscious whispered.

If you're so smart, then you tell me.

Simple, you want him.

Simple? He's responsible for Mark's murder. There is nothing simple about it.

Great, now she was talking to herself as if her subconscious was a separate entity.

Okay, girl, you are a scientist, and scientists search for solutions to problems instead of dwelling endlessly on the unfairness of them.

First, for the sake of clarity, she needed to define the problem from a rational standpoint rather than an emotional one. Perhaps it would be better to write it down.

The *Anna* would be mooring soon, but no one said Amanda needed to leave right away. And if Geneva had a problem with that, so be it. Amanda had paid the crew a hefty sum, a whole week of double wages, and had used only three days.

Fates, it felt as if she'd been gone for weeks.

Her tablet was in her purse and she pulled it out, then settled on the chaise lounge to write her *paper* on Dalhu. Staring into the color-infused ocean, she gathered her thoughts.

Dalhu was an ex-Doomer, who had decided to leave his old life behind and turn a new page on her account. He had kidnapped her only because she would've never given him a chance and gotten to know him otherwise.

The little time they had spent together had been the best she had ever experienced—and that was saying a lot considering that half of the time she'd been either terrified of him or plotting to clobber him over the head with a shovel and run.

He'd treated her with respect—more like reverence—and she had no doubt that he'd fallen in love with her. He'd been mostly honest with her and had told her about his past without trying to portray himself as a better man.

Not telling her about Mark qualified more as an omission than an outright lie. Except, if he'd omitted one thing, he might have omitted other incriminating stuff. On the other hand, the list of his crimes was probably too long for him to mention each one separately. After all, he'd been a mercenary—a killer.

His past wouldn't have troubled her so if not for Mark. There was a big difference between thinking of Dalhu's kills as casualties of war, and regarding his part in her nephew's murder the same way.

And yet, she had to concede that there were mitigating circumstances.

When he'd issued the order to kill Mark, Dalhu hadn't known

she even existed, or that Mark was an immortal. In his eyes, his intent, this was another casualty of war.

Except, Mark had been a programmer, not a warrior.

Then again, if Mark hadn't been a relative, it would've bothered her to a much lesser extent.

What did it say about her, though? What kind of woman was willing to accept a killer as her mate?

Why couldn't Dalhu have been a professor? Heck, anyone would've been better than a killer. Even an accountant.

Amanda chuckled. As if she would've ever been attracted to a boring number cruncher.

The embarrassing truth was that she liked dangerous boys, and mellow males left her indifferent. It was utterly stupid, especially since she was supposed to be this sophisticated woman and to know better. She was a professor, for heaven's sake.

Yeah, the sadistic Fates were probably cackling with glee at the havoc their machinations were wreaking. Why pair her with a nice guy, when an ex-Doomer provided so much more entertainment for them?

The Fates had been kind to Kian, though. Amanda couldn't imagine a better partner for him than his sweet Syssi. The girl was simply the best. But to be fair, Kian had waited an awfully long time for his fated mate. And while he'd waited, he'd been earning a shit-load of points by impressing the Fates with all the sacrifices he'd made—always putting the welfare of the clan before his own.

So yeah, Kian was definitely deserving of their benevolence. Amanda, on the other hand, had partied for most of her life, and when she'd finally decided to take herself more seriously and dedicate her time to solving her clan's most pressing problem—finding Dormants of other lines—it hadn't been an entirely selfless move. She'd sought recognition and respect.

And anyway, it wasn't as if nice, eligible, immortal bachelors were lined up for her. Except for Andrew, that is. But first of all,

Andrew wasn't an immortal, yet, and second, he wasn't an innocent lamb either—hence the initial attraction. But that attraction paled in comparison to what she felt for Dalhu.

"American, we've docked. Don't you want to go home?" Geneva's wide shoulders blocked the view.

"I need a few minutes. Half an hour tops. Why? Are you in a hurry, Ruska?"

"No, I let the crew off for the evening, but I'm staying. Care for some vodka while you stare at the blank screen of your tablet? You look like you need it."

"Actually, that's a splendid idea, though coming from you, somewhat suspicious. Why so nice all of a sudden?"

Geneva shrugged. "I don't like drinking alone."

"Fine, but mix mine with orange juice."

Geneva arched a brow. "That's a pussy drink, American. Good vodka should be drunk straight up."

"Yeah, yeah, whatever, I want a screwdriver."

"As you wish, pussycat."

Amanda flipped her the bird. It had been on the tip of her tongue to tell Geneva to go get drunk on engine oil, but it was never smart to offend someone who was bringing you food or drink—lest they spit in it.

Geneva flipped her back before taking the stairs down to the upper grand salon.

Okay, where was I?

Dalhu. Bad boy attraction. Fated mate. That about summed it up. Especially the fated mate part.

Was he, though? Her gut was saying yes, but her brain was refusing to accept it. Because if he were her fated mate, then she was screwed big time. She wouldn't be able to resist the pull, but her relationship with Dalhu would forever be tainted by Mark's blood.

"Here's your juice, American." Geneva handed her the tall glass, then walked over to the other side and sat down with the vodka bottle in hand.

Apparently, Amanda wasn't the only one having a tough time.

"What's wrong, Captain?"

"Everything. Nothing. Just life, you know, it sucks." She chugged an impressive quantity on a oner.

"Want to talk about it?"

"That's the problem with you, Americans—talk and talk and more talk. We Russians, we do not talk."

"Yeah? And what do you have to show for it? The last time I checked, nobody is rushing to your borders in hopes of a better life, chasing the *Russian* dream. While we can't keep them away."

"That is true. But the people who came here first and started your great country, they didn't spend their time talking, they were too busy building."

"Ha, but they came because they wanted to be free, and freedom is an idea, so they had to talk about it."

"Whatever, I'm not in the mood for a political discussion."

"You started it..."

"Just go back to staring at your tablet." Geneva waved with the almost empty bottle.

That's what I get for trying to be nice to a surly Russian. Amanda harrumphed.

But Geneva hadn't been entirely wrong. It was time to stop over-analyzing and overthinking. It was time for doing. Chickening out was the only reason Amanda was still on board instead of in a taxi on the way to the keep. And her sitting on her butt and pondering would resolve nothing.

She swung her legs over the side of the chaise and pushed up, then headed for the staircase, but stopped before descending and turned around.

"I'm leaving now. Come, give me a hug goodbye," she told Geneva.

As the woman regarded Amanda, her expression changed from her usual pissed one to something that approximated fondness. She got to her feet and pulled Amanda into a bear hug that would've crushed her ribs if she were a human. "You're okay, American. I like you." She let go with a slap on Amanda's shoulder.

"If that's how you are when you like someone, I wonder what you're like when you don't."

"You don't want to know."

"No, I guess I don't."

17

ANDREW

The gate to the clan's private garage was on the lowest level of the high-rise underground parking structure, and Andrew slowed his car before coming to a full stop in front of it. The sensor read the sticker on his windshield, and the thing slid open.

Kind of made a guy feel like he was part of the family. Except, as the only mortal among them, he was still an outsider, albeit one with a key to the front door—but no room of his own.

He eased into a vacant spot between Kian's SUV and someone's black Porsche. Hopefully, he wasn't taking somebody's parking space. But there were no markings on the concrete aside from those delineating the spots.

He was curious about whom the Porsche belonged to.

Perhaps Bridget? He wouldn't be surprised if it were hers. Last night, he'd found out that the doctor had an adventurous streak. A fast car suited her.

Reaching over to the passenger seat, he grabbed the grocery bag with the wine and Godiva chocolates box he'd bought for Bridget. It wasn't that he hadn't thought of buying a gift bag, or skimped on the few bucks it would've cost. It's just that he wasn't sure if Bridget wished for their relationship, or rather hookup, to become common knowledge.

That was also why he hadn't brought flowers. Nothing like a guy walking in with a bouquet to advertise that he was coming to see the woman and not the doctor for some medical advice.

As he walked toward the bank of elevators, he had the impulse to check whether his thumbprint would work on the one dedicated to the use of the penthouse occupants, namely Kian and Amanda. Obviously, they weren't the only ones with access to the thing. Their mother, the two butlers, and the Guardians had to have access too. But there was no reason for him to be granted that privilege, unless, as Syssi's brother and Amanda's rescuer, William considered him worthy of the honor.

Why not check it out? After all, he wasn't due at Bridget's for another twenty minutes.

As was his habit, Andrew had arrived early for his dinner date, but he had no intention of knocking on her door before it was time. It wouldn't be polite. He'd intended to check out the underground gym, but he could spare a few minutes for a quick ride up to the penthouse and then take the elevator down to the basement—if his thumbprint worked, that is.

By now, he had ridden up and down enough times to figure out the clever configuration of the private and public elevator banks. There were three doors that opened to the lobby, one of them serving the penthouse and the other two serving the guests of the rental floors. Three additional doors opened on the other side and served the clan. The two general use public elevators were back to back to two private ones while the penthouse had only one, but it opened both to the lobby and to the back. Of course, one needed a key or a thumbprint to be able to use it.

Andrew pressed his thumb to the reader, and a split second later the light turned on.

Nice, he was impressed. Well, too early to pound his chest and declare himself king of the elevators. He still needed to see if the thing would go where he told it to.

When the doors swished open, he stepped inside and glanced up —showing his face to the surveillance camera. If he were overstepping his bounds, the guys in security would tell him to get out.

The loudspeakers remained silent.

Still, he didn't want to appear as if he was snooping around uninvited. Maybe he should stop by the lobby and check with the guys if it was okay.

But as he was about to press his thumb to the L button, the elevator lurched into motion, and a moment later it came to a stop right where he wanted to go.

Probably the security guys' work—overriding the elevator's commands and bringing him up for a polite yet stern explanation of why he shouldn't be using the thing without an invitation from one of the penthouse occupants.

Damn, they'd think he was spying, and this little joyride would cause an incident.

The doors slid open.

"Oh, it's you..." Amanda's hand flew to her chest. "I'm sorry, Andrew, for a moment there, I thought you were Kian." She blew out a breath and stepped in, pulling behind her a carry-on. A matching duffle bag was slung over her shoulder. "Are you going up to Kian and Syssi's? Or going down to the underground? I must've hijacked you."

Hell, this was awkward. What was he going to tell her?

"That's okay, I just wanted to check if my thumbprint works on the penthouse elevator, but you beat me to it."

Amanda smiled. "I don't see why it wouldn't, but go ahead, press away." She moved aside.

"Thank you. Going up?"

"Where else? I just hope I can sneak into my apartment without bumping into Kian."

Andrew arched a brow and leaned to press the button for the penthouse level.

"Here, give me your bag." He lifted the thing off her shoulder and slung it over his. "So, you're still avoiding him?"

Amanda sighed. "Yeah, I don't want to see him, not yet."

"No worries, he's not here. He and Syssi are on a date—the same one they were supposed to go on the day her transition started and you got snagged—some fancy restaurant that one of your nephews runs. Syssi said he is going to help with the wedding menu. She wants to sample the dishes he suggested before finalizing it."

"Well, good for them."

Andrew detected the slight undertone of bitterness that she was working hard to hide. "Want to tell me what's going on with you?"

"It's complicated, and explaining would take a little longer than this ride." She looked away, but he caught her grimace reflected in the mirror.

"How about we go to your place, sit down, and you tell me what's on your mind? Sometimes, talking about it helps." He held the elevator door from closing as Amanda rolled out her carry-on.

He still had time before he was supposed to show up at Bridget's. Besides, if he arrived a little late, she'd understand—one of the advantages of dating a woman who wasn't ruled by emotions.

As Amanda regarded him, her pinched brows and the tight line of her lips implied that it was a no. Perhaps she didn't want to talk about it—with him—but didn't want to offend him by refusing.

"I see that you're not in the mood. We can catch up some other time." He moved to step back inside the elevator.

"No, wait." Amanda's hand closed around his bicep. "It's not that. It's just that my mother is staying at my place and I'd rather have this talk without her running commentary. I love her dearly, but sometimes she's just too much."

Amanda was right, the Goddess's overwhelming presence wasn't conducive to a heart-to-heart convo that didn't include her. "I know what you mean."

"We can sneak into Kian's."

"You think he'll be okay with us invading his home? And anyway, do you have a key?"

Amanda was already pulling the carry-on in a big arc as she turned toward the other door. "Okidu is probably home, and he won't mind. But even if he isn't, Kian leaves the door unlocked. It's not like there is any chance of thieves making it up here unnoticed."

She knocked once, then tried the handle. Just as she'd anticipated, the door swung open.

"Come on." She crossed into the living room, leaving her rolling suitcase by the door and heading for the bar.

Following Amanda's example, Andrew dropped her shoulder bag next to the luggage.

"I'm mixing myself a screwdriver. What would you like?"

"Same."

Amanda chuckled. "Earlier today, I was told by a surly Russian that a screwdriver is a pussy drink. I doubt she would've dared to say it to you."

"Why? Do I look so tough?" Andrew took the drink Amanda handed him.

"Very." She walked over to the sofa and plopped down—by some miracle not a drop of her drink spilling over.

"I'm not sure if I should be flattered or offended."

Definitely flattered.

Especially since his manliness had been put to the test by a tiny redhead and been found wanting.

Amanda shrugged. "I have a thing for tough guys, so coming from me it's a compliment."

Was she coming on to him? And if she was, what was he

supposed to say? Thank you? Instead, he took a big gulp from his drink and avoided her eyes.

"Everything okay? You seem… well, uncomfortable—for lack of a better word—like something is bothering you."

Yeah, time to fess up.

"You haven't asked me what I'm doing here."

Coward, just come out and say it.

Amanda arched a brow. "Okay… What are you doing here, Andrew?"

"Bridget invited me to a dinner date at her place."

"Our Bridget? Oh, Andrew, that's fantastic." Amanda put her drink on the coffee table and clapped her hands. "Tell me all about it. I want to hear all the juicy, romantic details."

Her eyes were sparkling with excitement as if he'd just told her the best of news as opposed to informing her that he was no longer vying for her affection.

Though truth be told, except for that first time they'd met in the restaurant, Amanda hadn't responded to any of his suggestive hints. Since hooking up with the Doomer, she simply hadn't been interested.

For a moment, Andrew experienced an ugly flare of jealousy. He was just too damn competitive to accept that he'd lost so handily to another man. Never mind that he already had come to the realization that Amanda wasn't the one for him.

He shrugged. "Nothing to tell, really. One thing led to another, and she invited me to a home-cooked dinner. So, here I am, bearing gifts of chocolates and wine." He lifted the grocery bag off the floor.

Amanda shook her head. "You men are hopeless. You can't show up for a date with a brown bag from a supermarket." She pushed up to her feet. "I'll go check if Kian has something you can use. Though I doubt he does. Worst case, you can ditch the bag and just hold the stuff in your hands."

He grabbed her hand and pulled her back. “Sit down, Amanda. I don’t need anything fancy. It’s not that kind of a date.”

“Oh.” Her face fell. She sat on the sofa and reached for her drink.

“So, tell me, where did you run off to?”

“I borrowed a boat from a friend.” She snorted at his surprised expression. “Not a fishing boat, a yacht with a crew.”

He chuckled. “That’s more like you.”

“I needed time to figure things out. Sort my feelings for Dalhu.” She sighed. “Not that it helped, much. I’m still having trouble deciding what I’m going to do about it.”

“Lay it on me.”

She scrunched her nose. “You sure? I know that you have something going on with Bridget now, but for a time you seemed interested in me, and I don’t know if you’re up to hearing about Dalhu and me. I don’t want you to feel awkward.”

“I was. Interested, that is. In fact, I was more than interested.” He chuckled nervously. It wasn’t something he was comfortable admitting. But if he expected her to open up and tell him private things, it was only fair for him to do the same—even if it came at the expense of his macho image.

“You are an exquisite woman, Amanda, but I’m ashamed to admit that this wasn’t the only reason I was obsessed with you.” He rubbed his palm over the back of his neck. “The truth is that I am an extremely competitive guy, and I just couldn’t bear to lose you to Dalhu. Especially since I truly believed I was the better choice for you. I couldn’t understand your infatuation with him. I thought, same as everyone else did, that your feelings weren’t real, that they were the result of a stressful situation and your survival instinct prompting you to gain the affection of your kidnapper.”

“What caused you to change your mind?”

“Dalhu.” Andrew finished his drink and got up to refill his glass.

“What do you mean?”

Andrew poured himself more vodka, omitting the orange juice this time. "You want the short version or the long one?"

"What do you think? Of course, I want the long one."

He sat down next to her. "Kian wanted me to be there while he interrogated Dalhu—mainly because of my lie-detecting skills, but also to help with the questioning." Andrew took a small sip of the vodka. Not very manly, true, but showing up drunk for a date was even less so. "Don't get me wrong, it's not that I think your guy is good, or even decent. He is a cold-blooded killer that doesn't give a damn about anybody or anything. Except you."

What he was going to tell her next was the toughest part, and Andrew took a more substantial sip this time. "I realized that his love for you wasn't a temporary flare, but a fire that burned bright and hot and steady, and I had no choice but to accept that my feelings for you were just a pale approximation in comparison. And while he would always choose you, not only over other women but over anything and everything else, I had to admit that it wasn't true for me. Not the other women part, because c'mon, none could compare, but I knew that there were things I would love to do even more than be with you." He braved a quick glance at her face and was relieved to find a small knowing smile and not a sad or disappointed one. In fact, her sagely benevolent expression made her look a lot like her mother.

But then, the mischievous spark that he was familiar with reappeared, combined with a heart-stopping grin. "Oh, yeah? Like what? What on earth could be more satisfying than worshiping at my feet?"

"For Dalhu? Apparently nothing. But give me a mission no one in his right mind would take and I'd be on it like there is no tomorrow." Andrew snorted. "I guess Kian wasn't wrong when he accused me of being an adrenaline junkie."

Amanda's brows shot up. "Really? You'd take on a deadly mission over me? I wasn't offended before, but now..."

Taking her hand, Andrew looked into her eyes. "Don't. You are beyond gorgeous and hot as hell, and to be frank, I think I'm a better man than your Doomer. But I would be deceiving myself as well as you if I pretend that you've touched my soul the way you've obviously touched Dalhu's. After witnessing the powerful connection between Kian and Syssi and then recognizing the same in Dalhu, I couldn't in good conscience dismiss him as unworthy of you. The enormity of his love proves him as worthy, and condemns me as not."

There were tears glistening in Amanda's eyes, and the hand he was holding was trembling.

She whispered, "What are you saying, Andrew?"

"When I had this epiphany, I wondered if your feelings for Dalhu were as strong as his were for you, and I made a wish."

"What was it?"

He leaned and kissed her cheek. "May you find the wisdom to realize your true heart's desire, the strength to acknowledge it, and the courage to pursue it."

Amanda's lip quivered, and tears glistened on her long, dark lashes. "That's so beautiful"—she sniffled—"but unfortunately, far from simple."

18

AMANDA

Sweet, sweet, Andrew. I wish that things were so straightforward.

But Dalhu's love wasn't enough to overcome his murderous past, or rather one specific murder.

"You're wrong," Andrew said.

With indignation drying her tears, fast, she crossed her arms over her chest and lifted her chin. "What? Am I supposed to forget and forgive the murder of my nephew?"

"No. But you shouldn't punish and torture yourself for it either. It had nothing to do with you."

Now, that was a convoluted way to look at it. Leave it to a male to try to simplify things to the level of absurdity.

Amanda chuckled. "Your interpretation of the situation is the equivalent of applying quantum physics to emotions and feelings."

"Huh?" Poor Andrew tilted his head like a dog trying to understand verbal communication.

Sliding into her teacher mode, Amanda put on a smile. "Our everyday reality, or the physics we are all familiar with, disintegrates at the quantum level—the level of elementary particles—where nothing makes straightforward sense. Einstein coined the phrase *spooky action at a distance* about what he thought was the improbability of quantum phenomena as presented by other scientists of his time. He also said that things should be made as simple as possible, but not any simpler."

"I must be dense because I'm not following."

"You are breaking it into its basic components while ignoring other relevant and limiting factors. The way you present it, all I need to do is figure out what I want, accept that this is indeed what I want, and go for it. As if nothing aside from my needs and wants matters."

"Because in the final analysis, nothing does. You cannot deny the powerful connection you have with Dalhu, one that even a dense guy like me has no choice but to acknowledge, and in the end, you are going to accept that there is no way you could go on without him. All you're doing in the meantime is suffering. God, or fate, or whatever you want to call it has decided that the two of you belong together, and to fight destiny is futile."

"Says Andrew the wise. How can you claim with such confidence that this is my fate or my destiny? How can anyone?"

Andrew shrugged. "Sometimes you just have to trust your gut."

"You sound like my mother."

"Who is very wise—a goddess, no less—with more than five thousand years of experience. I would listen to her if I were you."

He had a point. This was what she'd been planning to do anyway before he'd intercepted her and offered to play shrink.

"You're right, I will."

Andrew lifted his grocery bag and pushed to his feet. "Good luck," he said, offering his hand.

She pulled him into her arms and squeezed. "You're a great guy, Andrew. And I'm so lucky to have you as a brother-in-law. In fact, I consider Syssi a sister without the in-law and the same goes for you. From now on, for better or worse, you're my brother."

He grinned. "I never thought the day would come when I'd be

glad that a stunning woman has sisterly feelings for me, but here I am—happy as can be to have gained another sister."

As she reached for her carry-on, Andrew lifted her bag and slung it over his shoulder. He carried it the short distance across the vestibule. She didn't need his help; the bag was bulky but not that heavy, and by now he must've been aware that, as an immortal female, she was at least equal in strength if not stronger than him. But it seemed to be something he did without thinking, a behavior so ingrained that it was on autopilot.

Such a gentleman.

"Thank you." Amanda kissed his cheek before taking it from him.

"My pleasure."

"Say hi to Bridget for me."

Andrew grimaced. "I'm not sure she wants anyone to know about us."

"Why on earth not? If you were my boyfriend, I would've paraded you around, showing you off."

"That's the thing. I'm not sure she thinks of me as her boyfriend. It's, you know, more of a short-term thing. I think..."

"You mean a hookup?"

Andrew's ears got a shade darker, and he looked away. "Yeah, kind of."

He was probably reading Bridget's signals all wrong. The doctor would be insane not to sink her hooks into this yummy piece of a potential immortal male. The problem must've been with him.

"Well, I'm sure you're wrong about this. But whatever makes you comfortable. If you want me to keep this a secret, for now, I will."

"I'd appreciate it."

"Goodbye, Andrew." She waved her hand as he stepped into the elevator.

Okay, deep breath, big smile, and go... Amanda depressed the handle and pushed open the door. But Annani wasn't there.

"Ninni? Where are you?"

"I am outside," her mother called from the terrace. The sliding doors were closed, and the curtains were only partially parted to admit the weak moonlight.

Onidu rushed out from the kitchen, a big smile plastered on his face. "Mistress, you are back. Let me take care of your luggage."

She pulled him into a hug before he had a chance to grab her things and scurry away to unpack.

As always, he stood motionless without returning her hug. The poor thing's programming didn't include the proper response. Maybe she should teach him what to do when someone embraced him. On the other hand, his response—or lack thereof—was so familiar that she would've most likely found it disturbing if he ever hugged her back. Never mind that it was silly of her to do so in the first place. But there was something comforting about the peculiar feel of his hybrid too-solid body. Perhaps it was just that he'd been with her since she was a little girl, and in her subconscious his presence represented security and being cared for. Was it a wonder then that she often thought of him as family?

Letting go, she handed him her purse. "Please put it in my bedroom. When you unpack the luggage, take the clothes to the laundry. Everything is dirty and needs to be washed or dry-cleaned."

He bowed. "It will be done immediately, mistress."

Of course, it would.

As she made her way out to greet her mother, Amanda shook her head. Annani was probably lounging outside and hadn't felt like getting up to welcome her daughter home. And it had nothing to do with her being pissed at Amanda for leaving the way she had. It was just Annani's normal diva attitude.

Having a goddess for a mother had its advantages and disadvantages.

Not that Amanda had ever questioned her mother's love. Annani was very generous with her affections, both verbal and physical. It was just that sometimes, not often, Amanda secretly wished for a mother that wasn't so grand—one that would go shopping with her, or out for coffee, or just call to chitchat about things of no particular importance.

Would've been nice—would've alleviated some of Amanda's loneliness.

It was dark outside, but Amanda found Annani sprawled on a lounger as if she was sunbathing in the middle of the day. Her mother was holding a book, her own glow providing the illumination.

"Good evening, Mother, what are you reading?"

Annani lifted the book and turned it so Amanda could see the cover—*The Abbreviated History of Humankind.*

Amanda chuckled. "As someone who has witnessed humanity's formative years in person, you could write one yourself."

"Perhaps one day I will." Annani shook the book. "This one contains so many untruths and misconceptions while omitting some of the most critical events that changed the course of history, that I suspect no one would believe an account of how things really happened. They would think it was all fictional."

Amanda pulled out a chair and turned it to face Annani. "I bet." She sat down and leaned forward, bracing her elbows on her knees. "How mad are you at me? For running off on you?"

Annani put the book down and sighed. "You were not running away from me, my dear child. You were trying to run away from yourself. One cannot do that, you know."

Amanda snorted. "Tell me about it."

Annani lifted one red brow. "I thought I did."

"It's just an expression, it means that I know you are right."

"Of course, I am. I am never wrong."

This conversation was going nowhere fast. She'd better get to the point.

"If you're so wise, tell me what to do about Dalhu."

"I cannot. It is not my place to decide matters of the heart for you. Only you can do it."

Annani could be so frustrating at times.

"Can you at least help me figure things out?"

Annani inclined her head. "Certainly." In one fluid motion, she lifted her legs and swung them around to sit sideways, facing Amanda. "Would you care for some sparkling water?" She poured some from a carafe.

"Yes, thank you."

Annani filled another glass and handed it to Amanda, then took a few small sips before putting her glass down. She then leaned forward and rubbed her palms. "Let us figure out things together, my dear."

19

ANDREW

"Is this for me?" Bridget took the grocery bag from Andrew.

"My modest contribution to a meal that"—he inhaled deeply—"smells delicious."

"Thank you." Bridget stretched to plant a kiss on his cheek. "Please, come in." She pivoted on a very spiky high heel.

Damn, the same red fuck-me shoes from last night.

In response, his shaft punched out an erection that was about to pop his zipper. Apparently, he was like those Pavlov's dogs that salivated when the bell rang even when it no longer coincided with their meal delivery. Though in his case, it wasn't food, but a pair of spiky red heels on the feet of a deliciously compact female. They made her ass look so good that he felt like giving it a little love bite.

With an effort, Andrew managed to tear his eyes away from Bridget's sexy butt and take a look at the table that was set for a romantic dinner for two—including a fancy tablecloth, two crystal wine goblets, two lighted tapers, and a vase of fresh flowers.

Oh, hell, this doesn't look like a setup for a hookup.

Bridget had obviously put a lot of work into this dinner, and he was starting to think that maybe Amanda was right and he had somehow misjudged the doctor's intentions.

"Everything looks so nice," he mumbled, suddenly deeply embarrassed about the brown paper bag his gifts had arrived in.

Always listen to a woman's advice on matters like that.

Bridget's cheeks reddened. "I know that I went a little overboard with this. It's just that I've never had an opportunity to entertain a guy in my apartment before. Other than my son, that is. But he doesn't count." She took out the wine bottle from the bag and put it on the table. "Thank you for the wine." Next were the chocolates. "Ah, Godiva." She turned to Andrew. "You certainly know the way to a girl's heart." She licked her lips in a way that had his shaft pulsate—reminding him that it was still extremely uncomfortable and waiting to be taken care of.

But then what she'd said registered in his blood-deprived brain. "You have a son?"

And where was that son of hers? Sleeping soundly in one of the bedrooms? Damn, he hated hooking up with a mother—at her home. It was like having guerrilla sex, stealthy and rushed. Major bummer.

"Yes, Julian. He is a student at Johns Hopkins University School of Medicine. In fact, he's about to graduate."

For a moment, he was taken aback. It was hard to reconcile a woman that appeared to be in her late twenties with someone who had a son in medical school. But for all he knew, Bridget could've been hundreds of years old…

How was that for weird?

"Like mother, like son. You must be proud." He managed to sound conversational.

She beamed. "Very. And he is graduating at the top of his class. Though I'll be damned if I know how he pulled it off."

"Really?"

The boy must've been a genius to be at the top of a graduating class of a school that admitted only the best of the best.

"Julian still gets light-headed if I approach him with a needle in hand. He is like a baby when it comes to his own blood. But it seems that he is unaffected when it's someone else's."

"Do you visit him often?"

"Not really. It's hard to explain a mother that looks like me. We figured it would be best for him to come home when he can. But between the schoolwork, the lab work, and having a semblance of a social life, he doesn't have time—just the commute from Baltimore to LA takes half a day. Not to mention that he can't afford being jetlagged when he goes back to school."

"I bet you miss him."

"We talk on the phone and we video chat." She lifted her hands in the what-can-I-do sign.

Something started beeping in the kitchen.

"Take a seat, Andrew. I'll go check on the soup."

He did as he was told and waited for her to come back.

That beeping had sounded a lot like a microwave oven, and Andrew chuckled when a suspicious thought flitted through his mind. Bridget must've bought the meal from some restaurant and was just reheating it. Not that he minded. In fact, he was glad that she hadn't gone to all that trouble on his account.

And here I am, sitting like a schmuck instead of helping.

He started to get up. "Do you need help in there?"

"No! I've got everything under control." Bridget's panicky answer confirmed his suspicions.

As he lowered his butt to the chair, he couldn't help imagining Bridget burying restaurant containers deep under other trash to hide the evidence. Should he play along?

Yeah, he should. She would be so embarrassed if she knew he figured out her secret. But what would happen when he complimented her cooking? Which he'd have to do, or she'd think he didn't like the food.

He wondered how good of a liar she was. Not that she could ever deceive him. He was just curious to see her try. Would she avert her eyes? Blush? Fidget with her hands? There were so many telltale signs if one knew what to look for.

"Here is the soup, I hope you like it. It's cream of mushroom." She placed a steaming bowl in front of him and sat down on the other side of the table with her own.

The table was smallish in size, which was good because even across from him Bridget was still close and he liked the intimate setting. Scooping some of the thick, brown liquid together with the dried onion flakes she'd put in the center of each bowl, he brought it close to his mouth and blew on it to cool it. The soup was hot and he didn't want to risk burning his tongue.

It was important for that particular part of his anatomy to remain in good working condition because he was planning on using it expertly on her later tonight. Maybe if he gave Bridget several orgasms this way, she would be satisfied with his less than spectacular staying power. Even with the energy drinks he'd chugged, Andrew doubted he could keep up.

Damn, with the images this line of thinking was evoking, dinner was the last thing on his mind. Andrew would've gladly skipped straight to the main dish on tonight's menu, but Bridget was eyeing him from across the table, waiting to hear his opinion on her culinary skills.

"It's delicious," he said.

"I'm glad you like it. I used four different kinds of mushrooms. The texture is creamy, but there is no butter or milk in it, just the blended mushrooms."

She hadn't lied about cooking the soup.

After all the effort she'd put into this, he couldn't just tell her to forget it and drag her to bed. But he could sure as hell speed things up. It took him half a minute max to reach the bottom of the bowl, and he got up to carry it to the sink. "Are you done?" he asked and reached for hers even though it was still mostly full.

As she glanced up at him, Bridget's lips curled up in a knowing smile, and she handed him her half-eaten soup. "Impatient for the second course?" Her voice was husky.

Was he a lucky guy or what? A sharp brain and a lustful disposition were such a sexy combination. "You have no idea." He bent down and took her lips. They instantly parted in invitation. He entered. Her mouth was still hot from the soup, and the short kiss he'd intended turned into a lingering, passionate one, even though his back was painfully contorted from bending sideways while holding the two bowls up and away.

Eventually, she pulled back and smiled. "How about you put these in the dishwasher while I serve the beef Wellington with roasted fingerling potatoes." Bridget affected a British accent while describing the dish.

He moved to let her get up and followed behind her to the kitchen. "Sounds interesting, though I have no idea who that Wellington guy is, and what's his beef."

She chuckled. "It's a filet mignon and some other stuff put together and wrapped in puff pastry. I'm not exactly sure what goes in it, I didn't make it, I got it from a restaurant." She cast him an apologetic smile. "My cooking skills are limited to a few simple vegetarian recipes I can count on the fingers of one hand, none of which I thought would satisfy a manly man like you. But the soup and the salad are mine."

Well, she'd fessed up. Good girl. Not that it would've mattered to him if she hadn't, but he was glad that she had. Except, it made him even more uncomfortable realizing the extent of effort and thought she'd put into this dinner.

"That's very thoughtful of you, but you shouldn't have gone to all that trouble on my account. I'm not choosy about food. I would've eaten whatever you served."

"Think nothing of it. I do the same for Julian when he visits. He likes to eat steaks and ribs, and I can't stand to cook them." She shrugged. "Would you grab the salad bowl, please?" She lifted the tray with the fancy beef dish and carried it into the dining room.

Andrew followed, put down the salad bowl, and took his seat. "You know, I was under the impression that all of you guys stayed away from meat. Bhathian said something to that effect the other day when he invited me to share leftover lasagna with him. He said that that's all the cook serves. But then when I asked him if you had a cook he said not really. Not much for talking, that guy."

Well, that wasn't entirely accurate. The story Bhathian had told Andrew was still haunting him. He couldn't imagine carrying such a burden, not knowing whether he had a child or not. Finding closure for the guy was important to him.

He piled his plate with the beef, whatever it was called, and the tiny potatoes. Bridget had only salad.

"That's all you're going to eat?" he asked, motioning to her plate.

"Yeah, I would've eaten the potatoes if they weren't cooked together with the beef. But that's okay. I usually eat only salad for dinner. And as for the rest of the clan, some are vegan, some are vegetarian, and some are omnivorous. It's a matter of personal preference. Kian is vegan, and his butler Okidu cooks for him and sometimes for the other Guardians, but only stuff Kian eats." Bridget chuckled. "Bhathian eats everything—as long as someone else cooks it—so he really shouldn't complain."

Andrew cut a piece of the pastry-covered beef and put it in his mouth. It was so good that he closed his eyes and felt like moaning in pleasure.

"I see you like it."

"It's the best thing I've ever tasted. Well, food wise, that is." He winked.

"Oh, yeah? And what might that other thing be?" she teased.

"You'll find out after dinner."

"Oh, you're such a naughty boy."

Yes, he was.

20

SEBASTIAN

Clipboard in hand, Sebastian took the stairs down to the newly completed dungeon. Inspecting each of the small rooms and their compact attached bathrooms, he imagined them populated by beautiful girls and bursting with activity.

At first, he'd planned to simplify things by furnishing all of the rooms identically, but now that his vision was taking shape, he had second thoughts. Diversification would add spice to the clients' experience.

He pulled out his phone. "Tom, contact that hotel furniture supply store and tell them to cancel the order. I want to take another look at their catalog."

"Sure thing, boss. But I want to make sure that you're aware it will cause a significant delay. You wanted the dungeon to be ready as soon as possible."

"Good point. Have them ship four sets of what I've selected before. I'll let you know about the rest."

"How about the linens and towels and other small stuff? Do you want to change that order as well?"

"No, plain white will make handling cleanup and laundry simpler to manage. But I'm considering ordering a variety of colorful bedspreads and decorative pillows, as well as framed reproductions to hang on the walls. I want the girls to be able to personalize their rooms."

"That's very nice of you, boss. You want me to take care of it? Or do you want to make the selections yourself? It's in the same catalog as the furniture—under accessories."

"I'll make the selections and forward you the links."

"Good deal."

As Sebastian returned the phone to the back pocket of his jeans, his lips curled in a sardonic smile. His decision had nothing to do with being nice. It was about good business practices. And there was no better model to emulate than the success their exalted leader Navuh had achieved with *Passion Island*. Other than fear and intimidation, a little kindness and some degree of personal choice regarding inconsequential things went a long way toward ensuring the girls' cooperation.

Besides, Sebastian's team, as well as his future business contacts, would surely appreciate the variety, not only in the selection of girls providing services, but in their rooms' decor as well. For the place to function as an effective incentive, it had to provide an atmosphere of luxury and exclusivity. Esthetics were a crucial factor in creating that effect.

With this in mind, Sebastian had dedicated a sizable section of the dungeon to a bar and cigar lounge, sacrificing some of the space that could've been used for more private rooms. He'd had one hell of a ventilation system installed to suck out the smoke so the cigar fumes wouldn't poison the whole area. Personally, he wasn't overly fond of the things, but a lot of *Passion Island's* patrons were, and he wanted to provide his future clientele with a similar experience—his own miniature replica of Navuh's success story.

Robert's heavy footsteps on the concrete stairs announced his approach. The guy stomped like a gorilla. He was tall, but not as bulky as his footsteps implied.

"The first batch of soldiers has arrived, sir. Would you like a word with them before I show them to their quarters?"

What he would've liked was for Robert to drop the honorific. Perhaps punishment would drive the lesson home. "Robert, from now on I'll impose a one-hundred-dollar fine for each *sir*."

"Yes, S…Sebastian."

Sebastian sighed. The guy was hopeless. "How many have arrived?"

"Five, s…shit…" Robert dropped his head. "Why is it so hard?" he mumbled, addressing his boots.

"Tonight, after you're done with your duties, I want you to stand in front of the mirror and practice. Your trouble is that you're programmed to say sir after a yes; try responding with words like okay, sure, and no problem. Or even I got it, or I'm on it."

"I got it." Robert sounded like he was talking with a mouth full of spaghetti.

"That's a good start." Sebastian slapped the guy's shoulder.

They climbed the stairs, and as they reached the main level, Sebastian punched the code into the electronic lock. The new, reinforced steel door he'd had installed clicked open. Originally, the door to the basement had been visible to anyone walking down the hallway to the kitchen. He needed the new door hidden, so he'd had that part of the corridor sectioned off, enclosing it with a new wall and another plain-looking door. The corridor was wide, and the new enclosure created a small vestibule that was nevertheless sufficient in size for a guard station that included a desk with a monitor and a chair.

Robert pushed open the door, and as they emerged on the other side, the five new arrivals stood up from where they were seated around the dining table and saluted.

Sebastian smiled without returning the salute. "How was your trip? Good?" He shook hands with each one. "What do you think of the place? Nice, huh?" They kept nodding and mumbling their approval. "Robert will show you where everything is. The rooms are still unfurnished, but everything you need is in the containers outside. Each of you will be rooming with another warrior, and you are free to choose who you want to room with. The good news is that each room has its own bathroom."

That last bit got them excited. The facilities at their home base were communal. It wasn't as if the men had to stand in line for the showers or minded doing so in front of other males, but toilets were another story altogether. Having a semiprivate one must've seemed like the height of luxury to them.

"Tonight, after you get settled in your rooms, you're free to roam and acquaint yourself with the grounds. Tomorrow morning, you'll report to Robert. Your first task will be to prepare the base for the rest of the men, distributing furniture to the other rooms and whatever else Robert assigns to you. You are dismissed."

"Yes, sir." The men saluted.

Robert hesitated a moment before asking, "Should I tell them not to do it?"

"No, it's fine, Robert. It's not as if I'm planning on taking anyone other than you and Tom to meetings."

Robert nodded.

Well, that was one way to circumvent the compulsion—refrain from saying anything. He clapped the man's shoulder.

As the soldiers followed Robert to their ground-floor quarters, Sebastian waited a few seconds before climbing the stairs to his third-floor residence. Out of all the guys who'd worked on it throughout the day, only the tile man remained, applying gray grout to the gleaming white marble walls in the bathroom. But other than these last finishing touches, and the furniture Sebastian was still waiting for, the place was done. In the meantime, he had furnished his spacious quarters with standard issue items from the containers outside. One double bed took a small corner of his bedroom, and in the study, he'd positioned the simple student desk to face the tall, double glass doors leading out to the balcony. There was nothing in the living room aside from the built-in bar and the granite mantel surrounding the fireplace.

Sebastian dropped his clipboard on the desk and sat down. For a moment, he got distracted watching the setting sun reflected on the bookcases that had received their last coat of deep burgundy stain this afternoon. The fresh varnish was still wet, and its strong smell permeated the study. Breathing in the fumes, Sebastian contemplated taking his laptop down to the kitchen and working from there.

Except, he didn't want to interact with the soldiers who would no doubt frequent the place. His study was peaceful, and he found the pastoral view oddly tranquil.

The wholesaler's website selection of hotel room furniture and accessories wasn't extensive, and as Sebastian flipped through the limited assortment, he was tempted to look elsewhere for what he had in mind for the girls' rooms. Trouble was, he needed to bundle all of the purchases together and present them to headquarters as expenses related to housing his men. Buying nice things from a department store or some specialty bed-and-bath place would've raised suspicion. It was one thing to make these kinds of purchases for his private consumption; it was a different thing altogether to buy large quantities of the same.

The upside of the limited selection was that it didn't take him long to finalize his new list of items. Once he was done, he forwarded it to Tom with instructions for expedited shipping.

In a week, everything would be ready for the girls. It was time to make some phone calls and arrange for a timely delivery of the most important item on his supply list—the females themselves.

21

AMANDA

Annani's sage advice could've been condensed into one sentence—*follow your gut*—and Amanda had realized that talking with Andrew and her mother, although helpful, hadn't been all that illuminating.

It was still up to her to figure out a way to live with Dalhu, or conversely without.

If not for Annani's presence, Amanda would have done her thinking while pacing back and forth the length of her living room with short detours to replenish her drink. But doing so while her mother's wise and concerned eyes followed her every move wasn't going to work.

Soaking in a tub was the only other activity she found conducive to deep thinking. Not that it was doing her any good now. The only thing that kept going around in her head like a broken record was—*follow your heart.* No other thought managed to break through the never-ending cycle of that mantra, and the water was getting cold.

She reached for the hot water lever, but her hand landed on the drain knob instead. She twisted it open. It seemed that her subconscious had reached the same conclusion her conscious mind was beginning to form.

The time for thinking was over.

She needed to go down to that dungeon and confront Dalhu and his demons—or rather hers—head-on. Whatever came out of it would be better than this endless self-doubt and torment.

As she saw it, there were only two possible outcomes.

She would either jump his bones—and finally have the mind-blowing sex she'd been fantasizing about since the first time he'd touched her, or she'd be repulsed by him and leave—this time for good.

However, the first outcome presented a practical problem. With the unseen spectators monitoring what was going on in Dalhu's quarters, audio and visual, there was no privacy, and the bathroom's floor was definitely not part of her fantasy.

She had to figure out a way to circumvent the surveillance.

With the newfound resolution, Amanda stepped out of the tub and wrapped herself in a towel.

The idea of how to go about it came to her while applying mascara. She could render the cameras blind with black spray paint. Problem was, she had none and was too impatient to wait for Onidu to go down and get it from a building supply store. Maybe she could duct tape the lenses. Though that too was problematic. Even with her impressive height, and standing on top of a chair, she wasn't sure she could reach them. The ceilings in the dungeon were ten feet tall, if not more.

Spray paint, on the other hand, would work even from a couple of feet away. She had no choice but to send Onidu for it. If he hurried, he could be back with the stuff before she was finished dressing.

Still wrapped in the towel, she dashed out to her bedroom and pulled her phone out of her purse.

Please run down and buy me a can of black spray paint. Be back ASAP.

His reply was almost instantaneous. *Right away, mistress.*

She was so lucky to have him. Who else would've obeyed her wishes without a moment's hesitation or asking questions she didn't want to answer?

Standing inside her spacious walk-in closet, she dropped the towel and began sifting through the hanging garments, pulling out hangers and holding the outfits in front of her nude body as she examined herself in the mirror.

The outer layer determined the choice of undergarments.

No, and this one no, and that one... maybe, but no. Something super sexy...not slutty, but easy to take off... Aha!

The Diane von Furstenberg—classy and sensual.

The thing about a von Furstenberg wrap dress was that it rocked on someone tall and skinny but made everyone else look like crap. Lucky for her, she was tall, and although not rail thin, she wasn't busty either.

The dress looked fabulous on her.

The deep lapis blue complemented her eyes and the soft fabric molded beautifully to her figure. Problem was, the effect wouldn't be the same with underwear lines showing through. If Dalhu were the only one she was going to see, Amanda would've gone commando.

Just the thought of being bare under the dress—which could come undone with one tug on the loose knot holding it together—was so deliciously naughty that it was making her horny.

Regrettably, wrap dresses had a tendency of parting at the most inopportune moments, revealing more than a sexy thigh, and she still needed to get Anandur to take her to Dalhu.

With a sigh, she pulled on a black satin thong and matching bra. After putting the dress on and tying the belt in a loose knot, she did a couple of twirls in front of the mirror, enjoying the gentle caress of the fabric as it swished around her legs.

It turned her on.

Damn, evidently every little sensation was getting her all hot and bothered, and she wondered whether the culprit was her anticipated reunion with Dalhu or simply the result of going without sex for a few days.

Nah, it was Dalhu.

Fates, that male's pull was infuriating.

Her inability to resist Dalhu was so frustrating that she felt like punching him before making love to him. It wasn't a particularly noble sentiment, but perhaps the token revenge for Mark's murder would quiet her guilty conscience.

There was a gentle knock on her walk-in closet's door. "Mistress, I have the spray paint you requested," Onidu reported.

She stepped out and took the can. "Thank you, that was fast. How did you manage to get to the store and back so quickly?"

"I stopped by security to inquire about the whereabouts of the nearest paint supply store, and when I told the guard which item I was looking for, he suggested I visit the maintenance office first. Fortunately, they had the item in question." Onidu inclined his head.

"Wonderful." She gave him a quick hug before going back into the closet and closing the door behind her. A big purse was needed to hide the can from Anandur. Eventually he'd find out, but by then it would be too late for him to do anything about it.

Once she was done transferring everything from her smaller purse into the big satchel, she called Anandur.

"Good evening, Princess, how can I be of service?"

"What? No hi-how're-ya? Where have you been? Nothing?"

Anandur harrumphed. "The only reason you ever call me is because you need something. It's never just to chitchat."

Ugh, he was right. "I'm sorry. It's no excuse, but with everything that was going on, I kind of took it for granted that you'd be there for me. But that's just because you're such a great guy, and I know I can count on you." It was true, despite her not so subtle wheedling.

"Okay, you're forgiven. So, where have you been? And more

importantly, what have you been doing?" By the dip in his voice, it wasn't hard to guess the activity he was implying.

"Nothing exciting, Anandur. Get your head out of the porn flick. I borrowed Alex's boat and took it out for a short cruise to Catalina."

"Sweet, I heard she's a beauty."

"The *Anna* is, but her crew leaves a lot to be desired."

"What? No hunky sailors?"

"No, Alex's crew is all female."

"And you didn't invite me? I'm wounded."

"Trust me when I say it, even you wouldn't have found them particularly appealing."

"What do you mean—even me?"

She snorted. "I know your standards. If it's female and moving, it's kosher."

"That's not true. It has to be over twenty-five as well."

"Really?" Come to think of it, she had never seen Anandur approach the younger girls.

"I prefer experienced wenches."

"Yeah, I get it, same here—not the wenches part, but the experience. The younger ones are too emotional and tend to cling."

It took a lot of meaningless encounters to develop the necessary detachment to treat sex impersonally.

"That's part of it... Okay, but how did we get from talking about your love life to talking about mine? I guess your call has something to do with a certain frog."

"I need you to take me to him."

There was a moment of silence. "Had a change of heart?"

"Yes and no. I can't decide. I figure the only way to do it is to confront Dalhu. Not so much to hear what he has to say, but to see how he makes me feel. I haven't seen him since Kian shoved reality down my throat and made me face the fact that Dalhu is responsible for Mark's murder." Saying it out loud was akin to pricking a balloon and letting the air out—not in one explosive boom, but slowly in a quiet hiss.

The result was the same, though.

Feeling deflated, she walked over to the couch and plopped down with a sigh.

"It shouldn't have come as such a big surprise," Anandur said gently.

"I know. Some people have selective hearing; I have selective thinking. I don't let upsetting or inconvenient thoughts pass through the barrier of my conscious mind. I'm dimly aware of them floating somewhere in my subconscious, but that's all."

"Not good, Princess. You're not a child, and closing your eyes and plugging your ears to avoid ugliness will not make it disappear or protect you from its consequences. Better to face the demons and fight them head on than cower in the corner, hoping they'll go away. They never do, they just wait to ambush you when your guard is down. But if you acknowledge them, at least you have a fighting chance. The other way turns you into a helpless victim. Not a position I would have liked to find myself in."

Easy for him to talk.

Anandur hadn't had to mourn his own child or anyone else who'd been dearer to him than his own life. Except, she couldn't deny that he'd lost his fair share of friends—warriors that had been like brothers to him.

However, their respective miseries aside, he could no longer accuse her of hiding her head in the sand.

"Exactly. That's why I'm here and in need of your services. So, should we meet down at the dungeon, or do you want to come here and escort me there?" she asked.

"Stay put. I'm coming up."

22

KIAN

"I can't believe how good this is." Syssi's eyes practically rolled back with pleasure. "And the presentation, my God, each dish is like a mini work of art. How many people do you think he has, working in that kitchen?"

"I don't know. Would you like to take a peek? I'm sure Gerard wouldn't mind."

His nephew had greeted them when they'd gotten in and had spent a few minutes with Syssi, going over his menu suggestions for the wedding. But the busy restaurant required his stewardship, and he'd had to excuse himself.

Though not before Syssi had thanked him for his help about a dozen times. You'd think the guy had volunteered his services out of the goodness of his heart, and not because he was being paid through the nose.

It had been agreed that all of it would go to Gerard's private account instead of the restaurant's, which meant he'd get to keep it all without having to share profits with Kian. But whatever, Kian wasn't complaining. Gerard could've asked double what Kian had offered and would've gotten it. Because not only was he the only chef of his caliber willing to at least part-cater the wedding on such short notice, but also the best.

Not to mention Syssi's profound relief at having this major burden taken off her shoulders.

Syssi laughed. "Are you kidding me? Have you ever been inside a busy restaurant's kitchen? It's a madhouse in there."

"Oh, yeah? How would you know?"

Their date was turning out to be everything he'd hoped for and more. This was the perfect place for a romantic proposal—candle-light, soft music, and a procession of tiny but exquisite dishes. Syssi looked so happy that he wanted to kick himself for not taking her out more often. But he was intent on remedying his neglect from now on.

All dolled up, Syssi was wearing a short black dress that at first glance appeared plain but fit her like a second skin, and the earrings and necklace set Amanda had given her provided just the right sparkle to add some glamor to the simple outfit.

She was elegance and sophistication personified.

Spiky black heels added at least four inches to Syssi's petite figure, making her legs look a mile long. Kian was having a difficult time trying to banish the image of those legs, heels on, wrapped around his waist, and that clingy dress hiked all the way up.

Only his unwavering determination to make it a memorable evening for Syssi stopped him from taking her home. Hell, he wouldn't have even waited for them to get there. After all, they'd had some memorable adventures in the limo, and the elevator.

"After my second year of college, I tried waitressing during the summer break." She smiled sheepishly.

He hoped the restaurant's dim light hid his grimace as he adjusted himself as surreptitiously as possible. "And? What happened?"

Thankfully, Syssi was too wrapped up in her story to notice. "I discovered that holding several plates at once was harder than it looked. In fact, it was a tough balancing act that I had no talent for."

"Did you get fired?"

"No, it was my first day and they wanted to give me another chance. But I was too embarrassed to stay. I was already making decent money from tutoring and decided that it made more sense to stick with what I was good at. I printed a bunch of flyers and distributed them to a few local high schools. Soon, I was turning away students because I was maxed out. And I wasn't cheap." She sounded proud.

Kian leaned to take her hand. Clasping it, he rubbed his thumb over her palm. "My sweet, practical, levelheaded Syssi."

She blushed and lowered her eyes.

He chuckled. "And so demure..." He leaned to kiss the back of her hand before lifting his gaze to her smiling eyes. "But outward appearances are misleading, there is a whole other Syssi hiding under there, and I thank the merciful Fates each and every day that I'm the only one who gets to see that wildly passionate girl..." He leaned even closer. "And the one who gets to spank her gorgeous little behind," he whispered in her ear before catching her soft earlobe between his teeth.

"Oh...," she moaned involuntarily as a shiver ran through her.

He let go of her earlobe and smoothed his lips down her long neck.

Panting quietly, she closed her eyes, the flush on her face traveling down to paint her cleavage a rosy pink.

Beautiful.

To abandon that swan neck wasn't easy, and as he leaned back his words came out a little hissed. "Am I the luckiest guy on earth, or what?"

She opened her eyes and smiled. "I'm not sure about that, but I'm positive that I am the luckiest girl on the planet." She leaned toward him. "And every woman in this restaurant agrees with me. They are eating you up with their eyes and shooting murderous glares at me." She tilted her head and winked, pointing to a couple sitting across from them.

The man was a well-known businessman in his early sixties, and the young woman was his latest eye candy. Not that Kian was in any position to criticize.

Nearing his second millennial birthday, he was guilty of much worse. But at least he didn't look it.

The girl was the Barbie type. Though considering the vapid expression on her face, he would not have classified her as pretty. And as far as her Barbie-like figure, he didn't think it was attractive either. The pair of overinflated balloons that were filling her dress could've served as lifesavers in case of an emergency water landing. Vest not required.

"I have eyes only for you."

"I know."

"Good, because this kind of commitment comes with certain conditions and limitations."

"Oh, yeah? Like what?"

"You belong to me."

She waved a dismissive hand. "I know that, and you belong to me. Any other clauses?" Without even batting an eyelash she asked seriously, "Do you want a prenup?"

A prenup? I'll give you a prenup...

"In fact, I do." He smiled wickedly as he reached inside his suit jacket and pulled out two velvet-covered boxes. "First clause. I don't want to hear any arguments about these." He pushed the boxes to her side of the table.

Syssi's hand flew to her heart, and she blushed. "Is this what I think it is?"

He put his hand over the boxes. "You'll need to agree to the terms of my prenup first... if you want to open them and find out, that is."

"Okay." She reached for the ring box first, and he could tell she was holding her breath as she lifted the lid. Her eyes popped wide. "Please tell me this is a very shiny sapphire..."

Kian chuckled and took the box from her hand. "Let me do it right and put the ring on you."

Her hand was shaking as she held it up.

He slid the ring on her fourth finger. "Now it's official." He brought her ringed hand to his lips and gently kissed each digit.

"I don't want to know how much you paid for it."

"Good, because I'm not going to tell you. Now open the other one."

She smiled. "No more clauses before I open it?"

"Nope. This one is self-explanatory."

"I can just guess what's in it." She lifted the lid slowly, only half-way, and peered inside before letting it close. "You didn't..."

Kian pushed to his feet and walked over to stand behind Syssi. He opened the clasp of the necklace she was wearing and slipped it inside the inner pocket of his suit jacket. He then bent down and picked up the larger box.

The moment he lifted the lid, the choker he'd bought for Syssi reflected and refracted the candlelight, catching the attention of everyone in the vicinity. And the fact that the thing was studded with enough diamonds to render someone blind filled him with a sense of pure male satisfaction. He took it out, slipping the box into the same pocket as the other necklace.

As he gently fastened the choker around Syssi's slender neck, Kian leaned to whisper in her ear, "Just as I've promised."

23

SEBASTIAN

"I'm sorry, Mr. Shar, Sebastian, but I can't."

"Mr. Ax," Sebastian hissed through clenched teeth, "I'm sure you can arrange for at least one or two girls. I'm willing to pay premium for the first delivery."

The LA supplier of females for the island, who identified himself only by the unimaginative moniker Mr. Ax, was a tough and unyielding negotiator. Even without the benefit of a face-to-face conversation, Sebastian was starting to get the impression that the guy, although unwaveringly polite, was a most unpleasant fellow.

Which wasn't all that surprising considering Mr. Ax's chosen occupation.

Sebastian didn't like having to rely on someone nameless and faceless for something this important—regardless of the man's good reputation. There was something to be said for the way things used to be done when contracts and agreements had been finalized upon a handshake.

There was nothing like observing your associate's facial expressions and body language to determine if he was trustworthy. And seeing a man's interaction with his subordinates was another piece of crucial information. Usually, a guy like this would show up with a couple of bodyguards, and one could tell a lot from how they behaved around him. Respect and loyalty were good signs; fear less so.

He wondered what the Ax stood for, but the only options he could think of were either the tool or a tribute to Axl Rose.

"No can do. I just made a delivery of six new specimens five days ago, and I'm not due for another one until two months from now. Your bosses are not my only customers, and I have other clients who are waiting for merchandise that I've promised to deliver by certain deadlines. The best I can do for you is three weeks to a month, and even then only one or two girls. For larger orders, I need the info at least six months in advance—including half of the agreed price."

Lucky for the guy, Sebastian couldn't reach through the phone and tear his heart out.

Instead, he acquiesced in the most businesslike, calm tone, "I understand. I'm sure you're going to do your best. Let me know when you have something for me." After all, he still needed the guy's cooperation, and it wasn't going to happen if he antagonized his only supplier.

For now.

"I will, Mr. Shar. Good day."

Such a polite fellow.

Sebastian clicked off the phone and set it with deliberate care on the desk. Hurling it at the wall would've been so much more satisfying—but pointless and indicative of a lack of self-control.

Who else could he call? Maybe some of the drug or arms dealers would know who to refer him to?

Nah, it was bad business.

Smuggling drugs or weapons was one thing; trafficking in human sex slaves was another.

People found ways to morally justify an illegal business activity, even if their reasoning was convoluted. Evil was subjective. A crime lord who dealt in either drugs or arms could regard the activity as perfectly honorable, but he wouldn't necessarily extend the same rationale to slavers. Suggesting to a man that he had contacts with such *lowlives* could be seen as a grave offense.

With that avenue barred and no other leads, Sebastian had no choice but to find a solution himself.

There were the seven immortal males currently residing at his base to take care of, and more warriors were scheduled to arrive over the next couple of weeks. But until he came up with a plan of how to procure girls for his basement brothel, the men would have to seek sexual satisfaction the old-fashioned way—thralling random females and having their way with them.

A risky proposition at best.

In the old days, a woman who'd found herself lost and confused —with a sore cunt and semen dripping down her inner thighs— would have kept it to herself. Nowadays, she would run as fast as her shaky legs could carry her to the police. Some rape drug would be blamed, and every male she'd come in contact with around the time of the incident would be questioned.

Too many such reports would start a big stink.

Tapping his fingers on the desk, Sebastian gazed out the window at the dark sky. He would have no choice but to prohibit the practice. The men would have to work for a piece of ass, same as the males of Annani's clan. They'd have to seduce willing women in the places where such activity was welcomed, and then thrall the incriminating parts of the memory away.

Sebastian flipped his laptop open and googled dance clubs, but a sidebar ad caught his attention. Something about online dating.

Interesting.

Ha, if the site's ad copy were to be believed, men no longer needed to go out to meet women, they could do so from the comfort of their own homes. Online dating was what everyone was doing these days, and picking up women at bars and clubs was supposedly frowned upon.

Genius.

Problem solved.

His men, handsome immortals one and all, would have no trouble scoring dates on a site like this. And apparently, the rules of just a few decades ago, which had dictated a period of dating before having sex with a man, had evaporated with the last vestiges of Western morality.

Not that Sebastian had a problem with it. This part of Navuh's propaganda was meant for the consumption of his Eastern allies and the simple rank and file.

Navuh's inner circle had no such illusions.

The ultimate goal was world domination and everything else was just fodder for the ignorant masses.

Thinking of the interesting possibilities online dating presented, Sebastian leaned back in his chair. It would be so incredibly easy to find the perfect candidates for his brothel. Mr. Ax's services would no longer be needed. And a lot of money could be saved.

Between their online profiles and their Facebook pages, he could discover everything he needed to know—from how attractive a girl was, to what her financial situation was like, and whether she had family and friends who would notice that she went missing.

Come to think of it, Dalhu might have been wrong in his assumption that Annani's clansmen searched for sex partners in clubs and bars. As part of the Western society, they must've been exposed to this new dating phenomenon and were taking advantage of it.

But if this was indeed the case, it meant that Dalhu's plan was useless.

Still, Sebastian had no choice but to implement the plan regardless of his newfound doubts as to its chances of success. The alternative was giving up the hunt before it even began and it wouldn't fly with headquarters, no matter how well he justified his decision. After spending all this money and allocating the resources to its execution, he couldn't just abandon it without at least giving it a try.

Sebastian signed up as a member of the dating site and paid the fee, then set about creating a compelling profile for himself. Something that would lure the kind of girls he was looking for—young, pretty, lonely, and desperate.

24

AMANDA

"What's in the bag?" Not surprisingly, Anandur eyed her large tote with suspicion.

Amanda had hoped that being a guy he would dismiss it as just one of her peculiar fashion choices, but apparently he was more astute than that.

Luckily, she came prepared.

"If you really want to know, I packed an extra set of lingerie, a nightgown, a toothbrush, a hairbrush, a can of hairspray, perfume, lotions, and makeup. Want to search it in case I'm hiding a weapon there to spring Dalhu out of jail?" She opened the top and lifted it up to his face.

Unfazed by her sarcasm, he took a quick peek inside. But seeing the lacy red thong and matching bra that she'd put on top, he scrunched his nose and shoved the tote away. "How long are you planning on staying there that you're bringing all of this?"

"I don't know yet. I might leave right away. But in case I decide to stay the night, I came prepared." She wasn't lying. There was still a chance she would just walk out of there and never come back.

"Dream on, Princess, I can't babysit for so long. I can allow no more than an hour," he said as they entered the elevator.

We'll see about that. She shrugged and turned to the mirror to examine her makeup. *Perfect.*

"You look good, no need to check." Anandur's reflection was smirking at hers.

"Thank you."

"New dress?"

"No, I just haven't worn it in a while."

"Must have been a really long while…," he muttered as he eyed the outfit with a critical eye.

"Why? You don't like it?"

"Don't get me wrong, you look as stunning as always. It's just that this thing reminds of the seventies. Not a decade fondly remembered for its style." The elevator stopped and Anandur motioned for her to precede him.

With a raised eyebrow Amanda gave him a thorough up and down look over, taking in the worn-out Levis and plain green T-shirt. "I didn't know you followed fashion trends."

"I don't. But I know what I like and what I don't. The miniskirts were fine, more than fine, but everything else not so much."

"Well, this wrap dress is having a big comeback. It's the latest fashion trend."

"I'll take your word for it." He started to punch in the code, then stopped and turned to her. "I just wanted to warn you. You're in for a bit of a shock."

What the hell was he talking about? Had someone hurt Dalhu? "Why, what's wrong with him?"

The alarm in her voice prompted him to quickly qualify. "Nothing. It's a good thing." He pushed open the door and just let it swing all the way in while stepping aside to allow her an unobstructed view of the room.

"Oh, sweet Fates…" Her face was staring at her from at least a dozen portraits, if not more, covering every exposed stretch of wall in Dalhu's small living room. He'd drawn every possible expression —happy, aroused, contemplative, worried, challenging, argumentative, and there was even one of her sleeping. The simple charcoal sketches were so beautiful, so full of life, that she was tempted to get close and touch each one.

But where was the man who'd drawn them? She looked at Anandur.

"Probably in the bathroom. It's not like he can go anywhere."

The door to the bedroom was open, and as she was about to step inside, the bathroom's door banged opened and Dalhu emerged with a small towel still clutched in his wet hands.

Freezing in place, he whispered, "Amanda..." as if he saw an apparition.

Her heart felt as if it was swelling to monstrous proportions, choking her, then shattering, the broken pieces carving bloody furrows in her insides.

She was fighting for breath as desperately as she was fighting for a coherent thought. She wanted to run to Dalhu and hug him so hard that his ribs would crack, and then keep tightening her embrace until she squeezed him within an inch of his life.

Need and rage.

Love and hate.

Longing and loathing.

Compassion and cruelty.

No wonder her heart couldn't handle all of these contradicting feelings and was swelling and bursting in turns.

Why did I leave? How could I've stayed?

How could I've abandoned him when he needed me so desperately? He deserves much worse...

I love him... I detest him.

Amanda shook her head in a desperate attempt to dispel the disabling maelstrom of confusion and turned away from Dalhu. It took her a couple of seconds until she was able to breathe. She glanced at Anandur, who was still standing outside the opened door, watching her and Dalhu with an amused expression plastered on his face.

Nothing about this is funny, you moron.

Amanda grabbed the door and gave it a powerful shove with the intention of closing it in Anandur's smug face. But he blocked the door from slamming shut on him by wedging his boot against the doorjamb. She'd anticipated the move and leaned on the door.

Peering at him through the crack, she stated rather than asked, "Do you really think I need protection from this male?"

"No, but your brother doesn't share my opinion. I have my orders." He tried to push the door open again.

Anandur must've exerted a halfhearted effort because she had no problem preventing him from doing so. "Tell him I ordered you to leave. I'm sick and tired of him trying to run my life for me. I don't have to follow his orders in anything other than council business. I'm running this show from now on." She gave another shove, but the door didn't budge.

Anandur was quiet for a moment, then pushed back, just enough to make room for his big head to fit through the crack. "Good luck, Princess," he mouthed before jumping back and letting her shove the door closed.

What a pain in the ass, but a real prince of a guy nonetheless. She would thank him later.

Her hands still splayed on the closed door, she touched her forehead to the cool surface and just breathed. Getting rid of Anandur had been the easy part of her plan. Now that it was done, she was terrified by the prospect of facing the real challenge of confronting Dalhu and her warring feelings about him.

Amanda felt Dalhu rather than heard him come to stand behind her, and she turned, leaning her back against the door.

He was on her in a flash. Kissing, touching, groping. There was nothing gentle or loving about this. His mouth and his hands attacked her with bruising force. This was pure, desperate hunger.

There was no need for words—hell, there were no words to express what she was feeling, but this was a language they were both fluent in. She gave as hard as she got, pushing her hands under his T-shirt and clawing at his back with the intent of drawing blood.

He bit her then, his fangs two agonizing burning spots at the bottom of her neck. No venom came rushing into her through the entry points. Instead, he pulled back and bit her again at another spot. The pain was both excruciating and exquisite, and she snarled, digging her nails into his scalp to hold his mouth to the wound he'd inflicted. "Lick it!" she commanded.

He did, and the pain subsided immediately, as well as some of the frenzy. As she felt him reach for the loose knot holding her wrap dress together, she grabbed his hand to stop him. "Wait—"

"I can't—" He pushed his groin against her and rubbed, pulling his hand out of her grasp at the same time and going for the knot again.

She gave him a shove. "You have to stop."

He didn't move an inch, his wide chest heaving, but he forced his hand away.

"We are giving the guys in security one hell of a show," she whispered.

"I don't care."

"But I do. Now move so I can do something about it."

Reluctantly, he took a tiny step back, just an inch or so. "What now?" he hissed through his protruding fangs.

"Go to the bathroom and stay there while I handle this."

"Like hell, I will. I'm not going to make love to you on that bathroom floor, and have no doubt, this is going to happen even if I have to do it with them watching."

"Don't be an idiot, Dalhu. I have no desire for bathroom floor adventures either," she whispered. "I just want to keep you out of trouble. You need to stay out of it while I spray paint the camera lenses and order the guys to turn the audio off. I want it to be clear that you had nothing to do with it."

That shut him up, though he didn't move and was still crowding her.

As she tried to duck to the side, he stopped her with a hand on her shoulder. "Do I look like the sort of man who hides in the bathroom while his woman takes care of business?"

"Well, no, of course not. But you're in my territory, and I expect nothing more than a scolding for my actions. You, on the other hand, are a captive. And Geneva Conventions not only do not apply to you but are nonexistent here."

She might have not spoken at all as far as he was concerned. With a mulish expression on his handsome face, he extended his hand. "Give me the spray can. I'll take care of the cameras while you take care of the audio."

He was offering her a compromise.

There was no way Dalhu would do as she said, and anyway, he was taller and could probably spray the lenses without the benefit of a chair to stand on.

"Okay." Amanda reached into her tote and rummaged until she found the can all the way at the bottom. "Here, take it." She handed it to him.

"I'll start with the bedroom." Dalhu took the paint and headed for the door to the other room.

Amanda ambled to the center of the living room and glanced up at one of the camera lenses attached to the ceiling.

"Steve, I hope you're there, and if not, whoever is in charge, please listen carefully. From now on, I'll be staying down here, with Dalhu."

Up until that moment, she hadn't realized she'd already decided that she wasn't leaving. If Dalhu couldn't come live with her at her penthouse upstairs, she was going to move in with him down here.

The phone on the coffee table started ringing.

Fates, she was so stupid for not noticing it before and making a fool of herself—talking to the ceiling.

She grabbed the receiver. "Is that you, Steve?"

"Yes, ma'am."

She couldn't decide whether he sounded amused or worried. "Good, now listen and do as you're told. Surveillance of clan members' private quarters is not allowed, and as I consider this my personal residence from now on, I demand that all audio and video recording from inside this apartment be turned off. The cameras in the corridors will have to suffice as far as security goes."

Assuming an akimbo pose, she glanced at her wristwatch before narrowing her eyes at the camera. "Make no mistake, later on, I intend to make sure that you guys complied with my demand, and I will check if the recording stopped, starting five minutes from now. Noncompliance will result in severe consequences. Do you understand?"

"Yes, ma'am. I will turn everything off momentarily, but I have to notify Onegus."

There was no way to prevent him from doing so, but perhaps she could convince him to delay his report. "Listen, Steve, I know you have to, but could you wait a little? Like a couple of hours? I'll owe you big time…"

"I'll do my best."

"That's all I can ask for."

Hopefully, this would do the trick. But just to be on the safe side, painting the lenses black was a good precaution. She preferred being extra careful than later finding porn flicks of her and Dalhu circulating the keep.

Spray can in hand, Dalhu emerged from the bedroom. "That area is done."

"You can go ahead and spray these too." Amanda pointed at the three cameras near the ceiling. Maybe she was paranoid, but she couldn't help a suspicious glance at the large TV monitor. Grabbing two of Dalhu's creations from the corner they were propped against, she carried them over to the screen and attached them with the adhesive tape Dalhu had been using to hang those he couldn't fit on the walls.

Fates, there were so many of them. He must've been drawing like a madman to produce so many in such a short period of time. True, they were done in charcoal, some in simple black and white and others in full color, a medium which was not as time-consuming as oil paint or even acrylic, but still, the sheer number of them and the quality were awe-inspiring.

And humbling.

Not that she'd doubted Dalhu's love for her before, but it was more as an almost philosophical concept. She hadn't really internalized how fully he was consumed by it.

Would she ever be able to love him like this? Even if she found a way to forgive him about Mark? Was she even capable of feeling so much?

That was the problem with feelings. If she were to let go of the protective numbness and let the good ones bloom, the bad ones would inevitably emerge as well. And there was no way she could deal with those without the protection of a thick mental buffer.

She wasn't ready to discard her Teflon suit yet.

What she wondered, though, was how Dalhu had managed to shed his much thicker protective armor, one that must've grown over his nearly eight hundred years in the Brotherhood to the size of a nuclear-bomb shelter.

Evidently, he was much braver than she.

25

DALHU

After the last camera had been dealt with, Dalhu tossed the can into the trash bin and turned toward Amanda.

He was so proud of her. She'd dealt with the guys in security as effectively as an attorney, and he doubted they would dare disregard her orders. After all, if what she'd said about the mandatory exclusion of private clan members' quarters from surveillance was true, her case was perfectly valid. And he had no reason to doubt that Amanda knew what she was talking about. It was obvious that she'd come well prepared to wage war.

And what a fearsome warrior she made.

A tigress.

He could still feel the sting of the deep furrows she'd left on his back.

What a wildcat.

Apparently, he'd been wrong to think that she'd succumbed to her brother's diktat and had abandoned him without a fight. Amanda had done the smart thing, taking her time to devise an effective strategy for them to be together.

"I'm so proud of you." He pulled her into his arms and kissed her forehead.

"For what?" She regarded him as if she had no idea what he was talking about.

"For this." He waved his hand at the cameras. "For fighting for us."

She shrugged. "It's no big deal. All I want is some damn privacy, that's all."

Slowly, he was becoming aware that there was something off about Amanda's demeanor. The woman he had known would have been laughing and joking about her successful stunt, or even better, ripping off his clothes. But there was something dark clouding Amanda's expressive blue eyes, some sort of weariness or worry—he couldn't decipher her odd mood.

Was she afraid of her brother's reaction? Not that it was unwarranted. The moment Kian heard about this, he would come storming down here, and all hell would break loose. Except, Dalhu had gotten the impression that other than a cold shoulder there was nothing Kian would or could do to her. At least not as long as Amanda had her mother's unwavering support.

"What's wrong?"

Amanda looked up at him as if he was missing a screw. "What's right, is a better question."

"What do you mean?"

She sighed. "Sit down, Dalhu."

Why had it sounded so ominous? As he sat on the couch, Dalhu felt his whole body coiling up with tension, and a heavy, uncomfortable sensation was settling in the pit of his stomach.

Amanda walked over to the bar and opened the doors. Inspecting the small selection, she muttered, "Figures, nothing to make a margarita with. How about gin and tonic?" she asked.

"Whiskey, straight up, in a tall glass, please." He had a feeling he was going to need it.

She poured them both a drink and came to sit next to him on the couch. “Here you go.” She handed him his drink.

He was relieved that she sat beside him and not across from him.

For a while, Amanda just swished the ice cubes in her tall, clear drink, then took a small sip before setting it down on the coffee table.

She seemed nervous, which wasn’t like her, and he felt a chill of foreboding rush up his spine.

“Just spit it out. Whatever it is can’t be as bad as this damned suspense. You’re killing me.”

“Funny that you would phrase it like that.”

“What’s that supposed to mean?”

“My nephew, Mark, you were the one who ordered his murder.”

That heavy, uncomfortable sensation in his gut had just turned into a dark, bottomless pit of dread. He’d known that at one point or another Amanda would put two and two together and come to this rather obvious conclusion, but he’d hoped that by then she would be too deep into the relationship to just get up and leave. But nothing had gone down as he’d been hoping it would.

The way things had unfolded, he should be grateful for the few moments of grace he’d been granted with Amanda.

“Is that why you left?”

“Yes.”

“I thought Kian forbade you to see me.”

She snorted. “He did, but he can’t order me to do anything unless it has to do with safety issues. I can do pretty much as I please.”

“But you came back.”

“Yes.”

What did she expect him to say? That he was sorry? That he’d been following orders? Or maybe try to deny his part? There was absolutely nothing that he could do or say about her nephew’s murder that would make it less painful for her, or less damning for him.

Still, she was back, and it looked like she had every intention of staying, so she must've come to terms with the knowledge.

Otherwise, she wouldn't be here.

"I can say I'm sorry, and believe me, I am. But it would not change a thing. So tell me what you want to hear me say, or just scream at me, or scratch my eyes out. If it makes you feel better, I'll welcome it."

She chuckled. "You know me so well it's scary. I don't know what I want to do first, punch you in the face or screw you until we both see stars."

He raised two fingers. "I vote for the second one."

"I bet you do."

He took her hand, and she didn't object—a good sign. "I will do whatever it takes, but you need to tell me what's going on in your head."

She sighed. "A big mess, that's what's going on." She reached for her drink and took a few sips.

"Somehow, you've managed to get under my skin, to penetrate the protective shell I've built to keep emotions out. I wasn't aware of how much I grew to enjoy the intimacy we shared, and I'm not talking about the sex, although that too, until it got literally blown away by Kian and his rescue team. At first, I refused to give it up just because of my brother's conviction that Doomers are the worst filth to walk the earth. Not that I disagree with him, necessarily, but you're different, and he wasn't willing to give you a chance." Amanda paused to bring the drink to her lips and kept drinking until there was nothing but ice cubes left at the bottom of the glass.

"I'm not stupid, and the connection between you and Mark's murder wasn't something that I could've missed or not realized. But subconsciously, I must've repressed it. It shouldn't have come as a big shock when Kian shoved it in my face and forced me to acknowledge it, but it did. I had to get away. And I seriously thought that I could forget about you because there was just no way I could consort with my nephew's murderer...Trouble was, I couldn't stay away." She looked down at the melting ice cubes in her glass.

A pregnant silence stretched between them as Amanda gathered her thoughts. He gave her hand a squeeze for encouragement, and she squeezed back. "The truth is that I need you, and I hate myself for it," she whispered while avoiding his eyes.

"I'm not strong enough to sever this connection between us. And my only *smart* conclusion is that wishing for a perfect solution is futile. That real life is full of compromises. That I will have to learn to live with you and with my resentment."

She chuckled. "For a moment, I even considered asking my mother to tinker with my head and make me forget about Mark, but that would've been the ultimate betrayal, and also disrespectful to his memory."

Lifting her head, she looked up at him—her beautiful eyes gleaming with unshed tears. "As things stand now, I can't give you my heart, only my body and my company. But, perhaps, in time, my resentment will fade enough to release my heart."

She turned her head and glanced at the walls. "I know that you love me. Looking at all these pictures you drew of me, it scares me how well you've gotten to know me. Unfortunately, I can't say the same. I still have a lot to learn about you, and maybe what I'll discover will help me forgive you, but it might not. Right now it's the best I can offer you."

"I'll take it, even if you'll never return my love. To go on without you is a fate worse than death for me. I have to believe that my love for you burns strong enough to sustain us both."

Amanda smiled and wiped her eyes with the sleeve of her dress. "I knew you were going to say that. I must know you better than I thought I did."

26

AMANDA

"That predictable, huh? Must be boring...," Dalhu teased.

She felt lighter after getting that little speech off her chest. Dalhu had actually taken it better than she'd thought he would. Instinctively, he must've realized that trying to excuse his past would do him no good. After all, she had been well aware of the cold facts, and nothing he could've said would have been news to her.

It hadn't been personal.

Dalhu hadn't known her, or even of her, or Mark. He'd been doing his ugly job for an even uglier organization—following a cause he'd no longer believed in and taking orders from superiors he'd despised.

He should've left the Brotherhood long before he'd met her. But prior to that, he'd lacked the impetus to make such a radical change. He'd known nothing else, had believed in nothing at all, and had cared about no one.

In a way, she'd given him a new lease on life, a chance for an existence that wasn't as meaningless—bleak. For now, his love for her was like a flotation device in an ocean of hostility and indifference.

But in time, maybe her family would accept him, and he'd become part of the force for good. And the meaning he'd attach to his life would expand beyond his love for her to include a sense of belonging and purpose.

She winked at him. "You compensate in other departments."

He got closer, his hand resting innocently on her bare knee. "Yeah? Which ones?"

The hand traveled a little north, and the wrap dress parted farther, exposing her thighs to a little below her panties. An inch higher and they would be on full display.

She placed her palm over his large hand, halting his progress. "No more bathroom floors and no more couches. Take me to bed, big boy."

"With pleasure."

For such a large man Dalhu moved incredibly fast.

She was up and cradled in his arms before the second word left his mouth. Relaxing into his warm chest, she wrapped her arms around his solid neck as he carried her the few feet to the bedroom and kicked the door closed behind him.

With infinite care, he lowered her to the bed, then climbed on and straddled her hips with his knees.

"May I?" He reached for the knot holding her dress.

"Yes, you may."

Dalhu gave a gentle tug, and it unraveled. Slowly, he parted the dress—a look of reverence spreading over his harsh features.

Leaning back, he rested his palm on her soft belly—his large hand hot and heavy on her skin. For a moment, he didn't move, just looked at her—his eyes betraying his thoughts. The smoldering desire, the love, the unmistakable ownership his hand on her belly symbolized.

There was no question in his gaze, it was a statement—a claim he knew she wasn't ready to hear but was true nonetheless.

She wondered if he could read the truth in her eyes—that deep in her soul she'd known it from the start—from when she'd first seen him at that jewelry store. For a suspended moment in time, before her mind had taken over and the chasm of reality had opened between them, she'd reacted to him as a female would to her chosen male. And yet, she was still miles away from admitting it even to herself.

It seemed that he knew exactly what she'd been thinking. His harsh countenance softened, and the hand on her belly lightened and moved in a gentle caress—as if to say that it was okay, that there was no pressure, that he was going to wait for as long as she needed him to.

Damn, the man was reading her like an open book. She doubted even her own mother knew her so well. Amanda was just too good at putting up a show.

But for some reason, it didn't feel as intrusive or scary as she would've expected it to. Because Dalhu loved her unconditionally, and she knew that whatever he saw deep down in her heart wouldn't change it. Not a bit.

With him, she was free to be who she really was—imperfect, selfish, vengeful, hurting—and despite all the ugliness she worked so hard to hide from everyone, including herself, Dalhu would love her no less.

The silent communication between them must've lasted no more than a few seconds, but when Dalhu's hand finally reached up and his fingers snapped the fastener of her bra, it felt as if she'd been waiting a long time for him to make a move.

Her nipples stiffened in anticipation of his touch, and she couldn't help but arch her back in a long sinuous wave. He didn't reach for her breasts, though. Instead, he hooked his thumbs in her thong and pulled it down her legs. When they were off, she lifted her torso to let the bra straps slide off her shoulders, and got rid of it.

Completely bare now, she relaxed on her back with the fingers of her hands entwined behind her head.

"Your turn," she said. "And do it slowly, I want to watch the unveiling." Amanda hadn't seen Dalhu fully naked yet. She'd seen all the important parts, but not all at once, and she couldn't wait to see him in all his nude glory.

"Your wish is my command, Princess." He smiled before grabbing the bottom of his T-shirt and pulling it up in slow motion.

"You'd better believe it."

She watched him struggle with the slow pace. The poor guy wouldn't have much of a career as a stripper. He was kind of clumsy in his attempts to look sexy for her, but she didn't have the heart to tell him that. And anyway, if she hadn't insisted on him going slow, he would've been out of his clothes and pouncing on her in a heartbeat.

As it was, even his awkward moves had done nothing to detract from the sexiness of his amazing body as he bared it for her hungry eyes one piece of clothing at a time.

Dalhu kept the best for last, and her mouth watered in anticipation of the grand reveal. He hooked his thumbs in the elastic band of his shorts and shimmied out of them.

Oh, sweet Fates in heaven have mercy.

She remembered that magnificent shaft well, but that didn't stop her from drooling in appreciation as it sprung free out of his boxer shorts.

"Come here," she commanded, beckoning him to her with a crooked finger.

He came to stand by the side of the bed, and she seized him not too gently. This wasn't going to be tender lovemaking, at least not on her part. She still felt like hurting him, and if it meant that she was a vengeful bitch, so be it. Dalhu could take whatever she'd dish out and would probably beg for more.

She pulled, and he obediently climbed on the bed, kneeling in front of her. But if Dalhu thought that she was going to take him in her mouth, he should think again. Getting up on her knees, she pushed him back until he was spread out before her.

The man was huge, his long body barely fitting the length of the bed. He must've been sleeping diagonally across it because he sure as hell couldn't have slept comfortably otherwise.

It was a heady feeling to know that this fine exemplar of manhood was willingly submitting to her mercy, or lack thereof.

She used to think that there wasn't much difference between a bully and a dominant, but now it occurred to her that the resemblance between the two was only superficial. The bully thrived on fear, deriving pleasure from terrorizing and hurting a weak or meek partner, as opposed to the dominant who derived it from the submission of a strong, willing one who chose to participate in the game for his or her own pleasure. Still, she could easily see how the distinction could sometimes be blurred, and naïveté could be taken advantage of.

For a brief moment, a disturbing image of Dalhu tied to a post with whip welts marking his back flushed through her head. It disturbed her not only because she was the one wielding the whip, but because the image was making her wet.

When did I turn into a damn dominatrix?

No, she might scratch, and she might squeeze, and she might even bite, but she could never go that far.

Closing her eyes, she lowered herself on top of Dalhu. Her lips found his, and she kissed him, her tongue gently seeking entrance into his warm mouth. She felt his hands on her back, lazily caressing up and down until the kiss grew heated and he groaned, cupping her butt cheeks—each one fitting perfectly inside a large hand.

He was so hard and hot beneath her, swiveling his hips and grinding his erection against her pubic bone. She knew he was desperate to flip her under him and drive this hot rod inside her, but he was tolerating his subdued position for as long as he possibly could, waiting for her to give him permission to take over.

Not yet.

She kissed him deeper, her tongue caressing his elongated fangs in slow circles and driving him wild. His fingers were digging into her fleshy buttocks with bruising force, and his groans were getting louder. But then he must've realized he was hurting her and eased up, only to go on exploring the valley between them all the way down to her dripping wet, hot center. He lingered there for a moment, circling her opening with the tips of three fingers, but he didn't push in. Instead, he scooped some of her moisture and brought it up to her tight sphincter, shocking her with pleasure when he repeated the same move there.

Her eyes popped open, and she looked at his smug face. "What are you doing?"

"What does it feel like I'm doing?" He nipped her chin with his blunt front teeth, and she felt his finger apply light pressure as if seeking entry.

"Don't," she breathed, though what she really wanted to say was *please do.*

It wasn't that she was ignorant. Amanda was well aware that some people found this sort of thing pleasurable, but she had never tried it and had no desire to experiment. Except, although somewhat distasteful, it was also oddly arousing, and she was reluctant to insist that he stop his explorations.

"Please... I don't...," she mumbled into his neck.

Trouble was, the odd sensation wasn't restricted to the area in question. And the shockwave of intense heat sweeping through her made her sweat worse than one of her breakneck runs on the treadmill.

Fates, what's wrong with me?

27

DALHU

The fact that Amanda wasn't as experienced as she thought she was had taken Dalhu by surprise. Evidently, there still remained a thing or two he could teach her.

But this was probably not the right time.

Nevertheless, he was so damn thrilled at the prospect of being her first in yet another sexual experience.

So unexpected, yet so deeply satisfying.

Amanda's lithe body was hot and sweaty on top of his, and her breath was coming out in short, shallow puffs against his neck. Dalhu felt a wave of tenderness wash through him, and he wrapped his arms around her, hugging her to him gently.

Just for a moment, to let her regain her composure.

He had gotten a strong impression that Amanda didn't want gentle. She was too angry—with him for being who he was, and at herself for wanting him despite it—to tolerate tenderness.

It was a shame, really, because he wanted their first time to be about making love, not about angry sex. But he would take whatever she could give and would be thankful for it.

"I love you," he whispered against her damp temple.

She sighed and lifted her head to look at him. "Kiss me," she commanded.

He did, his lips just a light caress against hers before he slid his tongue into her mouth and began a lazy exploration, slowly rediscovering her, getting reacquainted.

At first, she followed his lead, her lips and tongue just as tender, but then a low growl started deep in her throat, and he knew the time for gentleness was over. She sucked his tongue into her mouth, forcefully, and when it was all the way inside she bit down.

The tangy taste was unmistakable—she'd drawn blood. But it had done nothing to cool his fervor; on the contrary, it had awakened the animal inside him. He felt an overwhelming need to flip her under him, to pin her hands over her head and ram himself inside her. But he squashed the impulse with all the force his willpower could muster. He had to allow her to be the aggressor this time, to take out all of her anger and frustration on him.

She let him withdraw his tongue from her mouth and licked his lips, smearing the few drops of blood she'd scooped up over them. "You taste good," she said with a smirk.

"So do you."

"Hmm, I wonder if the taste is the same all over." She dipped her head and bit a soft spot between his neck and shoulder, her sharp little fangs drawing blood again.

She licked the wound she'd inflicted and looked up at him, her blood-smeared lips looking cruel yet sexy as hell. "This tastes good too. Let's see if it's the same over here." She moved her lips up his neck and bit down there.

Dalhu's bonds of restraint were starting to unravel, and he was sweating with the effort of lying still and letting Amanda have her way with him. His damned fangs were throbbing with the urgent need of returning the favor.

But was he doing the right thing? Maybe she was spurring him on, on purpose, because she wanted him to overpower her? To take over so she could pretend that what was happening between them was out of her hands?

She'd bitten him two more times before he snapped and with a loud growl banded his arms around her and flipped her under him. She put up a half-hearted struggle when he caught her wrists and pinned them above her head, then held them there with one hand while the other one went behind her head and fisted her hair.

She was a strong female, but she was no match for him.

Gazing into her impossibly beautiful face, he read her expression to make sure that he'd not misunderstood her intentions, conscious or subconscious, and this was really what she'd been after. Her eyes were glowing, feral with a mixture of anger and need, and she was trying to free her head from his grasp so she could bite him again. He held on, tightening his grip on her hair and pulling back, which was no doubt causing her some pain.

And yet, she wasn't telling him to stop or let go.

Wedging a knee between her closed thighs, he forced her to spread for him and positioned his shaft at her entrance. But he refused to let himself shove inside her before ensuring she was ready—even though she was sopping wet.

"I'm going to let go of your hair, but if you bite me again, I'm going to bite back, and my fangs are longer." It wasn't much of a threat, considering the properties of what his fangs could deliver, but it worked. Apparently, Amanda didn't want to be out of it while experiencing his penetration for the first time any more than he wanted her to be.

He released her, waiting for a moment to see if she was going to behave before bringing his hand down to her wet center. He teased her a little, gently circling his finger around her engorged clit while his mouth went for one sweet nipple, and he repeated the same slow circling move with his tongue. Amanda groaned—though he wasn't sure if in pleasure or impatience.

Perhaps it wasn't such a good idea to stretch things out for too long, considering that she was already angry and frustrated.

"Ah…," she groaned and arched her back violently when he penetrated her with two fingers, then shuddered when he pressed on her clit with his thumb.

He'd managed about a minute of foreplay before his need became too great.

Amanda was more than ready for him, and there was no point in prolonging the wait for what they both so desperately wanted. Needed.

He reached for his shaft and fisted it, positioning at her entry. She closed her eyes, her lips slightly parted to allow her rapid breathing.

"Look at me," he growled. "Look at me when I take you." He pushed just an inch inside her and halted, waiting for her to obey.

"Oh, Fates," she groaned, peering at him with hooded eyes.

With a grunt, he rammed all the way inside her, eliciting an echoing sound from her.

He hadn't intended to do it like this, but going slow and penetrating her in increments had become impossible. The best he could manage was to refrain from moving until she grew accustomed to the intrusion.

Sweating, he held still on top of her, bracing his weight on one hand while his other was still shackling her wrists over her head with brutal force. He let go the moment he realized that he must be bruising her delicate skin, and probably restricting circulation to her hands as well.

Immediately, her hands went to his ass and her nails sunk into his flesh.

"Move," she hissed.

Wild…feral…stunning… his woman was beyond compare.

And he moved—like he'd never moved inside a female before for fear of breaking her. But he had no such concerns with Amanda.

She could take it.

Loving every battering ram, moaning and growling in turns, she spurred him on, her hands gripping his ass and guiding him to go deeper, faster, stronger.

28

AMANDA

Fates, this was a ride of a lifetime.

Dalhu was an animal—a wild alpha male in the midst of frenzied rutting. And she meant no insult by it. Coming from her, it was the best of compliments.

Their prior interludes had already raised the bar on her sexual expectations, but this was so much better than she could've imagined. It wasn't only that he was bigger than any male she had ever had inside her, or that he was pounding into her with the force and stamina of a locomotive—there was something additional in play. A chemistry, a coming together of two formidable forces so powerful, so all-consuming, that nothing else would ever do.

As she was losing her tenuous grip on lucidity, Amanda had the passing thought that this might be the start of the addiction.

A point of no return.

Or maybe this was a foregone conclusion from the moment she had decided to come back.

Too late for second thoughts now.

Dalhu's thrusts were becoming even faster, and she had to relinquish her hold on his ass to grab hold of the bed's headboard and brace against it to prevent him from driving her head into it.

As she felt him swell inside her, she began orgasming, and a moment later he roared his completion and sank his fangs into her neck.

Complete and total ecstasy.

This was how she would describe it later when verbal reasoning returned. In the meantime, she was floating in a haze of pleasure and euphoria and thinking of nothing at all.

When she came to, a few minutes later—or maybe longer? Who knew?—Dalhu was slumped on top of her, crushing her with his weight, and still out of it as if he'd been the one dosed with venom.

She pushed on his chest, first gently, and when that didn't help, forcefully, managing to lift him a bit, just enough to wiggle out from under him. But that effort had drained the last of her energy, and she just lay next to Dalhu spread-eagled as much as the space he wasn't occupying allowed.

After a moment, she regained enough strength to move her head and look at him. She smiled. Lying face down, the only indication that he was still alive and breathing was the slight up and down movement of his wide back.

"Are you alive, big guy, or have I drained all of your life force?" She teased with a smirk.

He turned his head toward her, his face the most relaxed and peaceful she'd ever seen it. "If you did, then I must've died a happy man."

"So that's it? You're done?"

He reached a long arm and pulled her to him, half turning to face her. "Not even close, I'm just taking a one-minute rest. After all, I was the one doing all the work..." He kissed her lips before collapsing again—dramatically.

"Well, it's not my fault that you wanted to be the big macho male. I was perfectly happy being the one on top."

"I'll tell you what, this time you can be." He flopped to his back, pulling her with him to lie on top of him.

Bracing her elbows on Dalhu's broad chest and her chin on her hands, she taunted, "Admit it, you're too wiped out to move a muscle and just want me on top to do all the work."

He smiled, not rising to the challenge. "I'll admit that I'm a red marshmallow if it makes you happy."

"A red marshmallow?"

He shrugged. "First thing that popped into my head, not very witty I'm afraid."

"Hmm..." She frowned. "I wonder what it means..."

"It doesn't mean anything, Professor, don't psychoanalyze me—especially not while we are engaging in sexual activity. It could have, potentially, a damaging effect on my fragile ego."

This was fun, this postcoital easy banter. She had never stayed with a guy long enough for small talk after she'd had her way with him.

As soon as she was done, she would thrall her partner, and the poor thing could barely remember his own name let alone conduct a conversation. And anyway, she doubted it could have been like this with anyone but Dalhu.

"Well, if your ego is that sensitive then it probably needs a little boost. You are a force of nature, absolutely magnificent."

He smiled. "Go on—"

"You want more? Okay. You're the best I ever had."

"Of course. Please continue—"

"Without compare."

"I'm all ears."

She narrowed her eyes at him and husked, "I'm ready for more."

"Are you now?"

She felt him stir beneath her. *Good boy.*

Her kiss was gentle this time, and attuned as he was to her, he responded in kind. Their tongues danced lazily around each other, and his hands on her back caressed and kneaded in turns before moving to her front and paying homage to her breasts.

He lifted and pulled her up, bringing one nipple into his mouth and lapping at it gently. Then he moved her, so the other one was hovering above his lips and repeated the treatment.

It felt so good to let him carry her weight, knowing that he was holding her up with ease, watching his incredible biceps flexing.

Once he had his fill of suckling and licking, and her sensitive nipples could take no more, he pulled her up even higher to worship her nether lips with his tongue.

She was indeed the one on top, but he was definitely still the one in charge. It was fine with her, though. His talented tongue was doing a fantastic job of bringing her to the verge of another orgasm. Incredibly dexterous for a tongue, it was somehow pushing and twisting inside her at the same time.

"You're going to make me come like this."

"I know," he mumbled and continued his assault.

She wasn't about to argue. Letting herself go, she climaxed with a soft gasp.

They made love a few more times, unhurriedly, learning each other's bodies, and the easy, gentle pace brought its own unique kind of pleasure—an intimacy that neither had experienced with anyone else before.

Other than that first time, Dalhu refrained from biting her, and she suspected that he didn't want her dopey from the effect of the venom because he wanted her to savor the closeness just as much as he did.

Amanda sighed contentedly as he pulled out and plopped beside her on the bed. She was so exhausted, it was a struggle to keep her eyes open, and after a moment she gave up, letting herself drift into sleep.

"I can't believe I'm saying it, but I think that you successfully drained the last drop of life out of me," she heard him say.

"Mm-hmm...," she murmured, not willing to lift her eyelids.

He turned sideways and draped his arm around her middle, turning her limp body around so he could snuggle up from behind. "Isn't it the guy who's supposed to turn around and go to sleep after?"

"Mm-hmm..."

29

SEBASTIAN

"Stay together and give Robert a buzz when you're done. He'll pick you up. Is everyone clear about what to do?" Sebastian eyed the small group of men he was dropping off at what was supposed to be a raunchy bar.

"I still don't understand about that Uber service. Why not use a taxicab?"

Sebastian rolled his eyes. "First of all, you might not need the service if you can take care of business in some secluded corner right here in the bar or in the alley behind it. But we don't want accidental witnesses, so in case privacy is a problem, you call up a car, using the Uber application on your phone like I showed you, and take the woman to one of the motels on your list. It's easier and cheaper than a taxicab, and the drivers do it as a part-time job and don't pay as much attention to their passengers."

The guy nodded, and the group headed for the bar's front door.

He really needed to solve the problem of females for his men, and the sooner, the better.

Sebastian eased into the sparse late-evening traffic and headed for the nearest coffee shop with Internet service. He had chosen the neighborhood carefully, searching for a lower-middle-class area that was becoming trendy, and had settled for Glendale. His research had yielded a few popular bars and clubs as well as coffee shops that were open late—a rarity in most of LA and its surrounding cities, whose residents apparently went to sleep with the birds.

As he spotted what he was looking for, Sebastian drove a little farther down the street until he found a parking spot big enough for his brand new Escalade. Tom had convinced him that it was best suited to his needs, but even though the car was pretty luxurious and surprisingly easy to drive despite its monstrous size, he would've preferred something more refined—like the Range Rover he had back home. Except, Tom's argument had been that Sebastian needed a car that could seat more passengers than the Rover and that the Escalade was in fact considered trendy. It remained to be seen. He would drive the thing for a week, and if he didn't like it, he'd fob it off on Tom and have the guy buy him something else.

The small coffee shop was almost deserted at only ten o'clock at night. He made his way down the narrow aisle separating the two rows of booths, benches that were covered in ugly burgundy Naugahyde and tables that were topped with cheap Formica, settling in the last one next to the front window. The only other customer was an older guy sitting in the booth across from him. The man was staring into space while mumbling something incoherent to his invisible companion.

A loon.

Sebastian pulled out his laptop from its leather carrying case and put it on the table. The Internet access code was printed on top of the plastic menu, and he logged in. Maybe some flies had been already caught in the dating web, and someone had responded to his ad, or profile as the dating service called it. He wondered if the other *profiles* were as fabricated as his. Probably. At least his picture wasn't fake. It was slightly altered, but not to make him look better, just to obscure his identity.

"What can I get you?" A waitress with a white apron and ratty sneakers, holding a little notepad and pencil, was giving him an appreciative look-over.

She didn't smile for him, though, or strike a pose like most girls would've done when they wanted to get noticed. Probably figured he was out of her league, and rightfully so. Too skinny, with a limp ponytail that looked like it needed shampooing. Perhaps with a little spiffing up and some meat on her bones she could've been pretty, not beautiful, but at least attractive.

He put on a charming smile and glanced at her name tag. "Tiffany, what a lovely name. How is your cappuccino? Any good?"

She shrugged. "I guess. A lot of the lunch regulars order it, so it must be good. I don't drink coffee, so I wouldn't know."

She didn't drink coffee?

Who didn't drink coffee? There must be something wrong with the girl. "I'll give it a try. How about those cakes over there?" As he tilted his head sideways to look at the pastries and cakes in the display case up front, he noticed the woman standing behind the tall counter.

Now, that was a looker.

Not as young as Tiffany, the woman was probably the proprietress. Only her face and a small part of her upper body were visible from behind the display, but unless she had a backside the size of his Escalade or crooked legs, she was definitely on the beautiful side of the scale. Except, she looked tired, with dark circles under her big brown eyes, and the expression on her face was decidedly unfriendly. In fact, she was eyeing him with almost open hostility.

It happened sometimes.

Here and there he'd encountered a woman who possessed some kind of a sixth sense about what was hiding under his charming veneer.

No big deal.

Very few females possessed this innate ability, and he had no problem ensnaring most others with his silver tongue and his charming smile.

However, it was a shame that this one was among those select few.

Even with that dour and tired expression, hair that was pulled back in a simple braid, and no trace of makeup, her face was arresting. Her features hinted at a mixed heritage, a combination of Hispanic, maybe Cuban, and Middle Eastern. Perhaps some Egyptian or even Ethiopian. It made her beauty unique.

Like a rare masterpiece.

One that he would've loved to possess.

"The cakes and pastries are to die for. I can say this with confidence because I've tasted most of them. I promise that anything you choose will be amazing—" He listened to the skinny waitress's gushing endorsement while locking gazes with the proprietress.

She didn't back down.

Gutsy bitch, he'd give her that.

"What's your favorite?" Sebastian smiled at the dark-haired beauty before turning his attention back to the waitress.

She hadn't returned his smile.

"Oh, I can't say, they're all so good." She leaned over a little as if to tell him a secret. "My boss makes them herself, and the recipes are a family secret."

"In this case, I must sample more than one. Bring me an assortment."

The waitress's face visibly brightened, probably calculating the tip she was going to get. "How many would you like?"

He glanced at the woman behind the counter and winked. "Let's start with six."

"Yes, sir!" she chirped. Tucking her small notepad inside her apron pocket, she hurried away to fill his order.

He'd definitely succeeded in winning the waitress over, but her boss's expression remained unchanged.

Oh well, he couldn't win them all. The waitress would do.

Come to think of it, with a little fattening and styling she might be good enough for his men.

30

KIAN

"I don't know what to say." Syssi touched her fingers to the choker.

Kian leaned over her shoulder and kissed her cheek. "A simple thank-you will suffice, my love." He walked back to the other side of the table and sat down.

Syssi looked like a queen, and for the first time in his life, he was truly thankful for his wealth. He felt a purely male sense of satisfaction at being able to buy his fiancée things few other men could. Never mind that it was unwarranted. After all, it wasn't as if he had slain a dragon or bested numerous opponents in a tournament to win her hand in marriage. But dragons didn't exist and knights no longer jousted for ladies' affections. Nowadays, acts of bravery and combat skills were replaced by business acumen, and battles were waged in the financial arena. The measure of success for men, and for women, was how well they managed to distinguish themselves in either politics or the art of money making.

"Thank you." She shook her head as she lifted her hand to examine the ring. "But seriously, Kian, these two pieces of jewelry can feed a small country. Don't get me wrong, I'm flattered, but I'm also somewhat perplexed. And even though I promised not to argue about accepting these, I just have to know; what in God's name possessed you to spend a fortune on diamonds for me?"

Luckily, he'd come prepared with an argument even his practical Syssi couldn't find fault with. "It's a sound investment. Diamonds of this caliber that come with authentication certificates appreciate in value. So in case we ever find ourselves in a situation where we need to feed a small country, and all our other resources are gone, we can sell them for more than their original cost." *Checkmate.*

Syssi opened her mouth to say something, but then closed it, slumping back in her chair. For a moment, she just gazed at him with narrowed eyes.

His lips twitched with the effort of stifling a smirk.

Crossing her arms over her chest, she finally smiled. "Very clever, aren't you? You had it all carefully planned."

"Obviously, I know who I'm dealing with. I have more."

"Oh, yeah?"

"You know, it's not very romantic to argue with your fiancé when he presents you with a ring."

"Oh, that's a good one, laying a guilt trip on me. But seriously, where am I going to wear these? I'll need armed guards to accompany me if I leave the keep with this on—to protect your *investment*."

Kian leaned forward and beckoned Syssi with his finger to get closer. "Remember my original proposal?" he whispered.

She blushed, "How could I ever forget?"

"So you know exactly where and how you're going to wear these."

Syssi grinned and leaned even closer. "With nothing on besides spiky high heels."

"You got it."

"Pervert."

"What else is new?"

"I love you."

He took her hands and kissed each one. "That's not new, and neither is how much I love you and how grateful I am for you. You make my life worth living."

Syssi's eyes shone, but he suspected that it wasn't the supernatural glow of his kind. She was tearing.

He gave her hands a gentle squeeze. "I hope those are happy tears."

"Oh boy, and here I thought I was doing such a good job of holding them back. But yes, these are happy tears... mostly."

Mostly?

"Why, what's wrong?"

Just as Syssi was about to answer, his phone buzzed in his pocket—again. He'd silenced the damned thing's ringer but the vibrate was still on, and every time an e-mail or a text message came in it buzzed. Which meant that it was buzzing almost continuously. It was like having a damned vibrator in his pocket. For a moment, he eyed his Perrier glass and considered drowning the phone in it.

But it probably won't fit.

"Give me a second." He took it out and shut it down completely. If a catastrophe struck in the next two hours, they'd have to manage without him.

"Okay, I'm listening."

Syssi glanced at his phone. "Are you sure that's smart? What if something happens and they can't get a hold of you. I didn't bring mine. It didn't fit in this tiny purse." She lifted what was the size of his wallet to show him.

Why the hell had she bothered to bring it with her at all? It could barely contain a lipstick. Though he remembered that Syssi had her driver license in there because she showed it to the waiter who had taken their drink order.

As if anyone would've asked to see it in a place like this.

"It's fine. The world will manage without me for a couple of hours. Now, tell me what troubles you before I start blowing smoke out of my nostrils."

"For real?"

"No! You're driving me crazy. Talk, woman."

"It's not about us, so you can relax. It's just that I feel guilty for being so happy—with you—planning our wedding, joking, having fun, while Amanda suffers because she can't be with the one she loves."

Aha, so that is her story. Well, at least she said she is happy and having fun.

"She was the one who sobered up and left. I had nothing to do with it." *Technically.*

"So what are you saying? That if Amanda comes back and wants to be with Dalhu, you will not stand in her way?"

"That, I didn't say."

Syssi pulled her hands out of his grip and crossed her arms over her chest. "You're not doing the right thing here, Kian. I know you think it's best for Amanda to forget about Dalhu, but you can't make this kind of a decision for her. And from what I hear Dalhu is a decent guy, for a Doomer, and he is cooperating with us. If they truly love each other, you should give them a chance."

He could've strangled that damned Doomer. The guy was intruding on Kian's perfect date.

"Can we not talk about this tonight? This evening is about us, and I don't want to think about anything other than you and how soon I can get you naked."

Syssi smiled and dropped her arms. She returned her hands to the table and slipped them inside his larger ones. "Do you ever think of anything else when you're with me?"

"Let me see… nope. And I don't think of much else when I'm not with you either. I'm just a simple guy with simple needs."

She snorted. "Yeah, right, and here is the evidence of that." She lifted her hand and twisted it around, so the big diamond was in his face.

He took her fingers and brought her hand closer for a kiss. "Did you forget already? Should I repeat my *pervy* proposal?"

Syssi threw her head back and laughed out loud. "Oh, God, you're right, this too is about getting me naked."

"Absolutely."

31

SEBASTIAN

"A pretty girl like you shouldn't be walking all by herself in the middle of the night." Sebastian sidled up to the little waitress. He'd said it jokingly, the street wasn't deserted, and people were still going in and coming out of the trendy cafés and restaurants that were still open. Only the boutiques and other small shops were closed, but their window fronts remained brightly illuminated.

It hadn't required a Sherlock-Holmes-caliber deductive skill to guess that the girl was dirt poor and didn't own a car. One look at her ratty sneakers and her old, threadbare jeans—and not the fashionable kind that just looked worn out—had told him all he needed to know.

He had waited outside the coffee shop until her shift had ended and followed her from a safe distance for a couple of blocks. After all, someone might have come to pick her up, a boyfriend or maybe even her lovely boss. But no one had.

"It's not that late, and I live just around the block," she said with a thin, nervous smile.

"You're right, it is definitely too early for calling it a night. How about a drink somewhere, you and me? Or are your legs killing you after your shift?" He flashed her his best shy smile, the one he had perfected over the years to lure countless females into his trap. Stuffing his hands in his pockets, Sebastian slouched a little, not because he was tall—his height was average for a male—but because he wished to appear as nonthreatening as possible.

She hesitated for about a second and a half. "Okay, there is a bar a few minutes' walk down the other way." She turned around and pointed to a red neon sign that read McClintock's.

The place was one block away from the coffee shop she worked in. It wouldn't have been his first choice, someone might know her there, but he'd gotten the impression that she wouldn't go with him anywhere else. He could've thralled her right there on the street, but that wasn't a good idea either. He needed to find out more about the girl before deciding if she was a good candidate for abduction.

"Sounds great, lead the way," he said.

The girl relaxed visibly.

"Do you go there often?" he asked.

"No, not at all. But I heard it's a nice place."

Perfect.

It was dark inside, for a human that is, and they settled into one of the intimate booths. He ordered them drinks, a plate of nachos, and fried calamari. The girl needed some fattening.

Over the next hour, he coaxed her to tell him her story.

After graduating high school, Tiffany had packed her meager belongings and left her miserable childhood home in Alabama to pursue an acting career in Hollywood. She'd covered the distance mostly by hitchhiking and only occasionally taking a bus. She'd made it to the *promised land* two and a half months ago, and until her big break arrived, she was waitressing and sharing a two-bedroom apartment with four other girls. What she made at her part-time job paid her share of the rent with little left over for other necessities. She was dedicating most of her time to an endless parade of auditions for any part that was open to nonunion members—she couldn't afford the fees.

No wonder she was so skinny.

Poor Tiffany was in over her head. Sooner or later someone was going to take advantage of her naivety and youth. She wasn't exceptionally pretty, or smart. Girls like her weren't likely to get their big break.

By providing her with shelter and food, he'd probably be doing her a favor—and saving her a lot of heartbreak.

32

KIAN

The blinking red light on the bedside phone was the first thing Kian saw when he cracked his eyes open the morning after his and Syssi's date.

Damn, I forgot to turn my cell phone back on.

Ignoring it, he rubbed his eyes and turned to his side. Syssi was snoring lightly beside him, nude save for the choker and the ring—a testament to last night's sexcapades. The poor thing had been too exhausted to take the jewelry off before falling asleep. He would have taken it off for her. Trouble was he'd passed out as well.

Syssi's stamina in bed had improved so dramatically since her transition that he had a nagging suspicion she was capable of outlasting him. But he'd be damned if he ever allowed this to happen. He'd keep on going until one of two things happened: either Syssi was done or he dropped dead.

Not a moment earlier.

He wrapped his arm around her and snuggled closer. Sleepily, she swept her voluminous hair to the side and over her shoulder, exposing her long neck. Kian frowned. There was a red indentation where the choker's clasp had been pressing into her skin. She shouldn't have slept with it on, must've been uncomfortable. In fact, it was probably dangerous. The thing was called a choker for a reason. He pinched the clasp open and gently removed it from Syssi's neck. The ring could stay.

"What time is it?" she rasped in her sexy morning voice.

"Seven fifteen."

Syssi bolted up and twisted to face him. "Really? We overslept?"

"Yep." He pulled her down to him and kissed her dry lips.

She covered her mouth with her hand and spoke through slightly splayed fingers. "How did it happen? And how come you're not freaking out?"

"I turned off my phone last night and forgot to turn it back on. And guess what? The keep is still standing, we are not under attack, and I feel damn good, relaxed." He kissed the fingers she was shielding her mouth with. "You're still obsessing about your morning breath? I told you it's all in your head, and even if it were bad, which it's not, I wouldn't mind. I'd rather kiss your mouth even when it's stinky, which it's not, than not kiss it at all."

She wiggled out of his arms and rolled off the bed, holding her hand in front of her mouth until she was a safe distance away. "I'm going to brush my teeth and get us something to drink. I'm thirsty." She disappeared into the bathroom.

With his excuse for not checking his messages gone, Kian picked up the receiver and punched the blinking button. There were a couple from Shai about rescheduling a meeting and one from William about some new equipment he wanted to order—as if he needed Kian's approval for that. He'd told the guy, countless times, to buy whatever he deemed necessary as long as it was within the budget allotted to him, and only to call if he ran out.

Kian suspected that William's calls were more about sharing his latest ideas than asking permission to spend money.

The last message was from Onegus.

"Eh, Kian, I know that you're out with Syssi, and I'd hate to ruin your date, that's why I'm leaving the message on your home phone instead of calling your cell phone. Steve from security called me. There is no way to sugarcoat it so, yeah, here goes. Amanda is back, and she moved in with the prisoner. She told Steve that from now on the cell apartment was going to be her residence and demanded that he cut the surveillance. He had no choice but to do as he was told because it is clearly stated in the bylaws that monitoring clan members' personal quarters is not allowed. I double-checked, and he is right, so there is nothing I can do about it either. It's up to you, tell me what you want to do."

Fuck, Amanda was one hell of a clever manipulator. But it was not going to help her with him. He would go down there and drag her out by her hair if need be. Playing house with a Doomer was not going to happen, not on his watch.

Kian was out of bed and in the bathroom before finishing his internal rant. Even Syssi's sumptuous naked butt, which was shaking enticingly as she brushed her teeth, failed to lighten his mood.

Syssi spat out the last of the toothpaste and wiped her mouth with a towel. "Why are you out of bed? I only wanted to freshen up and was coming back to you."

"Amanda is back." He grabbed his toothbrush and toothpaste. "Fuck!" He squeezed the tube too hard and a big blob landed in the sink. Struggling for control, he applied gentle pressure on his second try and got the right amount.

Syssi turned around and leaned against the counter, crossing her arms over her naked breasts. "You're not happy to have her back home?"

Kian spat out the paste. "She is down in the dungeon with that Doomer and has no intention of leaving anytime soon. She ordered security to cut surveillance to his cell."

Syssi was quiet for a moment. "Is it really so bad, Kian? Do you really believe he'll hurt her?"

"No, but that's beside the point and you know it." He wiped his face with a towel and headed for the closet to get dressed, hoping Syssi wouldn't follow. The last thing he wanted was to argue with her while he was fuming with rage.

The one who deserved his wrath was Amanda and not Syssi, but she was in the way.

Except, of course, she had to follow him. The girl had no sense whatsoever when her romantic ideas hijacked her otherwise sensible brain. In this, Syssi was the quintessential female.

"What are you going to do?" she asked.

"What do you think? I'm going to drag her out of there, lock her in her apartment, and reinstate the surveillance."

"You can't do this. She's a grown woman, and you can't behave like a caveman. What do you think is going to happen? You think you'll order her to get out and she'll meekly obey? Or are you planning on throwing her over your shoulder and carrying her up to her penthouse?"

Kian buttoned his jeans and grabbed a T-shirt off the shelf. "If she will not listen to reason, then yes, I have no problem with hauling her out of there caveman-style. I'm in charge of this keep, and everyone here answers to me, including the spoiled princess."

Syssi shook her head. "I can't believe how unreasonable you are. They are in love, Kian, let them be, for God's sake."

Slipping his feet into a pair of loafers, he turned around and pointed a finger at Syssi's chest. "Stay out of it, Syssi. I know you mean well, but I'm in no mood for silly arguments."

"Silly arguments?" She was the one fuming now. "You dare call me silly? When you're the one who is not thinking straight? What's wrong with you?"

"Nothing. This is who you're marrying, sweetheart. Deal with it." Kian was well aware that he was behaving like a monumental jerk, but he was too pissed off to control it. Why the hell was she antagonizing him? She should know him better by now.

"Maybe I shouldn't marry a man who was born in the Dark Ages and evidently has never left." Her voice quivered, and there was a sheen of tears in her eyes.

Damn! Kian gritted his teeth and summoned the last of his self-control, reaching for Syssi and pulling her into his arms. "I'm sorry, baby. Please, let's talk about it later, when I'm not so close to the edge."

Syssi's arms were still crossed over her chest, and she didn't return his hug, but her stiff shoulders relaxed a bit, and her voice was almost steady when she asked, "Don't you think it's also a good idea for you to calm down before confronting Amanda? You don't want to say or do something that you'll regret later."

"I'll try, that's all I can promise."

33

SYSSI

The moment Kian had left, Syssi collapsed onto the wardrobe's footstool and let the tears flow freely. She felt disappointed and disillusioned. Once again, she had discovered that Kian wasn't all that she'd built him up to be.

He wasn't perfect, far from it.

The dominant alpha tendencies that she found so arousing in bed were annoying as hell outside of it. The man was a Neanderthal. Living by some outdated notion of a man's supposed authority over his family.

Question was, would she be able to live with them?

Did she have a choice?

Kian was the love of her life, warts and all. Perfect or imperfect, it didn't really matter. She loved the big arrogant jerk too much to even think of leaving.

She'd have to learn to deal with him and his heavy-handed attitude.

He'd hurt her feelings, though, big time. The dismissive manner in which he'd talked to her—as if she was some silly little girl, a pest.

Where were his proclamations of appreciation for her intellect? Her common sense? Were they just empty compliments?

It certainly seemed like it. This morning, he'd showed her his real opinion of her, hadn't he?

Oh, I'm just overreacting, being melodramatic.

She needed to talk to somebody. But the only one she could confide in was Amanda, who, naturally, was otherwise engaged at the moment. True, Annani had promised to always have Syssi's back and box Kian's ears if he earned it, which he had, with interest, but running to Kian's mother every time she and Kian had a fight wasn't a good idea. Not in the slightest.

That left Andrew.

Oh, God, she needed to make more friends. Immortal female friends, so she could pour her heart out to someone other than Amanda without worrying about exposing the clan. Andrew loved her dearly, but he wouldn't understand, or worse, would get mad at Kian and initiate a fight. Who could predict how far men were willing to take their macho posturing and what idiotic things they might do?

Pulling on her soft yoga pants and a T-shirt, her comfort clothes, she plodded to the bedroom to get her phone.

She selected Andrew's name from her short list of favorites and waited patiently for him to pick up. Weird. Andrew almost always answered immediately, but this time, the phone kept ringing and ringing, and she was considering ending the call when he finally picked up.

"What's up, Syssi?"

"Nothing much, just wondered if you have a few minutes to shoot the breeze with your sister."

Andrew wasn't fooled by her casual tone. "I'm coming up. I'll be there in a minute. Start the coffee."

"What do you mean you're coming up? Are you here? In the

building?" She glanced at the bedside clock. "At seven thirty in the morning?"

"I'll tell you all about it when I get there."

What the hell was Andrew doing in the keep so early? Even if Kian had called him, perhaps summoning him to help with Amanda's situation, Andrew couldn't have made it here so fast. He must've crashed at someone's apartment overnight.

But who? Had he befriended one of the Guardians?

That was the most reasonable explanation. He'd probably gone drinking with some of the guys, and they'd brought him here because he'd been too wasted to drive home. If Amanda was a typical example of an immortal's drinking capacity, then Andrew was no match for them in that department. No wonder he had gotten drunk. And that's why he wanted coffee.

Mystery solved.

Syssi went back to the closet for a pair of clogs, then headed for the kitchen.

The doorbell rang just as the machine finished brewing and began spewing little steaming jets into the two tall porcelain mugs Syssi had placed under the twin spouts.

She opened the door with a smile. "You're right on time. The coffee is ready."

"Good, I need it." Andrew followed her to the kitchen counter and pulled out a stool.

She chuckled. "I can imagine."

His brows lifted in surprise. "So you know?"

"About what?" She placed a mug in front of him and sat down.

"Me and Bridget."

"You went out drinking with Bridget?"

"Drinking? Why would you think that I went out to a bar? And with Bridget?"

"You said Bridget, not me. I thought you went out drinking with the guys and crashed in one of their apartments." She turned to him, and a small smile bloomed on her face. "Wait a minute, so if you went out with Bridget and then crashed at her place, does it mean what I think it means?"

"Yes, just minus the drinking part. Bridget invited me to dinner at her place, and I fell asleep."

Syssi snorted. "I bet the interesting part of the story happened in the interval between eating and falling asleep, you naughty boy." She slapped his shoulder. "I like Bridget, and I'm very happy for you."

"It's nothing serious, so please don't make a big fuss about it. I don't think Bridget wants to advertise our whatever it is. Anyway, I came up here to talk about you, not me. What's going on? And who do I need to beat up?"

"I had a fight with Kian."

"You want me to rough him up for you?"

"Why does everything have to end up with you beating up somebody? I just need someone to vent to, and you happen to be the only one available."

He made a sweeping motion with his hand. "Vent away, I'm all ears. But after you're done venting, my offer still stands."

"Fine." She took a few sips from her mug while Andrew finished his. "Last night, while Kian and I were out, Amanda came back."

"I know, I met her on my way to Bridget's."

"Did you know that she was planning on moving in with Dalhu in his dungeon apartment?"

"No, but good for her."

"That's what I think too, but obviously Kian doesn't. As soon as he heard about it, he wanted to storm out and head over there. I barely managed to get in a few words, trying to convince him to calm down before he went to talk to her. But I only succeeded in annoying him even more, and he told me to stay out of it, very dismissively, as if my opinion was irrelevant. And now I'm thinking that maybe I'm making a mistake marrying him. He made it very obvious that he doesn't see me as his equal. What kind of marriage will I have? The little wife who is expected to say 'yes, sir'? I can't live like that." She was getting more and more agitated as her rant went on, and, of course, the tears came as well.

Andrew laughed—out loud—and she had to fight the strong urge to take off one of her heavy wooden clogs and chuck it at his head.

"I'm sorry," he said. "It's just that you were spouting one nonsense after the other, and your face looked so pouty, it was comical." He took her hands, and she let him, even though he was infuriating.

"I'm not pouting."

"Yes, you are. Now listen, you know perfectly well that most of what you said is not true. Kian worships the ground you walk on, and his opinion of you is probably higher than what you deserve."

"Hey," she objected.

"You're a twenty-five-year-old woman, who is smart and compassionate and loving and the best person I know. But, you cannot compare your life experience or your level of responsibility to Kian's. There will be times, probably many, that you'll have to defer to him and abide by his judgment. That being said, I'm sure there are many things that he can learn from you. In a good marriage, each partner contributes his or her strengths to the unit and trusts the other one to handle matters which he or she is more knowledgeable or is better equipped to deal with. It should be an equality of value, where one partner's contribution is deemed just as important as the other's. Both partners are equally valuable—but that doesn't mean that they have to share every responsibility equally. It doesn't make sense. It's like the CIA and the Air Force are both equally important, true? But pilots shouldn't go spying, and spies shouldn't go flying jet planes."

"In theory, you're absolutely right. But in real life, men used that same argument to excuse delegating inferior tasks to women, claiming that females were ill-suited to do this or that."

"All those mean, mean males. You girls should've gotten rid of us a long time ago," he mocked.

"Don't make fun of it, you know I'm right."

"I do. It's just that accusing Kian of misogyny is preposterous. His clan is headed by a woman."

"Yeah, I know." Syssi sighed and slumped her shoulders. "Here I am, feeling all sorry for myself when there is probably an all-out war going on down there. Maybe we should go and try to help. Amanda and Kian's relationship is already strained as it is, and I know Kian is going to make an even bigger mess of things."

"They are both big kids, and they'll figure it out. If not today, then tomorrow, or in a month, or a year from now. Putting yourself in the middle will only get you hurt."

Syssi chuckled as Andrew's argument evoked an image of Kian and Amanda as kids. Annani had been lucky to have them eons apart. Both were so hardheaded and stubborn that raising them together would've been a nightmare.

Suddenly, her vision blurred.

Oh no, here it comes.

It had been such a long time since her last premonition, but the sensation was unmistakable.

All outside stimuli receded. Vision, sound, smell, all of it was no longer there. A small swirl of intense bright color started filling the void, getting bigger and bigger until it completely filled her inner sight. Then it began to coalesce into a picture, or rather a movie—the image wasn't static.

It was a beautiful summer day in a park. Somewhere where the green was strong and vivid, the trees and the grass and everything that grew appeared healthy, like in Hawaii. Andrew and a little girl were the only ones there. He was tossing the giggling child up, or rather just pretending to throw her because his large hands never left her tiny waist, then pretending to catch her, sneaking hugs and kisses in between the tosses.

His daughter—Syssi had no doubt that the child in her vision was Andrew's—was a beautiful little girl. No more than two years old, she had long, thick dark hair that curled at the bottom, a rosebud of a mouth, and cheeks that were pink from exposure to the fresh air and from laughter. A perfect little girl. And Andrew looked so happy, the happiest she'd ever seen him.

The vision blurred, the child's laughter fading into the distance, and Syssi opened her eyes with a gasp.

"Are you okay?" Andrew was holding her shoulders with a worried look on his face.

"I'm fine. In fact, I'm better than fine." She smiled, but then her smile wilted when she reminded herself that her premonitions were mostly about impending disasters, and not about happy fathers and giggling daughters.

And yet, this time, it had been different. It had started the same as the others had, but then it had changed. And in the aftermath, she wasn't left with a dark cloud hanging over her head like with her other premonitions.

"What did you see?"

"You. And your little girl."

"My what?"

"Your daughter, Andrew. You're going to become the proud father of the most gorgeous and sweetest little girl."

Who was the mother, though? Was it Bridget? But the child had dark hair and a darker shade of skin than Bridget's white, translucent porcelain complexion. Maybe his daughter would take after Andrew, who was slightly darker than Syssi and had brown hair. Except, the girl's hair looked almost black, not brown. And even if Amanda were still a possibility for Andrew, her black hair wasn't her natural color. Amanda's real color was dark red like her mother's—and Bridget's.

A mystery.

"Are you sure? What exactly have you seen?"

"You and this little girl playing in a park."

"Maybe she was someone else's daughter? Like maybe yours?"

Not unless she ended up with a dark-haired husband instead of Kian. And that was not going to happen.

"No, she was yours."

"Damn."

34

KIAN

At the last moment, Kian punched the button for the gym's level instead of the dungeon's. Syssi was right, he should calm down if he hoped to have a civilized talk with Amanda. Not that it was likely to happen, they'd probably end up tearing at each other's throats, but then he could at least tell Syssi that he had done his best.

The loafers weren't suited for running, but he could release steam by lifting weights almost as well as by running on a treadmill. He was not about to go back for gym shoes.

The prospect of seeing Syssi and her disapproving expression wasn't something he was ready to face.

Not yet.

Maybe later, when he could report to Syssi how civilized he had been with Amanda so she'd be proud of him again.

Fates help me. How am I going to achieve that?

Buckets of sweat, that's how. Maybe if he pushed himself to a level of exhaustion that drained all of his energy, negative and positive alike, he'd be able to pull it off.

"Kian, over here," Anandur called out.

Great, he was hoping for Yamanu as a lifting partner. Today he was in a mood that could only be satisfied on the bench, pressing some serious weight. Yamanu was perfect for that. But the guy was usually done with his routine by six in the morning, and it was almost eight now. The only two left in the gym were Anandur and Bhathian. The clown and the undertaker.

Reluctantly, Kian walked over to Anandur's lifting station. "I need someone to spot me on the bench, you volunteer?"

Anandur cast a quizzical glance at Kian's loafers. "Last minute change of heart?"

"You can say that. So? Are you going to assist or not?"

"You know I can't say no to you, *boss*." Anandur replaced the kettlebells he'd been training with on the rack and wiped his hands with a towel. "Lead the way."

Kian lay on the bench, adjusting his position until his arms were at the right angle to the bar. "I'll start with four hundred for the warm-up."

"On each side or total?"

"Total, you smart ass."

"Yes, boss."

Kian gripped the bar, tightening his hold to create more tension in his lower arms and chest, then tucked his elbows to his sides and unracked the weight. He held it for a moment before bringing it down to his chest, then drove his feet downward and reversed the movement.

"So, how did your date with Syssi go?" Anandur asked.

"Great, not that it's any of your business."

"I was just wondering why you look so pissed." He chuckled. "For a moment, I was harboring hope that Syssi had smartened up and broken off the engagement."

The bastard, taking advantage of Kian's compromised position. Joking aside, though, after this morning this wasn't such a far-fetched possibility. "You're lucky my hands are busy."

"That's what I was counting on. But seriously, what has gotten your panties in a wad?"

"As if you have to ask. I'm sure Amanda didn't get into the Doomer's cell by materializing through the door," Kian bit out.

"Aha..."

"Did you know that she intended to move in with him?"

"No, I didn't. Before kicking me out, she said she was going to stay overnight, which wasn't all that surprising, but I had no idea she was planning on playing house with the dude."

Bloody Anandur hadn't sounded bothered at all, talking about the incident as if it was just another piece of gossip. And what had he meant by *not surprising*?

"What made you think she'd want to stay the night?"

"Really? You want me to spell it out for you?"

"To scratch her itch, she could've fucked him and left. No need to stay."

Anandur sighed melodramatically. "You still refuse to face the facts. She is in love with the dude, it's not only about the sex."

"She is not in love with him. If she were, she wouldn't have left. Fates know that I wanted to do the right thing by Syssi and let her go before she transitioned, when I didn't believe that she would, but I couldn't."

"Are you done with the warm-up? Or do you want to continue with the light weight?"

"No, put another two hundred on."

"On each side or total?"

"Total, you moron."

"Hey, no need for name calling, it was a legitimate question. After a good warm-up, I press eight hundred."

Show-off.

"Good for you."

Anandur was silent for a moment, but Kian had no illusions

about Anandur dropping the subject. The guy was a worse romantic sap than Syssi.

"I think Amanda is fighting it."

Yeah, Anandur was probably right. But it seemed that she was either making a half-assed effort or losing the battle.

"Not hard enough."

"It's like you couldn't resist Syssi. When it hits you, you're powerless against it, even if you know that it's not good for you or for the other person."

Damn, why is Anandur making sense?

"Well, if she is not strong enough to resist the pull, then I have to do it for her. There is no way in hell that I'll allow Amanda to shack up with a goddamned Doomer."

"If you want my honest opinion, I think you're being an ass about this."

"I don't."

Was he the only sane one in this place? Had they all lost their fucking minds? What were they expecting him to do? Welcome a murderer—a goddamned Doomer—into the family?

35

AMANDA

Waking up next to a man in her bed felt weird, but in a good way. After more than two centuries of sleeping alone and having the bed all to herself, it was an adjustment to share the space with someone else—especially someone as big as Dalhu who was taking up most of it and hogging the blanket.

Though why he needed it was a mystery. The man was a furnace. Amanda snuggled closer to get warm.

Smooth skin over hard muscle—yum.

She ran a hand down his impressive pectoral then followed it with a kiss. Even after all their rigorous activity of last night, Dalhu's scent was still mouth-watering like that of a rich wine—distinctively his, with a hint of the simple Irish Spring soap he'd showered with the day before.

"Good morning." He wrapped an arm around her and started caressing her back, up and down, all the way to her butt.

"Is it? How can you tell time in here? There are no windows."

"Inner clock… and this." He showed her his wristwatch.

She kept caressing his chest, checking out every ridge and valley. "I must say, I'm surprised Kian didn't show up yet. I was expecting him barreling in a long time ago, breaking down the door in the middle of the night and giving me hell."

"Shh... let me enjoy this with you. We'll deal with him when the time comes."

"I don't know about you, but I'd rather be showered and dressed when he comes. One naked showdown is enough for a lifetime."

He chuckled. "You're right. Although I think you were absolutely majestic. I can't imagine any other woman, or man for that matter, who'd have the guts to confront a room full of gawking members of the opposite sex in a butt-naked, akimbo pose. You're one of a kind." He ducked his head and kissed her lips.

Well, hello... That featherlight touch was enough to ignite the hungry beast lurking inside her, and she grabbed his head, holding him in place for a proper kiss—one that involved tongues and teeth, and lasted until she ran out of breath.

"I thought you wanted to shower and dress," Dalhu hissed through fangs that were growing longer in front of her eyes.

Amanda wrapped her arms around him and pulled him on top of her. "This will only take a minute. I want you inside me—right now."

He smiled, the long, protruding fangs making him look positively evil, but his big brown eyes were soft—full of love. "Your wish is my command." He sank into her wet heat in one smooth slide.

"Ah..." She wanted to tell him *you say the nicest things,* but all that came out was a groan of pleasure.

Now, this was a fabulous way to wake up in the morning and start a day—none better—even if a quickie was all they had time for.

She clawed his ass and drew him closer—the small hurt spurring him on—and she felt him twitch inside her as he bucked between her thighs.

Soon, his thrusts were becoming frantic and his chest slick with perspiration—the sparse hair on it rubbing her aching nipples. He growled against her neck, and as she felt his hot breath on her skin, she willed him to bite her.

"Do it," she hissed.

"Not yet," he snarled and drove into her harder, faster, his powerful body a perfect male breeding-machine at peak performance.

Magnificent.

His grip on her shoulders was bruisingly rough, as he held her in place, but so were her claws on his glutes, urging him on to go deeper, harder. It didn't take long until she felt the start of an orgasm bearing down on her, building up momentum.

Her channel spasmed around Dalhu's pistoning shaft, and he swelled inside her, impossibly thick as he neared his own climax.

"Now!" she screamed, and he obeyed, his fangs sinking into her neck on a snarl.

She was pinned to the mattress by Dalhu's powerful arms, immobilized by his twin incisors burning deep in her flesh, and yet she flew, soaring on the wings of incomparable pleasure to a place where nothing but euphoria existed.

Sometime later, she felt herself being picked up, gently cradled in those powerful arms that just a few moments ago held her down with such uncompromising brutality. Only partially cognizant, she realized that Dalhu had carried her into the bathroom when he took her with him into the shower. He sat on the bench while still holding her in his arms, then, somehow, managed to manipulate the faucets with one hand while holding her with the other, and began washing her with infinite care.

So, that's how it felt to be taken care of.

Nice, real nice.

She could get used to that, like on a daily basis.

Come to think of it, from now on it would be Dalhu's job to wash her. Her personal bathing slave.

He did a great job, soaping and washing everywhere, except her hair, which she told him not to touch. Though, next time, definitely. By the time he was done, she was back to herself, but a peaceful, satisfied feeling still lingered—a side effect of the venom she was becoming pleasantly accustomed to. If Kian were hankering for a fight, he would be deeply disappointed. She'd be the epitome of clever diplomacy while he would look like a raving lunatic.

Sweet.

"Thank you, that was lovely." She kissed Dalhu's cheek.

"Just lovely? I was hoping for earth-shattering, incomparable..."

"I was talking about the shower, you nitwit." She kissed him again. "But the sex was indeed incomparable. Happy?"

"Except for being called a nitwit, yeah."

She examined his expression, but he was still smiling. "I'll stop if it bothers you. But I hope you know that I say it jokingly, right?" She shrugged and waved her hand. "It's like a term of endearment for me, I mean nothing by it."

Dalhu pulled her into his arms and kissed her forehead. "I know. And when it's just the two of us alone, I don't mind. But if you ever call me names in front of other people, I'll have no choice but to give you a spanking." He smacked her bare bottom.

"Kinky...," she purred.

He chuckled. "Do you remember the first time you accused me of being kinky?"

Amanda paused with the fresh thong she'd pulled out from her tote in hand. "No, when was that?"

"Right after I'd kidnapped you, I was afraid that you'd try to jump out of the moving vehicle, so I handcuffed you to the handle."

Frowning, she pulled her underwear on. "I remember the handcuffs, but only in the motel, when you thought securing me to the wooden bed's slatted headboard would keep me from getting away."

Dalhu buttoned his jeans and opened a drawer to pull out a fresh T-shirt. "It worked, though, didn't it?"

"Only because you drugged me."

He threaded his fingers through his short hair. "Yeah, I forgot about that. Sorry."

"Sorry that you forgot? Or sorry for doing it?"

"Both, I guess. Though I had no choice. I had no idea how strong you were, so I wasn't concerned about escape, but you would have screamed bloody murder the moment I was out of there."

"True." She shrugged and pulled out a brush and a makeup case from her tote.

As she passed him on her way to the bathroom, Dalhu glanced at her equipment. "I see that you came prepared." There was no mistaking the happy note in his tone.

"For one night. I wasn't planning on staying for good. That decision came later when I was talking to Steve." She leaned closer to the mirror to apply mascara.

Dalhu followed her inside, and she got a glimpse of him through the mirror, leaning against the doorjamb with his arms crossed over his chest.

The guy had amazing biceps.

Look away, Amanda, before you get your fresh thong wet.

She returned to her own reflection and applied a little lip stain, then ran a quick brush through her hair.

"You should bring more of your things. Unless you want to stay naked, which is fine with me, or you can borrow my T-shirts. Anandur brought me a generous supply."

"I'll have my butler bring down a few items at a time. The closet in here is tiny."

She retied the wrap dress for a snugger fit and slipped her feet into the low-heeled mules.

"By the way, what do you do for coffee? Do you have a coffeemaker here?"

"No, a short, weird-looking butler brings in my meals, each with a fresh thermos of coffee, and it usually lasts me until the next one. If I get thirsty in between, there is orange juice and Perrier in the bar fridge."

"That must be Okidu, Kian's butler. Let's go check if he left anything in the living room for us." Amanda collected her beauty supplies and put them back in their case before heading out to the other room.

"Yay, we have coffee," she enthused. "Come, sit next to me."

Dalhu joined her on the couch, and she poured them coffee from the thermos.

"How did he know to bring two cups?" Dalhu lifted the delicate porcelain cup with two thick fingers. It looked like a child's plaything in his hand. "And these are not the type of cups he gets for me. He knew that you were here."

"Of course." Amanda drank gratefully, then picked up a piece of toast from the tray.

"Did you tell him? Or was it Anandur?"

"No one has to tell Okidu anything. He figured it out the moment he opened the door and saw my purse on the coffee table. He must've gone back upstairs for what he considered appropriate for a lady."

"Aren't you bothered that he might have heard us while he was here?"

"Nope."

"Okay."

She would tell him the real story about Okidu and Onidu some other time; now she wanted to be done with breakfast before Kian showed up.

A girl had to have her priorities straight.

Sex first, shower and makeup second, food third. All the rest could wait.

Or not.

The mechanical buzz of the door's interior mechanism engaging was their only warning before Kian blew in like an angry storm descending on a cloudless, sunny day.

36

ANANDUR

"Just stay calm, okay, my man?" Anandur cautioned Kian one last time before punching the code to Dalhu's cell. Correction, Amanda and Dalhu's love nest—as the guest suite was going to be known from now on.

People in love were doing strange things for even stranger reasons. Like Kian refusing to go home and change from his sweat-saturated clothes because he was scared shitless of Syssi—a little thing who weighed maybe a hundred and twenty pounds and was as gentle as a dove.

Instead, the guy had showered at the gym and sent Anandur to get him some of Brundar's clothes—adamantly refusing to let Anandur go to his and Syssi's penthouse for his own. Again, for no good reason other than being scared of Syssi's scorn.

It was good that Kian hadn't asked for Anandur's. After donating a large portion of his wardrobe to Dalhu, he was already running low. Another trip to Walmart was unavoidable. It was either that or doing laundry.

Guess which was more likely to happen.

Kian took a deep breath, held it in, then released it in a slow stream through his mouth. "Just open the goddamned door," he barked.

So much for calming down—

Let the games begin.

As Anandur pushed open the door, he implored the Fates that he'd find the lovebirds out of bed and decently attired. Neither Kian nor Amanda would survive a repeat of what had happened in the cabin.

It was a huge relief to see the two seated on the couch—busy doing nothing naughty—enjoying a civilized breakfast.

With a quick glance at the ceiling, he mouthed a heartfelt thank-you to the heavenly Fates.

But then Amanda had to open her big mouth.

"Hello, Kian, and welcome to my new place of residence. Though, please knock next time you visit."

"As if you ever knock on my door before barging in—uninvited!"

"Duly noted, from now on I promise I will. Please take a seat, brother mine."

Oh, boy, she is pushing it. Not smart, girl. Not smart at all.

Surprisingly, Kian did as she asked and planted his butt in a chair. Anandur took the opportunity to sidle behind him and mime to Amanda to cut it out, then plonked himself in the other armchair.

"You can't stay here, Amanda." Kian served the first ball in the match.

"I don't see why not," Amanda countered.

Pity that it was too early in the morning for a drink because this was going to take a while and Anandur would have loved one. Hell, he was sure all of them could use one.

Eh, what the hell. "Drink, anyone?" He got up and opened the bar.

"I'll have whatever you're having." Apparently Kian shared his opinion.

"Dalhu? Amanda?"

"I'll have what you're having too," Dalhu said.

"Nothing for me, I'm fine with coffee," said the one with the biggest set of balls in the room.

Anandur poured three shots of whiskey, and after handing the guys their drinks returned to his chair.

Kian took a small sip and grimaced. "It's really too early for that." He lowered the glass to the table. "I hate beating around the bush, so I'm going to be blunt. There is no way in hell I'm going to allow you to stay here with the Doomer. Is that clear?"

"And there is no way I'm leaving. Is *that* clear?"

A strained moment of silence stretched between the siblings as they locked eyes, each trying to stare the other down.

Damn, this could take a very long time.

Neither was going to relent.

Luckily, a soft knock on the door saved the day. Expecting Okidu and a tray loaded with an assortment of munchies, Anandur got up and opened the door. But instead of the butler, he found Syssi and Andrew, and what was worse, no food.

"I thought we should be here," Syssi said.

"I'm with her." Andrew pointed to his sister.

Well, this was going to get even more interesting…

Because there wasn't enough drama to begin with...

Anandur let the door swing all the way for the newcomers to come in.

Syssi's hand flew to her chest. "Oh my God! This is amazing. You're so talented, Dalhu." She walked around the room touching the various portraits of Amanda, before settling next to her on the couch.

"Thank you."

"Impressive," Andrew mumbled as he drew out one of the dinette chairs and swung it around so it faced the couch.

After that, no one said a thing. Andrew cleared his throat a couple of times, and Syssi kept glancing at the pictures and shaking her head in wonder.

Kian was the first to break the silence, training his eyes first on Syssi and then on Andrew. "I don't know what you were hoping to achieve by coming down here, but if you thought you'd be able to pressure me into changing my mind, you should think again."

Andrew raised his hands, palms out. "I'm just an impartial observer. I came to prevent unnecessary bloodshed and provide my lie detector services—if needed."

"And I want to ensure that you guys are civil to each other, and maybe help negotiate a compromise," Syssi said so quietly it was almost a whisper.

Brave girl. It took guts, putting herself in the middle of a showdown between the warring siblings. And the only reason someone as gentle as her would volunteer to referee between the snarling beasts was her love for both Kian and Amanda.

Amanda wrapped her arm around Syssi's shoulder and gave it a light squeeze. "Thank you, but I can manage Kian on my own."

"No one is managing me. My word is final."

"Oh, yeah? You're not the boss of me." The professor threw out her preschool challenge.

"The last time I checked, I'm still the regent of this keep, and it is my job to ensure everyone's safety, including my spoiled, bratty sister." Kian was making a valiant effort to keep his tone in the human range, and not to snarl like a beast, probably on account of Syssi. But with the way his eyes were glowing and his words slurring he was fooling no one.

"I'm perfectly safe with Dalhu." Amanda crossed her arms over her chest and slumped back into the couch.

Kian opened his mouth to answer when Syssi stopped him by raising her hand.

"This back and forth hurling of meaningless statements and insults is going to achieve nothing other than widening the rift between you." She leveled her eyes first on Kian, then on Amanda, and then back on Kian. "I suggest that you state your case, one at a time and without interjections from the other. Amanda, you go first. Only when she's done, you'll have your turn, Kian. Agreed?" Syssi looked at Kian until he gave her a tight-lipped nod.

"Thank you," Amanda said.

"Just try to be less antagonistic, deal?" Syssi rested her hand on Amanda's thigh.

"I'll do my best." Amanda plastered a pleasant expression on her gorgeous face.

What a pity that Kian was immune to his sister's looks as well as her antics.

"I wish Dalhu's past was different, but it is what it is." Her face turned somber, and her tone lost its playful shade. "It wasn't easy for me to come to terms with it. His part in Mark's assassination, in particular, was a hard nugget to swallow. It has taken a lot of thinking and soul-searching for me to realize what my gut has known all along."

Her voice was almost a whisper. "Dalhu and I share a connection, a strong one." She glanced at the guy before returning her focus to Kian. "I don't know what it means yet, but I need to find out. If I don't, I'll spend the rest of my life wondering what if."

She chuckled. "Who am I kidding, other than a lock and key, there is no way I can stay away, even if I wanted to. The pull is too strong. I don't know if it has been decreed by the Fates or if it's nothing more than powerful immortal pheromones, but the fact remains that I need to be with Dalhu." She leaned forward and picked up her coffee mug, taking a few sips before returning it to the table.

To Kian's credit, he waited to see if she was done.

But she wasn't. "It's not only a compulsion, though. During the short time I've known Dalhu, he's shown me a side of himself that he's never shown anyone—not since his transition. He's been sheltering that vulnerable part of himself behind heavy armor, one he's been forced to erect in order to survive in the Doomers' camp. But the fact that he managed to keep the spark alive, and not let the darkness infiltrate and consume this last shred of his soul, proves, to me at least, that he is worthy, and that he should be given a chance to prove himself. After all, since Dalhu has sworn allegiance to me, to us, he has demonstrated his commitment in every possible way."

Amanda took a deep breath and reached for Dalhu's hand. "Moving down here is the only solution I can think of. I know beyond a shadow of a doubt that Dalhu would never harm me or do anything to endanger the clan or me. But I understand that the rest of you are still wary of him, and I don't blame you. Therefore, even though I would've preferred for Dalhu to move into my comfortable penthouse, I'm willing to move down here and share with him this excruciatingly humble abode. I already asked Onidu to pack some of my things and bring them here. With the nonexistent closet space in this tiny apartment, my poor butler will have to schlep up and down every day." She harrumphed as if to emphasize the great sacrifice she was making.

In truth, though, for the princess to come slumming it in the dungeon it was probably a big one.

When no one said a thing, she announced, "That's it, I'm done."

"I kind of like the idea of a lock and key. I'd throw you in solitary confinement and wait for you to shake off the addiction. Tough love and all that, for your own good," Kian deadpanned.

If looks could kill, the dude would've been annihilated by the fury in Syssi's eyes.

Amanda emitted a deep throaty growl, something that sounded like a lioness readying for the kill.

Andrew shifted in his chair, probably getting ready to jump and defend Kian in case Amanda went for her brother's eyes.

The air in the room felt so dense that it could've been chopped into a salad, dressed with the bitter juices of resentment and garnished with a sprinkle of shredded nerves.

The knock on the door couldn't have been better timed.

Thank the merciful Fates for Okidu.

The snacks would provide a much-needed time out. And maybe chewing would help bring down the hostility.

37

DALHU

Hanging by a thread, Dalhu barely managed to contain the rage from bubbling up to the surface. It was so fucking damn hard to refrain from punching something or at least clenching his fists.

But he couldn't afford even the slightest show of anger.

Regrettably, as much as he craved to get his hands on Kian and throttle the asshole, it wouldn't be in his best interest—rather counterproductive. The whole thing was resting on Amanda's ability to prove that he was harmless.

A wolf turned sheep.

And for her he was even willing to go "baa."

Her heartfelt speech had helped convince Syssi and Andrew, but it had done nothing to Kian. The jerk just wasn't willing to listen. Dalhu must've been deluding himself thinking that Kian's attitude toward him had improved.

That last nasty remark proved that nothing would ever change the guy's opinion. For Kian, a Doomer was a hell-spawned creature that could never rise above his origins.

A creature he would never allow his sister to be with.

Amanda wouldn't go down without a fight, though, and right now she seemed on the verge of losing it and attacking her brother, which would only serve to escalate the situation from bad to catastrophic.

Should he wrap his arm around her?

Prevent her from lunging at Kian?

A gentle knock saved him the trouble, providing a much-needed distraction. Anandur got up to admit whoever it was, and everyone's eyes followed him to the door.

"Clan mother..."

"I was wondering where all of you were," Annani said as she glided into the room.

Kian stood up and offered her his chair.

The Goddess glanced at the walls, and a smile spread across her face. "Such beautiful portraits of my daughter. I feel the love practically radiating from the drawings. Could I have one, Dalhu?"

"Of course, as many as you want. I can always make more."

"That would be wonderful. Maybe I should have you draw mine as well." She sat down in the chair Kian had vacated. "Thank you, dear."

"I'd be honored." Dalhu finally regained control of his voice.

Was he worthy of such honor? Not really, he wasn't that good, but he would do his best.

"I tried to phone you, Kian, as well as you, Amanda, but instead got only that annoying voice mail thing. Is there a reception problem down here in the lower levels?" she asked, then continued without waiting for an answer. "I had to contact security, and this nice young man, Steven I believe is his name, told me I could find you here, and that Andrew and Syssi were with you as well."

Kian grimaced, looking guilty as if his mother was accusing him of deliberately ignoring her phone calls.

Amanda's brows drew tightly together. "How could Steven have known that Syssi and Andrew were here? I told him to turn off the surveillance."

"And I told him to turn it back on as soon as I was informed of your shenanigans," Kian said.

Amanda jumped to her feet and pointed a finger at Kian's face. "So you think you are above the law? That it doesn't apply to you because you are the almighty regent? I declared this as my new residence, and last I checked, no surveillance is allowed inside clan members' private lodging. You can call Edna and verify this if your memory is faulty." Her voice had been getting louder and louder until she was practically shouting.

But Kian wasn't impressed. "My memory functions perfectly, sister mine, and if you had done your legal research thoroughly, you would've realized that when a clan member's safety is in jeopardy, issues of privacy can be overridden."

The smug look on Kian's face was begging for Dalhu's fist.

Amanda placed her hands on her hips and leaned forward so her face was inches away from her brother's. "Oh yeah? And who decides which situation qualifies as jeopardy? You?"

"Yes."

Exasperated, Amanda threw her hands in the air and turned to Annani. "That's just great. Our code of law needs a serious rewrite, Mother. We preach the virtues of democracy while practicing a convoluted form of constitutional triarchy, for lack of better definition."

Annani regarded her daughter coolly. "Sit down, Amanda." She waited until her command was obeyed and turned to Kian. "Do not look so self-satisfied, Kian, I have had it with your pigheaded attitude as well."

The Goddess waved her hand, and Dalhu felt a containment field snap into place. Smart move. There was no need for the guys in security to witness Annani admonishing her children.

The Goddess's intense gaze returned to Amanda. "Our code of

law might need some small adjustments, but there is nothing fundamentally wrong with it or with the way we govern ourselves. We are not a country. We are a large family that is organized as a corporation because we also own a huge business conglomerate. Our clan members are treated as preferred stockholders who are entitled to a share of the profits but have no voting power. The main difference between us and other businesses is that we also hire our own shareholders for the higher up positions. Still, we do it based on their capabilities, not their popularity."

Amanda scoffed, "Do other corporations also police their shareholders?"

"I am sure they do so to enforce nondisclosure agreements and such. And, naturally, our unique situation dictates a deviation from the norm."

It seemed Amanda had exhausted her rebuttals. She slumped back, leaning slightly on Dalhu as if seeking comfort from his closeness. With a move that was guaranteed to infuriate Kian, Dalhu wrapped his arm around her shoulders and pulled her closer.

Let's see if the dickhead dares to say something derogatory in his mother's presence.

Annani waited for a moment, but when no one voiced an objection, she smiled magnanimously and continued. "Now that the legalities are cleared up, could you please tell me what the big fuss is all about, Amanda?"

Amanda perked up. "I want to be with Dalhu. I would like for him to move in with me, but if it's not possible"—she slanted a glare at Kian—"because some people are ultra paranoid, I would like to stay down here with him, and, naturally, I want the surveillance removed. There are enough cameras in the corridor outside this cell to assuage the fears of those who can see only the worst in people."

Brave behind her mother's protective shield, Amanda was once again goading her brother. Evidently, the smart professor wasn't a wise negotiator.

"I think this is a reasonable request. Kian? And please, try to be reasonable as well." Annani arched a brow in warning.

It was clear that the Goddess, bless her soul, was putting her little foot down, and Kian would be forced to accept the fact that Amanda was staying. But mindful of her son's position, Annani had left the door open for some negotiation.

Kian was a jerk and a hothead, but he was definitely not stupid. His mother's message wasn't lost on him.

"Fine, she can stay. But so does the surveillance."

"What?" Amanda blurted.

"Wait, I'm not finished. It's just a precaution. The recording will go straight to a dedicated server without anyone listening or watching—not unless there is a reason for alarm or something happens to you." Kian slanted a baleful look at Dalhu.

Annani beamed. "That sounds like a good compromise. You see? Amanda? Kian is being reasonable."

But Amanda didn't look happy. "Hold on. If you are insisting on cameras, then I see no reason why Dalhu can't come live with me in my penthouse. You can rig the whole place up to your heart's content, and we can live in the comfort of my apartment."

"That's a no, like a no way in hell."

"Why not? You can even have William put a cuff on Dalhu so you'll know where he is at all times."

"Not good enough. He'll still be able to communicate our location to his brethren. And even if you manage to convince me that the probability of him doing so is one in a million, I would still refuse to accept the risk. Too much is at stake."

"How about Edna giving Dalhu the probe? Like she did with me, see what's deep in his soul?" Syssi offered.

"And I can provide my humble services as a lie detector."

This was the second time Andrew had mentioned this. Was he a truth seeker? Dalhu had heard that one of Navuh's sons had the gift, but he thought it was just another piece of propaganda. Evidently, not this time.

"Please, Kian, just think about it. I'll be as much a prisoner in here as Dalhu. I'll have to get someone to open the door for me every time I want in or out."

"You'll survive. You should be grateful you're getting to stay at all."

"I know, and I am. But please, could you at least give it some thought? This is just a temporary solution—we can't stay here forever—you must realize that."

It broke Dalhu's heart to hear Amanda pleading, even though it was proving to be a better strategy when dealing with Kian than her previous attacks. The guy was guarded and hard to read, but Dalhu caught a slight whiff of guilt coming off him.

Maybe it was about time that he said something too. "What can I do to prove my loyalty? I'll do anything. Just tell me and I'll do it."

"Finish those goddamned profiles instead of wasting all your time on that"—he pointed to the walls—"and we'll pick it up from there."

"Consider it done."

38

SEBASTIAN

Sebastian woke up a couple of minutes before his alarm went off—concerned about his little waitress. She was sleeping a heavily thralled slumber in the basement room he had locked her in last night, and he needed to go check on her. If he didn't wake her, she would keep on sleeping and might get dehydrated.

He needed to feed her too.

Last night, she'd attacked the nachos and calamari like she hadn't seen food in a week. Though why she would go hungry when working in a pastry shop was beyond him. Hadn't that lovely boss of hers realized that Tiffany wasn't eating enough? Had the girl been too embarrassed to ask for a pastry or a sandwich?

Ironic, that a sadist like him had noticed and cared about a girl going hungry while the righteous American citizen had turned a blind eye to what had been glaringly obvious and could've been easily fixed.

Sebastian chuckled. Yeah, he was such a benevolent soul. He would beat her mercilessly but make sure she was fed.

Well, not Tiffany necessarily, she wasn't his type, but some other hypothetical hungry girl. He'd give Tiffany to his men. But first, some elaborate thralling and major beautifying was in order. The guys would not appreciate a reluctant girl—except for the few who enjoyed rape—and none would be thrilled about a mousy thing like her.

First, he'd thrall her to believe that she'd been doing this for a while and was very happy with her job. Good pay or something to that effect. Then, when she was agreeable and cooperative, he would take her to a beauty salon and buy her some clothes. Come to think of it, she'd need makeup and hairbrushes and a lot of other things big and small.

Maybe his next victim should be a beautician; it would be great to have one in-house.

He was so smart. Two birds with one stone. He'd take Tiffany to a hair salon and come out with another girl for his basement.

Today and tomorrow, more men were scheduled to arrive, and he needed to fill those underground rooms as soon as possible. Regrettably, the online thing was not going to work. He'd gotten plenty of fish on his digital hook, but for some reason they were either successful career women or college students and none had fit the profile of a destitute, lonely girl. He would have to do it the old-fashioned way—one at a time.

The good news was that it was more fun; the bad news was that it was more time-consuming.

Hopefully, he would stumble upon one or two he could keep for himself. Better make it three, or even four. If he wanted to keep his stock healthy and enthusiastic, he needed to limit the wear and tear. Thralling and venom were great, but he knew from experience that they only went so far. Human females were too fragile, and eventually, not even the healing properties of venom could counteract the damage of repeated injuries.

A human girl could handle no more than two of his men in a twenty-four-hour period, and him no more than once a week, two at the most, and only if she was very resilient.

As he waited for the coffee to brew in the small kitchenette he had installed in his suite, Sebastian's thoughts wandered to the attorney. Now, that was a human he would've loved to have for himself. She was special, despite being neither young nor particularly attractive. But what she lacked in looks she made up in wit and stamina.

He wanted to play with her again.

Having her for himself was out of the question, but from time to time he could still schedule club assignations with her.

In between, he would have to settle for the peasants.

39

KIAN

Kian's day had started shitty and had gone downhill from there.

First, the *lovely* message about Amanda, then, the blow up with Syssi, and lastly, his mother's intervention that forced his hand into allowing Amanda to shack up with the Doomer.

But wait, the day wasn't over yet. So it might not end at that.

Kian raked his fingers through his hair. He should go home and apologize to Syssi, but Bhathian and Onegus were keeping him in his office with reports he couldn't care less about.

"You should come to one of the self-defense classes," Onegus added at the end of his report. They were now running four of them a week, and soon they would need to double up because more and more people were joining every day.

All of a sudden everybody wanted to be a fucking warrior.

"I will, at some point, but don't expect it until after the wedding."

"Why? It's not as if the ladies need or want your help."

"I'm not sure about it. Syssi is going crazy, Amanda is no help at all because she is busy playing house with the Doomer, and we all know that my mother's idea of helping is giving advice and ordering everybody around."

He got a sympathetic look from Onegus. "So, go and help your girl instead of moping around."

"I will, right after I'm done here, as soon as you guys are done with the rest of your reports."

Bhathian rewarded him with a frown. "The sex-ed class went fine. From now on these boys are going to behave like perfect gentlemen."

"You threatened them with the whip."

"Naturally, after I explained everything that might be considered a sexual offense, of course, so there will be no misunderstandings." He crossed his arms over his chest.

"Good. What else?"

"That's it."

Thank the merciful Fates.

Shai took a look at Kian's face and expelled a defeated breath. "I know, take care of it or reschedule it. I already resort to pretending to be you when dealing with humans, but I can't pull it off with our people. And anyway, I'm supposed to be your assistant, not your CEO. I don't have the qualifications."

"Bullshit and you know it. You've been working with me for the past fifty years, and you have an eidetic memory. You can do my job no problem."

"No, I can't, and I don't want to. Too much responsibility and too much stress."

"You're telling me..."

Yeah, Kian didn't want the job either but was stuck with it. He got up and patted Shai's bony shoulder. Unlike the muscular Guardians, Shai was lanky, and his lifting routine was limited to hefty stacks of papers. "Did you join one of the self-defense classes?"

"No, you know I hate sweating."

"You should. In fact, I insist."

Shai grimaced as if Kian had ordered him to shovel manure. "With all the crap I have to do because you're busy with other things, I don't have the time or the energy."

"Fine, but after things return to normal, you're going."

"As if that's going to happen anytime soon."

40

SYSSI

I hate it. I absolutely hate it.

Syssi looked at the sample centerpiece the florist had delivered, but she wasn't addressing the flower arrangement. It was beautiful. After almost despairing of finding a flower shop that would take on the project, she was thrilled when this one called that they had a cancellation. She hadn't even checked which one it was. As long as they delivered on time and the flowers were not completely wilted she was good.

She hated the tension between Kian and her.

It was killing her. She was of a mind to take a page from Amanda's book and just throw it all to hell and go away somewhere.

Let Kian plan his precious wedding by himself.

After the meeting in the dungeon, he'd stormed out and disappeared into his office.

No I'm-sorry-I-was-rude, no please-forgive-me, nothing. And the worst part was that she was already making excuses for him in her head. He was under a lot of stress. Amanda was driving him crazy. He hated Doomers...yada, yada, yada.

But the truth was that there was no excuse for the way he'd

talked to her. And the only reason he'd allowed himself to act this way was because he'd known that she was a pushover and wouldn't retaliate.

God, was this whole wedding thing a mistake? With him acting like a jerk now, when theoretically she could still walk away, what would he be like after they were married? She let the tears flow freely and even allowed herself a couple of sobs before wiping her face with a kitchen paper towel.

Oh, please, stop being so dramatic. Kian wasn't a charmer before, he isn't now, and he isn't going to become one just because he loves me. But I know he loves me, and that's all that matters...

Still, for her own sense of worth, she had to make him pay for his behavior. Even if in the long run it achieved nothing—because come on, as if she had a chance in hell to change a guy that was nearly two thousand years old.

Question was, how?

Amanda would know the perfect payback.

I wonder if there really is a reception problem in the lower levels.

With William in charge, not likely, but on the other hand, she doubted that Kian and Amanda would have dared to ignore their mother's calls. Well, one way to find out. She selected Amanda's contact from the Favorites menu.

"I was just about to call you. Did you have one of your premonitions?" Amanda sounded like her old upbeat self again.

"In fact, I did, but not about you."

"Do tell..."

"Come up here and I will. If you can bear to part with your guy for a little bit."

Amanda chuckled. "I think I'll manage. Dalhu is busy with the profiles he promised Kian, and I feel guilty for abandoning you when you needed me most. I'll be there as soon as I get someone to open the door for me."

"I'll start the coffee."

Having Amanda back was such a tremendous relief, Syssi felt as if the boulder she had been carrying on her shoulders since the wedding plans had begun had lost at least half of its weight. Even her posture was markedly straighter and her step lighter as she headed toward the kitchen.

Amanda kept her promise to Kian and knocked on the door, except, she didn't wait to be admitted. Still, progress was progress.

"I owe you a big hug," she said, pulling Syssi into a bone-crushing embrace.

"It's good I don't break as easily now, or you would have cracked some ribs."

Amanda smiled as she drew out a stool and sat down, arranging her wrap dress so it didn't part. "I know. I was careful with you before, but it's no longer necessary."

"I love your dress."

"I'm glad you do. Anandur was giving me grief about it. He said it looked outdated."

"What does he know?"

"Exactly."

Syssi poured them both coffees. "I need you to use your devious mind for something." She took out the cream from the fridge and put it on the counter next to the sugar bowl.

"Oh, yeah? I'm all ears." Amanda perked up.

"Kian and I had a fight this morning, and he was really rude and dismissive toward me. I want to make him pay. Nothing big, just so he knows I don't forget and forgive that easily."

Stirring in a teaspoon of sugar, Amanda shrugged. "Easy, just don't have sex with him."

"And what? Punish myself? I was hoping for something clever, something original." Syssi made another trip to the fridge and pulled out a wedge of brie. "Cheese?"

"Sure. What have you been fighting about?"

It was a little awkward to admit that they had been fighting about her and Dalhu. But what the heck, there was no point trying to dance around it either.

"I tried to tell him to be reasonable and calm down, and he told me to mind my own business." The small plate with cut pieces of cheese clunked on the counter as Syssi let go of it instead of putting it down gently.

"Ouch… I think he deserves to sleep in the doghouse. I can send Onidu to get one, something big like for a Labrador, and we'll put it in your bedroom. After you have your way with him, just tell him to get in there."

Syssi snorted. "Yeah, like he would do as I say. Come on, Amanda, think of something devious, something he'll be forced to endure."

Amanda's eyes sparkled. "Oh, I have something. The word *endure* gave me a fabulous idea. Kian hates poetry, and he can't stand rap music. Download a playlist of this young kid, George Watsky. I saw him once on *Ellen*. He is a slam poet that raps. Just blast his stuff nonstop. If Kian complains, tell him it relaxes you when you're upset. That way he'll know he'll have to endure slam poetry every time he behaves like a jerk."

Spoken like a true master.

Syssi bowed her head in mock reverence. Well, not mock, this was brilliant. "I'm humbled by your genius, Sensei."

"I'm good, aren't I?"

"The best. And I happen to like slam poetry."

"Perfect. Now that this is settled, tell me about your vision. I'm dying to find out who it was about."

Syssi hesitated for a moment. Was it okay for her to share this with Amanda? Would Andrew mind? But now that she'd blurted it out, there was no way Amanda would let it go.

"It was about Andrew."

"Go on…" Amanda waved her hand in a circular motion.

"I saw him playing with a little girl in a park, tossing her up and catching her, then kissing and hugging her to him before tossing her up again. I knew without a shadow of a doubt that I was seeing him with his daughter."

"Was the girl a redhead?"

"So, you know about him and Bridget?"

"Yeah, he was on his way to her place when I came back yesterday, and he told me. So, was she?"

"No, she had dark brown hair, almost black. It was long and the strands curled at the bottom—very thick and lustrous for a small child. She was such a beautiful little girl, all giggles and smiling large eyes. They looked so happy together, I really hope this was a true vision." She sighed.

"I wonder who the mother is, or will be. Do you have a clue?"

Syssi took a sip of her coffee and concentrated for a moment, hoping her precognition would fire a clue. But no. "No idea."

"There is a pattern going on here. Everybody is hooking up. You with Kian, me with Dalhu, Kri with Michael, and now Andrew with some mystery woman that is probably not Bridget. By the way, what's going on with Michael and Kri, any new developments I should be aware of?"

"Michael is training with the Guardians, but Kri is pressuring him to go back to school. Oh, and they moved in together."

Amanda clapped her hands. "That's wonderful!" She grabbed her purse and pulled out her phone. "I'm going to call Kri and tell her to hop over, if she isn't busy with some Guardian business, that is." Her finger hovered over the phone's display. "How rude of me, I didn't ask if it's okay with you."

"Of course it is, anytime."

Amanda finished her text and put her phone down on the counter. "I'm going back to work on Monday. I guess I shouldn't expect you until after the wedding?"

"You guess right. And even after, I need to see what Kian wants to do. There was some talk about me helping him in the office. So we'll see."

Amanda scoffed. "Nonsense, he can get plenty of people with office skills to help him, but I have only one seer. You're coming back to work with me."

"Please, I don't want to discuss it now, I have enough on my plate as it is. We'll talk after the wedding. I still have to call my parents and need to preserve all of my cognitive power for the talk with my mother." Syssi grimaced.

"I'm glad you decided to invite them."

"Yeah, I don't know what I've been thinking. Evidently, stress makes me stupid. Of course I have to invite them, they would've never forgiven me if I got married without them. Though I'm sure my mom will refuse to believe that I'm rushing to the altar for any reason other than pregnancy. I even dreamt that she dragged me straight from the wedding, in my big white dress, to see a gynecologist, and I'm sitting in the waiting room with everybody staring at me, ugh." She shivered.

"That reminds me, Joanne said the dress designs are ready, and we should hurry up and pick one. I was thinking, though, that we should order all of them and do a fitting to see which one looks best on you. There is only so much you can discern from a drawing."

Nice try, Amanda.

"Forget it, I'm going to get my laptop and we are going to choose one."

"Party pooper."

41

ANDREW

Andrew was the first to arrive at Barney's, despite the fact that he and Tim had left the office at the same time. He secured a quiet table at the very back, under a good light fixture, so Tim would have enough illumination for his sketching.

Not that the guy had to have good light to do what he did. Drawing from verbal descriptions, Tim could probably do it blindfolded.

The table wasn't next to a window, which was a disadvantage, but at least he had an unobstructed view of the front door.

At quarter to seven, Barney's lunch crowd had already come and gone, while the late-evening customers were only starting to trickle in. A couple in their early thirties sat at a table near the front, each with a phone in hand, communicating with someone unseen while ignoring each other. Sad, but at least they were quiet.

The same could not have been said about the two guys sitting at the bar. The idiots were watching a rerun of a football game and hollering their encouragements at the screen. The thing was mounted above the display cabinet, and the colorful drink bottles seemed to rattle in response. They were obnoxiously loud, especially the one with the red baseball cap.

Ignoring the raucous cries, the bartender was busy eyeing the red cap's tats, which were prominently displayed on his biceps. The thing was, Andrew wasn't sure what she was more fascinated by—the guy's muscles or the tattoos.

Probably the tats.

The girl had one on her neck that went down to her shoulders and around her arms, disappearing behind the skimpy little shirt covering her back.

Andrew grimaced. As a soldier, it was almost a requirement to have a tattoo, and he wasn't an exception. He had a small one of a white phoenix on his upper arm—his old unit's emblem.

It wasn't showy, and those who examined it closely thought that it wasn't finished—because while most of the bird's feathers were solid, two were only outlined.

He never bothered to explain. It was nobody's business that he prayed every day that he never had to fill those—because it meant that the two remaining men from his unit were still alive.

He didn't want or need the pitying looks.

This wasn't about making a statement—this was about carrying his private memorial on his person.

Andrew glanced again at the bartender and her wallpaper designs. What a shame that a pretty girl like her had tarnished her young healthy skin with gaudy drawings. She must've believed they were attractive. Maybe to the baseball-cap guy they were, but Andrew didn't like them on a woman, at least not that extensive. Something small and inconspicuous was okay, even sexy—something only a lover would see—but not this.

And if it meant that he was a chauvinist, so be it. If he ever had a daughter, he would never allow her to do such a thing. Heck, he wouldn't allow a son to look like a walking cartoon either.

If he had a daughter...

According to Syssi he was going to. Surprisingly, the thought wasn't as scary as he would've expected it to be. He was more apprehensive about the prospect of a wife.

Could it be Bridget?

The girl in Syssi's vision had dark hair, but then red hair was a recessive gene.

Problem was, he didn't feel it.

Bridget was an amazing woman—smart, beautiful, funny, sexy, not to mention a hellcat in bed. He liked her, a lot, but the feeling was too damned similar to what he'd felt for Susanna—just a friend with benefits.

Perhaps it wasn't in him to love passionately—the way Kian and Syssi loved each other, or even Amanda and Dalhu. He wished he knew that for a fact, because if he accepted that there was no one special in his future, he would've proposed to Bridget in a heartbeat. She was as good as it was going to get, and he could envision himself spending his life with her.

It could be nice, comfortable.

It should've been enough. In fact, it was probably more than most folks got out of a marriage, but his gut wasn't in agreement. It rebelled against the idea. And frankly, Bridget would've probably said thank you, but no, because she didn't feel it either.

For both of them it was just a temporary thing—a pleasant pastime—just until the right one appeared in a glowing beam of celestial light with angels singing in heavenly harmony to announce the arrival.

Andrew chuckled. Hell, if he was going for a fantasy then why not go all the way? True?

He took a swig from his beer, then ate a few peanuts, and glanced at his watch. It was seven on the dot. He waved the waiter over and ordered a pizza.

Bhathian walked in a few minutes later.

"I'm not late, am I?" The guy frowned and glanced at the phone he was holding in his hand.

"No, you're not. My office is a short drive away, and I didn't have to battle traffic to get here. Beer?"

"Sure." Bhathian planted his butt in the chair, his bulk dwarfing the thing.

Andrew signaled the waiter and ordered two beers.

"Pizza is on the way, you want something else?"

"No." Bhathian eyed the almost empty bowl of peanuts. "Maybe more of those." He pointed.

They waited until the waiter brought the beers, then waited some more.

"Tim will be here shortly. If not, I'm going to break his fingers."

"Yeah," Bhathian concurred without a smile.

Had he taken Andrew seriously? It was hard to know what he was thinking or feeling. By now, Andrew had noticed that there were slight nuances to the guy's perpetual frown, but he still couldn't decipher their meanings.

Waiting, they took turns with the beers and the nuts until Tim finally showed up—a sketchpad under one arm and various pencils sticking out from his dirty shirt pocket.

"Tim." He offered his hand to Bhathian but then withdrew it quickly when the guy's huge paw made an appearance. "Sorry, my man, but I need these beauties in good working shape." He wiggled his slender fingers. "I don't let them anywhere near dangerous equipment, and that hand of yours should be classified as such." Tim sat down across from Andrew.

"That's okay." Bhathian managed something resembling a smile—more like a grimace—in a weak attempt to put Tim at ease.

The thing with Tim was, though, that the guy only looked small and harmless but was a real bastard who didn't know the meaning of fear. He carried a nine millimeter and was incredibly fast with it.

Rumor was that he'd been a sniper in the army before retiring and changing careers.

Tim flipped through his drawing pad to an empty page and pulled out one of the pencils from his pocket. "When is the pizza coming?"

"Should be ready any minute now."

"Good, I'm hungry. And get me a beer, will you?"

Andrew gritted his teeth and waved the waiter over. "Beer for my friend, *please*." Putting an emphasis on the please, he cast Tim a hard glance.

"Yeah, you can shove it." Tim flipped him off and turned toward Bhathian. "We'll start with the eyes."

An hour later Tim was done...with the pizza and the nachos and the third bottle of beer but not with the sketch. Bhathian kept shaking his head and trying to put into words what he saw in his head.

"Look, dude, I'm not a mind reader. I can't draw it if you can't verbalize it." Tim wasn't shy about expressing his impatience.

"The nose, it's too wide, and the lips, the bottom one should be a little plumper than the top one..."

Before, it was that the nose was too narrow and the lips too full. Andrew had a feeling that Bhathian didn't remember the woman as well as he thought he did. Or maybe he just had a tough time with descriptions.

In any case, he decided they could manage without him, at least for a little while, and excused himself to call Syssi.

"Hey, how are you holding up?" he asked.

"I'm good, what's up?"

"Nothing, you were upset this morning, and I wanted to see if you sweethearts kissed and made up."

"Not yet, but I talked to Mom." She said it as if it was a monumental achievement. "I invited them to the wedding. At first, she thought I was pranking her, as if I would ever, then she asked if I'm pregnant. But they are coming. I think that she agreed so readily to drop everything and come was because she was hoping to stop me from making a mistake. When I explained the travel arrangements, Mom realized that Kian isn't some schmuck that I just met, but someone with impressive resources, so she was somewhat mollified. But I still expect her to give me grief about it."

"Don't worry, I'll keep them occupied. What are you going to tell them when they start noticing the abnormalities?"

"I'm going to tell them the truth, and have Kian thrall that portion of their memory before they go home. I'll tell them, of course, that we are going to do it. "

Syssi was deluding herself if she thought their mother would agree to someone messing with her head. Their father was chill and would have no problem with it. Hell, he'd probably ask Kian to erase some of the things he didn't want to remember.

"It's not going to be easy."

"Tell me about it, but what other choice do I have?"

42

AMANDA

"Can you take a break? You've been working on these profiles since morning. I'm bored." Amanda eyed Dalhu's sketchpad. Done with the written profiles, he was now working on the portraits.

"I'll just finish this one." The furious scratching of pencil on paper intensified.

Amanda sighed. "Would you like something to drink? Eat?"

He lifted his head from the pad and glanced at his untouched dinner plate. It had gone cold more than an hour ago. "A drink would be nice, thank you." The scratching resumed.

Men. What was it about testosterone and disregarding basic needs—like nourishment and sex—for the sake of completing a task? It wasn't as if she had no work to finish, but whatever wasn't done by dinnertime could wait for tomorrow.

Amanda made herself a margarita and poured Lagavulin for Dalhu.

He reached for the drink without looking, took a gulp, and put it down on the coffee table.

"You know, for someone who was supposedly so desperate for my company, you're very neglectful."

That got his attention, his head snapped up, and he wiped his forehead with a dirty hand. "I'm sorry, but you heard Kian. I need to finish this thing for him."

Poor guy, once a soldier always a soldier. Dalhu hadn't realized yet that military rules no longer applied to him, and Kian's request didn't have to be obeyed to the letter, at least as far as the time frame for completion.

"Darling, Kian is not expecting you to deliver everything by tomorrow morning. There is no real urgency. It's not like he is planning an offensive. It's just information for the sake of information. For future use."

Dalhu still didn't look convinced, but he glanced at the plate again.

"Go wash your hands. I'll warm it up for you."

"Okay." He lowered the drawing pad to the floor, leaning it against the couch's side before heading to the bathroom.

She called after him, "And wash your face too, you have charcoal smeared all over your forehead."

While Dalhu had been busy, Amanda had not only gone over her lectures for the coming week but had also arranged for some necessary improvements to their apartment and had ordered crucial supplies—like a margarita mix.

The bar's counter now sported two new appliances—a microwave oven and a Nespresso coffeemaker.

If she was going to play house with Dalhu, she needed things that were easy to operate. Both appliances required no more skill than sticking something inside them and pressing a button—perfect for someone with a severe domestic disability.

A minute and a half later, the microwave beeped, and Dalhu came back, clean and smelling of cologne. She put the plate down on the round dining table and refilled his drink.

"Thank you." He pulled out a chair and sat down.

Watching him eat, she was reminded of their time in the cabin. He was a quick and messy eater, but she found it sexy rather than offensive.

"Do you always attack your food like this? Or only when you're hungry?"

Dalhu paused with the fork a few inches from his mouth and looked down at the mess he'd made. "I'm sorry. I'll clean it up." He put his fork down and started brushing crumbs off the table and into his cupped hand.

"Leave it, my intention wasn't to comment on your table manners. I was just curious."

"No, I need to learn to slow down." He cleaned the last of the crumbs, but instead of throwing them in the trash, he put them in his mouth.

When she arched a brow, he mumbled, "What? The table is clean."

"Do you remember how you told me to be myself and not censor what I say in front of you?"

He nodded.

"I want the same from you. Just be yourself. And if you want to change something, do it because you want to, not because you think I expect you to."

He grinned. "Do you know that I love you?"

"Yeah, I do." Avoiding Dalhu's eyes, Amanda lifted the margarita glass to her lips. She wasn't ready to say it back, not yet.

"What will it take? I'm willing to do anything, just tell me."

There was no point in pretending that she didn't know what he was talking about. "I don't know. Let's just take it one day at a time and see how it goes. I can't promise you anything more."

"How about a deadly challenge? Would that help? A chance for redemption, like in the old days—when fighting lions bare-handed or competing in an arena could atone for a crime and wipe the slate clean."

"That's barbaric." So why did some vengeful and bloodthirsty part of her quicken to the idea?

You're so bad, Amanda.

"It is, but it's better than this eternal damnation. I'd much rather rise to the challenge and get it over with than endlessly squirm like a maggot."

"You're such a male, and I don't mean it as a compliment. You guys are all morons. You think that everything can be solved with either violence or sex."

Dalhu smirked. "That's right, we prefer the simple, quick, and efficient, over the complicated and drawn out."

"I'll never understand the way men think. Take Alex for example—"

"Who's Alex?" Dalhu tensed, probably thinking she was talking about an ex-lover.

She waved a dismissive hand. "He's family. Anyway, he runs a successful nightclub, and he just bought this super expensive boat. But whom did he hire to run it? A bunch of unpleasant, ex-mud-wrestling Russian females. It makes no sense to spend so much money on a yacht and then try to save on wages. They are so unfriendly that he never even invites anybody onboard to show it off. I just don't get it."

Dalhu shrugged. "It's obvious. He's not using the boat for pleasure. He's smuggling something."

"That's what I thought. When I left here"—she cast him an apologetic look—"I needed some place quiet to think, and I asked Alex if I could borrow his boat. He wasn't too ecstatic about it, but he didn't protest too much either. He lent me the use of the yacht and her strange crew. Things didn't add up, so I went snooping around, but I could find no evidence of any illegal activity."

Except for the closet.

Amanda frowned. "There was just this weird thing in the master cabin's walk-in closet. It had a false wall, and behind it were very deep shelves." She spread her arms to show the size. "I sniffed for drug residue—because that's the first thing that came to mind as a potentially illegal activity—but all I could detect were very faint traces of female products. You know, shampoos and perfumes. But there was no trace of emotions. I assume that the shelves were used for storing female clothing—which makes sense—considering that it's a closet. But then, why section it off? And why install a fake partition?"

Dalhu grimaced. "I'm sorry to break it to you, but your relative is smuggling females."

"Look, I know my sense of smell is not as good as yours, but I gave it several good sniffs and detected no residual scents of emotions. If at any point in time people were hiding there, I would have found traces of fear, or anticipation, or even boredom, but there was nothing."

"There would be nothing if he thralled them into a deep sleep before stashing them in there."

The implications of what Dalhu was saying were starting to sink in, but they were too horrible to accept. "Maybe he is smuggling illegal immigrants?"

"Get real. He is trafficking sex slaves. I've seen enough young women arrive at the island in a thralled stupor. Think about it, it's so much easier to transport them like this."

"Shit, how could I have been so stupid? It's so damn obvious."

Dalhu shrugged. "You've led a sheltered life. You hear about things like this but think they happen in some faraway place to some backward people and have nothing to do with you. The last thing you want to acknowledge is that it's not only happening in your backyard, but that someone you know is doing it. People are very good at putting on blinders."

Like she had done with him. In the back of her mind, she'd been well aware of the connection between Dalhu and Mark's murder, but she'd refused to acknowledge it.

Shit, she had done the same thing with Alex.

"I need to tell Kian."

43

KIAN

Stretching like a satisfied cat, Syssi purred, "Make-up sex is the best."

It had taken Kian a good amount of groveling and artful seducing before she had agreed to forgive him, but it was worth it. The sex had been indeed mind-blowing. But more importantly, the uncomfortable gnawing sensation he'd had in his stomach since morning was gone, replaced by the glorious state of peacefulness that holding Syssi in his arms brought about.

He snuggled close behind her and closed his eyes. "I love you, kitten."

"Is this my new nickname?"

"Yes."

"I like it. I love you too, tiger."

Kian chuckled. "Tiger, I can live with that."

His phone buzzed. "What now?"

Syssi was closer to the damned thing, and she stretched to retrieve it. "Here you go." She handed it to him.

"Amanda? What the hell does she want?"

"Be nice." Syssi slapped his arm.

He touched the screen and brought the phone to his ear. "I'm in bed, is this important?" He managed a civil tone.

"Yeah, I think it is. Would you mind coming down here?"

Amanda didn't sound like herself, she sounded troubled, even distraught. Which, considering the fact that even their recent battles hadn't managed to rattle her, was cause for alarm.

"What happened? Are you okay?" Funny how all his animosity toward her evaporated the moment worry settled in. Behind him, Syssi sat up in bed and leaned against his back to listen in.

"I'm fine. It's not about me. But I think you were right about Alex. Though if my suspicions are correct, you've underestimated the severity of his crimes."

Hallelujah, how long had he been telling her that Alex was a scumbag? "I'm getting dressed. I'll be there in a few minutes."

"Can I come?" Syssi asked.

"Of course, what kind of a question is that?"

"Well, I don't want to be told that it's none of my business."

"You're not going to let me forget it, are you?" And here he thought that he'd been forgiven.

"Nope." She followed him into the shower.

He turned on the spray heads, the overhead one for himself and the handheld for Syssi. "How long are you going to lay the guilt trip on me?"

"You should be thankful that I decided against Amanda's idea." Syssi adjusted the setting of the spray and grabbed the soap.

"Oh, yeah? And what was her sage advice?"

"To blast slam poetry rap and annoy the hell out of you."

"That woman is evil and has a twisted sense of humor. So what happened, couldn't find any?"

Syssi chuckled. "I found it all right, but Amanda forgot to mention the amount of cussing in the guy's lyrics. I couldn't stand it myself."

"Thank the merciful Fates."

44

DALHU

"Unbelievable." Syssi shuddered.

Listening as Amanda recounted the last part of her story, the girl must've grown dizzy from shaking her head so much.

Before, while Amanda had entertained them with tales of her escapades with the Russian crew of former mud-wrestlers, Kian had chuckled a couple of times, but now he looked ready to commit murder.

Not that Dalhu disapproved. For a change, he was in full agreement with the guy.

There was no worse scum on earth than slavers, especially those who trafficked in girls and women—kidnapping and selling them into sexual slavery.

"If we can prove it, I'm going to have the large assembly vote on a sentence of entombment," Kian growled.

"That's too mild for a maggot like that. He needs killing," Dalhu blurted before considering that his opinion wasn't welcomed.

Kian's answer was surprisingly amiable. "I wish I could, but my hands are tied. Our law doesn't allow it." Evidently, at the moment all of his hostility was directed toward his own clansman, while Dalhu's status had been downgraded to the role of a lesser evil.

And rightfully so.

Compared to this Alex, Dalhu was a good guy, or at least tolerable as far as Kian was concerned.

Encouraged, he took it further. "I'll gladly do the dirty work for you—you don't have to soil your hands."

Kian shook his head. "Suspicions are one thing and proof another. First, we need evidence, and then he'll stand trial."

"What if you can't prove it?" Dalhu pushed.

"Then the bastard lives."

The clan and its lofty, but misguided, ideas of due process. Protecting the rights of murderers, rapists, and slavers came at a price—which was paid out from their victims' hides.

The thing was, once identified, filth like that should be cleansed in a timely fashion—before it had a chance to cause even more damage. Dalhu would rather have taken care of business right away, trading, in a heartbeat, the occasional mistakenly accused for the lives saved.

Unfortunately, now and for the foreseeable future, he was relegated to the peanut gallery.

"You could have the yacht watched," Syssi offered.

Amanda shook her head. "I still think our best bet is to get the Russians to talk. I suspect that at least one of them is troubled by what's going on and might be persuaded to talk. Let's face it, even if Alex brings a bunch of girls onboard, it doesn't mean that he plans to kidnap them. It proves nothing. If he makes the delivery out at sea, how are we going to catch him in the act?"

"But if he returns without them, isn't it proof enough?"

"He can always claim that he'd dropped them off somewhere." Kian took Syssi's hand and patted it.

"Why go to all this trouble and let the maggot get away with more trade while you're playing by the rules? My offer to off him still stands. It will be my pleasure, and it will give me something to do." Dalhu could feel his hands twitch with the need to kill.

Damn, he'd thought that he was better than that—that the killings he'd done were just part of a despised job. So why was he suddenly craving it like a goddamned addict?

Kian got up and walked up to a wall, his nose almost touching one of Amanda's portraits. "What's the matter, Doomer? Drawing not satisfying enough?" The sarcasm in his tone indicated that he knew exactly what was going on in Dalhu's head.

He needed to think about his answer carefully. "I like drawing, but it's only a hobby, something to pass the time while I'm locked down here. But I'm a warrior, not a fairy. I prefer doing a man's job."

Amanda cringed and shifted away from him.

Fuck, he was such an idiot.

The programmer had been gay.

"I'm sorry, I really should get whipped bloody, if not for my crimes then for my idiocy."

Kian perked up.

Syssi cringed.

Amanda snorted. "Only if I get to do the whipping in a dominatrix outfit. Thigh-high boots, leather bustier—the works."

She is joking, right? And if she is, does it mean that she's softening up?

He inclined his head in mock submission. "It would be my pleasure to humbly submit to your whip, mistress."

"Oh, you say the nicest things."

45

AMANDA

"What did you think about Kian's idea with the drone?" Amanda asked after Kian and Syssi had left.

Dalhu shrugged. "I don't know. I'm not a techie. In theory, it sounds good. The military uses them to spy on whatever and whoever, so if Kian gets his hands on a long range one, he can have it follow that boat out to sea."

Amanda sighed. "I wish I were wrong about this whole thing and Alex would be proven innocent. Well, at least of this offense. I almost hope we'll catch him selling drugs. As morally wrong as that is, it's not as bad as selling women."

"How about we change the subject? I can think of a much more pleasant use of our time." His smirk had sex written all over it.

"Oh, yeah? Like what?"

"I'll show you." He pulled her hand and placed it over his shaft. "I've been this hard ever since you mentioned that dominatrix outfit. I couldn't stop thinking about you in it."

Kinky Dalhu. "Should I look for a whip?"

His shaft twitched. "Do you want to?"

Did she? No.

Playing a dominatrix was one thing, but inflicting real pain was another. "No, but we can play." She leaned to nuzzle his neck, closing her eyes as his masculine scent filled her nostrils. "I can dress the part, tie you up, and torture you without damaging the goods."

"Your wish is my command."

Every time he said these words, her heart gave a little flutter. *My own as-you-wish guy.*

"Give me a minute, then go to the bedroom, remove your clothes, and wait for me in bed."

"Yes, mistress."

Grabbing the few items she needed from the closet, she ducked into the bathroom.

Once she was done, Amanda admired the results in the mirrored wall. *Damn, I look so hot I'm turning myself on.*

Dalhu was going to climax as soon as he saw her.

Thigh-high black stockings were held in place by a tiny, lacy garter. And the sheer, even tinier black thong was more of a decoration than an attempt to cover anything. The bra was an ingenious contraption that provided a little boost to her smallish breasts but left her nipples exposed. She'd painted a thick black line around her eyes and a blood-red rouge on her lips. With no boots to complete her outfit, she settled for a pair of black, four-inch stilettos that worked just as well if not better to make her legs look fabulous.

As Amanda opened the door and sauntered into the bedroom, Dalhu's indrawn breath was followed by an outpour of male pheromones enough to saturate a stadium let alone the small room, and a flagpole of an Olympian standard.

"Fuck, Amanda, it's good that I'm immortal or my heart would've stopped from lack of blood supply. It's all down in my cock."

So sweet, the man had a way with words.

But right now he needed to shut up. "Did I give you permission to speak?" She did her best to sound stern, stifling up the giggles that were threatening to ruin the game.

"No, mistress, my apologies." Dalhu's lips twitched, but he managed to keep a straight face.

As she turned to the dresser to get some nylon stockings to use as bonds, flashing Dalhu her bare derrière, she heard him take another hissed breath. Poor guy, at this rate he was going to asphyxiate.

"Spread your arms and your legs," she commanded.

He did, and she tied each appendage to a bedpost. The stockings were perfect bondage material, strong but flexible enough not to restrict circulation. Not that Dalhu would have any trouble getting free. Even if she were to secure him to the bed with titanium-reinforced handcuffs, he would have no trouble just yanking the posts out of the frame. Except, the last thing Dalhu seemed to want right now was to be released.

Okay, what to do now?

If she had known ahead of time that they would be playing this game, she would've made a quick Internet search to get ideas. Now she had to use her *devious* mind to come up with a plan.

Hm...

A quick sashay to the bathroom provided her first torture implement in the form of a makeup brush. Dalhu raised a brow but was smart enough not to open his mouth without permission.

With a wicked smile, Amanda sat at the foot of the bed and began to feather the wispy brush in an upward motion over Dalhu's inner thighs, stopping a hair short of his sensitive parts.

It didn't take long for him to start squirming and bucking. He was doing his best to remain quiet, but here and there a muffled groan or a growl escaped his throat.

What a shame that this game was not doing it for her.

Dalhu was turned on all right, but it might have been the effect of her sexy outfit and not necessarily what she was doing to him. She dropped the brush and slithered on top of him.

Now, this was definitely better. The feel of his big, strong body, his warmth. She craved his arms around her; she craved him on top of her. He must've read her mind because before she had a chance to notice that he'd gotten free, his large hands were on her back, her ass, stroking, cupping.

With a groan, she dipped her head and took his mouth in a hungry kiss.

"I hope you don't mind," he whispered in her ear before flipping her under him.

"Not at all." His weight was just perfect, heavy but not crushing. And those powerful arms of his, wrapped around her and holding her like he would never let go, well, that was a real turn on.

He lifted his head and bent his neck to admire her jutting nipples. "I wanted these in my mouth since the second I saw you coming out of the bathroom. This weird bra is sexy as hell." Sliding down, he did exactly that, licking, nipping, and blowing hot air on her little buds until she was squirming worse than he had a few moments ago.

Was he exacting revenge? Or just having fun?

She'd bet it was the former.

Except, it seemed that Dalhu didn't enjoy torturing her any more than she had enjoyed tormenting him. With a tender kiss goodbye to each pebbled nipple, he slid farther down her body and got busy eating her panties.

He had them shredded and off her in no time. "Spread your legs for me, my beauty," he commanded, then nipped at her inner thigh, his sharp fangs almost nicking her flesh.

She parted her legs wider, and he rewarded her with a lash of his tongue, painting a trail of scorching heat down to her slit. *So good.* He flicked her swollen clit, and her back arched on a throaty moan.

"You like?" He growled against her flesh, then thrust a finger deep inside her.

"Oh, oh, yes!" she cried when his lips closed around her swollen clit and he pushed back with two fingers. She was coming undone under the steady, gentle onslaught of his tongue and his lips and his fingers—the orgasm building up momentum like a tsunami.

He was playing her body like a master musician with his prized violin, with skill, love, and reverence.

On a scream, the tsunami crested and crashed toward shore. In a heartbeat, Dalhu pushed inside her with one powerful thrust, his fangs sinking into her neck at the same time.

Bliss.

46

AMANDA

"Where are you going?" Dalhu asked.

Damn, she thought he was sleeping. Bending at the waist, she kissed his bruised lips. That last ride had been a little wild. Surprising, considering that it had been their fourth, or perhaps fifth? She wasn't sure.

It hadn't been gentle.

The sex, the wonderful closeness and Dalhu's skillful and reverent touch had brought about feelings she wasn't ready for. And looking into his big, warm, chocolate-colored eyes, so adoring, so devoted, she'd felt herself falling for him big time. But while her heart had been swelling with love, her gut had been churning with guilt, and the two mixed together had produced a combustible attitude.

She'd hurt him, just a little, and he'd taken everything she'd dished out with relish.

What an amazing male—

"I'm going to see Edna, our legal expert."

"Why? Can't it wait till morning? Come back to bed."

"No, I need to ask her something."

He sat up and leaned his back against the headboard. "What's so urgent that you're going to bother her at this hour?" He glanced at his wristwatch. "It's after ten."

She didn't want to tell him her idea before running it by Edna. But since this was about him, he deserved to know.

Sitting on the bed beside Dalhu, Amanda clasped his hand. "Edna has a unique ability. We call her the Alien Probe because she can see and judge what's in a person's heart. Combined with Andrew's ability to discern truth from lie, she might be able to finally convince Kian that you're not harboring some secret evil intentions and are completely loyal to us. He trusts her judgment implicitly."

"Okay." He pulled her to him for a kiss and held her for a long moment flush against his warm chest. "I love you," he whispered.

"I know." It was hard to deny him the words he so desperately needed, even cruel, but she just couldn't.

He let her go and slipped back under the covers. "I'll be awaiting your return, mistress," he teased.

They were not playing that game again. Well, except for the dress up, that part had been fun.

With a sigh, she left him and ducked into the tiny closet. The thing was no more than five by five, not nearly adequate even for a modest selection.

Before getting dressed, she checked with Edna, and her text message received an immediate and concise reply. *Of course.*

The next text went to Okidu. He was on his way to let her out, which precluded lengthy preparations. Yoga pants, T-shirt, and a pair of flip-flops would have to do.

On her way up to Edna's, at the councilwoman's new secure apartment assigned to her after Mark's murder, Amanda wondered what she looked like when not dressed for her official duties. She'd always seen the woman in either a loose-fitting pantsuit or her ceremonial robe, her hair brushed back and secured in a severe bun.

As she knocked on Edna's door, Amanda was actually excited

about getting a glimpse of the formidable judge in her off time.

The improvement turned out to be minimal. Instead of a bun, Edna had pulled her hair into a ponytail, and instead of a pantsuit, she had on a dark blue jumpsuit that might have been fashionable in the late eighties but now belonged only in a Goodwill store.

Oh, well.

It seemed that Edna's appearance had nothing to do with looking professional for her job and everything to do with a complete lack of style.

Should she offer to help?

"Good evening, Amanda, please come in."

"Thank you so much for agreeing to see me so late." Amanda followed the judge into a living room that looked surprisingly well put together.

Oh, wait, that's Ingrid's doing.

"Not a problem at all, I'm always glad to help. Please, take a seat." She motioned to the couch and waited for Amanda to sit down before joining her.

"I'm sure the rumor machine has churned enough gossip to reach even your ears. You know about Dalhu and me?"

"The Doomer and you? Yes."

Edna's face didn't betray her opinion on the subject.

Amanda continued. "Ex-Doomer. Anyway, Dalhu left the Brotherhood and has sworn loyalty to us, but Kian is suspicious. We have Andrew, Syssi's brother, who is a human lie detector, or rather a Dormant lie detector, and he confirmed the veracity of everything Dalhu told Kian. But Kian remains unconvinced. I thought that since Kian trusts your judgment, and you have the ability to reach into Dalhu's soul and ascertain what's in his heart, your testimony might tip the scale in Dalhu's favor."

Again, there was no smile or frown or even inflection in her tone to hint at what she was thinking. "I don't see why not. I'll arrange with Kian to go see the Doomer, I'm sorry, Dalhu," Edna corrected.

Well, at last, a slight indication of her opinion, but it wasn't a good one. Edna thought of Dalhu first and foremost as a Doomer. She wouldn't be positively disposed toward him, and her probe would be intrusive and thorough. Which, on second thought, was better. If after such an invasive probe, Edna found no evidence of ill intentions on his part and saw that Dalhu was indeed loyal to the clan, her conclusions would carry more weight with Kian.

"Thank you, I appreciate it."

There was one more issue Amanda wanted Edna's opinion on, but wasn't sure how to approach it.

Thankfully, the Alien Probe was very good at guessing. "You want to ask me if there is a way for Dalhu to atone for his crimes. Correct?"

Amanda exhaled a relieved breath. "Yes, one crime in particular that I find extremely difficult to forgive. Dalhu was in charge of the unit that assassinated Mark. I'm aware of all the mitigating factors—that he didn't know me then or even that Mark was one of us; that he was just doing his accursed job. But still, I can't put it behind me. It's like a big ugly sore on our relationship. You know what I mean?"

Edna nodded. "Do you believe that by enduring some horrible punishment or trial he will gain your forgiveness?"

"I'm not sure. I've been thinking and rethinking this for days to no avail. I was hoping you could provide the insight I'm lacking."

"Let's start with a few questions, shall we?"

"Sure."

"Whose forgiveness do you think Dalhu should seek?"

Smart woman. When put this way, it was pretty obvious that it wasn't Amanda's place—kind of obnoxious of her to think that she should be the one granting it.

"Mark's immediate family to start with, then the rest of the clan—Mark's extended family."

"Okay. Who do you think should decide if Dalhu deserves to be offered the option of redemption by trial?"

"I guess Micah, Mark's mother."

"Exactly." Edna looked satisfied as if Amanda had just passed a test.

"Let's assume for a moment that Micah is willing to offer Dalhu a chance to redeem himself by some incredible feat of courage or endurance. Two questions need to be asked. First, would Dalhu accept the verdict and submit to whatever Micah might demand? And second, if he accepts and goes through it, would it be enough for you?"

"Yes, and yes. Dalhu is willing to do whatever it takes, and if Micah's demands are met, then I'll consider it done."

Edna nodded. "There might be a legal precedent. It's an old one, from the time of the gods, and it doesn't fit Dalhu's situation precisely. But I think we can use it as a base.

"If a servant killed another servant, the head of the victim's household could ask for retribution to compensate the family, either monetary or physical. If it was monetary, the other head of household would pay, but the perpetrator would lose his freedom and spend his life as a slave to repay the debt. His boss could either keep him to repay over time or sell him to collect the debt right away. The system was put in place to prevent blood feuds between the victim and perpetrator's families, and at the same time provide support for those who lost their wage earners."

"I hope you're not suggesting slavery for Dalhu."

"Of course not. When the killing was accidental, whether because the men were fighting or because of negligence on the part of the accused, and it was clear that it wasn't a premeditated murder, the killer was given the option to choose physical retribution."

Amanda arched a brow. "And that was considered a lesser punishment than keeping the same job and just working without wages?"

"Certainly. Being a slave was shameful. Only the worst of criminals were sentenced to a life of slavery, and they were marked by a notch in the left ear to identify them as such. Additionally, the killer's wages most likely supported his family, and their loss would've reduced them to beggars."

"I see. Tough choice."

"Yes. Those who weren't young or healthy most often opted for slavery—fearing that they wouldn't survive the punishment. Others took the challenge."

"I assume that the victim's family determined the punishment."

"It was the only way to prevent blood feuds that would've claimed numerous lives."

Edna deserved her reputation. The woman was brilliant. There were enough mitigating factors in Dalhu's involvement in Mark's death to qualify him for the physical option. The question was, whether Micah would agree to see it this way.

To draw equivalents between that old custom and Dalhu's case—Mark would be considered a clan employee and Dalhu, Navuh's. Kian, as head of the American arm of the clan, could demand retribution, and Micah, as the victim's mother, would have the right to decide what form it would take.

"After the physical punishment was delivered, what did the victim's family do? Did they sign a release form?"

"Something to that effect. They would witness the punishment, and once it was done, the head of their household would ask if their vengeance was satisfied. They were honor bound to say yes. Besides, one-third of the killer's wages went to the victim's family. A strong incentive."

"And that was it? Case closed?"

"In theory."

Yeah, Amanda found it hard to believe that the victim's mother or wife had been able to forgive. But then, those garnished wages must've been the only way to put food on the table.

In Micah's case, however, she had no need for Dalhu's money—even if he happened to have any.

47

DALHU

Last night, when Amanda had returned and crawled under the covers, snuggling up to him, Dalhu hadn't asked her about her talk with the legal expert. He'd pretended to sleep. Holding her close had felt too good to spoil by discussing unpleasant things.

It still did. Just watching her sleep in the bed they now shared suffused him with joy—a feeling he'd forgotten existed and was so foreign to him that it had taken Dalhu a while to recognize it for what it was.

She looked so beautiful sleeping—curled on her side with one hand under her cheek—that he just had to draw her like that.

One more pose for his collection.

He got out of bed, washed and dressed in a hurry, then grabbed his supplies. Leaning against the dresser, he captured her outline with a few fast charcoal strokes. This way, if she woke or flipped to her other side, he'd have the base and draw the rest from memory.

The scraping sound of charcoal on paper must've woken her, and she flipped onto her back. "Why are you drawing me? I don't want a picture with no makeup and hair that looks like a bird's nest."

Dalhu put the pad aside and sat beside her on the bed. "Good morning, my beauty." He leaned and planted a quick kiss on her pouty lips.

Amanda smiled and wrapped her arms around his neck, pulling him down to her. "Good morning to you too." She kissed him long and hard. "Why don't you get out of those clothes and come back to bed?"

She didn't have to ask twice.

Their lovemaking was lazy and unhurried, like that of lovers who were comfortable with each other. But although the sex was as gentle as a breeze on a sunny shore, the intimacy was intense. Overwhelming.

Dalhu wanted to tell Amanda how much he loved her, over and over again, but he didn't. It made her uncomfortable. She couldn't say it back.

When they reached completion, he didn't even bite her.

Last night, he'd sunk his fangs into her so many times, sampling different spots on her body, that apparently his venom glands were spent. It was good, though, that his balls hadn't suffered similar fate. It would've been embarrassing. Even worse, Amanda would've been disappointed.

His woman was insatiable.

He was the luckiest bastard on earth.

"Dalhu, sweetheart, could you brew us some coffee?" she asked as they stepped out of their shared shower.

"Your wish is my command."

The radiant smile he got in return was priceless.

Ten minutes later, he had Amanda's cappuccino ready as she emerged from the bedroom, looking as perfect as ever in a pair of tight jeans and a blue blouse, her black hair sleeked back and her makeup done. Though why such a beautiful woman bothered with painting her face baffled him.

Females were such strange creatures.

"My lady?" He pulled out a chair for her at the dining table, not that it qualified as such with a diameter of just a little more than three feet. Still, it was the perfect size for two.

Breakfast had been already on the table when he'd stepped out of the bedroom to make coffee—Okidu must've delivered it while they'd showered. Amanda reached for a slice of toasted bread and spread a generous dollop of almond butter on top.

"You haven't tasted the cappuccino yet." It had been his first attempt at making one.

She took a small sip, following with a bite of toast.

"Did I do it right?"

"Perfect."

"Good, I'm glad." He ran a nervous hand over the back of his neck. "So, what did the legal expert say? Is she willing to test me?"

Amanda finished chewing and put the rest of her toast down. "Yes, she is. She said she is going to talk to Kian, though I don't know if she means to clear it with him first or coordinate a time that works with both their schedules. I hope it will be today, and that they'll let us know ahead of time. Not that any preparations are required, she just does her thing, it feels weird for a couple of minutes and that's it. Piece of cake if you have nothing to hide and let her in without a struggle." Amanda lifted what was left of her bread and took a big bite.

"Did she do it to you?"

"Uh-huh."

"Why?"

Amanda shrugged. "I was very young, maybe fifteen, and I'd done something stupid. I don't even remember what it was. I think I sneaked out to see a boy. Anyway, I tried to wiggle out of getting punished by inventing some cockamamie story and stubbornly clinging to it. My mother brought me to Edna."

"And..." He motioned for her to finish the story.

"I got grounded for a month. But that was nothing. What killed me was that I managed to really disappoint my mother for the first time. It was a big deal because her approval meant a lot to me. Still does."

"I bet."

Amanda lifted her mug and cupped it in her hands, her expressive face showing an inner struggle. A couple of times it looked like she was about to say something, but then she frowned and shook her head.

Just spit it out, he wanted to say to her, *don't you know that you can tell me anything?*

"Remember how you said that you should get whipped for your crimes?" she finally asked.

"Yes, what about it?"

"Did you mean it?"

"For a chance of redemption? I'd submit to any kind of torture in a heartbeat. Right now, I'm in no man's land. I'm no longer part of the Brotherhood, but I don't belong here either, or anywhere else for that matter. I'm an unwanted interloper at best—a despised enemy in the eyes of most of your relatives. I want to have a life with you, Amanda, and I'm willing to do whatever it takes to become part of your world—if not accepted, then at least tolerated."

She nodded as if he'd affirmed what she'd already known. "I had to be sure before telling you Edna's idea."

A spark of hope ignited in Dalhu's chest. "What is it?"

"There is this ancient custom, from the time of the gods, that was originally put in place to prevent never-ending blood vendettas between human families. There were no jails, so punishments were either monetary or physical. If the perpetrator didn't have the money to pay, his boss would pay it for him. As compensation, the boss had the right to either enslave him entirely or only garnish a part of his wages until his debt was repaid. The length of the enslavement depended on the severity of the crime and the amount of money owed. For a killing, it was slavery for life. Except, when it wasn't a premeditated murder—then it was up to the head of the offender's household to offer him a choice of physical punishment combined with garnishment of wages. The victim's family had the right to choose a trial that would satisfy their vendetta. After it was done, and if the offender lasted through it, they were asked if they were satisfied. Custom demanded that they say yes."

"I no longer have a boss or wages, so I don't see how this applies to me."

"I need to talk it through with Kian, but I think that this is the only way for you to earn redemption. If Mark's mother agrees to put you through a trial of her choosing and then declare that her vengeance was satisfied, then the rest of the clan would have to accept it as a done deal."

The logic was solid, except for the part of the grieving mother giving her son's killer a chance of redemption.

"Do you think she'll agree?"

"Maybe. It's worth a try. As I see it, this will give Micah something she can't have any other way. She can't retaliate against the Doom Brotherhood, and the guy who committed the killing is already entombed in our crypt. This is the only chance for retribution she can sink her teeth into, so to speak."

"Okay, let's assume she agrees. What makes you think that this will change the clan's attitude toward me?"

Amanda didn't reply right away, and a slight whiff of shame tickled his nose. What was she ashamed of?

"Look, Dalhu, this is about altering perception, and it requires a measure of showmanship. We'll need to make a production out of it, have it witnessed by a good number of clan members. They'll see you submit willingly and they'll have to acknowledge your bravery and your sacrifice. And once Micah declares you redeemed, they'll have no choice but to follow suit. You should prepare a short speech. I'll help."

"A circus performance."

“Yes. I know it sounds awful, and Fates only know what torture Micah will demand, but I don’t see any other way. I won’t blame you if you don’t want to go through with it.” Avoiding his eyes, she looked down at her plate.

He leaned toward her and engulfed her hands—together with the coffee mug they were still wrapped around. “Didn’t I tell you? I will do anything and everything in my power to make a life with you. And if I die trying, at least I’ll know that I gave it all I have.”

48

AMANDA

If there ever was a man who deserved to hear her say *I love you*, it was the one sitting across from her. Tears stinging the backs of her eyes, she dipped her head and kissed his hands.

She felt like such a bitch for denying him this, and still the words could not leave her throat. Because to say them out loud was like spitting on Mark's sarcophagus and stomping on Micah's grief.

Still, there was no way she could admit to him that she needed his sacrifice almost as much as she imagined Micah did. On the other hand, if Dalhu was brave enough to go through hell for her, she should be brave enough to at least tell him the truth.

"Thank you, for doing this for me," she croaked, tears running freely down her cheeks.

"Anything, you know it." He got up and lifted her, then sat down in her chair, cradling her in his arms. "You're priceless to me," he whispered.

She chuckled. "I bet you'll change your mind once I tell you this..." She wiped her eyes with his T-shirt.

"Nothing you can say will affect how I feel about you."

This made her tear up again. "How about the fact that I need your sacrifice for myself? So I can finally tell you I love you without feeling like I'm desecrating Mark's memory?"

Dalhu grinned, his whole face lighting up as if she had just given him the best of news. "I've known all along that you'll need something to help you cross that bridge. I just didn't know what that something was, which was worse than any kind of torture Micah could ever invent. And to hear you say you love me? I'll crawl to hell and back for it."

"You just might. A grieving mother's pain is so excruciating, so all consuming, that I fear Micah has no compassion left in her. She might be extremely cruel in her demands."

Amanda could testify from personal experience.

When her son had died, Amanda would've destroyed the earth and everyone on it—if she'd had the power to do so. She'd gone insane with grief, and it had taken her years to claw her way out of the bleak place she had spiraled down into.

"I had a son, once, a long time ago," she whispered into Dalhu's chest.

He tensed, his arms wrapping more securely around her. "What happened?"

"One moment he was alive and joyful, and the next he was lying dead on the ground. A six-year-old boy riding his first horse. The animal got spooked by a snake and reared up. My boy fell and broke his beautiful little neck. That's the whole story. One horrible moment in time that changed everything."

She'd been repressing her sorrow for so long that once released it erupted like the faulty lid of a pressure cooker—it hit the ceiling with a bang and whatever was cooking inside the pot followed—her guts, her blood, splattered, slowly dripping back down.

Dalhu held her while she cried, rocking her as she sobbed and screamed, "Why?"

"Why him?"

"Why me?"

It had taken a while until the sobs subsided. Dalhu had said nothing throughout her outburst, just waiting it out, caressing, rocking.

Smart man. There was nothing he could've said anyway.

"Thank you." She hiccupped, and he offered her a napkin to blow her nose into. "You're a good listener."

"Is there anything I can do?" he said hesitantly.

"No, you've been perfect. I had a good cry and now I'm better." She managed a small smile. "I could use a margarita, but I don't want to leave the shelter of your arms. I've never felt safer than I do when you hold me."

Dalhu kissed the top of her head, then lifted her up and sat her down on the tiny stretch of bar counter that wasn't occupied by appliances. "You hold on to me, and I'll pour you a drink. I don't think I can manage a margarita, though."

She did, holding on tight and pressing her cheek to his solid chest. When he was done, he handed her the drink and carried her to the couch. Sitting down with her cradled in his lap, he held her gently while she sipped on the gin and tonic he'd made her.

"Better?" he asked.

"Much. But could you hold me for a little longer?"

"I would gladly hold you for the rest of my life."

49

KIAN

The oppressive silence in the Lexus was like a déjà vu of Kian's previous visit to Micah.

Fuck, why the hell had he agreed to Amanda's idea? This was cruel. They would be reopening Micah's wounds. Hell, those had probably never healed and were still bleeding.

Their visit would bring on a hemorrhage.

So why was he sitting in his car and driving to Micah's house?

Because he loved his sister.

He was one hell of a stubborn ox, so it had taken him longer than the others to realize the inconvenient truth. Fate had saddled Amanda with a despicable mate—not of her choosing—and she was powerless against the metaphysical forces conspiring against her.

Damn, I can't believe I'm buying into all this supernatural crap.

He'd considered severing the connection forcefully, but to do so to one's own sister was even more detestable than Amanda's Doomer. If Dalhu were indeed her fated mate, and it seemed he was, then getting rid of him would take away Amanda's one and only opportunity of a true love match.

It was rare to find your fated mate once; to find another was unheard of.

And besides, Kian had to admit that Dalhu had succeeded in chipping away at his hatred one tiny shard at a time. The profiles the guy had compiled were as thorough and complete as he could make them, including the sketched portraits. And his love for Amanda was so glaringly obvious that even a stubborn skeptic like Kian was forced to acknowledge it.

But what really tipped the scales heavily in Dalhu's favor was his willingness to submit to whatever punishment imaginable for a chance of redemption. Grudgingly, Kian admired the guy's courage and determination.

He deserved a chance, if only for Amanda's sake.

Kian cast a sidelong glance at his sister. Sitting in the passenger seat, Amanda hadn't uttered a word since they'd left the keep, but the scents of guilt and fear were doing the talking for her. He laid a hand on her shoulder and gave it a gentle squeeze.

"It's going to be tough, I'm not going to sugarcoat it, but we'll get through it together."

She turned to him, a small pitiful smile tugging at her lips. "Thank you. You don't know how much I appreciate that you're doing this for me."

"You're welcome."

From the back seat, Anandur sniffled audibly. "I'm so happy that you guys are no longer at each other's throats. Albeit entertaining, it was breaking my poor heart."

Brundar grunted, expressing his opinion that the comment didn't deserve a response.

A few minutes later they arrived at Micah's modest suburban house, and Kian eased the SUV into a spot a little farther down the street.

Leaving the three of them down on the walkway, Amanda climbed the two steps leading to the front door and knocked.

Otto, Micah's brother, opened the door. "Come in." He motioned for them to go ahead.

Mark's mother was sitting on a couch with an expression as hard as stone. Damn, this was going to be even more difficult than Kian had anticipated.

"Thank you for agreeing to see us." Amanda walked over and gave Micah a quick hug.

Micah didn't return it. "Please, sit down," she offered in a dead voice.

Fuck, this isn't going to work.

"Thank you," he said and took a seat in one of the armchairs. Brundar and Anandur joined Otto at the dining table.

Amanda sat next to Micah, her knees and torso turned sideways so she was looking straight at the woman.

Brave move.

"I know Kian already explained over the phone the purpose of our visit, but I would like to elaborate."

"Be my guest," Micah said, in a tone that suggested that her mind had already been made up, and her decision wasn't the one they were hoping for.

"I know that you don't want to hear what I came here to say, and that nothing could ever make up for your loss, but I beg of you to hear me out."

Micah seemed to soften a little, her rigid pose loosening. She slumped back into the couch. "Go ahead."

For a split second, Amanda's eyes fluttered closed in relief. "Thank you." She took Micah's hand.

"First, I need to tell you why this is so important to me. I'm not an impartial observer, and I didn't come here as a council member or in any other official capacity. I'm here as a woman seeking a chance of redemption for her mate."

Micah's gasp meant that the rumors hadn't reached her yet. "How can a Doomer be your mate?"

"I know, hard to believe. It took me a long while to accept it." Amanda smiled a sad smile. "The Fates work in mysterious ways. We can huff, and we can puff, but in the end we have no choice but to accept whatever they decree for us."

Micah sighed. "I guess you're right, and I feel sorry for you, but I won't pretend that I don't want that Doomer dead—because I do."

Amanda crossed her legs and licked her lips.

A long speech was coming.

"Let me lay out the facts. We don't execute prisoners. The worst punishment we have is entombment, and it is reserved for premeditated murder, which isn't the case here. Mark's actual killer is already entombed in our crypt as a result of a skirmish between his unit and the Guardians. Therefore, you were denied the satisfaction of witnessing his punishment—unless, you want us to revive him only to have him entombed again, which I doubt Annani would allow."

Micah harrumphed. "I'm not that bloodthirsty."

"I know, I was just stating the obvious. What I'm trying to say is that Dalhu's involvement was not direct. When he gave the order, he had no idea that Mark was one of us. Though I can't say that it would've made a difference. But in any case, I'm not suggesting that he is not to blame. He was a member of the Brotherhood and was expected to deliver their loathsome vengeance. Everything changed for him when he met me. He has forsaken the Brotherhood, sworn allegiance to the clan, and is providing us with invaluable information about Navuh's operation. And for better or worse, he is my mate."

Micah's gaze cut to Kian, and he nodded, affirming Amanda's statements.

"He wants to become one of us, but he will never be accepted unless he is redeemed in the eyes of the clan."

Micah shrugged as if to say—what do I care.

"Please understand, I know that no matter what punishment he'll endure, his pain will never match yours. Nothing ever will." Amanda choked up a little, and this time, it was Micah who squeezed her hand to provide comfort.

"But at least you'll get the satisfaction that you've exacted some measure of vengeance. When I lost my son, I felt like my rage was powerful enough to destroy the world, but I had no one to blame, no one to punish, so I turned on myself. You have a chance to do something—to see someone punished and in the process give him the gift of redemption."

This must've been the most difficult speech Amanda had ever delivered. For her to talk about her son was like plunging a knife into her own heart and twisting.

Silence stretched across the room as Micah pondered Amanda's words, the seconds ticking off one by one like on a game show.

"I want him entombed."

Amanda's shoulders sagged in resignation. Even Kian felt an unexpected twinge of disappointment.

But Micah wasn't done. "For a week, and then you can revive him. I want him to experience dying. But before that, I want him flogged, and I want Otto to be the one wielding the whip." She crossed her arms over her chest. "Don't look at me with those accusing eyes. Because he'll be injured, I'll allow for a venom-induced stasis instead of the agonizingly slow loss of consciousness in the tomb. That's the best I can offer, and I'm doing it mainly for you. It's obvious that you feel for that male, and I know you well enough to realize that if you believe him worthy of redemption, then he must be. But I want him to earn it with a meaningful sacrifice and not a token one."

"Thank you." Amanda pulled Micah into a hug and held on. "You're doing the right thing." She managed only a whisper.

50

AMANDA

What have I done?

That sentence had been going on a loop in Amanda's head all the way home. She might have signed Dalhu's death warrant. Entombment was horrible, but it was pretty safe. Venom-induced stasis wasn't. It had to be done with extreme precision. If not halted at the right moment, Dalhu's heart would be stopped for good.

She turned around to face Anandur. "I want you to do it." He was the most friendly with Dalhu—seemingly the only Guardian who didn't harbor ill feelings toward him.

"No problem, Princess, your frog is safe with me." He chuckled. "And when he awakens seven days later, you'll kiss him, and he'll turn into a prince. Here, I just invented a new fairy tale."

Leave it to Anandur to make fun of the most grievous of situations. "It's not funny."

"Don't worry. Dalhu is a resilient fellow, and he'll not only make it but come out stronger on the other side. Micah's trial is perfect for what he needs. Not too severe, but not too easy either. He'll gain respect by submitting to it and enduring it honorably."

Looking satisfied, Anandur crossed his massive arms over his chest.

Men had such a different outlook on things. She still remembered the games boys used to play when she was a teenager—like who could withstand the most punches to the stomach, or to the shoulder. Or wrestling in the dirt, beating the crap out of each other, and calling it fun.

Idiots.

But when she'd told Dalhu the news, it turned out that Anandur had been right on the money.

"That's great!" was his response.

Really?

The guy was happy about a whipping and an entombment and called it freaking great?

Fates, she felt like shaking Dalhu. What was wrong with him?

Not that it would've made a difference if he didn't like the result of her ill-advised meeting with Micah. The verdict was irreversible. Once decreed, Micah's decision was obligatory.

"Why the angry face?"

"This was a mistake, my mistake. Nothing is worth even the slim chance of you dying."

He took her into his arms. "Of course, it is, my beauty. This is exactly what I've been hoping for, and I have no intention of dying. I'm going to be fine."

"How can you say it? Venom-induced stasis is extremely dangerous. The tiniest of miscalculations and your heart might stop beating for good. I will never forgive myself if that happens. Oh, sweet Fates, how could I have painted us into this corner?" Her mascara-tinted tears were making a mess of his shirt.

"Sweetheart, you're just overreacting."

No, he didn't just say it. Overreacting? The condescending, chauvinistic male.

She pushed, and he let her leave the shelter of his embrace.

Pointing a finger at his chest, she lashed out at him, "Just because I'm a female, you automatically assume that I'm overreacting? That I'm hysterical? Does your life mean nothing to you?"

With a tilt of his head and an expression of a dog that didn't understand why his owner was shouting at him, Dalhu reached for her again, but she swatted his hand away. He dipped his head and wiped the back of his neck with his hand.

After a moment, he lifted his head, his big soulful eyes bathing her with so much love that she almost staggered. "Did it ever happen? Do you know of a precedent—an incident of a Guardian miscalculating and killing someone he was supposed to put into stasis?"

Did she?

Amanda shrugged. "Well, no. But I don't think the Guardians would've advertised it."

"Why don't you call and ask?"

She was ready to argue when it occurred to her that he was right. "That's actually not a bad idea," she mumbled.

Dalhu released a relieved breath and crossed the living room to the bar. The entire two steps. "Would you like a drink?"

"Yeah, the one you made me this morning was good," she said while her fingers flew over the phone's screen, composing a text to Anandur. On second thought, she copied it and sent it to Kian as well. Anandur was a great guy, but he might be inclined to twist the truth for her sake. Her brother would tell it exactly as it was.

Anandur's reply was—*No, stop obsessing!*

Kian's was—*Not recently.*

Not great, but better than she'd expected.

"The good news is that no one died of it recently. The bad news is that it happened in the past."

Dalhu handed her the drink. "When is it going to take place? And where?"

Amanda plopped down on the couch and took a few sips. "Three days from now, in the evening. I don't know exactly where, but probably somewhere in the basement, maybe the gym or perhaps the catacombs."

"Why wait?" Dalhu frowned and sat next to her, holding a tall tumbler that was filled to the brim with whiskey. "I would rather have it over and done with as soon as possible."

"That's what I said. But Anandur said it is customary to wait three days to allow for the announcement to reach whoever wants to witness it."

Dalhu nodded. "That makes sense."

"It does, right? But he later confessed to me that he pulled it out of his ass. He plans a surprise bachelor party for Kian and wants you to be there—since you're going to miss the wedding."

Dalhu snorted. "As if Kian would've invited me to his wedding."

"If we had more time, or if Micah hadn't demanded seven days, he would've. After you're considered redeemed, you will become part of the clan, maybe not a fully trusted member—yet—but certainly one who is invited to a clan-wide celebration like this."

"Then I'm double glad for Micah's demands. Attending a wedding with your entire clan present would've been a nightmare for me."

"You're being silly. Typical macho male—enthusiastic about enduring torture and proving his machismo but terrified of social interactions."

Dalhu laughed, a deep belly laugh that didn't really belong in the context of their conversation. Was it his way of dealing with fear?

"You got me there. I don't know if it has anything to do with being a male, though. I think it has more to do with what is familiar and what is not. Torture and excruciating tests of courage, those I'm well acquainted with. I know I can handle anything anyone throws at me. Celebrations? Acting all polite and pretending that I'm smart? Worldly? I have no clue how to pull it off, and it scares the crap out of me."

Amanda had never considered that Dalhu might be insecure about his lack of education, or his somewhat crude manners. She had no problem with either. In addition to loving her with everything he had, Dalhu was smart and treated her with respect. Everything else was inconsequential. Evidently, though, not for him.

"Make room." She motioned to his lap and then promptly positioned herself in the space he'd made. Wrapping her arms around his neck, she gazed into his lovely chocolate eyes. "You are smart, and worldly, never doubt this. However, I understand where you're coming from, and I'm going to help you. You've got yourself a very accomplished professor here, one who will have you sounding like a scholar in no time." She kissed his smiling lips.

"How about we start with you schooling me in the erotic arts?"

She smiled. "Your enthusiasm for furthering your education is admirable. Take me to bed, big boy."

51

SYSSI

"You sure you don't want me to come with you?" Kian asked again. He'd looked a little hurt when she'd told him that only Andrew would be coming with her to pick up her parents from the clan's private airstrip.

The reason wasn't that she didn't want Kian to be there, but because she didn't want to show up with his bodyguards in tow. Better introduce her parents to this strange world in stages, and certainly not right upon their arrival.

"If you can ditch Anandur and Brundar, you're welcome to accompany me."

"I can't."

"How about just one? We could take the limo, and Anandur could pretend to be the driver."

"I think I can get away with it. Let me call him."

Syssi danced a little victory dance. She hadn't really expected him to cooperate.

Kian arched a brow. "You look so cute, dancing in your underwear."

"Are we back to cute?" She pretended offense.

"Sexy cute."

"That's better." She stretched up on her toes, but he was so tall that she had to drag him down to reach his lips. "I need a stepping stool just to kiss you, you big lug."

"All I hear are complaints," he joked, lifting her up and holding her pressed against him as they kissed.

Half an hour later, as Anandur stopped the limo in front of Andrew's house, her brother was already waiting for them out on the street.

"Nice hat," he said, getting into the passenger seat next to Anandur.

"I'm playing a chauffeur. Your sister doesn't want to spook your parents by showing up with a bodyguard. But why a driver and not a beloved cousin? Huh?" He turned his head to cast her an accusing glare.

He had a point. Who was she going to introduce him as? Kian's driver? And then a cousin, only later to change it to a nephew?

"You're right, ditch the hat. I'm going to tell them that you're Kian's cousin."

"Who drives a limo? We should've taken the SUV."

"The limo is more comfortable. Just give me a break, okay? I'm nervous enough as it is."

Andrew turned around in his seat and stretched his neck to peer at Kian over the partition that separated the front of the limo from the back. It was lowered, but it didn't go all the way down. "Why are we driving all the way out to the boonies instead of using the helicopter to bring them straight to your rooftop?"

"It's being serviced."

"You have only one?"

"No, but the other two are simple cargo birds."

"Got it." Satisfied with Kian's answer, Andrew turned back around. This line of questioning wasn't like him. He must also be nervous about seeing their parents.

Would they look older? What would they think of Kian? How would they react to all the weirdness?

God, two days to the wedding.

Less, it was already afternoon. Thank God that everything was good to go. And if something didn't turn out as well as planned, tough. The important thing, as Amanda had said over and over again, was that Syssi's dress was stunning and she looked fantastic in it. The fifteen thousand dollar price tag had been a shocker, but Amanda had reassured her that it was a bargain price considering that it was made by a semifamous designer and was a rush order. Apparently, Joanne had pulled some strings to have it done quickly and at a *reasonable* price.

The clan's private airstrip was about an hour's drive out of the city. It wasn't much, just one long runway and a huge hangar. Parked inside, there was a small jet that looked almost like a toy in the cavernous space. The hangar had room enough for at least five more. An office, built on a raised ramp, was accessible by a simple metal staircase. Considering the industrial look of everything else, it was surprisingly elegant, with a sitting area, a counter that held a coffeemaker and two baskets with an assortment of refreshments. Several magazines were stacked on top of a rectangular wooden table.

She picked one and was almost done flipping through it when Anandur announced that the plane was landing.

Butterflies in her belly, Syssi got up and watched the approaching aircraft through the window. Once it landed, the plane continued down the runway until it stopped in front of the hangar, waiting like a car for Anandur and the guy manning it to open the doors, then eased inside.

Syssi took the stairs down, Andrew and Kian following close behind her. It took a couple of minutes for the double engines to power down and for the door with the built-in staircase to open.

The woman standing at the opening was either the pilot or the flight attendant, it was hard to tell—she wasn't wearing a uniform.

Her father was the first to emerge, and his face lit up with a big grin as he saw them standing below. Carry-on in hand, he quickly took the short flight of stairs, dropped the luggage and opened his arms.

"Come here, baby girl."

She ran into his welcoming embrace and squeezed, his groan reminding her too late that she was so much stronger than before.

She let go of him quickly. "Sorry, Daddy."

"You've been exercising, yeah? Good for you." He turned to Andrew, who was patiently waiting his turn, and the two did the manly hug with the mutual back slapping. "It's good to see you both. We've missed you so much."

Her mother came down next, and this time, Syssi was careful, hugging Anita gently. "I've missed you, Mom."

"I've missed you too, sweetie, and you, Andrew, come here and give your mother a hug."

Once the hugs and kisses were done, Kian introduced himself, extending a hand to her father. "Welcome, I'm Kian."

"Adam Spivak." Her father repeated the hug and clap ritual with his future son-in-law. "Pleased to meet you. And this is my better half, Anita."

Her mother was somewhat more reserved in her hug, but Syssi could tell that she was impressed.

Though, duh, what did she expect? Kian was one hell of an impressive guy.

"Mom, Dad, I want you to meet Anandur, Kian's cousin."

The three of them shook hands, and the introductions were done.

"Tall family," Anita remarked with an admiring up and down glance first at Kian and then Anandur. "Handsome too."

"Let me help you with that." Anandur grabbed the two pieces of luggage and carried them to the limo, holding them up as if they weighed no more than a cheerleader's pompoms.

Her mom arched a brow.

"He's a bodybuilder," Syssi muttered.

"That explains it. Is your Kian into the body building sport as well?" Anita wrapped her arm around Syssi's shoulders as they followed Anandur to the car.

"He works out, but just to stay in shape."

"And a great shape it is," Anita whispered in her ear.

Syssi blushed, slanting a quick glance at Kian, who was grinning like a satisfied cat. "Mom…"

"What? He can't hear me."

"You'd be surprised."

The drive back to the keep went by quickly, with Adam entertaining them with one outlandish story after the other. It seemed that her parents were having a great time in Africa, despite the harsh conditions and the lack of modern amenities. Both looked fit and tanned.

Back at the keep, the group took the elevator up to the eighteenth floor, where an apartment had been prepared for her parents.

"Oh, wow, this is really nice," her mother said. "Is this your place, Kian?"

"No, we are in the penthouse. This is just for you."

"Thank you," Adam said, sounding relieved.

Syssi chuckled. What was it about fathers having trouble with their little girls growing up and having a man in their lives? Mothers had no such qualms.

"I'll leave you here to freshen up and come back in an hour. Hopefully, you'll still be awake. How is the jet lag?"

"Not too bad, I think I have another couple of hours in me. How about you, Adam?"

"After a shower, I'll be as good as new."

Syssi glanced at her watch. "Okay then, I'll be back at seven."

52

ANDREW

Syssi was fidgeting, wrapping one long strand of hair after the other on her finger and generally looking like she was about to have a nervous breakdown. Not that he could blame her; their parents were about to meet the Goddess.

"I'll go get them," Andrew volunteered.

"No, that's okay, I'll go. I promised them."

"You sure? They wouldn't mind. I can drop a few hints on the way to prepare them for the shock."

"God, I can only imagine their reaction to Annani."

"You worry too much. They'll get over it, same way you and I did."

"You're probably right. Okay, you go and get Mom and Dad while I check on dinner." She snorted. "Not that Okidu would even allow me in the kitchen, but I want to have a peek at the dining room and see if anything needs rearranging."

"You do that." He patted her arm.

It was exactly two minutes before seven when Andrew knocked. His father opened the door, looking distinguished in a dark blue suit.

"We are ready, just let me call your mom." He turned around and called. "Anita, Andrew is here."

His mom emerged from the bedroom wearing a narrow black skirt, a beige blouse, and a string of pearls around her neck. The last time he'd seen her wearing anything other than pants was at his grandmother's funeral. It seemed that Anita was making an effort to impress Kian's mother.

"You look nice," he said.

"Thank you."

"Shouldn't we lock the door?" his father asked as they headed for the elevators.

"No need. This is a secure building, and there are cameras in the corridors. See?" He pointed up.

"So, what's the deal here, Andrew? Syssi didn't say much, but it's obvious just from the travel arrangements that her guy is loaded. However, the important question is whether Kian is a good man?"

"The best. I approve of him wholeheartedly."

"Really?" Anita looked surprised. "How well do you know him?" The elevator doors opened, and they stepped inside.

"Well enough. But listen, before we get there and before you meet Kian's mother, I wanted to warn you. Be prepared for surprises and keep an open mind. This evening will probably be the weirdest you've ever experienced."

Anita frowned. "What is that supposed to mean?"

"It's all good, nothing to worry about. Just keep an open mind, that's all I'm asking."

Exiting, she shrugged. "Fine."

His father's posture stiffened, but he said nothing until Andrew opened the door to Kian and Syssi's penthouse apartment. "Impressive," he muttered, glancing at the wall of glass overlooking the city.

Syssi gave each a quick hug. "You guys look so great. Africa is good to you."

"Welcome to our home." Kian had a big friendly smile plastered on his face as he motioned for them to proceed to the sitting area. "Would you care for a drink?"

"No, thank you." Anita walked over to the glass doors and peered outside. Kian had turned on all of the lights on the terrace, including those inside the pool. Evidently, he wasn't immune to wanting to impress the in-laws either.

"What do you have?" Adam followed Kian to the bar and looked over the display of expensive bottles.

Andrew joined them. "I'll have the Jack Daniel's." He pointed at the opened bottle.

"Me too," Adam said. His father would've probably preferred to try one of the fancier ones, but he wasn't comfortable enough to ask.

Drinks in hand, they headed to the sitting area.

"My mother will be here shortly."

"I can't wait to meet her." Anita joined Adam and Syssi on the couch.

"So, what do you do, Kian?" Adam began the interrogation—the one that every groom, since the beginning of time, had been subjected to by his future father-in-law.

This should be interesting, considering what and who Kian was. Andrew got comfortable to watch the show.

"I manage the family business."

Now, that must've been the understatement of the century.

Adam made a point of looking around the luxurious living room before returning his stare to Kian. "Must be one hell of a business."

"I can't complain."

There was a gentle knock on the door, and Kian jumped up to open the way for his mother. She was accompanied by one of her butlers, whatever his name was. They all looked the same.

Andrew leaned to get closer to his parents. "Remember what I said before," he whispered.

"Anita, Adam, my mother, Annani."

The Goddess glided into the room, her long purple dress swaying gently with each small step, her skin glowing with her natural luminescence.

"It's a pleasure to meet you," the Goddess chimed.

With a gasp, Anita's hand flew to her chest. Adam gaped.

With a graceful, fluid motion, Annani lowered herself into an armchair facing the couch and smiled.

Anita was the first to recover. "What's going on, Syssi?"

"Mom, Dad, Kian's mother, Annani, is the last surviving member of a race of gods. The people who brought knowledge and civilization to humanity and were the source of most ancient mythologies."

"Perhaps it would be better if I told the story," Annani offered.

Adam cleared his throat. "Yes, please do."

"Since we are all hungry, and I do not wish to hold up dinner, I am going to tell you only a very abbreviated version. Later, Syssi can fill in the details."

Anita nodded. "First, if you don't mind, could you please clarify the meaning of the term gods?"

Annani laughed, and if his parents had any doubts before that they were in the presence of a goddess, the heavenly sound of that laugh should've been enough to convince them.

"Not the creator, or creators of the universe, of course, just a different race of beings—a small group of either survivors from an earlier civilization or refugees from somewhere else in the universe. I was not privy to that information. You should be familiar with the general gist of the story from what you have learned reading the Hebrew Bible and the mythologies of the Sumerians, the Egyptians, the Greeks, the Romans, and so on."

Annani continued to tell them about the gods taking human mates and the immortal children that had been born from those unions. She told them about the Dormants and how her people had figured a way to activate them, about Mortdh and the cataclysm that had destroyed her people along with most of their immortal progeny. And lastly, she told them about Syssi's transition.

"You're immortal," Anita stated more than asked.

"Yes."

"I'll be damned." Adam loosened his tie.

Syssi sighed and took Anita's hands. "No one is supposed to know immortals exist, but I figured it would be impossible to explain about Annani without resorting to measures that would've made everyone uncomfortable. So, for the duration of your stay, you'll be privy to the secret, but we will have to thrall you to forget this before you go home."

"Why? Don't you trust us? Do you think we'll betray our own children?" Anita looked not only hurt but furious.

"Of course, I trust you. It's just that no one outside the clan is allowed to know. Right, Kian?" Syssi's tone was pleading for him to take over.

"I'm sorry, but this is how it must be done. The safety of my family depends on secrecy. I'm not suggesting that you would deliberately disclose information you shouldn't, but you can blurt out something accidentally, or if our enemies suspect your connection to us, the information could be tortured out of you. It's better for everyone if I suppress and muddle your memories. Don't worry, you'll still remember the wedding, just not the other stuff."

Adam seemed placated, but not Anita. "Are you sure there is no other way?"

Suddenly, Andrew remembered something that Dalhu had told them. "There might be. How about a strong compulsion thrall like the one Navuh uses on his human pilots? They have the knowledge but are unable to reveal any of it without their brains short-circuiting."

Kian shook his head. "First, I'm not sure I know how to do it. Second, highly intelligent people like Adam and Anita might be able to shake it off."

"I will perform the thrall," Annani offered. "If it is acceptable to you." She trained her glowing eyes on Anita, then Adam.

"Sure, that's better than forgetting all of this, right, Anita?"

"Definitely."

Annani clapped her hands. "It is settled then. Let us adjourn to the dining room. I am famished."

53

ANANDUR

"What? No strippers?" Michael complained.

Anandur winked and leaned to whisper in the kid's ear, "Who said there won't be?"

Not that there were going to be any. Holding the party in a prison cell precluded inviting pros. And anyway, Syssi would have disapproved, and he had no intentions of antagonizing the new First Lady. The thing with the quiet, supposedly demure types was that their vengeance was often cunning and more vicious than that of the loudmouths.

Andrew chuckled. "I'll believe it when I see it."

"Blow me."

"You're not my type."

"I know that I'm irresistible, but instead of hitting on me, go open the door. I left it unlocked." Andrew's human hearing failed to register the faint knock. It was probably Okidu with the food because none of the guys would've been so discreet. There was no need—it wasn't as if a knock would've alerted Kian all the way up in his penthouse and spoiled the surprise—but apparently the word *secret* had this effect on Okidu's logic circuitry.

Andrew flipped him off and went to open the door, letting in Okidu and the stack of trays he was carrying.

There wasn't enough space on the table, and some of the platters had to go on top of the dresser in the bedroom.

Anandur had only invited the Guardians, the two male council members, and Michael to Kian's bachelor party, so all together Dalhu's small apartment would have to accommodate ten super-sized guys. Not an easy feat, but this was the only way to include the dude in the celebration.

It was the least he could do for Dalhu. The guy was facing a whipping and subsequent entombment the following evening.

He'd make it work somehow. There was enough booze to drown a platoon, and the playlist on his iPod had the best of rock 'n' roll's oldies—none of the whiny crap today's bands were barfing out, or rap, which, with the exception of Eminem, Anandur didn't consider music.

A bottle of Snake Venom beer in hand, Bhathian made a thorough inspection of the many portraits of Amanda that Dalhu had taped to his living room walls. "We should take these down for the party. I don't think Kian would enjoy himself with his sister staring at him from every fucking wall."

He had a point.

Dalhu grimaced but nodded. "Just be careful not to damage them when you pull them off."

"Where do you want to stash them?" Bhathian asked.

"Under the bed."

Dalhu and Bhathian made quick work of liberating the walls and took the stack to the bedroom.

"And what do we have here?" Bhathian pulled out a nude of Amanda from under the bed and held it up for everyone to see.

It happened in a blink of an eye.

Dalhu's hands closed around Bhathian's neck in a deadly chokehold, and the large rectangular sheet of white paper fluttered to the floor like a discarded peace offering.

Even Bhathian's powerful arms were no match for Dalhu's fury—his face turning red as he grabbed Dalhu's thick wrists, trying to pull the grip free with all his formidable strength. But it was getting him nowhere.

His eyes blazing, the Doomer snarled, baring fangs that were already at their extended full length.

In one swift move, Anandur attacked, grabbing Dalhu from behind in a rear naked choke. "Let him go before I break your neck." He was already applying force that would've felled most guys on the spot, but Dalhu was not only still standing, but his grip wasn't slackening in the slightest.

"You fucking idiot," Anandur hissed in Dalhu's ear, "Amanda is like a sister to us. She could've been parading naked in here, and no one would've even gotten a rise out of it."

It was true.

Regarding all clan females as mothers or sisters had been drilled into them since infancy, and the only thing her nudity would've evoked were some snide remarks.

Something must've penetrated the lunatic's malfunctioning brain, and he let go. "I'm sorry," he said, sinking down to a sitting position on the bed.

Bhathian rubbed at his thick neck. "You're a strong motherfucker," he said in a tone that suggested respect rather than animosity. "If I didn't get what got you so pissed off, I would've killed you." Again, the guy didn't sound angry. It had been more of a statement than a threat.

"Come on, girls. Time to party." Anandur motioned for them to get back into the living room.

Dalhu followed, sidling up to Anandur. "Thanks, man, I owe you. But just to be clear, the sisterly attitude doesn't extend to him." He tilted his head toward Andrew.

True. Up until a few days ago, the dude had been pining for

Amanda, but being the smart operative that he was, Andrew had realized that it was a losing proposition and had hooked up with the good doctor. Not that it was supposed to be common knowledge, but there was little that escaped Anandur's notice.

"Relax, and go get yourself a beer. These beauties cost me eighty bucks a pop, so enjoy while Scotland's finest lasts." At just over 65 percent alcohol by volume, Brewmeister's Snake Venom was the strongest beer available commercially and was priced accordingly.

His plan was to get the guys drunk, fast, especially Kian who needed it most. Problem was, immortals had a high tolerance for alcohol; add to that his clansmen's Scottish roots, and a barrel of regular beer each would have achieved nothing other than filling the guys' bladders.

When all was ready and the rest of the guys had arrived, Anandur texted Kian. *Could you stop by Dalhu's cell for a moment? There is something he needs to show you. It's important.*

I'll be there in five.

"Get in the bedroom and close the door," Anandur instructed the men. "And take the table with you. I don't want him to see the food."

Brundar and Arwel lifted the thing and carried it to the other room. Dalhu closed the doors to the cabinet housing the bar, and that was it. All traces of party were gone.

A few moments later the door opened, and Kian strode inside.

"I'm here, so talk. I don't have much time."

"I need to show you something." Anandur put on a grave face. "Follow me." He stepped up to the bedroom's door. "Go ahead, take a look." He tilted his head toward the door.

Kian arched a brow, pushing the thing and letting it swing in.

Immediately, the party horns began blasting, and he was pelted with several pounds of hard candy.

"What the hell?"

"Party time!" Anandur clapped his back.

"What's the occasion?"

Sometimes the dude was dense.

"You—getting married."

"A fucking bachelor party?"

"What else?"

"The tailor is bringing my tux. I have to be there in ten minutes."

"No, you don't. Syssi rescheduled it for tomorrow morning."

"So, all of you are in cahoots." He finally smiled.

"Yep. Go get yourself a beer. I brought Snake Venom."

"Went all out, I see."

"Only the best of the best for my best buddy."

"I'm touched." Kian put a hand over his heart.

The rest of the guys spilled out from the other room, William and Yamanu carrying back the dining table. Once they put it back in place, William stayed nearby to sample the goodies. Yamanu grabbed a beer and parked his ass on the couch next to Brandon.

"Okay, so where is the stripper you promised?" Michael asked, his speech already slurred after only one beer.

Lightweight.

Anandur pretended to check the time on his watch. "Fifteen minutes."

A big grin on his puss, Michael saluted him with the bottle.

Ten minutes later, Anandur ducked into the bedroom and closed the door, locking it behind him.

Hopefully, Amanda had some sexy lingerie in there. Sifting through the contents of five out of the six dresser drawers that she had appropriated for herself, he found a pair of fishnets that seemed stretchy enough, a lacy bra, a thong, and several silk scarves.

If he wanted to pull this off, he needed to think creatively.

There was no way the thong would fit him, and the bra had to be extended by tying a scarf to each end. He tied another scarf around his hips to cover his briefs. The fishnets barely made it past his knees, and after all the tugging and pulling there were a few extra holes in them—with his red curly leg hair poking through.

Fuck, he'd have to buy Amanda new ones.

Anandur didn't even bother to look for Amanda's shoes. Obviously too small. Which was a shame because high heels would've worked better with the torn fishnets than his scuffed combat boots.

He found Amanda's makeup case in the vanity drawer and pulled out a red lipstick and a black eyeliner pencil. The thick line he'd painted around his eyes made him look like a raccoon, and he got some of the lipstick on his bushy mustache. He left the eyeliner alone but wiped the smeared lipstick off with a wet washcloth.

Damn, I look good. He blew a kiss at his reflection before heading out.

A firm shove had the door to the living room fly open with a bang that caught everyone's attention.

Andrew choked, then sprayed beer all over Onegus, who was unlucky enough to stand next to him.

"Hello, boys." Anandur sauntered into the room and grabbed his iPod, switching playlists to something slow and sexy.

"Are you ready?"

"No, go away, you ugly mutt!" Arwel shouted.

Anandur ignored him and began his version of a belly dance.

Between bursts of hoots and hollers, the guys were laughing their asses off. Kian included.

Anandur smirked and untied the knot holding the bra in place, making a production of slowly sliding the straps off his shoulders.

"No! Please! Stop! I'm too young to witness such horror!" Michael crouched down and grabbed a fistful of candy from the floor, then chucked it at Anandur. Soon, everyone joined the offensive, forcing Anandur to flee into the bedroom.

Their laughter continued long after he was gone.

Mission accomplished.

54

DALHU

"I can't. I just can't let you go through with it," Amanda said for the umpteenth time while pacing like a caged tigress in the confined space of their living room.

There were tears in her eyes, and the pungent scent of guilt emanating from her body permeated the small space, overpowering what had remained of their recent lovemaking. Which was saying a lot, since they had been at it for hours. The smells of sweat and sex had been so strong that he was sure they had percolated out to the corridor and adjoining cells. It was good that, as far as he knew, they were the only occupants of this basement floor.

"For the love of Mortdh, fuck!"—Dalhu shook his head—"I can't believe I invoked that name," he murmured. "Just give it a rest, will you?"

Amanda strode up to him. Tilting her head and sticking her chin out, she poked a finger at his chest. "How the hell am I supposed to do that? It's entirely my fault, my stupidity that underestimated Micah's thirst for vengeance. I never expected her to be this cruel." She let her head fall upon his chest.

Wrapping her in his arms, he kissed her forehead. "Anything less would not have been enough, and you know it."

"Enough for who?" she whispered.

"For the clan, for you…"

"I don't need it."

"Yes, you do. And I want it over and done with. I want nothing to cast shadows over our relationship. I want to be free of the accusing eyes and the hate-filled hearts, and I'm willing to pay any price for it. I will not get what I want by submitting to a punishment that is deemed insufficient by you or any other member of your clan. If I could've conceived of something harsher, I would've gladly paid an even greater price. Do you understand?"

She nodded, tears running in rivulets down her cheeks and onto his shirt.

"You don't have to watch."

"Yes I do, it's the least I can do."

He sighed, caressing her back in small circles. "It will go easier if I don't have to worry about your reactions. I'd rather spare you the anguish," he whispered, hooking a finger under her chin to tilt her head up. "Can you do this for me?" He gazed into her moist eyes.

After what seemed like long minutes, she nodded.

Dalhu released a breath he hadn't been aware of holding. "Thank you." He took her lips in a tender kiss.

"Can I at least accompany you there and then leave before it begins? Though if it makes things harder for you, I'll stay here."

"I would love for you to be with me at the start of the ceremony —just looking at you will lend me strength."

She reached for him, and her desperate kiss and crushing embrace were a mute declaration of love—nearly as good as a spoken one.

He was almost there. One whipping and seven days of entombment would get him this most coveted prize. The woman he loved more than anything, more than life itself, would tell him that she loved him back.

To finally hear her say the words, he would've endured this trial ten times over.

Later, when Kian and Anandur arrived to escort him to the catacombs, he was ready and anxious to get it over with.

"Shall we?" Kian asked.

"Lead the way."

Dalhu was wearing the attire he'd been given for the ceremony—a short, black robe and loose black pants resembling a judo uniform, but made from some thin silky material, and no shoes.

He wasn't the only one who was dressed up for the occasion. Fancy, long robes covered Amanda, Kian, and Anandur from head to toe, and he noticed that Anandur had exchanged his scuffed combat boots for a pair of shiny black dress shoes.

As they made their way in silence, the clicking of Amanda's heels on the concrete floor was the only sound echoing from the walls of the long, winding corridor. The large chamber they arrived at was surrounded on three sides by recessed niches that had been carved into the stone walls. They were empty, waiting like silent gaping mouths to swallow their future residents.

Dalhu glanced at the small group of people assembled to witness his trial and, hopefully, subsequent redemption. He recognized some as Guardians by the robes they were wearing, including a tall, muscular woman who must've been the Guardian friend Amanda had mentioned. There were two other females present. The one with the smart, sad eyes, wearing a robe in different colors than those of the Guardians, was most likely the legal expert. The one in civilian clothes—who was also the only one seated—was no doubt the bereaved mother, Micah.

He bowed his head to her, for the simple reason that he had no idea what else to do or say. Dalhu prayed that Kian would do the talking and get the ball rolling. Though he had no idea what to expect as far as procedure.

There were no chains in sight, no podium, not even chairs, and everyone aside from Micah was standing.

How were they going to whip him?

He was relieved when Kian clapped his back and pointed to the spot he wanted him to stand on. But then he realized he would be directly in front of Micah.

The man standing behind her with his hands on her shoulders looked just as grief-stricken—the pained expression and family resemblance identifying him as either a brother or another son.

Unable to look them in the eyes, Dalhu felt like the worst of cowards. But Amanda's presence and, surprisingly, Kian's gave him strength.

And there were others.

He was not alone.

At least two people in this crowd were rooting for him, Amanda and Anandur. And there was Andrew, who at least believed him to be forthright. Even Kian, who finally seemed resigned to give Dalhu a chance.

Could've been worse.

Kian raised a hand to get everyone's attention. "Before we begin Dalhu's trial, I would like Edna to come forward and search his soul. If she finds that he is harboring nefarious intentions toward us, we will not proceed with this ceremony, and he'll suffer the same fate as his fellow Doomers—a permanent resting place in our catacombs. If, however, Edna declares his intentions pure, Micah will extend him the offer of redemption through a trial of her choosing. If he accepts her challenge with gratitude and endures it with courage, Dalhu will earn redemption.

"He will then be granted conditional acceptance into our clan for a period of three years. During that time, he will be watched and tested. If he proves to be loyal and worthy by the end of this trial period, I'll personally welcome him as a full member of our family."

Edna wasn't a tall woman, and as she came closer and cranked her neck way up to look into his eyes, Dalhu dropped down on his knees, making it easier for her.

A small smile made a brief appearance on her austere face. "Thank you, that's very considerate."

He took her small, cold hand and placed it over his heart. "My life is in your hands. I wasn't a good man, and my past is dark, but I have nothing to hide. I'm an open book. My soul may not be worth much, but whatever there's left of it belongs to Amanda. I pledge my life and my loyalty to her and to you—her people."

Edna touched the fingers of her other hand to his cheek. "Don't resist, and it will go easier. The more you fight it, the more discomfort you'll feel."

"As I said, I'm an open book. I welcome your inquiry."

"Good, that's very good."

Her pale blue stare didn't faze him. On the contrary, he felt warmth and comfort as her ghostly fingers gently sifted through his memories, his feelings, going deeper and deeper until they reached the very essence of him. The place where Dalhu the warrior didn't exist—the small sheltered enclave where Dalhu the boy could still be found, a boy who'd been loved and cherished by his mother.

Time and space lost meaning as Edna's tender tendrils wove through the story of his life, and when she withdrew, he was startled to find himself back in the stone chamber.

She palmed his feverish cheeks with her chilly hands and kissed his forehead before turning to face the small crowd.

"The love in this man's heart burns brightly enough to purify his sins, and perhaps even restore his soul to the beautiful sapling it once was—before Navuh's tutelage shriveled it. He regrets his past deeds and wholeheartedly seeks redemption by paying any price Micah would demand of him. In light of his good intentions, I would have asked for mercy on his behalf, but he would not have welcomed it. Dalhu wishes the price he pays to be worthy of forgiveness and acceptance even by his most vehement detractors' standards."

There were tears in Amanda's eyes as Edna finished her unequivocal endorsement, and Anandur, who was standing behind the small group, smiled and lifted both hands with his thumbs up.

Andrew nodded to no one in particular.

The speech Amanda had helped Dalhu prepare was no longer needed. Edna had done a much better job of pleading his case than he and Amanda could have ever done.

Kian moved closer to Dalhu and pulled out a scroll made of parchment from inside his robe, unrolled it, and held it in front of Dalhu as if to show him what was written on it. Not that it did him any good—the writing was in some ancient script that looked like a strange hybrid of hieroglyphs, Hindu, and old Hebrew.

"Edna composed it in the old language. I'm going to translate," Kian clarified.

"On the fifth day in the month of Kislimu, in the year 3942 after the cataclysm, Micah mother of Mark is graciously extending to Dalhu, formerly of the Brotherhood of the Devout Order Of Mortdh, a chance to atone for his part in the crime perpetrated against her beloved son Mark. He is to be flogged by her brother Otto, until she says enough, then put into stasis and entombed for a period of seven days. If at any time during his atonement, Dalhu is unable to endure, and he asks for the punishment to stop or impedes it in any way, it will cease immediately, and the offer of redemption will forever be revoked. However, if he prevails, Micah will deem Dalhu redeemed and would seek no further vengeance against him."

Kian produced a pen from a pocket inside his robe and handed it to Dalhu. "By signing this document, you accept these terms."

Without a shred of hesitation, Dalhu scribbled his name on the line Kian had pointed to.

Kian took the pen and parchment back, walked over to Micah,

and handed her both. "By signing this document you accept these terms," he repeated.

As she held the pen, Micah's hand hovered over the parchment, her tormented expression revealing her inner struggle.

Please sign, please sign, please sign, Dalhu kept chanting.

The complete silence in the chamber was suffocating. It seemed as if no one dared to move, and all of them were holding their breath with him. Except, it was only his heart that was racing and only his palms that were sweating worse than if he were facing his own execution—and not the temporary one of entombment.

After what felt like an eternity, Micah's brother gave her shoulders an encouraging squeeze, and she released a breath, lowered her hand to the parchment, and signed her name on the dotted line.

As if someone had pressed play on a paused scene, a communal release of breath and the swishing of robes shattered the silence.

Kian took the parchment and lifted it for everyone to see. "The contract was signed and witnessed." He held it up for a few moments, moving it from side to side so everyone had a chance to see, then rerolled it and stashed it back inside his robe.

Turning to Dalhu, he asked, "Are you ready?"

"Yeah, I am. How do you want to do this?" He took another glance around to see if a whipping post had magically appeared.

"Nothing will hold you, it's part of the test. You're going to lean against that wall"—Kian pointed at a narrow stretch of wall that was free of niches and nearly smooth—"without a thing to grab onto—the only thing holding you up is going to be the power of your will."

This was going to be a lot tougher than he'd anticipated. To endure the pain while immobilized and restrained was one thing, to maintain position voluntarily was another.

"I can do it. I will do it."

"I know."

55

KIAN

On his way to Amanda's penthouse, Kian deliberated how much to tell her. On the one hand, he'd promised to give her a full account, on the other, he didn't think she could handle the uncensored, blow-by-blow report.

Damn, it had been hard to watch.

But he had to admit; Dalhu had gained his respect and then some. Kian couldn't think of a single man, himself included, who could've taken the whipping Dalhu had, without moving an inch, without crying out even once, and without collapsing from the massive blood loss and exhaustion.

To say that the guy had an iron will was an understatement—a will hard as a diamond was more like it.

Micah had chosen a vicious implement, a three-stranded whip with metal tips for added injury.

At first, Otto had seemed to relish wielding the thing, but after only a few blows he was looking at Micah before delivering the next one, hoping she'd give the signal to end it.

Dalhu's blood had formed a pool at his feet, and speckles of it as well as pieces of his flesh had landed on Otto's clothes and even as far as the line of spectators.

When she had finally raised her hand and given the signal, Otto had thrown the whip to the ground. "I want this evil thing destroyed —" had been his parting words before he'd stormed out, leaving his sister behind.

Anandur hadn't wasted any time before going over to Dalhu and taking him in his arms with infinite care for his injured back, then sinking his fangs into the guy's neck and ending his misery.

The one good thing about the brutal whipping was that the fangs of all immortal males present had been ready for action with no additional aggression required.

Dalhu had proven to be one of the strongest males Kian had ever encountered. But there was no way he could've offered even a token fight after the beating he'd taken.

As he reached Amanda's door and knocked, Kian pondered the peculiar feeling that had been on the edge of his awareness since Dalhu's trial had ended. He felt at ease for some reason, like there was one less thing he had to worry about. At first, he'd thought that he was simply relieved that Dalhu had prevailed and that he wouldn't have to deliver bad news to Amanda. But now, standing in front of her door, he realized that there was more to it.

The truth was that there was no stronger protector for Amanda than Dalhu. The guy would not only give his life for her without a moment's hesitation, but more to the point, he could single-handedly take down an army to save her.

The Fates hadn't been cruel to Amanda when they'd paired her with Dalhu. They'd given her exactly the kind of male she needed.

The door opened, and the woman standing before him looked like a wreck, emotionally and physically. Amanda's eyes were so red and puffy that he suspected that she'd been crying the entire time since leaving the chamber.

"It is done, and Dalhu passed with flying colors."

She stepped aside to let him in. "Is he okay?"

"He is in stasis."

"Thank you, merciful Fates." Amanda collapsed into a chair. There was a pile of used tissues on the floor next to it. "I want you to tell me everything."

Kian glanced at his mother who had the I-knew-he-would-be-fine expression on her face and was probably itching to say, "I told you so."

"Let's just say that you should be proud of your man. I don't know of anyone who would've taken Micah's punishment as well as he did."

His choice of words hadn't escaped Amanda's notice, and her eyes widened. "You called Dalhu *my man*."

"Yes, and I also said that you should be proud of him."

"So you have no more reservation about him and me? You accept Dalhu a hundred percent?"

"How about ninety-nine?"

"I can live with that."

56

AMANDA

The good thing about clan celebrations was that no one had partners. Otherwise, Amanda would've felt even worse than she did.

It didn't seem right to stand there in a designer evening gown and diamond jewelry, surrounded by her family's smiling faces, while her man was all alone in a dark, cold tomb. But there was no way she could've missed Kian and Syssi's wedding. After all, she was the matchmaker who had made it happen. Not to mention that her only brother was marrying her best friend and the whole clan was celebrating for the first time since its inception.

Her sisters, Sari and Alena, had arrived this morning and the three of them had a nice, tearful reunion. Kian had stopped by her apartment a little later, but hadn't stayed for long, so he'd escaped the guilt trip her sisters had laid on her.

There was really no good excuse for why she hadn't visited them more often. Sari had her hands full running the Scottish arm of their clan, and it had taken some juggling for her to get away for a couple of days to attend the wedding. And Alena was busy managing

Annani, which the three of them agreed was a much more challenging job than Sari's.

Searching for her sisters, she stretched her neck, which was all she needed to do to peer over the crowd. The four-inch heels she had on made her just as tall as most of the Guardians. She spotted Sari chatting up a storm with Brandon, while Alena was standing amidst a large group of females. Someone must've told her a joke because she was doubling over with laughter.

It was good to see them having fun, and Amanda felt the vise squeezing her heart loosen a notch, allowing her at least to fall back on her well-practiced routine.

Plastering a confident smile on her face, she sauntered over to where Syssi's parents and Annani were greeting the guests. She got there just in time to see Anandur and Brundar enter.

"I thought the day would never come. You? In a tux? And Brundar too? You guys look amazing."

Brundar's long blond hair was tied at his nape with a black leather cord, his fallen-angel face looking as austere as ever. Anandur must've spent time at the barber's because his wild, curly red hair was sleeked back away from his face with the help of plenty of hair product, and his beard and mustache were trimmed a lot shorter than usual. The brute looked almost civilized.

"Syssi made me do it," Anandur complained. "I can't even move my shoulders in this damned penguin suit." He demonstrated, the seams on the tux straining from the pressure of his muscles flexing beneath them.

Amanda slapped his shoulder. "Stop it, you big oaf. The tux was custom made for you and it fits perfectly. You are not supposed to play football in it, just stand next to Kian during the ceremony and look handsome."

"I'll play my part because Syssi asked me to, but I still think bridesmaids and groomsmen do not belong in this ceremony. It is not part of our tradition."

"What tradition? We have none. This is the first wedding we ever had. We are creating tradition tonight."

"Exactly. And from now on we'll be stuck with this stupid human custom." Anandur bunched his shoulders again.

Amanda rolled her eyes. "You'll get used to it. I don't see Brundar complaining."

Brundar shrugged.

The range of the guy's emotions spanned between indifferent and stoic, oscillating at the rate of once a month.

Someone tapped her bare shoulder. "Good evening, gorgeous." Drink in hand, Andrew, the third groomsman, looked much more comfortable in his fancy suit than the brothers. He kissed her cheek. "I'm taking advantage of the opportunity that your guy is not around."

She kissed him back. "Don't be silly, Andrew, you can kiss my cheek whenever you like. Dalhu is not the jealous type."

Andrew's quick reflexes saved her gown—he spun around before spewing his drink on the floor. His shoes, however, hadn't escaped the splatter. Anandur's deep belly laugh almost popped the buttons on his tux jacket. He fished out a folded kerchief from a back pocket and handed it to Andrew. "Here, buddy, for your shoes."

"Thanks." Andrew wiped his face before attending to his footwear.

"What's so funny?" What did they all know that she didn't?

"You are one clueless princess."

"Okay, just tell me. I can see that you're dying to."

"Your guy almost choked the life out of Bhathian at Kian's bachelor party. Dalhu had a nude picture of you stashed underneath his bed, and when Bhathian found it and showed it to everyone, he attacked him so viciously that even I couldn't pry him away—not until I explained to the idiot that your nudity has no effect on the males of your own family."

Oh, wow. Her guy was jealous.

Sweet. Amanda likes.

Syssi could cling to her opinions and regard ungrounded jealousy as offensive, but Amanda was flattered. Heck, if Dalhu were near she would've grabbed him and kissed him long and hard to show him that she was all his, and that he had nothing to be jealous about.

Regrettably, Dalhu wasn't there, and she couldn't show him or tell him anything. She would, though, in four days, eighteen hours, and fifty-three minutes.

57

SYSSI

"Are you ready, my love?" Kian smiled and offered Syssi his arm.

Taking a deep breath, she nodded.

It was time for their big entry.

She and Amanda had planned the ceremony, incorporating traditions they both liked and replacing the ones they didn't. After all, they were in charge of creating a new script that would provide the foundation for future clan weddings.

They had agreed that bridesmaids and groomsmen were nice to have, but there was no need for more than three each and the girls should choose their own gowns. Amanda had been adamant about that.

Kian had chosen Andrew, Anandur, and Brundar, and Syssi had chosen Amanda, Kri, and Bridget.

The walk down the aisle with a father giving away the bride had been thrown out the window. The obvious reason was that aside from Syssi, other clan females had no fathers to call on. Besides, it was an outdated custom that should've ended along with everything else that still stunk of patriarchy—like taking on the husband's last name.

Amanda had insisted, however, that a grand entry was necessary and that Syssi should walk down the aisle by herself.

Syssi had refused.

To make the walk alone while everyone was watching?

No way.

Not her style.

It was her wedding, and she was the one making the rules.

She would walk down the aisle with Kian by her side.

"You look stunning." Kian kissed her cheek, gently, careful not to mess up her makeup—per Amanda's instructions. She had warned him, threatening to unman him if he dared.

Syssi had to admit that this was the most beautiful she had ever looked. Her dress was long-sleeved and had a simple cut, the bodice following her contours without being too clingy, and a long train that she was certain would get stepped on—a lot. The décolletage was wide and low, leaving the tops of her shoulders bare but stopping short of her cleavage. Her concession to tradition was that the dress was white and long, but she refused a veil—another outdated custom that should've been tossed out a long time ago.

Kian had requested that she leave her hair down, and Armando, who had shown up with two assistants each carrying two cases filled to the brim with tools of his trade, had been so proud of the job he'd done with her hair and makeup that he'd cried. Not a few pretend teardrops for drama, but for real, claiming that this was his masterpiece and he would never achieve such perfection again. So he should quit and retire while at his peak.

The guy was no more than thirty.

And yet, after all the effort everyone had invested so she'd look her best, gazing at Kian, she doubted anyone would be looking at her while this Greek god in a tux walked beside her. There was no way she could compete with his perfection.

"Not to add to your already overinflated ego, but you must be the most good-looking man ever to exist." She took his hand.

Kian dipped his head in a slight bow. "Thank you, my lady. But I assure you that no one else shares your opinion. Beauty is in the eyes of the beholder."

Yeah, right.

There was a moment of quiet as the soft music that had been playing in the large assembly hall stopped.

A new, familiar tune began.

Ooga-Chaka Ooga-Ooga

Ooga-Chaka Ooga-Ooga

Kian grinned from ear to ear. "This is our cue."

Syssi laughed. "That's the song you've chosen? "Hooked on a Feeling?"

"Isn't it perfect?"

"It is."

"Then let's go." He pushed through the double doors, and they danced their way up to the podium to the beat of Blue Swede's *Hooked on a feeling* while their guests clapped, cheered, and sang along.

I can't stop this feeling deep inside of me.

58

ANDREW

It was after seven, and even the most diligent of his fellow agents had left—some to go home, others down to Barney's.

Like in the old days, before he'd gotten involved with the clan and had taken on an after-hours part-time job, Andrew was the last one in the office and wasn't expecting to be done anytime soon.

Tim's sketch had been sitting inside a large shopping bag next to Andrew's desk, calling to him throughout the entire day.

He couldn't wait to sink his teeth into the investigation.

Now that he was no longer on the clock, he could finally pull it out and start digging.

There was something very compelling about the woman in the picture. It wasn't her beauty, though she was a looker. It was something about her eyes—a mystery begging to be solved. Andrew had the odd feeling that she was staring at him from the paper and imploring him to find her.

Doubtless, it was all in his head. The expressive eyes were nothing more than testament to Tim's talent, and his interpretation of Bhathian's longing for a lover the guy had lost more than thirty years ago.

I'll do my best, he promised her anyway.

Trouble was, Patricia would be seventy-five years old. If she was still alive, that is. She could've died from natural causes by now, and there was always a possibility that someone other than herself had arranged her disappearance.

People disappeared all of the time—some voluntarily, some not.

Sadly, in the case of beautiful women, it was more often than not the latter.

Fuck, he hoped Patricia hadn't been the victim of some scumbag like Alex.

True, they had no proof yet that Amanda's cousin was engaged in the business of kidnapping and trafficking women for sexual slavery, but the circumstantial evidence Amanda had gathered during her trip aboard Alex's yacht, together with Dalhu's observation, suggested that he was.

This was going to be Andrew's next pet project.

He just needed to figure out the logistics first. There had been talk of using the clan's private satellite to spy on the boat, but William had shot it down. Their communication satellite wasn't designed for that purpose. However, the clan had the resources to build one, and it had been decided to hire a team to start working on it.

Obviously, the thing wouldn't be ready anytime soon.

He'd have to resort to more mundane means—like finding the weak link in the Russian crew and manipulating her, one way or the other, to cooperate with them.

Later.

Now, he needed to focus on finding Patricia.

There were several databases to go through. But first, he decided to run the social security number, even though he was certain it was fake. Government agencies issued them for various purposes, and if this were the case, then he would strike gold. They typically made use of a real, recently deceased person's social security number instead of producing an entirely fake one—which was the method most amateurs and small-time criminals used.

A minute later he found it. The number belonged indeed to a Patricia Evans, born September 1951 and deceased November 1987. For a moment, his heart sank. Patricia had died about a year after meeting Bhathian. But then he glanced at the year of birth again. The math didn't add up. Patricia had claimed to have been forty-five at the time, which would've put her birth year at somewhere around 1940, not 1951.

Was it possible that she'd lied about her age? Claiming to be a decade older than she actually was? Not likely.

And the fact that the year of death was not before, but after she had met Bhathian? A death certificate could've been falsified. The elaborate setup, however, was more appropriate for an undercover operative than someone in the witness protection or relocation service.

The year of birth didn't match Pat's real age, but it matched the way she'd looked at the time Bhathian had met her. The guy had thought she was in her late twenties. If Pat had been working undercover at the time, her assumed social security number wouldn't have not raised suspicion. If anyone had bothered to check, they would've found a Patricia Evans who matched the agent's perceived age—and who wasn't dead. The death certificate hadn't been entered into the system.

Andrew stretched his arms over his head before diving back in. This was going to make his job so much easier. Fewer databases to check.

Bingo! Pat was, or rather had been, a drug enforcement agent. Her real name was Eva Paterson. Funny, the guys in charge of producing the fake social security numbers must've liked that one. The real Patricia Evans, a name that would've been very easy for Eva Paterson to remember, had conveniently passed away at the right time.

A little more digging produced Eva Paterson's file and the rest of the pieces fell into place.

As a drug enforcement agent, she'd been working undercover as a flight attendant, investigating the involvement of airline personnel in drug smuggling. The setup had been long, and that particular stint had lasted more than three years. She had retired from the agency shortly after meeting Bhathian—for health related reasons. The government was still depositing monthly pension checks into her account.

Eva was still alive.

Okay, next step was to find out what she'd been up to.

Andrew switched to the IRS database. Other than Facebook, there was no better source of information about people's lives than their tax returns, which he had unrestricted access to.

Interesting.

A month after leaving the agency, Eva had married a guy named Fernando Vega, a Cuban immigrant, and seven months later the couple had a daughter, Nathalie. Five years after Nathalie was born, they'd moved from Florida to Los Angeles and had opened a bakery in Studio City.

Judging by the couple's tax returns, their small-business income combined with Eva's retirement checks had been just enough to provide their family of three with a comfortable middle-class living.

Nathalie had remained their only child.

Thirteen years ago, Eva had filed for a divorce.

Andrew had to look up both spouses' tax returns to continue.

Fernando kept filing as a single man, but three years later he'd apparently been declared mentally incompetent, and the daughter had been the one filing the returns since.

Eva's last tax return had been filed seven years ago.

Damn, what happened?

He ran her name again through a couple of other databases, and what he found wasn't good.

The daughter had filed a missing person's report with the police six years ago. With no evidence of foul play, the case had been closed even though Eva hadn't been found.

Fuck.

Andrew felt like punching the computer screen. He'd been so close to finding the woman, and she had to go and disappear. Again.

With a sigh, he pulled up the police report.

Damn! Eva must've had extensive plastic surgery done because the woman in the photograph looked exactly the same as the woman in Tim's forensic sketch. She hadn't aged at all...

It could've been the result of a skillful surgical knife, or... immortality...

But Bhathian had claimed that he hadn't bitten her.

Had any Dormant ever turned without the help of venom?

Searching his memory, Andrew sifted through everything he'd been told about a Dormant's turning, dimly recalling something about the little girls' turning facilitated by Annani's presence alone.

Under no circumstances, though, could Eva have been exposed to the Goddess as a child. He doubted the clan would've surrendered any of its precious children for adoption in case something had happened to the child's mother.

But just in case, he would check if they had lost track of any of their females. Maybe someone who had moved far away and hadn't kept in touch with her family had been abducted or killed, and her young child had been adopted by unsuspecting humans.

There was a more expedient way to find out, though; he could check Eva's birth record.

Thank God for Uncle Sam and the access to information Andrew had been granted. Adoption records and the birth certificates of adopted children were guarded better than the government's strategic secrets.

Eva's birth record, however, was easy to find and as fascinating as yesterday's porridge. She was born at Tampa General Hospital, previously known as Municipal Hospital Davis Islands, to Alfonso and Fawn Paterson.

Nevertheless, it wouldn't hurt to ask Kian if he was aware of a long lost female clan member.

Damn, Bhathian would be disappointed that Andrew hadn't found Eva. But at least he could deliver the news about the daughter.

Okay, Nathalie, let's see what we can tell Daddy about you.

Husband—none. Children—none.

Her father was the only dependent listed on her tax return.

She'd closed the Studio City coffee shop less than a year after her father had been declared mentally incompetent, and opened a new one in Glendale. Most years the profits hadn't been great. Nathalie was barely scraping by.

He wondered why she hadn't closed the place a long time ago. She could've been making more as an employee somewhere. Perhaps she was the type who valued being her own boss above everything else. Or maybe it had something to do with the father and preserving his business for sentimental reasons.

A closer look at her tax returns provided the answer. Her residence address was the same as her business, save for the suite number. Nathalie had moved the shop to an area that allowed mixed-use housing—business and living quarters combined. A perfect solution for someone who needed to work and at the same time keep an eye on a parent who had suffered a severe mental decline. Apparently, Nathalie was a very devoted daughter.

Did she know that Fernando wasn't her real father?

How would she react if she ever discovered who her biological father was?

Andrew pulled out his cell phone and selected Bhathian's number.

"You found something?" There was no mistaking the excitement in the guy's voice.

Andrew delivered the good news without preamble. "You have a daughter. Her name is Nathalie, and she lives right around the corner from you, in Glendale."

"Thank the merciful Fates," Bhathian breathed in a shaky voice. "And Patricia? Is she"—the guy swallowed—"you know..."

"As far as I know."

"What do you mean?"

"Patricia's real name is Eva Paterson, and she went missing six years ago. Nathalie filed a missing person's report, but the case was closed."

"What the hell? She disappeared again?"

"Meet me at Barney's in half an hour, and I'll tell you everything I was able to find."

"I'm leaving right now. I can be there in fifteen minutes."

"Good deal, see you there."

Eva's missing person's file was still opened on his screen, and he printed an enlarged version of the photograph Nathalie had given the police.

While his terminal was powering down, Andrew stashed both the forensic sketch and the printout in the shopping bag. Keys and wallet went into his jacket's inside pocket, and he switched off the lights on his way out.

The drive to Barney's took less than ten minutes, and as he entered the bar, Andrew felt an irrational rush of satisfaction that he'd made it there before Bhathian.

Selecting a quiet booth at the back, he ordered two beers and a platter of nachos.

It took Bhathian another fifteen minutes to storm into the bar, and people scurried to clear the path for the hulking guy with a murderous expression on his face.

"Goddamned LA traffic." He pulled out a chair, grabbing a beer as his butt landed in the seat.

"It's a bitch," Andrew agreed.

Bhathian sucked half the bottle on a oner, then pinned Andrew with a hard stare. "Lay it on me."

Andrew moved the nacho platter over to the edge of the table before leaning sideways and lifting the shopping bag. He pulled out the large forensic sketch and the letter-size printout, laying both side by side so they were facing Bhathian. He pointed to the photograph. "This is the picture Nathalie gave the police when she filed the report six years ago. I don't think she would've given them an old one."

Bhathian picked up the photocopy, his gloomy features softening as he caressed it with his finger. "She looks exactly as I remember her," he said quietly.

It seemed that the guy was so used to being around people who didn't age that the significance of what he was seeing escaped him.

"Does it not strike you as odd? Eva, your Patricia—a human—not aging in the slightest?"

Bhathian lifted his head, the momentary softening of his features giving way to a frown that was impressive even for him. "What are you implying?"

"Look"—Andrew pointed to the picture—"the woman hasn't aged in thirty years. So she is either an immortal or has undergone extensive plastic surgery. Frankly, though, I don't think any surgeon is that good."

"I didn't bite her."

"I know, I'm not saying that you did, there must be some other explanation."

"Like what?"

"Maybe she was already immortal when you met her? You said she looked a lot younger than what she claimed to be, and looking at this picture I agree. This woman looks like she's in her late twenties, not midforties."

Bhathian rubbed his neck. "Immortal females are supposed to smell different than humans when aroused."

"And she didn't?"

The guy shrugged. "All I can remember is that everything about her was amazing. My head was all into the sex and wanting to bite her. Then when I realized she wasn't responding to the thrall, all I could think of was how to refrain from sinking my fangs into her neck. It took all I had just to hide what I am from her."

"So there is a chance she was an immortal."

Bhathian shook his head. "There are no immortal females other than ours. Maybe the Doomers have some, but even if they do, there is no chance in hell even one managed to get away."

"Are all the clan females accounted for? Is it possible that you guys lost touch with one who had a young daughter? A child who was already turned and somehow ended up being adopted by humans?"

Bhathian kept shaking his head from side to side. "We know where every clan member is at all times."

"You sure? How can you keep tabs on everyone, every moment?"

"I didn't say every moment. But everyone who lives outside the keeps or travels for extended periods of time calls in once a week."

"What about before there were phones?"

"Back then hardly anyone lived outside the community and the few who did, lived nearby."

"Travelers?"

Bhathian shook his head. "Never alone, always in groups."

"Okay, I'm stumped. I can think of no other explanation."

Bhathian's neck rubbing intensified, the furrow in between his brows so deep that the bushy things became a unibrow. "There is one more possibility. But it's a one in a billion chance. She might have had sex with another immortal before me, and he turned her without him or her realizing it. Otherwise, he would've never let her go."

"Yeah, it does sound extremely far-fetched. There must be a simpler explanation. Like your daughter, for some reason, using an old picture. Maybe Eva was...is...one of those women who hate being photographed and this was the only picture Nathalie had of her."

"Yeah, that's sounds more likely." Bhathian sighed. "I would like to meet he… my daughter." There was wonder in his tone.

Andrew grimaced. "That's a really bad idea. Eva married a guy named Fernando Vega shortly after you'd last seen her, and Nathalie was born seven months later. She might not know that Fernando is not her real father. And anyway, you look too young."

Bhathian stared at Andrew. "So, there is a chance she isn't mine. Premature babies are not uncommon."

"Nah, she's yours. Too much of a coincidence."

"Do you have her picture?"

"No. What I know about her, I got mostly from her tax returns—she's not married, doesn't have children, owns a coffee shop, and takes care of her father—adoptive father that is—who suffers from mental decline. I didn't have time to dig any deeper. I can, if you want."

Bhathian's frown eased a fraction, relaxing the pissed-off expression he normally wore. "Can we go see her? You know, at her coffee place, like random customers. I just want to get a look, hear her voice."

"Sure, but you don't need me. I'll give you the address."

Bhathian swallowed a couple of times before spitting it out. "I don't want to go by myself."

The big guy was asking for moral support, and Andrew could think of no good reason to deny him. In fact, it would be better if he went with Bhathian. After all, a man who looked like that, sitting alone and staring at the woman for God knows how long, would scare the shit out of her. Andrew could provide a cover and soften the impact.

"No problem, when do you want to do it?"

"How late do you think her place is open?"

"Let me check."

59

AMANDA

The crypt was awfully quiet as Amanda waited for Anandur and Brundar to arrive and revive Dalhu.

Since she'd gotten there more than an hour early, she'd been breathing shallowly and barely moving, afraid of making any noise lest it disturbed the dead. Their ghosts might rise to haunt her.

Or rather one ghost—Mark's.

Please, dear Fates, let Mark be satisfied with Dalhu's sacrifice.

She wished Mark would give her a sign, let her know somehow that he was okay on the other side and that he had forgiven her.

This entire week, ever since Dalhu's atonement, she'd been going to bed early, hoping that Mark would visit her in her dreams. But, of course, he hadn't.

It was stupid. Just wishful thinking.

Fates, she was lonely.

Her mother and sisters had gone home the day after the wedding, as had Syssi's parents, while Syssi and Kian had left for their honeymoon in boring Dana Point. She had tried to convince them to pick Hawaii, but Kian had refused to go any farther—claiming that he needed to remain close by in case he was needed urgently.

Like the keep couldn't function without him for one measly week.

At least he'd been nice about leaving Anandur and Brundar behind, taking Onegus and Arwel as his bodyguards instead.

She didn't trust anyone other than Anandur to revive Dalhu.

Her man had already suffered so much.

He'd paid with his flesh and blood. And in a way—his life. Experiencing entombment came too damn close to dying.

And yet, there was a sense of poetic beauty to it—death and rebirth.

Dalhu would be reborn as a new man.

Both Andrew and Edna had vouched for him, and he'd provided the clan with loads of vital information about the Doomer organization that couldn't have been obtained in any other way.

Feeling like an idiot, she murmured, "Come on, Mark, this must be good enough, give me a sign that you've forgiven me."

Not that she was really expecting a response, but she couldn't help the pang of disappointment when the crypt remained silent. She wondered if Mark could hear her, wherever he was. Probably not, because otherwise he would've answered. Mark had been such a nice guy—he would not have let her suffer like this even if he was still angry with her. Come to think of it, she was pretty sure he would've forgiven her even without Dalhu's sacrifice.

The one who had been seeking retribution was she, not Mark.

Mark had been a good person, she wasn't.

Maybe that was why she was carrying around such tremendous guilt.

Her mind couldn't focus on anything, and even though she had gone back to work the day after Dalhu's trial, she had done nothing more than going through the motions—lecturing and supervising the standard university research. Using the convenient excuse of Syssi's absence, she hadn't conducted a single paranormal test—as if she hadn't done it for years before hiring Syssi.

She just hadn't been in the mood.

It was hard to concentrate while counting the seconds until Dalhu's *rebirth*.

She heard the brothers coming down the corridor even though they were making very little noise. The crypt magnified the slightest sound—she could hear the swish of their robes.

"Hi, guys," she greeted them as they entered the chamber. "Why the formality? Is there a ceremony involved that I wasn't aware of?" She was wearing jeans and a T-shirt.

Anandur shrugged. "I guess not, but I kind of like these." He waved a hand between his and Brundar's robes.

Brundar arched a brow as if to say, *really?*

Amanda sighed. "Okay, you had me scared for a moment there. I don't want to waste one more minute of Dalhu's life, and I would've hated to have to wait for Onidu to bring my robe."

"Well, then let's get down to business. Follow me."

Anandur led them down another corridor and into a smaller chamber, where a simple, unadorned sarcophagus was resting on top of a stone platform.

"Amanda, you stand over there." He pointed to the wall. "Brundar, you grab the lid from the other side, and we lift on a count of two."

He waited till his brother had a good grip on the stone lid.

"How heavy is that thing?" she blurted before thinking. "Sorry..."

Anandur gave her an exasperated look. "It's heavy. Not to say that I wouldn't have been able to lift it by myself, but you don't want that thing to accidentally fall and smash your frog. Broken bones take much longer to heal than broken skin."

"I'm sorry. I'm going to keep my mouth shut from now on."

Anandur's smirk implied that he doubted she could keep her promise.

"Okay, Brundar, on the count of two. One, two..." They lifted the lid simultaneously, then laid it carefully on the stone floor.

Anandur reached inside his robes and pulled out two large glass containers the size of a two-liter soft drink bottle each, filled with some clear liquid. Brundar produced a large box of saltine crackers.

"What's in the containers?"

"Holy water." Anandur winked.

"Really?" What the hell was he talking about? What holy water?

"Just plain water, Princess. Clear, uncontaminated, chemical free, spring water."

"Oh…can I come closer?"

"No," both brothers said at once.

"Wait over there." Anandur pointed a finger at where she was standing.

"Okay," she whispered. Dalhu must look awful if even Brundar didn't want her to see him.

Anandur lifted one of the containers over the sarcophagus and began pouring water over Dalhu's body in a thin steady stream, careful to wet him all over. She watched, expecting him to grab the second container once the first was emptied, but he didn't. Instead, he pulled out a piece of cloth from the inside of his robe and began rubbing Dalhu's body in circular motion.

"He's dehydrated, like a freeze-dried piece of fruit. Once his skin absorbs the water, his systems will gradually come online until he's able to drink on his own. I guess we could've used intravenous rehydration, but this is the way it has always been done."

"What the hell? Why didn't you?"

"Don't get your panties in a wad, he'll be fine. In fact, his pulse is already getting stronger."

Amanda could've punched him. Why stick to some old and outdated custom when modern medicine provided a safer, easier way?

Men were such idiots.

"Brundar, check if he can drink," Anandur instructed.

Brundar bent to reach into the sarcophagus, lifted Dalhu's head, and brought the container to his lips. Not that she was able to see what was going on inside the box, but it was easy to guess from Brundar's movements. What surprised her, though, was the gentleness with which the guy performed his task. She would've never suspected that the brutal weapons master had it in him.

"Good, keep giving him a little at a time." Anandur kept rubbing.

Thank you, merciful Fates, Dalhu was drinking on his own.

To say she felt relieved was an understatement. A massive weight had lifted off her chest.

He was okay.

A moment later his hands shot out and grabbed the container Brundar was holding. Brundar held his head up as he gulped loudly.

"Easy there, slow down, you don't want to choke or vomit." Anandur put pressure on the container's other end, reducing the tilt. "That's it, slow and steady," he encouraged in a soft voice.

Dalhu kept drinking for what seemed like forever—until all the water was gone.

"Good job. Brundar will help you sit up, slowly, we want all of that life-giving water to stay inside, okay?" He was talking slowly and quietly, as if to not frighten a child or spook an animal.

Amanda held her breath as she waited to get her first glimpse of Dalhu's face. When she finally did, a gasp escaped her throat. His skin looked gray and dry like that of a corpse, and there were crusted lines of brown blood on his bare back. But it seemed that his injuries had healed while he'd been in stasis.

At the sound of her voice, Dalhu turned his head and smiled, his dry, chapped lips cracking.

She ran to him and wrapped her arms around him, burying her nose in the crook of his neck. The tears came next, then the sobs, and soon her whole body was quaking. She sobbed even harder when Dalhu's once powerful arms hugged her limply.

"It's okay, don't cry, my love," he rasped in her ear. "I'm fine, just a little weak, it will pass."

Dear, merciful Fates, she loved this man. Even barely alive he was comforting her, putting her needs before his—always and without fail.

"I love you," she sobbed into his neck.

As if her words had given him strength, she felt his arms tighten around her. "Say it again," he whispered.

Amanda lifted her head and kissed his cheek. "I love you," she said aloud. "I love you," she repeated even louder. "And I'm so sorry for putting you through this," she added quietly.

"It was all worth it, and I'd do it again tonight, and tomorrow, and the day after that, just to hear you say you love me."

There were tears in his eyes, and she quickly kissed each one to hide it from the guys. "I promise to say it over and over again, so many times that you'll grow sick of hearing it."

He smiled, the sparkle in his eyes infusing life into his cadaverous visage. "Not going to happen, I'll never tire of hearing the woman I love say it back to me, never."

The sound of clapping reminded Amanda that they were not alone, and with one last kiss to Dalhu's forehead, she retreated a step.

Anandur's grin was so wide that his face looked like it was going to split in half. He went on clapping for a few more seconds. "This must be what true love is. Dude, you look like a corpse and stink like one too, and she kisses you and tells you she loves you. Damn." He shook his head.

Brundar opened the box of saltines and handed Dalhu a few. "Eat, you need the carbs and the salt."

Dalhu chewed obediently but refused more. "Help me get out of here, would you?"

The brothers assisted Dalhu, practically lifting him out, and Anandur held on while Brundar produced a folded white sheet from inside the folds of his robe, flopped it out of its square, and wrapped it around Dalhu's naked body. He tied it like a toga so it wouldn't unravel.

"Thank you," Dalhu murmured.

"No problem. Can you walk?"

"Not on my own, I need your help."

"That's what I'm here for. Lean on me, brother."

Wow, did Anandur just call Dalhu "brother"? Was it a joke?

From the expression on Dalhu's face, he wasn't sure either. "Thanks, you're the man, Anandur."

Brundar got on Dalhu's other side and wrapped his arm around his middle. "Put your arms on our shoulders, you need to distribute your weight between us."

Dalhu did as he was told. "I'm sorry for the stink, guys," he said as the three of them shuffled slowly toward the exit.

"Yeah, you owe us for this, big time. I think a nude of me in full color would do. What about you, Brundar, what would make you happy?"

"To burn it?"

"What? My nude? Why? I want to hang it in our living room."

"That's why."

Their banter continued as they made their way down the corridor at a snail's pace with Dalhu's feet dragging on the floor between them.

Walking behind the men, she felt her heart breaking at the sight of Dalhu's poor back. A week in stasis had taken care of his wounds, and even the scars were barely visible, though it was hard to tell under the layer of crusted brown blood.

"We are not going to the cell. I'm taking Dalhu up to my penthouse," she announced.

The procession halted, and both Anandur and Dalhu turned their heads to look at her.

"Kian would have our heads," Anandur said.

"He is not here. I'll deal with him when he returns."

"All I need is you, a shower, and a bed. I don't care where," Dalhu croaked through his dried out throat.

She put her palm on his sunken cheek. "I know, my love, but I will no longer tolerate anyone doubting the value and loyalty of my fated mate."

Dalhu nodded. "As you wish, my princess."

She smiled. Her guy was so smart. In a matter of mere weeks, Dalhu had figured out the key to a successful marriage—the three little words every male should know and use—

As you wish.

COMING UP NEXT

Michael & Kri's story

book 6.5: My Dark Amazon

Andrew's Story

Dark Warrior Tetralogy

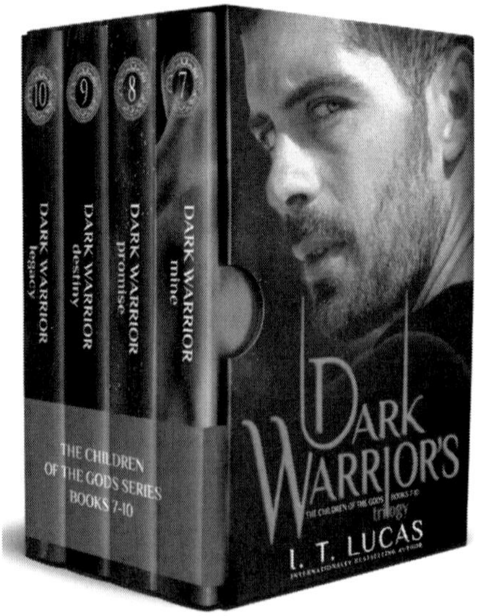

Turn the page to read an excerpt

INCLUDES:
7: DARK WARRIOR MINE
8: DARK WARRIOR'S PROMISE
9: DARK WARRIOR'S DESTINY
10: DARK WARRIOR'S LEGACY

Dear reader,

Thank you for joining me on the continuing adventures of the ***Children of the Gods***.
As an independent author, I rely on your support to spread the word. So if you enjoyed the story, please share your experience, and if it isn't too much trouble, I would greatly appreciate a brief review on Amazon.
Click here to leave a review
Love & happy reading,
Isabell

DARK WARRIOR TRILOGY EXERPT

PROLOGUE

Harvard-Westlake High school
Studio City, California
13 years ago.

"Hi, Nathalie." Leaning his hip against the metal door of his locker, Luke Bruoker produced his seductive smile. For her.

Walk away, the voice in her head commanded.

Shut up, Nathalie thought back.

Just do it. You know what he's thinking.

As if she needed Tut to freaking tell her what was on Luke's mind as he flashed her, *Nutty Nattie,* the perfect set of teeth that had all the other girls wetting their designer panties. With his good looks and rich daddy, Luke was one of the most popular guys in school, and for giving her the time of day, he probably expected her to fall at his feet in gratitude.

Not this girl, not going to happen, buddy.

Trying to ignore her too handsome and too full of himself locker neighbor, Nathalie stuffed the books she came to retrieve in her backpack.

But what if she was wrong? What if Luke was just being nice? And anyway, even if he wasn't, she didn't want to be rude.

"Hi, Luke." Nathalie lifted the corners of her lips in a tight smile and waved goodbye.

You're not wrong, Tut snickered. *But if it's any consolation, he thinks you're hot.*

It's not.

Unfortunately, there was no way to hide things from the stowaway sharing her cranium space.

You're such a liar. Tut's laugh echoed in her head before slowly fading away.

Well, what did he expect? She was only human and couldn't help but feel flattered.

He was such a pain, but if she was lucky, for the next few hours he'd leave her alone. Tut, or *tutor,* as he'd introduced himself after chasing all the other voices away, hated math class. In fact, the ghost in her head didn't like school, or homework, or tests—which was probably the main reason she was such a good student. The only time Nathalie could be alone in her own skull was while studying.

Tut claimed to be teaching her about life.

Yeah, right, more like ruining it.

Watching TV with him was a nightmare. He wouldn't shut up for a moment with his nonstop derisive commentary about everyone and everything. And hanging out with friends or going to the mall was more of the same.

Who was she kidding? As if anyone wanted to hang out with Nutty Nattie—the girl who talked to herself.

Nathalie pulled on the straps of her heavy backpack, hitching it higher on her back as she walked faster—pretending to rush so no one would notice that she always walked alone.

Mostly, she felt invisible. No one would look at her, except maybe for some of the nicer girls who would occasionally give her a pitying smile—as if she was retarded or deformed. The best she could hope for was to be regarded as the crazy genius. Unfortunately, even though she was smart and worked harder than most, she deserved only the first part of the title.

But at least her hard work had gotten her accepted into this overpriced private high school. Trouble was, her parents couldn't really afford it—not even with the generous financial aid they'd been awarded—and she knew for a fact that they were dipping into their equity line to finance the difference. The school called the discount a scholarship, but it wasn't. None of the rich kids were getting it, not even those who were excellent students.

Still, it wasn't as if anyone was privy to that information, but it wasn't hard to guess either. Her classmates arrived at school in Mercedes and BMWs while she drove a three-year-old Toyota Corolla hatchback.

Not that she was complaining, her car was great—the previous owner had hardly driven her, and she was almost as good as new. Besides, this was the best her parents could afford. God knew they had always given her everything they could, and probably more than they should—spoiling their only child.

When she was younger, she'd thought it was her due, but lately, it was making her feel guilty. It seemed as if by giving her all of their love, her parents were left with nothing for each other.

In fact, this morning, her mother told her that she'd filed for a divorce.

Oh, God, what is Papi going to do?

The coffee shop wasn't making much, and they would not have been able to afford much of anything without her mother's government pension.

How is Papi going to survive without it?

Thank God, it was her last year of high school, so at least this expense would be gone. And since she'd gotten a full-ride scholarship to the University of Virginia, college wouldn't cost her parents anything.

But savings aside, it meant that her father would be all alone once she left.

At sixty, her mother was still a knockout, while Papi, two years her junior, looked like a grandpa. It had to do with his love of baking—and eating. He was at least fifty pounds overweight and almost bald. But he was the sweetest guy. Which was probably why his business wasn't doing so well. He had never turned away anyone who was hungry, regardless of their ability to pay.

Not fair.

The God her father believed in so earnestly should've smiled upon a man like him, rewarded him for his good heart and generosity. But instead, his beloved coffee shop was barely staying afloat, and his beautiful wife was leaving him.

Nathalie had a feeling that her mother had just been waiting for her to finish school and go to college to make her move. Eva hadn't been happy for years—even when Papi had been much thinner and still had hair. She always looked troubled, almost fearful, though Nathalie couldn't figure out why.

Maybe her mother suffered from some mental disease—like Nathalie did. Though instead of hearing voices of dead people in her head, Eva might've been anxious or depressed.

It was about time she talked with her mother and cleared things up. She was definitely old enough for a grownup conversation. Perhaps they both could benefit from psychiatric help. And maybe, just maybe, with treatment, Eva might change her mind about leaving.

But even if she wouldn't, to be rid of Tut, it was worth a try.

Problem was, psychiatrists were expensive.

Maybe that was why her parents had never taken her to one, even though they must've known that her so-called imaginary friends had been very different than those of other kids.

But Papi had said that it was harmless, nothing to worry about, and her mother had agreed. They'd cautioned her that it was okay to play pretend at home, but she shouldn't be talking to herself in public.

Nathalie had tried.

As she had grown older, she'd realized that it wasn't normal and that the people talking to her in her head were probably just elaborate hallucinations. A mental disorder and not ghosts. She'd stopped telling even her parents about it.

But here and there, she would forget herself and respond out loud—hence the damn nickname. *Nutty Nattie.*

1

ANDREW

I've just landed, taxiing in, I can be at your place in an hour. Andrew texted Bridget as soon as it was okay to turn cell phones on.

She answered. *Waiting impatiently* (‘}~{‘)

It took him a few seconds to decipher the meaning.

Cute.

For an immortal, who was born God knew when, she was surprisingly well versed in current texting lingo and etiquette. Better than he was. He'd never asked Bridget how old she was, in part because he felt it was impolite, and in part because he was afraid to find out. For a forty-year-old man, it would've been beyond weird to know that his girlfriend was hundreds of years old.

Andrew wondered how Syssi dealt with her husband's age. His baby sister, thirteen years his junior, had fallen in love with Kian before finding out that her Greek-god-lookalike boyfriend was so ancient.

The few clan members Andrew had gotten to know since he'd been sucked into their world ranged in age from nearly two thousand, like his new brother-in-law, to Amanda, who was over two hundred. Not to mention their mother, the goddess, who was over five thousand years old or more.

This was another lady who Andrew would never dare ask for her age. He was an adrenaline junkie, but he wasn't stupid enough to court certain death.

After a day of endless meetings, followed by a five-hour flight from Washington back to L.A., Andrew would've preferred for Bridget to come over to his place. Trouble was, whatever was in the fridge had probably spoiled over the two weeks he'd been gone.

True, he could've ordered takeout, but there was also the issue of his bed being messy, and probably not quite fresh smelling. He couldn't remember the last time he'd changed the linens. Not that they were all the way into the gross category, but Bridget deserved better.

He'd thought about buying her a present in D.C. but eventually had given up on the idea. First of all, Bridget was loaded, just like all other clan members, and what Andrew defined as a reasonably-priced gift, she might consider trash. Secondly, he had no idea what to buy for a woman in general and for this one in particular. Dr. Bridget's tastes gravitated toward the practical.

Except, she had a thing for red.

Damn, just thinking about those spiky red heels of hers was enough to get him hard. But it wasn't as if he could buy her shoes. And even if he were one of those guys who could guess a woman's shoe size, hers were probably the kind that cost over a thousand bucks—not something he could afford on his government salary.

So yeah, the only things he felt confident buying for a woman were chocolates and flowers.

But at least he wasn't as clueless as Bhathian, who didn't even know how to behave around one, or what to say.

The guy had been terrified of going to see the long-lost daughter

Andrew had found for him. So much so that he'd asked Andrew to accompany him to her coffee shop, just so they could sit there, pretending to be customers. It hadn't been a good feeling to bail on the guy, but Andrew had had no choice. Her place had been closed on the evening he'd delivered the news of her existence, and the next day he'd been told to pack up a suitcase and hop on a plane to Washington.

The trip had been a total waste of time. He'd spent two fucking weeks in Homeland Security headquarters—stuck in boring meetings, listening to bureaucrats who believed they knew best how to devise a plan of action that could've been condensed into five paragraphs on one yellow-pad page. Actually, it was exactly what he'd brought back.

One fucking page.

They could've bloody emailed him. Anyway, no one had listened to what he'd had to say.

Fuck, he hoped Bhathian hadn't waited for him to go see the girl —correction, woman; earlier this year the guy's daughter had turned thirty.

An hour later, Andrew knocked on Bridget's door. Luckily, no one had hitched a ride with him on the elevator that had taken him from the clan's private parking level up to her floor. And by no one he meant Bhathian.

He planned to call the guy after his reunion with Bridget.

Andrew and the doctor had a lot of steam to release. The entire time he'd been away, he'd been preserving his energy for the insatiable immortal.

Today, he would show her staying power.

She opened the door, wearing a long white T-shirt, spiky red heels, and nothing else. "Andrew, you have no idea how happy I am to see you," she purred.

"Not as happy as I am." He lifted her up for a kiss, kicking the door closed behind him. She wrapped her legs around his hips.

Bridget was naked under that semi-sheer thing, every curve and shade of her generous breasts and aroused nipples clearly visible, and the bedroom was too far away.

Turning around, he pinned her against the nearest wall. "I can't wait," he groaned, holding her up with one hand and going for his belt buckle with the other.

"Let me." She pushed his hand away and opened things up for him. Freeing his shaft, she guided it into her moist heat. Bridget was drenched. He hesitated, but only for a split second, before ramming inside her with one powerful thrust.

On a groan, her head hit the wall behind her.

With the wall holding part of her weight and her thighs locked in a tight grip around his hips, he needed only one hand on her ass to keep going, and he put the other one to good use, pushing her shirt up and palming a breast.

Bridget did one better, pulling the thing over her head and tossing it on the floor. Now, she was completely bare save for the shoes.

They could stay on.

Damn, this was so fucking hot.

Thumbing one perky nipple, he pinched and tugged, taking turns and giving each the same loving attention.

Bridget's hands shot into his short hair, and she gripped his skull, bringing his head closer for a hungry kiss. As their tongues and teeth dueled, her sharp incisors were winning, and as she bit down on his lower lip, she drew blood.

Feisty immortal.

He brought his hand down on her butt with a loud slap, then gripped both cheeks and began pounding with gusto.

"Yes! Oh, dear Fates, yes!" Bridget seemed oblivious to the fact that she was being banged into the wall with such force that the plaster was cracking, and small particles of paint were flying in the air.

If she were mortal, she would've bruised badly.

Liberated by her resilience, Andrew kept going hard.

It was so fucking good to feel vital, strong, male. But as he neared his completion, Andrew had the passing thought that as amazing as this was, something was still missing.

"Now," Bridget hissed.

He obeyed her command, synchronizing his climax with hers and coming hard inside her—his shaft milked by the convulsing muscles in her sheath gripping him harder than any fist.

"God, Bridget…" He fumbled for words as he lowered her.

Her thighs trembled a little, but as her feet touched the floor, she was steady. "Come to bed." She bent and pulled his pants up but left them unzipped. "I don't want you to trip on the way. I still have a use for you." She winked and walked away.

To his relief, he saw that although her back was slightly reddened, the skin looked intact. But as she sauntered ahead of him, he noticed that one of her curvy butt cheeks still bore a faint outline of his handprint. That one, he didn't mind. Not at all.

In fact, he felt his shaft give a twitch. Good, the abstinence was paying off. Tonight, he would be able to last, hopefully for as long as it would take to satisfy the lustful immortal.

Two hours later, a Victoria's Secret lineup naked parade wouldn't have gotten a rise out of him. And if tongues could get sprains, his would've been sporting a brace.

The merry tune Bridget was whistling in the kitchen was like a slap to his manhood. She was going to kill him, pleasurably, but he'd be dead nonetheless.

Andrew closed his eyes and inhaled deeply. One didn't need an immortal's superior nose to smell the thick scent of sex on the bedding, and if he had an ounce of energy left in him, he would've gotten all domestic and taken them off for her.

Still naked, Bridget sauntered into the bedroom with a loaded tray and placed it on the side table. "Sit up. I'm going to nourish you. You look pale."

"I wonder why?" he said as he propped himself up on the pillows and took the coffee mug she'd handed him.

"Poor baby. Too much for you?"

Now, that was mean.

"Not at all. Give me an hour and I'm back up." *Not if my life depended on it…*

"Aha. Sure. Whatever you say." She handed him a pastry.

As he chewed, he was reminded of the call he still owed Bhathian. It would have to wait until he could move.

"This is good. Where did you get it?"

"I was on Fairfax earlier today, and the smells lured me into this new bakery. I don't remember the name, but it's on the box if you want to write it down. I bought an assortment to try it out, but I'm afraid this is the only one left." She smiled sheepishly.

"Oh, yeah? Who ate all the rest?"

"I did."

"How many?"

"Eleven. There were twelve in the box."

And here he'd thought that Bridget only ate veggies. With an appetite like this for baked goods, it was a miracle she wasn't fat.

He appraised her lean midsection. "Where do you pack it all?"

"Breasts and butt." She patted the aforementioned parts.

"Then by all means, eat more. I love your curves."

A sad shadow clouded her eyes, but only momentarily. She shook it off so fast Andrew wasn't sure if it had really been there or if he'd just imagined it.

She grinned. "You and the construction workers renovating that old office building on Olive. Every time I pass by, they whistle and comment."

"Want me to beat them up for you?"

She laughed. "Why on earth would I want that?"

"Some women find it offensive." He shrugged.

"I don't mind the whistling, but the comments they think I can't hear..."

"My offer is still on the table."

She leaned and kissed his cheek. "You're so sweet."

"What is it with immortal females and calling me sweet? Even my own mother never called me that."

She kissed him again, on the lips this time. "What's the matter? Your machismo got hurt?"

He crossed his arms over his chest. "Yes."

Bridget refilled his coffee mug and handed him a piece of an apple as a peace offering.

"Can you stay the night?"

And prove himself a liar when even three hours later he would remain as limp as a noodle? No way. "I wish I could, but I need to talk to Bhathian. There is something I'd promised him to do, and I didn't have a chance because of that damn useless conference my boss sent me on with barely any notice."

"You could come back later...I'm flying out to Baltimore tomorrow..."

"I thought Julian's graduation was next week."

"It is, but I wanted to spend some time with him, and he made plans with his roommates for a road trip after the graduation."

Damn, he hated to disappoint her, but he hated the prospect of staying even more. His suitcase was still in his car because he'd come here straight from the airport, and tomorrow was another long workday. He needed to go home.

Andrew pulled her into his arms and kissed her lips gently. "I'm sorry, but I just have to go home and unpack, check what alien life forms are growing in my fridge..." He tried for humor, and it worked.

She smiled. "Fascinating, save some samples for me."

"I promise to save something better than disgusting growth for you to play with."

"And what might that be?"

"Life force? Energy?" He made a face.

Bridget laughed. "After another ten days of nada, you'll need it."

"I know."

2

SEBASTIAN

Standing on top of the old monastery's newly added third-floor balcony, Sebastian leaned over the railing and glared at the cars parked outside. A damned parking lot was one more thing Sebastian realized he had neglected to plan for his new base of operation in the picturesque Ojai.

The front of the building looked like a junkyard, and in the daytime it was even worse.

From his balcony, he should be gazing at a grassy lawn and flowerbeds, not a bunch of used cars scattered on top of packed dirt.

A paved circular driveway and a fountain with a statue at its center, surrounded by rose bushes, would have made the place look grand.

But hiring workers now that the warriors were all in residence was problematic. Training would have to be suspended, and the guys would have to make themselves scarce.

The men hardly matched what one would expect of those visiting a restful *spiritual retreat*.

There was no helping the cars, though. The men needed vehicles to transport themselves to and from the clubs they were now scoping nightly in search of male clan members. Tom and Robert had gone shopping, and in a few days had managed to fill the lot with a bunch of used cars. Sebastian would've preferred to go into a dealership and lease a fleet, but Tom had insisted that buying from private owners was more discreet.

All in all, they now had twenty-nine vehicles at their disposal.

One was a big truck, for just in case, and the rest an assortment of minivans and SUVs. While the troops shared the used cars at a ratio of three to one, Sebastian had insisted that he and his two assistants each had their own brand new vehicle.

For obvious reasons, all had darkened windows.

The cars were serving dual purposes. The obvious one was transportation, but also, when needed, the back seats could be folded to provide a place for a quick fuck.

With his basement brothel's low occupancy rate, his troop's needs had to be satisfied off base.

Over the last two weeks, Sebastian had been able to find only five girls for his brothel. Not enough to take care of seventy-five immortal warriors, two assistants, and one sadist. But there was only so much he could do in a day, and snagging the right females required investigative work that took time.

Most hadn't been the right fit.

Which reminded him that there was another issue he hadn't accounted for. Human females required sunlight and fresh air to stay healthy and in a good mood. Thralling was not enough to counteract the underlying depression the lack of natural light and tiny jail rooms were causing.

He'd come to the conclusion that he couldn't keep them cooped up in the basement twenty-four hours a day.

On Pleasure Island, the women enjoyed several swimming pools, above-ground bars and restaurants, and the beautiful, tropical ocean. It was a gross oversight on his part to not realize the importance of those amenities.

Sebastian should have known that the exalted leader of *The Devout Order Of Mordth*, Lord Navuh, never did anything without a good reason. If Navuh had chosen to provide his whores with outdoor recreation, it had been only because it was crucial for the women's health and their ability to provide the exceptional services his secret island was known for.

Sebastian pulled out his phone and selected Robert's number. "Grab Tom and meet me outside."

"Yes, sir."

Sebastian rolled his eyes but didn't say anything. Robert was a lost cause. Jogging down the stairs, he glanced at the spacious recreation room. The men were done with their chores for the day, and several were taking a break playing pool or watching a movie before going to their rooms to get ready for the nightly club patrols.

There had been a lot of grumbling about the domestic chores they'd been assigned, but he had no intention of getting more humans on the premises to perform the cooking and housekeeping duties. Perhaps once the basement rooms were all filled, he would divert his attention to finding at least a decent cook. He was sick of the barbecued steaks and hamburgers the men were taking turns preparing.

Other than that, the lazy fuckers could keep on doing laundry, sweeping floors, and cleaning toilets. It wasn't as if they had that much to do during the day. Five hours of training was enough to keep them in shape, and the rest of their work was done at night.

Outside, the mountain air was crisp and cool, and other than the rumbling voices of the men inside, he could hear only the chirping of crickets and the hooting of the occasional owl. Even the coyotes didn't dare go anywhere near the compound.

"You wanted to see us, boss?" Tom said from behind him.

"Yes, I want to do something about the grounds." He waved his hand at the vehicles. In the weak moonlight, their colors were faded, all looking like different shades of gray and black. "I don't want to see this out of my window."

Robert glanced around at the gentle hills surrounding the former monastery. "This is the only flat area."

The problem with subordinates who were good at taking orders was that they didn't think independently, you had to chew everything for them.

"What do you have in mind?" Tom asked.

"I want the parking lot to be moved over there." Sebastian pointed to the side of the building. "And I want a circular driveway with a fountain in the center. The rest of the grounds need planting; grass, flowers, trees, the works." Sebastian began walking. "Come with me." He motioned for them to follow.

At some point, the back of the property had had grassy lawns with gravel paths meandering through them, but now there was nothing besides overgrown weeds and construction debris that hadn't been taken care of yet.

"I'm thinking of putting in a swimming pool over there, and an outdoor bar with shaded trellises on that side. We'll need to bring in large, mature trees to create a green canopy around the whole thing. Girls lounging in bikinis are not exactly what one expects to find in an 'Interfaith Spiritual Retreat'."

Robert looked intrigued.

"And how do you suggest we do it?" Tom asked.

"That's what I need to figure out. If it were only planting, I would've had the men do it, but for the pool and hardscaping we need a contractor with heavy equipment."

Robert crossed his arms over his chest and started pacing back and forth. "Curfew," he uttered a few moments later. "We need to coordinate several contractors with large crews to come and be done in a few hours. We'll have the men on lockdown in the house while the construction is going on."

"What about the cars?" Tom asked.

"We park them in a line on the side of the road, one behind the other."

Sebastian clapped Robert's back. "Great idea, Robert. We could tell the contractors that there are guests in the retreat and work needs to be confined to a predetermined number of hours a day. This will also explain the cars."

The guy, who was tall to begin with, seemed to grow a few inches. "Thank you, Sebastian," he said without stuttering or mumbling for the first time.

Clap, clap, clap. "Finally," Tom said.

3

ANDREW

I'm back and here in the building. Want to meet me downstairs? Andrew texted Bhathian.

Come to my place. 37 floor, #4.

I'm on my way.

Bridget's apartment was just one floor above Bhathian's, and Andrew opted to take the emergency stairs down.

They had already said their goodbyes. He'd offered to come get her and drive her to the airport, but she'd declined. Her flight was leaving in the afternoon, and she'd said that she saw no reason for him to take time off work. A taxi would do.

To his shame, he'd felt relieved. There was a big pile of files waiting for him in the office, and to catch up, he would need to not only work through his lunch break but stay overtime. His damn bosses still expected him to deliver a report despite sending him on that useless trip.

Andrew rapped his knuckles on the door and waited.

After a moment, Bhathian opened it. "Hey, my man, come in. How was your trip?" He clasped Andrew's hand.

"A waste of time." Andrew shook it then followed him inside.

The layout and furnishings were similar to Bridget's. But where hers had been personalized with all kinds of knickknacks, and everything was nice and tidy, the guy's place was typical of what one would expect to find in a bachelor's apartment.

There was an opened box of pizza on the dining table, and empty beer bottles littered every surface. It seemed that Bhathian had appropriated all that had been left from Kian's bachelor party because most of them were Snake's Venom, the expensive, super potent Scottish beer Anandur had bought for the occasion.

Bhathian followed his gaze. "Want one? I have plenty."

"Sure, why not?'

The guy ducked into the kitchen and returned with two cold ones.

Andrew took one. "I'm surprised so many were left. I thought we demolished all of them."

"There were none. But they were good, so the next day I went and bought two cases for myself."

"I thought they were pricey."

Bhathian shrugged his massive shoulders and planted his butt in a chair across from Andrew. "I have plenty of money and nothing to spend it on."

"You didn't go to see her." There was no need to specify which her he was talking about.

Bhathian winced. "The farthest I got was to stand outside her shop, but I didn't have the guts to go in."

"I'm sorry that I bailed on you."

"Not your fault."

"Do you want to go tomorrow?"

"If you can come, then yes."

"So, did you get a peek?"

Bhathian nodded. "She looks like her mother."

"Oh, yeah?"

"Beautiful." There was a definite note of pride in Bhathian's voice.

"Does she have anything from you?"

"Luckily for her, not much." Bhathian grimaced. "She has my thick eyebrows. Though, hers are pretty, not bushy like mine."

Andrew tried to picture a woman with Eva's exotic beauty and Bhathian's surly expression and came up blank.

Bhathian took a swig from his beer. "I need to find out what happened to Eva. Any idea how?"

Good question. The fact that the police hadn't found anything didn't mean much. Their investigation had probably been superficial at best.

"We can start by following the money trail. The government is still depositing her monthly pension checks into her bank account, and if she's still alive, I'm sure she is accessing it."

"And you can find out where she's making withdrawals?"

"Not easily, but yes. Unless the money is funneled through a Swiss bank. Then it's next to impossible."

Bhathian shook his head. "Just so you know, I'm forever in your debt. Whatever you need, whenever, just say the word."

"I appreciate it, but save your gratitude for when I actually find something."

"You already found my daughter, and for this alone I owe you big time. I'm not just blowing smoke up your ass, I mean it. Whatever, whenever."

"Okay, I got it, but it's really not necessary. If the roles were reversed, I'm sure you would've done the same for me." It seemed like the right thing to say, even though Andrew wasn't sure it was true. He was an outsider, tolerated only because his sister was married to the regent.

But Bhathian nodded solemnly, and leaned forward, extending his hand with the bottle. "That's what family is for."

Okay, so he might have been wrong. It seemed that Bhathian had really accepted Andrew as one of the clan. "To family." He clinked bottles with the guy.

"To family," Bhathian echoed.

Andrew emptied his bottle of Snake's Venom and put the empty on the coffee table before pushing up to his feet.

Damn, the thing must've gone to his head because he had a moment of vertigo. But it passed almost as soon as it started. It was probably only the fatigue catching up to him. "Tomorrow after work I'll come to get you, and we'll drive to Glendale. Seven okay?"

Bhathian got up and escorted him to the door. "Whatever works for you." The guy pulled Andrew into a crushing bear hug and clapped his back.

"Careful, my man. I'm still only a fragile human."

A rare smile brightening his gloomy features, Bhathian let go. "You might be a human, but from what I hear there is nothing fragile about you, tough guy."

And wasn't that good to hear.

On his way home, as he drove through the deserted streets of downtown L.A., Andrew reflected on his conversation with Bhathian.

Family.

For better or worse, the clan was now his family—independent of his decision regarding chancing the transition or not. They'd accepted him as is—the first human ever to be admitted into their tight, secret community.

He wondered if things would've been different if he hadn't brought all that he had to the table. If he were just an average Joe, with an average job, would they have entrusted him with their secrets?

Probably not.

The truth was that the clan needed him. Not that it was a bad thing necessarily, being needed was just as important as being accepted, maybe even more. Especially for a proud son-of-a-gun like him.

Which made him think of Dalhu.

The dude had done the impossible. His acceptance by the clan, however, had come at an unimaginable price. Andrew could not think of a single male that could've taken the torment Dalhu had gone through—not with the dignity and unparalleled willpower the guy had displayed.

One thing was for sure, if Andrew ever needed someone to fight by his side, Dalhu would be his first choice. Not that there was a chance the guy would be allowed to fight anytime soon. For all intents and purposes, Dalhu was still under house arrest—during his probation period as Kian had called it. True, he was no longer confined to the dungeon, and was sharing Amanda's spacious penthouse, but he wasn't allowed to leave.

The guy must be going crazy.

For a warrior to be cooped up in an apartment without the ability to release some steam must be hard. And it didn't matter that he was living in the lap of luxury with the love of his life.

Maybe Andrew should go spend some time with the dude, invite him for a sparring contest down in the gym.

Right.

Who was he kidding? As if he could offer any kind of a challenge to the powerful immortal. Even among the Guardians, Andrew suspected that only Anandur, or perhaps Yamanu, stood a chance against the ex-Doomer.

Amanda had gotten herself one hell of a protector.

Damn, it still stung.

Losing to the other guy hadn't been good for Andrew's ego. But he had to concede that despite his initial opinion of the guy, Dalhu had turned out to be the better man for Amanda.

God knew that with the kind of trouble the woman courted, Dalhu was probably the only male on earth capable of keeping her safe.

4

SYSSI

"Come here." Kian swiveled his chair and spread his knees in invitation.

It had been like this since the first day she had joined him in the office. The moment Shai would leave, Kian would turn his chair around and invite her for a kiss that would often end in nookie.

As it turned out, she was more of an impediment than help.

The only thing she'd managed to achieve so far, apart from keeping her hubby happy, was to reorganize one small section of the filing cabinet. One at a time, she replaced the old, worn files with new ones and created an electronic version, including making detailed spreadsheets and scanning the supporting documents. Since Kian and Shai were such old farts they were still doing things the old fashioned way, meaning like before the Industrial Revolution, her help was invaluable. Problem was, Kian and she were too busy necking to accomplish much.

"I'm waiting…" he growled.

Syssi rolled her eyes and punched one last number into the spreadsheet before obeying his command.

"Yes, sir." She pushed out of her chair and got between his spread thighs.

"That's what I like to hear." He closed his arms around her, pulling her in and kissing her, hungrily, as if they hadn't kissed just five minutes ago.

"You know, I was supposed to be helping you, but I don't think you're getting any work done." She moved to sit on one muscular thigh.

His hand snaked under her shirt, and he thumbed her nipple over her bra. "Yes, I love coming to work now. I didn't before."

He had a point there. Well, not really, but who could think straight with arousal short circuiting cognition?

"I don't want to be responsible for your conglomerate's demise… Oh, God…" she breathed as he snapped her bra open and tugged on the other nipple.

"Nonsense, you're providing an invaluable service." He pushed her shirt up and licked the engorged peak before closing his lips around it and sucking it in.

"Fuck…" she exclaimed.

Oh no... they had a rule about her using that kind of language. Because it wasn't part of her usual vocabulary, it had become an invitation to a game that she preferred to play in the privacy of their bedroom, and not in the office where anyone could walk in at any moment. And besides, the freaking place had glass doors, so anyone passing by could see what was going on inside. Never mind that she was already half naked. But for some reason, it wasn't as embarrassing as what was coming next.

As Kian lifted his head up from her breast, he had the wickedest smile on his handsome as sin face. "My sweet, naughty girl just earned herself a spanking."

"Not here," she whispered, feeling herself blush. But this wasn't the only heat that was spreading all over her body…

"Yes, here." In a heartbeat, she found herself face down over his other knee with her jeans yanked down and her butt exposed.

"Someone might come in," she hissed, struggling to get up without much success. Even with her new strength, the arm holding her pinned to his body was as unyielding as an iron band.

"Don't worry, no one is coming, and I'll hear if anyone is out in the corridor." With a loud crack, the first slap landed on her exposed behind.

As if he can hear anything over that...

But as the second and third fell in quick succession, she stopped thinking and stopped struggling and just gave in to the sensation. By the time Kian had delivered the tenth and last, she was so close to climax she was contemplating using another f-bomb to have him start over. There was no need, though. Thirty seconds later, as Kian penetrated her soaking sheath with two fingers and then added a thumb over her most sensitive part, she came all over his hand. And his jeans.

He lifted her limp, spent body and cradled her in his lap. "I love you so much." He kissed her lips.

"I'm going to sue my boss for sexual harassment," she croaked.

"Oh, yeah? And who is that wicked boss? You can't sue yourself, you know."

"So now I'm the boss?"

"Of course, you are."

"Didn't feel like it a moment ago when you were spanking me."

"Just fulfilling my matrimonial duties as promised."

She shifted up and kissed his lips. "I love you too. But seriously, now I need to go up and change underwear. Again. And you must be really uncomfortable." She wiggled her butt over his shaft.

"No problem. I'll accompany you upstairs, and we'll continue where we left off."

"For the second time today. This can't go on, Kian. We are like a couple of horny teenagers who can't keep their hands off each other."

"What's wrong with that? I think it's great."

"Because you have important work to do, you big lug. And frankly, although playing nookie with you is super fun, I'm wasting my time here. Anyone with basic computer skills could be doing my job."

"Don't you dare quit on me. For the first time that I can remember, I'm looking forward to my workday."

"What workday? You are not doing any work. Admit it, even when Shai is here, all you do is think about the next time he leaves so you can have your hands on me."

Kian ran his fingers through his chin-length hair, brushing it back. "I can't help it. Having you near me all day long is a temptation I can't resist. I'm just a simple man with simple needs. In fact, just one, you."

He was so sweet. "I love you, and I feel the same. But we are both adults with adult responsibilities. My time would be better spent helping Amanda find more Dormants. And you could actually accomplish something during the hours you spend here."

"I don't want to." He crossed his arms over his chest, pouting like a toddler.

She caressed his cheek. "I know, my love. How about this, you bring in another assistant, someone young who will modernize your ancient record keeping and help you finish your work in less time. I'll work with Amanda, but only until four in the afternoon. That way we'll still have plenty of time to spend with each other."

"What about the other stuff I need to do, besides office work? Like showing my face at meetings and classes, and visiting with people in my official capacity."

"I'll come with you to those."

"Okay, you won. But I don't like it."

"I know, neither do I. But it's for the best. Besides, it's not like it's carved in stone. If it doesn't work, we can reevaluate and make changes. Now let me go so I can pull my pants up. I've been sitting here bare-assed for far too long."

Kian helped her up and tugged her jeans back into place.

"Yikes, I hate wearing wet panties."

His smile was conceited. "Let's go. You can take them off in our private elevator. We have some unfinished business to take care of."

5

AMANDA

"So, what do you think?" Amanda crossed her arms over her chest.

"This bedroom is definitely better than the one facing the side of the building." Ingrid pushed the second layer of drapery aside. "If we position the easel next to the window, our resident artist will have plenty of natural light to draw by. We can knock out the dividing wall between this and the adjoining room, to give him more space."

Dalhu was in need of a studio, or rather Amanda was.

Her living room was a mess. With all kinds of drawings, completed and in various stages of progress, propped against the walls and couches and the coffee table. Soon, Dalhu would be spilling his mess into the dining room. Not to mention that there had been charcoal smears on her designer throw pillows before Onidu had rushed to hide the evidence, somehow managing to remove the stains and return her beautiful pillows to their previous pristine condition.

It seemed that her emotionless butler had taken a liking to Dalhu.

Figures, even a biomechanical creation and an ex-Doomer were doing the male bonding thing.

But the mess and the charcoal dust weren't the worst of it. A number of her clansmen were waiting in line for Dalhu to draw their portraits, and some had requested a full body nude. Well, just one. Anandur.

At first, she'd thought he was joking, but he'd kept nagging about it, and today he came over, thankfully posing only half naked. She could deal with him shirtless, but she drew the line there. Anandur's junk on full display wasn't something she wanted to see, which would be hard to avoid with Anandur posing for Dalhu in the middle of her living room.

Our living room...

Damn, after almost two centuries of living practically alone, it was one hell of an adjustment to live with someone other than Onidu. Having to be considerate, accommodating...

To keep the façade going twenty-four-seven.

It was such an ingrained habit that she just couldn't drop it no matter how hard she tried.

She kept telling herself that it wasn't needed, that Dalhu loved her unconditionally, and that he didn't expect her to act upbeat and smile all of the time. But it was no use. Wherever she had an audience, even if only of one, Amanda felt compelled to put on a performance.

She sighed. Small steps, one little thing at a time.

"What else do we need here?"

"Shouldn't you ask Dalhu what he wants?"

"Nah, he wouldn't know. It's not as if he has ever set foot into an art studio. And anyway, I want it to be a surprise."

"I was wondering where he was. What have you done with him?"

"I had Anandur take him down to the gym for a workout. After all, we can't have all those amazing muscles atrophy, can we?" She winked at Ingrid.

"Certainly not. The guy is such eye candy..."

"Watch it." Amanda pointed her finger at the covetous designer. "He is mine. Eyes and hands off."

Ingrid laughed. "Yes, ma'am. But you need to hurry up and find more male Dormants for us because there is talk among the girls of going down to the catacombs and reviving us some Doomers."

"You are joking, right?"

"Give it a little time and the joking will turn into doing. I'm not kidding. Some of us are green with envy."

"Listen, Ingrid, tell your horny friends to forget about it. Dalhu is the one and probably only exception to what we know is a typical Doomer. Should I remind you what we are dealing with? Brainwashed murderers who thrive on death and suffering. Minions of evil who will target a preschool and laugh with glee when children are blown up. That's what Doomers are. Tell them."

Damn, her outburst had gotten her so worked up that she needed a drink to calm down. "I'm going to make myself a margarita, do you want one too? Or are you in the mood for something stronger?"

"A margarita is fine." Ingrid followed her to the living room. "I'll send a couple of guys to clear that bedroom. Just tell me when is a good time."

Amanda mixed the two drinks and handed Ingrid hers. "Tomorrow, same time. I convinced Anandur that he needs to take Dalhu to the gym every day. My guy will go crazy if he stays cooped up here."

"Good deal. I'm going to do a little Internet search to see what he needs. Do you want me to run it by you? Or are you okay with me just going ahead and ordering whatever I see fit?"

"I don't want to waste time, just pick the most expensive stuff. You can't go wrong with that."

"Sweet, I like an open-ended budget." Ingrid took her drink for a walkabout to check out Dalhu's various creations. She stopped in front of the large canvas Dalhu was currently working on as a wedding present for Syssi and Kian. "Oh, wow. This is gorgeous. I didn't know Syssi posed for him in her wedding dress."

Amanda snorted. "Right, as if Kian would have been okay with her posing for a *Doomer*. Heck, the Doomer thing is secondary. He wouldn't want any male looking at her for a prolonged period of time let alone drawing her. Dalhu is using one of the wedding photos. His next one will be of them together at the altar with Annani presiding over the ceremony. Here, let me show you."

Amanda walked over to the media cabinet and pulled out a small wedding album, one of the hundreds that had been sent to every guest at the wedding. She flipped to the right page and showed it to Ingrid.

Ingrid sighed and put a hand over her chest. "They are so in love. Just look at how they gaze at each other as if nothing else exists. I want that."

"I'm working on it." *Not really*. For some reason, Amanda was reluctant to go back to the paranormal research without Syssi, the traitor who had abandoned her to go work for Kian. And anyway, Amanda was so behind on her formal research that she'd decided it was more important to catch up on that and not stress herself out by trying to do too much at once.

And as to working overtime? Forget it. She wasn't about to stay longer than was absolutely necessary when there was a hunk of a man waiting for her at home.

Priorities, priorities. Amanda first, the rest of the world second.

"What are you going to do with Syssi and Kian's portraits?"

"They are a present from Dalhu to Kian. A thank you for not making too much of a fuss over us moving up here. We were expecting a war when Kian came back from his honeymoon, but, apparently, the vacation had done him good, and he was in an uncharacteristically agreeable mood. Or perhaps it was all the sex. But in any case, all we got was a frown. And a cuff. William engineered a special contraption for Dalhu."

"I'm almost afraid to ask. Is it some kind of detonation device that is triggered if Dalhu tries to leave the building?"

Ingrid was such a weirdo.

"No, silly, you read too many suspense novels. There are no explosives in the cuff, but there is a transmitter that interferes with cellular signal. Dalhu can only use a landline, and as you know, all of them go through security."

Ingrid looked disappointed. "Oh."

"Of course, Dalhu couldn't care less. It's not like he has anyone he wants to call."

Well, it wasn't entirely true. He called her at work, about every thirty minutes—to tell her how much he loved her.

THE FATES' POST-WEDDING CELEBRATION

HOLLYWOOD CALIFORNIA

"It was such a beautiful wedding," Betty wiped tears from her host's cheeks. "Almost the entire clan was there."

Alba cast her an amused glance. "Haven't you cried enough?"

Not wanting to deprive anyone of enjoying the wedding, Betty had taken over the body of a female who had been too drunk to remember it anyway. The downside was the effect the alcohol had on Betty. She couldn't help but see the world through the prism of the biological host's impairment.

Betty shook her head. "To see Annani after all these years was very emotional for me. She has matured so well, and she looked so regal on that podium while presiding over the ceremony."

"I agree that she looked impressive." Alba scanned the place for hot guys but got distracted by a couple sitting on the other side of the bar. The woman was glaring daggers at her partner, but Alba couldn't see his face, just his back.

Oh, well. She couldn't help everyone's love life. Besides, she and her sisters were on a break.

Gamma popped a peanut into her mouth. "It's not like this was the first time you've seen her in ages. Since we've been allowed back, we've peeked in on her several times, and we can do that again anytime you want."

"Watching her while I'm in my incorporeal form is not the same as seeing her through a biological host's eyes." Betty reached for the peanuts. "I cried the hardest when she said all those lovely things about the bonds of love, the solid foundation of family, and how important it is to celebrate life's most important moments together. It was the best wedding speech I've ever heard."

Gamma put her drink down. "I liked Syssi's dress and that she and Kian walked down the aisle together. I also liked the unusual wedding song. I wonder who chose it."

"Kian, of course." Alba eyed the couple in the corner who were arguing quietly. "Do you think we should help them?" She tilted her head to indicate who she was referring to.

"We are on a break," Betty said. "After all that hard work, we deserve another vacation, and helping a silly human couple resolve their insignificant differences is not it. Besides, I'm tired. All that body-hopping was exhausting."

"There was no way around it." Alba sighed. "We wanted to attend the wedding in person, not in spirit form, so we had to take over bodies of guests. And since we didn't want anyone to miss the entire thing, we had to hop from one host to the next."

For a pure consciousness, there was nothing more tiring than that.

"And then we came over here and found human hosts so we could talk about it." Betty leaned back to take a look at the couple. "They'll be fine. It's just a lovers' spat."

"I know what we can do," Alba said. "You and Gamma can wind down with more drinks, and I'll take over that woman's body."

"You can't do that," Gamma said. "Our three hosts came into the bar together, and you can't leave yours until we leave ours."

"Right." If she did that, her host would want to talk to her friends whose souls were taking a snooze at the moment.

"I hope that Dalhu is alright after his week-long entombment," Betty said. "He was so brave."

And just like that, the waterworks started again.

That was the trouble with occupying bodies, whether human or immortal. As pure consciousness, Alba and her sister Fates were serene and logical, but while residing inside a biological host, their thoughts were affected by hormones, and they got overly emotional. But having emotions was also the beauty of wearing a body, and that was why they did it despite how exhausting it was.

There were advantages and disadvantages to both states, and just being bound to earth had its limitations too. As long as they weren't assigned to a physical realm, she and her sisters existed outside the space-time continuum. They could project themselves to any time and any place, but they couldn't interact with anyone in the places they visited. The only way to do that was by giving up their freedom and agreeing to exist inside the continuum and abide by its rules.

Except, giving up was not the right term. They were getting much more than they were losing.

The spectrum of what they were aware of while tethered to the four dimensions was an infinitesimal fraction compared to the vastness of universal knowledge, but what they were gaining in return was so much more intense.

It made them feel alive.

Just being tethered to earth amplified all the sensations, but nothing could compare to occupying a body. The difference between being a detached observer and experiencing all the thoughts and emotions through a biological entity's prism was like watching events reflected from a murky surface compared to living them.

And the most important part of it was caring.

Without the tether, there was no emotion, and with no emotion, there was no care. Perhaps that was the reason the boss assigned them to a specific time and place and allowed them the temporary use of bodies. They needed to learn about compassion and love, as well as hate and anger, and her favorite, lust.

For a transient entity like her, sex was the ultimate connection she could achieve to another.

The problem was that they were already working on their next pairing, which was not as difficult to orchestrate as Dalhu and Amanda's had been, but it wasn't easy either.

Given all the restrictions the boss had imposed on them, it was going to be just as challenging as the others, which meant that she couldn't indulge in any fun side activities.

Gamma patted Betty's arm. "Dalhu was very courageous, like we knew he would be. He will make a fine mate for Amanda, but more than that, he will prove to Kian that not all Doomers are evil, brain-washed lowlifes who are incapable of redemption, and that's crucial for our future plans."

Alba signaled the barmaid to refill her drink. "I can't believe that we've actually pulled that one off. My favorite part was taking over the waitress's body and telling Dalhu about the fancy club where he could meet Amanda."

Betty chuckled. "You were so mad at us for making you leave before he hooked up with her."

"Can you blame me? He's such a fine male specimen."

Gamma pinned her with a hard stare. "That would have been wrong on so many levels, and it's against the rules."

"Oh, I know, which could have made it so much more delicious."

Gamma huffed. "You are incorrigible."

The club hadn't been the real destination, and Dalhu ended up meeting Amanda on the street, but it wouldn't have happened if he wasn't planning on going to the club. That was what had brought him to look for clothes on Rodeo Drive, Amanda's favorite shopping destination.

Alba smiled at Betty. "Your plan was brilliant."

"Thanks. I'm very proud of how cleverly I plotted everything that day."

It had been indeed ingenious.

The success of the entire scheme had depended on Syssi giving Amanda her pendant, and to pull it off they had walked a very thin line between bending the rules and breaking them entirely. They'd had to give Andrew and Syssi tiny mental nudges to steer them in that direction, and hopefully, the boss wouldn't view it as a punishable offense.

They really couldn't afford another trip to purgatory.

Betty sighed. "My only regret is failing to convince Micah to show Dalhu mercy. The retribution she demanded for her forgiveness was vicious."

Gamma shook her head. "I think that given the circumstances, Micah was merciful."

As her friends continued talking about Micah's capacity for forgiveness or lack thereof, Dalhu's bravery, and their future plans for the clan, Alba tuned in to the couple in the corner once more.

It seemed like the arguing was done, and now the two were kissing passionately. Perhaps after she and her sisters left the bodies of their current hosts, she could take over the female's body.

The way things were going, the two were about to reconcile in bed, and it was a perfect opportunity for her to get her fix without putting too much effort into it.

Except, that would be unfair to the woman. She wouldn't be there for the sex, and the next morning she would have no idea what had happened and why she couldn't remember the reconciliation.

With a sigh, Alba picked up her glass and took another sip. She had to find a solution to the damn three-hour limit that would allow her to have fun but was also moral.

Perhaps there was a lonely soul in the bar waiting to find Mr. Right or even Mr. For Tonight, and she could help her do that.

Letting her senses flare, she started listening to other conversations. Most were the usual boring chitchat that people engaged in over drinks, but one caught her interest, especially since the two men talking in hushed voices were absolutely yummy.

"Do you really think that the best way to utilize our breakthrough technology is to use it for virtual hookups?" the guy on the left asked. "There are so many wonderful experiences our machine could provide. Virtual scuba diving, flying with a flock of birds, going to the moon, colonizing Mars, the possibilities are endless. Focusing on hookups just complicates things."

The guy on the right put his beer bottle down and leaned back. "Because all of these things are solo activities. They are fun, but that's nothing out of the ordinary. Many companies are working on the same technology. Our unique selling proposition is that we can offer a fully immersive shared experience. No one else is thinking in that direction."

"That's because it's so damn difficult to implement. We've been working on this for three years and sinking all of our money into it. Perhaps we should come out with the fully immersive solo activities first, recoup some of our investment, and use the money to keep developing the shared experience?"

"I don't know, Gabriel." The guy rubbed a hand over the back of his neck. "It's tempting, but I'm afraid that once the technology is out, someone will copy it and beat us to the finish line on the end product. That's where the real money is."

"It's not just about the money for you, Hunter. I know why you really want to do that, and I respect you for it, but I'm starting to think that it's just not doable."

Hunter nodded. "I promised Simon that I'd find a solution for him and Debra. He was so devastated after the accident, and I gave him hope that one day he and his wife could have sex again despite his paralysis. I feel like I've failed him."

"You haven't failed him yet."

Alba elbowed Gamma. "Are you hearing that?"

"What?"

"The two guys over there. They are working on virtual sex technology."

"So?"

"Maybe we can help them."

Gamma snorted. "We have enough on our plate with the clan. Besides, we are tethered to this particular time and space, and we can't hop into the future to bring back innovations."

"We don't have to. William already has access to the gods' technology, or at least parts of it. Maybe we can get him to help these guys. And while we are at it, we can help him find his mate."

William wasn't one of the key players in their grand scheme, but that didn't mean that they couldn't take care of him ahead of some of the others.

He was such a sweet guy, and he was lonely.

Gamma waved a dismissive hand. "William's mating is not a top priority. He is way down the list."

"We can push him ahead of some of the others whose matings are not crucial to our plan."

"I don't mind doing that, but the list of those who are pivotal to our grand scheme is so long that it will take a while until we can focus on the others."

That was unfortunately true.

Still, Alba would have loved to talk to Hunter and Gabriel, and if they were single, hook up with either one. Gabriel was more her type, but if he wasn't interested, she would take Hunter.

"Our time is almost up." Betty sighed. "We either find new hosts or call it a night."

Alba looked around the bar for another group of three ladies on their own, but she only found two. The good thing was that they were eyeing Hunter and Gabriel, so getting them to hook up with those guys wouldn't be a violation of their free will.

"How about the two over there?" She nudged Gamma. "They are looking at the guys with the virtual technology thing, and I would love to join them and see if they are available." And maybe use the opportunity to ask a few questions, but perhaps it would be better not to waste her precious time on that.

From what she'd heard so far, Gabriel and Hunter guarded their secret technology fiercely, and they would probably not volunteer any information. But now that she was aware of them, she could track them through the ether and ghost into their offices whenever she wanted.

Gamma looked at the men with unabashed interest. "I wish they had another friend with them."

Betty waved a dismissive hand. "You two go ahead. I've had enough excitement for one night, so I'll just ghost. But before I do, I want a group hug."

They always did that before ghosting. One of the best things about having a physical body was experiencing the wave of oxytocin that hugging produced.

It was addictive.

After they were done with their group hug, they sat back at the bar and gently extracted themselves from their hosts' bodies.

As their own consciousness took over, the three young women looked confused.

"What were we talking about?" asked the one whose body Gamma had occupied.

Alba's host rubbed her temples. "Something about virtual reality and hookups." She shook her head. "I must have been daydreaming. Ever since the new headsets came out, I've been dying to try one, but they are so damn expensive."

Betty's host looked at her empty glass. "I think that I had too much to drink. I don't remember anything about our conversation or even ordering this margarita."

The Fates next adventure is coming out soon in the Dark Enemy Warrior Quartet.

Also by I. T. Lucas

ALSO BY I. T. LUCAS

DARK ANGEL

14: DARK ANGEL'S OBSESSION

15: DARK ANGEL'S SEDUCTION

16: DARK ANGEL'S SURRENDER

DARK OPERATIVE

17: DARK OPERATIVE: A SHADOW OF DEATH

18: DARK OPERATIVE: A GLIMMER OF HOPE

19: DARK OPERATIVE: THE DAWN OF LOVE

DARK SURVIVOR

20: DARK SURVIVOR AWAKENED

21: DARK SURVIVOR ECHOES OF LOVE

22: DARK SURVIVOR REUNITED

DARK WIDOW

23: DARK WIDOW'S SECRET

24: DARK WIDOW'S CURSE

25: DARK WIDOW'S BLESSING

DARK DREAM

26: DARK DREAM'S TEMPTATION

27: DARK DREAM'S UNRAVELING

28: DARK DREAM'S TRAP

DARK PRINCE

29: DARK PRINCE'S ENIGMA

30: DARK PRINCE'S DILEMMA

31: DARK PRINCE'S AGENDA

DARK QUEEN

32: DARK QUEEN'S QUEST

33: Dark Queen's Knight
34: Dark Queen's Army

Dark Spy

35: Dark Spy Conscripted
36: Dark Spy's Mission
37: Dark Spy's Resolution

Dark Overlord

38: Dark Overlord New Horizon
39: Dark Overlord's Wife
40: Dark Overlord's Clan

Dark Choices

41: Dark Choices The Quandary
42: Dark Choices Paradigm Shift
43: Dark Choices The Accord

Dark Secrets

44: Dark Secrets Resurgence
45: Dark Secrets Unveiled
46: Dark Secrets Absolved

Dark Haven

47: Dark Haven Illusion
48: Dark Haven Unmasked
49: Dark Haven Found

Dark Power

50: Dark Power Untamed
51: Dark Power Unleashed
52: Dark Power Convergence

ALSO BY I. T. LUCAS

Dark Memories

53: Dark Memories Submerged

54: Dark Memories Emerge

55: Dark Memories Restored

Dark Hunter

56: Dark Hunter's Query

57: Dark Hunter's Prey

58: Dark Hunter's Boon

Dark God

59: Dark God's Avatar

60: Dark God's Reviviscence

61: Dark God Destinies Converge

Dark Whispers

62: Dark Whispers From The Past

63: Dark Whispers From Afar

64: Dark Whispers From Beyond

Dark Gambit

65: Dark Gambit The Pawn

66: Dark Gambit The Play

67: Dark Gambit Reliance

Dark Alliance

68: Dark Alliance Kindred Souls

69: Dark Alliance Turbulent Waters

70: Dark Alliance Perfect Storm

Dark Healing

71: Dark Healing Blind Justice

72: Dark Healing Blind Trust
73: Dark healing Blind Curve

Dark Encounters

74: Dark Encounters of the Close Kind
75: Dark Encounters of the Unexpected Kind
76: Dark Encounters of the Fated Kind

Dark Voyage

77: Dark Voyage Matters of the Heart
78: Dark Voyage Matters of the Mind
79: Dark Voyage Matters of the Soul

Dark Horizon

80: Dark Horizon New Dawn
81: Dark Horizon Eclipse of the Heart
82: Dark Horizon The Witching Hour

PERFECT MATCH

Vampire's Consort
King's Chosen
Captain's Conquest
The Thief Who Loved Me
My Merman Prince
The Dragon King
My Werewolf Romeo
The Channeler's Companion
The Valkyrie & The Witch
Adina and the Magic Lamp

TRANSLATIONS

DIE ERBEN DER GÖTTER

Dark Stranger

1- Dark Stranger Der Traum

2- Dark Stranger Die Offenbarung

3- Dark Stranger Unsterblich

Dark Enemy

4- Dark Enemy Entführt

5- Dark Enemy Gefangen

6- Dark Enemy Erlöst

Dark Warrior

7- Dark Warrior Meine Sehnsucht

8- Dark Warrior – Dein Versprechen

9- Dark Warrior - Unser Schicksal

10-Dark Warrior-Unser Vermächtnis

LOS HIJOS DE LOS DIOSES

EL OSCURO DESCONOCIDO

1: EL OSCURO DESCONOCIDO EL SUEÑO

2: EL OSCURO DESCONOCIDO REVELADO

3: EL OSCURO DESCONOCIDO INMORTAL

EL OSCURO ENEMIGO

4- EL OSCURO ENEMIGO CAPTURADO

5 - EL OSCURO ENEMIGO CAUTIVO

6- EL OSCURO ENEMIGO REDIMIDO

ALSO BY I. T. LUCAS

LES ENFANTS DES DIEUX
DARK STRANGER

1- Dark Stranger Le rêve

2- Dark Stranger La révélation

3- Dark Stranger L'immortelle

The Children of the Gods Series Sets

Books 1-3: Dark Stranger trilogy—Includes a bonus short story: **The Fates Take a Vacation**

Books 4-6: Dark Enemy Trilogy —Includes a bonus short story—**The Fates' Post-Wedding Celebration**

Books 7-10: Dark Warrior Tetralogy

Books 11-13: Dark Guardian Trilogy

Books 14-16: Dark Angel Trilogy

Books 17-19: Dark Operative Trilogy

Books 20-22: Dark Survivor Trilogy

Books 23-25: Dark Widow Trilogy

Books 26-28: Dark Dream Trilogy

Books 29-31: Dark Prince Trilogy

Books 32-34: Dark Queen Trilogy

Books 35-37: Dark Spy Trilogy

Books 38-40: Dark Overlord Trilogy

Books 41-43: Dark Choices Trilogy

Books 44-46: Dark Secrets Trilogy

Books 47-49: Dark Haven Trilogy

Books 50-52: Dark Power Trilogy

Books 53-55: Dark Memories Trilogy

Books 56-58: Dark Hunter Trilogy

Books 59-61: Dark God Trilogy

Books 62-64: Dark Whispers Trilogy
Books 65-67: Dark Gambit Trilogy
Books 68-70: Dark Alliance Trilogy
Books 71-73: Dark Healing Trilogy
Books 74-76: Dark Encounters Trilogy

MEGA SETS

The Children of the Gods: Books 1-6

INCLUDES CHARACTER LISTS

The Children of the Gods: Books 6.5-10

Perfect Match Bundle 1

CHECK OUT THE SPECIALS ON

ITLUCAS.COM

(https://itlucas.com/specials)

FOR EXCLUSIVE PEEKS AT UPCOMING RELEASES & A FREE I. T. LUCAS COMPANION BOOK

Join my *VIP Club* and gain access to the VIP portal at itlucas.com

To Join, go to:

http://eepurl.com/blMTpD

Find out more details about what's included with your free membership on the book's last page.

TRY THE CHILDREN OF THE GODS SERIES ON AUDIBLE

First published in the United States 2015

This paperback edition published 2024

ISBN: 978-1-962067-35-5

NOTE FROM THE AUTHOR:

Dark Enemy Trilogy & The Fates' Post-Wedding Celebration are works of fiction!
Names, characters, places, and incidents are products of the author's imagination or are used fictitiously and are not to be construed as real. Any similarity to actual persons, organizations, and/or events is purely coincidental.

FOR EXCLUSIVE PEEKS AT UPCOMING RELEASES & A FREE COMPANION BOOK

JOIN MY *VIP CLUB* AND GAIN ACCESS TO THE VIP PORTAL AT

ITLUCAS.COM

CLICK HERE TO JOIN

INCLUDED IN YOUR FREE MEMBERSHIP:

YOUR VIP PORTAL

- READ PREVIEW CHAPTERS OF UPCOMING RELEASES.
- LISTEN TO GODDESS'S CHOICE NARRATION BY CHARLES LAWRENCE
- EXCLUSIVE CONTENT OFFERED ONLY TO MY VIPS.

FREE I.T. LUCAS COMPANION INCLUDES:

- GODDESS'S CHOICE PART 1
- PERFECT MATCH: VAMPIRE'S CONSORT (A STANDALONE NOVELLA)
- INTERVIEW Q & A
- CHARACTER CHARTS

IF YOU'RE ALREADY A SUBSCRIBER, YOU'LL RECEIVE A DOWNLOAD LINK FOR MY NEXT BOOK'S PREVIEW CHAPTERS IN THE NEW RELEASE ANNOUNCEMENT EMAIL. IF YOU ARE NOT GETTING MY EMAILS, YOUR PROVIDER IS SENDING THEM TO YOUR JUNK FOLDER, AND YOU ARE MISSING OUT ON IMPORTANT UPDATES, SIDE CHARACTERS' PORTRAITS, ADDITIONAL CONTENT, AND OTHER GOODIES. TO FIX THAT, ADD isabell@itlucas.com TO YOUR EMAIL CONTACTS OR YOUR EMAIL VIP LIST.

Made in United States
North Haven, CT
13 April 2025

67927956R00420